Bolitho

Alexander Kent

Bolitho

With all Despatch

Honour This Day

The Only Victor

LONDON   NEW YORK   SYDNEY   TORONTO

This collected edition first published 1993
by BCA by arrangement with William Heinemann Ltd
an imprint of Reed Consumer Books Ltd
Michelin House, 81 Fulham Road, London SW3 6RB
and Auckland, Melbourne, Singapore and Toronto

With All Despatch © Highseas Authors Ltd 1988
Honour This Day copyright © Highseas Authors Ltd 1987
The Only Victor copyright © Highseas Authors Ltd 1990

CN 3983

Printed and bound in Great Britain
by Clays Ltd, St Ives plc

With All Despatch

For my Dormouse,
with all my love

Therefore with courage bold, boys, let us venture;
Like noble hearts of gold now freely enter
Your names on board the fleet, all friends forsaking,
That we may soon complete this undertaking.

Anon

Contents

1

A King's Officer

Rear-Admiral Sir Marcus Drew stood to one side of a window and idly watched the comings and goings of people and carriages outside the Admiralty. Like the other windows in his spacious room it was tall and broad and enabled him to distinguish the passers-by from the more regular visitors who daily, hourly even, thronged the Admiralty corridors in search of employment. Captains, young and not so young, some of whose exploits had once brought pride and hope to an England at war. Seeing the most persistent applicants, and having his subordinates turn the majority away, took much of the admiral's time. He studied some puddles in the road left by a sudden shower. Now they shone like pale blue silk, reflecting the April sky while the clouds receded across London.

For this was spring 1792, another year of uncertainty and threats of danger from across the Channel. But you would not think as much to watch the ladies in their frivolous gowns and bright colours, with their carefree, posturing escorts.

Two years back, when news of the bloody revolution in France had hit London like a broadside, many had feared that the butchering, the murderous mobs and their guillotines would somehow spread their horror across the Straits of Dover. Others, naturally enough perhaps, had found comfort in their old enemy's terrible change of circumstances.

It might have been better if England had put aside the rules of war for once and attacked the French when they were caught in their own turmoil. But that had not even been considered.

Drew turned away, his day, and the thought of dining later on in St James's with some whist afterwards, turned sour.

Their lordships of Admiralty expected miracles if they imagined that the fleet, left to rot in harbours and estuaries for most of the ten years since the American Revolution, could suddenly be rebuilt to anything approaching its old strength. Thousands of seamen and marines had been thrown on the beach, unwanted by a nation for which so many had died or been maimed in the King's name. Officers, too, left on half-pay if they were lucky, begging for berths in the merchant service, trying to return to the sea which had been their chosen life.

Rear-Admiral Drew was nevertheless content with his own lot. There was even the promise of a mistress on a permanent basis now that he had managed to obtain an appointment for her husband, a young captain, in the East Indies.

He stared hard at a huge painting on the opposite wall. It depicted Admiral Vernon's seventy-gun flagship *Burford* with all flags flying, her broadside battering a Spanish fortress, 'The Iron Castle' at Porto Bello, at almost point-blank range. It was how the public, the romantics, liked to imagine a sea-fight, he thought. No blood, no terror of a surgeon's blade, just the majesty of battle.

He permitted himself a small smile. Vernon's fight had been some half-century ago, but the ships had changed hardly at all since then. No, he decided, his appointment here at the Admiralty was better than any quarterdeck. He would have his mistress, and his elegant London rooms; he would, of course, need to be seen on Sundays in the family pew on his Hampshire estate, with his wife and children.

He returned to the ornate table and sat down without enthusiasm. His clerk had placed his papers in order. The clerk's duty was to interrupt him after a pre-arranged time during each interview. It never stopped.

Soon the French would declare war. One could hardly describe this uneasy pause on the fringe of the Terror as little better anyway. As always England would be unprepared. Ships and men. Ships and men.

2

His gaze fell on the name on the uppermost sheet. *Richard Bolitho Esquire.* It looked much-handled, and Drew wished that someone else could take his place today. Richard Bolitho, who had distinguished himself in the American Revolution, and a man luckier than most, had held two highly successful commands since, the last being the frigate *Tempest* in the Great South Sea. His final battle with the frigate *Narval* and supporting schooners had been legendary. The French *Narval* had been seized by the notorious pirate Tuke after an uprising within her own company. The *Bounty* mutiny, then the horrendous news from Paris had given Tuke mastery of the barely defended islands. Only Bolitho's command had stood between him and total control of the rich trade routes from the Indies.

And now Bolitho was here. He had, to all accounts, visited the Admiralty daily for several weeks. Like most professional sea-officers Drew knew a great deal about Bolitho. About his old Cornish background, and his fight against the shame which had cost his family dearly. His only brother Hugh had deserted from the navy after killing a fellow officer in a duel, and had then gone to seek his fortune in America; even worse, as a lieutenant, then the captain of a Revolutionary prize frigate.

No amount of courage and honour could completely wipe that stain away. And he had paid his debt in full, Drew thought as he turned over the papers. Wounded to the point of death; and then after the fight with Tuke's *Narval* Bolitho had been struck down by fever. He had not been employed for two years and, if half of what Drew had heard in the elegant rooms around St James's was true, he had nearly died many times during his fight to live.

Their lordships must have a reason for their change of heart, the admiral decided – although on the face of it, it would seem better if Bolitho turned down this appointment, and be damned to the consequences.

Drew's eyes sharpened as he recalled the rumour about Bolitho's attachment for a government official's lovely wife. She had died of fever and exposure after some desperate journey in an open boat. Drew covered the papers with a leather folder. *An official's lovely wife.* That would make a change from some of the dull, earnest faces he had seen across this table, with their high-sounding requests in the name of duty or the King, as the fancy took them.

He picked up a small brass bell and shook it impatiently. *Get it over with*. In the event of another war against France, without the standards of monarchy to guide the old enemy, there might be no room for yesterday's heroes. Admiralty agents in Paris had reported seeing whole families of alleged gentlefolk being dragged through the streets to lie beneath the blade of Madame Guillotine: even the children were not spared.

Drew thought of his serene estate in Hampshire and suppressed a shudder. It could not, must not happen here.

The clerk opened the door, his eyes downcast like a well-rehearsed player.

'Captain Richard Bolitho, Sir Marcus!'

Drew gestured expressionlessly to a chair which faced the table. As a captain he had taught himself the art of inscrutability, just as he had learned the skill of missing nothing.

Richard Bolitho was thirty-five but looked younger. He was tall and of slim build, and Drew observed that his white-lapelled coat with the buttons and gold lace of a post-captain hung just a bit too loosely on his frame. As he sat in the chair, Drew could sense his tension in spite of his efforts to conceal it. A shaft of sunlight played across his face and hair, a loose lock above the right eye barely hiding the great scar received when he had been hacked down as a youthful lieutenant in charge of a watering party on some island or other. The hair was black, like a raven's wing, and the eyes which watched him steadily were grey, and reminded Drew of the Western Ocean.

Drew came straight to the point. 'I am pleased to see you, Bolitho. You are something of an enigma, as well as one of England's heroes.' The grey eyes did not blink and Drew felt off-balance. Irritated, too, that he and not Bolitho had been suddenly put on the defensive. After all, Bolitho was the one who had been begging for a ship – *any* ship.

He began again. 'Are you feeling returned to fair health?'

'Well enough, Sir Marcus.'

Drew relaxed again. He was in command. He had seen the sudden anxiety which even Bolitho's impassive gravity could not contain.

4

Drew continued, 'You will know this tale of old, Bolitho. Too many captains, and not yet enough vessels to receive them. There are fleet transports and supply vessels, of course, but —'

Bolitho's eyes flashed. 'I am a frigate captain, Sir Marcus —'

The admiral raised one hand so that the frilled lace spilled over his cuff.

He corrected, '*Were* a frigate captain, Bolitho.' He saw the pain cross his face, the deeper lines which seemed to sharpen his cheekbones. The fever might still lurk there. He said smoothly, 'And a fine one to all accounts.'

Bolitho leaned forward, one hand grasping the hilt of his old sword so tightly that the knuckles were as white as bones.

'I am recovered, Sir Marcus. In God's name, I thought when I was admitted —'

Drew stood up and crossed to the window again. He had no sense of command or victory now. If anything he felt ashamed.

He said, 'We need men, Bolitho. *Seamen*, those who can reef and steer, fight if need be.'

He turned briefly and saw Bolitho staring down at the old sword. Another part of the story, he thought. It had been in the family for generations. Had been intended for Bolitho's brother. His disgrace and treachery had killed their father as surely as any pistol ball.

'You are being appointed to the Nore. As captain-in-charge of some small craft.' He waved his hand vaguely. 'We have had many deserters from the Nore — they see smuggling as a more profitable profession. Some have even decamped to the Honourable East India Company, although I —'

Bolitho remarked coldly, 'John Company has a record of treating its people like *men*, Sir Marcus, not as some will use them.'

Drew turned and said sharply, 'It is all I can offer. Their lordships believe you to be suitable for it. However —'

Bolitho stood up and held his sword tightly against his hip.

'I apologise, Sir Marcus. It is not of your doing.'

Drew swallowed hard. 'I *do* understand.' He tried to change the subject. 'You will have none of your past company with you from *Tempest*, of course. She came home well before you and is

5

now in service with the Channel Fleet. *Tempest*, and before that the – *Unicorn*, I believe?'

Bolitho watched him in despair. *Doing his best*. He heard himself reply, '*Undine*, sir.'

'Well, in any case –' It was almost over.

Bolitho said quietly, 'I shall have my coxswain. He is enough.'

Drew saw one of the gilt door-handles drop; the clerk was right on cue.

Bolitho added, 'It is history now, maybe forgotten entirely. But one ship, *my* ship, was all His Britannic Majesty's navy had in the whole ocean to meet with and destroy Tuke.' He turned and appeared to be studying the great painting, hearing perhaps the true sounds of war, feeling the pain of a ship under fire. He continued, 'I fell that day. It was then that the fever rendered me helpless.' He faced Drew again and smiled. The smile did not touch his grey eyes. 'My coxswain killed Tuke. So you could say that he saved the islands all on his own – eh, Sir Marcus?'

Drew held out his hand. 'I wish you well. My clerk will attend your orders. Be patient, Bolitho – England will need all her sailors soon.' He frowned. 'Does that amuse you, sir?'

Bolitho took his cocked hat from the hovering clerk.

'I was thinking of my late father, Captain James as he was to all who knew him. He once said much the same words to me.'

'Oh, when was that?'

Bolitho withdrew, his mind already grappling with the brief outline of his commission.

'Before we lost America, sir.'

Drew stared at the closed door, first with fury and then unwillingly, with a slow grin.

So it was true after all. The man and the legend were one.

Captain Richard Bolitho opened his eyes with a start of alarm, surprise too, that he had fallen into a doze as the carriage rolled steadily along a deeply rutted track.

He looked through a side window and saw the various shades of green, bushes and trees, all glistening and heavy from another rainfall. Springtime in Kent, the Garden of England as it was called, but there seemed precious little sign of it.

6

He glanced at his companion, who was slumped awkwardly on the opposite seat. Bryan Ferguson, his steward, who did more than anyone to direct the affairs of the house and estate in Falmouth. He had lost an arm at the Battle of the Saintes. Like Allday, he had been a pressed man aboard Bolitho's ship *Phalarope*, and yet the events then had joined them together. Something unbreakable. He gave a sad smile. Few would guess that Ferguson had only one arm as he usually concealed the fact with his loose-fitting green coat. From one outthrust boot Bolitho saw the gleam of brass and guessed that Ferguson was carrying his favourite carriage pistol. *To be on the safe side*, as he put it.

God alone knew, the Kentish roads were deserted enough, perhaps too much so for highwaymen, footpads and the like.

Bolitho stretched and felt the ache in his bones. It was his constant dread that the fever might somehow return despite all that the surgeons had told him. He thought of the two years it had taken him to fight his way back to health, and finding the strength to relive it once again. Faces swam in misty memory, his sister Nancy, even her pompous husband the squire, 'The King of Cornwall' as he had been dubbed locally.

And Ferguson's wife who was the housekeeper in the great grey home below Pendennis Castle where so many Bolithos had begun life, and had left to follow the sea. Some had never returned. But above all Bolitho remembered his coxswain, Allday. He had never seemed to sleep, had been constantly close by, to help in the struggle against fever, to fetch and carry, and too often, Bolitho suspected, to accept his delirious bursts of anger.

Allday. Like an oak, a rock. Over the ten years since he had been brought aboard by the press gang in Cornwall their relationship had strengthened. Allday's deep understanding of the sea, his impudence when need be, had been like an anchor for Bolitho. A friend? That was too frail a description.

He could hear him now, talking with Old Matthew Corker the coachman, while Young Matthew occasionally joined in with his piping tones from the rear box. The boy was only fourteen, and the old coachman's grandson. He was the apple of his eye, and he had brought him up from a baby after his father had been lost at sea in one of the famous Falmouth packet-ships. Old Matthew had always hoped that the boy would eventually follow in his footsteps. He was getting on in years, and Bolitho knew he had missed the right road on several occasions on the long haul from Falmouth, where weeks ago this journey had had its beginning. The old man was more used to the local harbours and villages around Falmouth, and as he had followed the road to London, pausing at inn after inn to change horses and pick up fresh post-boys to ride them, he must have wondered when he would eventually step down from his box.

The coach had been Bolitho's idea. The thought of being taken ill on some part of the journey, perhaps on a crowded mail coach, had haunted him. This carriage was old, and had been built for his father. Well sprung, with the motion more like a boat on these roads than a vehicle, it was painted dark green, with the Bolitho crest on either door. The motto too, *For My Country's Freedom*, picked out in gold scrollwork beneath.

He thought of that motion now as the carriage rolled past the endless bank of shining trees and fields. In his pocket were his written orders, the wording so familiar to him, and yet, in these circumstances, so barren.

To proceed to the Nore. The great River Medway, the towns which marked the miles to the Royal Dockyard at Chatham, and then on to the open sea.

To command what? As far as he could discover he was under the local control of a Commodore Ralph Hoblyn. His name at least was familiar, and he had served with distinction in the Americas before being badly wounded at the decisive battle of the Chesapeake in '81. Another misfit perhaps?

Ferguson yawned and then collected his wits.

'Must be close to Rochester, sir?'

Bolitho pulled his watch from his breeches and felt his jaw stiffen as he flicked open the guard. She had given him the watch to replace one lost in battle. Viola Raymond. He had tried to recapture her in his thoughts a million times. To hear her laugh, see the light dance in her eyes because of something he had said. Dear, lovely Viola. Sometimes in the night he would awake, sweating, calling her name, feeling her slip from his arms as she had on that terrible day in the open boat. She above all, who had shared the misery of what had appeared a hopeless passage under relentless sunlight, deprived of food and water with some of the men half-mad in their suffering. She had somehow sustained all of them, wearing his coat, bringing grins to their scorched faces and cracked lips. The Captain's Lady, they called her.

Then, on that final day, when Bolitho knew they had found *Tempest* again, she died without even a murmur. In the nightmares which had followed, one scene always stood out stark and terrible above all else. Allday, holding her slim body, and with a boat's anchor tied about her waist, lowering her into the sea. Her figure, white in the dark water, fading and fading, then nothing. But for Allday, he would have gone mad. He was still unable to think of her without pain.

He stared at the watch in his palm, the engraved inscription which he knew by heart.

> 'Conquered, on a couch alone I lie
> Once in dream's conceit you came to me
> All dreams outstripped, if only thou wert nigh –'

Bolitho said, 'We shall see the Medway directly.'

Something in the dullness of his voice made Ferguson watch him uneasily. The same dark, intelligent features, the eyes which could laugh or show compassion; and yet something was lost. Perhaps forever.

Old Matthew called out to the leading post-boy and the carriage came slowly to a halt where the road met with the gradient of a shallow hill.

Old Matthew disliked using post-boys when he had handled four horses, even six at a time, from the age of eighteen in the Bolitho service. But it was a long journey back to Falmouth, to the last inn where he would recover his own two pairs of chestnut horses, which he was said to love more than his wife.

Bolitho heard Allday mutter, 'Not here, matey. I can manage without *his* blessing!'

The carriage moved forward again, the horses scraping their shoes on the damp ground and shaking their harness like sleigh bells.

9

Bolitho lowered a window and saw the reason for his coxswain's agitation.

They were at a dreary crossroads; a stone which read, *To London, thirty miles* shared the deserted place with a gibbet which swung slightly in the wet breeze.

A tattered, eyeless thing hung in irons. It was hard to believe it might have once lived and loved like other men. A felon, a common thief, now denied even the dignity of burial.

Bolitho climbed down from the carriage and stamped his feet to restore the circulation. He could smell salt from here, and beyond a ragged procession of trees he saw the great curving outline of the river. It looked flat and unmoving, more like pewter than water hurrying to join the sea.

Through the haze of distant rain he saw the old town of Rochester, the ruins of some ancient fortification near the water's edge. A town which, like many others around this part of Kent, lived off the navy and its great dockyard and victualling jetties. In times of war the townspeople listened at their locked doors when darkness fell, for fear of the hated press gangs which roamed the streets in search of men for the fleet. To begin with they combed the inns and lodging houses for prime seamen, but as the toll of war mounted, and every King's ship cried out for still more hands, the press gangs had to be content with anyone they could find. Ploughmen and boys, tailors and saddle-makers, none was spared.

Many a ship would be forced to put to sea with only a third of her company trained seamen. The remainder, punched, threatened, and chased by boatswain's mates with their 'starters', learned the hard way. Many were killed or injured in the process long before their captain had to face an enemy. Falls from aloft in a screaming gale, bones broken by waves surging inboard to sweep a man against a tethered cannon, and those who merely vanished, lost overboard with nobody able to help, or even to hear them go.

And now, with the clouds of war rising above the Channel, the press gangs were out again. This time they were seeking deserters and unemployed seamen. The press would never be popular, but as yet there was no other way. England needed ships; the ships needed men. The equation had not altered in a hundred years.

Bolitho looked up and felt a shaft of watery sunlight touch his

10

cheek. *A captain of his own ship*. Once an impossible dream, the greatest step anyone could make from wardroom to the privacy of the great cabin. But to gain it and then have it taken away was even harder to accept.

His new command consisted of three topsail cutters, fast, highly manoeuvrable craft similar to those used by the Revenue Service. One was completing a refit in the dockyard, and the others doubtless awaited his arrival with curiosity or displeasure, and probably wondered why their world was to be invaded by a post-captain.

Bolitho had studied all the available reports with care, hoping to discover some glimmer of purpose which might make this appointment bearable. But it seemed as if in south-east England, and the Isle of Thanet in particular, the cat and the dog lived side by side. The revenue cutters hunted for smugglers, and the press gangs searched for unwilling recruits and deserters. The law-breakers, the smugglers who in many cases seemed better equipped and armed than their opposite numbers, seemed to do much as they pleased.

Bolitho remounted the coach and saw Allday watching him, his pigtail poking over the collar of his coxswain's blue jacket.

Their eyes met. 'Back again, Cap'n. Frigate or no, 'tis still the sea. Where we belong.'

Bolitho smiled up at him. 'I shall hold to that, old friend.'

Allday settled down again and watched the horses lean forward to take the strain.

He had seen the tightening of Bolitho's jaw. Like those other times when the deck had been raked with the enemy's iron, and men had fallen on every side. And when he had forced himself to accept that his lady had gone, fathoms deep, to a peace he had been too late to offer her. And like the times when they had ventured from the old grey house, for those first pitiful walks together after the fever had released its grip. A few yards at first, and the next day, then the next, until Bolitho had thrust him away, pleading with him to let him go the rest of the way unaided. Once he had fallen in sight of the headland where the sea surged endlessly amongst the rocks. He had cried out brokenly, 'She would have liked it here, old friend!'

11

And together they had won the battle. The hardest one Allday had ever shared.

Now he was back, and God help anyone who tried to stand against him. Allday touched the heavy cutlass beneath his seat. *They'll have to take me first, and that's no error.*

But they had not even driven into the outskirts of Rochester before trouble showed itself.

Bolitho had his orders spread on his knees as the carriage gathered speed down another hill when he heard Allday exclaim, 'On the road, by God – looks like a riot! Better turn back, Old Matthew!'

The coachman was yelling at the post-boys, and Bolitho thought he heard Allday groping for a loaded piece from the weapons box.

'*Stay!*' Bolitho swung out of the door and held on to the handrail. The carriage was almost broadside across the road, the horses steaming and agitated by the baying sound of voices.

Bolitho drew a small telescope from his coat and levelled it on the road. There was a surging crowd of people, some waving their arms and sticks, others laughing and drinking from flasks. Two of them were mounted. They were all men.

Allday laid a short, heavy-muzzled blunderbuss on the carriage roof and covered it with a piece of canvas from his seat.

He said harshly, 'I don't like it, Cap'n. Looks like a hanging mob.'

Ferguson was examining his small pistol and said, 'I agree, sir. We should pull back. There must be a hundred of them heading this way.' He did not sound frightened. The Saintes had taught him to overcome fear. It was more like concern.

Bolitho held the small telescope steady. It was much easier with the carriage halted.

In the centre of the yelling crowd two figures, each with a halter tied around his neck, were being dragged along, their hands pinioned, their feet bare and bloodied on the rough road. One was naked to the waist, the other had had his shirt almost ripped from his back.

Ferguson said, 'One of the mounted men, sir. He looks well dressed.'

Bolitho had already noted that. A heavy, bearded man with a fine hat and a cloak lined with scarlet. If anything he was inciting the mob, his words lost in distance.

Allday said, 'Maybe they've caught a pair of thieves, Cap'n.' He glanced back up the hill as if still expecting to see the gibbet with its ragged skeleton.

Bolitho snapped, 'Drive on!' He looked at Allday and saw his anxiety. 'Those two *thieves* are wearing sea-officers' breeches.'

Ferguson protested, 'But, sir! That may be nothing to do with it!'

Bolitho looked steadily at Old Matthew. 'When you are ready.'

The carriage rolled on to the road again. Even above the rattle of wheels and hooves Bolitho could hear the rising din of angry voices as they bore down on the procession.

'Whoa, there!' Old Matthew's voice was harsh with anger. 'Yew stand away from those horses, yew buggers!' Then the carriage halted.

Bolitho stepped down on to the road, aware of the sudden silence, the staring faces, many flushed with drink, others gaping as if he had just appeared from hell.

He could feel Ferguson watching from the carriage window, his pistol just out of sight. Allday too, measuring the distance to jump to the ground. By then it might be too late.

It was Young Matthew who unknowingly broke the spell. He ran from behind the carriage to help quieten the lead horses. It was as if the mob did not exist.

The mounted man with the beard spurred his horse through the watching figures.

'What have we here, sir? A King's officer, no less.' He made a mock bow in the saddle. 'On his way to take charge of a fine ship at Chatham, no doubt! To protect us all from the Frenchies, eh, lads!'

There was some derisive laughter, but many of them were studying Bolitho more closely, as if they expected a trap of some kind.

Bolitho said shortly, 'And what are *you* about, sir?' His hand dropped to his sword. 'I'll not be asking twice!'

The bearded man stared past him. Looking for an escort? It was hard to tell.

But he grinned confidently as he replied, 'I am the deputy sheriff of Rochester, *Captain*.'

'That is something. Now we know each other's rank.'

At that moment one of the captives threw himself to his knees and almost choked as someone dragged hard on the halter.

Bolitho recognised just one word. *Lieutenant*. It was enough.

'I would suggest you release these men at once. They are both sea-officers in the King's service.'

He saw the significance of his words sink in, the way that some of the mob were attempting to drift away and dissociate themselves from the incident.

But the bearded man yelled, 'And be damned to them *and* their bloody press gang, I say!' He stared around and showed his teeth as a few men shouted in support.

Like baying hounds at the kill, Bolitho thought.

He repeated, 'Remove their ropes.' He nodded to Young Matthew. 'Do it, boy.' He turned towards the deputy sheriff. 'And you, sir, will dismount. *Now*.'

The half-naked lieutenant, his face and body cut and bruised from several blows, staggered to his feet.

'They *attacked* us, sir.' He was almost incoherent. His companion was much younger, a midshipman probably. One sign of panic now, and the rioters might rush them. They would be swamped.

Bolitho watched the bearded man dismount. 'Where are their uniforms?'

He stared at Bolitho, then burst out laughing. 'You are a cool one, Captain – I'll give you that, for what it's worth!' His mood changed. 'They came without asking consent from the mayor. We taught them a lesson.' He tried to meet Bolitho's gaze and added thickly, 'They'll not forget it!'

Bolitho waited. 'Their uniforms?'

The man looked up at his mounted companion. 'Tell him, Jack.'

The other man shifted uneasily in his saddle. 'We threw 'em into a pigpen.' Nobody was laughing or jeering now.

14

Bolitho removed his hat and tossed it into the carriage.

'They are *King's* officers, sir.'

'I know that, damn it. We were just doing it –'

'Then I suggest you insulted the King.'

'*What?*' The deputy sheriff's eyes were bulging beneath his hat.

'You may take your choice. Draw that fine sword you wear so bravely.' He touched the old hilt at his side. 'I think this may be a good place for it.' His voice hardened. 'Nothing to say? No words for your courageous mob?'

A mist seemed to swirl across his eyes and for a moment he thought the fever had returned. Then he realised what it was. The same madness he had felt in the past when a battle had seemed hopeless and all but lost.

He had wanted to bluff this arrogant bully. Now he actually wanted him to take up the challenge, merely for the satisfaction of killing him. All the weeks of frustration, the anger and bitterness which had tested him throughout the months of despair, the waiting and pleading at the Admiralty, seemed to be joining in one terrible, vindictive force.

'I – I ask your pardon, Captain.' It was almost a whisper.

Bolitho eyed him with contempt. 'I do not pardon cowards.' He glanced at the two shivering victims who had probably believed they were about to be hanged. 'Get into the coach, gentlemen.'

He turned once more to the deputy sheriff. 'Your sword.' He took it from him. The man seemed twice his size and yet his hand was shaking as if with a palsy.

Even now the crowd might regain its temper. But something had cooled them – the sight of his uniform, or the knowledge of their own guilt? He would never know. He drove the splendid blade beneath the rear box of the carriage, then leaned on it until it snapped like a carrot. Then he tossed it at the man's feet.

'Cowards have no use for fine steel, sir. Now be off with you.'

The crowd parted and seemed to fade into the fields on either side of the road.

Bolitho climbed on to the step and looked up at his coachman. 'A brave lad you have there, Matthew!'

Corker wiped his brow with a red handkerchief.

'By God, Cap'n, yew 'ad me fair scared just then!'

Allday gently eased the hammer of his blunderbuss.

'You've made a bad enemy, Cap'n, an' that's no error.'

Bolitho closed the door and said, 'And so, by God, has he!'

Then, as the carriage gathered speed, he folded his arms and asked the rescued men gently, 'Now tell me in your own time what happened.'

As they spoke he had to clutch his arms tightly to his body to prevent them from shaking. It had been a near thing, although right from the beginning he had known instinctively that on such a deserted road the incident had been carefully planned for his benefit.

He smiled at his reflection in the rain-streaked glass. They had not been prepared for his reaction. *And neither was I.*

Ferguson saw the brief smile. For a few moments he had imagined everything was about to end. Now he saw that it was, for Bolitho, a beginning.

2

Trust

Captain Richard Bolitho stood with his shoes sinking into the wet sand of a sloping foreshore and stared across the widening stretch of the River Medway. The sun was hard and bright, so that the trees on the opposite bank were almost lost in steaming haze. But it was without warmth, although to look at it was like being reminded of a tropical shore elsewhere. He moved his shoulders inside his coat and wondered if he would ever feel warm again. Even the breeze from the river was cool and damp.

He tried to push the thought aside. It was a typical spring day; he had to keep remembering that. *He* was the one at fault with his memory forever rooted in another place, another time.

Allday, standing a little apart and a few paces behind him on the slope, remarked casually, 'Well, Cap'n, there's one of your brood right enough.' He waited, gauging the mood as he had since their arrival here.

Bolitho nodded and shaded his eyes to study the little ship which lay above her own reflection beyond an islet and two shining sandbars. A topsail cutter, *Telemachus*, the one which had been undergoing a refit in the dockyard upriver from here.

Bolitho looked at her spartan outline, a vessel so different when under full sail. It was hard to realise that these cutters, so small after a frigate, had for their size a bigger sail area than any other craft afloat. They might not be able to outrun all the rest, but in any sort of wind they could outmanoeuvre anything.

One of his brood. Allday, in spite of his forced casualness,

17

must know what he was thinking. Comparing her with *Tempest*, the Great South Sea, everything. Without effort he could picture the three tall pyramids of pale, fair-weather canvas, reaching up to the cloudless blue sky. The deck seams sticking to your shoes as you moved about in search of a shadow while the horizon lay sharp and empty in all directions. A *real ship*. A thoroughbred. Yes, Allday would know and feel it too.

Bolitho had reported his arrival to the admiral in command at the Royal Dockyard, a distant but affable man, who had seemed to regard the affair on the road with the two bound and humiliated officers as little more than an irritation.

He had said, 'The midshipman – well, he knew less than nothing, but the lieutenant in charge should have known better than to search premises and arrest suspected deserters without first informing the local authorities. I shall make my displeasure felt, of course, and I dare say that someone might be made to pay a fine, but –' He did not need to continue.

Bolitho had persisted, 'I am told that the same thing happened at Rochester last year, sir. Then it was no less than the mayor who led a mob to attack the guardhouse where some pressed men were awaiting an escort.'

The admiral had frowned. 'That's true. The devil even fined our officers heavily before he would release them.' He had become angry. 'But they'll sing a different tune when the Frogs are on the rampage again. It will be *good old Jack Tar* then, sure enough, when these self-righteous hypocrites think that their rotten skins are in danger once more and they whimper for sailors to defend them!'

Bolitho had not yet met Commodore Hoblyn. The admiral had explained that he was visiting some local shipyards with a view to the Admiralty's purchasing small, handy craft, in the event of war. The admiral had commented wryly, 'With letters of marque no doubt, to enlist a few more cutthroats for the King!'

Bolitho had left the admiral's house, his final words still in his ears. *'Don't take it so to heart, Bolitho. You have three fine cutters at your command. Use them as you will, within the scope of your orders.'*

It was strange, Bolitho thought, that in the two days since his

18

arrival here he had sensed more than once that every move he made was being watched. More so perhaps because of the efforts some had made to look away when he had passed. Which was why he had sent his carriage with a protesting Ferguson back to Falmouth. He had even arranged for the local dragoons to provide a small escort until they were out of Kent and on the road to London and beyond.

Bolitho looked down the slope again and saw the boy, Young Matthew, peering at the anchored cutter, barely able to stand still with his excitement.

That had been almost the hardest part, he thought. The boy had pleaded with his grandfather to be allowed to go with Bolitho as a servant, a groom, anything.

The old coachman had blown his nose and had said eventually, 'Well, sir, 'e's more trouble underfoot than 'e knows. Mebbee a bit o' time with some discipline will tame the little puppy!' But his eyes had told another story, and his voice had been as heavy as his heart.

Allday murmured, 'I'll go an' hail the vessel, Cap'n.'

'Aye, do that.' He watched Allday stride down the slope to join the boy at the water's edge. *Probably thinks I'm imagining all of it.* It was why Bolitho had asked for a carriage to bring him here, instead of joining the *Telemachus* in the dockyard. They knew too much already. He needed a few surprises of his own.

The other two cutters, named *Wakeful* and *Snapdragon*, were already lying downriver towards Sheerness, where the Medway surged out into the great estuary with the Thames.

Small ships perhaps, but each one a private world like every vessel in the fleet.

He shaded his eyes again. *Telemachus* was just a few inches short of seventy feet but had the surprisingly ample beam of twenty-four feet. Sturdily built with a rounded bow, the after part narrowed down to a typical mackerel-tail shape. How she shone above her own image, the cat's-paws rippling down her side, more like a toy than a ship-of-war. The sunlight played on her buff hull with its single, broad black wale below the gunports. But it was always the rig which took a sailor's attention, he decided. A single, large mainmast mounted forward of

19

midships, made even taller by a tapering fidded topmast. She had a long, horizontal bowsprit and a boom to carry the huge loose-footed mainsail which protruded well beyond her low counter. With all her canvas furled or brailed up to the topsail yard she looked unfinished. But once at sea . . .

Bolitho sighed. Enthusiasm, like warmth to his body, defied him.

Allday's powerful voice echoed across the water, and after a few seconds some faces appeared at the *Telemachus*'s bulwark. Bolitho wondered what the cutter's commander must think of this unorthodox arrival.

He saw a jolly-boat appear around the stern, the oars taking charge as a deceptively slow current carried them clear of the hull. There were already many more people on deck now. *A visitor, a break in the monotony.*

A fraction under seventy feet and yet she carried a complement of sixty souls. It was hard to accept that they could cram themselves into that hull and share it with guns, powder, shot and stores enough to sustain them, and still find room to breathe.

He saw Allday watching the jolly-boat with a critical eye.

'Well?'

Allday shrugged one massive shoulder. '*Looks* smart enough. Still –'

Then he glanced at the boy beside him and grinned. 'Like a dog with two tails, he is.'

'Can't think why. A safe bed, with nothing fiercer than horses to meet each day. In exchange for this –' He gestured towards the river and the other anchored men-of-war. 'It might help him to make up his mind, I suppose.' He sounded bitter.

Allday looked away. What was the point of piping up and offering an argument? Young Matthew worshipped Bolitho, just as his father had done after he had obtained a berth for him in the packet company. He shook his head. Later on perhaps. But right now the captain was all aback. Maybe they had only half-won the battle after all.

The boat lurched alongside a waterlogged piece of slipway and a young lieutenant splashed up towards Bolitho, his face astonished and full of apology.

He doffed his hat and stammered, 'Lieutenant Triscott, sir. I am the senior in *Telemachus*.' He stared round in disbelief. 'I – I had no idea that you were expected, sir, otherwise –'

Bolitho touched his arm. '*Otherwise*, Mr Triscott, you would have borrowed the admiral's barge and been planning a guard-of-honour for the occasion, am I right?' He looked again at the river. 'This way is better.' He gestured to the road. 'There is a chest yonder. Be so good as to have it brought over.'

The lieutenant stared at him blankly. 'You are staying aboard, sir?'

'It was my intention.' Bolitho's grey eyes settled on him and he added gently, 'If you have no objection, that is?'

Allday hid a grin. Mr Triscott was the senior. He had refrained from mentioning that apart from the commander he was the *only* commissioned lieutenant in the ship.

Bolitho watched the oars rising and falling, the way some of the seamen glanced quickly at him, then looked away when he saw them. Experienced, strong hands, every one.

He asked quietly, 'You have a good company, Mr Triscott?'

'Aye, sir. Most were volunteers. Fishermen and the like –' His voice trailed away.

Bolitho rested his chin on his sword hilt. Triscott was about nineteen at a guess. Another young hopeful, glad to serve in a lowly cutter rather than spend his most precious years on the beach.

He watched the tall, solitary mast rising to meet them. Well built, with her name in scrollwork across her counter. He noticed that a carved dolphin appeared to be supporting the name; a fine piece of craftsmanship, he thought.

Then he remembered. Telemachus, in legend, the son of Ulysses and Penelope, had been rescued from drowning by a dolphin.

The cutter might not be grand enough to warrant a proud figurehead in her bows, but the unknown carver had made certain she would be honoured all the same.

As they made for the chains Bolitho glanced at the closed ports. The sides were pierced for fourteen guns, originally only six-pounders, with a pair of swivels mounted aft by the tiller. But there were now two powerful carronades up forward, 'smashers' as the Jacks called them, a match for any vessel which drifted under their lee in a fight.

There was a bark of commands as the boat hooked on to the chains and Bolitho stood up to seize a small ladder. At any other time he would have smiled. Standing in the boat he was almost level with the entry port itself, where a tall lieutenant with a press of figures behind him waited to receive the post-captain.

Small fragments stood out like pieces of a partly cleaned painting. The lieutenant's grim expression, Allday rising from a thwart in case Bolitho should slip or feel suddenly faint. And the boy, Young Matthew Corker, with his round, open face shining with sheer pleasure at this moment when his fourteen years had suddenly changed.

Calls shrilled and then Bolitho found himself on deck. As he raised his hat towards the narrow poop where the White Ensign streamed out to a lively breeze, he said shortly, 'I am sorry for this lack of warning.'

Lieutenant Jonas Paice bit back a retort and said gruffly, 'I thought, sir, that is –'

He was a powerful man in every way. Bolitho knew the essentials about him. Paice was old for his rank, perhaps two years younger than himself, but had once commanded a collier-brig out of Sunderland before entering the King's service as a master's mate. It would be sufficient to begin with. Later, Bolitho intended to know the man behind every face in his small flotilla of three cutters.

'You imagined I might be spying on you.'

Paice stared at him as if he could scarcely believe it. 'I did think that you intended to take us unawares, sir.'

'I am glad to hear it.' Bolitho glanced over and beyond the silent figures. 'The flag stands out well from Beacon Hill, Captain. May I suggest you up-anchor and get under way without fuss.' He gave a slight smile. 'I can assure you I will attempt not to get under your feet.'

Paice tried again. 'You'll find this somewhat different from a fifth-rate, sir. A wild animal if she's not handled to her liking.'

Bolitho eyed him calmly. 'I served in a cutter years ago. The *Avenger*. She was commanded by my brother.'

22

A few seconds and he saw it all. The sudden prick of memory, the mention of his brother. Something like relief too. As if Paice was glad to know, or think he knew, why Bolitho had been given this humble appointment. Perhaps it was even true. Dead or not, Hugh had made too many enemies to be forgotten, or his family forgiven.

He looked forward along the deck again. It was full of people. They probably resented his arrival. He said, 'We will join *Wakeful* and *Snapdragon* without delay.'

Paice stared at Allday and then at the boy as if he could still not accept what was happening.

'But, sir, don't you need any others to assist you?'

Bolitho watched some gulls rising to circle lazily around the mainmast truck, their wings straight and motionless.

'I have all I need, thank you.' He grimaced at Allday. 'I fear the first lesson has begun.'

They all stared at Young Matthew. In those few minutes his face had changed to a startling green.

Paice cupped his hands. 'Man the capstan! Prepare to break out the anchor! Mr Hawkins, hands aloft, loose tops'l!'

Bolitho walked aft as the crowded figures surged into a new and ordered pattern. He half-listened to the squeal of blocks as men hauled on halliards and braces, while from the capstan the stamp of bare feet, accompanied by the groan of incoming cable, seemed to rouse him from a deep sleep.

Like hearing the sea calling to him without pain or mockery. He removed his hat and felt his hair ruffle in the damp air.

He recalled Rear-Admiral Drew's dry comment: '*Were* a frigate captain.'

A last show of pride would have cost him even this. He would still be haunting the corridors of the Admiralty, or returning beaten and sick to the grey house at Falmouth.

Allday said, 'I'll show you to the cabin, Cap'n.' He chuckled. 'Falmouth rabbits have more room!'

He watched as Bolitho groped his way to the small companion ladder near the tiller, beside which a master's mate and two helmsmen were already pointedly at their stations.

Once at sea things might seem better, he thought.

Allday heard the boy's desperate retching and hurried to find him. Once he paused, his chin just level with the deck coaming, and watched the land sway over as the anchor tore free from the ground.

Sails banged and thundered in confusion and he saw the great shadow of the boomed mainsail slice overhead like a banner.

They had done with the land. This was their place. It was enough.

Allday tapped on the cabin door and had to bend almost double to peer inside. He saw Bolitho with his back to the bulkhead, the three commanding officers of the anchored cutters packed in around the table as best they could.

'All secure, Cap'n.' Just a brief exchange of glances, but Bolitho understood that he would be outside the door and make sure that nobody should hear what he was not intended to. Allday knew from experience. Little ships had the biggest ears, and Bolitho needed his first meeting to be undisturbed.

Before he withdrew, Allday also noticed that Bolitho was wearing his old seagoing coat, with its tarnished buttons, displaying no epaulettes on the shoulders. A coat stitched and repaired so many times that, when his sister Nancy had held it up with dismay and tried to persuade him to get rid of it, Allday had realised just how close he had become to the family.

Nancy had been helping to pack two chests for Bolitho's journey to London to plead for an appointment. During the long illness which they had shared in their various ways Allday had stood firm, knowing it was his strength which Bolitho depended on. But the mention of the coat, such a simple thing, had broken his defences, taken him by surprise like boarders in the night.

'No, Miss Nancy! Leave it be!' Then in a defeated voice, his eyes downcast, he had explained, 'It was what the Captain's Lady wore in the boat, afore she –' He had been unable to go on.

Get rid of that coat? It would have to fall apart first.

The door closed and Bolitho glanced around at their various expressions.

On the short passage to this anchorage he had spoken to Paice as much as he could without interfering with his duties of ship-handling. A tall, powerful figure, but one who rarely raised his voice when passing commands. He did not seem to need it. The combined wardroom and cabin had no headroom at all, and only directly beneath the skylight was it possible to stand upright. But Paice had to stoop even there.

He was an excellent seaman, with a master's eye for wind and current. He seemed to *feel* the moods of his sturdy command even before the helmsmen who stood on either side of the long tiller bar. But he was slow to answer questions; not resentful, more defensive. As if he searched for any possible criticism, not of himself but of his *Telemachus*.

It was a perfect evening after all. Pink clouds as dusk moved across the headland which sheltered the anchorage, with the first lamps already glittering like fireflies from the homes of Queenborough.

The three cutters might look as alike as peas in a pod to any watching landsmen, but Bolitho had already marked their small differences, no more apparent than right here with their commanders. Lieutenant Charles Queely of the *Wakeful* was in his mid-twenties, a dark-haired man with a hooked nose and deepset eyes, ever-alert like a falcon. The face of a scholar, a clergyman perhaps; only his speech and dress marked him as a sea-officer. He hailed from the Isle of Man, and came of generations of deepwater sailormen. Lieutenant Hector Vatass of the *Snapdragon* was a direct contrast. Fair-haired, with a homely face and blue eyes which would deceive no one. An English sailor from almost any century. He was twenty-five, and had served originally in a frigate until she was paid off.

Bolitho said, 'Please light up your pipes if you wish; I am sure that *Telemachus* has a good store of tobacco!' They smiled politely but nobody moved. It was too soon for confidences.

Bolitho said, '*Snapdragon* will be entering the dockyard in a few days.'

He saw Vatass start with surprise. 'Er – yes, sir.'

'Make the most of it. It seems likely that overhauls will soon be a thing of the past, and I need – no, I *want* this flotilla to be ready for anything.'

Vatass prompted carefully, 'Will it be war, sir?'

Before Bolitho could answer, Queely snapped disdainfully, 'Never! The Frogs have their King and Queen in jail, but they'll let them out soon enough when their bloody-minded National Convention realise they need them!'

Bolitho said, 'I disagree. I believe there *will* be war, and very soon. Ready or not, it is not unknown for a country to provoke a conflict if only to cover its own failings.' His tone hardened. 'And England is even less prepared!'

Paice folded his arms. 'But where do we come into this, sir? We carry out patrols, stop and search some homebound vessels, and occasionally find deserters amongst their people. We also offer support to the revenue vessels when asked –'

Queely showed his teeth in a grin. 'Which ain't too often!'

Paice glanced at the sealed skylight. 'It's a mite hot, sir. Could I –'

Bolitho smiled. 'I think not. I need to speak without others lending their attention.'

He saw Paice's immediate, defensive frown and added bluntly, 'We can trust nobody. Even the most loyal seaman would be hard put to resist a few pieces of gold for what he might see as harmless information.'

Vatass said vaguely, 'But what *do* we know, sir?'

Bolitho looked at each face in turn. 'Smuggling is rife here, and on the Isle of Thanet in particular. From the Nore to the Downs the trade is barely checked, and there are insufficient revenue vessels to hunt them down.' He placed his hand flat on the table and added, 'From what I have seen and heard already, I am certain that smuggling is condoned, even aided, by some in authority. The lieutenant who was stripped and beaten when I found him on the London Road did not obey the letter of his orders. He *should* have applied for permission from the town before he raided houses and recaptured deserters, men who bad or not are desperately needed in the fleet.' He saw his words sinking in. 'Why did he not ask? Why instead did the young lieutenant choose to ignore his orders?' His hand rose and fell with a slap. 'He knew that the very authority he looked to would probably warn or offer refuge to the deserters. I have no doubt that there are many such prime seamen earning their keep in the Trade as we sit right here.'

Queely cleared his throat. 'With respect, sir, we have tried in the past to seek out smugglers. Perhaps, and I mean no offence for I know you to be a gallant officer, being away for so long in the Indies and the Great South Sea, you have –' He hesitated as Bolitho's eyes settled on his.

Bolitho smiled grimly. 'Lost touch? Is that what you meant?'

Paice said in his gruff voice, 'I hate the scum too, sir. But we are so few against so many, and now that you have spoken out, I'll say my piece if I may.'

Bolitho nodded. Their guard was down. He had spoken to them like companions, not as a senior officer to his subordinates. Low in rank maybe, but they were all captains, and had the right to be heard.

Paice said bluntly, 'It's as Charles Queely says.' He gave what might have been a cautious smile. 'You being a Cornishman, sir, will know a lot about the Trade and those who live by it. But with respect, it's nothing compared to this coast. And as you said, sir, it seems that there are more who commit these crimes outside the jails than in them!' The others nodded in agreement.

Vatass said, 'The revenue officers are often outnumbered, and outgunned by the smugglers. Many of their captains are loath to work close inshore for fear of being wrecked and overrun, and ashore their riding-officers risk their lives when there is a big haul being unloaded. They strike terror into anyone who raises a hand against them. Informers are butchered like pigs. Even revenue men are not safe any more.'

Bolitho asked, 'What information do we receive?'

Paice said, 'The coastguard help, so too the revenue officers *if* they get enough time.'

Bolitho stood up and banged his head sharply on a beam. He looked at Paice and gave a rueful smile. 'You are right. Quite different from a fifth-rate!' This time they all laughed.

It was a small beginning. He said, 'It takes too long. They hold all the advantages. Send for dragoons, and the beach will have been emptied by the time a courier is able to raise the alarm.'

Queely murmured angrily, '*If* the poor devil gets through without having his throat slit!'

Paice said, 'And the buggers watch us at anchor, sir. Out there at this moment there'll be one of them, a fast horse nearby. We'd need fifty cutters and even then –'

Bolitho stood up again to lift one panel of the skylight and felt the salt air on his lips.

'Then we will mark them down at sea, gentlemen. It may stir up a hornet's nest, but we shall have results. The more trouble we can make for them, the less interference we shall get with our work. We are ordered to obtain men for the fleet. That we shall do.' His eyes flashed in the reflected sunset. 'The navy has never taken second place to pirates. I see these smugglers as no different. We will press or prosecute, but first we will try a little action of our own.'

He rapped on the door and eventually Young Matthew bowed into the cabin with a tray of goblets and wine.

Bolitho looked at Paice. 'Some wine from my home in Falmouth, *not* smuggled, I trust!' *Telemachus* was after all Paice's command; it would be seen as high-handed to offer drinks when he was only a guest here. He glanced at the boy and saw that his face was almost back to normal, his cheeks like Devon apples again. But his gaze was glassy, and he had not been seen at all on the passage downriver. One of Allday's sworn-by remedies no doubt. A ship's biscuit ground up to a powder and soaked under a powerful measure of rum. Kill or cure, Allday claimed. Young Matthew was learning more every hour of the day.

Bolitho said, 'I can rely on all of you to share this discussion with no one. When the time is ripe, we will hit them.'

He lifted his goblet and thought he heard Allday leaning against the door.

'I give you a sentiment, gentlemen. To those across the Channel who are suffering terror which is not of their making, and to our three ships!' He saw Queely's surprised glance.

But they drank deeply, the air touched with rum as the boy refilled the goblets.

The wine was hock, chilled like a Cornish stream in the bilges. Young Matthew had often helped at table under Mrs Ferguson's watchful eye; he was proving that he had forgotten nothing.

28

Bolitho raised his goblet again and said simply, 'To His Majesty. Damnation to all his enemies!'

That night, while *Telemachus* swung easily to her anchor cable, Bolitho, cramped though he was in a small cot like any junior lieutenant, slept for the first time without the dream's torment. Near the cot, lying on a chest, was his old coat, the watch she had given him tucked carefully into a pocket.

A reminder, that with her memory he could never be alone.

3

Decoy

Lieutenant Jonas Paice stood with his legs spread while he watched *Telemachus*'s long running bowsprit as it lifted, then lunged forward again like a lance. It was as if the cutter was taking on the endless ranks of short, steep waves in personal combat.

The sky overhead was streaked with tattered clouds, all hurrying before a strong north-easterly breeze which felt more like autumn than spring.

It would soon be dusk. Paice shifted his position but barely staggered as his command heeled even further over, her huge mainsail, like the jib and foresail, set tightly almost fore-and-aft as she butted up to windward. How she could sail, he thought, and to confirm his appreciation the helmsman yelled, 'Full an' bye, sir! Nor' by West!' But for once the pleasure of sailing so close to the wind failed to sustain him. This was the third day of it, beating back and forth in a great triangle above the approaches to the north-east foreland of Kent.

Perhaps he should have held his tongue and waited for Captain Bolitho to grow tired of hunting smugglers and turn to a easier life in some shore-based headquarters like the commodore. Paice had received news from an old and trusted informant that there was to be a 'run', somewhere along the shores of Deal, either last night or tonight. He had been surprised at Bolitho's interest and immediate reaction. He had sent *Telemachus* to sea, while he himself had sailed in Queely's *Wakeful*. Then at a pre-arranged rendezvous Bolitho had changed back to Paice's own command.

Bolitho was down below now studying the chart, comparing his notes with the ship's log. Like a man being driven to the limit, Paice thought. He heard the acting-master, Erasmus Chesshyre, giving some instructions to the two helmsmen, then his slithering footsteps as he joined him at the bulwark.

Together they watched the grey-green sea lifting almost to the rail, spurts of spray coming through the sealed gunports as she heeled right over to the wind.

Chesshyre was a master's mate, with one other to assist him. But his skill had distinguished him long ago, and with luck he would soon be promoted to sailing-master. And if there was to be war, he would be snatched away from *Telemachus* to watch over the sailing and pilotage of some lively frigate.

Paice frowned. If Bolitho failed to recover more deserters or find more men for the fleet, the cutters would be the first to lose their people. It was unfair, just as it was unavoidable. The cutters were like a navy within a navy. Their companies were mostly volunteers from inlets and villages where the fishing had died out, and skilled seamen had turned to the navy for work. Many of the men had known each other before signing on, so that discipline rarely needed harshness, and the qualities of leadership were respected far more than gold lace.

Chesshyre gauged his moment. 'After tonight, sir –'

Paice turned towards him. 'We shall continue until ordered otherwise.'

Chesshyre nodded glumly. 'Aye, aye, sir.'

The deck fell beneath them and a deluge of spray from high over the side swamped the waterlogged jolly-boat which had been double-lashed at the beginning of the watch. Astern, far across the taffrail, was the Kentish coast, but it was completely shrouded in mist and spindrift and when night came it would be as black as a boot.

Paice urged, 'Look at the weather, man. Do you not see it?'

Chesshyre shrugged, unconvinced. 'I know, sir. A perfect night for a run. But out here we could ride past the buggers.'

'Aye.' Paice thought of Bolitho's elaborate care to disguise their movements, even changing ships so that any observer on the shore might pass the word that *Wakeful* was the cutter to be watched. He thought of young Vatass in *Snapdragon*, snug in the dockyard by now. He was well out of it.

Paice glanced around at the stooping figures of his men. Every one a seasoned sailor who did not have to be told when to splice a piece of frayed cordage, or take another turn on a halliard. They were even trusted to go ashore on the rare occasions when *Telemachus* was resting in harbour. That was more than could be said for most of their grander consorts in peace *or* war.

He squinted up at the topsail yard where two lookouts clung like bedraggled monkeys, the spray running from their bodies like rain. With her topsail tightly furled while she surged and lifted into the teeth of the wind, *Telemachus* stood a fair chance of seeing another vessel before she was sighted herself.

They had barely sighted anything since putting to sea. It was as if local traders and the merchantmen from the Channel were unwilling to move any distance without the visible presence of a man-of-war. Across the water France lay like a mad beast, resting one moment, spitting blood the next. There were few honest seafarers prepared to run afoul of that.

Chesshyre persisted, 'Everybody knows about the Trade in Kent, sir.' He faltered as Paice's eyes fastened on him and he could have bitten out his tongue for speaking.

When he had first joined *Telemachus* he had wondered why the master of a collier-brig, to all intents a free agent, would choose to enlist in the navy as a lowly master's mate. When Chesshyre had been accepted by *Telemachus*'s tight little company he had slowly learned the truth about this tall, powerful lieutenant.

Paice had been married a short time to a girl he had known for several years. On her way home from visiting her father and mother she had been horrified to see a dozen or more known smugglers attacking a solitary revenue officer. A crowd of people, too afraid or too indifferent to interfere, had watched them beating the man to death. Paice's wife had called the onlookers to assist, and when they had hung back she had tried to drag one of the smugglers off the revenue officer who was by then dead.

32

One smuggler had raised his pistol and shot her down. A savage warning to all those who watched, far more chilling than the death of a revenue man.

'I – I'm fair sorry, sir.' Chesshyre looked away. 'I was forgetting –'

'Well, *don't*! Not now – not ever, while you serve in my ship!'

There was a step on the companion ladder and Bolitho climbed up beside them. He was hatless, and his black hair rippled in the wind as he studied the hard press of canvas, the sea boiling along the lee-side. Like his brother's cutter *Avenger*, so long, long ago.

The acting-master touched his forehead. 'I'll attend the helm, sir.'

He made to move aft but Bolitho asked, 'You are from Kent?'

'Aye, sir.' Chesshyre watched him warily, Paice's heated outburst momentarily forgotten. 'Maidstone, sir.'

Bolitho nodded. His voice, the easy Kentish accent, had so reminded him of Thomas Herrick, who had been his first lieutenant; his firm friend. Even Chesshyre's eyes, clear blue, were much the same. So many times he had watched Herrick's eyes change. Stubbornness, concern, hurt; and Bolitho had been the cause of most of it. They had parted when *Tempest* had set sail for England after that last savage battle with Tuke's ships. Bolitho, half-dead from fever, had followed at a more leisurely pace in a big Indiaman. Where was Herrick now, he wondered? At sea somewhere. Remembering what they had done and suffered together.

He realised that he was staring at the acting-master. 'You reminded me of a friend. Did you ever meet a Lieutenant Herrick?'

For a brief moment Bolitho saw the man's caution change to warmth. Then he shook his head. 'No, sir.' The contact was broken.

Paice said, 'We can come about in two hours, sir.' He glanced at the sky. 'After that, it will be too dark to see anything.'

Bolitho glanced at his strong profile. 'You think me mistaken?' He did not wait for a reply; it was wrong to make Paice commit himself. He smiled tightly. 'Mad too, probably.'

33

Paice watched him although his mind was still grappling with his inner pain. Would he ever forget how she had died?

He said, 'There are some who may ask why you care so much, sir.'

Bolitho wiped his face with the sleeve of his old coat. 'I realise that smuggling is a great temptation and will remain so. You can hang for it, but in some parishes you can dangle from the gibbet for stealing a chicken, so where's the comparison?' He shivered as spray pattered against his shoulders. 'The navy must have men. Smugglers or not, a firm hand will soon break them to our ways!'

During his brief passage in *Wakeful* her commander with the falcon's features had told him about Paice's wife. Bolitho had heard Paice's voice as he had left the cabin, but had only guessed the content.

He said, 'Like me, you grieve. Some think it leaves you vulnerable.' He gripped a swivel gun on the bulwark as the deck slanted down again and added sharply, 'But I believe it makes you – care, as you put it.'

Paice swallowed hard. It was like being stripped and made defenceless. How did he know? What memory did *he* carry to distress him?

He said gruffly, 'Never fear, sir, I'm with you –'

Bolitho touched his arm and turned away. He seemed to hear the admiral's words in his brain. *Use them as you will within the scope of your orders.* Spoken words, not written ones. Valueless if things went wrong.

He said, 'You may live to regret that, Mr Paice, but I thank you.'

Allday appeared from the companionway, a tankard held carefully in one fist while he waited for the deck to rear upright again.

He held it out to Bolitho, his eyes swiftly examining the men nearby, Chesshyre the master, with his mate Dench who was shortly taking over the watch. Luke Hawkins the boatswain, a great cask of a man. It was hard to see him at the tender age of seven when he had been packed off to sea as a ship's boy. *Telemachus* carried no purser as she did not rate one. The clerk,

Percivale Godsalve, a reedy little man whose pale features had defied all the months at sea, did duty as purser too. Evans, a tough gunner's mate, had said to Allday, 'No passengers in this ship, matey! We all does a bit of everythin'!'

Allday knew most of what was said about Bolitho being aboard. They saw him as a threat, something from the *other navy* that only a few of the petty officers knew anything about.

Deep in his heart Allday thought Bolitho, a man he had nearly died for and would do so again without a second's thought, was wrong to press on with this task. He should take things quietly — hell's teeth, he had earned it ten times over. Let others take the risks and the blame, which, unlike prize money, were equally shared out.

Allday would never have returned to the sea but for Bolitho. But Bolitho loved the navy; it was his whole life. Only once had Allday seen that love waver, but now the Captain's lady was gone. Only the sea was left.

He watched Bolitho swallow the steaming coffee gratefully. They had seen so much. Allday stared out at the frothing yellow wave crests. They'd get another ship together. If only . . .

'Deck there! *Sail ho!*'

Paice stared up at the two waving lookouts, his face creased with disbelief.

The voice pealed down again. 'Fine on the lee quarter, sir!'

Bolitho saw the instant change in the tall lieutenant as he snatched a telescope from its rack and swung himself on to the weather ratlines with the agility of a cat.

Bolitho tried to contain the shiver of excitement as it coursed through him like icy water.

It was probably nothing, or a ship, alone and running for shelter before darkness closed in. The Channel was a treacherous place on any night, but in these times it was a blessing to hear the anchor safely down.

Bolitho recalled his own desperate efforts to go aloft without the awful fear of it. Many were the times he had had to force himself up the madly shaking ratlines, clinging to a stay and trying not to peer down at the deck and the creaming water far below.

Paice had no such qualms. But he was soon clambering on to the deck again, and his face, masklike in the dying sunlight, was composed by the time he had strode aft.

He said, 'She's the *Loyal Chieftain*, sir. A Deal vessel. Know her well.' He spat out the words. '*Loyal* – the last word I'd use for that pig!'

There was no time for further discussion. At any moment the other vessel would see *Telemachus*'s sails.

Bolitho said, 'Bring her about, Mr Paice. As fast as you will.'

'Hands aloft and loose tops'l!'

'Stand by to come about!'

Feet padded over the streaming planks, and more figures crowded up from between decks as the calls shrilled through the hull.

'Let go an' haul!' Hawkins's thick voice made the men lie back on the braces and halliards to bring the boom over.

'*Helm a-lee!*'

Bolitho gripped a stanchion and watched the sails flapping like insane banners as the rudder was heaved over, the helmsmen backed up by two more hands as the ship fought against sea and wind. Then all at once they were round, and running with the breakers, the spray bursting beneath the stem so that they seemed to be flying.

Paice mopped his face and shouted above the thunder of more canvas as the topsail filled and hardened from its yard like a breastplate. ''Nother minute and the bugger would have slipped across our stern!' He saw Bolitho's expression and said, 'Her master is Henry Delaval, a known smuggler, but he's never been taken with any evidence, God rot him! His vessel's a brig, well found and armed.' Here was the bitterness again. 'That's no crime either, *they* say!'

'There she is, sir, larboard bow!' It was Lieutenant Triscott, who had been preparing to take over the watch, and had run on deck with some butter and crumbs sticking to his lapel.

Paice thrust his big hands behind him. His eyes spoke volumes, but all he said was, '*Got you!*'

Bolitho wedged his hip against the companion hatch in an attempt to keep steady enough to train a telescope on the other vessel.

Above the leaping wave crests, broken here and there into ragged spectres by stronger gusts of wind, he saw the brig's topsails, now copper-coloured against the evening sky. Her hull was still hidden and he guessed that Paice had recognised her only after climbing aloft. Never before had he seen Paice show so much emotion, hatred even, and he guessed that the memory of his young wife was linked in some way with the man Delaval.

Hawkins bellowed, 'She's settin' 'er forecourse, sir!'

Bolitho nodded, oblivious to the spray which was soaking him from head to toe. The brig was using the wind to full advantage and was already standing away, her two masts seeming to draw closer together above the tumbling water.

Paice glanced at him, his eyes in shadow. 'Sir?' He could barely conceal his eagerness.

Bolitho lowered the glass. 'Aye, give chase.' He was about to add that the brig's master might have taken *Telemachus* for a French privateer, and was heading away to safety. But seeing Paice's intent expression killed the thought instantly. Paice knew this man, so Delaval would know him and his cutter equally well.

'Alter course, Mr Chesshyre! Let her bear up two points and steer South-West by West!'

As the men ran to braces to haul the long boom further out above the water, Dench the master's mate was already crouching by the compass box, his hair plastered to his forehead while the rudder went over.

One helmsman lost his footing on the tilting deck, but another took his place at the long tiller bar, his bare toes digging for a grip.

'Steady she goes, sir! Sou'-West by West!'

'Damn his eyes, he's making a run for it, Cap'n.' Allday seemed the calmest one on the deck as he watched the other vessel's blurred topsails with apparently little more than professional interest.

Bolitho knew him too well to be deceived. *Like me, perhaps?* Holding it all inside, showing just a mask to others who looked to you for hope or fear.

Paice heard Allday's comment and snapped, 'God, I'll not lose the bastard now!'

Bolitho said, 'Put a ball across her, Mr Paice.'

Paice looked at him, unused to anyone's methods but his own. 'We're supposed to fire well clear, sir, as a signal.'

Bolitho smiled briefly. 'As close as your gunner can arrange it. In a long chase we might lose her when the night finds us, eh?' From the corner of his eye he saw one of the seamen grinning and nudging his companion. Was it because they thought him mad, or because they were beginning to discover their true role as a man-of-war, albeit a small one?

George Davy the gunner supervised the foremost six-pounder personally, one horny hand on the gun-captain's shoulder while the crew worked with their handspikes and tackles until he seemed satisfied.

Paice cupped his hands. 'Load the larboard smasher as well, Mr Davy.'

Bolitho balled his hands into fists to discipline his shivering limbs. Paice was thinking for himself. If the brig was prepared to fight, even if she tried merely to cripple *Telemachus*'s rigging and sails, it was sensible to have the deadly carronade loaded and ready to rake her poop.

'*Fire!*'

Bolitho had been too long away from the sea, longer still from the harsh roar of a frigate's broadside; the crack of a six-pounder was sharp enough to bring pain to his ears.

Allday muttered, 'Bloody little popgun!'

Bolitho saw the boy Matthew Corker kneeling near the aftermost gun, his hands gripping a bucket of sand as he stared at the scene on deck where the six-pounder's crew were already tamping home another ball, each man very aware of the post-captain beside Paice.

Bolitho snapped, 'Keep down, boy!'

The youth peered up at him. No trace of fear. But it was because he knew nothing. Nor would he, Bolitho decided grimly.

There was far too much spray to see the fall of shot, but the angle of the *Loyal Chieftain*'s masts and topsails was unchanged, and she was moving fast with the soldier's wind right under her coat-tails.

Paice looked at Bolitho. 'Into her this time, if you please.'

The six-pounder hurled itself inboard on its tackles and as Bolitho lifted his glass he was in time to see the brig's main topsail jerk, then split from head to foot. The wind greedily explored the ball's puncture and reduced the whole sail to wildly flapping ribbons.

Someone gave a derisive cheer then Hawkins shouted, 'She's puttin' about, sir!'

Paice retorted, 'Even if she is heaving-to, Mr Triscott, I want her under our lee, do you understand?' Urgency had set an edge to his voice.

Bolitho stood aside as Paice strode this way and that, his tall frame moving with remarkable ease amongst his men and the litter of cordage and tackles.

'Load the larboard battery, Mr Triscott, but do not run out!' He pivoted round. 'Shorten sail, Mr Hawkins! Take in the fores'l!' His eyes moved across Bolitho and he exclaimed, 'If that suits, sir?'

The brig had taken in her forecourse, and under topsail and jib only was floundering round into the wind. She was much closer now, less than a cable away, her masts and rigging glowing warmly in the copper light.

There were not many hands on her yards, or indeed working about the deck. But she was under control, and as *Telemachus*'s gun-captains faced aft and held up their fists, Bolitho knew that the brig could be swept with grape and canister before she could hit back.

Paice loosened the hanger at his side and said, 'Lower the jolly-boat. Your best oarsmen, Mr Hawkins. It'll be a hard pull in this sea!'

Bolitho said, 'I would like to come with you.' Their eyes met and held. 'You *are* going yourself, I take it?'

Paice nodded. 'The first lieutenant can manage, sir.'

'It is not what I asked.'

Paice shrugged. 'It is my right, sir.'

'Very well.' He could feel the lieutenant's strength like something physical, barely controlled. He added, 'It were better I am present. For both our sakes, eh?'

The calmness of his tone seemed to stay Paice's emotion,

although Bolitho felt anything but calm. He knew that if this man Delaval was caught on board the brig with contraband Paice would likely kill him. Equally, as senior officer, he would be seen as having condoned a murder by a subordinate.

Bolitho watched the boat being swayed up and over the side. The brig's people might attack the boarders as soon as they climbed aboard and still make off in escape.

Bolitho said, 'Mr Triscott, if they attempt to make sail, fire into them.' His voice hardened. 'No matter what you may see.'

Triscott stared from him to his commander. He looked suddenly very young and vulnerable.

He stammered, 'Aye, aye, sir, if you so order.'

Paice said sharply, 'He does, and I am in agreement!'

The jolly-boat was manhandled alongside and once again Bolitho was impressed by the quality of the seamanship, the scarcity of spoken orders, let alone the use of a rope's end. He found himself wondering if all cutters were like this one. He glanced quickly at Paice as he scrambled down beside him in the sternsheets. Or was it just because of this impassive, haunted lieutenant?

'Out oars! Give way all!'

The sound of Allday's resonant voice brought a few stares from the boat's crew. But Allday had no intention of being left behind as a helpless onlooker. He was doing what he knew best. Nor would Bolitho deny him after all he had gone through.

The boat lifted and plunged wildly until Allday had steered her clear of the choppy water around the cutter's quarter. Bolitho saw the White Ensign streaming out from the gaff above his head and thought suddenly of Hugh, his dead brother. What a waste, and for no purpose. He turned to watch the brig's tapering topgallant masts spiralling against the sky and found that he was gripping the old sword closely against his thigh. Hugh had lost his chance to wear it, and now, perhaps within minutes, there would be no one left to carry it with pride. There were faces along the bulwark now, strangely silent, with no sign of defiance or fear.

Paice lifted a speaking trumpet. 'We are boarding! Do not resist!'

Allday said beneath his breath, 'It'll be now or never. They

40

could make a bloody gruel of us with one whiff of canister, an' that's no error!' He pushed it from his thoughts and shouted, 'Bowman! Lively there! Stand by!' He eased the tiller bar and saw the bowman's grapnel soar into the brig's main chains, clatter down and hook on.

'Boat your oars!' Allday supported Bolitho's arm as he crouched ready to leave the pitching boat. He hissed, 'Right with you, Cap'n!' He gave a throaty chuckle. 'Old times!'

Then they were taking their turn to leap from the boat and scramble their way through the small entry port.

Bolitho glanced quickly around. He saw the vessel's master, a short, neat figure in a fine blue coat standing almost indifferently by the wheel. He knew it was Delaval even before Paice opened his mouth.

Paice had his hanger drawn and strode aft, his voice carrying easily above the slap of canvas and the sea's protests beyond the bulwarks. 'Stand where you are!'

Delaval retorted, 'So it's you. By what *right —*'

Paice gestured to a seaman by the wheel and the cutlass he had seen in his belt clattered to the deck.

'In the King's name, so hold your noise.' He nodded his head to the petty officer who had accompanied the boat and the man hurried away, calling names, ignoring the brig's sailors as if they were not there.

Paice said, 'I intend to search this vessel. After that —'

'You are wasting your time. More important, you are wasting mine.' His dark eyes moved suddenly to Bolitho, taking in the plain blue coat, the outdated sword which was still sheathed at Bolitho's side. Delaval said, 'I will make the strongest protest. I was going about my lawful business.'

Bolitho asked, 'What cargo?'

Delaval's eyes flashed. There could have been triumph there. 'None. I am in ballast, as your worthy boarding party will soon discover.' He did not attempt to hide the sneer in his voice. 'I intended to sail for Amsterdam. You will see from the log that I have regular transactions with agents there.'

Bolitho could sense Paice's anger and impatience. He asked quietly, 'And you changed your mind?'

41

'The weather, news of more trouble in France, several things.'

The petty officer returned but stood so that Delaval could not see his face. He swallowed hard. 'Nuthin', sir. In full ballast.' He seemed almost afraid of his discovery.

Delaval said, 'I told you.' He lifted his chin and stared at Paice. 'You will pay for this.' His arm shot out and he pointed to an inert shape covered by a piece of canvas. He continued, his voice almost caressing, 'You fired on my ship –'

Paice snapped, 'You tried to run, you refused to heave-to! Don't pretend with me, damn you!'

A seaman pulled the canvas aside and Bolitho saw it was a man in sailor's clothing. Beside him lay a heavy block, its sheaves sticky with blood and hair. The man's forehead and skull had been crushed. Only the features were unmarked.

'I did not try to run away. But as you see, my vessel is short-handed, some of my men are working another. It took twice as long to bring her round and heave-to.' He nodded several times. 'I shall be certain to mention all this in my complaint to the proper authority!'

Bolitho gripped his sword to his leg again. It was bad luck. The ball must have severed some rigging and allowed the block to fall and kill the man. It happened often enough in any ship, but this could not have occurred at a worse time.

He said, 'We shall return to *Telemachus*, Mr Paice.'

Even a bloody hand-to-hand fight would have been better than this, he thought. Lady Luck, as Thomas always called it, had been against them from the beginning. He glanced at Paice and was surprised to see his face was stiffly controlled, his anger apparently gone.

Even when they clambered down to the jolly-boat nobody aboard the brig called out or abused them in any way. Delaval was not going to spoil his victory by putting a foot out of place.

Bolitho did not wait for the boat to be hoisted inboard before going below to the cabin.

He half-listened to the usual bustle and noise of a vessel getting under way once more, the creak of the rudder below the transom, a goblet clattering from the table as the cutter heeled over to the wind. Allday was outside the door, having made certain the boat was safely secured. Poor Allday; he would hate to see him disgraced. He bit his lip. There would be others who would be less displeased when he was sent back to Falmouth.

Paice ducked through the door, his coat still black with spray. It was his command but he waited for Bolitho to ask him to be seated. He looked tired and strained, a different person.

Bolitho did not waste time. 'I am sorry. You were right, I was mistaken. I shall see that no blame is attached to you. I ordered the chase –' He lifted his hand heavily as if his sleeve was filled with lead shot. 'No, hear me out. I told you to fire into her. It is enough. Perhaps I still thought –'

Paice waited and then said, 'No, sir, you were *not* mistaken. If anyone is to blame it's me for thinking, even for a moment, that Delaval would be stupid enough to be caught so easily.'

Bolitho looked across the small cabin with its leaping shadows made by the spiralling lanterns.

'Then tell me, what has changed your mind?'

Paice said calmly, 'Delaval *knew* we were out there, sir. And he needed us to know that he had outwitted us.'

'You mean it was all a lie?'

'Not all of it.' Paice clenched his fists several times, as if they were detached from the apparent calm he was displaying. 'That dead man was never killed by a falling block, sir. That's why the bastard wanted me to see his face.'

'You knew him?'

'He was my informant. The one who told me about the run.'

'And there's nothing we can do about it.'

Paice gave a deep sigh. 'Delaval is a Channel Islander by birth. It's rumoured he had to leave Jersey because of his cruelty when he commanded a privateer there.'

Bolitho tried to shut out the picture of the vicious mark Tuke had branded on Viola's naked shoulder when he had held her captive. But the picture would not fade, and he could still hear Tuke's sneers as they had circled around each other on *Narval*'s bloodied deck, their swords seeking an opening.

He heard himself say quietly, 'I knew another like that.'

Paice watched him for several seconds. 'Probably tortured him after they had discovered he was informing on the smugglers.

43

Then murdered him. Or maybe he was trading information to others. Either way they've done for him, and we can't prove a thing.' He took a long, deep breath which seemed to come from his shoes.

'So you see, sir, you *were* right. *Loyal Chieftain* acted as a decoy for something else, but Delaval couldn't resist putting his own touch to it for my benefit. But one day –' He did not continue. He had no need.

Paice groped his way bent double to the door. 'Do you wish to rendezvous with *Wakeful*, sir?'

Bolitho stared at him. '*Wakeful*? That's it, by God! Only *Wakeful* knew I was transferring back to your ship!'

Paice rubbed his chin fiercely even though he was still bent over in the doorway.

'Surely you don't think –'

Bolitho felt the shivers again up his spine.

'I don't know Delaval, but I *do* understand men like him. He showed no interest in me, not even curiosity – it was you he wanted to humiliate and impress – do you not see that?'

Paice nodded grimly. 'I'm afraid I do, sir.'

Bolitho said, 'Let us take a glass together before you change tack.' He reached over and impetuously touched the big lieutenant's arm.

'The battle's not lost after all. But I fear for the casualties when the fight is over!'

Allday heard the change in Bolitho's voice, could almost see his shoulders lifting again.

He gave a slow grin as Bolitho added, 'So let's be about it, eh?'

4

Divided Loyalties

The house which Commodore Ralph Hoblyn occupied and used as his personal headquarters was an elegant, square building of red brick with a pale, stone portico.

Bolitho reined in his horse and looked at the house for a full minute. It was not an old building, he decided, and the cobbled driveway which led between some pillared gates was well kept, with no trace of weeds to spoil it. And yet it had a air of neglect, or a place which had too many occupiers to care. Behind him he heard the other horse stamping its hooves on the roadway and could almost feel Young Matthew's excitement as he shared the pride and privilege of accompanying Bolitho on this warm, airless evening.

Bolitho recalled the angry waves and the brig's sail being ripped apart by it. It could have been another ocean entirely. There was a smell of flowers in the air, mixed as ever with that of the sea which was never far away.

The house was less than a mile from the dockyard at Sheerness where the two cutters had returned that morning.

A lieutenant had brought the invitation to Bolitho. It had been more like a royal command, he thought grimly.

He saw the glint of steel and the scarlet coats of two marines as they stepped across the gateway, attracted possibly by the sound of horses.

He had seen several pickets on the way here. It was as if the navy and not the local felons and smugglers were under siege. His

45

mouth tightened. He would try to change that – always provided Commodore Hoblyn did not order him to leave.

He tried to recall all he could about the man. A few years older than himself, Hoblyn had also been a frigate captain during the American Rebellion. He had fought his ship *Leonidas* at the decisive battle of the Chesapeake, where Admiral Graves had failed to bring de Grasse to a satisfactory embrace.

Hoblyn had engaged a French frigate and a privateer single-handed. He had forced the Frenchman to strike, but as he had closed with the privateer his own ship had exploded in flames. Hoblyn had continued to fight, and even boarded and seized the privateer before his ship had foundered.

It had been said that the sight of Hoblyn leading his boarders had been enough to strike terror into the enemy. His uniform had been ablaze, one arm burning like a tree in a forest fire.

Bolitho had met him only once since the war. He had been on his way to the Admiralty to seek employment. He had not even looked like the same man. His arm in a sling, his collar turned up to conceal some of the terrible burns on his neck, he had seemed a ghost from a battlefield. As far as Bolitho knew he had never obtained any employment. Until now.

Bolitho urged his mount forward. 'Come, Matthew, take care of the horses. I shall have some food sent to you.'

He did not see the awe on the boy's face. Bolitho was thinking of Allday. It was so out of character not to ask, to demand to accompany him. Allday mistrusted the ways of the land, and hated being parted from Bolitho at any time. Perhaps he was still brooding over their failure to catch the smugglers. It would all come out later on. Bolitho frowned. But it would have to wait.

He had spoken with Lieutenant Queely aboard *Wakeful* before leaving Sheerness. It was like a missing part of a puzzle. *Wakeful* had seen nothing, and the revenue men had had no reports of a run. Testing him out? Like Delaval's elaborate and calculated display of the dead man, Paice's informant. Cat and mouse.

He nodded to the corporal at the gate who slapped his musket in a smart salute, the pipeclay hovering around him in the still air. Bolitho was glad he had declined a carriage. Riding alone had given him time to think if not to plan. He smiled ruefully. It had also reminded him just how long it was since he had sat a horse.

Young Matthew took the horses and waited as a groom came forward to lead him to the stables at the rear of the house. Bolitho climbed the stone steps and saw the fouled anchor above the pillars, the stamp of Admiralty.

As if by magic the double doors swung inwards noiselessly and a dark-coated servant took Bolitho's hat and boat cloak, the latter covered with dust from the steady canter along an open road.

The man said, 'The commodore will receive you shortly, sir.' He backed away, the cloak and hat carried with great care as if they were heated shot from a furnace.

Bolitho walked around the entrance hall. More pillars, and a curved stairway which led up to a gallery. Unlike the houses he had seen in London, it was spartan. No pictures, and few pieces of furniture. *Temporary*, that described it well, he thought, and wondered if it also indicated Hoblyn's authority here. He looked through a window and caught the glint of late sunlight on the sea. *Or mine.* He tried not to think about Queely. He could be guilty, or one of his people might have found a way to pass word to the smugglers. News did not travel by itself.

It was like being in a dark room with a blind man. Uniform, authority, all meaningless. A fight which had neither beginning nor end. Whereas at sea you held the obedience and efficiency of your ship by leadership and example. But the enemy was always visible, ready to pit his wits against yours until the final broadside brought down one flag or the other.

Here it was stealth, deceit, and murder.

As a boy Bolitho had often listened to the old tales of the Cornish smugglers. Unlike the notorious wreckers along that cruel coastline, they were regarded as something vaguely heroic and daring. The rogues who robbed the rich to pay the poor. The navy had soon taught Bolitho a different story. Smugglers were not so different from those who lured ships on to the rocks where they robbed the cargoes and slit the throats of helpless survivors. He found that he was gripping his sword so tightly that the pain steadied his sudden anger.

He felt rather than heard a door opening and turned to see a slim figure framed against a window on the opposite side of the room.

At first he imagined it was a girl with a figure so slight. Even when he spoke his voice was soft and respectful, but with no trace of servility.

The youth was dressed in a very pale brown livery with darker frogging at the sleeves and down the front. White stockings and buckled shoes, a gentle miniature of most servants Bolitho had met.

'If you will follow me, Captain Bolitho.'

He wore a white, curled wig which accentuated his face and his eyes, which were probably hazel, but which, in the filtered sunlight, seemed green, and gave him the quiet watchfulness of a cat.

Across the other room and then into a smaller one. It was lined from floor to ceiling with books, and despite the warmth of the evening a cheerful fire was burning beneath a huge painting of a sea-fight. There were chairs and tables and a great desk strategically placed across one corner of the room.

Bolitho had the feeling that all the worthwhile contents of the house had been gathered in this one place.

He heard the young footman, if that was his station here, moving to the fire to rearrange a smouldering log into a better position. There was no sign of the commodore.

The youth turned and looked at him. 'He will not be long, sir.' Then he stood motionless beside the flickering fire, his hands behind his back.

Another, smaller door opened and the commodore walked quickly to the desk and slid behind it with barely a glance.

He seemed to arrange himself, and Bolitho guessed it came of long practice.

Just a few years older than himself, but they had been cruel ones. His square face was deeply lined, and he held his head slightly to one side as if he was still in pain. His left arm lay on the desk and Bolitho saw that he wore a white fingerless glove like a false hand, to disguise the terrible injuries he had endured for so long.

48

'I am pleased to see you, Bolitho.' He had a curt, clipped manner of speech. 'Be seated *there* if you will, I can see you the better.'

Bolitho sat down and noticed that Hoblyn's hair was completely grey, and worn unfashionably long, doubtless to hide the only burns which probed above his gold-laced collar.

The youth moved softly around the desk and produced a finely cut wine jug and two goblets.

'Claret.' Hoblyn's eyes were brown, but without warmth. 'Thought you'd like it.' He waved his right arm vaguely. 'We shall sup later.' It was an order.

They drank in silence and Bolitho saw the windows changing to dusky pink as the evening closed in.

Hoblyn watched the youth refilling the goblets.

'You've been luckier than most, Bolitho. Two ships since that bloody war, whereas –' He did not finish it but stared instead at the large painting.

Bolitho knew then it was his last battle. When he had lost his *Leonidas* and had been so cruelly disfigured.

Hoblyn added, 'I heard about your, er – misfortunes in the Great South Sea.' His eyes did not even blink. 'I'm told she was an admirable woman. I am sorry.'

Bolitho tried to remain calm. 'About this appointment –'

Hoblyn's disfigured hand rose and fell very lightly. *'In good time.'*

He said abruptly, 'So this is how they use us, eh? Are we relics now, the pair of us?' He did not expect or wait for an answer. 'I am bitter sometimes, and then I think of those who have *nothing* after giving their all.'

Bolitho waited. Hoblyn needed to talk.

'It's a hopeless task if you let it be so, Bolitho. Our betters bleat and protest about the Trade, while they filch all they can get from it. Their lordships demand more men for a fleet they themselves allowed to rot while they flung those same sailors on the beach to starve! *Damn them*, I say! And you can be sure than when war comes, as come it must, I shall be cast aside to provide a nice posting for some admiral's cousin!' He waited until his goblet was refilled. 'But I love this country which treats her sons so badly. You know the French as well as I – do you see them stopping now?' He gave a harsh laugh. 'And when they come we shall have to pray that those murderous scum have lopped off the heads of all their best sea-officers. I see no chance for us otherwise.'

Bolitho tried to remember how many times the youth had refilled his goblet. The claret and the heat from the fire were making his mind blur.

He said, 'I have to speak about the *Loyal Chieftain*, sir.'

Hoblyn held his head to a painful angle. 'Delaval? I know what happened, and about the man who was killed too.' He leaned forward so that his fine shirt frothed around the lapels of his coat. A far cry from the tattered veteran Bolitho had seen years ago on his way to the Admiralty.

Hoblyn dropped his voice to a husky growl. 'Someone burned down the man's cottage while you were at sea – I'll lay odds you didn't know *that*! And his wife and children have vanished into thin air!' He slumped back again, and Bolitho saw sweat on his face.

'Murdered?' One word, and it seemed to bring a chill to the overheated room.

'We shall probably never know.' He reached out to grasp his goblet but accidentally knocked it over so that the claret ran across the desk like blood.

Hoblyn sighed. 'Damn them all.' He watched his footman as he deftly mopped up the wine and replaced the goblet with a clean one.

'But life can have its compensations –'

Just for a brief instant it was there. The merest flicker of an exchange between them. The youth did not smile and yet there was an understanding strong enough to feel.

Hoblyn said offhandedly, 'You have *Snapdragon* in Chatham dockyard?'

Bolitho shook himself. Maybe he was mistaken. He glanced quickly at the footman's pale eyes. They were quite empty.

'Yes, sir. I thought it best –'

'Good thinking. There'll not be much time later on. Our lords and masters want results. We shall give them a few.' He smiled for the first time. 'Thought I was going to bite your head off, did ye? God damn it, Bolitho, you're what I need, not some knothead who's never heard a shot fired in bloody earnest!'

Bolitho pressed his shoulders against the chairback. There was something unnerving about Hoblyn. But under the bluster and the bitterness his mind was as sharp and as shrewd as it had ever been. If he was like this with everyone the slender footman must have heard every secret possible. Was he to be trusted?

Hoblyn added, 'The big East Indiamen are among the worst culprits, y'know. They come up-Channel after months at sea and they meet with smugglers while they're under way, did you know that?'

Bolitho shook his head. 'What is the purpose, sir?'

'John Company's captains like to make a little extra profit of their own, as if they don't get enough. They sell tea and silks directly to the Trade and so avoid paying duty themselves. The Customs Board don't like it, but with so few cutters to patrol the whole Channel and beyond, what can they expect?' He watched Bolitho calmly. 'Wine and brandy is different. Smaller runs, less chance of the buggers getting caught. But tea, for instance, is light but very bulky.' He tapped the side of his nose with the little white bag. 'Not so easy, eh?'

Bolitho waited, not knowing quite what he had expected.

'I have received information.' He must have seen doubt in Bolitho's grey eyes. 'From a better mouth than some wretched turncoat's.' Hoblyn calmed himself with an effort. 'There's a cargo being landed at Whitstable ten days from now.' He sat back to watch Bolitho's expression. 'It will involve a lot of men.' His dark eyes seemed to dance in the candlelight as the youth placed a silver candelabrum on the desk. 'Men for the fleet, *or* the gallows, we'll strike no bargains, and a cargo to make these bloody smugglers realise we're on the attack!'

Bolitho's mind was in a whirl. If it was true, Hoblyn was right. It would make all the difference to their presence here. He pictured Whitstable on the chart, a small fishing port which lay near the mouth of the Swale River. More proof if any were needed of the smugglers' audacity and arrogance. At a guess, Whitstable was no more than ten miles from this very room.

'I'll be ready, sir.'

'Thought so. Nothing like a bit of humiliation to put fire in your belly, eh?'

A clock chimed somewhere and Hoblyn said, 'Time to sup. The rest can keep. I know you're not one to loosen your tongue. Something else we have in common, I suspect.' He chuckled and then struggled around the desk while the youth waited to lead the way to another room.

As he bent over Bolitho saw the livid scars lift above his collar. He must be like that over most of his body. Like a soul banished from hell. They moved out into the same hallway where a servant waited at another pair of doors. There was a rich smell of food, and Bolitho noticed the cut and material of Hoblyn's clothes. His fortunes had changed if nothing else.

He was about to ask that a meal be sent for Young Matthew when he saw Hoblyn's hand brush against that of the footman.

Bolitho did not know if he felt disgust or pity.

As Hoblyn had said, *the rest can keep.*

Bolitho awoke shocked and dazed and for a few agonising seconds imagined that he was emerging from the fever again. His skull throbbed like hammers on an anvil, and when he tried to speak his tongue felt as if it was glued to the roof of his mouth. He saw Young Matthew's round face watching him in the gloom, only his eyes showing colour in a feeble glow from the cabin skylight.

'What is it?' Bolitho barely recognised his voice. 'Time?' His senses were returning reluctantly and he realised with sudden self-abhorrence that he was still fully clothed in his best uniform, his hat and sword on the table where he had dropped them.

Matthew said in a hoarse whisper, 'You bin sleeping, sir.'

Bolitho propped himself on his elbows. The hull was moving very sluggishly on the current, but there were only occasionally some footfalls on the deck above. *Telemachus* still slept although it must soon be dawn, he thought vaguely.

'Coffee, Matthew.' He lowered his feet to the deck and suppressed a groan. Blurred pictures formed in his mind and faded almost as quickly. The laden table, Hoblyn's face shining in the candlelight, the comings and goings of servants, one plate following the next, each seemingly richer than that which had preceded it. And the wine. This time a groan did escape from his lips. It had been a never-ending stream.

The boy crouched down beside him. 'Mr Paice is on deck, sir.'

He remembered what Hoblyn had revealed, the information he had gained on a Whitstable landing. The need for secrecy. How had he got back to *Telemachus*? He could remember none of it.

His mind steadied and he looked at the boy. 'You brought me here?'

'It were nothing, sir.' For once he showed no excitement or shy pride.

Bolitho seized his arm. 'What is it? Tell me, Matthew.'

The boy looked down at the deck. 'It's Allday, sir.'

Bolitho's brain was suddenly like clear ice. 'What has happened?'

Pictures flashed through his thoughts. Allday standing over him, his bloodied cutlass cleaving aside all who tried to pass. Allday, cheerful, tolerant, always there when he was needed.

The boy whispered, 'He's gone, sir.'

'Gone?'

The door opened a few inches and Paice lowered his shoulders to enter the cabin.

'Thought you should know, sir.' He added with something like the defiance he had shown at their first meeting, 'He's not borne on the ship's books, sir. If he was . . .'

'He's my responsibility, is that what you mean?'

Paice must have seen the pain in his face even in the poor light.

'I did hear that your cox'n was once a pressed man, sir?'

Bolitho ran his fingers through his hair as he tried to assemble his wits. 'True. That was a long while ago. He has served me, and served me faithfully, for ten years since. He'd not desert.' He shook his head, the realisation of what he had said thrusting through him like a hot blade. 'Allday would not leave me.'

Paice watched, unable to help, to find the right words. 'I could pass word to the shore, sir. He may meet with the press gangs. If I can rouse the senior lieutenant I might be able to stop anything

53

going badly for him.' He hesitated, unused to speaking so openly. 'And for you, if I may say so, sir.'

Bolitho touched the boy's shoulder and felt him shiver.

'Fetch me some water and fresh coffee, Matthew.' His voice was heavy, his mind still groping.

Suppose Allday *had* decided to leave? Bolitho recalled his own surprise when Allday had not insisted on accompanying him to the commodore's house. It was all coming back. Bolitho felt his inner pocket and touched the written orders which the commodore had given him. It was a wonder he had not lost them on the way back to the cutter, he thought wretchedly.

Allday might have felt the affair of the *Loyal Chieftain* badly. God knew he had put up with enough over the past months – and with what reward for his faith and his unshakeable loyalty?

Now he was gone. Back to the land from which Bolitho's own press gang had snatched him all those years back. Years of danger and pride, loss and sadness. Always there. The oak, the rock which Bolitho had all too often taken for granted.

Paice said, 'He left no message, sir.'

Bolitho looked up at him. 'He cannot write.' He remembered what he had thought when he had first met Allday in *Phalarope*. If only he had had some education Allday might have been anything. Now that same thought seemed to mock him.

Somewhere a boatswain's call twittered like a rudely awakened blackbird.

Paice said heavily, 'Orders, sir?'

Bolitho nodded and winced as the hammers began again. Eating and drinking to excess, something he rarely did, and all the while Allday had been here, planning what he would do, awaiting the right moment.

'We shall weigh at noon. See that word is passed to *Wakeful*.' He tried to keep his tone level. 'Do it yourself, if you please. I want nothing in writing.' Their eyes met. *'Not yet.'*

'All hands! All hands! Lash up an' stow!' The hull seemed to shake as feet thudded to the deck, and another day was begun.

'May I ask, sir?'

Bolitho heard the boy returning and realised that he would have to shave himself.

54

'There is to be a run.' He did not know if Paice believed him, nor did he care now. 'The commodore has a plan. I shall explain when we are at sea and in company. There will be no revenue cutters involved. They are to be elsewhere.' How simple it must have sounded across that overloaded table. And all the while the handsome youth in the white wig had watched and listened.

Paice said haltingly, 'I sent the first lieutenant ashore to collect two of the hands, sir. They were found drunk at a local inn.' He forced a grin. 'Thought it best if he was out of the way 'til I'd spoken with you.'

The boy put down a pot of coffee and groped about for a mug.

Bolitho replied, 'That was thoughtful of you, Mr Paice.'

Paice shrugged. 'I believe we may be of one mind, sir.'

Bolitho stood up carefully and thrust open the skylight. The air was still cool and sweet from the land. Maybe he no longer belonged at sea. Was that what Allday had been feeling too?

He glanced down and saw Matthew moving a small roll of canvas away from the cot.

Paice backed from the cabin. 'I shall muster the hands, sir. No matter what men may believe, a ship has no patience and must be served fairly at all times.'

Bolitho did not hear the door close. 'What is that parcel, Matthew?'

The boy picked it up and shrugged unhappily. 'I think it belonged to Allday, sir.' He sounded afraid, as if he in some way shared the guilt.

Bolitho took it from him and opened it carefully on the cot where he had lain like some drunken oaf.

The small knives, tools which Allday had mostly made with his own hands. Carefully collected oddments of brass and copper, sailmaker's twine, some newly fashioned spars and booms.

Bolitho was crouching now, his hands almost shaking as he untied the innermost packet and put it on the cot with great care.

Allday never carried much with him as he went from ship to ship. He had placed little importance on possessions. Only in his models, his ships which he had fashioned with all the skill and love he had gained over the years at sea.

He heard the boy's sharp intake of breath. 'It's lovely, sir!'

Bolitho touched the little model and felt his eyes prick with sudden emotion. Unpainted still, but there was no mistaking the shape and grace of a frigate, the gunports as yet unfilled with tiny cannon still to be made, the masts and rigging still carried only in Allday's mind. His fingers paused at the small, delicately carved figurehead, one which Bolitho remembered so clearly, as if it were life-sized instead of a tiny copy. The wild-eyed girl with streaming hair, and a horn fashioned like a great shell.

Young Matthew said questioningly, 'A frigate, sir?'

Bolitho stared at it until he could barely see. It was not just any ship. With Allday it rarely was.

He heard himself murmur, 'She is my last command, Matthew. My *Tempest*.'

The boy responded in a whisper, 'I wonder why he left it behind, sir?'

Bolitho turned him by the shoulder and gripped it until he winced. 'Don't you see, Matthew? He could tell no one what he was about, nor could he write a few words to rest my fears for him.' He looked again at the unfinished model. 'This was the best way he knew of telling me. That ship meant so much to both of us for a hundred different reasons. He'd never abandon it.'

The boy watched as Bolitho stood up to the skylight again, barely able to grasp it, and yet knowing he was the only one who was sharing the secret.

Bolitho said slowly, '*God damn him* for his stubbornness!' He bunched his hand against the open skylight. 'And God protect you, old friend, until your return!'

Marching in pairs the press gang advanced along yet another narrow street, their shoes ringing on the cobbles, their eyes everywhere as they probed the shadows.

At the head a tight-lipped lieutenant strode with his hanger already drawn, a midshipman following a few paces behind him.

Here and there the ancient houses seemed to bow across the lanes until they appeared to touch one another. The lieutenant glanced at each dark or shuttered window, especially at those which hung directly above their wary progress. It was all too common for someone to hurl down a bucket of filth on to the hated press gangs as they carried out their thankless patrols.

The lieutenant, like most of them in the local impressment service, had heard all about the two officers being stripped, beaten and publicly humiliated on the open road, with no one raising a hand to aid them. Only the timely appearance of the post-captain and his apparent total disregard for his own safety had saved the officers from far worse.

The lieutenant had been careful to announce his intentions of seeking prime seamen for the fleet, as so ordered. He slashed out angrily at a shadow with his hanger and swore under his breath. You might just as well ring the church bells to reveal what you were about, he thought. The result was usually the same. Just a few luckless ones, and some of those had been lured into the hands of the press gangs, usually by their own employers who wanted to be rid of them. A groom who had perhaps become too free with a landowner's daughter, a footman who had served a mistress better than the man who paid for her luxuries. But trained hands? It would be a joke, if it were not so serious.

The lieutenant snapped, 'Close up in the rear!' It was unnecessary; they always kept together, their heavy cudgels and cutlasses ready for immediate use if attacked, and he knew they resented his words. But he hated the work, just as he longed for the chance of a ship. Some people foolishly wrung their hands, and clergymen prayed that war would never come.

The fools. What did they know? War was as necessary as it was rewarding.

There was a sudden crash, like a bottle being smashed on the cobbles.

The lieutenant held up his hanger, and behind him he heard his men rouse themselves, like vixens on the scent of prey.

The midshipman faltered, 'In that alley, sir!'

'I know that!' He waited until his senior hand, a hard-bitten gunner's mate, had joined him. 'Did you hear that, Benzie?'

The gunner's mate grunted. 'There be a tavern through there, sir. Should be closed now, o'course. This be th'only way out.'

The lieutenant scowled. The idiot had left the most important fact to the end. He swallowed his revulsion and said softly, 'Fetch two men and –'

The gunner's mate thrust his face even closer and whispered thickly, 'No need, sir, someone be comin'!'

The lieutenant thankfully withdrew his face. The gunner's mate's breath was as foul as any bilge. Chewing tobacco, rum and bad teeth made a vile mixture.

'Stand to!' The lieutenant faced the narrow alley and cursed their lordships for the absurdity of it. The hidden figure with the slow, shambling gait was probably a cripple or as old as Neptune. What use was one man anyway?

The shadow loomed from the shadows and the lieutenant called sharply, 'In the King's name, I order you to stand and be examined!'

The gunner's mate sighed and tightened his hold on the heavy cudgel. How the navy had changed. In his day they had clubbed them senseless and asked questions later, usually when the poor wretch awoke with a split head to find himself in a man-of-war already standing out to sea. It might be months, years, and in many cases never, that the pressed man returned to England. Who would care anyway? There had even been a case of a bridegroom being snatched from the steps of a church on his wedding day.

But now, with regulations, and not enough ships ready for sea, it was unsafe to flout the Admiralty's rules.

He said, '*Easy*, matey!' His experienced eye had taken in the man's build and obvious strength. Even in this dawn light he could see the broad shoulders and, when he turned to stare at the press gang, the pigtail down his back.

The lieutenant snapped, 'What ship?' His nervousness put an edge to his voice. 'Answer, or you'll be the worse for it, man!'

The gunner's mate urged, 'There be too many o' us, matey.' He half-raised his cudgel. 'Tell the lieutenant, like wot 'e says!'

Allday looked at him grimly. He had been about to give up his hazy plan, when he had heard the press gang's cautious approach. Were it not so dangerous it might have made him smile, albeit secretly. Like all those other times when he had dodged the dreaded press in Cornwall, until the day when His Britannic Majesty's frigate *Phalarope* had hove into sight. Her captain had been a Cornishman, one who knew where landsmen ran to ground whenever a King's ship topped the horizon. It was strange when you thought of it. If a Frenchie ever drew close inshore every fit man would stand to arms to protect his home and country from an enemy. But they would run from one of their own.

Allday said huskily, 'I don't have a ship, sir.' He had spilled rum over his clothing and hoped it was convincing. He had hated the waste of it.

The lieutenant said coldly, 'Don't lie. I told you what would happen if –'

The gunner's mate gestured at him again. 'Don't be a fool!'

Allday hung his head. 'The *London*, sir.'

The lieutenant exclaimed. 'A second-rate, so you are a prime seaman! *Yes?*' The last word was like a whip-crack.

'If you say so, sir.'

'Don't be bloody insolent. What's your name, damn you?'

Allday regarded him impassively. It might be worth it just to smash in the lieutenant's teeth. Bolitho would have a useless pipsqueak like him for breakfast.

'Spencer, sir.' He had neglected to invent a name, and the slight hesitation seemed to satisfy the officer that it was because of guilt.

'Then you are taken. Come with my men, or be dragged in irons – the choice is yours.'

The press gang parted as Allday moved amongst them. Their eagerness to be gone from this deserted street was almost matched by their relief.

One of the seamen muttered, 'Never mind, mate, could be worse.'

Somewhere, far away, a trumpet echoed on the morning air. Allday hesitated and did not even notice the sudden alarm in their eyes. He had done it. At this moment Bolitho might be looking at the little *Tempest*. But would he see a message there? Allday felt something like despair; he might see only desertion and treachery.

Then he squared his shoulders. 'I'm ready.'

The lieutenant quickened his pace as he heard someone drumming on a bucket with a piece of metal. The signal for a mob to come running to free their capture.

But this patrol at least had not been entirely wasted. Only one man, but obviously an experienced sailor. No excuses either, nor the last-moment, infuriating production of a Protection like those issued to apprentices, watermen, and the likes of the H.E.I.C.

The gunner's mate called, 'Wot's yer trade, Spencer?'

Allday was ready this time. 'Sailmaker.' Chosen carefully, not too lowly, so that they might have disbelieved him, nor too senior, so that they might have sent him back to the *London*, a ship he had never laid eyes on.

The man nodded, well satisfied. A sailmaker was a rare and valuable catch.

They topped a rise and Allday saw the masts and crossed yards of several men-of-war, their identities still hidden in deep shadow. Bolitho was there. Would they ever meet again?

If not it will be because I am no longer alive.

Strangely enough the realisation brought him immediate comfort.

5

Out Of The Mouths Of Babes . . .

Bolitho gripped the swivel-gun mounting on the weather bulwark, and used it to steady himself as *Telemachus* dipped and
lifted to a steady north-easterly, her forward rigging running
with spray. Eight bells had just chimed out from the forecastle
and as in any man-of-war, large or small, the watches changed to
a routine as old as the navy itself.

Lieutenant Triscott touched his hat to Paice. 'The watch is aft,
sir.'

Bolitho sensed the stiffness in his manner, something unusual
for one so young and usually so buoyant.

'Relieve the wheel, if you please.'

The helmsman chanted, 'West Nor'-West, sir! Full an' bye!'

The members of the last dogwatch hurried to the hatchway
while the relief took over and began to check running rigging,
and the lashings of countless pieces of equipment and the guns
which lined either side.

It was not just the first lieutenant who was showing strain,
Bolitho thought. It was never easy in a small overcrowded hull at
the best of times, and he was well aware of their resentment as
day followed day, beating up and down, holding on to visual
contact with *Wakeful* running far down to leeward, and preparing for what most of them thought was another empty rumour.

Bolitho blamed himself for much of it. It was Paice's
command, but he watched everything himself, and tried to plan
for whatever lay ahead.

61

Paice had had little to do with Commodore Hoblyn and was unwilling to voice an opinion as to the value of his information. Perhaps he was still brooding over the murder of his own inform-ant and the calculated arrogance with which Delaval had dis-played the man's corpse. Or he might place Hoblyn in the category of senior officers who had been too long ashore to understand the stealth and cunning of this kind of work.

Whenever he was alone in his cot Bolitho was unable to lose himself in his plans. Allday would return to his thoughts again and again, so that he lay tossing and turning until he fell into an exhausted sleep, his anxieties still unresolved.

He noticed that neither Paice nor Triscott ever mentioned All-day in his presence. Either they were afraid to arouse his dis-pleasure, or, in the way of sailors, they were convinced that Allday was already dead.

Paice crossed the narrow poop and touched his hat, while his eyes watched the clear sky of evening.

'Might get some mist later, sir.' His gaze moved to Bolitho's profile, assessing the mood. 'But we can hold contact with *Wakeful* for a few more hours before we tell her to close with us for the night.'

Bolitho glanced up at the quivering mast where the lookouts squatted on the topsail yard. They had the other cutter in sight, but down here on deck the sea might have been empty.

They had twice met with a revenue lugger. Once she had carried a curt despatch from the commodore, a confirmation that his information was still valid.

The second time the lugger had carried news of a more disturb-ing nature. It seemed that there had been several daring runs made along the south coast, from as far afield as Penzance in Cornwall and Lyme Bay in Dorset. A revenue cutter had chased one schooner as far as the Isle of Wight before the smuggler had give her the slip in a sudden rain squall.

Paice had commented, 'Seems that all the excitement is else-where, sir.'

A criticism of Bolitho's strategy, perhaps, and the fact that their two cutters were placed as far as possible from any of the landings. The Customs Board had taken them very seriously, and had diverted every available vessel to seize or destroy any boats suspected of dropping smuggled cargoes. The navy had even loaned a thirty-two-gun frigate from Plymouth to offer support if the revenue vessels were outgunned or fought on to a lee shore.

Paice remarked, 'First of May tomorrow, sir.'

Bolitho turned and said shortly, 'I am aware of it. You may assure your people it is also the last day they will be required on this patrol.'

Paice held his gaze and replied stubbornly, 'I implied no lack of faith, sir. But it could mean that the commodore's intelligence, with all respect to him for I believe him to be a brave officer, was falsely offered. Any failure might be seen as something personal.'

Bolitho watched some fish leaping across the crisp wave which surged back from *Telemachus*'s plunging stem.

'You think the commodore would be ordered to withdraw our cutters?'

'It crossed my mind, sir. Otherwise why are we out here, and not even in the Strait of Dover? If it was a ruse, we are too far away to be of any use.'

'Is that the opinion of your whole command?' There was steel in his voice.

Paice shrugged heavily. 'It is *my* opinion, sir. I do not ask others while I command here.'

'I am glad to know it, Mr Paice.'

It was reaching him now, like the rest of the vessel. No room to escape, no place to hide from others at any time of the day or night. Only the masthead lookouts had any sort of privacy.

After this Bolitho knew he would have to go ashore and set up his own headquarters like Hoblyn. And without even Allday to make the sea's rejection bearable. He pounded his hand against the swivel gun's wet muzzle. Where was he now? How was he faring? Perhaps some press gang had already taken him to a ship at Chatham where his explanation had fallen on deaf ears. What could he have hoped to achieve anyway? The endless, unanswered questions seemed to roar through his head like surf in a cave.

He turned his thoughts to Hoblyn, and Paice moved away to consult with Scrope, the master-at-arms, who had been hovering

63

near the tiller for some time, trying to catch his commander's eye. Paice had probably taken Bolitho's silence as another rebuff, the slamming of a door which both had imagined was open between them.

→ What then of Hoblyn? He did not come from a successful family or even from a long line of sea-officers. He was, as far as Bolitho knew, the first to enter the navy which he had served without sparing himself until the terrible day he had been changed into a broken and disfigured *relic*, as he had described himself. Officially he was under the orders of the flag officer in command at the Nore, but like Bolitho was expected to act almost independently. Part of his work was making a list of vessels which in time of war could be purchased from their merchant service and used for the navy. Vessels under construction in the many yards around Suffolk and Kent would also have to be listed.

There were certainly openings for bribery. Money could soon change hands if a shipowner or builder could persuade a senior officer to pay a high price which could then be shared to mutual profit. Some vessels had changed hands several times in peace and war, and like the ill-fated *Bounty* had made good profits with each transaction.

If Hoblyn depended solely on a commodore's pay, he was certainly living far above it. The house was spartan Admiralty property, but the food and wine Bolitho had seen would have found favour on the table of the Lord High Admiral himself.

The yards Hoblyn visited would also be well known to the smuggling fraternity. Bolitho turned, and allowed the cold spray to dash across his face to clear his mind, like that first morning after Allday disappeared. His imagination was running wild, with a suspected felon in every shadow.

Hoblyn had tried to tell him in his own way; so had the admiral at Chatham. Let others fret over it, and content yourself with your daily lot until something better offers itself.

He was trying too hard. At the Admiralty he had been told in a roundabout way that he had been chosen because of his gallant record, something which might inspire young men to sign on, to wear the King's coat because of his own service. It was a bitter reward.

The Nore and Medway towns were known for their distrust in the stirring words of a recruiting poster. In other wars the harbours and villages had been stripped of their young men, some who had gone proudly to volunteer, others who had been dragged away from their families by the desperate press gangs. The aftermath had seen too many cripples and too few young men to encourage others to follow their example.

Relic. The word seemed to haunt him.

He watched some seamen clambering up the weather ratlines to whip some loose cordage which had been spotted by the boatswain's eagle eye.

This was their ship, their home. They wanted to be rid of the officer who had once been a frigate captain.

There was a slithering footfall on deck and Matthew Corker moved carefully towards him, his young face screwed up with concentration. He held out a steaming mug. 'Coffee, Cap'n.' He smiled nervously. ''Tis half-empty, I'm afraid, sir.'

Bolitho tried to return the smile. He was doing everything he could to please him, do the things which he had seen Allday do. He had even called him Cap'n, as Allday did and would allow no other. He had overcome his seasickness for most of the time.

'D'you still want to go to sea, Matthew?' The coffee was good, and seemed to give him strength.

'Aye, sir. More'n ever.'

What would his grandfather, Old Matthew, think of that?

A shaft of red sunlight ran down the mainmast, and Bolitho stared at it as the great mainsail rattled and boomed in the wind. A few more hours and all pretence would be over.

He would not be remembered as the frigate captain, but as the man who tried to use a cutter like one. *Relic.*

'I forgot to tell you something, sir.' The boy watched him anxiously. 'Us being so busy an' worried like.'

Bolitho smiled down at him. *Us*, he had said. It had not been easy for him either. The crowded hull, and doubtless some language and tales which he would barely understand after his sheltered existence at Falmouth.

'What is that?'

'When I took the horses to the stables at the commodore's

house, sir, I had a walk round, looked at the other horses an' that.' Bolitho saw him screwing up his face again, trying to picture it, to forget nothing.

'There was a fine carriage there. My grandfather showed me one once, when I was very young, sir.'

Bolitho warmed to him. 'That must have been a *long* time ago.'

It was lost on him. 'It's got a special kind of springing, y'see, sir – I've never seen another, until that night.'

Bolitho waited. 'What about it?'

'It's French, sir. A berlin, just like the one which came to Falmouth that time with some nobleman an' his lady.'

Bolitho took his arm and guided him to the bulwark so that their backs were turned to the helmsmen and other watchkeepers.

'Are you quite sure?'

'Oh yes, sir.' He nodded emphatically. 'Somebody had been varnishing the doors like, but I could still see it when I held up the lantern.'

Bolitho tried to remain patient. 'See what?'

'I forget what they calls them, sir.' He pouted. 'A sort of flower with a crest.'

Bolitho stared at the tilting horizon for several seconds.

Then he said quietly, 'Fleur-de-lys?'

The boy's apple cheeks split into a grin. 'Aye, that's what my grandad called it!'

Bolitho looked at him steadily. *Out of the mouths of babes . . .*

'Have you told anyone else?' He smiled gently. 'Or is it just between *us*?'

'I said nuthin', sir. Just thought it a bit strange.'

The moment, the boy's expression, the description of the fine carriage seemed to become fixed and motionless as the lookout's voice pealed down to the deck.

'Sail on th' weather quarter, sir!'

Paice stared across at him questioningly.

Bolitho called, 'Well, we know she's not the *Loyal Chieftain* this time, Mr Paice.'

Paice nodded very slowly. 'And we *know* there's naught 'twixt her and the land but –'

Bolitho looked at the boy. '*Us*, Mr Paice?'

66

'Aye, sir.' Then he raised his speaking trumpet. 'Masthead! Can you make out her rig?'

'Schooner, sir! A big 'un she is, too!'

Paice moved nearer and rubbed his chin with agitation.

'She'll take the wind-gage off us. It would be two hours or more before we could beat up to wind'rd, even in *Telemachus*.' He glanced meaningly at the sky. 'Time's against that.'

Bolitho saw some of the idlers on deck pausing to try and catch their words.

He said, 'I agree. Besides, when she sights *Telemachus* she might turn and run if she thinks we are about to offer a chase.'

'Shall I signal *Wakeful*, sir?' Once again that same hesitation.

'I think not. *Wakeful* will stand a better chance downwind if this stranger decides to make a run for the Dover Strait.'

Paice gave a tight grin. 'I'll say this, sir, you never let up.'

Bolitho glanced away. 'After this, I hope others may remember it.'

Paice beckoned to his first lieutenant. 'Call all hands, Andrew –' He glanced anxiously at Bolitho. 'That is, *Mr* Triscott. Clear for action, but do not load or run out.'

Bolitho watched them both and said, 'This is where *Telemachus*'s ability to sail close to the wind will tell. It will also offer our small broadside a better chance should we have to match the enemy's iron!'

He crossed to the lee side and looked down at the creaming wake. There was only this moment. He must think of nothing further. Not of Allday, nor that this newcomer might well be an honest trader. If that were true, his name would carry no weight at all.

He heard the boy ask, 'What'll *I* do, sir?'

Bolitho looked at him and saw him falter under his gaze. Then he said, 'Fetch my sword.' He nearly added *and pray*. Instead he said, 'Then stand by me.'

Calls trilled although they were hardly needed in *Telemachus*'s sixty-nine-foot hull.

'All hands! Clear for action!'

Tomorrow would bring the first day in May. What might it take away?

67

Bolitho lowered the telescope and spoke over his shoulder. 'What do you estimate our position, Mr Chesshyre?'

There was no hesitation. ''Bout ten miles north of Foreness Point, sir.'

Bolitho wiped the telescope with his sleeve to give himself time to digest the master's words.

Foreness Point lay on the north-eastern corner of the Isle of Thanet, and the mainland of Kent. It reminded him briefly of Herrick, as had Chesshyre's voice.

Paice said hoarsely, 'If he *is* a smuggler he'll be hard put to go about now, sir.'

Bolitho levelled the glass again and saw the big schooner's dark sails standing above the sea like bat's wings. Paice was right. The north-easterly would make it difficult, even hazardous to try and claw round to weather the headland. The lookouts would be able to see it from their perch, but from the deck it looked as if the two vessels had the sea to themselves.

Bolitho glanced at the sky, which was still cloudless and clear. Only the sea seemed darker, and he knew that sooner or later one of them would have to show his hand.

He pictured the coast in his mind. They were steering towards the old anchorage at Sheerness, but before that lay Whitstable, and as the two vessels maintained their same tack and speed they were slowly converging, drawing together like lines on the chart.

Paice said, 'He'll have to stand away soon, sir, or he'll end up with Sheppey across his bows.'

Bolitho glanced along the deck, at the gun crews crouching or lounging by the sealed ports, each captain having already selected the best shot from the garlands for the first loading.

Bolitho had been in so many actions that he could recognise the casual attitudes of the seamen, the way they watched the schooner's steady approach with little more than professional interest. With Allday it was different; but these men were not accustomed to real action. A few might have fought in other ships, but most of them, as Paice had explained, were fishermen and workers driven from the land because of falling trade.

Bolitho said, 'You may load now, Mr Paice.' He waited for the lieutenant to face him. 'He is not going to run, you know that, don't you?'

Paice swallowed. 'But I don't see that –'

'*Do it*, Mr Paice. Tell the gunner's mates to supervise each piece personally. I want them double-shotted but with no risk of injury from an exploding cannon!'

Paice yelled, 'All guns load! Double-shotted!'

Bolitho ignored the curious and doubtful stares as several of the seamen peered aft to where he stood by the taffrail. He raised the glass again and watched the big sails leap into view. People too, at the bulwarks, and moving around the tapering masts. How would *Telemachus* look to them, he wondered? Small and lively, her guns still behind their port lids. Just one little cutter which stood between them and the land.

'D'you know her?' Bolitho lowered the glass and saw young Matthew staring at him unblinkingly, as if fearful of missing something.

Paice shook his head. 'Stranger, sir.' To the master he added, 'What about you?'

Chesshyre shrugged. 'Never laid eyes on her.'

Bolitho clenched his fists. It had to be the right one. A quick glance abeam; the light was slowly going, the sun suddenly misty above the hidden land.

He said, 'Bring her up two points, Mr Paice.'

Men scampered to their stations, and soon the blocks squealed, and the great mainsail thundered from its long boom.

'Steady she goes, sir! Nor'-West!'

'Run up the Colours!'

Bolitho dragged his eyes from the schooner and watched the gun crews. Some of them were still standing upright, gaping at the other ship.

Bolitho snapped, 'Tell those bumpkins to stand to, damn them!'

He heard the big ensign cracking in the wind above the deck, then shouted, 'Fire one of the larboard guns, Mr Paice!'

Paice opened his mouth to dispute the order, then he nodded. By firing a gun from the opposite side they would keep the whole starboard broadside intact.

69

Moments later the foremost six-pounder banged out, the smoke dispersing downwind before the crew had begun to sponge its barrel.

Bolitho folded his arms and watched the schooner, like the boy at his side, not daring to blink.

Paice said, 'He's ignored the signal, sir.' He sounded dazed, as if he scarcely believed it was happening. 'Maybe he's —'

Bolitho did not know what Paice intended to say for at that second there was a great flash from the schooner's forecastle, and as smoke belched over the wave crests a ball smashed through *Telemachus*'s bulwark and burst apart on a six-pounder. Splinters of wood and iron shrieked away in all directions, and as the gun's echo faded the sound continued, but this time it was human.

One of the seamen was on his knees, his bloodied fingers clawing at his face and then his chest, his scream rising until it sounded like a woman in terrible agony. Then he pitched on his side, his life-blood pumping across the sloping deck and into the lee scuppers. Several of the other sailors stared at the corpse with utter horror; and there were more yells and screams as another ball crashed into the bulwark and hurled a fan of splinters across the deck.

'Open the ports! *Run out!*' Paice was standing silhouetted against the surging water alongside, his face like a mask as men whimpered and crawled across the shattered planking, marking the pain and progress with their blood.

Bolitho called, 'On the uproll, Mr Paice! It's our only hope at this distance!' So it had happened just as Hoblyn had predicted. His mind cringed as Triscott's hanger sliced down and the six guns on the starboard side crashed out in unison. The carronade was useless at anything more than point-blank range, and undoubtedly the schooner's master knew it.

He saw the sails dancing above the schooner's deck and watched as some blocks and cordage plummeted over the side to trail like creeper in the water.

'Reload! Run out!' Triscott's voice was shrill. 'As you bear, lads!' He dropped his hanger again. *'Fire!'*

Bolitho saw several of the men peering round at their fallen

70

comrades – how many had died or been cruelly wounded it was impossible to tell. At the same time Bolitho thought he saw their anxiety and sudden terror changing its face to anger, fury at what had been done to them.

Chesshyre yelled, 'Down here – take over from Quin!' The helmsman in question had been hit in the head and had slumped unnoticed and unheard across the tiller bar, his eyes fixed and staring as they lowered him to the deck.

Chesshyre caught Bolitho's glance and said, 'They've a bit to learn, sir, but they'll not let you down.' He spoke so calmly he could have been describing a contest between boats' crews.

Bolitho nodded. 'We must hit her masts and rigging.' He shouted in the sudden lull. 'Gun-captains! Aim high! A guinea for the first sail!'

'Fire!'

Paice said harshly, 'That bastard's using nine-pounders if I'm any judge!' He gasped as a ball smashed hard down alongside and flung spray high over the bulwark.

Bolitho saw his expression as men ran to the pumps. Like pain. As if he and not the cutter had been hit.

There was a wild cheer and Bolitho swung round to see the schooner's foresail tearing itself apart, the wind bringing her down as she fought against the confusion of sea and helm.

Bolitho bit his lip as another ball screamed overhead and a length of halliard whirled across the deck like a wounded snake. It could not last. One ball into *Telemachus*'s only mast would finish it.

Paice said wildly, 'He can't depress his nine-pounders, sir!'

Bolitho stared. Paice was more used to this kind of vessel and would know the difficulty of mounting a long nine-pounder on the deck of a merchantman.

'He's trying to put about!' Triscott waved at his gun crews. 'Into him, lads!' He watched as their grimy hands shot up. *'Fire!'*

Paice whispered, *'Holy Jesus!'*

Luck, the skill of an older gun captain, who could say? Bolitho saw the schooner's bowsprit shiver to fragments, the forecastle suddenly enveloped in torn shrouds and writhing canvas.

Paice searched through the drifting smoke for his boatswain.

71

'Mr Hawkins! Stand by the arms chest!' He tugged out his own hanger, his eyes back on the schooner. 'By God, they'll pay for this!'

Bolitho saw the distance dropping away as the crippled schooner continued to pay off downwind. His eyes narrowed and he heard the vague bang of muskets, the balls slamming against the cutter's hull. How long? He gestured urgently. 'Can you manhandle the other carronade to the starboard side?'

Paice nodded, his eyes blazing. 'Clear the larboard battery, Mr Triscott! Lay the smasher to starboard and prepare to fire!' He glanced at Bolitho and added, 'They may outnumber us, but not for long!'

Bolitho watched the punctured sails rising above the cutter as if to swoop down and enfold her, smother her into the sea. Fifty yards. Twenty yards. Here a man fell coughing blood, there another clapped one hand to his chest and dropped to his knees as if in prayer.

Bolitho pushed the boy down beside the companionway.

'Stay there!' He drew the old sword and pictured Allday right here beside him, his cutlass always ready.

'Stand by to board!' He saw their faces, some eager, others fearful now that the enemy was alongside. They could hear them yelling and firing, cursing while they waited for the impact.

Bolitho walked behind the crouching seamen, his sword hanging loosely from his hand.

Some glanced at him as his shadow fell over them, stunned, wild, filled with disbelief as he showed himself to the schooner's marksmen.

'Ready!' Bolitho winced as a ball cut through the tail of his coat. Like a gentle hand plucking at it. *'Now!'*

The two carronades exploded in adjoining ports with a combined roar which shook the cutter from truck to keel. As the smoke fanned inboard and men fell about coughing and retching in the stench, Bolitho saw that most of the schooner's forecastle had been ripped aside, and the mass of men who had been waiting to attack or repel boarders were entwined in a bloody tangle, which turned and moved as if one hideous giant had been cut down. The weight of grape with canister from the poop swivel had turned the deck into a slaughterhouse.

72

Bolitho gripped the shrouds and shouted, 'To me, lads! Grapnels there!' He heard them thudding on the schooner's bulwark, saw a crouching figure beside a upended gun, as if watching the attack. But it was headless.

The two hulls ground into each other, lurched apart, and then responding to the hands at the grapnels came together in a deadly embrace. *'Boarders away!'* Bolitho found himself carried across to the other vessel's deck, men thrusting past and around him in their need to get at their adversary.

Figures fell screaming and dying, and Bolitho saw *Telemachus*'s anger and jubilation change yet again to an insane sickness. With cutlass and pike, bayonets, even their bare hands, they fell on the schooner's crew with a ferocity which none of them would have believed just an hour earlier.

Bolitho shouted, *'That's enough!'* He struck down a man's cutlass with his own blade as he was about to impale a wounded youth on the reddened planks.

Paice too was yelling at his men to desist, while Hawkins the boatswain and a picked party of seamen were already taking charge of halliards and braces, to prevent the two hulls from destroying each other in the swell.

Cutlasses were being collected by the victors, and the schooner's company herded together, their wounded left to fend for themselves.

Bolitho said breathlessly, 'Send men below, Mr Paice – some brave fool might try to fire the magazine.' More orders and some cracked cheers rose around him, and he saw Triscott waving his hat from *Telemachus*'s poop. The boy was standing near him, trying to cheer but almost choked by tears as he saw the devastation and the hideous remains left by the carronades.

Hawkins squeaked through blood and pieces of flesh, his boots like a butcher's as he reported to his commander.

'All secured, sir.' He turned to Bolitho and added awkwardly, 'Some of us was no 'elp to you, sir.' He gestured with a tarred thumb. 'But you was right. The 'olds is full to the deck-beams with contraband. Tea, spices, silk, Dutch by the looks o' it.' He lowered his voice and watched without curiosity as a badly wounded smuggler crawled past his boots. 'I've set some armed

73

hands on the after 'old, sir. Spirits by the cask, Hollands Geneva I'll wager, and there may be more.'

Paice wiped his face with his sleeve. 'Then she *is* a Dutchie.'

Hawkins shook his head. 'Only the cargo, sir. The master is, or *was*, from Norfolk. Most of the others is English.' His lip curled. 'I'd swing the lot of 'em!'

Bolitho sheathed his old sword. Hoblyn had been right about that too. The cargo intended for Whitstable had probably begun its journey in the holds of some Dutch East Indiaman. A quick profit.

He looked at the dead and dying, then across at *Telemachus*, her own pain marked in blood. There had been little profit this time.

Paice asked anxiously, 'Are you well, sir?' He was peering at him. 'You're not hurt?'

Bolitho shook his head. He had been thinking of Allday, always close at times like these, and they had seen more than enough between them.

'I feel as if I have lost my right arm.' He shook himself. 'Have the vessel searched before nightfall. Then we shall anchor until we can attend to our repairs.' He watched as one of the smugglers, obviously someone of authority, was marched past by two seamen. 'That is good. Hold them apart. There is much we don't yet know.'

Paice said simply, 'My bosun spoke for us all, sir. We fought badly because we had no heart for it. But you are a man of war. We shall know better in future.'

Bolitho walked to the side, his whole being revolted against the sights and stench of death.

Hoblyn should be pleased; their lordships of Admiralty also. A fine schooner which after repair could either go to the prize court or more likely be taken into the navy. An illegal cargo, and desperate men who would soon hang in chains as a warning to others.

His glance moved over some of the huddled prisoners. A few of them might be pressed into service like their ship, provided they were found guiltless of murder.

It should have been enough. He felt a seaman offer his hard hand to assist him over the bulwark to *Telemachus*'s deck.

But if victory there was, it seemed an empty one.

6

The Brotherhood

John Allday sat on a stone bench with his back resting against the wall. There was only one window, small, and too high to see out of this damp, cell-like room, but he had kept his eyes open since he had surrendered to the press gang and knew that the lockup house was somewhere on the road to Sheerness. They had passed a small cavalry barracks, no more than an outpost for a handful of dragoons, but enough, it seemed, to allow the press gangs to come and go without fear of being attacked by those who might try to release their captives.

Allday guessed it was about noon and tried to disperse his own sense of uneasiness, the conviction that he had acted rashly and might find himself in worse trouble.

His companions, just five of them, were a poor collection, he thought. Deserters probably, but no loss to any ship of war.

Feet clattered on cobbles and somewhere a man laughed. There was an inn just a few yards from the lockup house, and he had seen two fine-looking girls watching from its porch as they had hurried past. He had thought of the inn he visited in Falmouth. He felt suddenly alone, and lonely.

He recalled too the time he had been taken by Bolitho's press gang in Cornwall. He had tried to lie his way out of it, but a gunner had seen the tattoo on his arm, the crossed cannon and flags which he had gathered along the way when he had served in the old seventy-four, *Resolution*. If what he had suspected was a fact, this same tattoo would help rather than hinder his hazy

75

plan. If not, he might find himself aboard a seagoing ship, outward bound to some hell on the other side of the world before he could make himself believed. Even then, a captain short of trained men would scarcely be willing to listen.

What would Bolitho do without him? He screwed up his brows in a deep frown. He had watched Bolitho's despair as he had met one barrier after another, and then the affair with the *Loyal Chieftain* had been more than enough.

He glanced at the door as a key grated in it and the same gunner's mate with the foul breath peered in at them.

He gestured with his key. 'Outside and get cleaned up. Then there's some bread and cheese, ale too if you behaves yerselves!' He looked directly at Allday. 'You stay 'ere. We need some more words about you.'

Allday said nothing as the others hurried away, already lost. Was the gunner's mate merely dragging it out for no purpose, or was there something behind his remarks?

But it was another who finally entered the dank room. Allday recognised him as a member of the press gang, the one who had spoken to him on the way here.

'Well, Spencer?' The man leaned against the wall and regarded him bleakly. 'Got yerself in a right pot o' stew, eh?'

Allday shrugged. 'I ran once. I'll do it again.'

'Mebbe, mebbe.' He cocked his head to listen to some horses cantering along the roadway.

'With them bloody dragoons on yer tail you'd not get far, matey!'

'Then there's no way.' Allday lowered his head, to think, to hide his eyes. It was something like a wild animal's sixth sense, an instinct which he had always possessed, and which had saved his skin too many times to remember. Something Bolitho admired and respected, and had told him as much.

The man said, 'Sailmaker, y'say?'

Allday nodded. He had no fears there. He had learned to stitch and use a sailmaker's palm before he was eighteen. There were not many tasks aboard ship he could not manage.

'Does it matter now?'

'Look, matey, don't take that tone with me –'

Allday sighed. 'You know how it is.'

The other hid his relief. For a moment he had felt something akin to fear when the big man had stirred from smouldering anger.

'Right then. There are ways. An' there's those who needs the likes o' you.' He gestured contemptuously at the closed door. 'Not like them bilge rats. They'd rob an' cheat anyone, gallows meat th' lot of 'em!'

He moved closer to Allday and added quietly, 'We're movin' tonight. So wot's it to be? Another poxy ship-o'-th'-line, or a berth in somethin' a bit more –' he rubbed a finger and thumb together '– *rewardin*', like?'

Allday felt cold sweat on his chest. 'Can it be done?'

'No questions. But yes, it can, an' it is!' He grinned. 'You be ready, see?'

Allday leaned over to pick up his old jacket and was careful that the other man saw his tattoo. 'I can't stomach being locked up.'

'Right you are. But make no mistake. If you betray those who might be willin' to 'elp you, you'll pray for death on a halter. I've seen things –' He straightened up. 'Just *believe* me, see?'

Allday thought of the corpse on the *Loyal Chieftain*'s deck, the rumours he had heard from some of the *Telemachus*'s hands that the murdered man's family had vanished too. It did not need a magician to discover why.

The door opened and the gunner's mate came in. 'You can get yer grub now, er – Spencer.'

Allday watched for a hint of understanding between them, but there was none. In this game nobody trusted anyone. Perhaps the gunner's mate was controlling this strange business?

Any deserter would probably take an offer of help, even if it landed him in the midst of a gang of smugglers. Being retaken by a press gang at best meant the same life from which he had tried to escape. At worst it could mean real hardship, plus a savage flogging as a warning to others.

The gunner's mate walked beside him to a long, scrubbed table where the others were already eating bread and cheese as if it was their last meal on earth.

He said, 'Stick to the sea, Spencer. Don't get like them scum.'

Allday asked casually, 'What did you want to talk about?'

The gunner's mate picked up a tankard and waited for a seaman to fill it with ale for him.

'Don't matter now. Your ship, the *London*, 'as sailed for the Caribbean. You'll just 'ave to take what you're given.'

When Allday had been pressed and taken to Bolitho's frigate *Phalarope* he had seen nothing like this. From a quiet Cornish road to the messdeck of a man-of-war. He smiled grimly. Him and Ferguson who had later lost an arm at the Saintes. Now they would serve no other. It was more like love than duty.

He glanced around the yard. Small groups of men were being mustered and checked by the lieutenant and some other members of a press gang.

His heart sank. Not a good seaman amongst them ... he almost laughed. How could he care about the needs of the fleet when at any moment his own life might be in danger?

But there *had* to be a way of doing it. If not the gunner's mate, then who? No ordinary seaman, press gang or not, could manage it alone. It would be more than his life was worth. A brief court martial, a few prayers, and then run aloft to some big ship's mainyard to kick your breath to the wind. No, there had to be more involved than that.

He watched the lieutenant, the same one who had called on him to stand and be examined. Allday knew ships, and he knew officers. This lieutenant would not have the brains even to be dishonest.

The lieutenant shouted, 'Pay attention. I'll not say it twice!'

Silence settled over the uneasy gathering.

He continued, 'In view of the situation here you must move at dusk to Sheerness. You will go in separate parties, and obey all orders without hesitation. I shall personally see that any disorder is treated as mutiny.' He glared around. 'I need not say more, I think?'

Allday heard someone whisper, 'Sheerness, up the road! Christ, Tom, we'll be signed into some ship afore the week's out!'

A tall figure with white patches on his collar moved from one of the outhouses.

Allday watched, his heart suddenly beating hard. The midshipman looked old for his lowly rank, about the same age as *Telemachus*'s Lieutenant Triscott. A pale, embittered face, the mouth turned down like someone permanently out of humour. Passed-over for lieutenant, or held back because of a senior officer's disfavour? There could be a dozen reasons.

Allday reached out to pick up some cheese and saw the midshipman give him a quick glance, then another at the seaman who had made him the offer.

So this was it. Allday tried to think clearly and calmly so that the chunk of dry cheese almost choked him.

There had to be an officer mixed up in it, even if it was an unimportant, passed-over midshipman.

The gunner's mate said, 'That's Mr Midshipman Fenwick. 'E'll be with your lot.' He glanced at him curiously. 'Between us, 'e's a pig, so watch yer step!'

Allday faced him. 'I'll remember.'

He returned to the cell-like room, his mind already busy on the next tack. If Bolitho discovered what was happening, it would be Mr bloody Fenwick who would need to watch his step.

Allday grinned. *And that's no error.*

Commodore Ralph Hoblyn climbed up from the schooner's cabin and leaned heavily on an ebony stick while he looked along the upper deck.

Bolitho watched him and tried to read his thoughts. The schooner, originally Dutch, had been renamed the *Four Brothers*, and, according to her papers, was used for general trading from the port of Newcastle. Her owner and master were one and the same, a man named Darley who had died in the brief but savage fight with *Telemachus*.

Now she lay at anchor off Sheerness, with the scarlet coats of a full marine guard at bow and stern in case anyone inside or outside the dockyard might be tempted to pilfer her cargo.

Hoblyn regarded the great bloodstain which had defied all attempts of the captured smugglers to remove it. The remains of those cut down by the carronades' devastating bombardment had been thrown unceremoniously overboard, but the stain, and the shattered timbers and planking were evidence enough of the battle.

Hoblyn wiped his mouth with his handkerchief. Bolitho had noticed that he seemed to tire very easily. Was it just that he had become unused to the sea, or did this schooner's deck act as a cruel reminder of his last command?

He said, 'I am extremely gratified, Bolitho. A full cargo, and a well-found vessel to boot.' He glanced up at the rigging, some of which had been spliced by Paice's hands for the passage to Sheerness. 'She'll fetch a good bounty at the next prize court, I shouldn't wonder. The dockyard can patch and paint her beforehand, of course.'

Bolitho asked, 'You'll not take her into the service, sir?'

Hoblyn shrugged and winced. 'I should be *delighted* to act on their lordships' behalf, naturally, Bolitho, but money first – theirs or someone else's.' He turned towards him. *'No favours.'*

Hoblyn walked to the vessel's wheel and touched it thoughtfully. 'I shall send word immediately. To the Customs Board too.'

'So there were no arrests at Whitstable, sir?'

Bolitho half-expected Hoblyn to show concern or discomfort. If he felt either he concealed it well.

Only two smugglers had been caught on the shore by a patrol of dragoons who had been forewarned by Hoblyn about the expected run. In the skirmish both had been killed.

'No, more's the pity. But you took the *Four Brothers*, and that will make these felons think before they try again.' He half-smiled. 'I'm afraid you'll not get many recruits from the prisoners, though.'

Bolitho stared across the water at the anchored cutter. He had never seen such a change in any vessel. The whole company seemed shocked and unable to believe what had happened. The fight had left five of their people dead and three more who were unlikely to recover from their wounds. In their small, tight company the losses had left a gap which new hands would be hard put to fill. Of the dead, the helmsman named Quin had been one of the most popular aboard. Ironically he had originally come from Newcastle, the *Four Brothers*' home port.

80

'Had we been able to take her by boarding, sir, then . . .'

Hoblyn made as if to touch his arm but withdrew it to his side. Another constant reminder.

He replied harshly, 'It was not to be. They fired on a King's ship. There's not a judge in the land who would let them escape the scaffold, and rightly so!' He seemed to overcome the passion in his tone and added, 'Be patient, Bolitho, you will have your men.' He waved his stick towards the shore. 'They're there, *somewhere*.'

Bolitho turned away as Allday returned to his thoughts. It was not the first time he had acted alone. But now it was different. This enemy flew no flag. It could be anyone.

He watched as Hoblyn limped to another hatch where some men were preparing tackles for hoisting smaller items of cargo on deck. His mind kept returning to the boy Matthew Corker's discovery. The berlin concealed in Hoblyn's stables. Where did it come from? Hoblyn had arrived at the dockyard in an expensive carriage of his own, so had proved once again, if proof was needed, that he was a rich man. There could be no connection between Hoblyn and the schooner. It was far too risky. Any one of her hands might have turned King's evidence to save his neck, and damn anyone who was left secure.

Hoblyn remarked, 'I suggest you do your utmost to get *Snapdragon* out of Chatham. I think you're going to need her. After your escapade with this schooner their lordships will likely feel more inclined to offload some of these patrols from the revenue cutters to *your* shoulders.' He turned so that the sunlight glittered in his eyes. 'Who knows? I may discover more intelligence for you to act upon.' He shaded his eyes with his disfigured hand and watched as his carriage moved slowly along the waterfront.

Bolitho followed his gaze and saw what he imagined was the white wig of Hoblyn's servant inside the carriage.

A lieutenant of the guard called to the boat alongside as Hoblyn limped carefully to the entry port.

Then he paused and glanced once more along the scarred decks.

'Speak to Paice's people, Bolitho. It would come better from you.' He gave him a searching stare. 'Your man was unhurt, I trust? I know how you value his services.'

So casually said. Or was it?

Bolitho replied, 'He is on an errand for me, sir.'

He felt something like sick relief as Hoblyn lowered himself into the boat.

I wish to God I knew where he was.

The marine lieutenant watched him impassively and said, 'We shall have a guardboat pulling around us until all the cargo is unloaded, sir.'

Bolitho looked at him. A young, untried face. He remembered Paice's words. A man of war. *Am I really like that?*

'Good. Keep your men away from the spirits too.' He saw the sudden indignation in his expression. 'Even marines have been known to *drink*, you know.' He saw *Telemachus*'s boat hooking on to the chains. 'I shall leave it to you, Lieutenant.'

On the short pull to the anchored cutter he noticed the way that the oarsmen watched him when they thought he was not looking. What was it now, he wondered? Respect, fear, or to learn what they were expected to become?

Paice greeted him at the cutter's side and touched his hat.

'All the wounded have been removed, sir. I fear that another of them died just before they left.' He shifted unhappily. 'His name was Whichelo, but then you'd not know him, sir.'

Bolitho looked at the tall lieutenant and said, '*Know* him? Yes, of course. The one who was standing in full view by his gun. I am sorry the lesson had to be learned in death.' He walked towards the companionway. 'May I have the aid of your clerk, or is he the purser today?' He stepped down and almost expected to see Allday on the deck below, watching and waiting. 'I have some despatches to be copied.' He turned on the companion ladder, his face warm in the sunlight. 'After *that*, prepare for sea, Mr Paice.'

Paice stared after him, his mind still grappling with Bolitho's cool acceptance of what had happened. Such a short while in their midst and yet he had even recalled the man who had just died.

Paice clenched his big hands. Bolitho had somehow managed to use that information like part of a lesson as well as a warning.

Perhaps what he had seen and done since he had first gone to sea as a twelve-year-old midshipman had honed all the pity and compassion from him.

Paice thrust through the throng of seamen who were working on repairs to seek out Godsalve the clerk, so he did not see the man who had just left him in turmoil.

Bolitho knelt in the small cabin, the uncompleted model ship grasped in both hands like a talisman.

A man of war?

Allday groped his way around the small timbered outhouse feeling for anything he might use as a weapon.

All afternoon the party of six prisoners with an armed escort of seamen had marched along the road towards Sheerness. When dusk came, the midshipman named Fenwick who commanded the group ordered a halt at a small inn where he was received with familiarity, although not with warmth. The other five prisoners were locked in an outbuilding with their legs in irons as an extra precaution. Allday, apparently because of his superior status as a sailmaker, was kept apart.

Allday returned to a crate where he had been sitting. The stage was set, he thought vaguely. He had heard the midshipman explaining just a bit too loudly to the seamen in the press gang why he was separating them in this fashion.

Once, the man who had first approached Allday came to the outhouse with some water and a hunk of bread.

'Is this all?' Allday had smelled the rum on the man's breath. It was what he needed more than anything.

The man had grinned at his anger. 'The others ain't gettin' nuthin'!'

Allday had tried to question him about the proposed escape. How would the midshipman explain it to his superior?

The man had held up his lantern to study him more closely. 'Leave it to us. Yer talks too much. Just remember wot I told yer!'

If only he could lay hands on a dirk or a cutlass. Maybe they had already seen through his feeble disguise? Someone might even have recognised him, and they were holding him apart so that he could be silenced for good when night came.

At sea Allday could tell the time almost by the pitch of a hull, and on land, when he had spent a short while guarding sheep in Cornwall, he had grown used to reading the stars and the moon's position for the same purpose.

But sealed up in this dark hut he had no way of telling and it made him more uneasy.

He wondered what Bolitho was doing. It worried him to think of him managing on his own. But something had to be done. He tensed as he thought he heard a slight sound through the door.

Now the truth. He could feel his heart pounding, and tried to control his breathing.

If it is to be murder – he would take one with him somehow.

Lanternlight made a golden slit up one side of the door, and a moment later a bolt was drawn. Then the seaman peered in at him.

Allday saw the midshipman's white collar-patches glowing beyond the lantern, and sensed the sudden tension. Even the seaman seemed ill at ease.

'Ready?'

Allday left the hut and almost fell as the lantern was shuttered into darkness.

The midshipman hissed, 'Stay together!' He peered at Allday. 'One foul move and by God I'll run you through!'

Allday followed the midshipman, his eyes on his white stockings. It was not the first time *he* had made this trip, he thought grimly. Rough ground, with scrub and bushes, the smell of cows from a nearby field. Then over a flint wall and towards a dark copse which loomed against the early stars like something solid. Allday's ears told him that nobody else from the press gang was coming with them. He heard the seaman behind him stagger, and tensed, expecting the sudden agonising thrust of steel in his back. But the man uttered a whispered oath and they continued on through the darkness. The trees appeared to move out and surround them like silent giants, and Allday knew from the midshipman's uneven breathing that he was probably doubly afraid because of his own guilt.

'This is far enough!' Midshipman Fenwick raised an arm. 'Here it is!'

84

Allday saw him stopping to peer at a large, half-burned tree trunk. The meeting point. How many others had come here to sell themselves, he wondered?

The seaman spat on the ground and Allday saw the glint of a pistol in his belt, a cutlass bared and held in his fist; no doubt he was ready to use both.

Allday pricked up his ears. The creak of harness, perhaps, but if so the horses must have muffled hooves. Where was it? He strained his eyes into the darkness, so that when the voice spoke out he was surprised at its nearness.

'Well, well, Mr Fenwick, another of your adventures.'

Allday listened. The speaker had a smooth, what he would call an educated voice. No accent which he could recognise, and Allday had heard most of them on all the messdecks he had known.

Fenwick stammered, 'I sent a message.'

'You did indeed. A sailmaker, you say?'

'That is so.' Fenwick was replying like a frightened schoolboy to his tutor.

'It had better be, eh?'

'There is just one thing.' Fenwick could barely form his words for trembling.

The voice snapped, 'More money, is it? You are a fool to gamble. It will be your undoing!'

Fenwick said nothing, as if he was unable to find the courage.

Allday watched the shadows. So it was gambling. The midshipman was probably being threatened because of debts. Allday stiffened and felt the hair rise on his neck. He had heard a footfall somewhere to his left, a shoe kicking against loose stones. He could still see nothing, and yet he sensed that there were figures all around them, unseen among the trees.

Fenwick must have felt it too. He suddenly blurted out, 'I need help! It's this man –'

Allday crouched, ready to spring, and then realised that Fenwick was pointing at his armed seaman.

'What about him?' The voice was sharper now.

'He – he's been interfering, doing things without coming to me. I remembered what you said, how it was planned –' The

85

words were pouring out in an uncontrollable torrent.

The voice snapped, 'Put down your weapons, *both of you!*' When neither of them moved, Allday heard the metallic clicks of pieces being pulled to full cock. Then two shadows emerged from the opposite side, each armed with what appeared to be a hanger or, perhaps, a cutlass.

The seaman dropped his own blade and then tossed his pistol to the ground.

He rasped, 'It's a bloody lie! The *young gentleman*'s gutless! You can't take 'is word fer nuthin'!'

Allday waited. There was defiance in the man's tone, anxiety too.

The voice asked, 'And Spencer, if that is your name, why are *you* here?'

'I'll repay my escape by working, sir.'

'Mr Fenwick, how have you left matters at the inn?'

Fenwick seemed completely stunned by the change of manner. The unseen questioner was smooth, even jocular again.

'I – I thought we could claim Spencer had escaped –'

The seaman sneered, 'See? Wot did I tell yer?'

'I have a better idea.' There was a creak, as if the man was leaning out of a window of his carriage. 'To have this sailmaker make good his escape, we need a victim, eh? A poor dead sailor-man murdered as he tried to prevent it!'

The two shadows bounded forward and Allday heard the seaman gasp in pain as he was beaten to his knees.

'Here!' Allday felt the cold metal of a cutlass grip pushed into his fingers.

The voice said calmly, 'Prove your loyalty to the Brotherhood – Spencer. That will bind both you and our gallant midshipman closer than ever to our affairs.'

Allday stared at the kneeling figure while the others stood clear. The cutlass felt like lead, and his mouth was as dry as a kiln.

The voice persisted, 'Kill him!'

Allday stepped forward but at that moment the seaman threw himself on one side, scrambling for the pistol which he had dropped.

The explosion and the flash which lit up the motionless figures by the burned tree was like a nightmare. It all happened in seconds and Allday gritted his teeth as he saw the pistol fall once more, still gripped by the sailor's hand, which had been severed at the wrist by one blow from a cutlass. Even as the man rolled over and gave one last shrill scream the same attacker raised his blade and drove it down with such force Allday heard the point grate into the ground through the man's body.

The sudden silence was broken only by the sudden muffled stamp of nervous horses, the far-off barking of a farm dog, then the sound of wheels on some kind of cart-track.

The figure by the corpse bent down and picked up the fallen cutlass, but left the pistol still gripped by its severed hand.

He stared at Allday, his expression invisible. 'Your turn'll come.' To Fenwick he added, 'Here, take this purse for your gaming table.' There was utter contempt in his voice. 'You can raise the alarm in an hour, though, God knows, some picket might have heard the fool shoot!'

Fenwick was vomiting against a tree, and the man said softly, 'I'd finish him too, but –' He did not go on. Instead he watched as Fenwick picked up his weapons and the small bag of coins before adding, 'We had best be moving.' He could have been grinning. 'You can keep the cutlass. You'll need it.'

Allday looked back at the untidy corpse and wondered if Fenwick would be the next victim.

He followed the other man through the trees, the shadowy figures of his companions already on the move.

Allday had had cause to kill several men in his life. In anger, and in the fury of battle, sometimes in the defence of others. So why was this any different? Would he have killed the seaman to give his story more value, if the other man had not struck first?

Allday did not know, and decided it was better to keep it that way until the danger was past.

How quickly fate could move. Soon the midshipman would raise the alarm, and later they would find the corpse. A common seaman who had been murdered by an escaping prisoner named Spencer.

Allday thought of the unseen man in the carriage. If he could only manage to learn his name – he shook himself like a dog. One thing at a time. At present he was still alive, but the knowledge he had gained so far was enough to change that just as quickly.

7

In Good Company

Lieutenant Charles Queely clattered down *Wakeful*'s companion ladder and after a small hesitation thrust open the cabin door. Bolitho was sitting at the table, chin in hand while he finished reading the log.

He glanced up. 'Good morning, Mr Queely.'

Queely contained his surprise. He had expected to find Bolitho asleep, not still going through his records and examining the chart.

He said, 'I – I beg your pardon, sir. I was about to inform you that dawn is almost upon us.' He glanced quickly around the cabin as if expecting to see something different.

Bolitho stretched. 'I would relish some coffee if you could provide it.' He knew what Queely was thinking, and found himself wondering why he did *not* feel tired. He had allowed himself no rest, and when *Telemachus* had sighted the other cutter he had arranged to be pulled across to Queely's command without delay or explanation.

Queely was usually well able to conceal his innermost feelings, and, despite his youth, had already slipped easily into a commander's role. But Bolitho's arrival, and the sight of *Telemachus* hove-to, displaying her powderstains, and areas of pale new timber where her carpenter and his crew had begun their repairs, had taken him all aback.

Queely had asked, 'Will they return to the yard, sir?'

'I think not. I have told Lieutenant Paice that working together at sea to complete their overhaul, even though they are short-handed because of those killed and wounded, will do far more good. It will draw them into a team again, keep them too busy to grieve or to fall into bad ways.'

Queely had been shocked to see the damage and had said immediately, 'I knew nothing about it, sir. I carried out my patrol as you ordered, and after losing signalling contact with you I decided to remain on station.'

That had been yesterday. Now, after a full night's sailing, they had continued to the south-east in spite of tacking again and again into the wind.

It was possible that Queely had been totally ignorant of the fierce close-action with the *Four Brothers*. With his studious features, hooked nose and deepset eyes he seemed to be a man who was well able to make up his own mind and act upon it. *I decided to remain on station*. What Bolitho might have said under the same circumstances.

As Queely pushed through the door to send for some coffee Bolitho looked around the cabin once more. *Telemachus* and this vessel had been built in the same yard with just a couple of years between them. How could they be so different? Even the cabin gave an air of intentional disorder, or temporary occupancy. As if Queely used it just for the purpose *Wakeful* was designed for, not as something to be coddled. Uniforms swayed from various hooks, while sidearms and swords were all bundled together in a half-open chest. Only Queely's sextant lay in pride of place, carefully wedged in a corner of his cot where it would be safe even in the wildest weather.

He thought of Paice's unspoken protest at being ordered immediately to sea after *Telemachus*'s first battle. Was it really the true reason he had sent him, the same explanation he had made to Queely? Or was it to protect Allday from sailors' casual gossip once they were able to get ashore?

If Allday was still alive . . . He ran his fingers through his hair with quiet desperation. *He was alive*. He must believe it.

The door opened and Young Matthew entered with a pot of coffee. His round face had lost its colour again, and his skin looked damp and pallid. He had been fighting his own battle with the motion. That was another difference between the two cutters. Paice *sailed* his *Telemachus*, Queely seemed to drive his command with the same lack of patience he exhibited in his daily routine.

Bolitho thought of Queely's second-in-command, a reedy lieutenant named Kempthorne. He came of a long line of sea-officers, and his own father had been a rear-admiral. Bolitho suspected that it was tradition rather than choice which had brought Kempthorne into the King's navy. Chalk and cheese, he thought. It was hard to see him having much in common with Queely. Bolitho had never seen so many, well-used books outside of a library. From them he had gathered that Queely was interested in many subjects, as widely ranged as tropical medicine and astronomy, Eastern religions and medieval poetry. A withdrawn, self-contained man. It would be useful to know more about him.

Bolitho looked at the boy over the top of his tankard. 'Feeling a mite better, Matthew?'

The boy gulped and gripped the table as the sea surged along the hull and brought an angry exchange between the watchkeepers around the tiller.

'*Easier*, sir.' He watched Bolitho drinking the coffee with despair. 'I – I'm trying –' He turned and fled from the cabin.

Bolitho sighed and then slipped into his old, seagoing coat. For a few moments he fingered a faded sleeve and its tarnished buttons. Remembering it around her sun-blistered shoulders, her beautiful body lolling against him in the sternsheets. *And then* . . .

He almost fell as the hull rolled again and did not even notice the pain as his head jarred against the deckhead. He stared round wildly, the anguish sweeping over and through him like a terrible wave.

Will it never leave me?

He saw Queely angled in the doorframe, his eyes watching warily.

Bolitho looked away. '*Yes?*' He may have called out aloud. But Viola would never hear him. The picture haunted him, of Allday lowering her over the boat's gunwale while the others stared, unbelieving, their burned faces stricken as if each and every man

90

had found and then lost something in her. And now Allday was gone.

Queely said, 'Land in sight, sir.'

They clambered up the ladder, the steps running with the spray which cascaded through the companionway each time *Wakeful* dipped her bowsprit.

Bolitho gripped a stanchion and waited for his eyes to accept the grey half-light. The sky was almost clear. It held the promise of another fine day.

The watch on deck moved about with practised familiarity, their bodies leaning over to the cutter's swooping rolls and plunges, some wearing rough tarpaulin coats, others stripped to the waist, their bare backs shining like statuary in the flying spray. The 'hard men' of *Wakeful*'s company. Every ship had them.

Bolitho wondered briefly what they thought about the *Four Brothers*. They had had no contact with *Telemachus* until yesterday, but he knew from experience that the navy created its own means of transmitting information: fact and rumour alike seemed to travel faster than a hoist from any flagship.

'Do you have a good lookout aloft?'

Queely watched his back, his hooked nose jutting forward like a bird of prey.

'Aye, sir.' It sounded like *of course*.

'Have a glass sent aloft, if you please.' Bolitho ignored Queely's angry glance at his first lieutenant and lifted a telescope from its rack beside the compass box.

As he wiped the lens with a handkerchief already damp in the spray, he said, 'I want to know if anything unusual is abroad this morning.'

He did not need to explain, but it gave him time to think.

He waited for a line of broken waves to sweep past the larboard beam, then braced his legs and levelled the glass beyond the shrouds. A shadow at first, then rising with the hull, hardening into an undulating wedge of land. He wiped his mouth and handed the telescope to Kempthorne.

France.

So near. The old enemy. Unchanged in the poor light and yet being torn apart by the Terror's bloody aftermath.

He heard the master say in a loud whisper, 'We'm gettin' a bit close.'

Queely raised his speaking trumpet and peered up at the lookout. 'D'you see anything? *Wake up*, man!'

He sounded impatient; he probably thought it a waste to send a good telescope aloft where it might be damaged.

'Nuthin', sir!'

Queely looked at Bolitho. 'I'd not expect much shipping here, sir. The Frogs maintain their inshore patrols all the way from the Dutch frontier, right down to Le Havre. Most ships' masters think it prudent to avoid arousing their attention.'

Bolitho walked to the bulwark and thought of Delaval, and the *Four Brothers*' dead captain. The smuggling gangs seemed to come and go no matter whose ships were on patrol.

Queely explained, 'The Frenchies have a stop, search and detain policy, sir. Several ships have been reported missing, and you'll get no information from Paris.' He shook his head. 'I'd not live there for a King's ransom.'

Bolitho eyed him calmly. 'Then we must ensure it cannot happen *here*, eh, Mr Queely?'

'With respect, sir, unless we get more ships, the smugglers will ignore us too. The fleet is cut to virtually a handful of vessels, and now that they see a richer living in the Trade, able-bodied seamen are becoming a rare commodity.'

Bolitho walked past the vibrating tiller bar and saw there were three men clinging to it, a master's mate nearby with his eyes moving from the mainsail's quivering peak to the compass and back again.

'That is why our three cutters must work together.' Bolitho saw Young Matthew run to the lee bulwark and lean over it to vomit although his stomach had been emptied long ago. A passing seaman grinned, seized his belt and said, 'Watch yer step, nipper, it's a long fathom down there!'

Bolitho looked past him but was thinking of *Telemachus*. 'You are all unique, and because of the trust and loyalty shared by your people you are an example to others.'

Queely watched him then said, 'You were examining the log, sir?'

'Is that a question?' Bolitho felt the spray soaking into his shirt, but kept his eyes on the far-off ridge of land. 'Whenever I have been given the honour of command I have examined the punishment book first. It always gives me a fair idea of my predecessor's behaviour, and that of his company. You should be grateful that your command is free of unrest and its inevitable repression.'

Queely nodded uncertainly. 'Aye, sir, I suppose so.'

Bolitho did not look at him. He knew his comment was not quite what Queely had expected.

Some of the hands working at the halliards were chattering to each other when Queely shouted, 'Belay that!' He held up his hand. '*Listen*, damn you!'

Bolitho clenched his hands together behind his back. Sharp hammer-like explosions. Small artillery, but firing in earnest.

'Where away?'

The master called, 'Astern, starboard quarter, sir.' The others stared at him but he faced them defiantly. 'No doubt in my mind, sir.'

Bolitho nodded. 'Nor mine.'

Queely hastened to the compass. 'What must I do, sir?'

Bolitho turned his head to listen as another series of shots echoed across the water.

'Bring her about.' He joined Queely beside the compass. 'In this wind you can run free to the south-west.' It was like thinking aloud. It was also like *Telemachus* all over again. The doubt, hesitation, opposition, even though nobody had raised a single protest.

Queely glanced at him. 'That will surely take us into French waters, sir.'

Bolitho looked at the straining mainsail, the way the long boom seemed to tear above the water with a mind of its own.

'Maybe. We shall see.' He met his eyes and added, 'It would seem that *someone* is abroad this morning after all?'

Queely tightened his jaw then snapped, 'All hands, Mr Kempthorne! Stand by to come about.' He glared at the master as if he had caused his displeasure. 'We shall steer south-west.'

The master's face was blank. 'Aye, aye, sir.'

Bolitho suspected he was used to Queely's moods.

93

'Ready ho!'

'Put the helm down!'

Bolitho gripped the companion head for support again as with her headsail sheets set free and the sails flapping in wild confusion, *Wakeful* butted around and across the wind's eye.

'Mains'l *haul*!'

Bolitho dashed the spray from his face and hair and could have sworn that the long fidded topmast was curving and bending like a coachman's whip.

Queely's impatience matched Paice's pride.

'Meet her! Steady as you go – *steady*, man!'

Heeling over on the opposite tack *Wakeful* responded again to wind and rudder, but with the lively north-easterly hardening her sails like armour plating, she held firmly to her course, the motion less violent.

'Sou'-West, sir! Steady she goes!'

Bolitho walked stiffly to the larboard side and watched the first thin sunlight touch the land. It looked much nearer, but it was a trick of light and colour which often happened in coastal waters.

Bolitho snatched up a telescope as the lookout yelled, 'Deck there! Ships on th' larboard bow!' He sounded breathless, as if the violence of the manoeuvre had almost hurled him down.

It was still too far. Bolitho watched the waves looming and fading as he trained the glass carefully on the bearing.

Smaller vessels. Perhaps three of them. One of them firing, the sound reaching him now through the planks under his feet. Like driftwood striking into the hull.

'Deck there! 'Tis a chase, sir! Steering sou'-west!'

Bolitho tried to picture it. A chase, using the same wind which made *Wakeful*'s canvas boom like thunder. What ships must they be?

'Let her fall off two points, Mr Queely. Steer south-south-west.'

He forced himself to ignore Queely's stifled resentment. 'Make as much sail as you can safely carry. I want to catch them!'

Queely opened and closed his mouth. Then he beckoned to Kempthorne. 'Loose the tops'l!'

Bolitho found time to think of his dead brother as under extra

94

canvas the cutter seemed to throw herself across the short crests. No wonder he had loved his *Avenger*. The picture faded. If he ever really cared for anything.

He looked up and saw the sunshine touching each sail in turn, the canvas already steaming in the first hint of warmth.

The guns were still firing, but when he raised the glass again he saw that the angle of the sails had increased, as if the furthest craft was being headed off and driven towards the land when before she had been making for open water. Like a sheep being tired and then harried by the shepherd's dog until all thought of escape was gone.

A voice said, 'We're overhaulin' the buggers 'and over fist, Ted!'

Another exclaimed, 'They ain't even seen us yet!'

The coastline was taking on personality, while here and there Bolitho saw sunlight reflecting from windows, changing a headland from purple to lush green.

'Deck there!' Everyone had forgotten about the masthead. 'Two French luggers, sir! Not certain about t'other, but she's in bad trouble! Canvas shot through, a topmast gone!'

Bolitho walked this way and that. Two luggers, perhaps after a smuggler. 'We shall discover nothing if the French take her.' He saw the others staring at him. '*More sail*, Mr Queely. I wish to stand between them!'

Queely nodded to the master then said in a fierce whisper, 'We shall be inside their waters in half-an-hour, sir! They'll not take kindly to it.' He offered his last card. 'Neither will the admiral, I'm thinking.'

Bolitho watched more men swarming aloft, their horny feet moving like paddles on the jerking ratlines.

'The admiral, fortunately, is in Chatham, Mr Queely.' He glanced round as more shot hammered over the crests. 'Whereas we are here.'

'It is my right to lodge a protest, sir.'

'It is also your duty to fight your ship if need be, to the best of your ability.' He walked away, angry with Queely for making him use authority when he only wanted co-operation.

'One of 'em's seen us, sir!'

The other lugger had luffed and was spilling canvas as she thrust over into the wind to meet *Wakeful*'s intrusion.

Queely watched the lugger, his eyes cold. 'Clear for action.'

Kempthorne strode aft from the mainmast, his gaze questioning.

'Sir?'

'Then stand by to shorten sail!'

Bolitho looked across the deck, feeling his displeasure, his resistance.

'Have your gunner lay aft, Mr Queely. I wish to speak with him.'

Something touched his coat and he turned to see the boy staring up at him, the old sword clutched in both hands.

Bolitho gripped his shoulder. 'That was *well* done, Matthew.'

The boy blinked and stared at the frantic preparations to cast off the gun's breechings without hampering the men at halliards and braces. There was no longer awe there, nor excitement. His lips quivered, and Bolitho knew that fear, and the reason for it, had replaced them. But his voice was steady enough, and only Bolitho knew what the effort was costing him. As he helped Bolitho clip the sword into place he said, 'It's what *he* would have done, sir, what he would have expected of me.'

Once again, Allday's shadow was nearby.

Luke Teach, *Wakeful*'s gunner, waited patiently while Bolitho described what he wanted. He was a thickset, fierce-looking man who hailed from the port of Bristol, and was said to boast that he was a true descendant of Edward Teach, or Blackbeard as he was known. He had also come from Bristol, a privateer who soon found piracy on the high seas was far more rewarding.

Bolitho could well believe it, for the gunner had a jowl so dark that had the King's Regulations allowed otherwise he might have grown a beard to rival that of his murderous ancestor.

Bolitho said, 'I intend to drive between the luggers and the other vessel. The French may not contest it, but if they do –'

Teach touched his tarred hat. 'Leave 'un to me, zur.' He bustled away, calling names, picking men from various stations because he knew their ability better than anyone.

96

Queely said, 'That ship is in a poor way, sir.' But his eyes were on the preparations around the carronades. 'I fear we may be too late.'

Bolitho took the telescope and examined the other vessels.

The luggers would be wary of the English cutter, for although they served their navy and were well-handled, probably by local men, like *Wakeful*'s, they would be unused to open combat.

He watched the nearest one tacking steeply under a full press of tan-coloured sails and saw the new French ensign flapping from her gaff, the little-known Tricolour set in one corner of the original white flag.

He glanced up and saw that Queely had already made his own gesture, although he doubted if the French would need to see an English flag to know her nationality and purpose.

The craft being chased had lost several spars and was barely making headway, some rigging and an upended boat trailing alongside to further pull her round. A fishing vessel of some kind, Bolitho thought, their own or English did not matter. It seemed very likely she might be employed in the Trade – few revenue officers dared to venture into the fishermen's tight community.

'God, she's taking it cruelly.' Kempthorne was standing on the mainhatch to get a better look as more shots pursued the stricken vessel, some striking the hull, others tearing through rigging and puncturing her sails.

'Run out, Mr Queely.' Bolitho rested his hand on his sword hilt and watched as the *Wakeful*'s men hauled and guided their guns up to their open ports.

The French lugger would know what that meant. *Baring her teeth*. Making it clear what she intended.

The lugger changed tack and began to fall downwind to draw nearer to her consort.

Teach the gunner was creeping along the bulwark like a crab, pausing to peer through every port, to instruct each man, a handspike here, a pull on a tackle there. *Wakeful* was no fifth-rate but at least she was prepared.

Queely exclaimed, 'The Frogs are hauling off!'

Bolitho thought he knew why but said nothing. The explosion when it came was violent and unexpected. A tongue of flame shot

97

from the fishing boat's deck and in seconds her canvas was in charred flakes, the rigging and upperworks savagely ablaze.

A boat was pulling away, and must have been in the water, hidden by the shattered hull before the explosion was sparked off. One of the luggers fired, and a ball passed above the little boat to hurl a waterspout high into the air.

Queely stared at Bolitho, his eyes wild. '*Engage*, sir?'

Bolitho pointed to the fishing boat. 'As close as you dare. I don't think –' The rest was lost in a second explosion as a ball crashed directly into the oared boat, and when the fragments had finally ceased splashing down – there was nothing to be seen.

Queely banged one hand into his palm. '*Bastards!*'

'Shorten sail, if you please.' Bolitho trained his glass on the sinking fishing boat. By rights she should have gone by now, but some trick of buoyancy defied both the fire and the gashes in her hull.

Kempthorne whispered to his commander, 'If there is another explosion we shall be in mortal danger, sir!'

Queely retorted, 'I think we are aware of it.' He looked hotly at Bolitho. '*I* certainly am.'

There was a far-off, muffled bang, and it seemed an eternity before a great fin of spray cascaded across the sea near the capsizing hull. Fired at maximum range from some shore battery which was watching the drama through powerful telescopes. Probably a thirty-two-pounder, a 'Long Nine' as the English nicknamed them, an extremely accurate gun, and the largest carried by any man-of-war. For that purpose it was also used on both sides of the Channel to determine the extents of their territorial waters.

Wakeful was out of range for any accurate shooting. But it would only need one of those massive iron balls, even with the range all but spent, to dismast her, or shatter her bilges like a battering ram.

It was why the luggers were keeping well clear, and not just because they were unwilling to match the cutter's carronades.

Bolitho said, 'No time to put down the boat. I want grapnels.' He looked at the men not employed at the guns. '*Volunteers* to board that wreck!'

98

Nobody moved, and then one of the half-naked seamen swaggered forward. 'Right ye be, sir.'

Another moved out. 'Me too, sir.'

A dozen hands shot up, some of the gun crews too.

Bolitho cleared his throat. Allday might have got volunteers; he had not expected to do it himself with total strangers.

'Take in the mains'l!' Queely had his hands on his hips, pressing against his waist to control his agitation.

'Tops'l and jib, Mr Kempthorne, they will suffice!'

Bolitho walked amongst the volunteers as they prepared their heaving lines and grapnels.

The first volunteer peered at him and asked, 'Wot we lookin' fer, sir?' He had the battered face of a prize-fighter, and Bolitho's mind clung to yet another memory, that of Stockdale, his first coxswain, who had died protecting his back at the Saintes.

'I don't know, and that's the God's truth.' He craned over the bulwark and watched the sinking hull moving dangerously near. The surrounding sea was covered with dead fish and shattered casks, flotsam, charred remains, but little else.

There was another distant bang and eventually the ball slammed down just a few yards from the wreck. The fishing boat was an aiming mark for the invisible shore battery, Bolitho thought. Like a lone tree in the middle of a battlefield.

The shock of the heavy ball made the wreck lurch over and Bolitho heard the sudden inrush of water as the seams opened up to speed its end.

'Grapnels!'

Four of them jagged into the wreck and within seconds the seamen were clawing their way across, urged on by their messmates, the luggers all but forgotten except by Teach and his handpicked gun crews.

The shore battery fired again, and spray fell across the sinking vessel and made the seamen there peer round with alarm.

Queely said hoarsely, 'They'll catch us at any moment, sir!'

A grapnel line parted like a pistol shot; the wreck was starting to settle down. There was no point in any further risk.

'Cast off! Recall those men!'

Bolitho turned as the man with the battered face yelled, ''Ere, sir!'

He floundered through a hatchway where the trapped water already shone in the sunlight like black glass. If the hull dived nothing could prevent it, and he would certainly go with her.

'*Call him back!*'

Bolitho watched, holding his breath as the man reappeared. He was carrying a body over his bare shoulders as effortlessly as a sack.

Queely muttered, 'God's teeth, it's a woman!'

Willing hands reached out to haul them on board, then as the wreck began to dip, and another line snapped under the strain, Bolitho said, 'Carry on, Mr Queely, you may stand your ship out of danger.'

A ball smashed across the water and hit the wreck beneath the surface.

'*Loose the mains'l! More hands aloft there!*'

Wakeful gathered way, flotsam and dead fish parting beneath her long bowsprit.

When Bolitho looked again, the fishing boat had vanished. He walked slowly through the silent seamen then felt his head swim as he saw the woman lying on the deck. She was just a girl, wearing rough, badly made clothing, a coarse shawl tied under her long hair. One foot was bare, the other still encased in a crude wooden *sabot*.

They stood around staring until Queely pushed between them, and, after glancing questioningly at Bolitho, knelt beside her.

The man who had carried her aboard said, 'She be *dead*, sir.' He sounded stricken, cheated.

Bolitho looked at her face. The eyes tightly shut, with saltwater running from them like tears, as if she was asleep, trapped in some terrible dream.

Some poor fishergirl probably, caught up in a conflict in which she had no part.

But looking at her pale features reminded Bolitho of only one thing, that moment when Viola had been given to the sea.

Queely opened the front of the girl's clothing and thrust his hand underneath and around her breast.

Apart from the wind in the sails there was no other sound.

Queely withdrew his hand and tidied her wet garments with unexpected care.

'Dead, sir.' He looked up at him dully. 'Shall I have her put over?'

Bolitho made himself move closer, his hands bunched so tightly that he could feel the bones cracking.

'*No*. Not yet.' He looked at the watching faces. 'Have her sewn up.' He lowered himself to the deck and touched her hair. It was like sodden weed.

Then he looked at her bare, outthrust foot. 'What are those marks?'

Queely glanced at him. He had been looking at the sails, and the men at the tiller, to make certain there was no chase, no further threat from the battery.

'Sir?'

Bolitho made himself hold her ankle. It was like ice. There were scars on the skin, raw, like the marks of irons.

Queely explained. 'The wooden *sabots*, sir. They did it. Look at the other one.'

'Yes. I see.' Bolitho wanted to cover her. To hide her pain from their eyes.

Then he stared at the lieutenant across her body. 'I should have seen it.' He ignored Queely's surprise and took her bare foot in his fingers. It was all he could do not to cry out as the memory probed through him.

Her foot was soft, and not from the sea. Too soft for a rough wooden shoe, and one more used to happier times, to dancing and laughter. He lowered his face until it was almost touching hers. 'Come here.' He felt Queely kneel beside him. 'Can you smell it?'

Queely hesitated. 'Aye, sir. Very faint.' He pushed the wet hair from the girl's stricken face so that it still seemed it might awaken her, open her eyes to his touch. He said, 'Perfume, sir.'

Bolitho examined her small hands, stiffening now in spite of the warm sunlight. Dirty, but smooth and well kept.

Queely said quietly, 'No fishergirl, this one, sir.'

Bolitho stood up and held on to a backstay for support. He looked abeam but the luggers were partly hidden in low haze, the land already meaningless.

He knew Queely was searching her body but could not watch.

Queely stood up and held out a lace-edged handkerchief. It had the initial *H* in one corner. Soaked in seawater but quite clean. A last link perhaps with a life which had rejected her.

Queely said heavily, 'That's all, sir.'

Bolitho took it. 'One day perhaps –' He could not go on.

Later at the lee bulwark the small, canvas-sewn body was raised on a grating.

Lieutenant Kempthorne had asked if a flag was required but Bolitho had replied, 'She has been destroyed by her own, and ours cannot help her now.'

With heads uncovered the seamen stood about and watched in silence.

Bolitho steeled himself, then turned as Queely, his hat crushed beneath one arm, said something aloud in French.

Then he repeated to his men around him, 'We cannot kneel beside her grave, but we commend her to the sea from which she came.'

There was a brief slithering sound, a splash alongside, and in twos and threes the men broke up and returned to their duties.

Queely replaced his hat and said, 'Well, sir?'

'How strange it should be a young, unknown French girl who has become our first ally in this wretched business.'

Watched by Queely he took out the handkerchief and shook it in the warm breeze.

'She *will* be remembered.' He stared astern at *Wakeful*'s frothing progress. 'She is safe now, and in good company.'

8

By Sea And By Stealth

The hoofbeats of the three horses became more muffled as they turned off the narrow road and on to rough moorland, the grass still glittering from overnight rain.

Bolitho kneed his horse forward and watched the sunlight uncovering the trees and some scattered farm buildings. Opening up the land, like the sunshine of that morning when they had sighted the pursued fishing boat.

Wakeful had anchored before dawn and within the hour Bolitho had been mounted, and with Young Matthew following close behind had set off to this place.

In the early sunlight he saw the trooper of dragoons pausing to peer back at them, his scarlet coat and white crossbelt very bright against the dripping trees.

The man had been waiting to escort him as soon as the cutter was anchored. The commodore's aide had sent the message, although he had been unable to offer any more intelligence regarding the reason. Hoblyn it appeared was away again visiting some boatyard.

He heard the boy yawning hugely behind him. Half-asleep still, dazed by the events he had shared and witnessed, and obviously grateful to feel the land under him again.

The trooper called, 'Not much further, sir.' He eyed Bolitho curiously. 'Am I ridin' too fast for 'e, sir?'

'I'm a Cornishman.' Bolitho's voice was unusually curt. 'I am used to riding.'

103

The trooper hid a grin. 'Oi be from Portsmouth, sir, but Oi knows nowt about ships!' He spurred his horse into a trot.

Bolitho noticed that the trooper had a short carbine, favoured by the dragoons, already drawn and resting across his saddle. Like a skirmisher in enemy territory. In such peaceful country-side it seemed unreal.

Again and again Bolitho's mind returned to the dead girl. She was his only link, and yet he still did not know how to use it. Instead he saw her face, tight with shock when she must have realised she had only seconds to live. He imagined he could still feel the icy skin of her ankle in his grip. *Viola*.

Whom could he trust? Who would believe him, or even want to believe him?

''Ere we be, sir.'

Bolitho gave a start and realised that they were cantering into a widespread copse of tall trees. There was a clearing now, almost circular, with a burned-out tree in the centre. The perfect place for a duel, he thought grimly.

Amongst the trees he saw several scarlet-clad figures, the occasional nervous swish of a horse's tail. There was something sinister about the clearing. A place of danger.

An officer was sitting on a small stool, drinking from a silver tankard while his orderly stood attentively at his elbow. He saw Bolitho and handed his man the tankard before rising to his feet.

His uniform was beautifully cut, but could not disguise his slight belly. A man who lived well, despite his calling, Bolitho thought.

The officer raised his hat and smiled. 'Major Philip Craven, 30th Regiment of Dragoons.' He gave a slight bow. 'Would you care for a taste?'

He had an easy, pleasant manner, and was younger than Bolitho had first imagined.

Bolitho noticed that, despite his relaxed air, his eyes were rarely still. On his men, the horses, or the track which they had just left.

Bolitho replied, 'I should enjoy that.' It surprised him, for he was usually ill-at-ease with the army, foot *or* cavalry.

As the orderly busied himself with a basket on the ground,

104

Bolitho noticed a naval lieutenant and a tall, pale-faced midshipman for the first time.

The major gestured. 'Two officers of the press.'

Bolitho took the proffered tankard and was glad he could keep it so steady.

More trouble. Was it Allday?

He asked, 'Why was I informed?'

The major shrugged. 'I've heard of your – er, exploits of course. When the commodore is away, I try to keep in contact with the navy and the civil authority.' He frowned suddenly. 'God, you'd think we were an army of occupation!' He beckoned for the orderly to refill his tankard and added, 'One of the sailors was murdered here, trying to retake a man who had escaped from their custody.'

Bolitho sipped the wine. It was, he suspected, very expensive claret.

The major explained, 'The midshipman was here too, but they were rushed by some mob or other, and his sailor was cut down.' He walked slowly to a patch of trampled grass. 'Found his severed hand just here, the pistol still in it. It had been fired, so he may have winged one of the scum. But luck in that direction is thin on the ground. I've had my fellows search the area.' He added bitterly, 'By God, they're getting used to that, I can tell you, sir! But there was nothing. I did not expect there would be.' He looked around at the watching trees, the way that the sunlight seemed shut out, beyond reach.

Then he said, 'I can see that you feel it too. This is a place of ill repute. Nobody comes here now.' His eyes sparked in a memory. 'However there was a carriage here recently. But we lost the tracks as soon as it left the copse.'

'A local man of importance?'

The major observed him shrewdly. 'I have my own ideas. But what can I do? To think that within a year perhaps, I shall be ordered to lead my dragoons –' he waved vaguely in the direction of the sea, 'against French invaders, to protect the same people who lie, cheat, and if necessary murder anyone who stands up to them!'

'Is it really as bad as that?'

105

The major smiled. 'My colonel will tell you, given half a chance. He was in Thanet, about eight years ago when he was a captain. He was ordered to Deal, with a troop of fifty dragoons, to put down a smugglers' gang and burn their boats.' His eyes hardened as he saw it in his mind, imagining himself and not his colonel. 'They were set upon by an armed mob of well over a thousand, and were cut off. But for the timely arrival of the 38th Regiment of Foot, who, God bless 'em, had marched all the way from Canterbury to assist, my colonel's troop would have been massacred. I am a soldier, and I have seen some terrible sights, just as you have. But this kind of work leaves me sick with disgust.'

Bolitho saw Young Matthew leading his horse towards the trees, then pausing as a dragoon held up his hand and shook his head.

'Why don't people come here?'

The major shrugged. 'You see that burned-out tree? A smuggling gang caught a man from the nearby village. He had been spying on them, was well known for it apparently. Sometimes he was said to have sold information to the revenue officers, even to the army.'

'So they killed him here?' Bolitho looked hard at the clearing.

'No. They set fire to that tree, then burned out his eyes. A warning to others, if one such were needed!'

Bolitho felt his shirt clinging clammily to his body. 'Thank you for telling me all this.' He beckoned to the two watching sea-officers. 'I'll be quick.'

The major smiled. 'I'm willing to fight in the open. But here? I'd prefer to use infantry!'

The lieutenant touched his hat and explained that he had been in charge of a press gang, and had ordered his midshipman to march some prisoners to Sheerness.

Bolitho said sharply, 'I will attend to that matter presently.' The lieutenant's obvious eagerness to shift any blame to his subordinate's shoulders was sickening.

'Who are you?' Bolitho eyed the pale midshipman, and immediately sensed his fear. 'Tell me exactly what happened.'

'Midshipman Fenwick, sir.' He looked anywhere but at

106

Bolitho's eyes. 'I – I had halted my party at a small inn, as is customary, sir, and whilst doing rounds I discovered that one of my charges had escaped. There was no time to rouse the guard, so I decided to give chase along with –' His eyes moved nervously to the trampled grass. 'We were outnumbered. They were everywhere –'

The major interrupted gently, 'It was at *night*, Captain Bolitho.'

'I see.' Bolitho watched the midshipman's hands. Fingers opening and twitching. More like an old man than one at the start of his chosen calling. Passed over for promotion, failed his lieutenant's examination, but opportunity was still with him, something too often denied others altogether.

Bolitho asked, 'Who was the man who escaped?'

'He – he was a sailmaker, sir, we'd kept him apart from the rest because –' His voice trailed away, then he exclaimed, 'I did my best, sir!'

The lieutenant stared at Fenwick angrily. 'He should have known better, sir. The one good man we'd been able to catch, a deserter from the *London*, and this fool let him run!'

Bolitho snapped, 'Pray be silent.' Then to the midshipman he said, 'Can you recall the sailmaker's name?' He did not really care, but there was more to this than was out in the open. The midshipman was hiding something. Perhaps he had run away and left the seaman to die alone, a memory which would haunt him for the rest of his life.

The midshipman screwed up his eyes. 'I – I –' Then he nodded. 'Yes, sir. It was Spencer. I recall it now!'

The major remarked, 'Probably already at sea in some smuggling vessel.'

Bolitho turned away to conceal his expression from them. He walked a few paces, feeling their eyes following him. Perhaps Allday could not read or write, but he knew and loved animals. Especially the old sheepdog at the great grey house in Falmouth, whom Bolitho had named Spencer.

He turned abruptly and said to the lieutenant, 'You will place this midshipman under open arrest, and you will remain with him at the dockyard, until a proper enquiry has been carried out.'

He ignored the lieutenant's dismay and Fenwick's shocked gasp. If they were involved it would be better if they were safely under supervision. Either way they would lose if implicated. A court martial, and death at a yardarm, or – he looked at the burned-out tree – much worse if others discovered they had been unmasked.

The major followed him to the horses and said admiringly, 'I *liked* that.'

Bolitho glanced at him and smiled briefly. He might not like it so much if he knew the real reason.

He raised his boot to the stirrup and saw Young Matthew watching him from the other horse.

Allday was alive. Was risking his life once again, for him.

It was all he could do to keep his voice normal.

'I shall go to the commodore's residence, Major. He may have returned.'

'Then I shall escort you, sir.' The major was pleased to leave.

As they moved out of the trees into the welcoming sunshine, and the dragoons formed into pairs behind their officer, Bolitho turned in his saddle and looked back towards the sinister copse. He saw rooks circling above the trees, their raucous voices breaking the stillness like taunting cries.

No wonder people avoided the place. He felt his jaw tighten as he saw the dead girl's face in his mind again.

She may have died alone when the fishing boat had blown up, but he doubted it. His heart rebelled against it as he recalled the small boat pulling frantically away before the explosion had blasted the fisherman apart. Whoever they had been must have locked the girl on board before lighting a fuse, something prepared long in advance should they be found by one of the French patrol vessels.

There may have been only a few terrified people; there could have been hundreds who had fled the Terror, selling all their possessions, even themselves, for the chance to escape.

Smugglers? Slavers would be a closer description, and that was too good for them.

Wakeful had been the only witness, and now, because of it, Allday's own life was doubly at risk.

He waited until the major had cantered up beside him and then asked, 'That man you mentioned to me.' He looked at him directly. 'Is he still alive?'

The dragoon nodded, his eyes on the surrounding hedges. 'In his own crazed world. People give him food, though they are careful to keep secret their Christian generosity. My own men toss him some scraps, I suspect. He were better dead. Alive he is a living reminder of what will happen to those who inform on the Brotherhood.'

Bolitho asked, 'Could you find him for me?' He saw the disbelief in his eyes. 'It is just a straw. I can ignore nothing, no matter how futile it may appear.'

The major nodded. 'I shall *try*.' He glanced at Bolitho's profile. 'I am with you in this affair, sir, for I too am heartily sick of waiting.'

Bolitho reached out and impetuously took his gloved hand. 'So be it!'

He shivered despite the warm air. The time for caution was over.

Apart from the usual marine sentries, the commodore's residence appeared to be deserted, but after asking the corporal of the guard point-blank, Bolitho said, 'He's back.'

Major Craven's orderly stood with Young Matthew holding the horses' heads, and Bolitho noticed that the rest of the small detachment of dragoons remained mounted in the road outside the gates.

The door swung inwards noiselessly and Bolitho saw it was Hoblyn's personal footman.

'I must see the commodore.'

The youth glanced beyond the two officers as if he was about to deny that Hoblyn had returned. Bolitho saw his hazel eyes widen with alarm at the sight of the mounted dragoons, then he said, 'I shall take you to him.' He drew back from the steps, then led the way towards that same room.

The major grimaced. 'Like a tomb. Needs a woman's touch.'

The commodore was sitting behind his massive desk but made no attempt to rise as they were ushered in.

Hoblyn said in his clipped fashion, 'Why the urgency? I've much to accomplish. There are not enough hours in the day.'

Bolitho began, 'I sent a report –'

'Did you indeed?' Hoblyn glanced coldly at the major. 'Do *you* wish to see me too?'

Craven stood firm. 'Captain Bolitho thinks it might be better for all of us if I did, sir.'

'I see.' Hoblyn waved towards two chairs and shuffled some papers on his desk. 'Ah yes, the *report*. I did see it, I remember now. The fishing boat and the two French luggers.' He looked up suddenly, his eyes hard. 'You moved too hastily, Bolitho. The French will swear you acted unlawfully in their waters. Right or wrong, they will certainly use the incident to endanger peace, something that His Majesty is trying to preserve. He does not wish to antagonise the French, no matter what state their country is in.'

Bolitho retorted, 'I would have thought that His Majesty might have an even greater desire to retain his head on his shoulders!'

Hoblyn snapped, 'That is *impertinent*! In any case, why should it matter about one fishing boat? Surely you can use your talents to better advantage?' He was becoming angrier by the minute, his maimed hand tapping the desk to emphasise each point.

Bolitho said, 'I believe they were smuggling émigrés across the Channel, sir. Human cargo, with no thought for the consequences.' Even as he told Hoblyn about the dead girl he saw the commodore's eyes give just the briefest hint of anxiety.

Then Hoblyn snapped, 'Who will say, one way or the other? It is just your word, Bolitho, which I am afraid will carry little weight in Admiralty.' He leaned forward and stared at him, the major ignored or forgotten. 'They will break you if you persist with this obsession. You know from your own experience in London that there are a hundred captains who would grasp your appointment and be grateful!'

Bolitho replied stubbornly, 'I cannot believe that you think that the tolerance of a crime should be in the same boat as the fear of annoying the French government. If so, then I want no part of it. I will return to London and resign.' He heard the major's boots

110

squeak as he shifted his position in the chair. It was surprising he could hear anything above the pounding of his own heart.

Hoblyn dabbed his brow with his handkerchief. 'Let us not be hasty, Bolitho.'

Bolitho said simply, 'I am asking you, sir, *pleading* if you will, that you will forget the security of this appointment and use your influence to intervene. It seems that every man's hand is against us here, and the smugglers laugh at our attempts to run them to earth.'

Hoblyn stared at his desk. 'You have so much passion, Bolitho, yet so little trust in authority.'

'I have no cause to be trusting, sir.'

Hoblyn appeared to be wrestling with his innermost thoughts. 'You are quite determined to continue in this fashion, regardless of the hornets' nest you will most surely rouse?'

'I have no choice, sir, but I must have support.'

'Yes.' Hoblyn moved his shoulder as if it was hurting him. 'You may be correct to assume that there is a direct link between the smugglers and the oppression in France. It is certainly true that our prime minister has been urging stronger action against these gangs.' He added bitterly, 'I fear that William Pitt has done precious little to supply the money to enforce the necessary prevention!'

Major Craven murmured, 'Everyone sends for the dragoons, sir.'

Hoblyn gave a deep sigh. 'I will send a despatch to the Admiralty, Bolitho. It will be up to their lordships, of course, but I shall explain that I am in favour of a more aggressive policy.'

Bolitho said, 'Thank you, sir.' He hoped that his surprise did not show in his voice. From anger to agreement; it was too sudden, too easy. Not like the captain who had once stormed an enemy privateer with his body ablaze.

Hoblyn pressed his fingertips together and stared at him impassively.

'Draw your three cutters to Sheerness.'

'They are here, sir. *Snapdragon* left Chatham dockyard in my absence.'

Hoblyn gave a thin smile. 'I hope you can continue to stay

ahead of events, Bolitho. There are some who will wish you dead. I suggest you move ashore as soon as is prudent. I will arrange quarters inside the dockyard here at Sheerness. It will be safer for you.'

The door opened silently and the slim footman stood watching from the hallway. It was as if he could read his master's thoughts.

'Jules will show you out, gentlemen.'

Bolitho and the major got to their feet. Apparently there was to be no wine this time.

Hoblyn said, 'Inform me of your every intention.' He eyed both of them for several seconds. 'My head will not rest on any block because of your personal ambitions!'

The interview was over.

Outside on the cobbles Bolitho said grimly, 'A victory or a reverse, I am uncertain which.'

The soldier frowned. 'Far better than sitting still. It is high time that the authorities understand what we are facing. You need men for the fleet –'

Bolitho saw Young Matthew leading the horse towards him. 'If and when a fleet is refitted in time!'

'Either way, you'll not get the men until you scatter the Brotherhood and lessen their power over ordinary people.'

The major climbed into his saddle and looked down at him. 'I am with you.'

Bolitho smiled. 'Do not forget what I asked of you.'

The soldier grinned. 'I said, I shall *try*!' Then he cantered from the yard, touching his hat to the sentries as he rejoined his troop on the road.

A good officer, Bolitho thought, and for some reason one he knew he could trust.

At the dockyard they left the horses with a marine, and walked to the jetty where some boats were loitering.

For a moment longer Bolitho stared at the three anchored cutters, riding above their reflections like graceful seabirds. *His little brood.* Even that reminded him of Allday.

He said to a waterman, 'Take me to *Telemachus*.'

As the boat moved slowly amongst the anchored vessels Bolitho saw the glint of sunlight on a raised telescope from

Wakeful's taffrail. He looked away. It was most likely to be Queely, watching his progress, glad to be rid of him – or was he?

Paice greeted him at the entry port and touched his hat. Bolitho was surprised to see his apparent pleasure.

'I was not certain you would return to us, sir.' He grinned. 'Welcome.'

He waved one big hand around the busy figures on deck. 'You were right, sir. They've all worked so hard together that most of the pain is behind them.'

Bolitho nodded approvingly. Apart from the strong smells of tar and paint, there was virtually nothing to show of the damage.

As he caught the glances of some of the seamen he saw them nod self-consciously, before turning back to their tasks. Like a homecoming.

Paice became serious again. 'No news of your cox'n, sir.'

'What do you know?' Bolitho met his gaze.

'Only that he is on a mission for you, *officially* that is.' He glanced at his men. 'But news has wings. The longer it takes . . .' He did not finish.

Bolitho touched his arm. 'I know. Please let it lie, for his sake if not for mine.'

He glanced at the waterfront, the bright sunshine, the sense of peace.

'I shall write some fresh orders for you.' He turned and looked at him steadily. 'You will command here if anything happens to me.'

Paice's strong features were a mixture of pleasure and anxiety. 'They'd not *dare*, sir!'

Bolitho's gaze seemed to embrace all three cutters. 'I might lose this appointment at the whim of some quill-pusher in Admiralty. I might even fall in a fight. It is *our way*, Mr Paice, so be ready for anything.'

Paice walked with him to the companionway. 'Hell's teeth, sir, you've changed the people here and in the other cutters. You'll not find us wanting next time.'

Bolitho closed the door of the cabin behind him and stared up at the open skylight.

Was Hoblyn guilty of some conspiracy, or did he really not

care for involvement of any kind? Bolitho thought of the graceful footman, and grimaced. *Jules*. It suited him well.

He did not remember falling asleep, but awoke with his forehead resting on his arm, the pen still in his fingers from the moment he had signed Paice's new orders.

Paice was sitting opposite him on a sea chest, his eyes doubtful.

'You've not slept for two days, I'll wager, sir.' It sounded like an accusation. 'I was most unwilling to rouse you, but –'

Bolitho saw the wax-sealed envelope in his fist and was instantly alert. Since the tender age of twelve his mind and body had been hardened to it. Years of watchkeeping in all weathers, moments of anxiety to banish any craving for sleep when the watch below was turned up to reef sails in a screaming gale, or to repel enemy boarders. It was the only life he had ever known.

'What is it?'

He slit open the envelope and first read the signature at the bottom. It was from Major Craven, the hand neat and elegant, like the man. He read it through twice very carefully. He was aware that the cutter was moving more than she had been when his head had dropped in sleep, just as he was conscious of Paice's measured breathing.

He looked up and saw the gleam in the lieutenant's eyes.

'Where is "the old abbey"?'

Paice withdrew a chart from a locker without questioning him. He jabbed the coastline with one big finger. 'Here, sir. 'Bout three miles to the east'rd. A quiet, dismal spot, if you ask me.'

Bolitho peered at it and nodded. The ideal place for a meeting. To move by road, as Craven had pointed out, would soon draw somebody's notice, and the words would go out like lightning. The troublesome Cornish captain was on the move again.

By sea then, and by stealth.

He said, 'We will weigh before dusk and steer for the Great Nore.' He moved some brass dividers to the north-east from Sheerness. 'Once in the dark we will come about and make a landfall here –' the dividers rested on the point marked as an ancient abbey. 'Nobody must see us, so you will anchor offshore.'

Paice's hand rasped over his chin. 'Beg pardon, sir, but I *am* in

114

the dark right now. Are you intending to send a press gang ashore? Because if so –'

Bolitho stared at the much-used chart. 'No, I am meeting someone. So I shall need a good boat's crew and someone who knows these waters like his own right arm.'

Paice replied without a second's hesitation, 'The master, Erasmus Chesshyre, sir. Feel his way inshore like a blind man.'

Bolitho glanced sharply at him, but Paice's remark was an innocent one.

Paice added, 'I'd like to go with you, sir.'

'No.' It was final. 'Remember what I told you. If anything should happen –'

Paice sighed. 'Aye. I know, sir.'

'One last thing, Mr Paice. If the worst should happen, send Young Matthew back to Falmouth, with an escort if need be.'

'Aye, sir.' He stood up carefully, bowed beneath the deckhead beams. 'I'll tell Mr Triscott to prepare the hands.' He hesitated in the low doorway. 'An' I'm *right proud* to serve alongside you, sir.'

The sentiment seemed to embarrass him and he hurried to the companion ladder, calling names as he went.

Bolitho drew a fresh sheet of paper towards him and decided he would write a letter to his sister Nancy. If he did fall, her husband the squire, known around Falmouth as the King of Cornwall, would soon get his hands on the big grey house below Pendennis Castle, the home for generations of Bolithos.

The thought disturbed him more than he thought possible. No more would the local people see a Bolitho returning from the ocean, or hear of another who had died in some far-off battle.

He glanced momentarily at Craven's instructions, then with a sad smile held the note up to a candle and watched it dissolve in flames.

He had recalled something which his father had made him and his brother Hugh learn by heart before they had left that same house for the navy.

> 'They have outlived this fear, and their brave ends
> Will ever be an honour to their friends.'

It could have been written for them.

'Out yer get, matey!'

Allday groaned and rolled painfully on to his side, and felt somebody guiding his feet over the back of a cart.

If they trusted him, it was the wary trust of one wild animal for another. He had no idea how far he had been carried, and as the cart had bumped and staggered over rutted tracks, once through a field, he had felt as if every bone was broken.

He stood upright and felt his hands being untied, a rough bandage being removed from his eyes.

One of his escorts grinned and handed him the cutlass. 'No 'ard feelin's, matey. Under this flag you takes no chances, see?'

Allday nodded and looked around him. It was dawn, another day, the air busy with birdsong and insects. His nostrils dilated. The strong smell of saltwater and tar, oakum and freshly hewn timber. A boatbuilder's yard.

He was pushed, rather than guided, into a long shed where a crude slipway ran the full length and vanished through some heavy canvas awnings at the lower end. Newly built or repaired boats could be launched straight into the water from here, he supposed.

He blinked his eyes as he saw some twenty or more men sitting at tables wolfing food and draining jugs of ale as if they had been here all night. They all looked up as the man who had accompanied Allday said harshly, 'This 'ere's Spencer, sail-maker. It's all you need to know. Get 'im some grub.'

Allday crossed his leg over a bench and regarded his new companions thoughtfully. A mixed bunch, he decided. Some had been honest sailormen; others would have been rogues in any marketplace.

As his eyes grew accustomed to the windowless shed he realised that the man who had been with him in the cart had been the one who had hacked off the sailor's hand. Now he was laughing and sharing a joke with one of his companions as if he hadn't a care in the world.

Allday took a jug of ale and grunted his thanks. It would be wise to say as little as possible.

The ale was tasteless but strong on an empty stomach; it made him feel slightly better.

Another step. He eyed his new companions warily. Deserters to a man. If what he had seen of his 'rescuers' was anything to judge by, they had stepped from one captivity into another.

He leaned over and asked casually, 'What now?'

The man at his side darted him a suspicious glance. 'We waits, see? We'll be part of a crew.' He nodded, reassured by Allday's massive presence. 'We'll all be stinkin' rich!'

Allday took another swallow of ale. Or bloody dead, he thought darkly. Then he looked around the boatshed, probably well guarded too. It was so simple. A boatyard, the last place you would expect to find seamen on the run. But where was it? He had to discover that or all the risks were pointless. The Captain must be told where –

He stiffened as a voice rapped, 'I'll let you know when *I'm* ready. You just do as you're told, damn your eyes!'

Allday raised his head very slowly and stared between two men who were in deep conversation.

The sunlight was stronger now, and he could see a half-completed hull standing amidst a litter of planks and wood shavings, and beyond that a line of tall trees. He knew the incisive, irritable voice – but how could he?

He heard someone murmuring what sounded like an apology and then part of a canvas awning was pulled aside like a curtain.

Allday held his breath as the dark eyes moved over the listless figures around the tables.

The man said, 'Well, they'd better show more steel than the last lot!'

When Allday dared to look again the awning had fallen back into place. *He didn't see me*. He almost gasped his relief out loud.

The face had been that of *Loyal Chieftain*'s master, Henry Delaval . . .

It was all that Bolitho needed to know. But the plan would not settle in his mind.

All he could hear was a scream. All he could see was the smoking pistol in a severed hand.

9

Enemy Territory

Bolitho gripped the jolly-boat's gunwale and looked up at the endless canopy of small stars. Only an undulating black shadow which broke the foot of the pattern gave a true hint of land, and he could sense Chesshyre's concentration as he peered above the heads of the oarsmen, or directly abeam.

Once he said, 'Tide's on the ebb, sir.'

Bolitho could hear it rippling and surging around the boat's stem, the deep breathing of the oarsmen as they maintained a regular stroke without an order being passed.

The man in the bows called aft in a loud whisper, 'Ready with the lead, sir!'

Chesshyre came out of his concentrated attention. 'Is it armed, Gulliver?'

'Aye, sir.'

'Start sounding.'

Bolitho heard the splash of the boat's lead and line being dropped over the bows, then the man named Gulliver calling, 'By th' mark three!'

Chesshyre ordered, 'Pass it aft!' He waited for the leg-of-mutton-shaped lead to be handed from thwart to thwart, then he rubbed the tallow in its base between his fingers before holding it up to his nose. He passed the lead back again and muttered, 'Shell and rough sand, sir. We're making headway. So long as we stand away from the sandbars at low water we shall —'

The bowman called, 'By th' mark *two*!'

Chesshyre swore silently and eased over the tiller bar. 'Like *that*, sir!'

Bolitho understood. It was common enough in his own West Country for sailors to be able to feel their way by using a lead and line, know the state of the seabed by what they found on the tallow which 'armed' it. In another twenty years he guessed it would be a lost craft of seamanship.

'How far?'

Chesshyre raised himself slightly as something white broke the pitch-darkness. Then he sank down again. It was not a rock or sandbar but a leaping fish.

''Nother half-hour, sir.' He kept his voice low so that the oarsmen would not know the extent of their labour. They were used to it, but the boat was crowded with extra hands and weapons, including a heavy bell-mouthed musketoon already packed with canister and metal fragments, in case they were attacked.

Bolitho listened to the creak of oars – how loud they sounded despite being muffled with greased rags. But he knew from experience that it would be swallowed completely in the other noises of sea and wind.

Suppose it was a wasted journey? Perhaps the man would take fright and hide when he heard the sailors with their weapons?

Chesshyre hissed, 'There, sir! See the old abbey?'

Bolitho strained his eyes and saw a sharper shadow rising amongst the stars.

Chesshyre breathed out. 'Better'n I thought.'

Bolitho thought how like Herrick he sounded. Another memory. A different ship.

'Less than a fathom, sir!'

'Haul in the lead, Gulliver. Stand by, boys!' Chesshyre crouched half-upright, his silhouette like a dark gargoyle. 'Be ready to beach!'

The bowman was busy with his boathook and called, 'Comin' in now, sir!'

'*Oars!* Lively there!' After that it all happened in seconds.

The extra hands leaping outboard and splashing in the shallows to guide the hull safely on to a small, unusually steep

119

beach. Oars lowered with great care across the thwarts while Christie, one of Paice's boatswain's mates, growled, 'Drop that bloody gun an' I'll see yer backbones!'

In spite of the tension Bolitho heard somebody chuckle at the threat. Then he was out of the boat, the receding water dragging at his shoes, clawing him back as if to claim him.

Chesshyre passed his instructions and two men hurried away in either direction, while others grouped around the beached boat to make certain it could be quickly launched, but was in no danger of drifting away.

Bolitho found a moment to recall the other times when he had seen it done. *The sailor's way.* Give him a boat or even a raft and he is in good heart. But with only the sea at his back it is a different story.

Chesshyre rejoined him and said, 'There's a small track to the left, sir. That'll be the one.'

Shadows moved in around them and Bolitho said, 'Draw your blades, but do not cock your pistols. One shot by accident, and we'll awaken the dead.'

Somebody murmured, 'An' there are plenty o' them round 'ere, sir!'

Another jester.

Chesshyre waited as Bolitho drew his old sword and balanced it in his fist.

'You must be an old hand at this, sir?'

It was strange coming from him, Bolitho thought, as they were the same age.

'I admit it's more like landing on enemy soil than I expected in England.'

He tested his bearings and then walked carefully towards the track. It was little more than a fox's path, but the sandy soil made it easy to follow.

He half-listened to the sea's lazy grumbling as it laid bare rocks in the falling tide, and pictured Paice somewhere out in the darkness, unable to help, unwilling to be left out.

The sea sounds suddenly faded and Bolitho felt the warm air of the countryside fanning his face. The smells of the land. The old abbey lay to the left although he could see less of it now than from the boat.

Chesshyre touched his arm and stopped in his tracks. *'Still!'*

Bolitho froze and heard someone gasp, feet kicking in the long grass. Then two figures loomed from the darkness, one with his hands above his head, the other, a small, darting man with a drawn cutlass, pushing him none too gently ahead of him.

Bolitho said, 'I have good ears, but –'

Chesshyre showed his teeth. 'Inskip was a poacher afore he saw the light, sir. Got ears in his arse, beggin' your pardon.'

The man with raised hands saw Bolitho, and perhaps recognised some sort of authority when seconds earlier he had been expecting his life to be cut short.

He exclaimed, 'I was sent to meet you, sir!'

Chesshyre rapped, 'Keep your voice *down* for Christ's sake, man.'

Bolitho gripped his arm; it was shaking so violently that he knew the man was terrified.

'Where is the blind man? Did he not come?'

'Yes, yes!' He was babbling. 'He's here, right enough. I did just what the major told me – now I'm off afore someone sees me!'

A seaman strode along the path. ''Ere 'e is, sir.' He directed his remarks to the master but they were intended for Bolitho.

'Don't go too close, sir. 'E stinks like a dead pig.'

Bolitho walked away from the others, but heard Chesshyre following at a careful distance.

The blind man was squatting on the ground, his head thrown back, his eyes covered by a bandage.

Bolitho knelt beside him. 'I am Captain Bolitho. Major Craven said you would help me.'

The man moved his head from side to side, then reached out and held Bolitho's arm. Through the coat sleeve his fingers felt like steel talons.

'I need your aid.' Bolitho's stomach rebelled, but he knew this contact was his only hope. The blind man stank of filth and dried sweat, and he was almost grateful for the darkness.

'*Bolitho?*' The man moved his head again as if trying to peer through the bandage. 'Bolitho?' He had a high piping voice, and it was impossible to determine his age.

Chesshyre said thickly, 'The poor bugger's off his head, sir.'

121

Bolitho retorted, 'Wouldn't *you* be?'

He tried again. 'That night. When they did this to you.' He felt the hand jerk free, as if it and not its owner was in terror. 'What did you see? I wouldn't ask, but they took a friend of mine – you understand?'

'See?' The blind man felt vaguely in the grass. 'They took a long while. All th' time they laughed at me.' He shook his head despairingly. 'When the fire was lit they branded my body, an' – an' then –'

Bolitho looked away, sickened. But he was so near to Allday now. This poor, demented creature was all he had. But he felt as if he were applying torture, as they had once done to him.

'I used to watch for 'em. Sometimes they come with pack-horses – bold as brass, they was. Other times they brought men, deserters. That night –'

Chesshyre said, 'He knows nowt, sir.' He peered around at the trees. 'He should be put out of his misery.'

The man turned as if to examine the *Telemachus*'s master, then said in a flat, empty voice, 'I bin there since, y'know.' He wrapped his arms around his ragged body and cackled. 'I was that well acquaint with the place!'

Bolitho kept his voice level. 'What place? Please help me. I shall see you are rewarded.'

The man turned on him with unexpected venom. 'I don't want yer stinkin' gold! I just wants revenge for what they done to me!'

Chesshyre bent over him and said, 'Captain Bolitho is a fine an' brave officer. Help him as you will, and I swear he'll take care of you.'

The man cackled again. It was an eerie sound, and Bolitho could imagine the small party of seamen drawing together nearby.

Chesshyre added, 'What's your name?'

The man cowered away. 'I'm not sayin'!' He peered towards Bolitho and then seized his arm again. 'I don't 'ave to, do I?' He sounded frantic.

'No.' Bolitho's heart sank. The link was too fragile to last. It was another hope gone wrong.

In a surprisingly clear voice the blind man said, 'Then I'll take you.'

Bolitho stared at him. 'When?'

'Now, o' course!' His reply was almost scornful. 'Don't want the 'ole o' Sheppey to know, does we?'

Chesshyre breathed out loudly. 'Well, I'll be double-damned!'

That, too, was what Herrick said when he was taken aback.

Bolitho took the man's filthy hand. '*Thank* you.'

The bandaged head moved warily from side to side. 'Not with nobody else though!'

Christie the boatswain's mate murmured, 'Not bloody askin' for much, is 'e?'

Bolitho looked at Chesshyre. 'I must do as he asks. I must trust him. He is all I have.'

Chesshyre turned away from his men. 'But it's *asking* for trouble, sir. He may be raving mad, or someone might have put him up to it, like the fellow who brought him here, eh, sir?'

Bolitho walked to the men who were guarding the messenger. 'Did you tell anybody about this?' To himself he thought, *more to the point, will he tell someone after he has left us?*

'I swear, sir, on my baby's life – I swear I've told nobody!'

Bolitho turned to Chesshyre. 'All the same, take him aboard when you leave. I think he is too frightened to betray anyone at the moment, but should the worst happen and you discover it, see that he is handed to Major Craven's dragoons.' His voice sharpened. 'He can join the other felons at the crossroads if it comes to that.'

Chesshyre asked desperately, 'What shall I say to Mr Paice, sir?'

Bolitho looked at him in the darkness. Then he raised his voice and saw the bandaged head move towards him again. 'Tell him I am with a friend, and that we are both in God's hands.'

Chesshyre seemed unable to grasp it. 'I just don't know, sir. In all my service –'

'There is always a first time, Mr Chesshyre. Now be off with you.'

He watched as the sailors began to fade away into the shadows and noticed how they seemed to pass him as closely as they could before they groped their way to the fox's path. To see for themselves, as if for the last time.

Chesshyre held out his hand. It was hard, like leather. 'May God indeed be at the helm this night, sir.' Then he was gone.

Bolitho reached down and aided the man to his feet. 'I am ready when you are.'

He felt light-headed, even sick, and his mouth was suddenly quite dry. This man might only think he knew where he was going, his mind too broken to distinguish fact from fantasy.

The blind man picked up a heavy piece of wood, a branch found somewhere in the course of his despairing ramblings.

Then he said in his strange, piping voice, 'This way.' He hesitated. 'Watch yer step. There's a stile up yonder.'

Bolitho swallowed hard. Who was the blind one now?

An hour later they were still walking, pausing only for the bandaged head to turn this way and that. To gather his bearings, to listen for some sound, Bolitho did not know. Perhaps he was already lost.

He heard dogs barking far away, and once he almost fell with alarm as some birds burst from the grass almost under his feet.

The blind man waited for him to catch up, muttering, 'Over yonder! Wot d'you see?'

Bolitho stared through the darkness and discovered a deeper blackness. His heart seemed to freeze. A different bearing, but there was no doubt about it. It was the same sinister copse, which they were passing on the opposite side.

The blind man could have been studying his expression. He broke into a fit of low, wheezing laughter. 'Thought I'd lost me way, did ye, Captain?'

About the same time, Chesshyre was explaining to Paice and his first lieutenant what had happened, the jolly-boat's crew lolling on the deck like dead men after the hardest pull they had ever known.

Paice exploded, 'You *left* him? You bloody well left the captain unsupported!'

Chesshyre protested, 'It was an order, sir. Surely you know me better than –'

Paice gripped his shoulder so that the master winced. 'My apologies, Mr Chesshyre. Of *course* I know you well enough for that. God damn it, he wouldn't even let me go!'

Triscott asked, 'What shall we do, sir?'

'Do?' Paice gave a heavy sigh. 'He told me what I must do if he sent back the boat without him.' He glanced at Chesshyre sadly. 'That was an *order* too.' Then he gazed up at the stars. 'We shall haul anchor. If we remain here, dawn will explain our reasons to anyone who cares to seek them.' He looked at the messenger who was sitting wretchedly on a hatch coaming under guard. 'By the living Jesus, if there is a betrayal, I'll run him up to the tops'l yard myself!'

Then in a calmer voice he said, 'Hoist the boat inboard, Mr Triscott. We will get under way.'

A few moments later there was a splash, and a voice yelled with surprise, 'Man overboard, sir!'

But Paice said quietly, 'No. I was a fool to speak my mind. That was the lad – Matthew Corker. He must have heard me.'

Triscott said, 'Even the jolly-boat couldn't catch him now, sir.'

Paice watched the regular splashes until they were lost in shadow.

He said, 'Good swimmer.'

Chesshyre asked, 'What can he do, sir?'

Paice made himself turn away from the sea, and from the boy who was going to try and help the man he worshipped above all others.

He was like the son Paice had always wanted, what they had prayed for, before she had been brutally shot down.

He said harshly, 'Get the ship under way! If anything happens to that lad, I'll –' He could not go on.

Thirty minutes later as the glass was turned, *Telemachus* spread her great mainsail and slipped out into the North Sea, before changing tack and steering westward for Sheerness.

Paice handed over to his second-in-command and went aft to the cabin. He opened the shutter of a lantern and sat down to complete his log when his eye caught a reflection from the opposite cot.

He leaned over and picked it up. It was a fine gold watch with an engraved guard. He had seen Bolitho look at it several times, and not, he guessed, merely to discover the hour. The parcel containing the uncompleted ship-model was nearby.

125

With great care he opened the guard. Somehow he knew that Bolitho would not mind. Afterwards he replaced it beside All-day's parcel.

In the navy everyone thought a post-captain was junior only to God. A man who did as he pleased, who wanted for nothing.

Paice thought of him now, out there in the darkness with a blind man. Apart from this watch he had nothing left at all.

Bolitho lay prone beside a thick clump of gorse and levelled his small telescope on a boatyard which lay some fifty yards below him. He winced as a loose pebble ground into his elbow, and wondered if this really was the place which the blind man had described.

He laid the glass down and lowered his face on to his arm. The noon sun was high overhead, and he dared not use the glass too much for fear of a bright reflection which might betray their position.

He would have to go down as soon as it was safe. How could he lie here all day? He cursed himself for not thinking of a flask when he had left the *Telemachus*. His mind shied away from water and he placed a pebble in his mouth to ease his parched throat.

He raised himself briefly on one elbow and glanced at his companion. The blind man was a pitiful sight, his clothing stained and in rags, the bandage covering his empty sockets foul with dirt.

The man remarked, 'You gets used to waitin'.' He nodded firmly. 'When it's dark –' He shook with silent laughter. 'Dark – that's rich, ain't it?'

Bolitho sighed. How did he know night from day? But he no longer doubted him after that demonstration of his uncanny abilities.

He stiffened and raised the small telescope again, but was careful to hold it in the shade of a clump of grass.

A few figures were moving through the boatyard. Two were armed, one carried a stone jar. Probably rum, he thought. Nobody was working there, and tools lay abandoned near an uncompleted hull, an adze still standing on a length of timber.

The men walked like sailors. They showed no sign of fear or wariness. There had to be a reason for such confidence.

Bolitho closed the little telescope, recalling how he had used it on the road from London when he had confronted the mob and the two frightened press gang officers. He watched some tiny insects busying themselves around his drawn sword. He *must* decide what to do next. If he left this place to fetch help, he might miss something vital. He glanced again at his ragged companion, and was moved by what he saw. He was rocking back and forth, his voice crooning what sounded like a hymn. Once a gentle man, perhaps. But when he had said he wanted his revenge for what they had done to him, he had been like a man from the fires of Hell.

When he looked again he realised that he was alone, but not for long. The blind man crawled through some bushes, a chipped mug in his clawlike hand. He held it out in Bolitho's direction. 'Wet yer whistle, Captain?'

It must be from some stream, Bolitho thought. It tasted rancid, and was probably used by sheep or cows. Bolitho drank deeply. It could have been the finest Rhenish wine at that moment.

The blind man took the empty mug and it vanished inside one of his tattered coats.

He said, 'They brings 'em 'ere sometimes, Captain. Men for the Trade. From 'ere they goes to smugglin' vessels, see?' He cocked his head, like a schoolmaster with some backward pupil.

Bolitho considered it. If it was so easy, why did the authorities not come and search the place? Major Craven had hinted at powerful and influential people who were more interested in profit than the enforcement of a law they insisted could not be maintained.

'Whose land is this?'

The blind man lay down on his side. 'I'll rest now, Captain.'

For the first time since their strange rendezvous there was fear in his voice. The true, sick fear of one who has been on the brink of a terrible death.

He could almost envy the man's ability to sleep – perhaps he only ventured out at night. For Bolitho it was the longest day. He busied his thoughts with the commodore and the three cutters, until he felt his mind would crack.

And then, quite suddenly, or so it seemed, the light began to fade, and where there had been green trees and the glittering sea beyond, there were shadows of purple and dark pewter.

A few lights appeared in the boatyard's outbuildings, but only once or twice had he seen any movement, usually an armed man strolling down to the waterfront to relieve himself.

Bolitho examined every yard of the distance he would have to cover. He must avoid catching his foot or slipping in some cow dung. Surprise was his only protection.

He realised that the blind man was wide awake and crouching beside him. How could he live in such filth? Or perhaps he no longer noticed even that.

'What is it?'

The man pointed towards the sea. 'A boat comin'.'

Bolitho seized his telescope and swore under his breath. It was already too dark, as if a great curtain had been lowered.

Then he heard the creak of oars, saw a shaded lantern reflecting on the water where a man stood to guide the boat in.

The blind man added, 'A *ship*, Captain.'

Bolitho strained his eyes into the darkness. If ship there was, she showed no lights. Landing a cargo? He dismissed it instantly. The blind man knew better than anyone what they were doing – he had more than proved it. They were collecting sailors: men who had been marked *run* in their ships' logs; others who had managed to escape the gibbet; soldiers of fortune. All dangerous.

He heard the creak of oars again. Whatever it was, it had been quickly done, he thought.

He stood up, the cooler air off the sea making him shiver. 'Wait here. Don't move until I return for you.'

The blind man leaned on his crude stick. 'They'll gut you, sure as Jesus, if they sees you!'

'I have to know.' Bolitho thought he heard a door slam. 'If I don't return, go to Major Craven.'

'I ain't goin' to no bloody redcoats! Not no more!'

Bolitho could hear him muttering querulously as he took the first steps down the grassy slope towards a solitary lighted window. He heard laughter, the sound of a bottle being smashed, then more laughter. So they had not all gone. Perhaps Allday . . .

He reached the wall of the building and leaned with his back against it, waiting for his breathing to steady.

Then, very slowly he peered around the edge of the window. The glass was stained and covered with cobwebs, but he saw all he needed. It was a shipwright's shed, with benches and fresh planks piled on racks. Around a table he saw about six figures. They were drinking rum, passing the jar round, while another was cutting hunks of bread from a basket. Only one man was armed and stood apart from the rest. He wore a blue coat with a red neckerchief and an old cocked hat tilted rakishly on thick, greasy hair.

Bolitho glanced behind him. There was no other sound. So these men were also deserters, awaiting the next boat which could use them? There was an air of finality about the place, as if once they had gone, it would be abandoned, or returned to its proper use. Then there would be no evidence. *Nothing.* And Allday would be just as lost as ever.

Bolitho licked his lips. Six to one, but only the armed man, who was obviously one of the smugglers, presented real danger. He found that his heart was beating wildly, and he had to lick his lips repeatedly to stop them being glued with dryness.

They were all together, but any second one might leave the building and raise the alarm. They would soon arm themselves then.

Bolitho moved carefully along the wall until he reached the door. He could see from the lantern's flickering light that there were no bolts or chains.

It seemed to taunt him. *Have you been stripped of your courage too?* He was committed, and knew that he had had no choice from the beginning.

Bolitho eased the pistol from his belt and tried to remember if he had kept it clear of the water when he had waded ashore. He winced as he cocked it. Then he stood clear of the door, held his sword angled across his body, and kicked it with all his strength.

'In the King's name!' He was shocked at the loudness of his voice in the confined space. 'You are all under arrest!'

Someone yelled, 'God damn, it's the press!'

Another gasped, 'They told us we was *safe*!'

The armed man dropped his hand to the hanger at his belt and rasped, 'He's not the press! I knows who he is, damn his eyes!'

Bolitho raised his pistol. 'Don't move!' The man's face was twisted with anger and hatred and seemed to swim over the end of the muzzle like a mask.

Then he seized his hanger and pulled it from its scabbard.

Bolitho squeezed the trigger and heard the impotent click of a misfire. The man crouched towards him, his hanger making small circles in the lanternlight, while the others stared in disbelief, probably too drunk to register what had happened.

The man snarled, '*Get out! Fetch weapons!* He's alone – can't you see that, you gutless swabs?'

He lunged forward but held his legs as before. Sparks spat from the two blades, and Bolitho watched the man's eyes, knowing that whatever happened now, he could not win. They would set upon him like a pack, more afraid of the gallows than of killing a King's officer.

He could hear the rest of them clambering through a window, one already running through the darkness yelling like a madman. They would soon return.

He said, 'You have no chance!'

The man spat at his feet. 'We'll see!' Then he laughed. 'Blade to blade, Captain bloody Bolitho!'

He slashed forward, and Bolitho parried it aside, locking hilts for a second so that he could thrust the man away, and hold him silhouetted against the lantern.

The man yelled, 'Kill him, you bilge-rats!' He had sensed that despite his strength he was no match for Bolitho's swordsmanship. He vaulted over a bench, then faced Bolitho across it, his hanger held out like a rapier.

Not long now. Bolitho heard running feet, a man falling over some obstruction in the darkness, the rum making him laugh insanely. Then there was a single shot, and for an instant Bolitho thought one of them had fired at him through the window. He heard somebody sobbing, the sudden trampling thud of horses, and Major Craven's voice rising above all of it.

The door burst open and the place was filled suddenly with scarlet coats and gleaming sabres.

130

Craven turned as a sergeant shouted, 'One o' the buggers 'as done for Trooper Green, sir.' Craven looked at Bolitho and gave the merest nod, then faced the armed smuggler. 'You heard that? My men will be happy to end your miserable life here and now, *unless –*'

The man tossed his hanger on the bench. 'I know nothing.'

Bolitho took Craven's arm. 'How did you know?'

Craven walked to the door. 'Look yonder, Captain.'

A dragoon was helping a small figure to climb down from his saddle. The boy walked slowly and hesitantly into the lantern-light, his eyes running with tears, Fear, relief, it was all there.

Craven said quietly, 'Lift your foot, boy.'

Aided by the dragoon Young Matthew raised one bare foot. It was ripped and bloody, almost to the bone.

Craven explained, 'One of my pickets found him running along the road.' He looked at his men outside as they rounded up the deserters and bound their wrists behind them. One trooper lay dead on the ground.

Bolitho seized the boy and held him against his coat, trying to ease away the shock and the pain.

'There's no harm done, Matthew, thanks to you. That was a brave thing you did.'

Craven nodded. 'Damned dangerous, too.'

Bolitho looked at the dragoon who had carried the boy from his horse. 'Care for him. I have something to do.' He confronted the man who minutes earlier had been urging his companions to arm themselves and cut him down, and said, 'If you tell me what I want to know, I might be prepared to put in a word. I can promise nothing.'

The man threw back his head and roared with laughter. 'D'you think I fear the hangman?'

Craven murmured, 'He is far more frightened of his masters, the Brotherhood.'

He offered no resistance as the sergeant tied his hands behind him and sneered, 'They'll have you yet – *Captain!*'

A dragoon shouted, ''Ere – where d'you think you're goin', mate?'

Then, like the others, he fell silent as the ragged figure with the broken branch held out before him moved slowly into the circle of light.

Bolitho sensed it immediately, like a shaft of lightning between them.

The blind man whispered, 'It's 'im, Captain!' There was a sob in his voice now. 'I 'ad to come, then I 'eard 'is laugh. 'E's the one wot did this to me!'

The man shouted, 'You bloody liar! Who'd take the word of a blind lunatic?'

Bolitho had an overwhelming desire to strike him. To kill him, tied and helpless though he was.

'*I* would, whoever *you* are.' How calm his voice sounded. It was like hearing a complete stranger. 'When all this was begun, *this man* – who has become my friend, let it be known – asked no reward.'

There was absolute silence now and Bolitho saw the bound man staring at him uncertainly, the bluff gone out of him.

'He asked only for revenge, and I think I know what he meant.' Bolitho glanced at the others. 'Major Craven, if you will take your men outside?' The dragoons filed out, some shocked at what they had witnessed, others with the light of cruel revenge in their faces. They had just lost one of their own. What did outsiders understand of loyalty, and their sacrifice?

Bolitho watched as the realisation crossed the man's cruel features. Spittle ran from a corner of his mouth. '*You lie! You wouldn't dare!*' When Bolitho walked towards the door he screamed, '*Don't leave me!*'

The blind man felt his way around the seated prisoner, and then touched his eyes from behind. Very gently, as he crooned, 'Like trapped butterflies.'

The man screamed and struggled. '*Christ, my eyes!*'

Bolitho opened the door, his throat retching.

Then he heard the man shriek, 'I'll tell you! I'll tell you! Call him off, for Christ's sake!'

Bolitho crossed the room in two strides. 'I want names. I need to know things which only you will be a part of.'

The man's chest was heaving as if he was drowning. 'I felt his claws in my eyes!'

132

'I am waiting.' He rested one hand on the blind man's scrawny shoulder and saw him turn his bandaged eyes towards him. In his own way he was telling Bolitho he had already had his revenge. Perhaps he had found no reprieve in it.

Together they listened to the man's desperate flood of information. The hangman's halter, or death in a sea-fight were commonplace. But against the prospect of torture at the hands of someone he had blinded and broken he had had no defences.

Bolitho said, 'You will be kept in the barracks, alone and under guard at all times. If one word you have told me is false, you will have this man as your sole companion.'

He reached out and slammed the smuggler's head back against the chair. '*Look at me, damn you!* Do you see any bluff in *my* eyes?'

There was naked terror in the man's face now and Bolitho could smell the stench of it. Then he said quietly, 'So be warned.'

He walked out of the building and leaned against the wall, staring at the tiny stars.

Craven said, 'Thank God I was in time.'

'Aye.' He watched the blind man touching the muzzle of one of the horses. 'There's much we have to thank him for tonight.' He knew that in a few more minutes he would have vomited. 'Now where is that boy?'

But Young Matthew had fallen asleep across the dragoon's saddle.

Craven said, 'Time to leave. I sent word for assistance before I came. I felt this would be the place. My men have never been allowed to come here.' He glanced at the sky. 'There's a troop of fifty horse or more on the road from Chatham by now, but we'll take no chances.'

He watched his dead dragoon being tied across an empty saddle. 'Is it worth the cost this time?' He removed his hat as the horse was led past.

Bolitho nodded. 'I believe so.' He waited for the major to order a spare mount for him. 'You have done so much.' His tone hardened. 'Now it is up to me.'

The blind man waited beside the horses as Bolitho leaned down and touched his arm. 'Will you come with us?'

The man shook his head. 'I'll be close by if you needs me, Captain.'

As the troop, with the prisoners running beside the horses, moved away from the buildings, the blind man looked into his perpetual darkness and murmured, ''E called me 'is *friend*.'

Then, like a ragged shadow, he too was swallowed up.

10

The Spark Of Courage

The brig *Loyal Chieftain*, drifting and rolling under close-reefed topsails, was a death-trap for any landsman or the unwary. In pitch-darkness she lay between two sturdy luggers while men from all three crews hauled on tackles, levered, and stowed an endless collection of cargo. In the brig's forward hold, Allday marvelled at the speed of the transfer from the two luggers in spite of several stupid blunders. The brig carried twice her normal company, but most of them had never worked together before, and he had heard more kicks and obscenities than in any man-of-war.

Each time he went on deck he looked hopefully towards the land. But there was no sign of it, not even a light to reveal how near or far it lay. He knew they were lying-to off the Dutch coast, somewhere near Flushing, but it might easily have been on the other side of the world.

His prowess as a seaman had soon been noted, and Allday had found himself thanking his Maker more than once that Delaval was not aboard. The brig *Loyal Chieftain* was under the charge of his lieutenant and mate, a tight-lipped man called Isaac Newby who hailed from Dorset. He had been arrested twice for smuggling but each time he had been released for lack or loss of evidence.

He had remarked to Allday, 'I've friends in high places.' Otherwise he had said little, and after they had made contact with the two luggers there had been no time even to eat or drink.

135

Men fumbled over unfamiliar tackles, or were knocked senseless by a cargo net of brandy casks. In the holds, another team was busily lashing hemp halters and floats to ranks of casks almost before they had been stowed for the passage. A man Allday had befriended, once a foretopman named Tom Lucas, had explained that once off the English coast the casks would be dropped overboard in moored trots, like lobster pots, to be collected later by some of the long, oared smuggling galleys. After that, the cargo would be distributed in caves and small inlets, to be carried to the next 'drops' by packhorse or donkey.

Lucas was a tall, grave-faced sailor, very much the landsman's idea of a typical Jack Tar of Old England. Once, on passage from Kent, he had been stitching a patch on his shirt. Allday, watching, was used to the navy's ways and harsh discipline, but Lucas's bare back was scarred and mangled beyond recognition. He had been serving in a seventy-four at the Nore, a ship plagued by a bad captain, undermanning and appalling food.

He had complained on behalf of his mess to the first lieutenant who to all accounts had been a fair man. He in turn had approached the captain. The result: three dozen lashes at the gangway for mutinous behaviour. Lucas had made up his mind to desert but had been surprised by another lieutenant on the night he had chosen. He had struck the officer only with his fist, but he had fallen from the gangway to the gundeck below. Lucas did not know if the lieutenant was dead or alive, and had no intention of returning to find out.

He had stared at Allday grimly. 'A flogging round th' fleet? Well, you knows what that means. I couldn't take it. An' if the lieutenant died, it'll be the yardarm dance anyway!'

But it was obvious to Allday that he had no heart for smuggling. It was an escape, without hope or future, until fate caught up with him. Allday had heard some of the others discussing it in the dogwatches. So far, there had been plenty of backbreaking work, and precious few rewards. It did not balance the scale, but it was some consolation, he thought.

Allday was with Lucas tonight, supervising the hold, and in some cases putting the right lines into unfamiliar hands while the hulls groaned and lurched together in a steep offshore swell.

Allday muttered, 'Black as a boot on deck.'

Lucas paused and sniffed the air, which was heavy with brandy. 'I could use some o' that.' He seemed to realise what Allday had said. 'Yeh. Well, I've done a couple of runs in this brig. The captain always 'as a decoy. So if our –' He seemed to grin in the gloom. 'I mean, if *their* patrols or revenue cutters appear, it gives 'im time to stand clean away.'

Allday lowered his head to conceal his expression. So that was how it was done. Maybe the smuggling fraternity took turns to play decoy, then shared the spoils afterwards?

Isaac Newby, the mate, peered down past the shaded lanterns. 'Ready below?' He sounded on edge, impatient.

Allday raised his fist. 'Soon enough. One more net to be stowed.'

Newby vanished, probably to examine the other hold.

Lucas said bitterly, 'What next, I wonder? Gold for the captain, an' a gutful of rum for us, eh?'

Allday watched him thoughtfully. How many good seamen had gone rotten because of uncaring officers and ruthless captains? It was a pity there were not many more like Our Dick, he thought.

A voice yelled, 'Stand by to cast off, starboard! Lively, you scum!'

Lucas swore. 'Just like home.'

First one lugger was cast off, then the other, with more curses and squealing blocks, the canvas unmanageable with the brig floundering downwind. Then just as suddenly she had set her topsails and jib and was leaning over to the larboard tack. Hatches were battened down, and the disorder removed.

Lucas stared out at the heaving, black water and gritted his teeth. 'Christ, they've brought women aboard!' He seized the ratlines and hung on them despairingly. 'God, *listen* to 'em. Don't the buggers know it's bad luck?'

Allday listened and heard someone cry out. It was little more than a sound, like a gull's mew, soon lost in the thunder of spray-soaked canvas.

The boatswain shouted, 'You lot! Stand by to loose the fore-course! Hands aloft, and shift your bloody selves!' A rope's end found its target and a man yelped with painful resentment.

The boatswain joined Allday at the weather shrouds. 'Fair wind.' He squinted aloft but the men strung out on the forecourse yard were hidden in darkness. 'Should be a good run this time.'

Allday heard it again, and asked, 'Women, eh?' For some reason it disturbed him.

The boatswain yawned. 'The captain likes to have his way.' He gave a hard laugh. 'It's all money, I reckon, but –' He shrugged as a piercing scream broke from the after skylight.

Allday tried to moisten his lips. 'Delaval, d'you mean?'

The boatswain glared impatiently as the big foresail flapped and writhed out of control. 'Yeh, he came aboard from one of the Dutchie luggers.' He cupped his hands. 'Catch a turn there, you idle bugger! Now *belay*!'

But Allday scarcely heard him. Delaval was here. But he might not remember. He had had eyes only for Bolitho and Paice at their last meeting. Even as he grasped the hope, Allday knew it was a lie.

More bellowed orders, and one watch was dismissed below for another foully cooked meal.

Allday walked aft, his powerful frame angled to the slanting deck, his mind in great trouble. He saw the faces of the helmsmen glowing faintly in the binnacle light, but it was too weak to be seen more than yards beyond the hull.

What should he do now? If he stayed alive long enough he might –

A larger wave than the previous one swayed the deck hard over. He saw the spokes of the wheel spin, heard the two helmsmen cursing as they fought to bring the vessel back under command.

Allday gripped a rack of belaying pins, and found himself looking directly down through the cabin skylight. There was a girl there – she could not be more than sixteen. One man, Newby the mate, was pinioning her arms, another, hidden by the skylight's coaming, was tearing at her clothes, laying her breasts naked while she struggled and cried out in terror.

Too late did he feel the closeness of danger.

'So this is the sailmaker? I never forget a face, *Mister* Allday!'

The blow across the back of his head brought instant darkness. There was no time even for fear or pain. *Oblivion.*

Bolitho loosened his shirt and stared around at the intent faces. *Telemachus*'s small cabin was packed to bursting-point with not only the lieutenants from all three cutters but their sailing-masters as well.

He spread his hands on the chart and listened to the wind sighing through the rigging, the regular creak of timbers as the hull tugged at her cable.

It was evening, but the air was humid rather than warm, and the sky broken by ridges of heavy-bellied clouds.

He found time to compare it with his first meeting with the cutters' commanders. In so short a while they had all changed. Now there was no doubt, no suspicion; events had somehow welded them together in a manner Bolitho had first believed impossible.

The others had also rid themselves of their coats and Bolitho wondered how they would appear to some landsman or outsiders. More like the men they were hunting than sea-officers, he thought.

'We will weigh at dusk, and have to risk arousing interest –' His glance fell on Chesshyre. 'I see that you have already noted the change?'

Chesshyre nodded, startled to be picked out before all the others. 'Aye, sir, wind's backed two points or more.' He shivered slightly as if to test the weather. 'I'd say fog afore dawn.'

They looked at each other, the suggestion of fog moving amongst them like an evil spirit.

Bolitho said, 'I know. When I consulted the glass –' He glanced up at the open skylight, plucking his shirt away from his body. It felt like a wet rag, like the moment he had kicked open the door and had faced the men around the table. It seemed like an age past instead of days. He hurried on, 'The information is that two vessels are heading for the Isle of Thanet from the Dutch coast. One will be deep-laden, the other a decoy.' He saw them exchange glances and added, 'I have no doubt that this intelligence is true.' He pictured the smuggler tied to a chair, his

139

screams of terror as the blind man's hands had touched his eyes. No, he had little doubt of this information.

Paice said, 'May I speak, sir?' He looked at the other lieutenants and Queely responded with a curt nod, as if they had already been discussing it. Paice said, 'If this fails, and we lose them, what will happen to *you*?'

Bolitho smiled; he had been half-expecting an objection to his plan. 'I shall doubtless be ordered to a place where I can no longer disrupt matters.' Even as he said it, he knew he had never uttered a truer word. Even with Midshipman Fenwick under close arrest, and the smuggler in the hands of Craven's dragoons, his evidence would leak like a sieve without Delaval and a cargo.

He pushed the thought from his mind and said flatly, 'I believe that the information which led to the capture of the *Four Brothers* was deliberately offered to us to allay suspicion. Probably a competitor anyway, a most suitable sacrifice with the stakes so high.'

He held his breath and watched their expressions. If they accepted this, they were implicating themselves. Only Commodore Hoblyn had known about the *Four Brothers*. By accepting Bolitho's word they too could be charged with conspiracy.

Paice said resolutely, 'I agree. We've been held away from that piece of coastline for as long as I can recall. There are several small boatyards there, most of 'em on the land which belongs to –' He looked at Bolitho and said bluntly, 'Sir James Tanner, a person of great power and authority.' He gave a slow grin as if to show he was aware of his own disloyalty and added, 'Some of us *suspected*. Most saw only the hopelessness of any protest with us against so many.' His grin widened, 'Until, with respect, sir, you came amongst us like a full gale of wind!'

Lieutenant Vatass of *Snapdragon* pulled at his crumpled shirt and said, 'I think that speaks for us all, sir. If we *are* to stand alone?' He gave an elegant shrug. 'Then let us get on with it.'

There was a muttered assent around the airless cabin.

Bolitho said, 'We will leave as arranged. I have left word with Major Craven, and sent a despatch to our admiral at the Nore.' He would have smiled but for Allday. Even the admiral would have to climb down from his eyrie when this news was exploded

140

before him. If Bolitho failed he would face a court martial. That he could accept. But these men, who had accepted his arrival only under pressure, he must shield at all costs.

The three sailing-masters were comparing notes and making last adjustments to their chart. Their navigation would have to be better than ever before. There was not even room for luck this time. Just three small cutters in search of a will-o'-the-wisp. Bolitho had sent word to Chatham in the hopes of calling a frigate to intervene should Delaval slip through their tightly stretched net. Even if the admiral agreed to his wishes, it was quite likely that no frigate was available.

Bolitho recalled his meeting with Sir Marcus Drew at the Admiralty. He had left him in no doubt where responsibility would lie if Bolitho misused his commission.

If Hoblyn was guilty of conspiracy with the smugglers, no matter for what reason, he could expect no mercy either from the navy or from the men he had served for his own profit.

Bolitho's mouth hardened. Allday's life was at stake because of all this. If anything happened to him he would deal with Hoblyn and the unknown Sir James Tanner in his own fashion.

As evening closed in across the anchorage Bolitho went on deck and watched the unhurried preparations to get under way.

He could sense the difference here too. The unspoken acceptance by men he had come to know in so brief a time. George Davy the gunner, even now crouching and ducking around his small artillery. Scrope, master-at-arms, with Christie the boatswain's mate, checking the heavy chest of axes and cutlasses below the tapering mast. Big Luke Hawkins, the boatswain, was hanging over the bulwark gesturing to some men in the jolly-boat to warp it closer to the tackles for hoisting inboard.

Slow, careful preparations – for what? To risk death at the hands of smugglers whom most people condoned, if not admired? Or was it out of *loyalty*? To Bolitho, or to one another, as was the navy's way with pressed man and volunteer alike.

Bolitho glanced at the waterfront and wondered if there was already a fine mist spreading towards the many anchored vessels. And although the wind still buffeted the furled sails, the sea seemed flatter, milkier out towards the Isle of Grain and Garrison

141

Point. He shivered and wished he had brought his coat on deck.

He heard dragging footsteps and saw Young Matthew Corker resting by a six-pounder, his eyes on the land.

Bolitho said quietly, 'We owe you a great deal, Matthew. One day you will realise it. What do you wish for yourself after this?'

The boy turned and faced him, his expression unusually sad and grave. 'Please, Captain, I'd like to go *home.*' He was near to tears but added with sudden determination, 'But only when Mr Allday is back.'

Bolitho watched him walk forward, soon hidden by the busy seamen. It was the right decision, he thought. One he had to make for himself.

Paice joined him by the bulwark and said, 'Good lad, that one, sir.'

Bolitho watched him, and guessed the reason for Paice's hurt.

'Aye, Mr Paice. But for him –' He did not need to continue.

With the wind filling and puffing at the great mainsails the three cutters weighed and headed out to open water. Many eyes watched them leave, but with the mist moving slowly out to embrace the three hulls, there was little to reveal their intentions.

Major Philip Craven of the 30th Dragoons was enjoying a glass of claret when the news of their departure was brought by a hard-riding trooper.

Craven folded the message and finished the claret before calling his orderly to fetch his horse.

Commodore Ralph Hoblyn paced his great bedroom alone, his eyes everywhere whenever he reached a window. And as darkness fell, he was still striding back and forth, his stooped shoulder even more pronounced in shadows against the walls.

A messenger brought word to the gates about the cutters' leaving without fresh orders, but the corporal of the guard retorted sharply, 'The commodore's made it plain in the past! 'E's not to be disturbed, *no matter wot!*'

And away in Chatham itself, the one person who had been the hinge of all these events, Midshipman Fenwick of the local impressment service, made the only firm decision of his miserable nineteen years. While the guards were changing their duties, he took his belt and hanged himself in his cell.

Down in *Telemachus*'s cabin once more, Bolitho changed into a fresh shirt and placed his watch carefully in his pocket. Around and above him the hull muttered and groaned, and he felt the wash alongside losing its power with each dragging minute.

He stared at the chart until his head throbbed.

It was now or never. He glanced at the parcel with the ship model inside. For both of them.

It seemed like an eternity before understanding returned. Even then it was a battle, against pain, and a sick unwillingness to believe what had happened.

Allday tried to open his eyes but with shocked horror realised that only the right one would obey. His whole body ached from bruises, and when he tried again to use his other eye he thought for an instant it had been put out.

He stared at the hazy picture which reached only to the perimeter of light cast by a gently spiralling lantern. It was barely a few feet away, and he thought he was going mad because of the confined space. He emitted a groan of agony as he tried to move. For the first time he realised that his legs were braced apart by irons bolted to the deck, his wrists dragged above his head by manacles so tight that he could no longer feel them.

He made himself wait, counting the seconds, while he attempted to muster his thoughts. He could remember nothing. But when he moved his head again he felt the force of the blow and guessed how he had come here. They must have beaten him almost to a point of death after that, although he had felt nothing. Not then.

He eased his legs and felt the irons dragging at them. He was naked to the waist, and when he peered down he saw blood, dried and stark on his body, like black tar in the lantern light.

A tiny pinprick flickered in his damaged eye and he felt more pain when he tried to open it. It must be clotted with his own blood, he thought despairingly, but what was the difference now? They would kill him. He tensed his legs in the irons. But not before they had made him suffer more.

Voices came faintly through the hull and he realised suddenly

143

that the motion had eased; for another few dazed seconds he believed the brig was in harbour.

But as his mind tried to grasp what was happening he heard the irregular groan of the tiller, the clatter of tackle on deck. He peered round the tiny space again, each movement bringing a fresh stab of pain. No wonder it was small and low. It must be the lazaret, somewhere below the after cabin where the master's stores were usually held. Here there was nothing but a few dusty crates. Delaval – Allday sobbed at the sudden discovery of his name. It was surging back in broken pieces. The girl, half-naked in the cabin, screaming and pleading, and then . . .

That was why the tiller movements were so loud and near. His sailor's instinct forced through the despair and the pain. The brig was barely making headway. Not becalmed, so that – it came to him then. It must be a fog. God, it was common enough in these waters, especially after wind across a warm sea.

He craned his neck again. There was a small hatch from the cabin above, and another even smaller door in the bulkhead. Probably for a carpenter to inspect the lower hull if the vessel was damaged.

Allday sat bolt upright. She was the *Loyal Chieftain*, and was loaded with contraband to the deck beams. He felt close to shouting out aloud, all his distress and anguish pinned into this one small prison. It was for nothing. *Nothing*.

He dragged himself out of the sudden self-pity and resignation, and listened to a new movement on deck. A brief rumbling that he had heard a thousand times, in a thousand places – the sound of gun trucks as a carriage was manhandled across deck planking. It was the long nine-pounder he had seen when he had helped to load the ship.

Suppose Bolitho was nearby? He fought against the sudden hope, because there was none. He tried to think only of dying without pleading, of escaping it all like the Captain's lady had done in the Great South Sea.

But the thought persisted, shining through the mists of pain like St Anthony's Light at Falmouth.

Just suppose Bolitho was searching this area . . .

More thuds echoed through the decks as if to prod his thoughts into order.

Allday had never trusted a topsail cutter, or any other vessel which relied on a single mast, no matter how much sail she carried. He peered with his sound eye at the deckhead as if to see the gun-crew who were manoeuvring the nine-pounder, probably towards the quarter in readiness for a stern-chase. One good shot, and a cutter would be rendered useless. She would be left to fend for herself. Allday gritted his teeth. Or more likely, Delaval would round-up on her and loose every gun he had into the wreckage until not a soul was left alive.

He moved his arms and legs but was helpless. He must be content, accept that death was close by.

To fall in battle as old Stockdale had done was one thing – to die screaming under torture was another. Allday did not know if he could face it.

He closed his eyes tightly as the hatch in the deckhead was flung open. He heard angry voices, and then a coarse laugh as someone was pushed down into the lazaret. The hatch banged shut and Allday opened his eye once again.

The girl was crouching on her knees, whimpering and gasping like a savaged animal. There was blood on her face, and even in the poor light Allday saw the scratches on her bare shoulders as if talons had torn at her body. It was the same girl he had seen in the cabin. Close to, she was even younger than he had first thought. Fifteen or less. He watched despairingly as her hands fluttered about her torn clothing as she tried to cover her breasts.

As the lantern swung suddenly she stared up and saw him for the first time. It was all there in her face. Revulsion, terror, disgust at what had been done to her.

Allday swallowed hard and tried to think of words to calm her. God alone knew what they had done. From all the blood he guessed she had been raped several times. And now, like him, she was waiting to be disposed of.

He began carefully, ''Ere, Miss, be brave now, eh?' His voice was little more than a croak. He added, 'I *know* what you've been through –' He groaned and felt the manacles tearing at his wrists. What was the use? She didn't understand what he was saying, not a bloody word; and what if she did?

145

The girl crouched in the same position, her eyes still and unblinking.

Allday murmured, 'I hope it's quick for you.' He groaned again. 'If I could only *move!*' His words seemed to bounce from the curved sides to mock him.

More voices echoed through the decks, and feet padded overhead as men ran to trim the sails yet again.

Allday's head drooped. Fog, that was it. Must be.

He glanced at the girl. She sat quite still, one breast bared. As if hope and life had already left her.

Footsteps thudded above, suddenly close, and Allday gasped hoarsely, 'Come here to me, Miss! *Please!*'

He saw her eyes widen as she stared up at the small hatch, then at him with the brightness of terror. Something in his tone, perhaps, made her crawl over the filthy deck and huddle against his body, her eyes tightly closed.

Legs appeared through the hatch, then Isaac Newby the mate dropped into full view. He drew a cutlass from his belt and stabbed it into the deck out of reach where it swayed from side to side like a gleaming snake.

He looked at the girl and said, 'Soon be time to drop you outboard, *Mister* Allday. But the cap'n 'as 'is own ideas, y'see —' He was grinning, enjoying it. 'We shall 'ave to leave a souvenir for your gallant captain to remember you by, to remind 'im of the time he tried to outrun the Brotherhood, *right?*' He tapped the knife at his belt. 'Delaval thinks your fine tattoo would make the proper sort of gift!' He threw back his head and laughed. 'So the arm will have to come off, like.'

Allday tasted bile in his throat. 'Let *her* go. What can she do?'

Newby rubbed his chin as if in thought. 'Well, seein' as you're not long for this world —' His arm shot out and he dragged the girl from the side, one hand tearing off the last covering from her shoulders. 'Feast yer eyes on *this!*' He gripped the girl's hair and pulled her face roughly to his own, his free hand ripping away the remainder of her clothing like some savage beast.

Allday had no way of knowing what happened next. He saw the girl slump back beside him, her breasts rising and falling in fear, while Newby propped himself on his hands and stared

146

straight ahead. Allday watched as Newby's utter disbelief changed to sudden emptiness while he pitched forward and lay still. Only then did he see the knife protruding from his side. She must have seen it before he had tried to rape her again, had dragged it from its sheath, and then . . .

Allday bobbed his head towards the dead man's belt. He had seen the screw there beside the empty sheath.

'*Get it for me!*' He struggled to make himself understood by dragging at his leg irons. 'Help me, *for God's sake!*'

She reached out and touched his bruised face, as if they were a million miles from this terrible place. Then she bowed over the man's body and unhooked the screw from his belt.

Allday watched with sick fascination as she unfastened first the leg irons then reached up to release the manacles, oblivious to her breasts brushing against him, to everything but the moment, the spark of courage which when offered she had used without hesitation.

Allday rolled over and gasped aloud in agony as the blood forced through his veins again. He felt light-headed, and knew that if he did not keep moving he might lose his wits completely.

He jerked the cutlass from the deck and gasped, 'That feels better!' Then he hobbled over to the corpse and plucked the knife from it. It did not come out easily, and he muttered, 'You did for that pig well enough!'

He stared up as shouts filtered down to them from that other world of sea and canvas. He heard the clatter of handspikes and tackles. They were moving the nine-pounder again. There could only be one reason. He gripped the girl's shoulder and wondered why she did not pull away. Maybe she was beyond that, beyond everything real and decent.

Allday gestured towards the little door in the bulkhead and made a sawing motion with the knife. He noticed there was still blood on it, but she watched his gestures without fear or revulsion.

He explained carefully, 'You get through there an' cut the lines to the rudder, see?' He groaned as her eyes remained empty and without understanding. They would soon come looking for Newby, especially if they intended to close with another vessel.

147

Allday levered open the little door with his cutlass and held the lantern closer so that she could see into the darkness of the afterpart. Controlled by unseen hands, the rudder's yoke lines squeaked and rubbed through their blocks, the sea beyond the transom gurgling so loudly it seemed just feet away. Allday started as he felt her fingers on his wrist. She looked at him just once, her glance searching as if to share their resources, then she took the proffered knife and slithered through the small doorway. Once inside that confined space Allday saw her body suddenly pale in the darkness, and knew that she had tossed aside the last of her covering, as if that too was part of a nightmare.

He loosened his arms and winced as the pain probed through them. Then he peered up at the hatchway. It was the only way anyone could approach. He listened to the girl's sharp breathing as she sawed up and down on one of the stout hemp lines. It might take her a long while, a strand at a time. He spat on his palm and gripped the cutlass all the tighter. Now she had the strength of hatred and fear to help her. A few moments ago he had been expecting death, but only after the brutal severing of his arm.

Now, if only for a short while, they were both free, and even if he had to kill her himself, she would suffer that and nothing more.

A voice bellowed, 'Where the *hell* is he?'

Allday bared his teeth. 'Here we go then!' A shaft of light came down from the cabin and a voice called angrily, 'Come on deck, you mad bugger! The cap'n's waitin'!'

A seabooted leg appeared over the coaming and Allday could feel the wildness surging through his mind and body like a raging fire.

He snarled, 'Won't I do, matey?' The cutlass blade took the man's leg just above the knee with all his power behind it, so that Allday had to lurch away to avoid the blood and the terrible scream before the hatch was dropped into place.

As his breathing steadied he heard the regular scrape of the knife and murmured, 'You keep at it, my lass. We'll show these bastards a thing or two!' He licked his dried lips. After that . . . But afterwards no longer mattered.

Bolitho walked aft to the compass box, aware of the loudness of his shoes on the damp planking. The *Telemachus*'s deck was filled with silent figures, but in the drifting mist he could have been with a mere handful of companions.

Chesshyre straightened up as he recognised him and said, 'Barely holding steerage way, sir.' Even he spoke in a hushed whisper. Like all sailors he hated sea-mist and fog. Bolitho watched the tilting compass card. North-North-East. He watched it move again very slightly under the tiny lamp-glow. Chesshyre was right. They were holding on course, but making barely two knots, if that. It couldn't have been at a worse time.

Someone up forward began to cough, and Hawkins the boatswain rasped, 'Stick a wad down yer gullet, Fisher! Not a squeak out of you, my son!'

Paice's tall shadow moved through the mist. Perhaps more than any other he understood Bolitho's predicament, the agony of seeing his one remaining chance slip away. To the smugglers it meant very little. Any landfall would do. They could rid themselves of their cargoes with ease once they were within sight of home waters.

Bolitho watched the winding tendrils of mist creeping through rigging and shrouds, while even in the darkness the big mainsail seemed to shine like metal from the moisture. It appeared as if the cutter was stationary, and only the mist was moving ahead.

It would be first light soon. Bolitho clamped his jaws together to contain his despair. It might just as well be midnight.

It was impossible to guess where the other two cutters lay. They would be lucky to regain contact when the mist cleared, let alone run down the decoy or Delaval.

Allday was out there somewhere. Unless he already lay fathoms deep, betrayed by his own loyalty and courage.

Paice remarked, 'We *could* change tack again, sir.'

Bolitho could not see his face but could feel his compassion. He had wanted Delaval more than anyone. Was there nothing they could do?

He replied, 'I think not. Attend the chart yourself and try to estimate our position and drift.' He spoke his anxiety aloud. 'I know it's unlikely but there may be a ship just out there. Otherwise I would suggest more soundings. Anything is better than not knowing.'

Paice thrust his big hands into his pockets. 'I shall put a good man aloft as soon as there is some daylight, sir.' He turned away, the mist swirling between them, the compass light vanishing. 'I will check the chart.'

Lieutenant Triscott shifted uneasily, unwilling to break into Bolitho's thoughts.

Bolitho said, 'What is it, Mr Triscott?' He had not meant to sound so sharp. 'You are all on edge today!'

Triscott said lamely, 'I was wondering, sir. Should we meet with the smuggler, I – I mean –'

'You are asking if we can overpower him without the other cutters?'

The youthful lieutenant hung his head. 'Well, yes, sir.'

Bolitho leaned on the bulwark, the woodwork like ice under his fingers even though his body felt hot and feverish.

'Let us *find* him, Mr Triscott. Then you may ask me again.'

Chesshyre cupped his hands behind his ears. 'What was that?'

Bolitho stared aloft but soon lost the shrouds and running-rigging in the mist, as if they led up to nowhere.

The boatswain called hoarsely, 'Not *riggin'*, sir!'

Bolitho held up his hand. 'Quiet!' Like Chesshyre he had thought for just a few seconds that the sound had come from above, like a line parting under stress, or being too swollen with damp and carrying away inside a block. But it was not. It had come from outside the hull.

Men stood and swayed between the six-pounders; others clambered into the shrouds as if to listen more easily, all weariness and disappointment forgotten. At least for the while.

Paice appeared on deck, hatless, his thick hair moving in the wet breeze like a hassock of grass.

He said thickly, 'I know *Telemachus* better'n I know myself, sir. Every sound carries down there to the cabin.' He peered angrily into the darkness. 'That was a musket shot, or I'm a bloody nigger!' He glanced awkwardly at Bolitho. 'Begging your pardon, sir!'

This time they all heard it. Muffled, the sound barely carrying

150

above the shipboard noises within the confines of the deck.

Chesshyre nodded, satisfied. 'Close, sir. Downwind of us. No doubt about it. The wind's poor enough, but it'll deaden the sound.'

Bolitho frowned with concentration. Chesshyre's observations were good ones. Who would be firing into mist without some kind of retaliation?

'Let her fall off a point.' He gripped Paice's sleeve as he made to move aft. 'Pass the word to load both batteries. Gun by gun.' He let each word hang in the air. 'I don't want anyone making a noise. We've not much time, but we've time enough for caution.'

Triscott and the gunner moved up either side, whispering instructions, gritting their teeth at the slightest creak or thud.

Bolitho walked forward between the busy, groping figures and stood in the eyes of the vessel, his fingers gripped around a stay with the tiny gurgling bow-wave directly beneath him. Once when he looked aft he thought the mist was thicker, for he could barely see the mast. It was like standing on a pinnacle, moving ahead, seeing nothing. One slip, and they would never find him.

There was another muffled shot and he felt a new disappointment. It seemed further away, on a different bearing. Mist distorted most things at sea, even a trained seaman's judgement. Suppose – he thrust it from his mind. *There was a ship there.* He could sense it. And if that someone kept firing, the sound would lead them to it. He tried to control his sudden anger. If only the mist would depart. He stared up at the sky. It was surely brighter now? It had to be.

Triscott called softly, 'All loaded, sir.'

Bolitho climbed down from the stemhead and used the lieutenant's shoulder to support himself as he groped his way over the inboard end of the bowsprit.

As they walked aft between the guns a voice whispered, 'We gonna fight, Cap'n?'

Another said, 'There'll be prize money if we takes this 'un, eh, Cap'n?'

Someone even reached out to touch his arm as he passed, as if to regain a lost courage, to find comfort there.

Not for the first time was Bolitho grateful they could not see his

151

face. He reached the compass-box and saw one of the helmsmen leaning backwards, his whole weight on the tiller bar, his red-rimmed eyes watching steadily for the tell-tale peak of the mainsail.

Bolitho stared at him, realising that he could see the man's stubbled face when moments earlier he had been hidden completely.

Paice exclaimed, 'I'll go myself, sir!' Then he was away, swarming up the lee ratlines with the ease of a young topman.

Bolitho watched him until his outline merged into the remaining mist. His wife must have been proud of him, just as she had been ashamed of the people who had stood by and allowed a man to be murdered. She had probably been thinking of the tall lieutenant even as the pistol had cut short her life.

Paice slithered down a stay. 'She's a brig, sir!' He did not seem to feel the cuts on his hands from the hasty drop. 'I can just make out her tops'l yards.' He stared at Bolitho without seeing him. 'Must be her! That bastard Delaval!'

Bolitho could feel the power of the man, the reborn force of his hatred.

'Two good hands aloft!'

Then Paice said in a more controlled voice, 'No sign of any other sail, sir.' He clenched his hands and stared with disbelief at the blood on his wrists. 'But by God, I'd walk on water to take that swine!'

There were more shots now and Bolitho offered silent thanks. If *Telemachus* could close the range and use her smashers it might compensate for the smuggler's heavier armament. The musket fire must be keeping them busy. Too busy even to put a lookout at the masthead.

A mutiny? He saw Delaval's cruel features in his mind. It was unlikely. A cold hand seemed to close around his heart and squeeze the life out of it.

It was Allday.

He was stunned by the flat calmness in his voice. 'Alter course to engage, Mr Chesshyre. Pass out the weapons.'

He looked up at a small handkerchief of pale sky, and thought of the dead girl on *Wakeful*'s deck.

A long, painful journey. When the mist eventually cleared, it would be settled. He loosened the old sword at his hip.

For some it would be over.

Allday flung himself against the curving side and ducked yet again as a musket ball slammed through the partly open hatch.

He heard them calling to one another, the scrape of ramrods as they reloaded. He was sweating despite the chill air of the lazaret, and his whole body was streaming as if he had just dragged himself from the sea.

He gripped the cutlass and squinted up through the trapped powder smoke. It was just a matter of time. He shouted over his shoulder towards the small door, 'Keep sawing, my lass! You'll get through!' Only once had he been able to watch the girl's progress. Even with a sharp blade it was hard work to cut through the stout rudder-lines. He had seen her pale outline rising and falling above the creaking lines, everything else forgotten, unimportant. She probably didn't even know why she was doing it, Allday thought despairingly, just as she understood not a word he said to her.

The hatch moved an inch, and the muzzle of a musket pointed blindly through the opening. Allday reached up and seized it, winced as he felt the heated metal, then tugged it hard, catching the man off balance so that he fell across the hatch, the musket exploding within a foot of Allday's head. Before the smuggler could release his grip Allday thrust upwards with his cutlass and yelled, 'One for the pot, you bastards!'

He fell exhausted against the side, his eyes too raw from smoke to care about the blood which poured through the hatch like paint.

The people in the cabin suddenly froze into silence, and above the creak of rudder lines Allday heard a voice yell, 'Stand to! Man the braces there! A King's ship, by Jesus!' And then another, calmer, more controlled; Delaval's. 'It's Paice's *Telemachus*, I'll swear. This time we'll do for him and his bloody crew, eh, lads?'

Allday did not know or care about any response. The words stood out before all else. Paice's *Telemachus*. Bolitho was here.

The deck was slanting down so that the corpse of Newby rolled on one side as if awakening to the din.

153

Allday heard the shouted orders, the slap of canvas, and then the too-familiar sound of the nine-pounder being hauled into position.

He peered through the little door and pleaded, 'Keep at it, lass. I can hold 'em off until –'

He stared blindly at the pale figure sprawled across one of the timbers. Either the last shot had caught her, or someone had fired down through the slits which held the sheaves of the rudder lines.

He reached over the sill and dragged her up and through, held her naked body against his own, turning her face with sudden tenderness until the swaying lantern reflected from her eyes.

Brokenly he whispered, 'Never mind, young missy, you bloody well tried!'

The deck bounded to a sudden recoil and he heard somebody yelling directions even as the discharged gun ran inboard on its tackles.

Allday crawled over the deck and dragged the coat from Newby's back. Then he covered her with it and with a last glance at her face lifted her to the open hatch and pushed her into the abandoned cabin.

Another minute or so and she might have cut the rudder lines, then Paice's cutter would have stood a good chance of outsailing her, crossing her stern and raking her with those deadly carronades.

The deck heaved again and dust filtered down from the poop as the gun fired across the quarter.

Allday wrapped the girl's body in the coat and put her across his shoulder. For just those seconds he had seen her face in the pale light. No fear, all anguish gone. Probably the first peace she had known since the Terror had swept through her country.

Allday glanced round the cabin until his eyes fell on a bottle of rum which was about to slide from the table. With the girl's body carried easily over his shoulder he drank heavily from the bottle before picking up the reddened cutlass again and making for the companion ladder.

They could not hurt her or him any more. Out in the open he would die fighting. He shuddered as the gun crashed inboard again and the deck shook to the concussion.

154

There was a ragged cheer. 'There goes 'er topmast, by God!'

Allday blinked the sweat from his eyes and left the cabin. At the foot of the ladder he saw the man whose leg he had nearly severed when he had climbed through the hatch. His bandage was sodden with blood, and he stank of vomit and rum. Despite his pain he managed to open his eyes, his mouth ready to scream as he saw Allday rising over him.

Allday said, 'Not any more, matey!' He jammed the point of his cutlass between the man's teeth and drove it hard against the ladder. To the dead girl he muttered, 'Keep with me, lass!'

As his eyes rose above the coaming he saw the backs of several men who were standing at the bulwarks to point at the other vessel. Between them Allday saw *Telemachus*, his heart sinking as he saw her despoiled outline, the topmast gone, like a great crippled seabird. The gun's crew were already ramming home another charge, and past them Allday saw Delaval watching his adversary through a brass telescope. All the fury and hatred seemed to erupt at once and Allday yelled,

'I'm here, you bloody bastard!'

For those few moments every face was turned towards him, the approaching cutter forgotten.

'Who's going to be brave enough, eh, you scum?'

Delaval shouted, 'Cut him down! Bosun, take that man!'

But nobody moved as Allday bent down and laid the dead girl on the deck in the dawn's first sunlight.

'Is *this* what you want? All you have guts for?' He saw the seaman Tom Lucas staring at the girl before he shouted, 'We didn't bargain for this!'

They were his last words on earth. Delaval lowered his smoking pistol and drew another.

He snapped, 'Put up the helm! We'll finish this now!'

Allday stood alone, his chest heaving, barely able to see out of his uninjured eye, or keep his grasp on the cutlass.

As if through a haze he watched the helm going over, saw sudden confusion as the spokes spun uselessly and a voice cried, *'Steerin's gone!'*

Allday dropped beside the girl on the deck and grasped her hand, the cutlass held ready across her body.

155

'*You done it, girl!*' His eyes smarted. 'By Christ, we're in irons!'

The brig was already losing steerage way and heeling unsteadily downwind. Allday looked at the gun's crew, their expression dazed as the distant cutter seemed to slide away from their next fall of shot.

'Well, lads!' Allday waited for the sudden, agonising impact. He knew Delaval was aiming his other pistol, just as he knew that men were moving away from the sides to stand between them.

He repeated, 'Is *this* what you want?'

Delaval screamed, 'Cut him down! I order it!'

Still no one moved, then some of the seamen Allday had seen at the boatyard tossed down their weapons, while others defiantly faced aft towards Delaval.

Allday watched *Telemachus*'s splintered topmast rise above the *Loyal Chieftain*'s weather bulwark, knew he would have seen Bolitho were his eyes not so blind.

It seemed like a year before a grapnel lodged in the bulwark and the deck was taken over by some of Paice's armed seamen.

There was no resistance, and Paice himself walked aft until he confronted Delaval by the abandoned wheel.

Delaval faced him coldly, but his features were like chalk.

'Well, Lieutenant, your greatest triumph, I dare say. Will you murder me now, unarmed as I am, in front of witnesses?'

Paice glanced across to Allday and gave a brief nod before removing the unfired pistol from the other's hand.

'The noose is for scum like you.' He turned aside as a voice yelled, '*Wakeful* in sight, sir!' Someone gave a cheer but fell silent as Bolitho climbed over the bulwark past the levelled muskets and swivels on *Telemachus*'s side.

He looked around at their tense faces. He had seen Paice's expression, his features torn with emotion when seconds earlier he might have hacked Delaval to the deck. Perhaps, like the blind man, he had discovered that revenge would solve nothing.

Then he walked to Allday, who was kneeling again beside the dead girl. Two unknown young women. A twist of fate.

He saw the cuts and cruel bruises on Allday's body and wanted to say so much. Maybe the right words would come later.

Instead he said quietly, 'So you're safe, John?'

156

Allday peered up at him with his sound eye and felt his face trying to respond with a grin, but without success.

One truth stood out. Bolitho had called him by his first name. Something which had never happened before.

11

Faces In The Crowd

The Golden Fleece Inn which stood on the outskirts of Dover was an imposing, weatherbeaten building, a place to change post horses, to rest a while after the rough roads around and out of the port.

Rear-Admiral Sir Marcus Drew waited for the inn servants to place his travelling chests in the adjoining room and walked to the thick leaded windows overlooking a cobbled square. He stared with distaste at groups of townsfolk who were chattering in the hot sunshine, some buying fruit or Geneva from women with trays around their necks.

It was just possible to see the harbour, or part of it, reassuring to know, as Drew did, that there were several small men-of-war at anchor there. On the way to the inn he had also found some comfort in the presence of scarlet-coated marines, or an occasional troop of stern-faced dragoons.

Nevertheless he felt uneasy here. But for a direct order he would still be in London, perhaps even with his young mistress. He turned away from the window as his secretary entered and paused to stare at him, wiping his small gold-rimmed spectacles with a handkerchief at the same time.

'Is it satisfactory, Sir Marcus?' He peered around the spacious room, and considered it a palace.

Drew snorted, 'I dislike this place – the whole situation in fact.' Coming here had stripped him of confidence, his accustomed sense of being in control. Usually he spent his days choosing officers for certain appointments; at other times he bowed to their lordships' whims and fancies by providing favours for others he might inwardly have regarded as useless.

Now here, to Dover. He scowled. Not even Canterbury where there was at least some social life, or so he had heard. Dover seen from within and not through the eyes of some homeward-bound sailor was too rough and ready, with an air of instability to match it. But for the great castle which cast its timeless gaze across the harbour and the approaches, he would have felt even more uncertain.

The secretary offered, 'Captain Richard Bolitho has arrived, Sir Marcus.' He laid his head on one side. 'Shall I –'

'*No!* Have him wait, dammit! Fetch me a glass of something.'

'Brandy, Sir Marcus?'

The rear-admiral glared at him. 'Don't make mock of me, sir! The brandy is quite likely contraband – I want no part of it!'

He controlled his temper. It was not his secretary's fault. Another thought pressed through his mind. Besides, the man knew about his little affair. He said in a more reasonable tone, 'Fetch me what you will. This place . . . it downs my heart.'

The elderly secretary moved to the windows and stared at the crowd, which within half-an-hour had doubled. There was music down there, some masked dancers bobbing through the crowd, probably picking pockets as they went, he thought.

At the far side of the square was a great cluster of horses, each held by a red-coated soldier. They looked wary, while their two officers paced back and forth in deep conversation.

He shifted his gaze to the crude scaffold, a man who was obviously a carpenter putting finishing touches to it. The secretary noticed that, as he worked, his foot was tapping in time to the cheerful music. No wonder the rear-admiral was uneasy. In London you were spared this sort of thing unless you counted the ragged scarecrows which dangled in chains on the outskirts, along the King's highway.

Sir Marcus joined him and muttered, 'By God, you'd think they'd have heard enough about France to –' He said no more. He was always a careful man.

Two floors below, Bolitho walked into a small parlour and rested his back in a cool corner.

The inn seemed to be full of naval people, none of whom he knew. But he had been away from England a long while. A young lieutenant had jumped to his feet and had stammered, 'I beg your attention, Captain Bolitho! Should you require a junior lieutenant –'

Bolitho had shaken his head. 'I cannot say. But do not lose heart.' How many times had he himself been made to beg for an appointment?

The landlord served him personally, carrying a tall tankard of local ale to his table.

'We're not used to so many senior persons, sir, and that's no mistake! War must be comin' soon, it's a sure sign!' He went off chuckling to himself.

Bolitho stared at the blue sky through one of the tiny windows. It kept coming back. Memory upon memory, and most of all, Allday kneeling on deck, his poor bruised face turned to greet him. There had been no sort of disbelief or surprise. As if they had both known in their hearts they would be reunited.

That had been weeks ago. Now he was here, summoned to Dover by the same flag officer who had offered him this appointment.

He heard shouts of laughter from the square outside and considered his feelings. Was it coincidence or purpose which had brought them here today?

At least the rear-admiral had come to him. Had it been the other way round Bolitho would have known his attachment was over.

A servant hovered by the door. 'Sir Marcus will see you now, sir.' He gestured towards the stairway which wound upwards past some old and stained paintings of battles, ship disasters, and local scenes. A sailors' haunt – smugglers too, he thought grimly.

He was breathing hard by the time he had reached the top floor. A shortage of breath or patience? Perhaps both.

An elderly man in a bottle-green coat ushered him into the first room, and he saw Drew sitting listlessly by one of the open windows. He did not rise, but waved for Bolitho to take a chair.

Bolitho began, 'I was called here, Sir Marcus, because –'

The admiral retorted wearily, 'We were *both* called here, man.

160

Have some claret, though after the journey it may taste like bilge!' He watched Bolitho as he poured a glass for himself. The same grave features, level eyes which looked like the North Sea in the reflected sunlight. Cold, and yet ... Drew said, 'It was a lengthy report which you sent their lordships, Bolitho. You spared nothing, added no decoration.' He nodded slowly. 'Like your Cornish houses and their slate roofs – hard and functional.'

'It was all the truth, sir.'

'I have no doubt of it. In some ways I would have wished otherwise.' He dragged the report across his table and ruffled through it, words or sentences sparking off pictures and events, as if he had been listening to Bolitho's voice while he had read it.

Drew said, 'You had a free hand and you used it, as many knew you would. The result? Most of those deserters, and many others who were in hiding, *volunteered* to return to the navy.' He glanced at him severely. 'I am not so certain that I would have permitted them to return to different vessels from which they had originally run, or accepted them without an example of punishment to deter others.' He sighed and continued, 'But you gave them your word. That had to be sufficient. All told we gained two hundred men; perhaps others will take your word as a bond. It will encourage wider areas, I hope.'

He cleared his throat. 'I would like you to tell me about Commodore Hoblyn.'

Bolitho got to his feet and walked to a side window overlooking a narrow street, like the one which Allday had described, where he had been taken by the press gang.

He said bitterly, 'That too is in my report, Sir Marcus.'

He expected a rebuke but Drew said quietly, 'I know. I would like you to tell me, as man to man. You see, I served with Hoblyn in that other war. He was a different being then.'

Bolitho stared at the empty street and tried to shut out the mounting buzz of voices from the crowd which waited to observe the spectacle of a man being hanged.

'I did not know, Sir Marcus.' He knew the admiral was watching his back but did not turn. 'It was too much for him in the end.' How could he sound so calm and casual? Like all the events which had led up to taking the *Loyal Chieftain*, and which

161

now lay safe in memory. Like being in a calm in the eye of a typhoon where everything was sharp and clear, desperately so, perhaps, while you waited to enter the second path of the storm. 'I suspected Hoblyn was involved with the smuggling gangs, although I wanted to disbelieve it. He was a poor man, rejected by the one life for which he cared, and then all at once he was rich. Gifts which he treasured as acts of friendship – perhaps he too refused to see them as bribes. A carriage from a French nobleman, a world in which he thought he held control. They needed him, and when they thought he had betrayed them they took their revenge.'

Bolitho rested his hand on the sill, praying that the admiral had had enough, that he could let the pieces fall into distance like the moment you lower a telescope from another craft.

But the room was still, and even the distant voices in the square seemed afraid to intrude.

'I had told Major Craven what I intended before we weighed anchor.' He stared into the little street, his grey eyes very still. 'When he saw us return with our prizes –' That too had been like a dream, *Snapdragon* following them to the anchorage, her jubilant prize-crew aboard the smuggling schooner intended as a decoy. That unknown seaman aboard *Telemachus* who had called to him through the fog would get his prize money after all. Bolitho continued, 'Craven had two troops of his men and a magistrate to read the warrant.' He barely listened to his own voice as he relived that night, when he had reached Hoblyn's house to join Craven's dragoons and a magistrate who had been almost too terrified to speak.

The marine picket was outside the gates, and most of Hoblyn's servants had been clustered in the gardens in their night attire. They had described how Hoblyn had ordered them from the house, and when one had requested a few moments to return to his room he had fired a pistol point-blank into a chandelier.

Craven had said, 'The doors are locked and bolted. Can't understand it, Bolitho. He must know why we're here.' He added with sudden anger, 'By God, some of my own men have died because of his treachery!'

Bolitho had been about to ring the bell himself when he had

seen Allday walking carefully between the dragoons.

Bolitho had said, 'You should be resting, old friend. After this –'

But Allday had replied stubbornly, 'I'm not leaving you again, Cap'n.'

Craven had settled it by calling for his farrier sergeant. A tall, bearded dragoon who had marched up to the doors with his huge axe, the one he sometimes used for slaughtering animals to feed the soldiers, and in just two minutes he had laid both doors on the ground.

It had been a macabre scene which had greeted their eyes. In the light of guttering candles Bolitho had seen the shattered fragments of a chandelier, and then when he had approached the great staircase he had seen the blood, on the carpets, against the wall, even on a banister rail. They had halted halfway up the staircase, and Major Craven's drawn sabre had glinted in the flickering candles as he had gripped Bolitho's arm. 'In God's name what was that fearful sound?'

No wonder the servants had been terrified out of their wits, and the picket had stayed by the gates until Craven's men had arrived in force. It was a terrible, inhuman cry, rising and falling like a wounded wolf. Even some of the older dragoons had glanced at one another and had clutched their weapons all the tighter.

Bolitho had hurried to the big door at the top of the stairs, Allday limping behind him, that same cutlass still in his hand.

Craven had shouted, 'In the King's name!' Then he had kicked the door inwards with his boot.

Bolitho knew he would never forget the sight which had waited in that room. Hoblyn crouching beside the huge bed, rocking from side to side, his hands and arms thick with dried blood. For a moment longer they had imagined that he was injured, or had attempted to kill himself without success. Until a sergeant had brought more candles, and together they had stared at the bed, at what was left of the naked body of Jules, the youthful footman and companion.

There was not a part of his body which had not been savagely mutilated or hacked away. Only the face was left unmarked, like

163

the murdered informer aboard the *Loyal Chieftain* when Bolitho had first confronted Delaval. From the youth's contorted features it was obvious that the horrific torture had been exercised while he had been alive. The bed, the floor, everything was soaked in blood, and Bolitho had realised that Hoblyn must have carried the corpse in his arms round and round the room until he had collapsed, broken and exhausted.

The Brotherhood had thought that he had betrayed them, not realising that Bolitho's search for Allday had provoked the attack on the boatyard.

From all the rewards Hoblyn had gained from them by his help and information, they had selected the possession he had prized the most, and had butchered the youth, then left him like a carcass at the gates.

Craven had said huskily, 'In the King's name you are charged this day —' He had broken off and had choked, 'Take him. I can stand no more of this charnel house!'

It had been then that Hoblyn had come out of his trance and stared at them without recognition. With a great effort he had got to his feet, and almost tenderly covered the mutilated corpse with a blanket.

In a steady voice he had said, 'I am ready, gentlemen.' He had turned only briefly to Bolitho. 'You *would not heed* me.' Then he had tried to shrug his shoulders, but even that had failed him.

At the door he had said, 'My sword. I am entitled.'

Bolitho and Craven had looked at one another. Maybe each had known in his own way.

They had waited outside the door, while the dragoons lined the hallway below, where some dazed servants were peering in at the bloodstains and the plaster which had fallen to Hoblyn's pistol.

The bang of the shot brought more cries and shouts from the waiting servants. They had found Hoblyn lying on the bed, one arm over the blanketed shape, the other crooking the pistol which had blown away the back of his skull.

Bolitho realised he had stopped speaking, that the din outside the inn was louder now.

Sir Marcus Drew said quietly, 'I am distressed to learn it, Bolitho, and I grieve that you should have been forced to witness it. In the long run, it will have been the best way out. Perhaps the only way for him.'

Bolitho moved to the large window and watched the scene below. The pattern had changed, and the dragoons were mounted now, lined, saddle to saddle, across the square, each sabre drawn and shouldered, the horses restless, uneasy in the presence of death. A mounted major was patting his own horse's neck, but his eyes were on the swaying crowd. It could have been Craven, but it was not.

Drew stood beside him and sipped at his claret, his mind still with the image of Hoblyn's death.

'He was a fool, not the man I once admired. How did he come to –' He could not continue.

Bolitho eyed him coldly. 'Come to *love* that youth? It was all he had. The woman who had waited for him during the war would not even look at him when she was told of his terrible scars. So he searched elsewhere, and found that boy.' Bolitho was again surprised at the emptiness of his voice. 'He learned too late that there are no pockets in a shroud, no money box in a coffin.'

Drew licked his lips. 'You are a strange fellow, Bolitho.'

'Strange, sir? Because the truly guilty go free, or hide in safety behind rank or privilege?' His eyes flashed. 'One day –'

He stiffened as he saw Delaval's slight figure mounting the scaffold, a trooper on either side. Dressed in a fine velvet coat, his dark hair uncovered, his appearance brought a chorus of cheers and jeers from the expectant crowd.

Bolitho looked down and saw Allday directly below him, leaning against one of the inn's pillars, a long clay pipe held unlit to his mouth. In the ensuing weeks he had lost the scars and his eye was as clear as before. But he had changed nonetheless; he seemed quieter, less ready to make a joke of everything. In one way he had not changed. Like dog and master, Bolitho had often thought, each fearful that the other might die first. Loyalty? That was no description of it. Probably Paice was there too, watching, remembering.

The horses were more restless, and the major raised his arm to steady the line.

Drew said softly, 'A rogue, but you can pity him this moment.'

165

Bolitho retorted equally quietly, 'I pray he rots in hell.'

It was nearly done. An official from the sheriff's office, a quavering clergyman whose words, if there were any, were quite lost in the hubbub of shouts and jeers.

Bolitho had seen hangings before – too many, and mostly those of sailors, men found guilty of mutiny or worse, run up to the mainyard by their own messmates.

But this display was little better than Madame Guillotine across the Channel, he thought.

The noose was placed around Delaval's neck but he shook his head when one of the executioners made to blindfold him.

He looked composed, even indifferent as he called something to those nearest the scaffold.

At that last moment an elegant, dark red phaeton with a fragile gold crest painted on the door, cantered around the fringe of the crowd until the coachman reined it to a halt.

Delaval must have seen it too, for he stared until his eyes almost bulged from his head. He tried to scream something, but at that instant the trap was sprung and his legs thrashed wildly in space, the air choked from his lungs while excreta ran down his fine nankeen breeches.

Bolitho saw the phaeton move away, but noticed a man's face watching from the open window. The face was smiling until it withdrew out of sight, and the fine carriage gathered speed away from the square.

The crowd was silent now in a mixture of disgust and disappointment that the spectacle was almost over. The puppetlike figure still twisted and flinched on the rope, and it would take another few minutes for the man who had been murderer, rapist, and smuggler to snuff out his life completely.

Delaval's last bravado might have carried him across the threshold of darkness but for that face in the carriage window.

Bolitho turned away from the window, his limbs shaking uncontrollably. He had seen it before, on the road to Rochester when it had been in company with the deputy sheriff and his mob. The missing piece of the pattern.

He faced the rear-admiral and asked calmly, 'So, may I ask why I am here, Sir Marcus?'

Bolitho watched the purple shadows standing out across the square and felt the cooler air of evening against his face. It had been a long day spent with Rear-Admiral Drew, a man so obviously worried by the prospect of implicating himself in anything which might damage his secure position in Admiralty that conversation had been stilted and fruitless.

All he had discovered of any value was that they were here to meet a man of great importance. His name was Lord Marcuard.

Bolitho had heard Marcuard discussed in the past, and seen brief mentions of him in the Gazette. Someone of supreme influence, above the rules of Parliament, who was called frequently to offer his advice on matters of policy to no less than the King himself.

Drew had said at one point, 'Do not provoke or irritate His Lordship, Bolitho. It can do nothing but harm and you will be the poorer.'

Bolitho saw some men working on the empty scaffold. Two highwaymen who had prowled together on the Dover Road would share Delaval's fate tomorrow. They might attract an even larger crowd. Yet another myth, that highwaymen were somehow different from murderers and thieves.

Drew was so typical, he thought bitterly. When war came, young captains would be expected to obey the commands and instructions of men like him. Admirals who had gained their advancement in times of peace, who had become soft in the search for their own advantages.

The old secretary opened the door and darted a quick glance between them.

'Lord Marcuard's carriage approaches, Sir Marcus.'

Drew twitched his neckcloth and glanced at himself in a mirror.

'We are to wait here, Bolitho.' He sounded incredibly nervous.

Bolitho turned away from the window. The carriage had not arrived by the square. The meeting was to be a secret affair. He felt his heart beat faster. He had imagined it might be one of routine, a few words of encouragement perhaps for future aggressive tactics against the smugglers. Lord Marcuard was rarely known to leave his grand house in Whitehall. Even when he did he usually remained secure in his great estate in Gloucester-shire.

He heard boots on the stairs and saw two grooms, each armed with a pistol and sidearm, take up a position on the landing beyond the open door. Despite their livery they looked more like seasoned soldiers than servants.

He murmured, 'It seems we are to be *protected*, Sir Marcus.'

The admiral turned on him. 'Don't be so damned flippant!'

A shadow crossed the doorway and Bolitho bowed his head. Marcuard was not what he had expected. He was tall and slender, of middle age, with a finely chiselled nose and chin, and eyes which turned down in a fixed expression of melancholy disdain. He was dressed in a finely cut coat and breeches of pale green which Bolitho guessed to be pure silk, and carried an ebony stick. His hair, which was gathered to the back of his collar in an un-English fashion was, Bolitho noticed, heavily powdered. It was a small enough vanity, but Bolitho had always disdained men with powdered hair. This was most certainly a man of the Court, and not of any field of battle.

Drew stammered, 'I am *honoured*, m'lord.'

Lord Marcuard seated himself carefully on a chair and arranged the tails of his elegant coat.

'I would take some chocolate. The journey – most tiresome. And now this place.' His eyes turned to Bolitho for the first time. He sounded bored, but his glance was as sharp as any rapier.

'So you are the man of whom I have heard so much. Splendid exploit. Tuke was a dangerous threat to trade.'

Bolitho tried not to show his surprise. He had imagined that Marcuard was referring to the seizure of the *Loyal Chieftain*. At the same time he guessed that he had been intended so to think. Like being tested.

Drew was flushing badly, taken aback by the switch from hot chocolate to Bolitho's last command in the Great South Sea.

Bolitho was glad that unlike the rear-admiral he had taken hardly any wine during the day. Marcuard might dress and act like a fop, but he was nobody's fool.

He said, 'I had a good company, m'lord.'

Marcuard gave a cool smile. 'Perhaps in their turn they were

168

fortunate in having an excellent captain?' He touched his chin with the knob of his stick. 'But I doubt that would occur to you.' He did not wait for a reply.

'His Majesty is concerned about France. William Pitt is attempting to take precautionary steps, of course, but –'

Bolitho watched the stick's silver knob. Fashioned like an eagle, its claws around a globe – the world perhaps? Marcuard had not said so, but Bolitho felt he did not like Pitt very much.

Marcuard added in the same bored tones, 'His Majesty's perspective does tend to alter from day to day.' Again the faint smile. 'Like the winds to France.' He gave a small frown. 'Do see if you can distract someone long enough to procure the chocolate.'

Bolitho made to move for the door but he snapped, '*No*. I must hear your voice in this.'

Bolitho felt almost sorry for Drew. Was the snub real, or only another demonstration of this man's immense authority?

As Drew hurried away Marcuard said, 'I was too late to see Delaval swing. The roads. I'd have laid a wager otherwise.' Then he said sharply, 'Your taking of the brig and the decoy schooner was brilliant. A frigate captain you once were, and no matter what fate awaits you, I suggest that in your soul you will remain one until you are in your grave!'

Bolitho knew his remarks were not casual. He had not come to Dover for idle conversation.

He replied, 'I was determined, m'lord. Much was at stake.'

'Yes.' The eyes passed over him again without curiosity. 'So I have heard. The matter of Commodore Hoblyn, well –' He gave a slight grimace. 'Once a brave man. A knave nonetheless. You are still troubled, Bolitho, that I can see without difficulty. Speak out, man.'

Bolitho glanced at the door. Drew would have a seizure if he knew he was being asked to reveal his thoughts like this.

He said, 'I was convinced that Delaval expected to be saved from the gallows, m'lord. Despite all the evidence and the discovery of his foul murders of young Frenchwomen, he was confident to the end.' He paused, expecting Marcuard to silence him, pour scorn on his ideas as Drew had tried to do. But Marcuard said nothing.

Bolitho continued, 'Sir James Tanner owns much of the land where deserters and smugglers were given shelter between their runs across the Channel. I obtained evidence that he, and only he could have controlled the organisation which such movements required. He *bought* people, anyone who could offer duplicity, from that wretched midshipman to the commodore, and many others respected in high places.'

'I can see why you are oft unwelcome here, Bolitho. What are you telling me now?'

'This man Tanner has been able to ignore every suggestion of involvement. There is not a judge or magistrate who will listen to any criticism. How can the government expect, no, *demand* common seamen to risk their lives, when they see the guilty flouting the same laws which have impressed them?'

Marcuard nodded, apparently satisfied. 'I was influenced by your last action. In a fog too. Your three cutters must think most highly of you now.'

Bolitho stared at him as if he had misheard. Had all the rest fallen on deaf ears?

Marcuard said, 'If, nay, *when* war comes, we cannot depend upon the French remaining a leaderless rabble. Many of their best officers have been beheaded because of the lust and madness of this present revolution. But there will always be other leaders, as there were in England when Charles lost his head on the block.' He reached out with the long ebony stick and tapped the floor to emphasise every word. 'Perhaps there will be a counter-revolution; only time will allow this. But France must have her King on his rightful throne.' He saw Bolitho's astonishment and smiled openly for the first time. 'I see I have confused you, my gallant captain! That is good, for if others penetrate my mind, our hopes will be dashed before we are begun!'

Marcuard stood up lightly and crossed to a window. 'We need an officer we can trust. No civilian will do, especially a man of Parliament who sees only his own advancement no matter what his tongue might proclaim!' He turned on his toes, like a dancer, Bolitho thought dazedly. 'I have chosen you.'

'To go where, m'lord? To do what?'

Marcuard ignored it. 'Tell me this, Bolitho. Do you love your King and country above all else?'

'I love England, m'lord.'

Marcuard nodded slowly. 'That at least is honest. There are people in France who are working to release their monarch. They need to be assured they are not alone. They will trust no spy or informer. The slightest flaw, and their lives end under the blade. I have seen it. I *know*.' He eyed him steadily. 'I am partly French, and your report of the two girls who died at sea interested me very much. My own niece was guillotined in the first month of the Terror. She was just nineteen. So you see –' He turned irritably as voices came from the landing. 'Damn their eyes, they make chocolate too fast in Kent!'

Then he said evenly, 'You will be advised, but will tell nobody until a plan is made. I am sending you to Holland.' He let his words sink in. 'When war comes, Holland will fall to the French. There is no doubt of that, so you must be doubly careful. Spain will throw in her lot with France for her own good.'

Bolitho stared at him. 'But I thought that the King of Spain –'

'Was against the Revolution?' He smiled faintly. 'The Dons never change, and I thank God for it. They value their Church and gold above all else. His most Catholic Majesty will soon convince himself where his loyalty lies.'

The door opened and Drew followed by two inn servants bowed his way forward.

'I regret the delay, m'lord!' Drew's eyes moved like darts between them.

'It will be worth it, Sir Marcus.'

As Lord Marcuard leaned forward to examine the tray his eyes met Bolitho's and he added softly, 'It *has* to be worth it.'

Then he looked away as if it was a dismissal.

'You may leave us, Bolitho. Your admiral and I have weighty matters to discuss.'

Bolitho walked to the door and turned to give a brief bow. In those seconds he saw Drew's relief, shining from his face like a beam of light, in the knowledge that Marcuard, the King's man, was not displeased, that life might continue as before.

He also saw Marcuard's final gaze. It was that of a conspirator.

12

The Power And The Glory

For Bolitho, the weeks which followed the capture of the *Loyal Chieftain* and the decoy schooner were uneventful and frustrating. Commodore Hoblyn was not replaced by a senior officer; instead, a studious official came from the admiralty to supervise the purchase of suitable vessels, and to list possible applicants for letters of marque should war be declared in the near future.

The house where Hoblyn had killed himself remained empty and shuttered, a landmark of his disgrace and final grief.

Bolitho found himself with less and less to do, and had to be content with his three cutters acting without his personal supervision, while they carried out their patrols or assisted the revenue vessels in the continuing fight against smugglers.

He found little comfort in the varying successes of his recruiting parties and the press gangs although there had been a surprising increase in volunteers for the fleet, especially from the more inland villages where news of Bolitho's victory over Delaval's ships and gangs had preceded his visits.

The news of the murdered girls had spread like wildfire, and fresh information had come from many different sources to prove that their wretched deaths had not been isolated incidents.

After the first bloodbath in the streets of Paris the mobs had turned their hatred towards the professional classes, then lower still to mere shopkeepers and artisans. Anyone who was branded as a traitor to the revolution, a lackey to the feared and loathed *aristos*, was dragged to prison for harsh interrogation and the

172

inevitable journey through the streets to the waiting guillotine. Some parents had tried to assist their children to escape by selling all they owned; others had attempted to bribe their way into small vessels in the hope of reaching safety in England. Some smugglers like Delaval had found the latter the most profitable of all. They would take everything from these poor, terrified refugees, then murder them in mid-Channel or in the North Sea. Dead men told no tales. If young girls were amongst their human cargo they could expect no mercy at all.

Once, when supping with Major Craven at his small barracks, Bolitho had said angrily, 'We are dealing with the scum of the earth. Any enemy who sails under a known flag, no matter what cause he represents, has more respect and honour.'

And now there was not even the major to pass the time with. He and most of his regiment had been ordered to Ireland, in readiness for disturbances there after an overall famine had failed to produce food and warmth for the approaching winter.

And winter was coming early, Bolitho thought. You could see it in the tide-race, and in the tossing white horses of the Channel.

The new detachment of soldiers was composed mainly of recruits and some of the freshly-formed militia, more concerned with their drills and exercises than they were with Bolitho's warnings about smugglers. But the Trade had slackened, if not died, since the *Loyal Chieftain* incident. It should have given him satisfaction, but when he walked the shoreline with Allday a constant companion, he found little consolation.

From the urbane Lord Marcuard he had heard nothing. That had been the biggest disappointment of all. Perhaps it had been another ruse to keep him quiet. Even Craven's removal might be connected in some way, although it was impossible to prove it. Officers and officials whom he was forced to meet if only to maintain the co-operation he had painstakingly built up, treated him with a certain wariness – respect or awe, he did not know.

To some he seemed to represent the man of war, to others an interference with a life they knew would soon change but still refused to abandon.

Rear-Admiral Drew's departure had been swift after the meeting at Dover. He had left with an air of profound relief and

173

perhaps a new determination to remain uninvolved in anything beyond the walls of Admiralty.

There had been one hope when Drew had left written orders that he should not invade the property or privacy of Sir James Tanner without express instruction from higher authority. There was little point anyway, for it was said that Tanner was elsewhere, maybe out of the country altogether. But Bolitho had nursed the idea that the orders had come through Drew from Lord Marcuard. Even that was difficult to believe now.

Late one afternoon Bolitho stood on a bluff watching a frigate working her way downstream towards Sheerness. Her paintwork shone in the grey light; the gilt gingerbread around her stern windows and counter was proof that the lucky man who commanded her had money to spare to present such a fine display. Like Bolitho's *Undine* and *Tempest* had been when he had assumed command first of one, then the other, after the American Revolution.

He watched her resetting her topsails, the men strung out like black dots on her braced yards. A ship to be proud of. The greatest honour of all. He thought of Viola's animation and interest when she had made him speak freely of his ship, as he had done to no one before, or since.

He heard Allday murmur. 'A good 'un, Cap'n.'

Bolitho smiled, moved by the supply of ruses which Allday used to prevent him brooding, or remembering too much.

Suppose Allday had been killed? He felt a pain in his chest like a stab. Now he would have been quite alone.

Bolitho turned and looked at him, his hat tugged down to cover his scar. She had touched and kissed that scar and had told him more than once that it was a mark of pride and honour, not something to shame him.

'I wonder if she carries any of the people we gained as volunteers after we had offered them a choice?'

Allday gave a lazy grin. 'Just so long as their cap'n knows how to treat 'em!'

Bolitho turned up the collar of his boat-cloak and watched the frigate again as she changed tack towards more open water. It was tearing him apart. Where bound? Gibraltar and the Mediter-

174

ranean? The West Indies and the dark green fronds which lined each perfect beach?

He sighed. Like the young lieutenant who had offered himself for a ship, any ship, he felt cut off. Discarded, as Hoblyn had been. He ground his heel on the loose sand. *No. Not like Hoblyn.*

He asked, 'And you never saw the man in the carriage that night, the one who ordered you to kill the sailor from the press?'

Allday watched the rebirth of something in those searching, grey eyes.

'Not a peep, Cap'n. But his voice? I'd recognise that even in hell's gateway, so to speak. Like silk it was, the hiss of a serpent.' He nodded fervently. 'If I hears it again I'll strike first, ask the wherefores afterwards – an' that's no error!'

Bolitho stared towards the frigate but her lee side was already clothed in deepening shadows. By tomorrow, with favouring winds, she would be abreast of Falmouth. He thought of the great house. Waiting. Waiting. How small the family had become. His sister Nancy, married to the 'King of Cornwall', lived nearby, but his other sister Felicity was still in India with her husband's regiment of foot. What might become of her, he wondered?

There were too many little plaques and tablets on the walls of Falmouth Church which recorded the women and children who had died of fever and native uprisings, in places few had even heard of. Like the Bolitho tablets which filled one alcove in the fine old church, each one reading like part of the navy's own history. From his great-great-great-grandfather, Captain Julius, who had died in 1646 during the Civil War which Lord Marcuard had touched upon, when he had been attempting to lift the Roundhead blockade on Pendennis Castle itself. And his great-grandfather, Captain David, who had fallen to pirates off the shores of Africa in 1724. Bolitho's fingers reached under his cloak and touched the old hilt at his side. Captain David had had the sword made to his own specifications. Tarnished it might be, but it was still lighter and better-balanced than anything which today's cutlers could forge.

Bolitho walked towards the sunset, his mind suddenly heavy. After his own name was added to the list, there would be no more

Bolithos to return to the old house below the headland and its castle.

Allday's eyes narrowed. 'Rider in a hurry, Cap'n.' His fist dropped to the cutlass in his belt. The land had made him wary and suspicious. In a ship you knew who your friends were, whereas – he exclaimed, 'By God, it's Young Matthew!'

The boy reined his horse to a halt and dropped lightly to the ground.

Bolitho asked, 'What is it, lad?'

Young Matthew fumbled inside his jerkin. 'Letter, sir. Came by courier.' He was obviously impressed. 'Said it must be handed to you, an' you only, sir.'

Bolitho opened and tried to read it but the dusk had made it impossible. But he picked out the gold crest at the top, the scrawled signature, *Marcuard*, at the foot of the page and knew it had not all been a figment of imagination, or some plan to keep him in the background until he could be discreetly disposed of.

The others were staring at him, the horse looming over the boy's shoulder as if it too wanted to be a part of it.

Bolitho had managed to read just three words. *With all despatch.*

Afterwards he remembered that he had felt neither anxiety nor surprise. Just a great sense of relief. He was needed again.

Wakeful's gangling first lieutenant groped through the waiting figures and eventually found Queely standing beside the compass.

He said quietly, 'I have been right through the ship, sir, as ordered. All lights doused.' He peered blindly across the bulwark at the occasional fin of white spray and added, 'I'll not argue when we come about for open water!'

Queely ignored him and stared first at the reefed mainsail, then the tiny flickering glow of the compass light.

The air was cold like steel, and when spray and spindrift pattered over the deck he could feel winter in it.

He said, 'My respects to Captain Bolitho. Please tell him we are in position.'

'No need. I am here.' Bolitho's shadow detached itself from the

176

nearest group and moved closer. He wore his boat cloak, and Queely saw that he was hatless, only his eyes visible in the gloom.

It was halfway through the middle watch, as near to two o'clock as their cautious approach to the Dutch coastline could make possible.

Queely turned away from the others and said abruptly, 'I am not content with these arrangements, sir.'

Bolitho looked at him. From the moment he had stepped aboard Queely's command and had ordered him to the secret rendezvous, this scholarly lieutenant had not once questioned his instructions. All the way across the bleak North Sea to a mark on the chart, and he had held his doubts and apprehensions to himself. For that Bolitho was grateful. He could only guess at the danger he was walking into, and was glad that whatever confidence he retained was not being honed away. Paice might have tried to dissuade him, but *Telemachus* was still in the dockyard completing the refitting of her rigging, and the replacement of her lost topmast. He saw Paice's strong features in his thoughts in the moments which had followed *Loyal Chieftain*'s capture.

Paice had exclaimed, 'We didn't lose a man, sir! Neither did *Wakeful*!'

It was strange, but nobody else had even asked him about that, not even Drew. He smiled grimly as he recalled the rear-admiral's agitation; *especially* him, might be more apt.

It was like the reports in the newsheets after a great battle or a storm's tragedy at sea. A flag officer or individual captains might be mentioned. The people and their cost in the ocean's hazards were rarely considered.

He replied, 'It is all we have, Mr Queely.' He guessed what he was thinking. Lord Marcuard's information had taken weeks to reach him, longer again to be studied and tested. In the meantime anything might have happened. Holland was still standing alone, but it would not be difficult for French spies to infiltrate even the most dedicated circle of conspirators. 'I shall remain ashore for four days. You will stand away from the land until the exact moment as we planned. That will prevent any vessel becoming suspicious of your presence and intentions.' He did not add that it would also stop anyone aboard *Wakeful* from spreading gos-

177

sip, willingly or otherwise. Queely was a quick-witted officer. He would recognise the unspoken reason.

He persisted, 'I think you should be accompanied to the shore at least, sir.'

'Impossible. It would double your time here. You must be well clear before dawn. If the wind should back or drop —' There was no point in further explanations.

Queely held his watch close to the feeble compass glow.

'We will soon know.' He peered around for his lieutenant. 'Mr Kempthorne! Silence on deck.' He raised a speaking trumpet and held it to his ear to try to shut out the restless sea.

Bolitho felt Allday beside him and was glad of his company, moved that he should be prepared to risk his life yet again.

Allday grunted. 'Mebbe they've changed their minds, Cap'n.'

Bolitho nodded and tried to remember each detail of the chart and the notes he had studied on the passage from Kent.

A small country, and not many lonely places suitable enough for a secret landing. Here it was supposed to be a waterlogged stretch of low land, not unlike the marshes and fens of south-east England. Eventually the hard-working Dutch would reclaim the land from the sea and perhaps farm it. They rarely wasted any of their overcrowded resources. But if the French came —

Bolitho tensed as a light shuttered across the heaving water. In the blackness of night it seemed like a beacon.

Queely muttered, 'Hell's teeth! Why not just fire a welcome salute!'

It was the first hint that he was more anxious than his manner had revealed.

'Bear up a point! Stand by, forrard! We don't want to run them down!' In a whisper he added, 'Depress that swivel, Robbins! If it's a trick we'll leave a card to be remembered by!'

The other boat seemed to rise from the seabed itself, and several attempts to take heaving lines and stave off a collision made even more noise, although Bolitho doubted if it would carry more than a few yards.

He noticed muffled figures rising and falling in the swell, a stumpy mast with a loosely brailed-up sail. Above all, the stench of fish. Something was handed to one of the seamen and passed swiftly aft to Bolitho. It was part of an old bone coat-button. Bolitho withdrew his piece from his pocket and held them both together. They were parts of the same button. He wondered what might have happened if one of the sailors had dropped it in the darkness. Would trust have overcome suspicion? It was a crude but tested form of recognition, far less complicated or dangerous than a written message.

Bolitho said, 'I am leaving now, Mr Queely.' He gripped his arm tightly. 'You know what to do if –'

Queely stepped aside. 'Aye, sir. *If.*'

Then they were scrambling down the cutter's side and into the small fishing boat. Rough hands reached out to guide them through the dangerous traps of nets and pots, stacked oars, and what felt like the entrails of gutted fish.

The sail banged out from its boom and the boat swayed steeply in a welter of fine spray.

When Bolitho looked again, *Wakeful* had disappeared, without even the disturbed white horses to betray her position.

Allday settled down on a thwart and muttered, 'I'll never grumble at a King's ship again!'

Bolitho glanced at the purposeful figures around them. Nobody had said a word, or offered any sort of greeting.

Marcuard's words seemed to ring out in his ears. *Be doubly careful.*

As he strained his eyes for a first glimpse of land Bolitho knew he would not need reminding again.

The journey to the rendezvous took longer than Bolitho had expected. He and Allday were transferred to a different craft, the final one being so cramped that it was necessary to remain almost bent double in the forepeak.

From the chart and what he had gathered from his sparse orders Bolitho knew they had passed Walcheren Island before the transfer, then after they had entered the Ooster Scheldt River they had touched sides with the second boat, barely pausing even to exchange a grunted greeting. The place seemed to be a mass of waterways and inlets although the crew were careful not to encourage Bolitho to look closely at their route.

179

A desolate, flat landscape, Bolitho thought, marked here and there by tall windmills, like giants against the sky. There were plenty of small craft on the move, but he had seen nothing of any uniforms which might indicate a naval or military presence.

When night closed in for the second time, the boat was pulled and manhandled into some long reeds, so that but for the gentle motion they could have been on a patch of dry land. It was too dark to see anything, with just a few tiny stars showing occasionally between the clouds. The wind had changed slightly, but not too much to concern *Wakeful*, he thought.

Allday craned his head over the side and listened to the regular creak of another great windmill. There was a strong smell too. 'Pigs,' he said without enthusiasm. 'Are we here, Cap'n?'

Bolitho heard voices, then two figures approached the boat – so there must be a spit of land hereabouts, he thought.

One figure was the boat's skipper, a round-faced Dutchman with an eye-patch. The other was stepping delicately over the wet reeds, a handkerchief clasped to his nose.

He stared down at them and then said, 'Er, Captain Bolitho? You are most prompt!' His English was almost flawless but Bolitho knew he was French.

Bolitho climbed from the boat and almost slipped into deeper water. As he eased his cramped muscles he asked, 'And whom do I have the honour –'

The man shook his head. 'We have no names, Captain. It is ·safer that way.' He gave an apologetic shrug. 'And now I am afraid I must blindfold you and your –' he glanced warily at Allday's powerful figure, '– companion.' He sensed their instant caution. 'You might see something, no matter how unimportant it may be in your eyes, which could be dangerous for us all, yes?'

Bolitho said, 'Very well.' The man was nervous. One of gentle breeding. Certainly no soldier. An experienced campaigner would have blindfolded them hours ago. He shivered. If he had to, he knew he could find his way back here without difficulty. Boyhood in the county of Cornwall, and years of service in small vessels had left him its own heritage.

They sloshed through the reeds and then on to rough ground, the windmill's regular groans then being joined by another.

180

Bolitho knew that someone from the boat was walking in the rear. Apart from the wind it was very still, the air as keen as sleet.

The man held Bolitho's elbow, murmuring occasional warnings about their progress. Bolitho sensed they were close to a large building, but not one of the windmills.

His guide whispered, 'You are meeting Vice-Amiral Louis Brennier.' He seemed to feel Bolitho's sudden attention. 'You know him?'

He did not reply directly. 'I thought there were to be no names, m'sieu?'

The man hesitated, then said, 'It is what he wishes. His life has no value but to this great cause.'

He sounded as if he was repeating a lesson.

Bolitho fell in step again. Vice-Amiral Louis Brennier, an officer of distinction during the American Revolution when he had directed the operations of French privateers and, later, men-of-war who were working alongside the rebels. He had been taking passage for Jamaica in de Grasse's flagship *Ville de Paris* when he had met up with Admiral Rodney's fleet off the little islands called the Saintes. The battle had been devastating and complete, with the French ships either destroyed or taken. It had seemed only right that the mighty *Ville de Paris* should have struck to the *Formidable*, Rodney's own flagship.

Brennier had been a mere passenger at the time, a hard role for a man of action like him, Bolitho had thought. It had been the French intention to attack and seize Jamaica and for Brennier, a very senior officer, to be installed as governor. The Saintes had changed all that, as it had for so many on such a fine April day. Ordinary, decent men. Like Stockdale who had fallen without a word, Ferguson who had lost an arm; the list was endless. His own ship, *Phalarope*, had only stayed afloat by working the pumps all the way to the dockyard at Antigua.

He heard a door being unbolted, felt sudden warmth in his face. The blindfold was removed and he found that he was in a broad stone-built room. It was a farm, although the true owners were nowhere to be seen.

He faced the old man who sat across the scrubbed table from him and bowed his head.

'Vice-Amiral Brennier?' He knew he must be old now, but it was still a shock. The admiral's hair was white, his skin wrinkled, his eyes half-hidden by heavy lids.

He nodded slowly, his eyes never leaving Bolitho's.

'And you are Capitaine Bolitho.' His English was not so good as his aide's. 'I knew your father.' His face crinkled into a tired smile. 'That is, I knew *of* him. It was in India.'

Bolitho was taken off balance. 'I did not know, m'sieu.'

'Age has its compensations, Capitaine, or so they tell me.'

He raised his thin hands towards a roaring fire and said, 'Our King lives, but matters worsen in our beloved Paris.'

Bolitho waited. Surely the hope of the King's reclaiming the French throne was not being entrusted to Brennier? He had been a gallant officer, and an honourable opponent, trusted by the King and all who had served him. But Brennier was an old man, his mind wandering now over the disaster which had overtaken his country.

Bolitho asked, 'What will you have me do, m'sieu?'

'*Do?*' Brennier seemed reluctant to rejoin him in the present. 'It is our intention and sworn duty to obtain the King's release, by any means, no matter the cost!' His voice grew stronger, and despite his doubts Bolitho could see the younger man emerging. 'Here in the Low Countries we have amassed a fortune. Precious jewels, gold –' He lowered his forehead on to one hand. 'A King's ransom, the English might call it.' But there was no mirth in his tone. 'It is close by. Soon it must be moved and put to work.'

Bolitho asked gently, 'Where did it come from, m'sieu?'

'From the many whose families have suffered and died under the guillotine. From others who seek only a return to a cultured, inventive life.' He looked up, his eyes flashing. 'It will be used to free the King, by bribery, by force if it must be so, and some to mount a counter-revolution. There are many loyal officers in the South of France, m'sieu, and the world shall witness such a reckoning! We will do to these vermin what they have done to us!' His outburst seemed to weaken him. 'We shall speak further when some of my friends arrive.' He gestured towards another door. 'Go there, Capitaine, and meet your fellow *agent-provocateur*.'

His aide entered again and waited to assist him to some stairs.

At their foot he turned and said firmly, 'France lives! Long live the King!'

The aide gave what might have been a small shrug. To Allday he said curtly, 'Wait here. I will send for some food and wine.'

Allday muttered, 'Little puppy! It's them like him who lost France, if you ask me, Cap'n!'

Bolitho touched his arm. 'Be easy, old friend. There is much we have yet to understand. But do as he says, and keep your eyes open.' He did not have to say any more.

Then he pressed on the other door and walked into a more comfortable room.

As the door closed behind him, a figure who had been sitting in a high-backed chair facing another lively fire, rose and confronted him.

'Bolitho? I trust the journey was none too arduous?'

Bolitho had only seen the man twice before and each time at a distance. But there was no mistaking him. About his own age, with the arrogant good looks and cruel mouth he remembered from the Rochester Road, and that brief moment in the coach window at Dover.

He felt his hand fall to his sword. 'Sir James Tanner.' He was calmed by the flatness in his voice. 'I never thought I'd meet a cur like you here!'

Tanner's face tightened but he seemed to control his immediate reaction with a practised effort.

'I have no choice. It is Lord Marcuard's wish. Otherwise –'

Bolitho said, 'When this is over I intend to see you brought to justice.'

Tanner turned his back. 'Let me tell you things, Bolitho, before your damned impertinence puts us both in jeopardy. Be assured, I would like nothing better than to call you out *here and now*.'

Bolitho watched his squared shoulders. 'You will find me ready enough, *sir!*'

Tanner turned and faced him again. 'Your life is so clean and well charted, Bolitho. It lies 'twixt forecastle and poop with no bridge in between, where a captain's word is law, when no one shall defy it!' He was speaking faster now. 'Why not try stepping outside and into the real world, eh? You will soon discover that

183

the politics of survival tend to create strange bedfellows!' He seemed to relax slightly as he gestured casually between them. 'Like us, for instance.'

'It sickens me even to share the same room.'

Tanner eyed him thoughtfully. 'You would never prove it, you know. Never in ten thousand years. Others have tried before you.' He became suddenly reasonable. 'Take yourself, Bolitho. When you returned from the American War you discovered your family estate pared away, sold to pay for your brother's debts, is that not correct?' His voice was smooth and insistent. 'You fought bravely, and that was your reward.'

Bolitho held his expression as before but only with difficulty. At every corner, in every turn, there was always Hugh's disgrace, the memory used to shame or belittle the family as it had killed their father.

Tanner was saying, '*My* father lost nearly everything. His debtors were measured in leagues, believe me. But I got all of it back on my own.'

'By organising a smuggling trade that was unrivalled anywhere.'

'*Hearsay*, Bolitho. And even if it were so, nobody will stand up and swear it.' He leaned over the chair and tapped the leather with his hand. 'D'you imagine I want to be here, involved in a wild scheme which has about as much chance of succeeding as a snowman in a furnace!'

'Then why are you?'

'Because I am the only one Lord Marcuard trusts to execute the plan. How do you imagine you reached here unscathed? You do not know the country or its language, and yet here you are. The fishermen are in my employ. Oh yes, they may be smugglers, who can say? But you came here in safety because *I* arranged it, even to suggesting the exact point at which to bring you ashore.'

'And what of Delaval?'

Tanner became thoughtful. 'He worked for me, too. But he had grand ideas, became less and less prepared to take orders. So you see –'

'He thought you were going to gain his discharge.'

'Yes, he did. He was a boaster and a liar, a dangerous combination.'

184

Bolitho said, 'Is that all there is to it?'

'Not completely. Lord Marcuard will have his way. You still do not understand this real world, do you? If he chose, Marcuard could use his power against me, and all my land and property would be forfeit. And if you are thinking I could still live at ease elsewhere, then I beg you to dismiss the idea. From Marcuard there is no hiding place. Not on this earth anyway.'

They faced each other, Tanner breathing hard, his eyes watchful, a man too clever to reveal the triumph he now felt.

Bolitho was still numbed by the fact that he was here. Had even planned his arrival.

Tanner said easily, 'We have to work together. There was never any choice for either of us. I wanted to meet you before that old man did, but he suggested it might be *difficult*.'

Bolitho nodded, in agreement for the first time. 'I'd have killed you.'

'You would have tried to do so, I dare say. It seems to run in your family.' He spread his arms. 'What can you hope for? If you go to the Dutch Customs House they will laugh at you. If French spies discover what you are about here, many will die, and the treasure will go to the revolutionary government.' He tapped the chair with his hand again. 'To use for supplying ships and weapons which *your* sailors will have to face before much longer!'

He seemed to tire of it. 'Now I shall take my leave. M'sieu will wish to speak at length about this matter, and of course on the *glory which was France*.' His voice was still smooth as he added, 'Do not delay too long. *My* men will not wait forever.'

He used a small side-door, and Bolitho heard horses stamping on some sort of track.

Bolitho left the room and saw Allday staring at him. Despite his bronzed features his face looked ashen.

'What is it? Speak, man!'

Allday watched the closed door.

'That man you just met. *His voice.* It was him. I'd not forget that one in a lifetime!'

Bolitho saw his eyes spark with memory. It was as he had suspected. The man in the carriage who had ordered Allday to

185

kill the sailor from the press gang, and Sir James Tanner, were one and the same.

Bolitho touched his arm and said, 'It is well he did not know it. At least we are forewarned.' He stared into the shadows. 'Otherwise he would see us both dead before this is over and done with.'

'But what happened, Cap'n?'

Bolitho looked up as voices floated from the stairway. *The glory which was France.*

He said quietly, 'I was outmanoeuvred.' He clapped him on the arm. Allday needed *him* now. 'This time.'

13

Last Chance

The footman took Bolitho's dripping cloak and hat and regarded them disdainfully.

'Lord Marcuard will receive you now, sir.'

Bolitho stamped his shoes on the floor to restore the circulation, then followed the servant, a heavy-footed man with stooped shoulders, along an elegant corridor. He was a far cry from the wretched Jules, Bolitho thought.

It had been a long and uncomfortable journey from Sheerness to London. The roads were getting worse, deeply rutted from heavy rain, and now there was intermittent snow, touching the grand buildings of Whitehall like powder. He hated the thought of winter and what it might do to his health. If the fever returned – he closed his mind to the thought. There were too many important matters on his mind.

When *Wakeful* had moored at the dockyard, Bolitho had left immediately for London. There had been a brief message awaiting his return from Marcuard. He would meet him on his own ground this time.

He heard sounds from the hallway and said, 'That will be my coxswain. Take good care of him.' He spoke abruptly. Bolitho felt past even common courtesy. He was heartily sick of the pretence and false pride these people seemed to admire so much.

He thought of the old admiral in Holland, of the great fortune amassed and ready to be used for a counter-revolution. It had

187

seemed like a dream when he had outlined it; back in England the plan seemed utterly hopeless.

Bolitho's silent guides had conveyed him to the rendezvous on time but only with minutes to spare. Even in the darkness there had been shipping on the move, and the fishermen had almost given up hope when *Wakeful*'s wet canvas had loomed over them.

Lieutenant Queely's relief had been matched only by his eagerness to get under way and head for open waters. He had confirmed Bolitho's suspicions; there were men-of-war in the vicinity, Dutch or French he had not waited to discover.

Some of Bolitho's anger at Tanner's involvement had eased on the journey to London. Noisy inns, with more talk of Christmas than what might be happening across the Channel. As the coach had rolled through towns and villages, Bolitho had seen the local volunteers drilling under the instruction of regular soldiers. Pikes and pitchforks because nobody in authority thought it was yet necessary to train them to handle muskets. What was the matter with people, he wondered? When he had commanded *Phalarope* the navy's strength had stood at over one hundred thousand men. Now it was reduced to less than a fifth of that number, and even for them there were barely enough ships in commission and ready for sea.

He realised that the footman was holding open a tall door, Bolitho's cloak held carefully at arm's length.

Marcuard was standing with his back to a cheerful fire, his coat-tails lifted to give him all the benefit of the heat. He was dressed this time in sombre grey, and without his ebony silver-topped stick looked somehow incomplete.

Bolitho examined the room. It was huge, and yet lined on three walls with books. From floor to ceiling, with ladders here and there for convenience, like the library of a rich scholar. Queely would think himself in heaven here.

Marcuard held out his hand. 'You wasted no time.' He observed him calmly. 'I am needed here in London. Otherwise –' He did not explain. He waved Bolitho to a chair. 'I will send for some coffee presently. I see from your face that you came ready for an argument. I was prepared for that.'

Bolitho said, 'With respect, m'lord, I think I should have been told that Sir James Tanner was involved. The man, as I have stated plainly, is a thief, a cheat and a liar. I have proof that he was engaged in smuggling on a grand scale, and conspired with others to commit murder, to encourage desertion from the fleet for his own ends.'

Marcuard's eyebrows rose slightly. 'Do you feel better for that?' He leaned back and pressed his fingertips together. 'Had I told you beforehand you would have refused to participate. Not because of the danger, and I better than you know there is danger aplenty on either side of that unhappy border. No, it was because of your honour that you would have refused me, just as it was because of it that I chose you for the mission.'

Bolitho persisted, 'How can we trust that man?'

Marcuard did not seem to hear. 'There is an hypocrisy in us all, Bolitho. You offered your trust to Vice-Amiral Brennier, because he too is a man of honour. But a few years ago, or perhaps even next week, you would kill him if the need arose because war has dictated how you shall think, and what you must do. In affairs like this I trust only those whom I need. Tanner's skills may not appeal to either of us but, believe me, he is the best man, if not the only man, who can do it. I sent you because Brennier would recognise you as a King's officer, someone who has already proved his courage and loyalty beyond question. But what do you imagine would occur if I had directed others to Holland? I can assure you that the Admiralty of Amsterdam would have been displeased, and would have closed every port against us. They have cause to fear the French and would likely confiscate the Royalist treasure to bargain with them.'

Despite his hatred of the man, Bolitho thought of Tanner's words about the possibility of the vast hoard of jewels and gold being used to strengthen French power to be thrown eventually against England.

Marcuard said, 'You look troubled, Bolitho. What do you feel about this affair, and of Brennier's part in it?' He nodded very slowly. 'Another reason why I selected you. I wanted a thinking officer, not merely a courageous one.'

Bolitho stared through one of the tall windows. The sky was

growing darker, but he could see the roof of the Admiralty building where all this, and so many other ventures in his life, had begun. Full circle. The roof was already dusted with snow. He gripped his hands together to try and stop himself from shivering.

'I believe that the prospect of an uprising is hopeless, m'lord.' Just saying it aloud made him feel as if he had broken a trust, that he was being disloyal to that old man in Holland who had been captured by Rodney at the Saintes. He continued, 'He showed me one of the chests. I have never seen the like. So much wealth, when the people of France had so little.' He glanced around at the fine room. An equation which should be learned here, he thought bitterly.

'Are you not well, Bolitho?'

'Tired, m'lord. My cox'n is with me. He is finding quarters for us.'

It was to sidestep Marcuard's question.

Marcuard shook his head. 'I will not hear of it. You shall visit here, while you are in London. There are some who might wish to know your movements. And besides, I doubt that there are many – *quarters* – as you quaintly describe them, freely available this near to Christmas.'

He regarded Bolitho thoughtfully. 'While you were in Holland, I too was forming opinions.'

Bolitho felt his limbs relaxing again. Perhaps it was the fire.

'About the treasure, m'lord?'

'Concerning it.' Marcuard stood up and tugged gently at a silk bell rope. There was no sound but Bolitho guessed it would reach one of the many servants who were needed for such an extensive residence.

Bolitho did not trust the so-called 'real world' as described by Sir James Tanner, but he had learned a lot about people, no matter what their rank or station might be. From a tough fore-topman to a pink-faced midshipman, and Bolitho knew that the bell rope was to give him time, to test his own judgement before he shared any more secrets.

Marcuard said bluntly, 'There is no hope for the King of France.'

Bolitho stared at him, and was struck by the solemnity of his

190

voice. While the King was alive there had always been hope that somehow things might return, halfway at least, to normal. In time, the murder of aristocrats and innocent citizens in the name of the Revolution might fade into history. The death of a King would have the brutal finality of the guillotine itself.

Marcuard watched him, his eyes smoky in the reflected flames. 'We cannot rely on Brennier and his associates. That vast fortune belongs here in London, where it will be safe until a counter-revolution can be launched. I could tell you of lasting loyalties which would rise up against the National Convention once a properly managed invasion was mounted.'

'That would cause a war, m'lord.'

Marcuard nodded. 'The war is almost upon us, I fear.'

'I believe that Admiral Brennier understands the danger he is in.' Bolitho pictured him, a frail old man by the fire, still dreaming and hoping when there was no room left for either.

The door opened and another footman entered with a tray and some fresh coffee.

'I know you have a great liking for coffee, Captain Bolitho.'

'My cox'n –'

Marcuard watched the servant preparing to pour.

'Your Mr Allday is being well taken care of. He seems a most adaptable fellow, to all accounts. Your right arm, wouldn't you say?'

Bolitho shrugged. Was there nothing Marcuard did not know or discover from others? *No hiding place*, Tanner had said. That he could believe now.

He said, 'He means all that and more to me.'

'And the young lad, Corker, wasn't it? You packed him off to Falmouth, I believe.'

Bolitho smiled sadly. It had been a difficult moment for all of them. Young Matthew had been in tears when they had put him on the coach for the first leg of the long haul to Cornwall, the breadth of England away.

He said, 'It seemed right, m'lord. To be home with his people in time for Christmas.'

'Quite so, although I doubt that was your prime concern.'

Bolitho recalled Allday at that moment, his face still cut and bruised from his beating aboard the *Loyal Chieftain*. He had said, 'Your place is on the estate, my lad. With your horses, like Old Matthew. It's not on the bloody deck of some man-o'-war. Anyway, I'm back now. You said you'd wait 'til then, didn't you?'

They had watched the coach until it had vanished into heavy rain.

Bolitho said suddenly, 'I fear he would have been killed if I had allowed him to stay.'

Marcuard did not ask or even hint at how the boy's death might have come about. He probably knew that too.

Marcuard put down his cup and consulted his watch. 'I have to go out. My valet will attend to your needs.' He was obviously deep in thought. 'If I am not back before you retire do not concern yourself. It is the way of things here.' He crossed to a window and said, 'The weather. It is a bad sign.'

Bolitho looked at him. He had not said as much, but somehow he knew Marcuard was going to have a late audience with the King.

Bolitho wondered what the prime minister and his advisers thought about it. It was rumoured more openly nowadays that His Majesty was prone to change his mind like the wind, and that on bad days he was totally incapable of making a decision about anything. He might easily be prepared to discuss his anxieties with Marcuard rather than Parliament. It would make Marcuard's authority all the greater.

He was standing by the window now, looking down at the road, his eyes deep in thought.

'In Paris it will be a bad winter. They were near to starvation last year; this time it will be worse. Cold and hunger can fire men to savage deeds, if only to cover their own failings.'

He looked deliberately at Bolitho, like that time at The Golden Fleece in Dover.

'I must make arrangements for the treasure to be brought to England. I feel that the sand is running low.' The door opened silently and Marcuard said, 'Have the unmarked phaeton brought round at once.' Then to Bolitho he said softly, 'Leave Brennier to me.'

192

'What of me, m'lord?' Bolitho was also on his feet, as if he shared this new sense of urgency.

'As far as I am concerned, you are still my man in this.' He gave a bleak smile. 'You will return to Holland only when I give the word.' He seemed to relax himself and prepare for his meeting. 'Anyone who opposes you will have me to reckon with.' He let his gaze linger for a few more seconds. 'But do not harm Tanner.' Again the bleak smile. 'Not yet, in any case.' Then he was gone.

Bolitho sat down and stared at the wall of books, an army of knowledge. How did men like Marcuard see a war, he wondered? Flags on a map, land gained or lost, investment or waste? It was doubtful if they ever considered it as cannon fire and broken bodies.

Below his feet, in the long kitchen Allday sat contentedly, sipping a tankard of ale while he enjoyed the pipe of fresh tobacco one of the footmen had offered him.

In any strange house the kitchen was usually Allday's first port of call. To investigate food, and also the possibilities of female companionship which most kitchens had to offer.

He watched the cook's assistant, a girl of ample bosom and laughing eyes, her arms covered in flour to her elbows. Allday had gathered that her name was Maggie.

He took another swallow of ale. A proper sailor's lass she would make. He thought of Bolitho somewhere overhead, alone with his thoughts. He had heard his lordship leave in a carriage only moments ago, and wondered if he should go up and disturb him.

He thought of the dead girl in his arms, the touch of her body against his. Poor Tom Lucas had sworn it would bring bad luck to take a woman aboard against her will. That had been true enough for both of them. Allday tried to see into the future. Better back in Falmouth than this shifty game, he thought. You never knew friend from foe. Just so long as they didn't go back to Holland. Allday usually clung to his same old rule. *Never go back*. The odds always got worse.

The cook was saying, ''Course, our *Lady* Marcuard's down at the estate. 'Is lordship'll not be 'ome for Christmas this year, *I* reckon!' She looked meaningly at Allday and added, 'Young

Maggie's 'usband is there too, as second coachman, see?'

Allday glanced at the girl and saw her blush faintly before she returned her attention to her work.

The cook watched them both and added encouragingly, 'Pity to waste it, *I* always says!'

His Britannic Majesty's Ship *Ithuriel*, a seventy-four-gun two-decker, made a handsome picture above her reflection on the flat water of the Royal Dockyard. Her black and buff hull and checkered gunports, her neatly furled sails and crossed yards shone with newness, as did the uniforms of her lieutenant and midshipman, facing inboard from their divisions of silent seamen. Across her poop the marines stood in scarlet lines, and above their heads a matching ensign curled listlessly against a washed-out sky in the hard sunlight.

There was pride and sadness here in Chatham today. *Ithuriel* was the first new man-of-war of any size to be commissioned since the American Revolution, and now, stored and fully manned, she was ready to take her place with the Channel Fleet.

Below her poop Bolitho watched the official handing-over of the new ship, her captain reading himself in to the assembled officers and men he would lead and inspire for as long as their lordships dictated, or as long as he remained in command.

Nearby, the officers' ladies stood close together, sharing this alien world of which they could never truly become a part. Some would be grateful that their husbands had been given appointments after all the waiting and disappointment. Others would be cherishing each passing minute, not knowing when, or if, they would see their loved ones again.

Bolitho looked at the sky, his heart suddenly heavy. He was only an onlooker. All the excitement and demands of a newly commissioned ship were cradled here, and would soon show their true value and flaws once the ship began to move under canvas for the first time.

He saw the admiral with his flag lieutenant standing a little apart from the rest, dockyard officials watching their efforts become reality as the company was urged to cry their *Huzzas* and wave their hats to honour the moment.

If only the command were his. Not a frigate, but a newly born ship nonetheless. The most beautiful creation of man yet devised; hard and demanding by any standards. He dropped his eyes as the captain finished speaking, his voice carrying easily in the still January air.

That too was hard to accept, Bolitho thought. Danger there had certainly been, but the promise of action had sustained him. Until now. In his heart he believed he had ruined his chances by his dogged and stubborn attack on Sir James Tanner. Marcuard must have found him wanting.

He looked up as he heard the new captain speak his name.

He was saying, 'A fine ship which I am proud to command. But for the inspiration and leadership given by Captain Richard Bolitho over the past months I doubt if we would have enough hands to work downstream, let alone put to sea and face whatever duty demands of us!' He gave a slight bow in Bolitho's direction. '*Ithuriel* shall be worthy of your trust, sir.'

Bolitho flinched as all the faces turned towards him. Pressed and volunteers, men who had accepted his offer to quit the smuggling gangs and return to their calling, but now they were of one company. It was only their captain's qualities which could carry them further. And Bolitho would be left far behind and soon forgotten.

Perhaps there would be no war after all? He should have felt relief, but instead was ashamed to discover he had only a sense of loss and rejection.

The ship's company was dismissed and the boatswain's mates refrained from their usual coarse language with so many ladies gathered on the quarterdeck and poop. Extra rum for all hands, and then, when the honoured guests had departed, the hovering bumboats and watermen would come alongside and unload their passengers under the watchful eyes of the first lieutenant and afterguard. Trollops and doxies from the town, the sailor's last freedom for a long while. For some, it would be forever.

The admiral was making a great fuss over the captain, which was not surprising as he was his favourite nephew. The groups were breaking up and making for the entry port below which the many boats thronged like water beetles. There were desperate

195

embraces and tears, brave laughter, and, from the older ones, resignation, a lesson learned from many repetitions.

Allday emerged from the shadows beneath the poop and said, 'I've signalled for the boat, Cap'n.' He studied him with concern, recognising all the signs. 'It'll *come*, Cap'n, just you see –'

Bolitho turned on him, and relented immediately. 'It was only that I had hoped –'

The senior officers had gone now; calls trilled and barges glided away to other ships and to the dockyard stairs.

Bolitho said wearily, 'I would that they were my men and our ship – eh, old friend?'

Allday made a passage to the entry port. In many ways he felt vaguely guilty. He should have done more. But in London while they had been staying in that great house, he had soon found his time fully occupied with the amorous Maggie. It was just as well Bolitho had been ordered back to Kent, he thought. It had been a close-run thing.

'Captain Bolitho?' It was the flag lieutenant, poised and eager, like a ferret. 'If you would come aft for a moment, sir?'

Bolitho followed him and saw the curious stares, heads drawn together in quick speculation. Rumour was firmer than fact. They would be speaking of Hoblyn and Delaval, even Hugh, and the strange fact that men who had managed to evade the dreaded press gangs had openly volunteered for service whenever Bolitho had been seen in their locality. Myth and mystery. It never failed.

In the great cabin, still smelling of paint and tar, new timber and cordage, Bolitho found another unknown captain waiting for him. He introduced himself as Captain Wordley; the papers he produced proved that he had been sent by Lord Marcuard.

Wordley watched him impassively as he examined his bulky envelope and said, 'You may read them at leisure, Bolitho. I am required to return to London forthwith.' He gave a wry smile. 'You will know his lordship's insistence on haste.'

Bolitho asked, 'Can you tell me?' He could still scarcely believe it.

'You are to return to Holland. All details are listed in your orders. There is some *urgency* in this matter. Information is hard to come by, but Lord Marcuard is convinced that time is short.

Very short. You are to supervise the removal of the . . . stores . . .
from Holland, and see them safely to these shores.' He spread his
hands unhappily. 'It is all I can tell you, Bolitho. In God's name it
is all I know!'

Bolitho left the cabin and made his way to the entry port where
Allday was waiting by the side-party and marine guard.

Like walking in the dark. A messenger-boy who was told only
the briefest facts. But excitement replaced the bitterness almost
immediately. He said, 'We are returning to Holland, Allday.' He
eyed him keenly. 'If you wish to stand fast I shall fully understand, especially so because of your – recent attachment.'

Allday stared at him, then gave a self-conscious grin. 'Was it
that plain, Cap'n? An' I thought I was keeping hull-down, so to
speak!' His grin vanished. 'Like I said afore. We stay together this
time.' His eyes were almost desperate. *'Right?'*

Bolitho gripped his thick forearm, watched with astonishment
by the marine officer of the guard.

'So be it.'

He doffed his hat to the quarterdeck and lowered himself to
the waiting boat.

Only once did Bolitho glance astern at the shining new
seventy-four, but already she seemed like a diversion, part of that
other dream.

Now only Holland lay ahead. And reality.

Lieutenant Jonas Paice placed his hands firmly on his hips and
stared resentfully at the anchored *Wakeful*. In the harsh January
sunlight she was a hive of activity, her sails already loosened, the
forecastle party working the long bars of the windlass, their
bodies moving in unison as if performing some strange rite.

'I'll not be in agreement, sir. Not now, not ever.'

Bolitho glanced at his grimly determined features. Time was
all-important, but it was just as vital he should make Paice
understand.

'I explained why I had to go before. It was a secret then. I could
not share it at the time, you must realise that.'

'This is different, sir.' Paice turned and stared at him, using his
superior height to impress each word. 'Half the fleet will know

197

what you're about.' He waved his hand towards *Wakeful*. 'You should let me take you if go you must.'

Bolitho smiled. *So that was it*. He said, 'Lieutenant Queely knows that coast well. Otherwise –' He saw *Wakeful*'s jolly-boat cast off and pull towards *Telemachus*. He said, 'Try to pass word to *Snapdragon*. She is working her station off the North Foreland. Either the revenue people or the coastguard might be able to signal her. I want her back here.' He studied his stubborn features. It was Herrick all over again. 'We are in this together.'

Paice replied heavily. 'I know, sir. I have read your instructions.'

He tried again. 'In any case, apart from the risks, there is the weather. Last time you had mist and fog. A hazard maybe, but also a protection.' He added scornfully, 'Look at this! As bright and clear as the Arctic! Even a blind man could see you coming!'

Bolitho looked away. He had been thinking as much himself. *Bright and clear*, the waves outside the anchorage pockmarked with choppy white horses from the cold south-westerly. 'I must go now.' He held out his hand. 'We shall meet again soon.' Then he was climbing down to the boat where Lieutenant Kempthorne removed his hat as a mark of respect.

'Cast off! Give way all!' Allday sat by the tiller, his hat pulled down to shade his eyes from the reflected glare. He had seen the light in Bolitho's eyes, the way that the call to action had somehow strengthened him. Allday had watched him aboard the new two-decker. The longing and the loss, side by side.

He gave a long sigh. Allday had no liking for what they were doing and it had cost him dearly not to speak his mind, that privilege he valued above all else. Bolitho could strike back with equal conviction and his anger had been known to hurt as well as sting. But he had never once used his rank and authority when others would have thought of nothing else. Now, as he watched the set of Bolitho's shoulders, the black hair gathered above the fall-down collar of that old, faded coat, he was glad he had kept his peace, no matter what.

They climbed aboard the cutter, and the boat was hoisted up and inboard almost before Bolitho had reached the narrow poop where Queely was in deep conversation with his sailing-master.

198

Queely touched his hat and nodded. 'Ready when you are, sir.' He looked at the green elbow of land, the rime of frost or recent snow dusting some of the port buildings. The air was like a honed knife, but it roused a man from the boredom of routine, put an edge on his reactions. Queely said, 'Doesn't much matter who sees us leave this time, eh?'

Bolitho ignored it. Like Paice, he was trying to dissuade him. It moved him to realise it was not for their own sakes, but for his.

Allday strode aft, then drew his cutlass and aimed its blade at the sun. 'I'll give this a sharpen, Cap'n.' He held out his hand. 'I'll take the sword, if I may?'

Bolitho handed it to him. Others might see and think they understood. But how could they? This was a ritual shared with nobody else, as much a part of each man as the moment before a battle when the ship was cleared for action, screens down, the people standing to their guns. Allday would be there. *Always*. After clipping the old sword to his belt. As his father's coxswain must have done for him and those who had gone before.

'Anchor's hove short, sir!'

'Loose mains'l! Stand by heads'l sheets!' Feet padded on the damp planking, bare despite the bitter air.

Bolitho saw it all. If only more of the people at home could have seen them, he thought. Men who had so little, but gave their all when it was demanded of them. He thought of the faces he had seen aboard the new *Ithuriel*. It might be months before her company worked even half as well as the men of his three cutters.

'Anchor's aweigh, sir!'

Wakeful came round into the breeze, her huge mainsail scooping all of it without effort and filling out with a crack of taut canvas.

'Hold her steady!' Queely was everywhere. 'Let go and haul. Mr Kempthorne, they are like *old women* today!'

Bolitho heard one of the helmsmen chuckle. 'Wish they was, matey!'

He turned and looked for *Telemachus*. How tiny she looked when set against the tall buff-and-black hull of the new two-decker.

Allday saw the look and gave a rueful grin.

199

There would be no stopping him now.

By evening the wind still held steady enough from the south-west, and the sea showed no sign of lessening. Spray swept regularly over the duty watch, reaching for the hands working aloft on the yards. When it caught you unawares it was cold enough to punch the breath out of your body.

Bolitho was in the cabin, going over Queely's calculations, the notes which he had made from their last rendezvous. Nothing must go wrong. He thought of Tanner and tried not to let his anger break out again. Tanner was under Lord Marcuard's orders, and on the face of it had far more to lose than Bolitho if things went badly wrong. Unless you counted life itself, Bolitho thought. He was surprised he could face it with neither qualms nor surprise. It might mean that he was truly restored, that the fever which had all but killed him had finally released him, as a receding wave will toss a drowning sailor to safety, as if for a last chance.

He heard shouts on deck and Queely clattered down the companionway, his body shining in a long tarpaulin coat.

'Sail to the nor'-east, sir.'

More yells came from above. Queely remarked, 'I'm changing tack. No sense in displaying our intentions.' He smiled faintly. 'Yet, anyway.'

The hull staggered and then reared upright again, and Bolitho heard the sea rushing along the lee scuppers like a bursting stream.

'What is she?'

'I've got Nielsen aloft, a good lookout.' Again the ghostly smile. 'For a Swede, that is. He reckons she's a brig. Square-rigged in any case.'

They looked at each other. Bolitho did not have to consult the chart to know that this stranger stood directly between them and the land.

'Man-of-war?' It seemed unlikely to be anything else out here and at this time of the year.

Queely shrugged. 'Could be.'

They heard the helmsman yell, 'Steady she goes, sir! Nor' by East!'

200

Queely frowned, seeing the complications in his thoughts. 'Don't want to bring her up too much, sir. I know the nights are long, but we've precious little room for mistakes.'

Bolitho followed him on deck. The sea was covered with leaping white clusters of spray, but beneath them the water looked black, a vivid contrast to the sky which despite some early stars was still clear and pale.

The hull plunged her long bowsprit down like a hunting marlin and the water surged over the forecastle and hissed aft between the gleaming guns.

Queely cupped his reddened hands. 'Where away, Nielsen?'

'Same bearing, sir! She changed tack when we did!'

Even from the deck amidst the din of spray and wind Bolitho could hear the man's Swedish accent. What was *his* story, he wondered?

Queely swore. 'In God's name, sir! That bugger is on to us!'

Bolitho gripped a stay and felt it quivering in his hand as if it were part of an instrument.

'I suggest you steer more to the east'rd as soon as it's dark. We should cross his stern and lose him.'

Queely eyed him doubtfully. 'So long as we can beat clear if the wind gets up, sir.'

Bolitho gave a dry smile. 'There is always *that* provision, of course.'

Queely beckoned to his first lieutenant. 'We shall hold this tack until –' The rest was lost in the boom of canvas and the creak of steering tackles as the helmsmen forced over the tiller bar.

Allday stood by the companionway and listened to the rudder. It was all to easy too picture the girl's pale shape as she had sawed frantically at the lines. *If only she had been spared.*

He tossed the stupid thought from his mind and groped his way to the ladder. There was always tomorrow. But now a good 'wet' of rum was all he needed.

When darkness closed in, and their world had shrunk to the leaping crests on either beam, *Wakeful* came about and under reefed topsail thrust her bowsprit towards the east. Immediately before that Queely joined Bolitho in the cabin and shook his hat on the littered deck.

201

'That bugger's still there, sir.' He stared at his cot but shut the picture of sleep from his thoughts. 'I shall call you when it's time.' Then he was gone, his boots scraping up the ladder and on to the streaming deck above.

Bolitho lay down and faced the curved side. Just once he spoke her name aloud. '*Viola*.' And then, with his eyes tightly shut as if in pain, he fell asleep.

14

Fair Wind . . . For France

H.M. Cutter *Wakeful* rolled heavily in the offshore swell, the motion made worse by a swift current at odds with a falling tide. Hove-to and with her flapping canvas in wild disorder, it felt as if she might easily dismast herself.

Queely had to shout above the din of rigging and wind. Caution was pointless; the clatter of loose gear and the sluice of water alongside seemed loud enough to wake the dead.

He exclaimed, 'It's no use, sir! They're not coming! I have to suggest that we turn back!'

Bolitho held on to the shrouds and strained his eyes through the wind-blown spray. Queely was in command; he had plenty of reasons to be alarmed, and had been right to speak his mind.

Bolitho cursed the unknown vessel which had made them take a more roundabout course towards the Dutch coast. But for that they would have reached the rendezvous in good time. He felt Queely peering at the sky, imagining it was already getting lighter.

Bolitho said tersely, 'They have orders to return on the hour.'

But they were fishermen, smugglers too, not disciplined sailors like those who stood or crouched around him.

Queely said nothing in reply. He was probably thinking much the same.

The wind had veered overnight, which made it even harder for Queely to maintain his position without the risk of being driven onto a lee-shore.

Bolitho tried to think what he must do. *What is the point? There is no other way.*

Allday stood close by, his arms folded as if to show his contempt for the sea's efforts to pitch him to the deck. Occasionally he glanced up at the furled mainsail, the huge mast which leaned right over him, then staggered away to the opposite beam as the cutter rolled her gunports under.

He could tell from Bolitho's stance, the way he barely spoke, that he was tackling each of his problems in turn. Earlier Allday might have been satisfied to know this might happen. But now, having come this far, he wanted to go ahead, get it over with, like Bolitho.

Men scampered down the larboard side as a line parted and the boatswain called for them to make it fast.

Bolitho wondered what Tanner was doing, how he would react when he discovered he had been delayed.

'Boat, sir! *Lee bow!*'

Bolitho tried to moisten his lips but they felt like leather. A few more minutes, and then –

Queely rasped, 'The same one as before! By God I thought they'd cut and run!'

Bolitho wrapped his boat-cloak around him, able to ignore the busy seamen with their ropes and fenders, pointing arms and angry voices as the two hulls swayed together for the first impact.

He said, 'You know what to do. I'd not ask you to risk your command, but –'

They clung together as the two hulls lifted and groaned in a trough, men falling, others heaving on ropes, their bare feet skidding on the wet deck.

Queely nodded. 'I'll be here, sir. If the Devil himself should stand between us.'

Then Bolitho followed Allday into the fishing boat. This time, her skipper gave him what might have been a grin. With the sea surging over the two vessels it could have been a grimace.

Bolitho sat inside a tiny hutchlike cabin and was thankful that the hold was empty of fish. Experienced though he was in the sea's moods, after the buffeting out there any stench might have made him vomit. Like when he had first gone to sea at the age of twelve.

The arrangements were exactly as before, although he sensed the Dutch crew's haste and nervous anxiety whenever they passed an anchored vessel, or riding lights betrayed the nearness of other craft. Merchantmen sheltering for the night, waiting for a favourable wind, men-of-war – they might have been anything. The final part of the journey was quieter, the sounds of sea and wind suddenly banished, lost beyond the endless barrier of waving rushes.

It was so quiet that Bolitho held his breath. Nobody bothered to conceal their approach and Allday whispered, 'Even the mills are still, Cap'n.'

Bolitho watched a tall windmill glide above the rushes, stiff and unmoving. It was eerie, as if nothing lived here.

The crew exchanged comments and then one clambered over the gunwale, his sea-boots splashing through shallows before finding the spur of land. One man ran on ahead, but the skipper stayed with Bolitho and waited for Allday to join them.

Bolitho felt a chill run up his back. The skipper had drawn a pistol from his coat and was wiping it with his sleeve. Without looking he knew that Allday had seen it too and was ready to cut the man down if need be. Was the Dutchman frightened – did he sense danger? Or was he waiting for the chance to betray them, as Delaval had done to so many others?

Allday said, 'Someone's coming, Cap'n.' How calm he sounded. As if he was describing a farm cart in a Cornish lane. Bolitho knew that he was at his most dangerous.

He heard feet slipping on the track and saw the shadowy figure of Brennier's aide stumble, gasp aloud as the other Dutchman pulled him to his feet again.

He stopped when he saw Bolitho and turned back towards the house. *No blindfold*. He seemed close to panic.

Bolitho and the Dutch skipper pushed open the door, and Bolitho stared at the disorder around him. Cupboards ransacked, contents spilled on the floor, even some of the charred logs raked from the fire. The search had been as thorough as it had been quick.

Bolitho looked at the Dutch skipper. They were totally separated by language.

205

Then he turned towards the aide and was shocked at his appearance as he revealed himself beside a lantern.

His clothes were filthy, and there were pale streaks down the grime on his cheeks, as if he had been weeping.

'What is it, man?' Bolitho unbuttoned his old coat to free the butt of his pistol. '*Speak out!*'

The man stared at him with disbelief. Then he said in a broken whisper, '*Il est mort! Il est mort!*'

Bolitho seized his arm; it felt lifeless in his grip. 'The admiral?'

The aide gaped at him as if only now did he realise where he was, that Bolitho was the same man.

He shook his head and blurted out, '*Non! It is the King!*'

Allday rubbed his jaw with his fist. 'God, they've done for him after all!'

The Dutchman thrust his pistol into his belt and spread his hands. It needed no language. The blade had fallen in Paris. The King of France was dead.

Bolitho wanted to find time to think. But there was none. He shook the man's arm and asked harshly, 'Where is Vice-Amiral Brennier? What has become of him?' He hated to see the fear in the man's eyes. All hope gone. And now apparently left to fend for himself in a country which might be unwilling to offer him shelter.

He stammered, 'To Flushing. We could wait no longer.' He stared at the disordered room. 'You were late, Capitaine!'

Bolitho released his hold and the aide almost collapsed on to a bench. He was wringing his hands, stunned by what had happened.

Allday asked, 'What do we do, Cap'n?'

Bolitho looked at the broken man on the bench. Somehow he knew there was more. He asked quietly, 'And the treasure, m'sieu, what of that?'

The aide stared up at him, surprised by the change in Bolitho's tone.

'It is in safe hands, Capitaine, but it was *too late*!'

Safe hands. There was only one other who knew about it. Now he was gone, taking the old admiral Brennier and the treasure with him. To Flushing. The name stood out in his mind like

206

letters of fire. About twenty miles from here at a guess. It might as well have been a thousand.

He recalled Marcuard's remarks about the weather. News would travel slowly with the roads bogged-down or hidden in snow. Nobody here would know for certain when the King had been executed. He felt the sense of urgency running through him, chilling his body from head to toe. Anything might be happening. There was nobody here to ask. Even the farmer who owned this place had vanished – perhaps murdered.

The Dutch skipper said something to his companion, who was guarding the door, and Bolitho snapped, 'Tell that man to remain with us!'

The aide murmured a few halting words in Dutch then added, 'He wants paying, Capitaine.'

Allday muttered harshly, 'Don't we all, matey!'

'If you help me, m'sieu, I will take you to England. Maybe you will discover friends there –'

He looked at Allday's grim features as the man threw himself on his knees and seized his hand, kissing it fervently.

When he looked up, his eyes were streaming, but there was steel in his voice now as he exclaimed, 'I know the ship, Capitaine! It is called *La Revanche*, but flies the English flag!' He cowered under Bolitho's cold gaze. 'I heard him talk of it.'

Bolitho allowed himself to speak his name aloud. 'Sir James Tanner.' The aide's fear told him everything he had not already guessed.

How apt a name. *The Revenge.* Tanner had outwitted them all.

Allday asked, 'What can *we* do, Cap'n? Without a ship of our own –' He sounded lost and bewildered.

Bolitho said, 'We had better be gone from here.' He strode to a window and threw back the shutter. The sky seemed paler. He must think of the present, not anguish over what had happened. *Wakeful*'s near encounter with the stranger had been deliberate, a delay engineered by Tanner. It had given him time to execute the rest of his plan. 'We must try to explain to the Dutchman that we need to be taken downriver to his fishermen friends.' He stared at the aide again. 'Tell him he will be well paid.' He jingled

207

some coins in his pocket to give the words emphasis. 'I'll brook no argument!'

Allday tapped the floor with the point of his cutlass. 'I reckon he understands, Cap'n.' Again he sounded very calm, almost casual. 'Don't you, matey?'

It would be a full day before *Wakeful* would dare to approach the rendezvous. Even then it might be too dangerous for Queely to draw near enough. Bolitho felt sick, and rubbed his eyes to rouse himself from despair.

Why should Tanner take the admiral, if his main intention concerned the treasure?

He walked out into the stinging air and looked up at some fast-moving cloud. It hit him like a clenched fist, as if the answer had been written in those same stars.

He heard himself say tightly, 'The wind has veered yet again, Allday.' He glanced at the familiar, bulky shadow framed against the fading stars.

'It blows fair, old friend.' He added bitterly, 'For France!'

Snapdragon's jolly-boat snugged alongside her anchored consort, and with the briefest of ceremony her commander, Lieutenant Hector Vatass, climbed aboard.

For an instant he paused and peered towards the shore. The wind was fresh to strong, but here in the Sheerness anchorage its force was lessened by the land, so that the snow flurries swirled around in an aimless dance. For a moment Vatass could see the headland beyond the dockyard; in the next it was all blotted out, with only his own vessel still visible.

Telemachus's first lieutenant guided him to the companionway and said, 'Good to see you, sir.'

His formality was unexpected and unusual. But Vatass's mind and body were too strained from the rigours of his entrance to the anchorage in the early morning to make much of it. He had received a message from the coastguard that he was required back at Sheerness. The order had come from Captain Bolitho. It was not one to question, even though Vatass had been fretting already over losing a speedy schooner which had evaded him in a heavier snowsquall off the Foreland.

He found Paice sitting in the cabin, his features grave as he finished writing laboriously in his log.

Vatass lowered himself on to a bench seat and said, 'I wish the damned weather would make up its mind, Jonas. I am heartily sick of it.' He realised that Paice was still silent and asked, 'What is wrong?'

Paice did not reply directly. 'Did you not meet with the courier-brig?' He saw Vatass shake his head. 'I thought as much.'

Paice reached down and produced a bottle of brandy, half-filling two glasses. He had been preparing for this moment as soon as *Snapdragon* had been reported tacking around the headland.

He held up his glass and regarded the other man thoughtfully. 'It's war, Hector.'

Vatass swallowed the brandy and almost choked. 'Jesus! Contraband, I'll wager!'

Paice gave a wintry smile. Vatass was very young, lucky to command a topsail cutter, to command anything at all. That would soon change now. Commands would go to officers who were barely used to their present junior ranks. *Good old Jack again.* He knew that the enormity of his announcement had taken Vatass completely aback. The weak joke was all he had to give himself time to accept it.

Paice said, 'I don't care if it's stolen from Westminster Abbey.' He clinked glasses solemnly. 'War. I received a signal late last night.' He waved his large hand across a pile of loose papers on the table. 'These are from the admiral at Chatham. It has them all jumping. They should have been damned well expecting it!' He stared around the cabin. 'They'll be asking *us* for men soon, you know that? *We* shall be using green replacements while our seasoned people are scattered through the fleet!'

Vatass was only half-listening. He did not share Paice's anxiety over the prospect of his *Telemachus* being pared away by the needs of war. All he could think was that he was young and once again full of hope. A new command – a brig perhaps, or even a rakish sloop-of-war. That would surely mean promotion.

Paice watched his emotions. Vatass had still not learned how to conceal them.

209

He said, 'Captain Bolitho is across the water in Holland, or he could be anywhere by now.' He looked at his log, and the chart which was beneath it. '*Wakeful* is with him.' He downed the brandy in one swallow and refilled his glass immediately. 'At least I trust to God she is.'

Vatass allowed his mind to settle. Which had touched him more? Paice's news of Bolitho, or the fact he had never seen the tall lieutenant drink in this fashion before. He had heard that, after his wife had been killed, Paice had rarely been without the bottle. But that was past. Another memory.

Vatass began, 'I do not understand, Jonas. What can we hope to do?'

Paice glared at him, his eyes red with anxiety and anger. 'Don't you see it yet, man? What the *hell* have you been doing?'

Vatass replied stiffly, 'Chasing a suspected smuggler.'

Paice said in a more level voice, 'The King of France has been executed. Yesterday we were told that their National Convention has declared war on England and Holland.' He nodded very slowly. 'Captain Bolitho is in the midst of it. And I doubt if he knows a whisper of what has happened!'

Vatass said unhelpfully, 'He left you in command of the flotilla, Jonas.'

Paice gave what could have been a bleak smile. 'I intend to use it.' He stood upright with his head inside the skylight and unclipped one of the covers.

Vatass saw tiny flakes of snow settle on his face and hair before he lowered the cover and sat down again.

'We're putting to sea as soon as makes no difference.' He held up one hand. 'Save the protests. I know you've only just come to rest. But at any moment I may receive a direct order from the admiral, one I cannot ignore, which will prevent our going.' He lowered his voice as if to conceal an inner anguish. 'I'll not leave him unsupported and without help.' He kept his eyes on the young lieutenant's face as he poured him another glass, some of the brandy slopping unheeded across the neatly written orders. 'Well, Hector, are you with me?'

'Suppose we cannot find *Wakeful*?'

'Damn me, we'll have tried! And I shall be able to hear that

210

man's name without the shame of knowing I failed him, after the pride he returned to me by his own example.' He waved vaguely over the chart. 'The frontiers will be closed, and any alien ship will be treated as hostile. *Wakeful* is a sound vessel, and her commander a match for anything. But she's no fifth-rate.' He glanced around the cabin. His command and his home; as if he could already see *Telemachus* facing up to a full broadside, with only her carronades and six-pounders to protect herself.

Vatass knew all this, and guessed that, whatever happened, his chances of an immediate promotion were in serious jeopardy. But he had always looked up to Paice's old style of leadership, even more, his qualities as a true sailor. Rough and outspoken, it was easy to picture him in his original role as master of a collier-brig.

'I'm with you.' He considered his words, his young face suddenly serious. 'What about the admiral?'

Paice swept the papers from his chart and picked up some dividers.

'I have the feeling that there is someone more powerful than that fine gentleman behind our captain!' He looked across at Vatass and studied him for several seconds.

Vatass tried to laugh it off. It was war anyway. Nothing else would count now. But Paice's stare made him feel uneasy. As if he did not expect they would ever meet again.

'More vessels lying ahead, Cap'n!' Allday ducked beneath the boat's taut canvas and peered aft through the snow. It was more like sleet now, wet and clinging, so that the interior of the small boat was slippery and treacherous.

Bolitho crouched beside the Dutch skipper at the tiller and narrowed his eyes to judge the boat's progress under her two lugsails. One side of the river was lost in sleet and mist, but here and there he could see the lower portions of hulls and taut cables, probably the same ships he had passed in the night after leaving *Wakeful*. Even in the poor light the small fishing boat was a pitiful sight. Scarred and patched, with unmatched equipment which had been salvaged or stolen from other boats. He guessed that it had been used more as a link between the larger vessels for

211

carrying contraband than for genuine fishing. The four
Dutchmen who made up the crew seemed anxious to please him
despite the stilted translations which passed through Brennier's
aide. Perhaps they imagined that, with Tanner gone, their chance
of any reward was remote, and Bolitho's promise of payment
was better than nothing at all.

Bolitho glanced at the aide. He had still not revealed his name.
In the gloom he looked pinched up with cold and fear, his sodden
clothes clinging to his body like rags. He was gripping a sword
between his grimy fingers, the contrast as stark as the man's own
circumstances, Bolitho thought. It was a beautiful, rapier-style
weapon, the scabbard mounted in silver with a matching hilt and
knuckle-bow. Like the dead French girl's handkerchief, was it his
last connection with the life he had once known?

He ducked beneath the sails and saw the anchored ships up
ahead. Three or four, coastal traders at a guess, their red, white
and blue flags making the only stabs of colour against the drifting
sleet and mist: Dutchmen waiting for the weather to clear before
they worked out of their anchorage. No wonder they called
Holland the port of the world. Who held the Low Countries
enjoyed the rich routes to the East Indies and beyond, to the
Caribbean and the Americas. Like the English, they had always
been ambitious seafarers, and greatly admired, even as enemies
when they had sailed up the Medway, attacking Chatham and
firing the dockyards there.

He saw the Dutch skipper murmur to one of his crew, then
pull out a watch from his tarpaulin coat. It was the size of an
apple.

Bolitho said, 'Find out what they are saying.'

Brennier's aide seemed to drag himself from his despair, and
after a slight hesitation said, 'Very soon now, Capitaine. The
other vessel is around the next . . . how you say . . . *bend*?'

Bolitho nodded. It had been quicker downstream, and using
the sails, small though they were, to full effect. Once aboard the
other boat they would rest, perhaps find something hot to eat
and drink before putting to sea when darkness fell. They might be
unable to make contact with *Wakeful*. But they would have tried.
To wait and think over what had happened would have been

212

unbearable. Anyway, where would they have gone when the waiting was over and still nothing had been solved?

He thought of Hoblyn, the terrified midshipman, the bearded braggart on the Rochester Road, and of Delaval's anguish when he had seen Tanner even as the trap had fallen beneath his frantic legs.

Through and above it, Tanner had manipulated them all. Bolitho bit his lip until it hurt. *Even me.*

Allday said, 'Over to larboard, matey!' The words meant nothing to the man at the tiller but Allday's gesture was familiar to sailors the world over.

'What is it?' Bolitho wiped his face and eyes with an old piece of bunting for the hundredth time to clear his vision.

'Bit o' bother, starboard bow, Cap'n.'

Bolitho wished he had brought his small telescope, and strained his eyes as he stood upright in the boat to follow Allday's bearing.

There was a smart-looking brig anchored in the deepwater channel, and her lack of heavy tackles or lighters alongside meant she was most likely a small man-of-war, or perhaps a Dutch customs vessel.

He saw the skipper staring at her too, his face creased with sudden anxiety.

Bolitho kept his own counsel. There were no boats on the brig's deck, and none in the water unless they were tied on the opposite side. So where were they?

He called quietly, 'Any movement?'

'No, Cap'n.' Allday sounded on edge. 'We only need half a mile and then –'

Bolitho watched as the weather decided to play a small part. A tiny shaft of watery sunlight came from somewhere to give even the drenching sleet a sort of beauty, and lay bare a part of the nearest land.

The Dutch skipper gave a sigh and raised his arm. Bolitho saw the fishing boat anchored a little apart from the others, and, even though he had not seen her before in daylight, he knew it was the one. He touched the Dutchman's arm and said, 'That was well done!'

The man showed his teeth in a smile. From Bolitho's tone he had guessed that it was some kind of compliment.

'Prepare to shorten sail.' He reached out with one foot and tapped the aide's leg. 'You can give the word.' The man jumped as if he had been stabbed.

Bolitho rubbed his hands together. They were raw with cold. Then he glanced at the dirty, patched sails and tried to gauge the final approach in this unfamiliar craft.

The sunlight was already fading, smothered by the approach of more sleet. But not before he had seen a sudden glint of metal from the fishing boat's deck, and even as he watched a figure in uniform with a white cross-belt rose into view, staring upstream for a few seconds before vanishing again below the bulwark.

'*Belay that!*' Bolitho seized the Dutchman's shoulder and gestured towards midstream. 'Tell him the boat has been boarded – *taken*, you understand?'

The tiller was already going over, the skipper crouching down, his eyes fixed unblinkingly on the open channel beyond.

Allday exclaimed, 'God Almighty, that was close!'

Bolitho kept his eyes level with the bulwark and watched for another sign from the anchored fisherman. Boarded, it did not really matter by whom. The Dutch navy, customs men searching for contraband; or perhaps it was merely an unhappy coincidence, a routine search.

Unhappy was hardly the right description, Bolitho thought. It had seemed almost hopeless before. Without some kind of vessel, it was impossible. He glanced along the boat, shielding his face with one arm as the sleet hissed and slapped across the sails and rigging. In open water it would be more lively, even rough, if the angle of the sleet was any measure of it. He thought of *Wakeful*, plunging and rolling in the offshore swell while she waited to make the rendezvous.

This boat had nothing. Just a compass and a few pieces of old equipment. He could not even see a pump.

He looked hard at Allday's crouching shoulders in the bows. Another risk. Was it still worth that?

Bolitho said suddenly, 'A good day for a shoot, Allday.' He spoke quickly as if his common sense might change his mind for him.

214

Allday turned as if he had misheard. '*Shoot*, Cap'n?' Their gaze met and Allday nodded casually. 'Oh, yes, I s'pose it is, Cap'n.'

When he had turned away he unbuttoned his coat and loosened the pistol in his belt where he had wedged it to keep it dry.

Bolitho glanced at his companions. The aide was staring emptily into nothing, and all the Dutchmen were watching the fishing boat which by now had drawn almost abeam.

Bolitho felt for his own pistol, then freed his sword. Two of the Dutchmen were visibly armed, the others might be too.

He waited for the aide to look up at him then said, 'In a moment I am going to take this boat away from here, m'sieu. Do you understand me?' The man nodded dully.

Bolitho continued carefully, 'If they refuse to obey, we must disarm them.' His voice hardened. 'Or kill them.' He waited, trying to guess what the man's broken mind was thinking. 'It is your last chance as well as ours, m'sieu!'

'I understand, Capitaine.' He crawled aft towards the tiller, his beautiful sword held clear of the filth and swilling water below the bottom boards.

Bolitho watched the oncoming curtain of sleet. It had blotted out some anchored vessels which moments earlier had been close enough to see in every detail. Once past the last few craft there would be nothing between them and the open sea.

'Be prepared, m'sieu!' Bolitho's fingers closed around the pistol. Against his chilled body it felt strangely warm, as if it had recently been fired.

Allday shouted, 'Larboard bow, Cap'n! A bloody boatload!'

Bolitho saw a long, double-banked cutter pulling out from behind some moored barges, the scarlet-painted oars rising and falling like powerful wings as it swept towards them.

There were uniforms aft in the sternsheets, naval, as well as the green coats of the Dutch customs. A voice boomed over the choppy wavelets, magnified by a speaking trumpet.

The aide whispered, 'They call us to stop!' He sounded completely terrified.

Bolitho prodded the Dutch skipper and shouted, 'That way! *Quickly!*'

There was no need to show their weapons. The Dutchmen were, if anything, more eager to escape authority than Bolitho.

They threw themselves to work on the two flapping sails, and Bolitho felt the hull tilt to the wind's wet thrust and saw sheets of spray burst over the pursuing cutter's stem, drenching the crew and throwing the scarlet oars into momentary confusion.

Allday yelled, 'They've got a gun up forrard, Cap'n!'

Bolitho tried to swallow. He had already seen the bow-gun in the eyes of the cutter. Probably a swivel or a long musketoon. One blast from either could kill or wound every man in this boat.

But the range was holding; the small fishing boat was better handled and rigged for this kind of work, and the wilder the sea the harder it would be for the cutter's coxswain to maintain his speed through the water.

Allday clung to the gunwale and choked as water reared over the bows and soaked him from head to foot.

The voice pursued them, crackling and distorted through the speaking trumpet.

Allday shouted, 'They're taking aim!'

'Down!' Bolitho pulled the nearest crew member to the deck and saw Allday peering along the boat towards him, his body half-hidden by floats and nets.

The bang of the gun was muffled by the wind and sleet, so that the charge of canister hit the afterpart of the hull with unexpected violence. Bolitho heard metal fragments and splinters shriek overhead and saw several holes punched through the nearest sail. He held his breath, waiting for something to carry away, a spar to break in half, even for a sudden inrush of water.

The Dutch skipper clambered to his knees and nodded. There was something like pride in his face. Even in this sad old boat.

Allday gasped, 'We've lost 'em, Cap'n!'

Bolitho peered astern. The sleet was so thick that even the mouth of the river had vanished. They had the water to themselves.

He was about to rise to his feet when he saw Brennier's aide staring at him, his eyes bulging with pain and fear.

Bolitho knelt beside him, then prized the man's hands away from his body. Allday joined him and gripped his wrists while

216

Bolitho tore open his waistcoat and then his finely laced shirt, which was bright with blood. There were just two wounds. One below the right breast, the other in the stomach. Bolitho heard the Dutch skipper tearing up some rags which he handed over his shoulder. Their eyes met only briefly. Again, language was no barrier. For a fisherman as well as a sea-officer, death was commonplace.

Allday murmured, 'Hold hard, matey.' He looked at Bolitho. 'Shall I lay him down?'

Bolitho covered the dying man with some canvas, held a hat over his face to protect him from the sleet. 'No.' He dropped his voice. 'He's drowning in his own blood.' He looked at the bottom boards where the trapped sleet and seawater glittered red now. Another victim.

He could not wait here. But when he got to his feet he saw the man's eyes follow him, terrified and pleading.

Bolitho said quietly, 'Never fear, m'sieu. You will be safe. We will not leave you.'

He turned away and stared down at the swaying compass card without seeing it. Stupid, empty words! What did they mean to a dying man? What had they ever done to help anyone?

Bolitho swallowed again, feeling the rawness of salt in his throat like bile.

'Nor' West!' He pointed at the sails. 'Yes?'

The man nodded. Events had moved too swiftly for him. But he stood firmly at his tiller, his eyes reddened by sea and wind; it must have felt like sailing his boat into nowhere.

Each dragging minute Bolitho expected to see another vessel loom out of the sleet, no challenge this time, just a merciless hail of grape or canister. Tanner repeatedly came to his mind and he found himself cursing his name aloud until Allday said, 'I think he's going, Cap'n.'

Bolitho got down on his knees again and held the man's groping fingers. So cold. As if they had already died.

'I am here, m'sieu. I shall tell your admiral of your courage.' Then he wiped the man's mouth as a telltale thread of blood ran unheeded down his chin.

Allday watched, his eyes heavy. He had seen it too often

217

before. He saw Bolitho's hand moving to make the man comfortable. How did he do it? He had known him at the height of battle, and flung to the depths of despair. Few but himself had seen this Bolitho, and even now Allday felt guilty about it. Like stumbling on a special secret.

The man was trying to speak, each word bringing more agony. It was just a matter of minutes.

Allday stared across Bolitho's bowed head. *Why doesn't the poor bastard die?*

Bolitho held the man's wrist but it moved with sudden strength and determination. The fingers reached down and unclipped the beautiful sword from his belt.

In a mere whisper he said, 'Give – give . . .'

The effort was too much for him. Bolitho stood up, the rapier in one hand. He thought of the sword which hung by his side, so familiar that it was a part of him.

He looked at Allday's stony features and said quietly, 'Is this all that is left of a man? Nothing more?'

As the minutes passed into an hour, and then another, they all worked without respite to hold the boat on course, to bale out the steady intake of water and constantly retrim the two patched sails. In a way it saved them. They had neither food nor water, and each man ached with cold and backbreaking labour; but there was no time to despair or to give in.

In darkness, with the boat pitching about on a deep procession of rollers, they buried the unknown Frenchman, a rusting length of chain tied about his legs to take him down to the seabed. After that, they lost track of the hours and their direction, and despite the risk of discovery Bolitho ordered that the lantern should be lit and unshuttered, as arranged, into the sleet which was once again turning to snow.

If no one found them they could not survive. It was winter, and the sea too big for their small vessel. Only Allday knew that there was barely enough oil left in the lantern anyway. He sighed and moved closer to Bolitho's familiar outline in the stern. It was not much of a way to end after what they had done together, he thought. But death could have come in a worse guise, and very nearly had on board Delaval's *Loyal Chieftain*.

Bolitho moistened his lips. 'One more signal, old friend.'

The lantern's beam lit up the snow so that the boat appeared to be hemmed in and unmoving.

Allday muttered hoarsely, 'That's the last of it, Cap'n.'

It was then that *Wakeful* found them.

15

No Hiding Place

Queely and his first lieutenant watched Bolitho with silent fascination as he swallowed his fourth mug of scalding coffee. He could feel it warming him like an inner fire and knew someone, probably Allday, had laced it heavily with rum.

They had been unable to do anything for the small fishing boat which had given them the chance to escape, and despite protests from the Dutch skipper it had been cast adrift; it seemed unlikely it would remain afloat for much longer.

Queely waited, choosing the moment. 'What now, sir?' He watched Bolitho's eyes regaining their brightness. It was like seeing someone come alive again. When *Wakeful*'s seamen had hauled them aboard they had been too numbed by cold and exhaustion even to speak.

As he had drunk his coffee, Bolitho had tried to outline all that had happened. He had ended by saying, 'But for you and your *Wakeful*, we would all be dead.' He had placed the silver-mounted sword on the cabin table. 'I suspect this poor man had already died when he heard that his King had been executed.'

Queely had shaken his head. 'We knew nothing of that, sir.' His jaw had lifted and he had regarded Bolitho with his dark, hawklike face. 'I would still have come looking for you no matter what the risk, even if I had.'

Bolitho leaned back against the side and felt the cutter rolling steeply in a cross-swell as she prepared to change tack. The motion seemed easier, but the wind sounded just as strong.

220

Perhaps his mind was still too exhausted to notice the true difference.

He replied, '*Now?* We shall lay a course for Flushing. It is our only chance to catch Tanner with the treasure.'

Lieutenant Kempthorne made his excuses and went on deck to take charge of the hands. Bolitho and Queely leaned on the table, the chart spread between them beneath the madly swinging lanterns. Bolitho glanced at the serious-faced lieutenant. Even in his seagoing uniform he managed to make Bolitho feel like a vagrant. His clothing stank of fish and bilge, and his hands were cut and bleeding from handling the icy sheets in the boat which they had abandoned astern.

Queely said, 'If, as you say, Tanner has loaded the treasure into this vessel, *La Revanche*, would he not make haste to get under way immediately? If so, we can never catch him, despite this soldier's wind.'

Bolitho peered at the chart, his grey eyes thoughtful. 'I doubt that. It would all take time, which is why I believe he was the one to cause our delay at the rendezvous. Any suspicious act might arouse the Dutch authorities, and that is the last thing he would want.'

A voice seemed to cry out in his mind. Suppose Brennier's aide had been mistaken? Or that he had heard them speaking of another vessel altogether?

Queely took his silence for doubt. 'She'll likely be armed, sir. If we had some support –'

Bolitho glanced at him and smiled sadly. 'But we do not have any. Armed? I think that unlikely, except for a minimum protection. Which was why Delaval and his *Loyal Chieftain* laid offshore whenever he was making a run. The Dutch were searching vessels in the river. Any heavily armed ship would draw them like bees to honey.'

'Very well, sir.' He gave a rueful grin. 'It is little enough, but I too am anxious to see what so much treasure looks like!' He pulled on his heavy coat and turned in the doorway to the companion ladder. 'I thank God we found you, sir. I had all but given up hope.'

Bolitho sat down wearily and massaged his eyes. The cabin

221

was tiny and, as usual, littered with the officers' effects. But after the fishing boat's squalor it seemed like a ship-of-the-line.

Just hours later, Bolitho was roused from his sleep. Allday found him sprawled across the chart, his head resting on one arm.

'What is it?'

Allday stood balancing a steaming basin. 'The cook managed to boil some water.' He gave a broad grin. 'I thought to meself a good shave an' a rub-down'll make the Cap'n feel his old self again.'

Bolitho slipped out of his coat and peeled off his shirt. As Allday shaved him with practised ease, legs braced, one ear attuned to every sound as the cutter rolled and plunged about them, he marvelled that the big man could always adjust, no matter what ship he was in.

Allday was saying, 'Y'see, Cap'n, 'tis always the same with you at times like this. *You* feel better – that makes it better for the rest of us.'

Bolitho stared up at him, the realisation of Allday's simple philosophy driving away the last cobwebs of sleep.

He said quietly, 'Today, you mean?' He saw him nod: the old instinct he had always trusted. Why had he not known it himself? 'We'll fight?'

'Aye, Cap'n.' He sounded almost buoyant. 'Had to come, as I sees it.'

Bolitho dried his face and was amazed that Allday could shave him so closely with the deck all alive beneath him. He had rarely even nicked him with his formidable razor.

Allday wiped down his shoulders and back with a hot cloth and then handed him a comb. '*That's* more like it, Cap'n.'

Bolitho saw the freshly laundered shirt on the bunk. 'How did you –'

'Compliments of Mr Kempthorne, Cap'n. I – mentioned it, like.'

Bolitho dressed unhurriedly. A glance at his watch told him all he had to know for the present. Queely and his company were doing what they could and needed no encouragement or criticism. He wondered what had become of the four Dutchmen,

222

and where they would end up. Probably on the next ship bound for Holland, even at the risk of being greeted by the Customs.

The shirt made him feel clean and refreshed, just as Allday had promised. He thought of all those other times, under the blazing sun, the decks strewn with dead and dying, the brain cringing to the crash and recoil of cannon fire. Like Stockdale before him, Allday had always been there. But with that something extra. He always seemed to understand, to know when the waiting was over, and smooth words were not enough.

Queely came down from the deck and peered in at him.

'Dawn coming up, sir. Wind's holding steady, and the snow's eased to almost nothing.' He noticed the clean shirt and smiled. 'Oh, you honour us, sir!'

As his feet clattered up the ladder again Bolitho said, 'There is still something *missing*, Allday. Fight we may, but –' He shrugged. 'He might have outfoxed us again.'

Allday stared into the distance. 'When I heard that silky voice of his –' He grinned, but no humour touched his eyes. 'I wanted to cut him down there and then.'

Bolitho half-drew his sword then let it fall smoothly into its scabbard again. 'We make a fine pair. I wanted that too.'

He picked up his boat-cloak. It was filthy also. But it would be like ice on deck. He must not fail, would not let the fever burst in and consume him like the last time.

Some of his old despair lingered on. He said, 'Hear me, old friend. If I should fall today –'

Allday regarded him impassively. 'I'll not see it, Cap'n, 'cause I shall already have dropped!'

The understanding was there. As strong as ever.

Bolitho touched his arm. 'So let's be about it, eh?'

Bolitho felt his body angle to the tilting deck as the wind forced *Wakeful* on to her lee bulwark. It was colder than he had expected, and he regretted taking shelter in the cabin's comparative warmth.

Queely touched his hat and shouted above the noise, 'Wind's veered still further, sir! Nor'-West by North or the like, by my reckoning!'

223

Bolitho stared up at the masthead and thought he could see the long pendant streaming towards the larboard bow, curling, then cracking like a huge whip. He even imagined he could hear it above the wild chorus of creaking rigging, the slap and boom of canvas.

Wakeful was steering south-south-west, close-hauled on the starboard tack, her sails very pale against the dull sky. Dawn was here and yet reluctant to show itself.

Bolitho felt his eyes growing accustomed to the poor light and recognised several of the figures who were working close at hand. Even the 'hard men' of Queely's command looked chilled and pinched, but for the most part their feet were bare, although Bolitho could feel the bitter cold through his shoes. Like most sailors, they thought shoes too expensive to waste merely for their own comfort.

Queely said, 'According to the master, we should be well past Walcheren Island and Flushing by now. If the weather clears we will soon sight the coast of France.'

Bolitho nodded but said nothing. *France.* Once there, Tanner would make his trade. A share of the treasure and probably a sure protection from the French Convention to enable him to continue his smuggling on a grand scale. He tried not to think of the old admiral, Brennier. Tanner's mark of trust, then humiliation before the mob, and the last steps up to the guillotine. Any other leading patriot would think again before he considered lending support to a counter-revolution with Brennier dead.

Bolitho watched the sky giving itself colour. The driving wind had swept the snow away; he could see no clouds, just a hostile grey emptiness, with the faintest hint of misty blue towards the horizon.

Queely was speaking to his first lieutenant. Bolitho saw Kempthorne bobbing his head to his commander's instructions. Despite his uniform and his surroundings he still managed to look out of place.

Queely walked up the slanting deck and said, 'He's going aloft with the big signals glass in a moment, sir.' He saw Bolitho's expression and gave a quick smile. 'I know, sir. He'd be happier as a horse-coper than a sea-officer, but he tries!'

224

He forgot Kempthorne and added, 'We shall draw near to the French coast again, sir. If Tanner intends to change allegiance and steal the King's ransom, he may stand inshore as soon as it's light enough.' He was thinking about that last time, the French luggers, the boat blowing up, and the dead girl they had returned to the sea.

Bolitho said, 'We shall take him anyway. I'll brook no interference from French patrol vessels!'

Queely studied him curiously. 'Strange how a man of influence like Tanner could change loyalties.'

'I have always seen him as an enemy.' Bolitho glanced away. 'This time he'll have no hope of escaping justice because of his damned toadies in high places!'

Kempthorne was hauling his lanky frame up the weather shrouds, his coat flapping in the wind as it pressed his body against the ratlines. Bolitho watched, conscious that he could now see the masthead sharply etched against the sky, the vibrating shrouds, even a solitary lookout who was shifting his perch as the lieutenant clawed his way up beside him.

Queely remarked unfeelingly, 'Just the thing to clear your head on a day like this!'

He looked at Bolitho's profile and asked abruptly, 'Do you regard this as a day of reckoning, sir?' He sounded surprised, but without the doubt he had once shown.

Bolitho replied, 'I believe so.' He shivered and pulled his boat-cloak more tightly about his body. Suppose he was mistaken, and Tanner's ship still lay at Flushing, or had never been there at all?

He added in a hard tone, 'It is a premonition one has from time to time.' He saw Allday lounging beside the companionway, his arms folded. There was nothing careless or disinterested in his eyes, Bolitho thought.

'As I see it, Tanner has nowhere else to run. Greed and deceit have made escape impossible.'

He thought again of Tanner's own words. *No hiding place.* Even then he had lied, must have laughed as Brennier and his companions played directly into his hands.

'Deck there!'

225

Queely peered up. 'Where away?'

Kempthorne called lamely, 'Nothing yet, sir!'

Several of the seamen nearby nudged one another as Queely snorted, 'Damned nincompoop!'

Bolitho took a telescope from the rack and wiped the lens carefully with his handkerchief. As he lifted it and waited for the deck to rear upright again, he saw the sea tumbling away across the larboard bow, reaching further and still further, individual banks of crested rollers and darker troughs forming into patterns in the growing daylight. A grey, blustery morning. He thought of Falmouth and wondered how young Matthew had enjoyed his Christmas. Probably had had the household enthralled with his tales of smuggling and sudden death. Bolitho was glad he was back where he belonged. The land needed boys who would grow into men like his father had been. He glanced at Allday. Let others do the fighting so that they could build, raise animals, and make England safe again.

'*Deck there!*'

Queely scowled.

Kempthorne's voice cracked with excitement. 'Sail on the lee bow, sir!'

Queely's dark eyes flashed in the poor light. 'By God, I'd never have believed it!'

'Easy now. Let us hold on to caution, eh?' But his face made a lie of his words. It was the ship. *It must be.* No other would risk running so close to the French coast.

Queely yelled impatiently, 'What is she?' His foot tapped on the wet planking. 'I'm waiting, man!'

Kempthorne called hoarsely, 'A – a brigantine, I think, sir!'

Bolitho said, 'It must be difficult to see, even from that height.'

Queely turned. 'You think I'm too hard on him, sir?' He shrugged. 'It may save his life and a few others before long!'

Bolitho moved to the narrow poop and clung to a dripping swivel gun. A brigantine. It seemed likely. They and schooners were most favoured in the Trade, and Tanner had probably selected this one as soon as Marcuard had taken him into his confidence. He thought of the grand house in Whitehall, the servants, the quiet luxury of day-to-day life in the capital. This

226

was a far cry from Marcuard's careful planning, but Bolitho had no doubts as to where the blame would be laid if Tanner and the treasure disappeared.

The master said to nobody in particular, 'A spot o' sunshine afore the glass is turned.'

Queely glared at him, but knew him well enough to say nothing.

Kempthorne, his voice almost gone from shouting above the wind and sea, called, 'Brigantine she is, sir! Holding same tack!'

Bolitho grasped his sword beneath his cloak. It felt like a piece of ice.

'I suggest you prepare, Mr Queely.'

Queely watched him, his features more hawklike than ever. 'The people know what to do, sir. If we are wrong, they might lose confidence.'

'Not in you. You can blame it all on the mad captain from Falmouth!'

Surprisingly they were both able to laugh.

Then Queely shouted, 'Pipe all hands! Clear for action!'

It was still strange for Bolitho to see the preparations for battle completed without drums, the rising urgency of a ship beating to quarters. Here, it was almost by word of mouth, with only the watch below summoned by the squeal of calls.

'Cast off the breechings!'

The master let out a sigh. *'Told you.'*

A shaft of watery sunlight plunged down through the spray and sea-mist, giving the water depth and colour, personality to the faces and figures working around the guns.

From his dizzy perch Lieutenant Francis Kempthorne wrapped one arm around a stay until he felt it was being torn from his body. As the sturdy hull lifted and dipped beneath him, the mast itself reached out and across the surging crests far below, and he saw the mainsail's shadow on the water, as if it were rising to snatch him down. The motion was sickening although the look-out at his side seemed indifferent to it.

He gulped and tried again, counting the seconds while he levelled the heavy telescope, not even daring to think what Queely would say if he dropped it. The bows lifted streaming from a jagged breaker and Kempthorne held his breath. The brigantine must have risen at exactly the same moment. He saw her forecourse and topsail, the big driver braced hard round as she steered on the same tack as her pursuer.

Just for those few seconds he saw her name across the counter, the gilt paint suddenly sharp and bright in the feeble glare.

He shouted, 'La Revanche, sir!' He was almost sobbing with relief, as if it would have been his fault had she been another vessel entirely.

The lookout watched him and shook his head. Kempthorne was popular with most of the hands, and never took it out of offenders like some. The seaman had been in the navy for twelve years but could still not fathom the minds of officers.

Kempthorne was glad, pleased that he had sighted the other vessel. Yet within hours he might be dead.

Of course there might easily be prize money if things went well . . .

Down on the streaming deck Queely stared at Bolitho and exclaimed, 'We've found her, sir!' His eyes flashed with excitement, Kempthorne's part in it already forgotten.

Bolitho levelled his glass, but from the deck the sea still appeared empty.

'And now, we'll *take* him!'

Kempthorne shouted, 'She's shaken out another reef, sir! Making more sail!'

Queely strode to the compass box and back to Bolitho's side. 'They're wasting their time,' he said confidently. 'We've got the bugger by the heels.' He cupped his hands. 'Be ready to run out the stuns'ls if she opens the range!'

Bolitho trained his glass again. Now in the growing light he could see the brigantine's forecourse and topsail, her driver filled to full capacity and making the vessel's two masts lean over towards the cruising white horses.

Even in this short interval, since Kempthorne had read her name, the distance between them had fallen away considerably. It was true what they said about topsail cutters. They could outrun almost anything.

228

'Run up the Colours, if you please.' Queely looked at Bolitho. 'He may not have recognised us, sir.'

Bolitho nodded. 'I agree. Let's see what he does next. Have the four Dutchmen brought on deck.'

The Dutchmen stood swaying below the mast, staring from Bolitho to the brigantine, wondering what was about to happen to them.

Bolitho lowered the glass. If he could see the other vessel's poop, then they, and most likely Tanner himself, would be able to recognise his erstwhile partners. He would know then that this was not some casual encounter, a time when he might risk turning towards the French coast to avoid capture. He would know it was Bolitho. It was personal. It was now.

'Fire a gun, Mr Queely!'

The six-pounder recoiled on its tackles, the thin whiff of smoke gone before the crew had time to check the motion with handspikes.

Queely watched the ball splash into the broken crests some half-a-cable from the brigantine's quarter.

He said, 'She does not seem to be pierced for any large artillery.' He glanced admiringly at Bolitho. 'You reasoned to perfection, sir.'

A man yelled, 'Somethin's 'appenin' on 'er deck, sir!'

Bolitho raised his glass in unison with Queely, and tensed as he saw the little scene right aft by her taffrail. He did not recognise the others, but in the centre of the small group he saw Brennier's white hair blowing in the wind, his arms pinioned so that he was forced to face the cutter as she continued to overhaul *La Revanche*.

Queely said savagely, 'What is his game? Why does he play for time? We'll be up to him in a moment – if he kills that old man it will be the worse for him!'

Bolitho said, 'Rig four halters to the mainyard.' He saw Queely look at him with surprise. 'Tanner will understand. A life for a life. So too will his men.'

Queely yelled, 'Come down, Mr Kempthorne! You are needed *here*!' He beckoned to his boatswain and passed Bolitho's instructions. Within minutes, or so it seemed, four ropes, each with a noose at one end, flew out from the mainyard like creeper, as if they were enjoying a macabre dance.

Bolitho said, 'Keep him to lee'rd of you. Run down on his

229

quarter.' He was thinking aloud. But all the time, Queely's question intruded. *Why does he play for time?* The game must surely be played out.

The truth touched his heart like steel. *He wants me dead. Even in the face of defeat he sees only that.*

He raised the glass again. Brennier's face loomed into the small silent picture, his eyes wide as if he was choking.

Bolitho said, 'I intend to board. Prepare the jolly-boat.' He silenced Queely's protest by adding, 'If you try to drive alongside in this wind, you'll likely dismast *Wakeful*. We'd lose Tanner, the treasure, everything.'

Queely shouted to the boat-handling party, then said stubbornly, 'If they fire on you before you board, what then? We have no other boat. Why not risk the damage, I say, and damn the consequences!' He shrugged; he had seen the fight lost before it had begun. 'Mr Kempthorne! Full boarding party!' He turned his back on the men by the tiller. 'And if —'

Bolitho touched his elbow. '*If?* Then you may act as you please. Disable her, but make certain they understand they will go down with the ship if they resist further!'

He watched the jolly-boat rising and dipping like a snared shark as the seamen warped it slowly aft to the quarter.

He took a last glance at the brigantine's poop as *Wakeful* bore down on her. The figures had gone. The threat of instant retribution which they had seen in the four halters run up to the yard might have carried the moment. The sight of *Wakeful*'s carronades and run-out six-pounders would demonstrate that there was no quarter this time, no room to bargain.

Allday dropped into the boat and watched the oarsmen as they fended off the cutter's hull, and prepared to fight their way over the water which surged between the two vessels.

Bolitho clambered down with Kempthorne and as the bowman shoved off, and the oars fell noisily into their rowlock, Allday shouted, 'Give way all!'

Kempthorne stared at *La Revanche*, his eyes filled with wonder. 'They're shortening sail, sir!'

Bolitho replied grimly, 'Don't drop your guard, my lad, not for a second.'

Faces appeared along the brigantine's bulwark, and Bolitho raised his borrowed speaking trumpet and shouted, 'Do not resist! In the King's name, I order you to surrender!'

He could ignore the sweating oarsmen, Allday crouching over his tiller bar, Kempthorne and the other boarders jammed like herrings into the sternsheets and amongst the boat's crew.

At any second they might open fire. It only needed one. Bolitho wanted to look round for *Wakeful* and gauge her position, how long it might take Queely to attack if the worst happened.

Allday said between his teeth, 'One of 'em's got a musket, Cap'n.'

Bolitho shouted again, his heart pumping against his ribs as his whole body tensed for a shot.

'Stand by to receive boarders!'

Allday breathed out slowly as the raised musket disappeared. 'Bowman! *Grapnel!*'

They smashed hard into the brigantine's side, lifted over her wale and almost capsized as another trough yawned beneath the keel.

Bolitho seized a handrope and hauled himself up to the entry port, with Kempthorne and some of the seamen scrabbling up beside him. Allday stared helplessly while the boat plunged down into another trough, leaving him and the rest of the crew momentarily cut off from the boarding party. Bolitho flung himself over the bulwark and in the next few seconds saw the scene like a badly executed painting. Men gaping at him when they should have been attacking or yelling defiance; Brennier beside the wheel, his hands apparently tied behind him, a sailor with a cutlass held close to his throat.

And in the centre stood Tanner, his handsome features very calm as he faced Bolitho across the open deck.

The jolly-boat ground alongside again and broken oars spilled out into the sea. But Allday was here, with three more armed men, their eyes wild, ready to fight – no, wanting to kill now that the moment had arrived.

Tanner said, 'You are making another mistake, Bolitho!'

Bolitho glanced at Brennier and nodded. He was safe now. The man who was guarding him jammed his cutlass into the deck and stood away.

231

Bolitho said, 'Well, Sir James, you once invited me to enter your world.' He gestured toward the horizon. 'This is mine. On the high seas you will find no bribed judges or lying witnesses to save your skin. If you or one of your men raises his hand against us, I will see him dead – here, today – be certain of that.' He was astonished that he could speak so calmly. 'Mr Kempthorne, attend the admiral.'

As the lieutenant made to cross the deck, Tanner moved. 'I shall see you in *hell*, Bolitho!'

He must have had a pistol, a long-barrelled, duellist's weapon, concealed beneath his coat. Too late Bolitho saw his arm swing up and take aim. He heard shouts, a grunt of fury from Allday, then even as a shadow passed across his vision came the sharp crack of the shot. Lieutenant Kempthorne swung round and stared at Bolitho, his eyes wide with disbelief. The ball had penetrated his throat directly below his chin, and as he fell forwards the blood welled from his mouth and he was dead.

In the immediate silence the sea's sounds intruded like an audience, and only the man at the wheel seemed able to move, his eyes on the compass and the straining driver. What he was trained to do, no matter what.

He wants me dead.

There was a faint splash as Tanner flung the pistol over the side. He watched Bolitho's expression and said softly, '*Next time.*'

Bolitho walked towards him, men falling back to let him through. It was then that he saw *Wakeful*, creeping along the side, near enough to fire directly at individual targets, but still keeping her distance to avoid collision.

Somebody shouted, 'Th' chests is in the 'old, sir!'

But the others ignored him. It no longer seemed to matter.

Allday tightened his grip on the cutlass. Remembering the silky voice from the hidden carriage, when Tanner had ordered him to kill the sailor from the press gang. He could feel the flood in his veins like thunder, and knew that if any one so much as moved towards Bolitho he would hack him down.

Bolitho faced Tanner and said, 'The next time is now, *Jack* – isn't that what they call you?'

232

'You'd kill an unarmed man, Captain? I think not. Your sense of honour –'

'Has just died with young Kempthorne.' He had his sword in his hand faster than he had ever known before. He saw Tanner gasp as if he expected the point to tear into him instantly; when Bolitho hesitated, he recovered himself and jeered, 'Like your brother after all!'

Bolitho stood back slightly, the point of his sword just inches above the deck.

'You did not disappoint me, Sir James.' He watched the arrogance give way to something else. 'You insulted my family. Perhaps on land, in "your world", you might still go free despite your obscene crimes!'

He was suddenly sick of it. The sword moved like lightning, and when it returned to the deck there was blood running from Tanner's cheek. The blade had cut it almost to the bone.

Quietly Bolitho said, 'Defend yourself, man. Or *die.*'

Gasping with pain Tanner dragged out his sword, his face screwed up with shock and fear.

They circled one another, figures hurrying away, *Wakeful*'s men standing to their weapons, one near the wheel with a swivel gun trained on the brigantine's crew.

Allday watched, shocked by Bolitho's consuming anger, the glint in his eyes which even he had never seen before.

Clash-clash-clash. The blades touched and feinted apart, then Bolitho's cut across Tanner's shirt, so that he screamed as blood ran down his breeches.

'For pity's sake!' Tanner was peering at him like a wounded beast. 'I surrender! I'll tell everything!'

'You lie, damn you!' The blade hissed out once more, and a cut opened on Tanner's neck like something alive.

Vaguely Bolitho heard Queely's voice, echoing across the water through his trumpet.

'Sail to the Nor'-West, sir!'

Bolitho lowered his sword. 'At last.'

Allday said, 'They might be Frogs!' Bolitho wiped his forehead with his arm. It was like the blind man. Exactly the same. He had wanted to kill Tanner. But now he was nothing. Whatever happened he could not survive.

He said wearily, 'They'll not interfere with two English ships.'

Again, it was like a stark picture. Brennier's faded eyes, his hoarse voice as he called with astonishment, 'But, Capitaine, our countries are at war!'

It was the missing part of the pattern which fate, or his own instinct, had tried to warn him about. At war, and they had not known. No wonder Tanner had been prepared to wait, to play for time. He had known the French ship was on her way. She was probably the same vessel which had stood between *Wakeful* and Holland such a short while ago.

But he did not see the sudden triumph and hatred in Tanner's eyes as he came out of his trance of fear and lunged forward with his sword. Bolitho ducked and made to parry it aside, but his foot went from under him and he knew he had slipped in poor Kempthorne's blood.

He heard Tanner scream, *'Die then!'* He sounded crazed with pain and the lust to kill.

Bolitho rolled over, and kicked out at Tanner's leg, taking him off balance so that he reeled back against the bulwark.

Bolitho was on his feet again, and heard Allday roar, 'Let me, Cap'n.'

The blades parried almost gently, and then Tanner lunged forward once again. Bolitho took the weight on his hilt, swung Tanner round, using the force of his attack to propel him towards the side, just as his father had taught him and his brother so long ago in Falmouth.

Bolitho flicked the guard aside and thrust. When he withdrew the blade, Tanner was still on his feet, shaking his head dazedly from side to side as if he could not understand how it could happen.

His knees hit the deck, and he slumped and lay staring blindly at the sails.

Allday gathered him up and rolled him over the bulwark.

Bolitho joined him at the side and watched the body drifting slowly towards the bows. He leaned against Allday's massive shoulder and gasped. 'So it's not over.'

234

Then he looked up, his eyes clearing like clouds from the sea. 'Was he dead?'

Allday shrugged and gave a slow grin of relief and pride. For both of them.

'Didn't ask, Cap'n.'

Bolitho turned towards the white-haired admiral. 'I must leave you, m'sieu. My prize crew will take care of you.' He looked away towards Kempthorne's sprawled body. He had intended to make him prize master of *La Revanche*, give him a small authority which might drive away all his uncertainties. He almost smiled. Prize master, as he had once been. The first step to command.

Brennier was unable to grasp it. 'But how will you fight?' He peered at *Wakeful*'s tall mainsail. 'Tanner was expecting something bigger to come after us!'

Bolitho walked to the entry port and looked down at the pitching jolly-boat. To the master's mate who had accompanied the boarding party he said, 'Put the men you can trust to work and make sail at once. Those you can't put in irons.'

The master's mate watched him curiously. 'Beg pardon, sir, but after wot you just done I don't reckon we'll get much bother.' Then he stared across at his own ship. He knew he would probably not see her again. 'I'll bury Mr Kempthorne proper, sir. Never you fear.'

Allday called, 'Boat's ready, Cap'n!'

Bolitho turned and looked at their watching faces. Would he have killed Tanner but for that last attack? Now he would never know.

To the admiral he said, 'Our countries are at war, m'sieu, but I hope we shall always be friends.'

The old man who had tried to save his King bowed his head. He had lost everything but the ransom in the hold, his King and now his country. And yet Bolitho thought afterwards that he had never seen such dignity and pride in any man.

'*Give way all!*'

Allday swung the tiller bar and peered at the men along *Wakeful*'s side ready to take the bowline.

Then he looked at the set of Bolitho's shoulders. So it's not over, he had said back there. He sighed. Nor would it be, until –

Allday saw the stroke oarsman watching him anxiously and shook himself from his black mood. Poor bugger'd never been in a sea-fight before. Was likely wondering if he would ever see home again.

He glanced at Bolitho and grinned despite his apprehensions.

Our Dick. Hatless, bloody, the old coat looking as if he had borrowed it from a beggar.

His grin broadened, so that the stroke oarsman felt the touch of confidence again.

But you'd know Bolitho was a captain anywhere. And that was all that counted now.

16

A Sailor's Lot

Luke Hawkins, *Telemachus*'s boatswain, shook himself like a dog and waited for Paice to loom out of the wet darkness.

'I've sent four 'ands aloft, sir!' They both squinted towards the masthead but the upper yards were hidden by swirling snow. 'Some o' that cordage 'as carried away!'

Paice swore. 'God damn all dockyards! For what they care we could lose the bloody topmast!' It was pointless to worry about the half-frozen men working up there, their fingers like claws, their eyes blinded by snow.

Hawkins suggested, 'We could reef, sir.'

Paice exclaimed, '*Shorten sail?* Damn it to hell, man! We've lost enough knots already!' He swung away. 'Do what you must. I shall let her fall off a point – it might help to ease the strain.'

Paice found Triscott peering at the compass, his hat and shoulders starkly white in the shadows.

The first lieutenant knew it was pointless to argue with Paice about the way he was driving his command. It was so unlike him, as if the flames of hell were at his heels.

Paice took a deep breath as water lifted over the bulwark and sluiced away into the scuppers.

When daylight came there would probably be no sign of *Snapdragon*. In these conditions station-keeping was almost a joke. Perhaps Vatass would use the situation to go about and beat back to harbour. Paice toyed with the thought, which he knew was unfair and uncharitable.

The helmsman yelled, 'Steady as she goes, sir! Sou' by East!'

Chesshyre said, 'We'll be a right laughing stock if we have the sticks torn out of us.' He had not realised that Paice was still in the huddled group around the compass.

He winced as Paice's great hand fell on his arm like a grapnel.

'You are the acting-master, Mr Chesshyre! If you can't think of anything more useful to offer, then *acting* you will remain!'

Triscott interrupted, 'We shall sight land when the snow clears. Mr Chesshyre assured me that it will by dawn.'

Paice said hotly, 'In which case it will probably turn into a bloody typhoon!'

Triscott hid a smile. He had always liked Paice and had learned all he knew from him. Nevertheless he could be quite frightening sometimes. Like now.

Paice strode to the side and stared at the surging wake as it lifted and curled over the lee bulwark.

Was he any better than Vatass, and was this only a gesture? He raised his face into the swirling flakes and stinging wind. He knew that was not so. Without Bolitho the ship even felt different. Just months ago Paice would never have believed that he would have stood his ship into jeopardy in this fashion. And all because of a man. An ordinary man.

He heard muffled cries from above the deck, and guessed that some new cordage and whipping were being run up to the masthead for their numbed hands to work on.

He shook his head as if he was in pain. No, he was never an ordinary man.

Paice's wife had been a schoolmaster's daughter and had taught her bluff sea-officer a great deal. She had introduced him to words he had never known. His life until she entered it had been rough, tough ships and men to match them. He smiled sadly, reminiscently, into the snow. No wonder her family had raised their hands in horror when she had told them of her intention to marry him.

He tried again. What was the word she had used? He nodded, satisfied at last. *Charisma.* Bolitho had it, and probably did not even guess.

He thought of Bolitho's mission and wondered why nobody

238

had listened to him when he had spoken his mind on Sir James Tanner. Like a hopeless crusade. It had been the same between Delaval and Paice himself: not just a fight between the forces of law and corruption, but something personal. Nobody had listened to him, either. They had been *sorry*, of course – he felt the old flame of anger returning. How would they have felt if their wives had been murdered like . . . He stopped himself. He could not bear even to use her name in the same company.

Now Delaval was dead. Paice had watched him on that clear day, every foot of the way to the scaffold. He had heard no voices, no abuse or ironic cheering from the crowd who had come to be entertained. God, he thought, if they held a mass torture session on the village green there would not be room to sit down.

He had spoken to Delaval silently on that day. Had cursed his name, damned him in an afterlife where he hoped he would suffer, as he had forced so many others to do.

Paice was not a cruel man, but he had felt cheated by the brevity of the execution. Long after the crowd had broken up he had stood in a doorway and watched Delaval's corpse swinging in the breeze. If he had known where it was to be hung in chains as a gruesome warning to other felons, he knew he would have gone there too.

He looked up, caught off balance as a dark shape fell past the mainsail, hit the bulwark and vanished over the side. Just those few seconds, but he had heard the awful scream, the crack as the living body had broken on the impact before disappearing outboard.

Scrope the master-at-arms came running aft. 'It was Morrison, sir!'

The thing changed to a real person. A bright-eyed seaman from Gillingham, who had quit fishing and signed on with a recruiting party after his parents had died of fever.

Nobody spoke, not even the youthful Triscott. Even he knew that it was impossible to turn the cutter or lie-to in this sea. Even if they succeeded they would never find the man named Morrison. It was a sailor's lot. They sang of it in the dogwatches below, in the ale shops and the dockside whorehouses. Rough and crude they might be, but to Paice they were the only real people.

239

He said harshly, 'Send another man aloft. I want that work finished, and lively with it!'

Some would curse his name for his methods, but most of them would understand. *A sailor's lot.*

Paice stamped his feet on the deck to bring back some warmth and feeling. He wanted to think about Bolitho, what steps he should take next if they failed to find him when daylight came. But all he could think of was the man who had just been chosen to die. For that was what he and most sailors thought. *When your name is called.* He gripped a backstay and felt it jerking and shivering in his fingers. All he had to do was lose his handhold. How would he feel then, as his ship vanished into the night, and he was left to choke and drown?

He came out of his brooding and snapped, 'I'm going below. Call me if –'

Triscott stared at his leaning shadow. 'Aye, aye, sir.'

Paice stumbled into the cabin and slammed the door shut behind him. He stared at the other bunk and remembered All-day's model ship, the bond which seemed to shine between those two men.

He spoke to the cabin at large. 'I must find him!' He glanced at the battered bible in its rack but dismissed the idea immediately. That could wait. Charisma was enough for one watch.

On the deck above, Triscott watched the comings and goings of men up and down the treacherous ratlines. In a few weeks' time he would be twenty years old. And now it was war. Only after he had seen and spoken with Bolitho had he grasped some inkling of what war, especially at sea, might mean. Paice had hinted that their lordships at the far-off Admiralty would be pruning out trained officers and men from every ship which had been fully employed. Why, he wondered, had they not kept a powerful fleet in commission if they knew war was coming?

Hawkins strode aft and said gruffly, 'All done, sir. The blacking-down will have to wait till this lot's over.'

Triscott had to shout over the hiss and patter of water. 'Morrison never stood a chance, Mr Hawkins!'

The boatswain wiped his thick fingers on some rags and eyed him grimly. 'I 'ope that made 'im feel better, sir.'

240

Triscott watched his burly shape melt into the gloom and sighed.

Another Paice.

Figures groped through the forward hatch and others slithered thankfully into the damp darkness of the messdeck as the watches changed. Dench, the master's mate, was taking over the morning watch and was muttering to Chesshyre, probably discussing the failings of their lieutenants.

Triscott went below and lay fully clothed on the bunk, the one which Bolitho had used.

From the darkness Paice asked, 'All right up top?'

Triscott smiled to himself. Worrying about his *Telemachus*. He never stopped.

'Dench is doing well with the watch, sir.'

Paice said fiercely, 'If I could just make one sighting at first light.' But he heard a gentle snore from the opposite side.

Paice closed his eyes and thought about his wife. He had the word *charisma* on his lips when he, too, fell into an uneasy sleep.

The morning, when it came, was brighter than even Chesshyre had prophesied. A bitter wind which made the sails glisten with ice-rime, and goaded every man's resistance to the limit.

Paice came on deck and consulted the chart and Chesshyre's slate beside the compass box. They did not always agree, but Paice knew Chesshyre was good at his work. It was enough.

He looked up at the curving topmast, the streaming white spear of the long masthead pendant. Wind on the quarter. So they had to be doubly careful. If they covered too many miles they would be hard-put to beat back again for another attempt to seek out the missing cutter.

Paice thought about Queely and wondered if in fact he had found Bolitho for the second part of their hazy plan. *Wakeful* might be in enemy hands. His mind hung on the word. *Enemy.* It somehow changed everything. Perhaps Bolitho was taken too, or worse.

He pounded his hands together. Bolitho should never have been sent to Kent, for recruiting, if that was truly the reason, and certainly not for a wild scheme like this one.

He should be in command of a real man-of-war. A captain

others would follow; whose subordinates would learn more than the rudiments of battle but also the need for humility.

Triscott came aft from inspecting the overnight repairs and splicing, a boatswain's mate close at his heels. He looked even younger in this grey light, Paice thought. His face all fresh and burned with cold.

Triscott touched his hat, testing his commander's mood. 'All secure, sir.' He waited, noting the strain and deep lines on Paice's features. 'I've had the gunner put men to work on the six-pounder tackles. The ice and snow have jammed every block.'

Paice nodded absently. 'As well you noticed.' The usual hesitation. Then, 'Good.'

Paice turned to the master's muffled figure beside the tiller. 'What do you make of the weather, Mr Chesshyre?'

Triscott saw them face one another, more like adversaries than men who served together in this tiny, cramped community.

Chesshyre accepted the flag of truce.

'It should be clear and fine, sir.' He pointed across the bulwark, below which some men were manhandling one of the stocky six-pounders behind its sealed port.

'See yonder, sir? Patch o' blue!'

Paice sighed. Nobody had mentioned it, but there was no sign of *Snapdragon*.

Triscott saw him glance at the masthead and said, 'I've put a good man up there, sir.'

Paice exclaimed, 'Did I ask you?' He shrugged heavily. 'Forgive me. It is wrong to use authority on those who cannot strike back.'

Triscott kept his face immobile. *Bolitho's words.* He was still fretting about it. He offered, 'There is a lot of mist, sir. In this wind –'

Paice stared at him. 'Did you hear?'

Chesshyre dragged the hood from over his salt-matted hair. *'I did!'*

Men stood motionless at their many and varied tasks, as if frozen so. The cook halfway through the hatch on his way to prepare something hot, or at least warm, for the watchkeepers. Big Luke Hawkins, a marlinspike gripped in one iron-hard hand, his eyes alert, remembering perhaps. Maddock the carpenter, clutching his old hat to his wispy hair as he paused in measuring some timber he had brought from the hold for some particular task. Chesshyre and Triscott, even Godsalve the clerk, acting purser and, when required, a fair hand as a tailor, all waited and listened in the chilling air.

Paice said abruptly, 'Six-pounders, eh, Mr Hawkins?'

His voice seemed to break the spell, so that men began to move again, staring about them as if they could not recall what they had been doing.

Triscott suggested, 'Maybe it's *Wakeful*, sir.'

Chesshyre rubbed his unshaven chin. 'Or *Snapdragon*?'

The air seemed to quiver, so that some of the men working below deck felt the distant explosion beat into the lower hull as if *Telemachus* had been fired on.

Paice wanted to lick his lips but knew some of the seamen were watching him. Gun by gun, booming across the water.

He clenched his fingers into fists. He wanted to yell up to the masthead lookout, but knew the man needed no persuading. Triscott had chosen him specially. He would be the first to hail the deck when he could see something.

Paice heard the boatswain's mate murmur, 'Could be either, I suppose.'

He thrust his hands beneath his coat-tails to hide them from view.

The regular explosions boomed across the sea's face once again, and he said, 'Whoever it is, they're facing the enemy's iron *this* day!'

Spray burst over *Wakeful*'s weather side and flooded down the steeply sloping deck. Even the most experienced hands aboard had to cling to something as the hull laid hard over until to any novice it would seem she must turn turtle.

Queely yelled, 'She's close as she'll answer, sir!' His salt-reddened eyes peered at the huge mainsail, then at the foresail and jib. Each one was sheeted hard-in until they were laid almost fore-and-aft down the cutter's centre line, forcing her into the wind, every other piece of canvas lashed into submission.

Bolitho did not have time to consult the compass but guessed that Queely had swung *Wakeful* some five points into the wind; the lee gunports were awash, and the water seemed to boil as she plunged across the lively crests. When he looked for the brigantine she already seemed a long way astern, her sails retrimmed while she bore away on the opposite tack.

As he had been hauled aboard Bolitho had said, 'We must stand between *La Revanche* and the Frenchman. The brigantine is fast enough, and given time she might reach safety, or at least lie beneath a coastal battery until help can be sent.'

He had seen Queely's quick understanding. No talk of victory, no empty promise of survival. They were to save the brigantine, and they would pay the price.

Bolitho stared up at the masthead as the lookout yelled, 'Corvette, sir!'

Queely grimaced. 'Twenty guns at least.' He looked away. 'I keep seeing Kempthorne. I used him badly. That is hard to forgive.'

Bolitho saw Allday moving carefully aft from the forehatch, his cutlass thrust through his belt. The words seemed to repeat themselves. *Of one company.*

Queely watched the sails shaking and banging, taking the full thrust of the wind.

He said, 'Must have veered some more. From the north, I'd say.' He puffed out his cheeks. 'It feels like it too!'

They all heard the sudden crack of cannon fire, and then the lookout shouted, 'Sail closin' the corvette, sir!'

There were more shots, the sounds spiteful over the lively wave crests.

Queely said guardedly, 'Small guns, sir.' He glanced at his men along either side, drenched with spray and flying spindrift, trying to protect their powder and flintlocks. 'Like ours.'

Bolitho frowned. It would be just like Paice. Coming to look for them. He tensed as a measured broadside thundered across the water. He saw the sea-mist waver and twist high above the surface, and for those few moments the other vessel was laid bare. Even without a telescope he saw the lithe silhouette of a square-rigged man-of-war, gunsmoke fanning downwind from

244

her larboard battery. The other vessel was beyond her, but there was no mistaking the great mainsail, its boom sweeping across the waves as she bore down on the French corvette.

Bolitho gritted his teeth. The corvette was like a small frigate, and probably mounted only nine-pounders. But against a cutter she was a leviathan.

Queely yelled, 'Another point!'

The helmsman shouted, 'West-Nor'-West, sir!' He did not have to add that she was as close to the wind as she had ever sailed; there was hardly a man who could stand upright.

Bolitho said, 'Bring her about.' He saw Queely's indecision. 'If we turn back, we may stand across his course, and still have time to turn again.'

Bangs echoed against the hull as Queely yelled, 'Stand by to come about! *Let go and haul!*'

As the helm went over, the cutter seemed to rise towards the sky, her bowsprit and flapping jib lifting and lifting until the sea boiled over the side and swept aft like breakers. Men fell cursing and gasping, others seized their friends and dragged them to their feet as the receding water tried to sweep them over the bulwarks.

But she was answering, and as she swayed over on the opposite tack Bolitho felt like cheering, even though each minute was one gone from his life.

Queely shouted, 'Hold her! Steady as you go!' He beckoned frantically – 'Two more hands on the tiller!'

The master glared at him, then called, 'Steady she is, sir! East by North!'

Bolitho snatched up a glass and sought out the corvette.

There she was, now on the larboard quarter, as if their whole world had pivoted round. *La Revanche* was almost lost in mist and spray, standing away as fast as she could. Queely's master's mate had even managed to set her topsail and royal.

He waited for the deck to steady again and tried to ignore the bustle of figures around and past him as the mainsail was sheeted home on the opposite tack.

He trained the glass with care and saw the corvette fire again, the smoke momentarily blotting her out but not before he had found the other cutter, and had seen the sea around her bursting with waterspouts and falling spray. The cutter was still pressing closer, and he saw her side flash with bright orange tongues as she fired her small broadside.

Queely said savagely, 'Vatass has no chance at that range, damn it!' He saw the question in Bolitho's eyes and explained, 'It's him. *Snapdragon* has a darker jib than the rest of us.' He winced as another fall of shot appeared to bracket the cutter. But *Snapdragon* pushed through the falling curtain of spray, her guns still firing, although, as Queely suspected, it was doubtful if a single ball would reach the French corvette.

Bolitho tried to ignore the twisting shape of the cutter and concentrated on the enemy. She was maintaining the same tack as before and steering almost south-east. Her captain had seen *La Revanche* and would let nothing stand in his way.

Queely exclaimed, '*Snapdragon* must have sighted us, sir!' He sounded incredulous as he raised his glass again, his lips moving as he identified the pinpricks of colour which had broken from *Snapdragon*'s topsail yard.

He said hoarsely, 'Signal reads, *Enemy in sight*, sir!'

Bolitho looked at him, sharing his sudden emotion. It was Vatass's way of telling them that they were at war. Trying to warn him before it was too late.

Bolitho said, 'Run up another flag.' He looked along the crowded deck, at the men who waited for the inevitable. 'It will give him heart!'

With two White Ensigns streaming from gaff and masthead, *Wakeful* prepared to come about yet again. The manoeuvre would stand her across the enemy's path and make it impossible for the corvette to avoid an embrace. Once in close action, *Snapdragon* might be able to attack her stern, with luck even rake her with a carronade as she crossed her wake. He held his breath as a hole punched through *Snapdragon*'s topsail and the wind tore it to ribbons before it could be reefed.

The corvette fired again, each broadside perfectly timed. No wonder this captain had been selected for the task, Bolitho thought. He raised the glass, but mist and gunsmoke made it impossible to see the horizon.

He looked at Allday by the compass box. *Where is Paice?*

Allday saw his expression and tried to smile. But all he could think of was the man-of-war which was closing on them with every sail set and filled to the wind. He looked at the men on *Wakeful*'s deck. Popguns against nine-pounders, an open deck with no gangways or packed hammock nettings to protect them from the splinters. How would they face up to it? Would they see there was nothing but death at the end of it?

He thought of Lieutenant Kempthorne and all the others he had seen drop in a sea-fight. Proud, brave men for the most part, who had whimpered and screamed when they were cut down. The lucky ones died then and there, and were spared the agony of a surgeon's knife.

Here there was not even a sawbones. Maybe that was all to the good. Allday watched Bolitho's fingers close around the sword at his side. It had to end somewhere, so why not here?

He winced as the guns thundered yet again, closer still, the shots churning the sea into jagged crests, or whipping off the white horses like invisible dolphins at play.

He tried to think of his time in London, the nights in Maggie's tiny room, with her buxom body pressed against his in the darkness. Perhaps one day – the guns roared out across the shortening range and he heard several of the watching seamen give groans of dismay.

Queely shouted harshly, 'Stand to, damn you! Prepare to come about! Topmen aloft, lively now!'

Bolitho heard the edge in his voice. Its finality. It was not even going to be a battle this time.

Lieutenant Paice yelled at the masthead, '*Repeat that!*' The last roll of cannon fire had drowned the man's voice.

The lookout shouted, '*Snapdragon*'s signallin', sir! *Enemy in sight!*'

Paice released his breath very slowly. Thank God for a good lookout. It was what they had planned should they find *Wakeful*. Where she was, so would be Bolitho.

Paice lifted his glass and saw the mist moving aside, even the smoke thinning to its persistent thrust. He saw the French vessel some two miles directly ahead, framed in *Telemachus*'s shrouds as if in a net. She was running with the wind directly under her coat-tails, her sails iron-hard. Paice saw *Snapdragon* for the first time, her frail outline just overlapping the enemy's quarter and surrounded by bursting spray from that last fall of shot. Her topsail had been shredded, and there were several holes in her mainsail; otherwise she appeared to be untouched, and as he peered through the glass until his eyes watered he saw Vatass's guns returning fire, their progress marked by thin tendrils of foam, well short of a target.

There was another vessel moving away from the embattled ships. Paice guessed it was either an unwilling spectator, or the one Bolitho was expected to escort back to England. Then he saw *Wakeful*, sweeping out of the mist, her sails flapping then filling as she completed her tack and swung once more towards the enemy.

Triscott broke into his thoughts. 'Why does the Frog stay on that tack, sir? I'd go for *Snapdragon*, if I were her commander, and lessen the odds. He must surely see us by now?'

Somebody dropped a handspike and Paice was about to shout a reprimand when he remembered what Triscott had told him about the six-pounders.

'The Frenchman has been under way all night, up and down, searching for Captain Bolitho, I suspect. My guess is that her running rigging is so swollen she can barely change tack – her blocks are probably frozen solid!' He gestured towards *Telemachus*'s spread of canvas. 'Here the wind does the work for us.' There was contempt in his tone. 'Over yonder even musclepower won't shift those yards until the day warms up!' He sounded excited. 'So they'll have to reef, or stand and fight!'

There was a great sigh from some of the hands and Paice saw *Snapdragon* stagger as some of the enemy's balls slammed home. But she came upright again and pressed on with her attack.

Paice swore angrily. 'Fall back, you young fool!' He swung on Triscott. 'Set the stuns'ls and shake out every reef! I want this cutter to *fly*!'

As the studding-sail booms were run out from the yard, the mast bent forward under the additional strain. The sea seemed to rush down either beam, so that some of the gun crews stood up and cheered without knowing why.

Paice folded his arms and studied the other vessels. *Hounds around a stag.* He swallowed hard as the tall waterspouts shot skyward along *Snapdragon*'s engaged side. The damage was hidden from view, but Paice saw rigging curling and parting, then, slowly at first, the tall mainmast began to reel down into the smoke. In the sudden lull of firing he heard the thundering crash of the mast and spars sweeping over the forecastle, tearing men and guns in its wake of trailing shrouds and rigging until with a great splash it swayed over the bows like a fallen tree. Tiny figures appeared through the wreckage where nobody should have been left alive, and in the weak sunlight Paice saw the gleam of axes as Vatass's men hacked at the broken rigging, or fought their way to messmates trapped underneath.

Some of the corvette's larboard battery must have been trained as far round in their ports as they could bear. Paice watched through his glass and saw the shadows of the enemy's guns lengthen against the hull as they were levered towards the quarter. He shifted his horrified stare to *Snapdragon*. It was impossible to see her as another graceful cutter. She was a listing, mastless wreck already down by the bows, her shattered jolly-boat drifting away from the side amidst the flotsam of planking and torn canvas.

Triscott exclaimed in a strangled voice, 'They'd not fire on her now!'

The after divisions of guns belched out flame and smoke together. It was like a single, heart-stopping explosion. Paice could even feel the weight of the iron's strength as *Snapdragon* was swept from bow to stern, timber, decking, men and pieces of men flung into the air like grisly rubbish. When it finally fell it pockmarked the sea with white feathers, strangely gentle in the pale sunlight.

Snapdragon began to capsize, her broken hull surrounded by huge, obscene bubbles.

Paice watched with his glass. He did not want to forget it, and knew he never would.

He saw the deck tilting towards him, a corpse in a lieutenant's coat sliding through blood and splinters, then rising up against the bulwark as if to offer a last command. Then *Snapdragon* gave a groan, as if she was the one who was dying, and disappeared beneath the whirlpool of pathetic fragments.

Paice found that he was sucking in the bitter air as if he had just been running. His head swam, and he wanted to roar and bellow like a bull. But nothing came. It was too terrible even for that.

When he spoke again his voice was almost calm.

He said, 'All guns load, double-shotted!' He sought out Triscott by the mast; his face was as white as a sheet. 'Did you see that? The Frenchie made no attempt to bear up on –' he hesitated, unable to say the name of the ship he had just seen destroyed. Vatass, so keen and unworldly, hoping for promotion, wiped away like the master's calculations on his slate. *Because of me. I forced him to put to sea.* He faced Triscott again. 'She'd have been in irons if she had. I reckon her running rigging is frozen as solid as a rock!'

Triscott wiped his lips with the back of his hand. 'But how long –'

He was close to vomiting.

'It don't matter, and it don't signify, Mr Triscott! We'll rake that bugger an' maybe Captain Bolitho can put a ball or two through *him*!'

Triscott nodded. 'Prepare to shorten sail!' He was glad of something to do. Anything which might hold back the picture of *Snapdragon*'s terrible death. It was like watching his own fate in a nightmare.

Paice moved aft and joined Chesshyre beside the helmsmen. From here he could see the full length and breadth of his small command. Within the hour she might share *Snapdragon*'s grave. He was surprised that he could face the prospect without pain. His fate, his *lot* would be decided for him. There was no choice open to any one of them.

He saw the master-at-arms and Glynn, a boatswain's mate, passing out cutlasses and axes from the chest, and below the raked mast another handful of men were loading muskets under the watchful eye of a gunner's mate. It kept them busy as the enemy vessel grew in size, lying in their path like a glistening barricade. He saw the gunner's mate gesturing towards the mast,

250

doubtless explaining that a good marksman could play havoc with men crowded together on a ship's deck. He had picked the men himself, each one an excellent shot.

Paice nodded as if in agreement; a seaman called Inskip had held up his fist and then hurried to the weather shrouds. A good choice. Inskip had been a poacher in Norfolk before he had found his way into the navy by way of the local assizes.

Chesshyre said dryly, 'Better him than me, sir.'

Paice knew that Inskip would be more than mindful of *Snapdragon*'s mast plunging down into the sea. Nobody working aloft or around it would have survived. The corvette's captain had made certain of those who had.

Chesshyre muttered, *'My God!'*

Paice walked to the side as *Telemachus*'s stem smashed through some drifting wreckage. A torn jacket, what looked like a chart, splinters as thick as fingers, and the inevitable corpses, bobbing and reeling aside as *Telemachus* surged through them.

He said roughly, 'I'll lay odds you wish you was in the East India Company!'

A puff of smoke drifted from the corvette's side, and seconds later a ball sliced across the sea before hurling up a waterspout half-a-cable beyond the bows.

Paice growled, 'Close enough, Mr Chesshyre.' He crossed to the compass box and peered at the card. 'Bring her up two points.' He eyed him impassively. 'We'll go for his flanks, eh?'

Chesshyre nodded, angry with himself because his teeth were chattering uncontrollably.

He said, 'Ready aft! Put the helm down! Steer South by West!' Then he watched as the corvette showed herself beyond the shrouds as if she had only now begun to move.

Paice watched the enemy loose off another shot, but it was well clear.

Shorten sail or stand and fight.

He saw *Wakeful*'s jib and foresail hardening on the new tack, the canvas clean and pale in the early sunshine.

Chesshyre called, 'We don't even know why we're here!'

Paice did not turn on him. He knew Chesshyre was afraid, and he needed him now as never before.

251

'D'you need a reason, then?'

Chesshyre thought of *Snapdragon*, the corpses bobbing around her like gutted fish.

Paice was right. In the end it would make no difference.

17

Ships Of War

Bolitho mopped his streaming face for the hundredth time and watched *Wakeful*'s seamen sheeting the mainsail home, while others swarmed aloft in the freezing wind to execute the next command.

Yet again *Wakeful* had fought round in a tight arc to her original course, with the approaching corvette lying directly across the starboard bow. The enemy would have the wind-gage, but for *Wakeful*'s small guns it might be their only advantage.

'*Loose tops'l!*' Queely was everywhere, never more acutely aware of Kempthorne's loss.

Bolitho could see it, the gangling lieutenant swinging around, the gaping hole in his throat. Then nothing. He plucked the sodden shirt away from his skin, another reminder of the man who had stopped a ball which had been intended for him.

Queely came aft again, his chest heaving. 'What now, sir?'

Bolitho pointed to the scarred jolly-boat. 'Drop it outboard.'

The boatswain glanced at Queely as if for confirmation. Queely nodded curtly. 'Do it!'

Bolitho watched the spare hands hoisting the boat up and over the lee bulwark. Like all sailors they were reluctant, fearful even of letting go of their only boat. Bolitho knew from experience it would have been the same had there been ten times as many people in the company, and still only one boat. Always the last hope.

Queely understood although he lacked experience of it.

He was saying, 'We'll have enough splinters flying about before too long, man!'

Bolitho waited for the boatswain to hurry away to tend to some frayed rigging. The choppy sea and freezing wind could play havoc with even the best cordage.

He glanced around the deck. 'Have all the hammocks brought up and lashed around the after gratings. It will give the helmsmen some protection.' He did not add that an unprotected deck could be swept into a bloody shambles by one well-aimed burst of grape. It gave every man something to do. After *Snapdragon*'s destruction they needed to be busy even in the face of the oncoming corvette.

La Revanche had seemingly vanished, tacking back and forth, each precious minute taking her away from the drifting smoke which still floated above the sea where *Snapdragon* had dived for the bottom.

They had not been able to see much of the encounter, but the broadside which had followed *Snapdragon*'s last futile shots had stunned all of them.

Bolitho saw Allday supervising the stacking and lashing of the tightly lashed hammocks. In battle, even a strip of canvas gave an impression of safety to those denied protection.

Allday crossed to his side and said, 'She'll be up to us in twenty minutes, Cap'n.' He sounded unusually desperate. 'What can we hit her with?'

'*Telemachus* has run out her stuns'ls, sir!' Another voice muttered, 'Gawd! Watch 'er go!'

Bolitho saw the other cutter surging across the diagonal ranks of angry white horses, her hull dominated by her sails, her stem and forecastle rising and dipping in great banks of bursting spray.

Bolitho took a telescope and rested it against Allday's shoulder. It took time to train it on *Telemachus* and as soon as he had found her he saw one empty gunport, like a missing tooth. Paice had forgotten none of the things Bolitho had brought to their small flotilla. He was at this moment manhandling his second carronade over to larboard so that both could be laid on the corvette.

254

The enemy fired again, but the ball fell outside his vision. It was strange that the corvette did not alter course just long enough to pour a full broadside on the approaching cutter. It was unlikely that such a compact man-of-war would mount stern-chasers, and she could not fail to miss as the range dwindled away between the two vessels.

Queely shouted, 'She's coming for us, sir!'

Bolitho watched the corvette. She was almost bows-on now, her canvas tall above *Wakeful*'s starboard bow. He could see her flag whipping from the gaff, and was glad Brennier had at least been spared that.

'Shall I shorten, sir?' Queely was watching him, as if trying to shut out the menace of the oncoming enemy.

'No. Speed is all we have. Hold her on this tack, then put the helm up when we cross their path. We can luff, but only with speed in the sails!' He looked along the crouching gun crews. 'I suggest you bring the men from the larboard battery.' Their eyes met and Bolitho added gently, 'I fear we will take heavy losses if they manage to rake us. The weather bulwark will give them some cover at least.'

A whistle shrilled and the men scampered across from the other battery. They ran half-crouching as if already under fire, their faces stiff and pinched, and suddenly aged.

Queely made himself turn and stare at the corvette. He said, 'Why does she hold so straight a path?'

Bolitho thought he knew. In this icy north wind and after the snow and sleet it was likely that every piece of her rigging was packed solid. It was also possible that the corvette had spent most of the past months in harbour while the loyalty or otherwise of France's sea-officers was decided. Her company would be unused to this kind of work. *Wakeful*'s company was also new to it, but each and every hand was a prime seaman. It was pointless to mention his thoughts to Queely. It might offer a gleam of hope where there was none to be had. If the corvette was able to destroy or cripple the remaining cutters she could still chase and catch *La Revanche* before she reached a place of safety.

He hardened his heart. It was their sole reason for being here. To delay this enemy ship no matter what.

Bolitho raised the telescope again and saw *Telemachus*'s topsail yard brace round, her hull merge then vanish beyond the corvette. Above the sounds of sea and wind he heard the faint crackle of musket fire, the harder bang of a swivel.

Then there was a double explosion and for a moment longer Bolitho imagined that the corvette did after all carry stern-chasers, and had fired directly into the cutter as she veered wildly across her quarter.

Queely muttered thickly, 'Hell, he's damned close!'

Bolitho saw smoke billow over the corvette's poop and knew Paice had fired both of his carronades into her stern. If one of those murderous balls managed to pierce the crowded gundeck it would keep them occupied until *Wakeful* was able to engage.

He heard the crack of Paice's six-pounders and saw a hole appear in the enemy's main topsail, some rigging part and stream out in the wind. But she was still coming, and Bolitho could see the details of her beakhead without the need of a glass, the white painted figure beneath it holding some sort of branch in one outthrust hand.

'*Stand by on deck!*' Queely swung round, his eyes angry as if searching for Kempthorne. He saw Bolitho watching him and gave a small shrug, but it said everything.

Then he drew his hanger and held it above his head. 'We fire on the uproll, my lads!'

Bolitho saw their despairing faces. The way they pressed close together, friend with friend, waiting to fight and die.

The corvette was sliding across the starboard quarter, and marksmen were already firing from her forecastle, one insolently straddling a cathead with his legs to obtain a better aim.

A musket banged out from below the mast and Bolitho saw the Frenchman hurl his weapon into the sea below as if it had become red-hot, before toppling from the cathead and plunging down the side.

Allday muttered, 'Good shot, matey!'

The tiller went over and as blocks squealed and the forecourse and topsail yards were hauled taut, *Wakeful* seemed to pivot round to windward when minutes before it had seemed she would be run down by the enemy.

256

'*Fire!*' The six-pounders cracked out in a ragged salvo, the double-shotted muzzles spitting their orange tongues as the trucks squealed inboard on their tackles.

Queely yelled, '*Stand fast!*' He waved down some of the gun crews who were about to sponge out and reload. '*Take cover!*' The hanger gleamed in the smoky sunshine as Queely signalled to the carronade crew. '*As you bear!*' The gun captain jerked his lanyard and the ugly, snub-nosed 'smasher' lurched back on its slide, the heavy ball exploding against the corvette's gangway, blasting one of the nine-pounders from its port, and flinging splintered woodwork and ripped hammocks over the side.

Bolitho watched the corvette's exposed battery recoil. The two attacks had broken their timing, and the broadside was ragged, each one firing independently.

Bolitho tensed as a ball smacked through the mainsail and another parted some rigging and struck the sea far abeam. One gun had been loaded with grape and canister and Bolitho ducked as the charge exploded over the maindeck, hurling shattered planking into the air, and thudding into the opposite bulwark where the gun crews would otherwise have been crouching.

Queely shouted, 'Reload!' He stared wildly at his men. Not one had been hit, although a splintered piece of wood had been hurled into the hammocks around the helmsmen with the accuracy of a spear.

And there was *Telemachus*. As *Wakeful* charged past the enemy's poop, they all saw the other cutter tacking around to follow the corvette on the same course.

It took longer to bring *Wakeful* about and under control again. With so much sail, it was like trying to slow a runaway team of horses. The corvette lay directly ahead of them, with the cutters using wind and rudder to hold station on either quarter as if they were escorting her rather than forcing another engagement.

The corvette's captain seemed unwilling to wear ship and confront them. But the cutters were unable to damage the enemy vessel without overhauling her. And the next time the French captain would be ready.

Bolitho watched Paice manoeuvring his cutter closer and closer, the occasional stab of musket fire exchanged between the

257

ill-matched vessels. *Telemachus* had been badly mauled, and Bolitho had seen there was a hole punched through her hull, just a few feet above the waterline, before she had changed tack to continue her attack.

Sunlight flashed across the corvette's stern-windows and Bolitho raised his glass to read the name painted on her counter.

La Foi. So the girl's figurehead must be Faith. In the stained lens he saw heads moving on the corvette's poop, the flash of muskets, an officer pointing with his speaking trumpet. He also saw the massive scars on her lower hull where one of Paice's carronades had found its mark. A foot or so higher and – he stiffened as two of the stern-windows shattered and pitched into the vessel's frothing wake.

For one more moment he thought a lucky shot had hit the stern, although reason told him that none of Paice's guns would yet bear.

Then he stared with sick realisation as another window was smashed out, and the black muzzle of a nine-pounder thrust into view.

'Signal *Telemachus* to stand away!' Bolitho had to seize Queely's arm to make him realise what was happening. 'They'll blow him out of the water!'

But *Wakeful* was a good cable's length astern of Paice's cutter, and nobody aboard was bothering to look and see what she was doing. Paice had at last realised what was happening. Bolitho saw the yards coming round, the mainsail suddenly free and flapping wildly as Paice let her sway over while she took the wind across her beam.

Bolitho watched anxiously. Paice was doing what he thought was best. Lose the wind, but stand away from the onrushing *Wakeful* and so avoid a collision.

Bolitho snapped, 'We'll engage to larboard!' He did not want to take his eyes from the two vessels ahead, but needed to watch the mast and bulging topsail. *Wakeful* was tearing through the waves; the mast must be curving forward under such a pressure and weight of canvas and spars.

He turned his head, and at that very moment *La Foi* fired her hastily-rigged stern-chaser.

258

Queely shouted, 'More grape!' He wiped his eyes wildly. 'She's still answering, sir!'

Telemachus was certainly under command, but her sails were pockmarked with holes, and, as he lifted his glass again, Bolitho saw bodies on her deck, a man on his knees as if he was praying, before he too fell lifeless.

He wanted to look away but watched as two thin threads of scarlet ran from the washports to merge with the creaming sea alongside. Like seeing a ship bleeding to death, as if there was no human hand aboard.

Wakeful's men were staring over the bulwark, the gun crews from the opposite side hurrying to join their comrades for the next embrace.

Bolitho said, 'It'll take time to load and train that gun with makeshift tackles.' He looked at Queely, his gaze calm. 'We must be up to her before she can use it on us.'

They bore down on *Telemachus* and Bolitho saw men working like demons at halliards and braces, others clawing their way up broken ratlines to discard or repair damaged rigging.

He saw a lieutenant amongst some fallen rigging and knew it was Triscott. Then right aft near the tiller, Paice's tall figure, with one hand thrust inside his coat. He might have injured it, Bolitho thought, but it was somehow reassuring to see him there, in his place. As *Wakeful* swept past Bolitho saw Paice turn and look across the tumbling waves, then very slowly raise his hat. It was strangely moving, and some of *Wakeful*'s men raised a ragged cheer.

Allday stepped nearer, his cutlass over his shoulder while he watched the other ship's stern rise above the larboard bow. He had been a gun captain himself aboard the old *Resolution* before he had met up with Bolitho. But then Allday had turned his hand to most things.

He knew better than most that if they overhauled the French ship they would be destroyed by her main battery. At close quarters like this, *Wakeful* would be pounded to fragments in minutes. Their only hope of delaying the corvette long enough to be worthwhile was to hit her with a carronade with no chance of a miss. For if they remained on the enemy's quarter, the impro-

259

vised stern-chaser would finish them just as brutally.

He saw a musket fire from the French ship and heard a spent ball slap into the deck nearby. In minutes, each ball could be deadly, and he stood close to Bolitho, just so that he would know he was here when it happened.

Bolitho said, 'I would that we were in *Tempest*, old friend.' He spoke quietly, so that Allday could barely hear him above the chorus of wind and sea.

He added in the same unemotional voice, 'I shall always remember her.'

Allday watched him grimly. Who did he mean? *Tempest* or his lady, Viola?

He heard Queely shouting to his gun crews, saw a terrified ship's boy dash past with fresh charges for the six-pounders, and one of the seamen of the boatswain's party staring at the deck, his lips moving as though in prayer, or repeating someone's name.

He saw all and none of it. Bolitho had shared something with him, as he always did.

Allday lifted his chin and saw a movement in the corvette's stern-windows. It was almost over. He stared up at the sky. *Please God, let it be quick!*

Lieutenant Andrew Triscott tore his eyes from *Wakeful*'s straining sails and made himself turn inboard again. He had thought he was prepared for this, had trained himself to accept the inevitable when it came. Instead he could only stare at the utter chaos on *Telemachus*'s deck, fallen rigging and scorched pieces of canvas, and worst of all the blood which ran unchecked into the scuppers. He had never believed there could be so much blood.

Faces he had come to know, some dead, others screwed up in agony, like strangers.

He heard Paice's strong voice forcing through the noise and confusion. 'Clear those men from the guns!'

Triscott nodded, still unable to speak. He clung to Paice's strength like a drowning man groping for a piece of flotsam in the sea. He saw Chesshyre by the tiller, two helmsmen down, one gasping with pain as his companion tied a rough bandage around his arm to staunch the bleeding. Triscott retched helplessly. The second man was headless, and he saw some of his blood and bone spattered across Paice's breeches.

The boatswain swam into Triscott's blurred vision, his face smeared with powder smoke, his eyes like coals.

'You all right, sir?' He did not wait for an answer. 'I'll muster some spare 'ands!'

Triscott stared round, half-expecting to find nobody alive, but Paice's powerful voice and the burly boatswain's angry gestures with a boarding axe brought them from cover, while others dragged themselves from beneath fallen sails and cordage. Obedient even in the face of death, from fear or from habit, or because they did not know how else to act.

Triscott lurched away from the bulwark and saw some of the bloodied corpses being dropped over the side. The wounded were taken to the main hatch or aft to the companionway, their cries and screams ignored as they were hauled to some kind of safety.

Triscott had seen Paice raise his hat to the other cutter, and wondered how he could stand there, with the ship shaking herself apart around him.

Paice seemed to read his mind from half the deck's length away.

He shouted, 'Stand to the guns again, Mr Triscott! Point the carronades yourself!'

Triscott realised that he was still gripping his hanger, the one his father had given him when he had passed for lieutenant.

He saw the gunner's body being toppled over the side. A dour but dedicated man, who had helped Triscott many times when he had learned the ways of handling the cutter's weapons. Now he was drifting away from the hull, no longer a face at gun-drill, or yelling threats to his own special party of seamen. Triscott stuffed his fist into his mouth to prevent himself from crying out aloud.

Hawkins rejoined him and said harshly, 'It's up to you, sir.' He regarded him steadily and without sympathy. 'We must engage again. *Wakeful's* trying to close with the enemy. She'll never manage unsupported!'

Triscott stared aft, seeking the aid which had always been there.

261

Hawkins said flatly, 'You'll get no 'elp there, Mr Triscott. 'E's badly wounded.' He watched his words sink in and added relentlessly, 'The master's as scared as shite, 'e'll not be much use.' He stood back, forcing himself to ignore the shouts and demands which came from every side. He had to make Triscott understand if only for a moment longer. '*You're* the lieutenant, *sir.*'

Triscott stared at Paice who was gripping the compass box, one hand still thrust inside his coat. His eyes were tightly shut, his teeth bared as if to bite back the pain. Then he saw the blood which had soaked the left side of Paice's breeches, all the way from beneath his coat to the deck around him. He had been hit in the side.

Hawkins persisted, 'Took a piece of iron the size of three fingers in his ribs. God dammit, I tried to get 'im to let me –' He watched the lieutenant, his voice suddenly desperate. 'So act like *'im*, sir, even if you does feel like runnin' to yer mother!'

Triscott nodded jerkily. 'Yes. Yes, thank you, Mr Hawkins.' He looked at the watching faces. 'We shall follow *Wakeful*, and attack to –' He hesitated, thinking of the dead gunner. 'To larboard. There's no time to transfer the carronades this time.'

The boatswain frowned and then touched his arm. '*That's* more like it.' He turned to the others nearby. 'The lieutenant says we'll engage to larboard!' He brandished the axe. 'So stand to, lads! Man the braces there!'

From aft Paice watched the sudden bustle, with even injured men limping to their stations, the sudden response as the punctured mainsail tugged at the long boom and filled reluctantly to the wind. He dragged himself to the tiller, the remaining helmsmen moving to give him room.

He gripped the well-worn tiller bar and felt his *Telemachus* answering him through the sea and rudder. His head dropped; he jerked up his chin, suddenly angry, and doubly determined.

God Almighty, what a bloody mess. He did not know or care if he had spoken aloud. A terrified lieutenant, and a third of his company killed or wounded. Two guns upended, and so many holes in the remaining sails they would be hard put to put about when the worst happened.

262

He closed his eyes and gasped while the agony lunged through him. Each time it was worse, each one like the thrust of a heated blade. He had bunched his waistcoat and shirt into a tight ball against the wound, and could feel his blood soaking his side and leg. It felt warm while the rest of his body was shaking and icy cold.

'Steady, men!' He peered forward but the compass seemed too misty to read. He said thickly, 'Steer for the bugger's quarter!'

Chesshyre cried, '*Wakeful*'s nearly there!'

Paice leaned hard on the tiller and growled, 'Get up on your feet, man! D'you want the people to see you cringing like a frightened cur?'

Chesshyre scrambled upright and stared at him wildly. '*God damn you!*'

'He most likely will!'

He heard Triscott yell, 'All loaded, sir!' Paice hoped that nobody else had guessed just how terrified Triscott really was. But his was the true courage, he thought. More afraid of showing fear than of fear itself.

Hawkins hurried toward him, his gaze taking in the blood and Paice's ashen features.

He said, '*Wakeful*'s goin' to engage, sir! But I reckon the Frogs 'as got their chaser rigged again!'

Paice nodded, for a moment longer unable to speak. Then he asked, 'What can you see now, Mr Hawkins?'

Hawkins turned away, his eyes burning. He had served with Paice longer than anyone. He respected him more than any other man, and to see him like this was worse than the stark death which had torn the decks open in a merciless bombardment. Now he could barely see. Hawkins said, 'She's up to 'er starboard quarter!' He slammed his hands together and shouted, 'The stern-chaser is runnin' out, sir!'

The explosions seemed joined as one, the stern-chaser's sharper note almost lost as *Wakeful*'s carronade belched fire at point-blank range even as her bowsprit outreached the enemy's quarter.

Paice asked, '*Well?* What's happened?'

Hawkins said, 'Not sure, sir. *Wakeful*'s payin' off.' He could

263

not bear to look at Paice. 'Their jib and fores'l are shot away.'

'And the enemy – speak up, man!'

Hawkins watched the other vessel. The carronade had blasted away the stern windows and must have completely destroyed the makeshift stern-chaser. But otherwise she seemed intact, with only her foresail in disarray. Some of her hands were swarming aloft, and he saw the corvette begin to change course for the first time.

Then he said with chilled disbelief, 'I think 'er steerin's gone, sir!'

Paice gripped his shoulder and shook him. *'Thank God!'* He peered along the torn and littered deck. 'Ready there?'

Triscott called aft, 'Aye, sir!'

Paice forced a grin. 'We'll close with her now, before the buggers can rig new steering-gear!'

Hawkins asked urgently, 'Will you let me fix a bandage?'

Their eyes met and Paice said, 'You bloody fool. We both know the truth.' Then he grimaced as the pain came back. 'But I thank you, and I plead to my Maker that you see another dawn break, Mr Hawkins!'

Hawkins swung away and waved his axe at some unemployed gun crews.

'To me, lads! Stand by to wear ship!'

He thought he heard faint cheering, and when he peered through the drifting smoke he saw *Wakeful* falling with the wind, temporarily out of control, her forecastle torn and splintered by that last charge of grapeshot.

He turned on his heel and shouted, 'They'm cheerin' you, sir!' Then he waved his hat and yelled to his own men, *'Huzza,* lads! *A cheer for Wakeful!'*

They probably thought him mad, with death lurking so close. But it helped to save Hawkins's last reserve of strength. When he had turned aft he had seen that for Paice, victory, like defeat, was already out of reach.

Bolitho crouched on his hands and knees, his mind and ears cringing to the twin explosions. He had felt the massive charge of grapeshot smash into the bows, the screams and yells of men who

264

had been scythed down even as the carronade had crashed inboard on its slide.

Then Allday's hand was beneath one armpit, lifting him to his feet, and he saw Queely offering him the old sword, which must have been cut from his belt by a single iron splinter. He felt his breeches, the jagged tear. The splinter had been that close.

Then he stared at the enemy's blackened stern. All windows demolished, the counter stove in like wet felt, the ornate taffrail high overhead splintered and unrecognisable.

Queely said hoarsely, 'I think we got her steering, sir!' He looked at him with sudden desperation. 'It's still not enough, is it?'

Bolitho watched the small figures swarming up the corvette's ratlines. Soon they would have a jury-rig, and be ready to face them once more. He shifted his glance to *Wakeful*'s foredeck. Six men dead, several more crawling to safety, or being carried to the hatchway. It was a miracle that anyone had survived.

It would take Queely's men an hour or more to re-rig the foresail and jib, and it was obvious that most of the forward rigging was rendered quite useless.

He watched the corvette turning very slowly, wind, and not rudder, carrying her off course. At this range she would use her broadside to bombard *Wakeful* until she followed *Snapdragon* to the seabed.

Allday exclaimed harshly, 'Here comes *Telemachus*, Cap'n! By God, haven't they taken enough?'

Bolitho saw the other cutter bearing down on the drifting corvette for another attack, her sails in rags, her bulwark and forecastle looking as if they had been torn and gnawed by some nightmare monster.

He said quietly, 'Give them a cheer, Mr Queely. I'd not thought to see such valour this day.'

The cheers echoed across the lively wave crests to the men on the other cutter, and probably to those working aloft aboard *La Foi* whose captain had ordered his stern-chaser to fire just seconds too late. Men were running aft and shooting towards the oncoming cutter, but once under the corvette's quarter there was not a single nine-pounder which could be brought to bear.

265

The two carronades fired within seconds of one another. More debris burst from the stern and up through the deck beyond. The force of the explosion flung men from the gangways, while some even fell from the foresail yard to the deck below.

Bolitho stared until his eyes throbbed. Was it the constant strain, the agony of seeing men cut down, who had never known the savage demands of sea warfare? He seized Queely's arm. '*Is it going?*'

Queely nodded, unable to answer. The corvette's main mast was beginning to topple, held for a while by stays and shrouds until the weight of spars and wind-filled canvas took control. In those few seconds Bolitho saw some of the French sailors who had been sent aloft to free each frozen block by hand, stare down as they realised too late that there was no escape or survival.

Then, with rigging parting like pistol shots, the mast thundered over the side, to be snared by the remaining lines and dragged alongside to make any chance of steering impossible.

Bolitho watched the confusion, and knew that *Telemachus*'s last shots must have exploited the damage left by Queely's carronade.

Queely stared along the deck, his eyes wild, hungry for revenge. For Kempthorne and the others who lay dead and dying, for *Snapdragon*, and for his own command.

He said huskily, 'We can still close with them, sir! God damn them, they'll not be able to move before nightfall!'

The sailing master called anxiously, '*Telemachus* is standing away, sir!' He hesitated, as if he too shared Bolitho's mood. 'She's dipped 'er Ensign, sir!'

Bolitho looked across the smoky water to where *Telemachus* was tacking very slowly away from her crippled adversary.

So Jonas Paice was dead. After all he had suffered, or perhaps because of it, he was now at peace.

Aloud he said firmly, 'There's been enough killing. I'll not countenance cold-blooded murder and smear our name.' His grey eyes lingered on the other battered cutter. No tall figure at her bulwark. He must have been dying then, even as he had doffed his hat in a last salute. 'Or *his* especially. A worthy and honourable man.'

Queely watched him dully, shoulders heaving from the madness of battle.

Bolitho looked at him and added, 'We have saved Brennier and his treasure.' He did not even glance at the drifting corvette which moments earlier had been ready to destroy them all. 'Her captain will pay a more terrible price for his failure – so why fire on his men, who cannot defend themselves?'

He saw Allday watching him, his hands crossed over the hilt of his cutlass.

Bolitho said, 'I'll board *Telemachus* as soon as we can work alongside. I shall take command and pass you a tow.'

'*You* in command, sir?'

Bolitho smiled sadly. 'Mine is the honour this time, Mr Queely.'

Later, as *Wakeful* tugged reluctantly at her towing warp, Bolitho stood by *Telemachus*'s taffrail and looked at the damage, the bloodstains, the *hurt* of this vessel, where it had all begun for him.

Paice's body had been carried below and laid in the cabin. Hawkins the boatswain had asked about burying him at sea with the others. Bolitho had seen the boatswain's rough features soften as he had replied, 'No, Mr Hawkins. We'll lay him with his wife.'

Allday heard and saw all of this, his mind dazed by the impossible shift of events.

The sky was even bluer than when he had looked up and offered his prayer. But his senses refused to accept any of it.

Only when Bolitho drew near him and said gently, 'Look yonder, old friend. Tell me what you see.'

Allday slowly raised his eyes, afraid of what might be there. Then in a small voice he murmured, 'White cliffs, Cap'n.'

Bolitho nodded, sharing the moment with him, and with Paice. 'I never thought to see them again.'

Allday's face split into an unexpected grin.

'An' *that's* no error, Cap'n!'

At eight bells that evening, they saw the murky silhouette of Dover Castle.

The two little ships had come home.

Epilogue

Allday glanced at the rigid marine sentry posted outside the frigate's stern cabin and after a brief hesitation thrust open the door.

He had been surprised to discover that leaving England again had been so easy. There was no knowing what lay ahead, or what the war might mean to him and to his captain. But on the nine days' passage from Spithead aboard this frigate, the thirty-six-gun *Harvester*, it had felt more like a homecoming than some of the anxious moments they had shared in the past.

For a few seconds he stood by the screen door and saw Bolitho framed against the tall stern windows, with a sunlit panorama of sea and hazy coastline turning very slowly beyond as the frigate was laid on her final tack for the anchorage.

In the vivid light the Rock itself was a hint of land, rather than a solid reality; but just the sight of it made Allday tense with excitement, something else he found difficult to explain. Gibraltar was not merely the gateway to the Mediterranean this time. It opened for them a new life, another chance.

He nodded with slow approval. In his best uniform with the white lapels, and the newly adopted epaulettes gleaming on either shoulder, Bolitho was a far cry from the man in the shabby coat, facing the smugglers', then the corvette's, cannon fire with equal determination, and with a defiance which had never left him despite the setbacks, the suffering and the procession of disappointments which had taken them both to the Nore.

Bolitho turned and looked at him. 'Well? What do you see?'

Allday had served with him for eleven years. Coxswain, friend, a right arm when need be. But Bolitho could still surprise him. Like now. The post-captain, a man envied not a little by *Harvester*'s young commanding officer; and yet he was anxious, even afraid, that he would fail, and betray all the hopes he had nursed since his return to duty.

'Like old times, Cap'n.'

Bolitho turned and gazed at the glistening water below the counter. Nine days' passage. It had given him plenty of time to think and reflect. He thought of the frigate's young captain – not even posted yet, about his own age when he had been given *Phalarope*, when his and Allday's lives had crossed and been spliced together. It could not be easy to have him as a passenger, Bolitho thought. He had spent much of his time in these borrowed quarters, alone, and cherishing that precious moment when the orders had at last arrived for him.

'To proceed with all despatch and upon receipt of these orders, to take upon you the charge and command of His Britannic Majesty's Ship Hyperion.'

He smiled wistfully. *The Old Hyperion*. Once something of a legend in the fleet. But what now after all those years, so many leagues sailed in the King's service?

Was he still disappointed that he had not been offered a frigate? He bit his lip and watched some Spanish fishing boats idling above their images on the clear water.

It was not that. For Bolitho it was still too easy to recall the months of illness, then his daily pleading at the Admiralty for a command, any sort of ship they might condescend to provide. No, it was not that. Failure, then? The lurking fear of some weakness, or of the fever which had almost killed him with no less skill than an enemy ball or blade?

A muscle jumped in his cheek as the frigate's salute crashed across the bay, shaking the hull gun by gun like body blows. He heard the timed response from one of the Rock's batteries, and wondered why he was not even now on the quarterdeck seeking out his new command from the many vessels moored beneath the Rock's changeless protection.

269

He moved to a mirror which hung above one of his sea chests and studied his reflection, dispassionately, as he might a new subordinate. The uniform coat, with its broad white lapels and gilt buttons, the gold lace and epaulettes, should have offered immediate confidence. He knew from hard experience that no matter what kind of ship lay ahead, her company would be far more concerned about their new lord and master than he should be about them. But it failed to repel the uncertainty.

He thought of his last appointment and wondered still if the thankless task of recruiting at the Nore had been the true reason behind it. Had Lord Marcuard known even then that Bolitho was his choice for the other, deeper trust? Using his desperation for an appointment, a chance, no matter what, of returning to the one life he knew, and after losing Viola, needed more than ever. Perhaps he might never learn the complete truth.

He had found himself thinking of Paice very often. *That worthy man*, as he had described him in his despatch to the Admiralty. Many hundreds would die in this war, thousands, before it was ended in victory or defeat. Names and faces wiped away; and yet there were always the solitary men like Paice, whose memory never died.

He thought too of Vice-Amiral Brennier. He had received barely a mention in the newssheets, and Bolitho guessed that Marcuard's powerful hand was in that too. Perhaps Brennier would after all be involved in some counter-revolution.

The last gun thundered, and he heard voices calling commands as they were sponged out and prepared for the final cable or so of the frigate's entrance. Many eyes would be watching her. Letters from home – fresh orders – or simply the sight of a visitor from England to prove that Gibraltar was not entirely alone.

Allday crossed the cabin, the old sword held in his hands. 'Ready, Cap'n?' He offered a grin. 'They'll be expecting to see you on deck.'

Bolitho extended his arms and heard Allday muttering to himself as he clipped on the sword.

'You needs a bit o' fattenin' up, Cap'n –'

'Damn your impertinence!'

270

Allday stood back and hid a smile. The fire was still there. It just needed coaxing out.

He ran his eyes over Bolitho's slim physique. Smart as paint. Only the cheekbones, and the deeper lines at his mouth betrayed the grief and the illness.

Bolitho picked up his hat and stared at it unseeingly.

It was very strange, he had often thought, that at no time since the French treasure had been landed at Dover and put under guard, had it ever been publicly mentioned. Perhaps Marcuard, or even the prime minister, Pitt, had their own ideas as to how it might be used to better advantage?

How things had changed, just as he had known they would; just as Hoblyn had so bitterly prophesied. Especially with Pitt, he thought. The man who had cursed and condemned the smuggling gangs, who had used dragoons and the gibbet to keep their 'trade' at bay if not under control, had now been quoted as paying tribute to the very same scum. 'These men are my eyes, for without them I am blind to intelligence of the enemy!' It was so incredible that it was all the harder to believe, and to stomach.

As Queely had remarked dourly, 'Had Delaval stayed alive he might well have held a letter of marque from the King!'

Queely: another face in memory. He had been appointed to command a sturdy fourteen-gun brig at Plymouth. Bolitho wondered if he would take all his books with him to this different ship and different war.

He turned to Allday. In his blue coat and flapping white trousers, the tarred hat in one big fist, he would stir the heart of any patriotic landsman, or woman. Bolitho thought of the song he had heard when he had boarded *Harvester* from Portsmouth. 'Britons to Arms'. How poor Hoblyn would have laughed at that.

He heard a yell from the quarterdeck, the instant creak of the rudder as the wheel was put over. He could see it in his mind, as clearly as if he had been there on deck. The cluster of figures around the cathead ready to let go one anchor. The marines lined up on the poop in neat scarlet ranks. Captain Leach, anxious that everything should be right on this fair June morning, and justifiably proud of his fast passage from Spithead.

Bolitho shrugged and said quietly, 'I can never find words to thank you, old friend.' Their eyes met and he added, 'Truly, heart of oak.'

Then he walked through the screen door, nodding to the sentry before moving out into the sunlight, the expectant seamen who were waiting to furl every sail with only seconds between them when the anchor splashed down.

Leach turned to greet him, his expression wary.

Bolitho said, 'You have a fine ship, Captain Leach. I envy you.'

Leach watched him cross to the nettings, unable to conceal his astonishment. Surely Bolitho wanted for nothing? A post-captain of distinction who was almost certain to reach flag rank before this war showed signs of ending, unless he fell out of favour or was killed in battle . . .

'Ready, sir!'

Leach held up his arm. 'Let go!'

Spray burst over the beakhead as the great anchor splashed down, but Bolitho did not see it.

I am a frigate captain.

And that gentle, remembered correction. *Were – a frigate captain.*

He ignored the voice in his memory and stared at the large ships-of-war anchored astern of one which wore a vice-admiral's flag at the fore.

One of them is mine.

He looked at Allday and smiled freely for the first time.

'Not a lively frigate this time, old friend. We've much to discover!'

Allday nodded, satisfied. The smile gave light to the grey eyes once more. It was all there, he decided. Hope, determination, and a new strength which her death had once taken away.

He breathed out slowly.

The Old Hyperion. So be it then.

Honour This Day

For Kim, with so much love

Mourn, England, mourn and complain
For the brave Lord Nelson's men
Who died upon that day
All on the main. . . .

Broadsheet ballad, 1805

Contents

Antigua
1804

1

Memories

English Harbour, in fact the whole island of Antigua, seemed to crouch motionless as if pinned down by the noon sun. The air was humid and oppressively hot, so that the many vessels scattered at anchor were blurred in heavy haze, like reflections in a steamy looking-glass.

This October in 1804 was only days old, the middle of the hurricane season, and one of the worst on record. Several ships had been lost at sea, or driven ashore when they had been caught in some dangerous channel.

English Harbour was the important, some said vital, headquarters for the fleet which served the Caribbean and to the full extent of the Leeward and Windward Islands. Here was a fine anchorage, a dockyard where even the most serious damage and refitting could be carried out. But peace or war, the sea and the weather were constant enemies, and whereas almost every foreign flag was assumed to be hostile, the dangers of these waters were never taken for granted.

English Harbour was some twelve miles from the capital, St John's, and so the social life in and around the dockyard was limited. On a flagged terrace of one of the better houses flanking the hillside behind the harbour, a group of people, mostly officials and their ladies, stood wilting in the unmoving air watching the approach of a man-of-war. It seemed to have taken an eternity for the newcomer to gain substance and shape through the shimmering haze, but now she stood, bows-on to the land, her sails all but flat against her stays and yards.

Ships of war were too commonplace for mention. After years of conflict with France and her allies, such sights were part of these people's daily lives.

This one was a ship-of-the-line, a two-decker, her rounded black and buff hull making a sharp contrast with the milky water and the sky which seemed without colour in the unwavering heat. The sun stood directly above Monk's Hill and was encircled with silver; somewhere out at sea there would be another storm very soon. This ship was different in one respect from other comings and goings. News had been brought by a guardboat that she was from England. To those watching her painstaking approach, just the name of England created so many images. Like a letter from home, a description from some passing sailor. Uncertain weather, shortages, and a daily fear of a French invasion across the Channel. As varied as the land itself, from lush countryside to city squalor. There was hardly a man or woman watching the two-decker who would not have traded Antigua for a mere glimpse of England.

One woman stood apart from the others, her body quite still, except for her hand, which used a fan with economical care to revive the heavy air.

She had tired long ago of the desultory conversation of the people she had come to know and recognise out of necessity. Some of their voices were already slurred with overheated wine, and they had not even sat down to eat as yet.

She turned to conceal her discomfort as she plucked the ivory gown away from her skin. And all the while she watched the ship. *From England*.

The vessel could have been quite motionless but for a tiny feather of white foam beneath her thrusting, gilded figurehead. Two longboats were leading her inshore, one on either bow; she could not see if they were attached to their mother ship by line or not. They too were barely moving, and only the graceful rise and fall of their oars, pale like wings, gave a hint of effort and purpose.

The woman knew a great deal about ships; she had travelled many hundreds of leagues by sea, and had an eye for their

4

complex detail. A voice from the past seemed to linger in her mind, which had described a ship as man's most beautiful creation. She could hear him add, *and as demanding as any woman.*

Someone behind her remarked, 'Another round of official visits, I suppose?' No one answered. It was too hot even for speculation. Feet clattered on stone steps and she heard the same voice say, 'Let me know when you get any more news.'

The servant scurried away while his master opened a scrawled message from somebody in the dockyard.

'She's the *Hyperion*, seventy-four. Captain Haven.'

The woman watched the ship but her mind was drawn to the name. Why should it startle her in some way?

Another voice murmured, 'Good God, Aubrey, I thought she was a hulk. Plymouth, wasn't it?'

Glasses clinked, but the woman did not move. Captain Haven? The name meant nothing.

She saw the guardboat pulling wearily towards the tall two-decker. She loved to watch incoming ships, to see the activity on deck, the outwardly confused preparations until a great anchor splashed down. These sailors would be watching the island, many for the first time. A far cry from the ports and villages of England.

The voice commented, 'Yes, she was. But with this war spreading every day, and our people in Whitehall as unprepared as ever, I suspect that even the wrecks along our coastline will be drummed into service.'

A thicker tone said, 'I remember her now. Fought and took a damned great three-decker single-handed. No wonder the poor old girl was laid up after that, eh, what?'

She watched, hardly daring to blink as the two-decker's shape lengthened, her sails being brailed up while she swung so slowly into whatever breeze she could discover.

'She's no private ship, Aubrey.' Interest had moved the man to the balustrade. 'God, she wears an admiral's flag.'

'*Vice*-Admiral,' corrected his host. 'Very interesting. She's apparently under the flag of Sir Richard Bolitho, Vice-Admiral of the Red.'

The anchor threw up a column of spray as it fell from the

cathead. The woman flattened one hand on the balustrade until the heat of the stone steadied her.

Her husband must have seen her move.

'What is it? Do you know him? A true hero, if half what I've read can be believed.'

She gripped the fan more tightly and pressed it to her breast. *So that was how it would be*. He was here in Antigua. After all this time, after all he had endured.

No wonder she had remembered the ship's name. He had often spoken so affectionately of his old *Hyperion*. One of the first ships he had ever commanded as a captain.

She was surprised at her sudden emotion, more so at her ability to conceal it.

'I met him. Years ago.'

'Another glass of wine, gentlemen?'

She relaxed, muscle by muscle, aware of the dampness of her gown, of her body within it.

Even as she thought about it she cursed herself for her stupidity. It could not be like that again. *Never*.

She turned her back on the ship and smiled at the others. But even the smile was a lie.

Richard Bolitho stood uncertainly in the centre of the great stern cabin, his head cocked to the sudden thud of bare feet across the poop. All the familiar sounds crowded into the cabin, the muffled chorus of commands, the responding squeal of blocks as the yards were braced round. And yet there was hardly any movement. Like a phantom ship. Only the tall, shimmering bars of gold sunlight which moved along one side of the cabin gave any real hint that *Hyperion* was swinging slowly into the off-shore wind.

He watched as the land edged in a green panorama across the first half of the stern windows. *Antigua*. Even the name was like a stab in the heart, a reawakening of so many memories, so many faces and voices.

It was here in English Harbour where, as a newly appointed commander, he had been given his very first command, the small, lithe sloop-of-war, *Sparrow*. A different kind of vessel, but then

6

the war with the rebellious Americans had been different also. How long ago it all seemed. Ships and faces, pain and elation.

He thought of the passage here from England. You could not ask for a faster one – thirty days, with the old *Hyperion* responding like a thoroughbred. They had stayed in company with a convoy of merchantmen, several of which had been packed with soldiers, reinforcements or replacements for the chain of English garrisons throughout the Caribbean. More likely the latter, he thought grimly. Soldiers were known to die like flies out here from one fever or another without ever hearing the crack of a French musket.

Bolitho walked slowly to the stern windows, shading his eyes against the misty glare. He was again aware of his own resentment, his reluctance at being here, knowing the situation would require all the diplomacy and pomp he was not in the mood to offer. It had already begun with the regular crash of salutes, gun for gun with the nearest shore battery, above which the Union Flag did not even ripple in the humid air.

He saw the guardboat riding above her own reflection, her oars stilled as the officer in charge waited for the two-decker to anchor.

Without being up there on the poop or quarterdeck Bolitho could visualise it all, the men at braces and halliards, others strung out along the great yards ready to fist and furl the sails neatly into place, so that from the land it would look as if every stitch of canvas had vanished to the touch of a single hand.

Land. To a sailor it was always a dream. A new adventure.

Bolitho glanced at the dress coat which hung across a chairback, ready for the call to commence his act. When he had been given command of *Sparrow* all those years ago he would never have believed it possible. Death by accident or in the cannon's mouth, disgrace, or the lack of opportunity to distinguish yourself or gain an admiral's favour, made any promotion a hard climb.

Now the coat was a reality, bearing its twin gold epaulettes with their paired silver stars. And yet . . . He reached up to brush the loose lock of hair from above his right eye. Like the scar running deep into his hairline where a cutlass had nearly ended his life, nothing changed, not even uncertainty.

He had believed that he might be able to grow into it, even though the step from command to flag rank was the greatest stride of all. Sir Richard Bolitho, Knight of the Bath, Vice-Admiral of the Red, and next to Nelson the youngest on the List. He gave a brief smile. The King had not even remembered his name when he had knighted him. Bolitho had also managed to accept that he was no longer involved with the day-to-day running of a ship, *any* ship which flew his flag. As a lieutenant he had often glanced aft at the captain's remote figure, and had felt awe, if not always respect. Then as a captain himself he had so often lain awake, fretting, as he listened to the wind and shipboard noises, restraining himself from dashing on deck when he thought the officer of the watch was not aware of the dangers around him. It was hard to delegate; but at least the ship had been his. To the ship's company of any man-of-war their captain was next only to God, and some said uncharitably that that was only due to seniority.

As a flag officer you had to stay aloof and direct the affairs of all your captains and commanders, place whatever forces you controlled where they would serve to the best effect. The power was greater, but so too was the responsibility. Few flag officers had ever allowed themselves to forget that Admiral Byng had been shot for cowardice by a firing party on the deck of his own flagship.

Perhaps he would have settled down to both his rank and unfamiliar title but for his personal life. He shied away from the thought and moved his fingers to his left eye. He massaged the lid and then stared hard at the drifting green bank of land. Sharp and clear again. But it would not last. The surgeon in London had warned him. He needed rest, more treatment, regular care. It would have meant remaining ashore – worse than that, an appointment at the Admiralty.

So why had he asked, almost demanded, another appointment with the fleet? Anywhere, or so it had sounded at the time to the Lords of Admiralty.

Three of his superiors there had told him that he had more than earned a London appointment even before his last great victory.

Yet when he had persisted, Bolitho had had the feeling they were equally glad he had declined their offers.

Fate – it must be that. He turned and looked deep into the great cabin. The low, white deckhead, the pale green leather of the chairs, the screen doors which led to the sleeping quarters or to the teeming world of the ship beyond, where a sentry guarded his privacy around the clock.

Hyperion – it had to be an act of Fate.

He could recall the last time he had seen her, after he had worked her into Plymouth. The staring crowds who had thronged the waterfront and Hoe to watch the victor returning home. So many killed, so many more crippled for life after their triumph over Lequiller's squadron in Biscay, and the capture of his great hundred-gun flagship *Tornade* which Bolitho was later to command as another admiral's flag captain.

But it was this ship which he always remembered. *Hyperion*, seventy-four. He had walked beside the dock in Plymouth on that awful day when he had said his last farewell; or so he had believed. Battered and ripped open by shot, her rigging and sails flayed to pieces, her splintered decks darkly stained with the blood of those who had fought. They said she would never stand in the line of battle again. There had been many moments while they had struggled back to port in foul weather when he had thought she would sink like some of her adversaries. As he had stood looking at her in the dock he had almost wished that she had found peace on the seabed. With the war growing and spreading, *Hyperion* had been made into a stores hulk. Mastless, her once-busy gundecks packed with casks and crates, she had become just a part of the dockyard.

She was the first ship-of-the-line Bolitho had ever commanded. Then, as now, he remained a frigate-man at heart, and the idea of being captain of a two-decker had appalled him. But then, too, he had been desperate, although for different reasons. Plagued by the fever which had nearly killed him in the Great South Sea, he was employed ashore at the Nore, recruiting, as the French Revolution swept across the continent like a forest fire. He could recall joining this ship at Gibraltar as if it was yesterday. She had been old and tired and yet she had taken him to her, as if in some way they needed each other.

Bolitho heard the trill of calls, the great splash as the anchor plummeted down into the waters he knew so well.

His flag captain would come to see him very soon now for orders. Try as he might, Bolitho could not see Captain Edmund Haven as an inspiring leader or his personal adviser.

A colourless, impersonal sort of man, and yet even as he considered Haven he knew he was being unfair. Bolitho had joined the ship just days before they had weighed for the passage to the Indies. And in the thirty which had followed, Bolitho had stayed almost completely isolated in his own quarters, so that even Allday, his coxswain, was showing signs of concern.

It was probably something Haven had said on their first tour of the ship, the day before they had put to sea.

Haven had obviously thought it odd, eccentric perhaps, that his admiral should wish to see anything beyond his cabin or the poop, let alone show interest in the gundecks and orlop.

Bolitho's glance rested on the sword rack beside the screen. His own old sword, and the fine presentation one. How *could* Haven have understood? It was not his fault. Bolitho had taken his apparent dissatisfaction with his command like a personal insult. He had snapped, 'This ship may be old, Captain Haven, but she has out-sailed many far younger! The Chesapeake, the Saintes, Toulon and Biscay – her battle honours read like a history of the navy itself!' It was unfair, but Haven should have known better.

Every yard of that tour had been a rebirth of memory. Only the faces and voices did not fit. But the ship was the same. New masts, and most of her armament replaced by heavier artillery than when she had faced the broadsides of Lequiller's *Tornade*, gleaming paint and neatly tarred seams; nothing could disguise his *Hyperion*. He stared round the cabin, seeing it as before. *And she was thirty-two years old.* When she had been built at Deptford she had had the pick of Kentish oak. Those days of shipbuilding were gone forever, and now most forests had been stripped of their best timber to feed the needs of the fleet.

It was ironic that the great *Tornade* had been a new ship, yet she had been paid off as a prison-hulk some four years back. He felt his left eye again and cursed wretchedly as the mist seemed to drift across it. He thought of Haven and the others who served this old ship day and night. Did they know or guess that the man whose flag flew from the foremast truck was partially blind in his left eye? Bolitho clenched his fists as he relived that moment, falling to the deck, blinded by sand from the bucket an enemy ball had blasted apart.

He waited for his composure to return. No, Haven did not seem to notice anything beyond his duties.

Bolitho touched one of the chairs and pictured the length and breadth of his flagship. So much of him was in her. His brother had died on the upper deck, had fallen to save his only son Adam, although the boy had been unaware that he was still alive, at the time. And dear Inch who had risen to become *Hyperion*'s first lieutenant. He could see him now, with his anxious, horse-faced grin. Now he too was dead, with so many of their 'happy few'.

And Cheney had also walked these decks – he pushed the chair aside and crossed angrily to the open stern windows.

'You called, Sir Richard?'

It was Ozzard, his mole-like servant. It would be no ship at all without him.

Bolitho turned. He must have spoken her name aloud. How many times; and how long would he suffer like this?

He said, 'I – I am sorry, Ozzard.' He did not go on.

Ozzard folded his paw-like hands under his apron and looked at the glittering anchorage.

'Old times, Sir Richard.'

'Aye.' Bolitho sighed. 'We had better be about it, eh?'

Ozzard held up the heavy coat with its shining epaulettes. Beyond the screen door Bolitho heard the trill of more calls and the squeak of tackles as boats were swayed out for lowering alongside.

Landfall. Once it had been such a magic word.

Ozzard busied himself with the coat but did not bring either sword from the rack. He and Allday were great friends even though most people would see them as chalk and cheese. And Allday would not allow anyone but himself to clip on the sword. Like the old ship, Bolitho thought, Allday was of the best English oak, and when he was gone none would take his place.

11

He imagined that Ozzard was dismayed that he had chosen the two-decker when he could have had the pick of any first-rate he wanted. At the Admiralty they had gently suggested that although *Hyperion* was ready for sea again, after a three-year overhaul and refit she might never recover from that last savage battle.

Curiously it had been Nelson, the hero whom Bolitho had never met, who had settled the matter. Someone at the Admiralty must have written to the little admiral to tell him of Bolitho's request. Nelson had sent his own views in a despatch to Their Lordships with typical brevity.

Give Bolitho any ship he wants. He is a sailor, not a landsman.

It would amuse Our Nel, Bolitho thought. *Hyperion* had been set aside as a hulk until her recommissioning just a few months ago, and she was thirty-two years old.

Nelson had hoisted his own flag in *Victory*, a first-rate, but he had found her himself rotting as a prison hulk. He had known in his strange fashion that he had to have her as his flagship. As far as he could recall, Bolitho knew that *Victory* was eight years older than *Hyperion*.

Somehow it seemed right that the two old ships should live again, having been discarded without much thought after all they had done.

The outer screen door opened and Daniel Yovell, Bolitho's secretary, stood watching him glumly.

Bolitho relented yet again. It had been easy for none of them because of his moods, his uncertainties. Even Yovell, plump, round-shouldered and so painstaking with his work, had been careful to keep his distance for the past thirty days at sea.

'The Captain will be here shortly, Sir Richard.'

Bolitho slipped his arms into the coat and shrugged himself into the most comfortable position without making his spine prickle with sweat.

'Where is my flag lieutenant?' Bolitho smiled suddenly. Having an official aide had also been hard to accept at the beginning. Now, after two previous flag lieutenants, he found it simple to face.

'Waiting for the barge. After that,' the fat shoulders rose

cheerfully, 'you will meet the local dignitaries.' He had taken Bolitho's smile as a return to better things. Yovell's simple Devonian mind required everything to remain safely the same.

Bolitho allowed Ozzard to stand on tip-toe to adjust his neck-cloth. For years he had always hung upon the word of admiralty or the senior officer present wherever it happened to be. It was still difficult to believe that this time there was no superior brain to question or satisfy. He *was* the senior officer. Of course in the end the unwritten naval rule would prevail. If right, others would take the credit. If wrong, he might well carry the blame.

Bolitho glanced at himself in the mirror and grimaced. His hair was still black, apart from some distasteful silver ones in the rebellious lock of hair covering the old scar. The lines at the corners of his mouth were deeper, and his reflection reminded him of the picture of his older brother, Hugh, which hung in Falmouth. Like so many of those Bolitho portraits in the great grey stone house. He controlled his sudden despair. Now, apart from his loyal steward Ferguson and the servants, it was empty.

I am here. It is what I wanted. He glanced around the cabin again. *Hyperion. We nearly died together.*

Yovell turned aside, his apple-red face wary. 'The Captain, Sir Richard.'

Haven entered, his hat beneath one arm.

'The ship is secured, sir.'

Bolitho nodded. He had told Haven not to address him by his title unless ceremony dictated otherwise. The division between them was already great enough.

'I shall come up.' A shadow moved through the door and Bolitho noticed just the briefest touch of annoyance on Haven's face. That was an improvement from total self-composure, he thought.

Allday walked past the flag captain. 'The barge is alongside, Sir Richard.' He moved to the sword rack and eyed the two weapons thoughtfully. 'The proper one today?'

Bolitho smiled. Allday had problems of his own, but he would keep them to himself until he was ready. Coxswain? A true friend was a better description. It certainly made Haven frown that one so lowly could come and go as he pleased.

13

Allday stooped to clip the old Bolitho sword to the belt. The leather scabbard had been rebuilt several times, but the tarnished hilt remained the same, and the keen, outmoded blade was as sharp as ever.

Bolitho patted the sword against his hip. 'Another good friend.' Their eyes met. It was almost physical, Bolitho thought. All the influence his rank invited was nothing compared with their close bond.

Haven was of medium build, almost stocky, with curling ginger hair. In his early thirties, he had the look of a sound lawyer or city merchant, and his expression today was quietly expectant, giving nothing away. Bolitho had visited his cabin on one occasion and had remarked on a small portrait, of a beautiful girl with streaming hair, surrounded by flowers.

'My wife,' Haven had replied. His tone had suggested that he would say no more even to his admiral. A strange creature, Bolitho thought; but the ship was smartly run, although with so many new hands and an overload of landsmen, it had appeared as if the first lieutenant could take much of the credit for it.

Bolitho strode through the door, past the rigid Royal Marine sentry and into the glaring sunlight. It was strange to see the wheel lashed in the midships position and abandoned. Every day at sea Bolitho had taken his solitary walks on the windward side of the quarterdeck or poop, had studied the small convoy and one attendant frigate, while his feet had taken him up and down the worn planks, skirting gun tackles and ringbolts without any conscious thought.

Eyes watched him pass, quickly averted if he glanced towards them. It was something he accepted. He knew he would never grow to like it.

Now the ship lay at rest; lines were being flaked down, petty officers moved watchfully between the bare-backed seamen to make sure the ship, no longer an ordinary man-of-war but an admiral's flagship, was as smart as could be expected anywhere.

Bolitho looked aloft at the black criss-cross of shrouds and rigging, the tightly furled sails, and shortened figures busily working high above the decks to make certain all was secure there too.

14

Some of the lieutenants moved away as he walked to the quarterdeck to look down at the lines of eighteen-pounders which had replaced the original batteries of twelve-pounders.

Faces floated through the busy figures. Like ghosts. Noises intruded above the shouted orders and the clatter of tackles. Decks torn by shot as if ripped by giant claws. Men falling and dying, reaching for aid when there was none. His nephew Adam, then fourteen years old, white-faced and yet wildly determined as the embattled ships had ground together for the last embrace from which there was no escape for either of them.

Haven said, 'The guardboat is alongside, sir.'

Bolitho gestured past him. 'You have not rigged winds'ls, Captain.'

Why could he not bring himself to call Haven by his first name? *What is happening to me?*

Haven shrugged. 'They are unsightly from the shore, sir.'

Bolitho looked at him. 'They give some air to the people on the gundecks. Have them rigged.'

He tried to contain his annoyance, at himself, and with Haven for not thinking of the furnace heat on an overcrowded gundeck. *Hyperion* was one hundred and eighty feet long on her gundeck, and carried a total company of some six hundred officers, seamen and marines. In this heat it would feel like twice that number.

He saw Haven snapping his orders to his first lieutenant, the latter glancing towards him as if to see for himself the reason for the rigging of windsails.

The first lieutenant was another odd bird, Bolitho had decided. He was over thirty, old for his rank, and had been commander of a brig. The appointment had not been continued when the vessel had been paid off, and he had been returned to his old rank. He was tall, and unlike his captain, a man of outward excitement and enthusiasm. Tall and darkly handsome, his gipsy good looks reminded Bolitho of a face in the past, but he could not recall whose. He had a ready grin, and was obviously popular with his subordinates, the sort of officer the midshipmen would love to emulate.

Bolitho looked forward, below the finely curved beakhead where he could see the broad shoulders of the figurehead. It was what he had always remembered most when he had left the ship

15

at Plymouth. *Hyperion* had been so broken and damaged it had been hard to see her as she had once been. The figurehead had told another story.

Under the gilt paint it may have been scarred too, but the piercing blue eyes which stared straight ahead from beneath the crown of a rising sun were as arrogant as ever. One outthrust, muscled arm pointed the same trident towards the next horizon. Even seen from aft, Bolitho gained strength from the old familiarity. *Hyperion*, one of the Titans, had overthrown the indignity of being denigrated to a hulk.

Allday watched him narrowly. He had seen the gaze, and guessed what it meant. Bolitho was all aback. Allday was still not sure if he agreed with him or not. But he loved Bolitho like no other being and would die for him without question.

He said, 'Barge is ready, Sir Richard.' He wanted to add that it was not much of a crew. *Yet.*

Bolitho walked slowly to the entry port and glanced down at the boat alongside. Jenour, his new flag lieutenant, was already aboard; so was Yovell, a case of documents clasped across his fat knees. One of the midshipmen stood like a ramrod in the sternsheets. Bolitho checked himself from scanning the youthful features. It was all past. He knew nobody in this ship.

He looked round suddenly and saw the fifers moistening their pipes on their lips, the Royal Marines gripping their pipeclayed musket slings, ready to usher him over the side.

Haven and his first lieutenant, all the other anonymous faces, the blues and whites of the officers, the scarlet of the marines, the tanned bodies of the watching seamen.

He wanted to say to them, 'I am your flag officer, but *Hyperion* is still *my* ship!'

He heard Allday climb down to the barge and knew, no matter how he pretended otherwise, he would be watching, ready to reach out and catch him if his eye clouded over and he lost his step. Bolitho raised his hat, and instantly the fifes and drums snapped into a lively crescendo, and the Royal Marine guard presented arms as their major's sword flashed in salute.

Calls trilled and Bolitho lowered himself down the steep tumble-home and into the barge.

His last glance at Haven surprised him. The captain's eyes were cold, hostile. It was worth remembering.

The guardboat sidled away and waited to lead the barge through the anchored shipping and harbour craft.

Bolitho shaded his eyes and stared at the land.

It was another challenge. But at that moment it felt like running away.

2

A Sailor's Tale

John Allday squinted his eyes beneath the tilted brim of his hat and watched the inshore current carry the guardboat momentarily off course. He eased his tiller carefully and the freshly painted green barge followed the other boat without even a break in the stroke. Allday's reputation as the vice-admiral's personal coxswain had preceded him.

He stared along the barge crew, his eyes revealing nothing. The boat had been transferred from their last ship *Argonaute*, the Frog prize, but Bolitho had said that he would leave it to his coxswain to recruit a new crew from *Hyperion*. That was strange, he had thought. Any of the old crew would have volunteered to shift to *Hyperion*, for like as not they would have been sent back to sea anyway without much of a chance to visit their loved ones. He dropped his gaze to the figures who sat in the sternsheets. Yovell who had been promoted from clerk to secretary, with the new flag lieutenant beside him. The young officer seemed pleasant enough, but was not from a seagoing family. Most who seized the chance of the overworked appointment saw it as a sure way for their own promotion. Early days yet, Allday decided. In a ship where even the rats were strangers, it was better not to make hasty decisions.

His eyes settled on Bolitho's squared shoulders and he tried to control the apprehension which had been his companion since their return to Falmouth. It ought to have been a proud homecoming despite the pain and the ravages of battle. Even the

18

damage to Bolitho's left eye had seemed less terrible when set against what they had faced and overcome together. It had been about a year ago. Aboard the little cutter *Supreme*. Allday could recall each day, the painful recovery, the very power of the man he served and loved as he had fought to win his extra battle, to hide his despair and hold the confidence of the men he led. Bolitho never failed to surprise him although they had stayed together for over twenty years. It did not seem possible that there were any surprises left.

They had walked from the harbour at Falmouth and paused at the church which had become so much a part of the Bolitho family. Generations of them were remembered there, births and marriages, victories at sea and violent death also.

Allday had stayed near the big doors of the silent church on that summer's day and had listened with sadness and astonishment as Bolitho spoke her name. *Cheney.* Just her name; and yet it had told him so much. Allday still believed that when they reached the old grey stone house below Pendennis Castle it would all return to normal. The lovely Lady Belinda who in looks at least was so like the dead Cheney, would somehow make it right, would comfort Bolitho when she realised the extent of his hurt. Maybe heal the agony in his mind which he never mentioned, but which Allday recognised. *Suppose the other eye was somehow wounded in battle?* The fear of so many sailors and soldiers. Helpless. Unwanted. Ferguson, the estate's steward who had lost an arm at the Saintes what seemed like a million years back, his rosy-cheeked wife Grace the housekeeper, and all the other servants had been waiting to greet them. Laughter, cheers, and a lot of tears too. But Belinda and the child Elizabeth had not been there. Ferguson said that she had sent a letter to explain her absence. God knew it was common enough for a returning sailor to find his family ignorant of his whereabouts, but it could not have come at a worse moment or hit Bolitho so hard.

Even his young nephew Adam, who now held his own command of the brig *Firefly*, was not able to console him. He had been ordered back to take on supplies and fresh water.

Hyperion was real enough, though. Allday glared at the stroke

19

oarsman as his blade feathered badly and threw spray over the gunwale. Bloody bargemen. They'd learn a thing or two if he had to teach every hand separately.

The old *Hyperion* was no stranger, but the people were. Was that what Bolitho wanted? Or what he needed? Allday still did not know.

If Keen had been flag captain – Allday's mouth softened. Or poor Inch even, things would seem less strange.

Captain Haven was a cold fish; even his own coxswain, a nuggety Welshman named Evans, had confided over a *wet* that his lord and master was without humour, and could not be reached.

Allday glanced again at Bolitho's shoulders. How unlike their own relationship. One ship after the other, different seas, but usually the same enemy. And always Bolitho had treated him as a friend, *one of the family* as he had once put it. It had been casually said, yet Allday had treasured the remark like a pot of gold.

It was funny if you thought about it. Some of his old messmates might even have jibed him had they not been too respectful of his fists. For Allday, like the one-armed Ferguson, had been pressed into the King's service and put aboard Bolitho's ship, the frigate *Phalarope* – hardly an ingredient for friendship. Allday had stayed with Bolitho ever since the Saintes when his old coxswain had been cut down.

Allday had been a sailor all his life, apart from a short period ashore when he had been a shepherd, of all things. He knew little of his birth and upbringing or even the exact whereabouts of his home. Now, as he grew older, it occasionally troubled him.

He studied Bolitho's hair, the queue tied at the nape of his neck which hung beneath his best gold-laced hat. It was jet-black, and in his appearance he remained youthful; he had sometimes been mistaken for young Adam's brother. Allday, as far as he knew, was the same age, forty-seven, but whereas he had filled out, and his thick brown hair had become streaked with grey, Bolitho never appeared to alter.

At peace he could be withdrawn and grave. But Allday knew most of his sides. A tiger in battle; a man moved almost to tears and despair when he had seen the havoc and agony after a sea-fight.

20

The guardboat was turning again to pass beneath the tapering jib-boom of a handsome schooner. Allday eased over the tiller and held his breath as fire probed the wound in his chest. That too rarely left his mind. The Spanish blade which had come from nowhere. Bolitho standing to protect him, then throwing down his sword to surrender and so spare his life.

The wound troubled him, and he often found it hard to straighten his shoulders without the pain lancing through him as a cruel reminder.

Bolitho had sometimes suggested that he should remain ashore, if only for a time. He no longer offered him a chance of complete freedom from the navy he had served so well; he knew it would injure Allday like a worse wound.

The barge pointed her stem towards the nearest jetty and Allday saw Bolitho's fingers fasten around the scabbard of the old sword between his knees. So many battles. So often they had marvelled that they had been spared once again when so many others had fallen.

'*Bows!*' He watched critically as the bowman withdrew his oar and rose with a boathook held ready to snatch for the jetty-chains. They looked smart enough, Allday conceded, in their tarred hats and fresh checkered shirts. But it needed more than paint to make a ship sail.

Allday himself was an imposing figure, although he was rarely aware of it unless he caught the eye of some girl or other, which was more often than he might admit. In his fine blue coat with the special gilt buttons Bolitho had presented to him, and his nankeen breeches, he looked every inch the Heart of Oak so popular in theatre and pleasure-garden performances.

The guardboat moved aside, the officer in charge rising to doff his hat while his oarsmen tossed their looms in salute.

With a start Allday realised that Bolitho had turned to look up at him, his hand momentarily above one eye as if to shield it from the glare. He said nothing, but there was a message in the glance, as if he had shouted it aloud. Like a plea; a recognition which excluded all others for those few seconds.

Allday was a simple man, but he remembered the look long after Bolitho had left the barge. It both worried and moved him.

21

As if he had shared something precious.

He saw some of the bargemen staring at him and roared, 'I've seen smarter Jacks thrown out of a brothel, but by God you'll do better next time, an' that's no error!'

Jenour stepped ashore and smiled as the solitary midshipman blushed with embarrassment at the coxswain's sudden outburst. The flag lieutenant had been with Bolitho just over a month, but already he was beginning to recognise the strange charisma of the man he served, his hero since he had been like that tongue-tied midshipman. Bolitho's voice scattered his thoughts.

'Come along, Mr Jenour. The barge can wait; the affairs of war will not.'

Jenour hid a grin. 'Aye, Sir Richard.' He thought of his parents in Hampshire, how they had shaken their heads when he had told them he intended to be Bolitho's aide *one day*.

Bolitho had seen the grin and felt the return of his sense of loss. He knew how the young lieutenant felt, how he had once been himself. In the navy's private world you found and hung on to friends with all your might. When they fell you lost something with them. Survival did not spare you the pain of their passing; it never could.

He stopped abruptly on the jetty stairs and thought of *Hyperion*'s first lieutenant. Those gipsy good looks – *of course*. It had been Keverne he had recalled to mind. They were so alike. Charles Keverne, once his first lieutenant in *Euryalus*, who had been killed at Copenhagen as captain of his own ship.

'Are you all right, Sir Richard?'

'*Damn you, yes!*' Bolitho swung round instantly and touched Jenour's cuff. 'Forgive me. Rank offers many privileges. Being foul-mannered is not one of them.'

He walked up the stairs while Jenour stared after him.

Yovell sighed as he sweated up the steep stone steps. The poor lieutenant had a lot to learn. It was to be hoped he had the time.

The long room seemed remarkably cool after the heat beyond the shaded windows.

Bolitho sat in a straight-backed chair and sipped a glass of hock, and marvelled that anything could stay so cold. Lieutenant

Jenour and Yovell sat at a separate table, which was littered with files and folios of signals and reports. It was strange to consider that it had been in a more austere part of this same building that Bolitho had waited and fretted for the news of his first command.

The hock was good and very clear. He realised that his glass was already being refilled by a Negro servant and knew he had to be careful. Bolitho enjoyed a glass of wine but had found it easy to avoid the common pitfall in the navy of over-imbibing. That could so often lead to disgrace at the court martial table.

It was too easy to see himself in those first black days at Falmouth, where he had returned there expecting – expecting what? How could he plead dismay and bitterness when truthfully his heart had remained in the church with Cheney?

How still the house had been as he had moved restlessly through the deepening shadows, the candles he held aloft in one hand playing on those stern-faced portraits he had known since he was Elizabeth's age.

He had awakened with his forehead resting on a table amidst puddles of spilled wine, his mouth like a birdcage, his mind disgusted. He had stared at the empty bottles, but could not even remember dragging them from the cellar. The household must have known, and when Ferguson had come to him he had seen that he was fully dressed from the previous day and must have been prowling and searching for a way to help. Bolitho had had to force the truth out of Allday, for he could not recall ordering him out of the house, to leave him alone with his misery. He suspected he had said far worse; he had later heard that Allday had also drunk the night away in the tavern where the inn-keeper's daughter had always waited for him, and hoped.

He glanced up and realised that the other officer was speaking to him.

Commodore Aubrey Glassport, Commissioner of the Dock-yard in Antigua, and until *Hyperion*'s anchor had dropped, the senior naval officer here, was explaining the whereabouts and dispersal of the local patrols.

'With a vast sea area, Sir Richard, we are hard put to chase and detain blockade-runners or other suspect vessels. The French and

23

their Spanish allies, on the other hand –'

Bolitho pulled a chart towards him. The same old story. Not enough frigates, too many ships-of-the-line ordered elsewhere to reinforce the fleets in the Channel and Mediterranean.

For over an hour he had examined the various reports, the results which had to be set against the days and weeks of patrolling the countless islands and inlets. Occasionally a more daring captain would risk life and limb to break into an enemy anchorage and either cut out a prize or carry out a swift bombardment. It made good reading. It did little to cripple a superior enemy. His mouth hardened. Superior in numbers only.

Glassport took his silence for acceptance and rambled on. He was a round, comfortable man, with sparse hair, and a moon-face which told more of good living than fighting the elements or the French.

He was to have been retired long since, Bolitho had heard, but he had a good rapport with the dockyard so had been kept here. Judging by his cellar he obviously carried his good relations to the victualling masters as well.

Glassport was saying, 'I am fully aware of your past achievements, Sir Richard, and how *honoured* I am to have you visit my command. I believe that when you were first here, America too was active against us, with many privateers as well as the French fleet.'

'The fact we are no longer at war with America does not necessarily remove the threat of involvement, nor the increasing danger of their supplies and ships to the enemy.' He put down the chart. 'In the next few weeks I want each patrol to be contacted. Do you have a courier-brig here at present?' He watched the man's sudden uncertainty and astonishment. The upending of his quiet, comfortable existence. 'I shall need to see each captain personally. Can you arrange it?'

'Well, er, ahem – yes, Sir Richard.'

'Good.' He picked up the glass and studied the sunlight reflected in its stem. If he moved it very slightly to the left – he waited, sensing Yovell's eyes watching, Jenour's curiosity.

He added, 'I was told that His Majesty's Inspector General is still in the Indies?'

Glassport muttered wretchedly, 'My flag lieutenant will know exactly what –'

Bolitho tensed as the glass's shape blurred over. Like a filmy curtain. It had come more quickly, or was it preying on his mind so much that he was imagining the deterioration?

He exclaimed, 'A simple enough question, I'd have thought. Is he, or is he not?'

Bolitho looked down at the hand in his lap and thought it should be shaking. Remorse, anger; it was neither. Like the moment on the jetty when he had turned on Jenour.

He said more calmly, 'He has been out here for several months, I believe?' He looked up, despairing that his eye might mist over once more.

Glassport replied, 'Viscount Somervell is staying here in Antigua.' He added defensively, 'I trust he is satisfied with his findings.'

Bolitho said nothing. The Inspector General might have been just one more burden to the top-hamper of war. It seemed absurd that someone with such a high-sounding appointment should be employed on a tour of inspection in the West Indies, when England, standing alone against France and the fleets of Spain, was daily expecting an invasion.

Bolitho's instructions from the Admiralty made it clear that he was to meet with the Viscount Somervell without delay, if it meant moving immediately to another island, even to Jamaica.

But he was here. That was something.

Bolitho was feeling weary. He had met most of the dockyard officers and officials, had inspected two topsail cutters which were being completed for naval service, and had toured the local batteries, with Jenour and Glassport finding it hard to keep up with his pace.

He smiled wryly. He was paying for it now.

Glassport watched him sip the hock before saying, 'There is a small reception for you this evening, Sir Richard.' He seemed to falter as the grey eyes lifted to him again. 'It hardly measures up to the occasion, but it was arranged only after your, er, flagship was reported.'

Bolitho noted the hesitation. Just one more who doubted his choice of ship.

Glassport must have feared a possible refusal and scampered on, 'Viscount Somervell will be *expecting* you.'

'I see.' He glanced at Jenour. 'Inform the Captain.' As the lieutenant made to excuse himself from the room Bolitho said, '*Send* a message with my cox'n. I need you with *me*.'

Jenour stared, then nodded. He was learning a lot today.

Bolitho waited for Yovell to bring the next pile of papers to the table. A far cry from command, the day-to-day running of a ship and her affairs. Every ship was like a small town, a family even. He wondered how Adam was faring with his new command. All he could find as an answer to his thought was envy. Adam was exactly like he had been. More reckless perhaps, but with the same doubtful attitude to his seniors.

Glassport watched him as he leafed through the papers while Yovell stooped politely above his right shoulder.

So this was the man behind the legend. Another Nelson, some said. Though God alone knew Nelson was not very popular in high places. He was the right man to command a fleet. Necessary, but afterwards? He studied Bolitho's lowered head, the loose lock above his eye. A grave, sensitive face, he thought, hard to picture in the battles he had read about. He knew Bolitho had been badly wounded several times, that he had almost died of a fever, although he did not know much about it.

A Knight of the Bath, from a fine old seafaring family, looked on as a hero by the people of England. All the things which Glassport would like to be and to have.

So why had he come to Antigua? There was little or no prospect of a fleet action, and provided they could get reinforcements for the various flotillas, and a replacement for − He wilted as Bolitho touched on that very point, as if he had looked up quickly to see right into his mind with those steady, compelling grey eyes.

'The Dons took the frigate *Consort* from us?' It sounded like an accusation.

'Two months back, Sir Richard. She drove aground under fire. One of my schooners was able to take off most of her company before the enemy stood against her. The schooner did well, I thought that −'

'The *Consort*'s captain?'

26

'At St. John's, Sir Richard. He is awaiting the convenience of a court martial.'

'Is he indeed.' Bolitho stood up and turned as Jenour re-entered the room. 'We are going to St. John's.'

Jenour swallowed hard. 'If there is a carriage, Sir Richard –' He looked at Glassport as if for guidance.

Bolitho picked up his sword. 'Two horses, my lad.' He tried to hide his sudden excitement. Or was it merely trailing a coat to draw him from his other anxiety? 'You are from Hampshire, *right?*'

Jenour nodded. 'Yes. That is –'

'It's settled then. Two horses immediately.'

Glassport stared from one to the other. 'But the reception, Sir Richard?' He sounded horrified.

'This will give me an appetite.' Bolitho smiled. 'I shall return.' He thought of Allday's patience, Ozzard and the others. '*Directly.*'

Bolitho peered closely at his reflection in an ornate wall mirror, then thrust the loose lock of hair from his forehead. In the mirror he could see Allday and Ozzard watching him anxiously, and his new flag lieutenant Stephen Jenour massaging his hip after their ride to St. John's and back to English Harbour.

It had been hot, dusty but unexpectedly exhilarating, and had almost been worthwhile just to see the expressions of passers-by as they had galloped along in the hazy sunshine.

It was dark now, dusk came early to the islands, and Bolitho had to study himself very carefully while his ear recorded the sound of violins, the muffled murmur of voices from the grand room where the reception was being held.

Ozzard had brought fresh stockings from the ship, while All-day had collected the fine presentation sword to replace the old blade Bolitho had been wearing.

Bolitho sighed. Most of the candles were protected by tall hurricane glasses so the light was not too strong. It might hide his crumpled shirt, and the stain left by the saddle on his breeches. There had been no time to return to *Hyperion. Damn Glassport and his reception.* Bolitho would much rather have stayed in his cabin and sifted through all which the frigate captain had told him.

Captain Matthew Price was young to hold command of so fine a vessel. The *Consort* of thirty-six guns had been working through some shoals when she had been fired on by a coastal battery. She had been that close inshore when she had unfortunately run aground. It was much as Glassport had described. A schooner had taken off many of *Consort*'s people, but had been forced to run, her task incomplete, as Spanish men-of-war had arrived on the scene.

Captain Price was so junior that he had not even been posted, and if a court martial ruled against him, which was more than likely, he would lose everything. At best he might return to the rank of lieutenant. The worst did not bear thinking about.

As Price sat in a small government-owned house to await the calling of the court martial he had plenty to ponder about. Not least that it might have been better had he been taken prisoner, or killed in battle. For his ship had been refloated and was now a part of His Most Catholic Majesty's fleet at La Guaira on the Spanish Main. Frigates were worth their tonnage in gold, and the navy was always in desperate need of them. When Bolitho had been in the Mediterranean there were only six frigates available between Gibraltar and the Levant. The president of Price's court martial would not be able to exclude that fact from his considerations.

Once, in desperation, the young captain had asked Bolitho what he thought of the possible outcome.

Bolitho had told him to expect his sword to point towards him at the table. To hazard his ship was one thing. To lose it to a hated enemy was another entirely.

There had been no sense in promising Price he could do something to divert the court's findings. Price had taken a great risk to discover the Spanish intentions. Laid beside what Bolitho already knew, his information could be invaluable. But it would not help the *Consort*'s captain now.

Bolitho said, 'I suppose it is time.' He looked at a tall clock and added, 'Are our officers present yet?'

Jenour nodded, then winced as the ache throbbed through his

thighs and buttocks. Bolitho was a superb horseman, but then so was he, or so he had believed. Bolitho's little joke about people from Hampshire being excellent riders had acted as a spur, but at no time had Jenour been able to keep pace with him.

He said, 'The first lieutenant arrived with the others while you were changing, Sir Richard.'

Bolitho looked down at the immaculate stockings and remembered when he had been a lowly lieutenant with only one fine pair for such occasions as this. The rest had been darned so many times it had been a wonder they had held together.

It gave him time to think about Captain Haven's request to remain aboard ship. He had explained that a storm might spring up without warning and prevent his return from the shore in time to take the necessary precautions. The air was heavy and humid, and the sunset had been like blood.

Hyperion's sailing master, Isaac Penhaligon, a fellow Cornishman by birth at least, had insisted that a storm was very unlikely. It was as if Haven preferred to keep to himself, even though someone at the reception might take his absence as a snub.

If only Keen was still his flag captain. He had but to ask, and Keen would have come with him. Loyalty, friendship, love, it was something of each.

But Bolitho had pressed Keen to remain in England, at least until he had settled the problems of his lovely Zenoria. More than anything else Keen wanted to marry his dark-eyed girl with the flowing chestnut hair. They loved and were so obviously *in* love that Bolitho could not bring himself to separate them so soon after they had found each other.

Or was he comparing their love with his own house?

He stopped his thoughts right there. *It was not the time.* Maybe it never could be now.

Perhaps Haven did not like him? He might even be afraid of him. That was something Bolitho had often found hard to believe in his own days as a captain. When he had first stepped aboard a new command he had tried to hide his nervousness and apprehension. It had been much later when he had understood that a ship's company was far more likely to be worried about him and what *he* might do.

Jenour asked politely, 'Shall we go, Sir Richard?'

Bolitho wanted to touch his left eye but stared instead at the nearest hurricane glass and the tendril of black smoke which rose straight up to the ceiling. It was clear and bright. No shadows, no mist to taunt him and take him off-guard.

Bolitho glanced at Allday. He would have to speak to him soon about his son. Allday had said nothing about him since the young sailor had left *Argonaute* on their return to England. *If I had had a son perhaps I would have wanted too much. Might have expected him to care about all the same things.*

A pair of handsome doors were pulled open by footmen who had hitherto been invisible in the shadows.

The music and babble of voices swept into the room like surf on a reef, and Bolitho found himself tensing his muscles as if to withstand a musket ball.

As he walked down the pillared corridor he pondered on the minds and the labour which had created this building on such a small island. A place which through circumstances of war had many times become a vital hinge for England's naval strategy.

He heard Jenour's heels tapping on the floor, and half-smiled as he recalled the lieutenant's eagerness to ride neck-and-neck with him. More like two country squires than King's officers.

He saw the overlapping colours of ladies' gowns, bare shoulders, curious stares as he drew closer to the mass of people. They had had little notice of his coming, Commodore Glassport had said, but he guessed that any official visitor or a ship from England was a welcome event.

He noticed some of *Hyperion*'s wardroom, their blues and whites making a clean contrast with the red and scarlet of the military and Royal Marines. Once again he had to restrain himself from searching for familiar faces, hearing voices, as if he still expected a handshake or a nod of recognition.

There were some steps between two squat pillars, and he saw Glassport peering along the carpet towards him. Relieved no doubt that he had actually arrived after his ride. One figure stood in the centre, debonair and elegant, and dressed from throat to ankle in white. Bolitho knew very little of the man he had come to meet. The Right Honourable the Viscount Somervell, his Majesty's

Inspector General in the Caribbean, seemed to have little which equipped him for the appointment. A regular face at Court and at the right receptions, a reckless gambler some said, and a swordsman of renown. The last was well-founded, and it was known that the King had intervened on his behalf after he had killed a man in a duel. To Bolitho it was familiar and painful territory. It hardly qualified him for being here.

A footman with a long stave tapped the floor and called, 'Sir Richard Bolitho, Vice-Admiral of the Red!'

The sudden stillness was almost physical. Bolitho felt their eyes following him as he walked along the carpet. Small cameos stood out. The musicians with their fiddles and bows motionless in mid-air, a young sea-officer nudging his companion and then freezing as Bolitho's glance passed over him. A bold stare from a lady with such a low-cut gown that she need not have covered herself at all, and another from a young girl who smiled shyly then hid her face behind a fan.

Viscount Somervell did not move forward to greet him but stood as before, one hand resting negligently on his hip, the other dangling at his side. His mouth was set in a small smile which could have been either amusement or boredom. His features were of a younger man, but he had the indolent eyes of someone who had seen everything.

'Welcome to –' Somervell turned sharply, his elegant pose destroyed as he glared into a trolley of candelabra which was being wheeled into the room behind him.

The sudden glare of additional light at eye-level caught Bolitho off-balance just as he raised his foot to the first of the steps. A lady dressed in black who had been standing motionless beside the Viscount reached out to steady his arm, while through the mass of candles he saw staring faces, surprise, curiosity, caught like onlookers in a painter's canvas.

'I beg your pardon, Ma'am!' Bolitho regained his balance and tried not to shade his eye as the mist swirled across it. It was like drowning, falling through deeper and deeper water.

He said, 'I am all right –' then stared at the lady's gown. It was not black, but of an exquisite green shot-silk which shone, and seemed to change colour in its folds and curves as the light that

31

had blinded him revealed her for the first time. The gown was cut wide and low from her shoulders, and the hair he remembered so clearly as being long and as dark as his own, was piled in plaits above her ears.

The faces, the returning murmur of speculative chatter faded away. He had known her then as Catherine Pareja. *Kate.*

He was staring, his momentary blindness forgotten as he saw her eyes, her sudden anxiety giving way to an enforced calm. She had known he was to be here. His was the only surprise.

Somervell's voice seemed to come from a great distance. He was calm again, his composure recovered.

'Of course, I had forgotten. You have met before.'

Bolitho took her proffered hand and lowered his face to it. Even her perfume was the same.

He heard her reply, 'Some while ago.'

When Bolitho looked up she seemed strangely remote and self-assured. Indifferent even.

She added, 'One could never forget a hero.'

She held out her arm for her husband and turned towards the watching faces.

Bolitho felt an ache in his heart. She was wearing the long gold filigree earrings he had bought her in that other unreal world, in London.

Footmen advanced with trays of glittering glasses, and the small orchestra came to life once again.

Across the wine and past the flushed, posturing faces their eyes met and excluded everyone.

Glassport was saying something to him but he barely heard. After all that had happened, it was still there between them. It must be quenched before it destroyed them both.

3

King's Ransom

Bolitho leaned back in his chair as a white-gloved hand whisked away the half-emptied plate and quickly replaced it with another. He could not remember how many courses he had been offered nor how many times the various goblets and fine glasses had been refilled.

The air was full of noise, the mingled voices of those present, at a guess some forty officers, officials and their ladies with the small contingent from *Hyperion*'s wardroom divided amongst them. The long room and its extended table was brightly lit by candles, beyond which the shadows seemed to sway in a dance of their own as the many footmen and servants bustled back and forth to maintain a steady supply of food and wine.

They must have garnered servants from several houses, Bolitho thought, and he could gather from the occasional savage undertones of the senior footman that there had been several disasters between kitchen and table.

He was seated at Catherine's right hand, and as the conversation and laughter swirled around them he was very aware of her, although she gave little hint of her own feelings at his presence. At the far end of the table Bolitho saw her husband, Viscount Somervell, sipping his wine and listening with apparent boredom to Commodore Glassport's resonant and thickening tones. Occasionally Somervell appeared to glance along the table's length, excluding everyone but his wife or Bolitho. Interest, awareness? It was impossible to determine.

As the doors swung open from time to time to a procession of sweating servants Bolitho saw the candles shiver in the smoky air. Otherwise there was little hint of movement, and he pictured Haven, safe in his cabin, or brooding over his possible role in the future. He might show more animation when he learned what was expected of him and his command.

She turned suddenly and spoke directly to him. 'You are very quiet, Sir Richard.'

He met her gaze and felt his defence falter. She was just as striking, more beautiful even than he had remembered. The sun had given her neck and shoulders a fine blush, and he could see the gentle pulse of her heart where the silk gown folded around it.

One hand lay as if abandoned beside her glass, a folded fan close by. He wanted to touch it, to reassure himself or to reveal his own stupidity.

What am I? So full of conceit, so shallow that I could imagine her drawn to me again after so long?

He said instead, 'It must be seven years.'

Her face remained impassive. To anyone watching she might have been asking about England or the weather.

'Seven years and one month to be exact.'

Bolitho turned as the Viscount laughed at something Glassport had said.

'And then you married *him*.' It came out like a bitter accusation and he saw her fingers move as if they were listening independently.

'Was it so important?'

She retorted, 'You delude yourself, Richard.' Even the use of his name was like the awakening of an old wound. 'It was not so.' She held his gaze as he turned again. Defiance, pain, it was all there in her dark eyes. 'I need security. Just as you need to be loved.'

Bolitho hardly dared to breathe as the conversation died momentarily around him. He thought the first lieutenant was watching them, that an army colonel had paused with his goblet half-raised as if to catch the words. Even in imagination it felt like a conspiracy.

'Love?'

34

She nodded slowly, her eyes not leaving his. 'You need it, as the desert craves for rain.'

Bolitho wanted to look away but she seemed to mesmerise him.

She continued in the same unemotional tone, 'I wanted you then, and ended almost hating you. *Almost.* I have watched your life and career, two very different things, over the past seven years. I would have taken anything you offered me; you were the only man I would have loved without asking for security in marriage.' She touched the fan lightly. 'Instead you took another, one you imagined was a substitute —' She saw the shot strike home. '*I knew it.*'

Bolitho replied, 'I thought of you often.'

She smiled but it made her look sad. 'Really?'

He turned his head further so that he could see her clearly. He knew others might watch him for he appeared to face her directly, but his left eye was troubled by the flickering glare and the swooping shadows beyond.

She said, 'The last battle. We heard of it a month back.'

'You knew I was coming here?'

She shook her head. 'No. He tells me little of his government affairs.' She looked quickly along the table and Bolitho saw her smile as if in recognition. He was astonished that the small familiarity with her husband should hurt him so much.

She returned her gaze to his. 'Your injuries, are they —?' She saw him start. 'I helped you once, do you not remember?'

Bolitho dropped his eyes. He had imagined that she had heard or detected his difficulty in seeing her properly. It all flashed through his mind like a wild dream. His wound, the return of the fever which had once almost killed him. Her pale nakedness as she had dropped her gown and folded herself against his gasping, shivering body, while she had spoken unheard words and clasped him to her breasts to repulse the fever's torment.

'I shall *never* forget.'

She watched him in silence for some moments, her eyes moving over his lowered head and the dangling lock of hair, his grave sunburned features and the lashes which now hid his eyes, glad that he could not see the pain and the yearning in her stare.

35

Nearby, Major Sebright Adams of *Hyperion*'s Royal Marines was expounding on his experiences at Copenhagen and the bloody aftermath of the battle. Parris, the first lieutenant, was propped on one elbow, apparently listening, but leaning across the young wife of a dockyard official, his arm resting against her shoulder which she made no attempt to remove. Like the other officers, they were momentarily free of responsibility and the need to keep up any pretence and the posture of duty.

Bolitho was more aware than ever of a sudden isolation, the need to tell her his thoughts, his fears; and was revolted at the same time by his weakness.

He said, 'It was a hard fight. We lost many fine men.'

'And *you*, Richard? What more did you have to lose that you had not already abandoned?'

He exclaimed fiercely, 'Let it be, Catherine. It is over.' He raised his eyes and stared at her intently. 'It must be so!'

A side door opened and more footmen bustled around, but this time without new dishes. It would soon be time for the ladies to withdraw and the men to relieve themselves before settling down to port and brandy. He thought of Allday. He would be out there in the barge with his crew waiting for him. Any petty officer would have been sufficient, but he knew Allday. He would allow no other to wait for him. He would have been in his element tonight, he thought. Bolitho had never known any man able to drink his coxswain under the table, unlike some of the guests.

Somervell's voice cut along the littered cloth although he seemed to have no problem in making it carry.

'I hear that you saw Captain Price today, Sir Richard?'

Bolitho could almost feel the woman at his side holding her breath, as if she sensed the casual remark as a trap. Was guilt that obvious?

Glassport rumbled, 'Not captain for long, I'll wager!' Several of the guests chuckled.

A black footman entered the room and after the smallest glance at Somervell padded to Bolitho's chair, an envelope balanced carefully on a silver salver.

Bolitho took it and prayed that his eye would not torture him now.

36

Glassport was going on again. 'My only frigate, by God! I'm dashed hard put to know —'

He broke off as Somervell interrupted rudely, 'What is it, Sir Richard? Are we to share it?'

Bolitho folded the paper and glanced at the black footman. He was in time to see a strange sympathy on the man's face, as if he knew.

'You may be spared the spectacle of a brave officer's dishonour, Commodore Glassport.' His voice was hard and although it was directed at one man it gripped the whole table.

'Captain Price is dead.' There was a chorus of gasps. 'He hanged himself.' He could not resist adding, 'Are you satisfied?'

Somervell pushed himself back from the table. 'I think this may be a suitable moment for the ladies to retire.' He rose effortlessly to his feet, as if it was a duty rather than a courtesy.

Bolitho faced her and saw the concern stark in her eyes as if she wanted to tell him out loud.

Instead she said, 'We will meet.' She waited for him to raise his head from a brief bow. 'Soon.' Then with a hiss of silk she merged with the shadows.

Bolitho sat down and watched unseeingly as another hand placed a fresh glass by his place.

It was not their fault, not even the mindless Glassport's.

What could I have done? Nothing could interfere with the mission he intended to undertake.

It might have happened to any one of them. He thought of young Adam instead of the wretched Price sitting alone and picturing the grim faces of the court, the sword turned against him on the table.

It was curious that the message about Price's death had been sent directly from St. John's to *Hyperion*, his flagship. Haven must have read and considered it before sending it ashore, probably in the charge of some midshipman who in turn would hand it to a footman. It would not have hurt him to bring it in person, he thought.

He realised with a start that the others were on their feet, glasses raised to him in a toast.

Glassport said gruffly, 'To our flag officer, Sir Richard Bolitho,

37

and may he bring us fresh victories!' Even the huge amount of wine he had consumed could not hide the humiliation in his voice.

Bolitho stood up and bowed, but not before he had seen that the white-clad figure at the opposite end had not touched his glass. Bolitho felt his blood stir, like the moment when the topsails of an enemy revealed their intentions, or that moment in early dawn when he had faced another in a duel.

Then he thought of her eyes and her last word. *Soon.*

He picked up his own glass. *So be it then.*

The six days which followed *Hyperion*'s arrival at English Harbour were, for Bolitho at least, packed with activity.

Every morning, within an hour of the guardboat's delivery of messages or signals from the shore Bolitho climbed into his barge and with a puzzled flag lieutenant at his elbow threw himself into the affairs of the ships and sailors at his disposal. On the face of it, it was not a very impressive force. Even allowing for three small vessels still in their patrol areas, the flotilla, for it was no more than that, seemed singularly unsuited for the task in hand. Bolitho knew that their lordships' loosely-worded instructions, which were locked in his strongbox, carried all the risk and responsibility of direct orders given to a senior captain, or a lowly one like Price.

The main Antigua squadron, consisting of six ships-of-the-line, were reported as being scattered far to the north-west in the Bahama Islands, probably probing enemy intentions or making a show of force to deter would-be blockade runners from the Americas. The admiral was known to Bolitho, Sir Peter Folliot, a quiet, dignified officer who was said to be sorely tried by ill-health. Not the best ingredients for aggressive action against the French or their Spanish ally.

On the sixth morning, as Bolitho was being carried across the barely ruffled water towards the last of his command, he considered the results of his inspection and studies. Apart from *Obdurate*, an elderly seventy-four, which was still undergoing storm repairs in the dockyard, he had a total of five brigs, one sloop-of-war, and *Thor*, a bomb-vessel, which he had left until last. He could have summoned each commander to the flagship; it would have been what they were expecting of any flag officer, let alone one of Bolitho's reputation. They were soon to learn that he liked to discover things for himself, to get the feel of the men he would lead, if not inspire.

He considered Somervell, and his failure to visit *Hyperion* as he had promised after the reception. Was he making him wait deliberately, to put him in his place, or was he indifferent to the final plan, which they would need to discuss before Bolitho could take decisive action?

He watched the rise and fall of the oars, the way the bargemen averted their eyes whenever he glanced at them, Allday's black shadow across the scrubbed thwarts, passing vessels and those at anchor. Antigua might be a British possession, one so heavily defended that a need for more ships was unnecessary, but there were plenty of traders and coastal sailing-masters, who, if not actual spies, would be ready and willing to part with information to the enemy if only for their own free passage.

Bolitho shaded his eyes and looked towards the nearest hillside, to a battery of heavy guns marked only by a rough parapet and a lifeless flag above it. Defence was all very well, but you won wars by attacking. He saw dust along the coast road, people on the move, and thought again of Catherine. She had been rarely out of his thoughts, and he knew in his heart he had worked himself so hard to hold his personal feelings at bay where they could not interfere.

Perhaps she had told Somervell everything which had happened between them. Or maybe he had forced it out of her? He dismissed the latter immediately. Catherine was too strong to be used like that. He recalled her previous husband, a man twice her age, but one of surprising courage when he had tried to help Bolitho's men defend a merchant ship from corsairs. Catherine had hated him then. Their feelings for each other had grown from that animosity. Like steel in the livid heat of a forge. He was still not sure what had happened to them, where it might otherwise have led.

Such a short climax in London after their meeting outside the Admiralty, when Bolitho had just been appointed commodore of his own squadron.

Seven years and one month. Catherine had forgotten nothing. It was unnerving, and at the same time exciting, to realise how she had managed to follow his career, and his life; two separate things as she had put it.

Allday whispered, 'They've manned the side, Sir Richard.'

Bolitho tilted his hat and stared towards the bomb-vessel. His Britannic Majesty's Ship *Thor*.

Small when compared with a frigate or line-of-battleship, but at the same time heavy-looking and powerful. Designed for bombarding shore installations and the like. *Thor*'s main armament consisted of two massive thirteen-inch mortars. The vessel had to be powerfully built to withstand the downward recoil of the mortars, which were fired almost vertically. With ten heavy carronades and some smaller six-pounders, *Thor* would be a slow sailer. But unlike many of her earlier consorts which had been ketch-rigged, *Thor* mounted three masts and a more balanced ship-rig, which might offer some improvement in perverse winds.

A shadow passed over Bolitho's thoughts. Francis Inch had been given command of a bomb-vessel after he had left *Hyperion*.

He looked up and saw Allday watching him. It was uncanny.

Allday said quietly, 'The old *Hekla*, Sir Richard – remember her?'

Bolitho nodded, not seeing Lieutenant Jenour's mystified stare. It was hard to accept that Inch was dead. Like so many now.

'*Attention on deck!*'

Calls trilled and Bolitho seized a ladder with both hands to haul himself through the low entry port.

The vessels he had already visited in harbour had seemed startled by his arrival on board. Their commanders were young; all but one had been lieutenants just months ago.

There was no such nervousness about *Thor*'s captain, Bolitho thought as he doffed his hat to the small quarterdeck.

Commander Ludovic Imrie was tall and narrow-shouldered, so that his solitary gold epaulette looked as if it might fall off at any moment. He stood over six feet, and when you considered

Thor's headroom, four feet six inches in some sections, it must have seemed like being caged.

'I bid you welcome, Sir Richard.' Imrie's voice was surprisingly deep, with a Scottish burr which reminded Bolitho of his mother. Bolitho was introduced to two lieutenants and a few junior warrant officers. A small company. He had already noted their names, and sensed their reserve giving way to interest or curiosity.

Imrie dismissed the side-party and after a brief hesitation ushered Bolitho below to his small stern-cabin. As they stooped beneath the massive deck beams, Bolitho recalled his first command, a sloop-of-war; how her first lieutenant had apologised for the lack of space for the new commander. Bolitho had been almost beside himself with glee. After a lieutenant's tiny berth in a ship-of-the-line it had seemed like a palace.

Thor's was even smaller. They sat opposite one another while a wizened messman brought a bottle and some glasses. A far cry from Somervell's table, Bolitho thought.

Imrie spoke easily about his command, which he had held for two years. He was obviously very proud of *Thor*, and Bolitho sensed an immediate resentment when he suggested that bombs, for the most part, had achieved little so far in the various theatres of war.

'Given a chance, sir –' He grinned and shrugged his narrow shoulders. 'I beg your pardon, Sir Richard, I should have known.'

Bolitho sipped the wine; it was remarkably cool. 'Known what?'

Imrie said, 'I'd heard you tested your captains with a question or two –'

Bolitho smiled. 'It worked this time.' He remembered some of the others he had met in Antigua. He had felt something akin to hostility, if not actual dislike. Because of Price, perhaps? After all, they had known him, had worked in company with his frigate. They might think that he had killed himself deliberately because Bolitho had refused to intervene. Bolitho could think of several occasions when he had felt much the same.

Imrie stared through the skylight at the empty sky.

'If I could lie near a good target, sir, I'd put down such a

41

barrage, the enemy'd think Hell had dropped amongst them. The Dons have never faced –' He faltered and added apologetically, 'I mean, that is, if we were against the Spaniards at any time –'

Bolitho eyed him steadily. Imrie had worked it out all by himself. Why else would his vice-admiral bother to call on him? Price's exploits and disaster on the Spanish Main linked with *Thor*'s obvious advantages in the shallows where *Consort* had run aground had formed their own picture in his mind.

Bolitho said, 'That is well thought, Commander Imrie. I will trust you to keep your suppositions to yourself.' It was odd that none of the others, not even Haven, had once questioned their motives for being here.

Bolitho rubbed his left eyelid and then withdrew his hand quickly. 'I have studied the reports, and have re-read the notes my aide took down when I spoke to Captain Price.'

Imrie had a long face with a craggy jaw and looked as if he could be a formidable opponent in any circumstances. But his features softened as he listened to Bolitho. Perhaps because he had referred to the dead man by his full rank. It offered some small dignity, a far cry from the lonely grave below the East Battery.

Bolitho said, 'The approaches are too well protected for what I must keep in mind. Any well-sited artillery can destroy a slow-moving vessel with ease, and with heated shot the effect would be disastrous.'

Imrie rubbed his chin, his eyes far away. As Bolitho had noticed, they were unmatched, one dark and the other pale blue.

He said, 'If we are both thinking of the same patch of coast, Sir Richard, and of course we can't be *sure* of that –'

Jenour watched, fascinated. These two officers, each a veteran in his own field, yet able to discuss something he still could not grasp, and chuckle over it like two conspiring schoolboys. It was unbelievable.

Bolitho nodded. 'But *if* –'

'Even *Thor* might have to lay-off too far to use the mortars, Sir Richard.' He scanned his face as if expecting an argument or disappointment. 'We don't draw much less than *Consort* did.'

A boat thudded alongside and Bolitho heard Allday barking at someone for interrupting their conference.

Then his face appeared in the skylight. He said, 'Beggin' your pardon, Sir Richard. Message from *Hyperion*. The Inspector General is come aboard.'

Bolitho concealed a tremor of excitement. Somervell had given in to curiosity at last. Or was he imagining that also? That there was already some kind of contest between them?

Bolitho stood up and winced as his head struck one of the beams.

Imrie exclaimed, 'God damn it, Sir Richard, I should have warned you!'

Bolitho reached for his hat. 'It acted as a reminder. It was less painful than the memory.'

On deck, the side-party had assembled and Bolitho saw *Hyperion*'s jolly-boat already pulling back to the ship. Allday clambered fuming down to the waiting barge. He had sent that pink-faced midshipman off with a flea in his ear. Young puppy. He glared at the bargemen. 'Stand by in the boat, damn you!'

Bolitho made a decision. 'Tell your senior to take over, Imrie. I wish you to accompany me directly.'

Imrie's jaw dropped open. 'But, Sir Richard –'

Bolitho saw his first lieutenant watching them. 'He is just aching to take command, albeit for a day – it is every first lieutenant's dream!' He was amazed at his own good humour. It was like a dam holding all the worries here and at home back and out of view.

He stooped over as if to examine one of the snout-nosed twenty-four pounder carronades. It gave him time to massage his eye again, to drive off the mist which the sharp sunlight had thrown at him as if to crack his confidence.

Imrie whispered to Jenour, 'What a man, eh? I think I'd follow him to hell *and* back!'

Jenour watched Bolitho's shoulders. 'Aye, sir.' It was only a guess, but he saw more than anyone of Bolitho apart from Allday and the cabin staff. It was strange that they never mentioned it. But Jenour's uncle was a physician in Southampton. He had spoken of something like this. Jenour had seen Bolitho caught off balance, like the moment when the Viscount's beautiful wife had reached out to aid him, and other times at sea before that.

43

But nothing was ever said about it. He had to be mistaken.

All the way across the anchorage Bolitho pondered over his mission. If he had frigates, even one at his disposal, he could plan around the one, formidable obstacle.

La Guaira, the Spanish port on the Main and gateway to the capital Caracas, was impregnable. That was only because nobody had ever attempted it before. He could feel Imrie's curiosity and was glad he had visited the *Thor* before discussing the venture with Haven and the others.

Imrie would be confident but not reckless. Price had believed he could do it, although for different reasons. Had he succeeded, it was unlikely that even a tiny fishing dory could slip through the Dons' defences afterwards.

Allday muttered, 'We have to put round t'other side, Sir Richard.' He sounded irritated, and Bolitho knew that he was still brooding over his newly-discovered and as quickly lost son.

Jenour stood up and swayed in the barge. 'The water-lighters are alongside, Sir Richard. Shall I signal them to stand away for you?'

Bolitho tugged his coat. 'Sit down, you impatient young upstart.' He knew the young lieutenant was smiling at his rebuke. 'We need fresh water, and *Hyperion* does have two sides to her!'

They pulled around the bows and past the out-thrust trident. Bolitho glanced up at the figurehead's fierce stare. Many a man must have seen that lancing through the gunsmoke and felt a last fear before he was cut down in battle.

He found Haven agitated and probably worried that Bolitho would berate him.

'I am sorry about the lighters, sir! I was not expecting you!'

Bolitho crossed the deck and looked down. Again, it was to test his eye, to prepare it for the cool shadows between decks.

'No matter.' He knew Haven was watching Imrie with suspicion and said, 'Commander Imrie is my guest.' He rested his hands on the sun-baked woodwork and regarded the nearest lighter. They were huge, flat-bottomed craft, their open hulls lined with great casks of water. One line of casks had already been hoisted up and lowered inboard on tackles; and Bolitho saw Parris, the first lieutenant, one foot resting negligently on a hatch

44

coaming, watching Sheargold the beaky-faced purser check each cask before it was sent below. He was about to turn away and then said, 'The lighter is still on even keel, yet all the casks are on the outboard side.'

Haven observed him warily, as if he thought Bolitho had been too long in the sun.

'They are so constructed, sir. Nothing will tilt them.'

Bolitho straightened his back and looked at Imrie.

'*There you have it*, Imrie. A platform for your mortars!' He ignored their combined astonishment.

'*Now*, I must meet the Inspector General!'

In the bars of bright forenoon sunlight, The Right Honourable the Viscount Somervell lounged against a leather-backed chair and listened without interruption. He was dressed in very pale green with brocade and stitching which would put any prince to shame. Close-to and in the brilliant glare Somervell looked younger, mid-thirties, her age or perhaps less.

Bolitho tried not to think beyond the outline of his plan, but Catherine seemed to linger in the great cabin like a shadow, as if she too was making comparisons.

Bolitho walked to the stern windows and looked out at some passing fishing boats. The anchorage was still flat and calm, but the mist was drifting seawards, and the pendant above an anchored brig was lifting occasionally to a lifeless breeze.

He said, 'Captain Price –' He paused, expecting Somervell to interrupt, or to voice some scathing comment. He did not. '– made a practice of patrolling that section of the Main where he was eventually forced to abandon *Consort*. He took careful note of everything he saw, and searched or destroyed some twenty enemy vessels in the process. Given time –'

This was Somervell's cue. 'It ran out for him.' He leaned forward in his chair, his pale eyes unblinking despite the harsh glare. 'And you have actually *discussed* some of this secret matter with, er, a Commander Imrie?' He spoke the man's name indifferently, as a landowner might speak of a lowly farm labourer. 'That is surely an extra risk?'

Bolitho replied, 'Imrie is an intelligent officer, shrewd too.

45

When I spoke to my other commanders earlier I had the impression that they were convinced I intended to try and cut out the *Consort*, or *Intrépido* as she has been renamed.'

Somervell pressed his fingertips together. 'You *have* done your work well, Sir Richard!'

Bolitho continued, 'Imrie would guess immediately that I had something else in mind. He knew that his *Thor* is too heavy and slow for a cutting-out expedition.'

'I am relieved to know that you have told him no more at present.'

Bolitho lowered his eyes to the chart, unnerved that Somervell could get under his skin so easily.

'Every year, Spanish treasure convoys set sail from the Main with each ship carrying a King's ransom. Between them, the church and the army have raped the continent, and now the King of Spain needs gold all the more. His French masters are making certain of their share.'

Somervell stood up and walked casually to the chart. Everything he did looked bored and unhurried, but his reputation as a swordsman made a lie of that.

He said, 'When I first came out here at His Majesty's *direction* –' He dabbed his mouth with a silk handkerchief and Bolitho thought it was to hide a small smile, 'I considered that the capture of such treasure might be just another dream. I know that Nelson has had some luck, but that was at sea where the chance of finding such booty is even more difficult.'

He traced the lines with one finger. 'La Guaira is well defended. It is where they will have taken the *Consort*.'

'With respect, my lord, I doubt that. La Guaira is the gateway to the capital, Caracas, but it is not suitable to refit a man-of-war, and it seems likely she will have been damaged after driving ashore.' Before Somervell could disagree he touched the coast away from La Guaira. 'Here, my lord, Puerto Cabello, seventy miles to the west'rd. It would be a far more likely destination.'

'Hmm.' Somervell leaned over the chart and Bolitho noticed a livid scar below his ear. A close call, he thought grimly.

Somervell continued, 'It is rather near to your intended operation. I am really not convinced.' He stood up and walked around the cabin as if pacing out a rectangle. 'Price saw vessels at anchor, and I have had reports that treasure-ships are using La Guaira. The place is well defended, with at least three fortresses, and as *Consort* discovered to her cost, some other batteries, probably horse-artillery, for good measure.' He shook his head. 'I don't like it. If we still had the frigate it might, and I only say *might*, be different. Should you attack, and the Dons repulse you, we shall toss away every chance of surprise. The King of Spain would lose a fleet, rather than surrender his gold. I am *not* convinced.'

Bolitho watched him and felt strangely calm. In his mind the hazy plan had become suddenly real, like a shoreline hardening through a dawn mist. War at sea was always a risk. It took more than skill and plain courage; it took what his friend Thomas Herrick would describe as the work of Lady Luck. Friend? Was he still that after what had happened?

'I am prepared to take that chance, my lord.'

'Well, maybe I am not!' Somervell swung round, his eyes cold. 'There is more than glory at stake here!'

'I never doubted it, my lord.'

They faced one another, each testing the other's intentions.

Somervell said suddenly, 'When I first came to this damned place I imagined that some well-tried and gallant captain would be sent to seek out and capture one of the *galleons*.' He almost spat out the word. 'I was informed that a squadron would eventually come and seal off the escape routes which these Spanish *ladies* take on their passage to the Canaries and their home ports.' He held out one hand as if about to bow. 'Instead, *you* are sent, like a vanguard, to give the matter weight, to carry it through *no matter what*. So if we fail, the enemy victory will seem all the greater – what do you say about that?'

Bolitho shrugged. 'I think it can be done.' It came to him like a cry in the night. Somervell needed it to succeed more than anyone. Because of disfavour at court or because he was in some sort of trouble which a share of the prize money would readily take care of?

He said flatly, 'There is no time left, my lord. If we wait until reinforcements arrive from England, and I must stress that I am

47

only expecting three more liners, the whole world will be after us. A victory may help our finances, but I can assure you that it will more than damage the Franco–Spanish alliance.'

Somervell sat down and carefully arranged his coat to give his thoughts time to settle.

He said irritably, 'The secret will out anyway.'

Bolitho watched him pout his lips and tried not to imagine them touching her neck, her breast.

Then Somervell smiled; it made him appear momentarily vulnerable. 'Then I agree. It shall be done as you describe. I am empowered to get you any assistance you need.' The smile vanished. 'But I cannot help you if –'

Bolitho nodded, satisfied. 'Yes, my lord, that word *if* can mean so much to a sea-officer.'

He heard someone hailing a boat, the clatter of oars nearby and guessed that Somervell had planned his departure, like his visit, to the minute.

Bolitho said, 'I shall tell Captain Haven at once.'

Somervell was only half-listening but he said, 'As little as possible. When two men share a secret, it is no longer a secret.' He looked at the screen door as Ozzard entered carrying his hat with elaborate care.

Somervell said quietly, 'I am glad we met. Though for the life of me I cannot imagine why you insisted on taking this mission.' He eyed him quizzically. 'A death-wish perhaps? You must surely have no need for more glory.' Then he turned on his heel and strode from the cabin.

At the entry port he glanced indifferently at the rigid marines and waiting side-party, then at Imrie's lanky shape by a poop ladder.

'I would imagine that the Lady Belinda is displeased about your zest for duty so soon after your recent victory?' He smiled wryly, then walked to the entry port without another glance.

Bolitho watched the smart launch being pulled away from *Hyperion*'s shadow and pondered what they had discussed; more, what they had left unsaid.

The reference to Belinda, for instance. What had Somervell expected to incite? Or was it merely something he could not

48

restrain when neither of them had once mentioned Catherine?

Bolitho looked at the nearest anchored brig, the *Upholder*. Very like Adam's command, he thought.

Haven moved nearer and touched his hat. 'Any orders, Sir Richard?'

Bolitho pulled out his watch and snapped open the guard. Exactly noon, yet it felt like no time since he had left to visit *Thor*.

'Thank you, Captain Haven.' Their eyes met, and Bolitho could feel the other man's reserve, a wariness which was almost physical. 'I shall require all our captains on board at the close of the afternoon watch. Bring them aft to my quarters.'

Haven swallowed. 'The rest of our vessels are still at sea, sir.'

Bolitho glanced round, but the guard was dismissed, and only a few idlers and the master's mate of the watch were nearby.

He said, 'I intend to up-anchor within the week, as soon as there is wind enough to fill our canvas. We shall sail southwest to the Main and stand off La Guaira.'

Haven had ruddy, sunburned cheeks which matched his hair, but they seemed to pale. 'That's six hundred miles, sir! In this ship, without support, I'm not certain –'

Bolitho lowered his face and said, 'Have you no stomach for it, man? Or are you seeking an early retirement?' He hated himself, knowing that Haven could not hit back.

He added simply, 'I need you, and so does this ship. It has to be enough.' He turned away, despairing at what he saw in Haven's eyes.

He noticed Imrie and called, 'Come with me, I wish to pick your brains.'

Bolitho winced as a shaft of sunlight lanced down through the mizzen shrouds. For just those few seconds his eye was completely blind, and it was all he could do not to cry out.

A death-wish, Somervell had said. Bolitho groped into the poop's shadows and felt the bitterness coursing through him. Too many had died because of him, and even his friends were damaged by his touch.

Imrie ducked his head beneath the poop and walked beside him into the gloom between decks.

'I have been thinking, Sir Richard, and I've a few ideas –'

He had not seen the dismay on his admiral's face, nor could he guess how his simple remarks were like a lifeline for him.

Bolitho said, 'Then we shall quench our thirst while I listen.'

Haven watched them leave the quarterdeck and called for the signals midshipman. He told the boy the nature and time of the signal for the other captains to repair on board, then turned as the first lieutenant hurried towards him.

Before the lieutenant could speak Haven rasped, 'Do I have to perform your duties too, damn you?' He strode away adding, 'By God, if you cannot do better, I'll see you cast ashore for good!'

Parris stared after him, only his tightly bunched fists giving a hint of his anger and resentment.

'*And God damn you too!*' He saw the midshipman staring owlishly at him and wondered if he had spoken aloud. He grinned wearily. 'It's a fine life, Mr Mirrielees, provided you hold your tongue!'

At eight bells that afternoon, the signal was run up to the yard. It was begun.

4

Storm Warning

Bolitho stood in the centre of the deserted boatshed and allowed his eyes to grow accustomed to its shapes and shadows. It was a great, ramshackle building, lit by just a few guttering lanterns which swayed on long chains to reduce the risk of fire, and which gave the impression that the place was moving like a ship.

It was evening outside, but unlike the previous ones the darkness was alive with sounds, the creak and slap of palm fronds, the uneasy ripple of wavelets beneath the crude slipway upon which the water-lighter had been prepared for its passage south. The boatshed had been a hive of activity, with shipwrights and sailors working against time to rig extra bilge pumps and fit iron crutches along the bulwarks so that it could be manhandled by long sweeps when required.

Bolitho felt the loose sand in his shoes from his walk along the foreshore while he went over his plans for the hundredth time. Jenour had kept him close company, but had respected his need to be alone, at least with his thoughts.

Bolitho listened to the lap of water, the gentle moan of wind through the weather-worn roof. They had prayed for wind; now it might rise and turn against them. If the lighter was swamped before it could reach the rendezvous he must decide what to do. He would either have to send *Thor* inshore unsupported, or call off the attack. He thought of Somervell's eyes, of the doubt he had seen there. No, he would not back down from the attack; it was pointless to consider alternatives.

He glanced around at the black, inert shadows. Skeletons of old boats, frames of others yet to be completed. The smells of paint, tar and cordage. It was strange that it never failed to excite him even after all the years at sea.

Bolitho could recall the sheds at Falmouth, where he and his brother, Hugh, and sometimes his sisters had explored all the secret places, and had imagined themselves to be pirates and princesses in distress. He felt a stab in his heart as he pictured his child, Elizabeth. How she had plucked at his epaulettes and buttons when he had first seen her, had picked her up so awkwardly.

Instead of drawing him and Belinda closer, the child had done the opposite. One of their disputes had been over Belinda's announcement that she wanted her daughter to have a governess and a proper nurse to care for her. That, and the proposed move to London, had sparked it off.

She had exclaimed on one occasion, 'Because you were raised in Falmouth with other village children, you cannot expect me to refuse Elizabeth the chance to better herself, to take proper advantage of your achievements.'

It had been a difficult birth, while Bolitho had been away at sea. The doctor had warned Belinda against having another child, and a coldness had formed between them which Bolitho found hard to accept and understand.

She had said sharply on another occasion, 'I told you from the beginning, I am not Cheney. Had we not looked so much alike I fear you would have turned elsewhere!'

Bolitho had wanted to break down the barrier, take her to him and pour out his anguish. To tell her more of the damage to his eye, admit what it might mean.

Instead he had met her in London, and there had been an unreal, bitter hostility which both of them would regret.

Bolitho touched his buttons and thought of Elizabeth again. She was just sixteen months old. He stared around with sudden desperation. Would she never play in boatsheds like this one? Romp on the sand and come home filthy to be scolded and loved? He sighed, and Jenour responded immediately. '*Thor* should be well on her way, Sir Richard.'

52

Bolitho nodded. The bomb-vessel had sailed the previous night. God alone knew if spies had already gleaned news of her proposed employment. Bolitho had made certain that rumours had been circulated that *Thor* was taking the lighter in tow to St Christopher's, and even Glassport had put aside his resentment to provide some deck cargo with the senior officer's name and destination plainly marked.

Anyway, it was too late now. Perhaps it had been so when he had insisted on sailing in advance of his new squadron, to deal with the King's need for gold in his own way. *Death-wish*. It stuck in his mind like a barb.

He said, 'Imrie will doubtless be glad to be at sea.'

Jenour watched his upright figure and saw that he had removed his hat and loosened his neckcloth as if to draw every benefit from this last walk ashore.

Bolitho did not notice the glance, but was thinking of his other commanders. Haven had been right about one thing. The remaining three vessels of his small force had not yet returned to English Harbour. Either Glassport's schooner had been unable to find them, or they had separately decided to drag out their time. He thought of their faces when they had gathered in the great cabin. Thynne, of the third-rate *Obdurate* which was still completing repairs to storm-damage, was the only post-captain amongst them. Bolitho's main impression had been one of youth, the other that of polite wariness. They had all known the dead Price, and perhaps they saw in Bolitho's strategy something stolen, by which their admiral intended to profit.

He had remarked as much to Jenour, not because his young flag-lieutenant had either the experience or the wisdom to comment, but because he needed to share it with someone he could trust.

Typically, Jenour had insisted, 'They all know your record, Sir Richard. That is enough for any man!'

Bolitho glanced at him now. A pleasant, eager young man who reminded him of no one. Maybe that was the reason for his choice. That and his unnerving knowledge of his past exploits, ships and battles.

The three brigs, *Upholder*, *Tetrarch* and *Vesta*, would weigh tomorrow and sail with their flagship. It was to be hoped they did not run down on some enemy frigates before they reached the Main. The brigs mounted only forty-two pop-guns between them. If only the one sloop-of-war had received his recall signal. The *Phaedra* at least looked like a small frigate, and in proper hands could double as one. Or was he again thinking of his first command, and the luck he had enjoyed with her?

Bolitho walked slowly to the end of the slipway where it dipped into the uneasy catspaws. The water looked like ebony, with only occasional shadows and reflections from riding-lights, or as in *Hyperion*'s case, the checkered lines of open gunports. He felt the warm breeze stir his coat-tails and tried to picture his chart, the uncertainties which marked each of the six hundred miles as surely as any beacons.

Bolitho tried not to become irritated when he thought of Haven. He was no coward, but had shown himself to be beset by other, deeper anxieties. Whatever he really believed about being given command of a veteran like *Hyperion*, Bolitho knew differently. Old she might be, but she was a far better sailer than most. He smiled sadly, recalling her as she had been when he had first taken command as a young captain. She had been in commission so long without entering harbour for a refit that she was unbearably slow. Even with her copper-sheathing, the weed on her bottom had been yards long, so that under full sail she could only manage half the speed of her companions.

It was unusual for any captain to antagonise his admiral, whether he hated him or not. The climb to promotion was hard enough without flinging down more obstacles. Haven refused every offer of personal contact, and when, on the passage from England, tradition had insisted on his presence at table while Bolitho had entertained some of the junior officers, he had kept to himself. Alone amongst so many. He thought of the picture of Haven's pretty wife. Was she the cause of his moods? Bolitho grimaced in the darkness. *That* he would understand well enough.

A shadowy fishing-boat slipped past the nearest anchored brig. She could be carrying a message to the enemy. If the Dons found out what they intended, the admiral in Havana would have a whole squadron at sea within hours of receiving the news.

It was time to return to the jetty where his barge would be waiting, but he felt a reluctance to leave. It was peaceful here, an escape from danger and the call of duty.

The fishing-boat had vanished, unaware of the thoughts it had roused.

Bolitho stared at *Hyperion*'s glowing lines of open ports. As if she was still hanging on to the angry sunset, or was burning from within. He thought of the six hundred souls packed into her rounded hull and once again felt the pain of his responsibility, which wrongly directed could destroy them all.

They did not ask for much, and even the simplest comforts were too often denied them. He could picture these faceless men now, the Royal Marines in their *barracks*, as they termed their section of the deck, polishing and cleaning their equipment. At other mess tables between the guns where sailors lived out their watches below, some seamen would be working on delicate scrimshaw, or making tiny models of bone and shell. Seamen with hands so roughened by cordage and tar, yet they could still produce such fine results. The midshipmen, of which *Hyperion* carried eight, would be performing their studies for promotion to the godly rank of lieutenant, sometimes working by the smallest light, a glim set in an old shell.

The officers had not yet emerged except for brief contact on deck, or at dinner in his cabin. Given time they would show what they could or could not do. Bolitho swung his hat at some buzzing insect in the darkness. *Given leadership*. It all came down to that. He heard Jenour's shoes scrape on the rough ground as he turned towards the top of the boatshed.

Then he heard the carriage wheels, the stamp of a restless horse, and a man calling out to calm it.

Jenour whispered hoarsely, ' 'Tis a lady, Sir Richard.'

Bolitho turned, only his heart giving away his feelings. Not once did he question who it might be at this hour. Perhaps he had inwardly been expecting her, hoping she might find him. And yet he knew otherwise. He felt off-guard, as if he had been stripped naked.

They met below the propped-up bow of an old boat and Bolitho saw that she was covered from head to toe in a long

55

cloak; its cowl hung loosely over her hair. Beyond her he could see a carriage on the road, a man at the horse's head, two small lamps casting an orange glow across the harness.

Jenour made to leave but she waved his apology aside and said, 'It is well. I have my maid with me.'

Bolitho stepped closer but she did not move towards him. She was completely hidden by the cloak, with just the oval of her face and a gold chain at her throat to break the darkness.

She said, 'You are leaving very soon.' It was a statement. 'I came to wish you luck with whatever –' Her voice trailed away. Bolitho held out his hand, but she said quickly, 'No. It is unfair.' She spoke without emotion, so that her voice seemed full of it. 'You met my husband?'

'Yes.' Bolitho tried to see her eyes but they too were in deep shadow. 'But I want to speak about you, to hear what *you* have been doing.'

She lifted her chin. 'Since you left me?' She half turned away. 'My husband spoke to me of your private meeting. You impressed him. He does not admire others very often. The fact you knew of the frigate's new name . . .'

Bolitho persisted, 'I need to talk, Kate.' He saw her shiver.

She said quietly, 'I once asked you to call me that.'

'I know. I do not forget.' He shrugged and knew he was floundering, losing a battle he could not fight.

'Nor I. I read everything I could, as if I expected that with time I could lose what I had felt. Hatred was not enough. . . .' She broke off. 'I was hurt – I bled because of you.'

'I did not know.'

She did not hear him. 'Did you imagine that your life meant so little to me that I could watch years of it pass and *not* be hurt? Years I could never share . . . did you think I loved you so little?'

'I thought you turned aside, Kate.'

'Perhaps I did. There was nothing offered. More than anything I wanted you to succeed, to be recognised for what you are. Would you have had people sneer when I passed as they do at Nelson's whore? How would you have ridden *that* storm, tell me?'

Bolitho heard Jenour's shoes as he moved away, but no longer cared.

56

'Please give me the chance to explain –'

She shook her head. 'You married another and have a child, I believe.'

Bolitho dropped his hands to his sides. 'And what of you? You married him.'

'*Him?*' She showed one hand through the cloak but withdrew it again. 'Lacey needed me. I was able to help him. As I told you, I wanted security.'

They watched each other in silence and then she said, 'Take care in whatever madness you are involved. I shall probably not see you again.'

Bolitho said, 'I shall sail tomorrow. But then he doubtless told you that too.'

For the first time her voice rose in passion and anger.

'Don't you use that tone with me! I came tonight because of the love I believed in. Not out of grief or pity. If you think –'

He reached out and gripped her arm through the cloak.

'Do not leave in anger, Kate.' He expected her to tear her arm away and hurry back to the coach. But something in his tone seemed to hold her.

He persisted, 'When I think of never seeing you again I feel guilty, because I know I could not bear it.'

She said in a whisper, 'It was your choice.'

'Not entirely.'

'Would you tell your wife you had seen me? I understand she is quite a beauty. Could you do that?'

She stepped back slightly. 'Your silence is my answer.'

Bolitho said bitterly, 'It is not like that.'

She glanced round towards the carriage and Bolitho saw the cowl fall from her head, caught the gleam of the lamps on her earrings. The ones he had given her.

She said, 'Please leave.' When he made to hold her again she backed away. 'Tomorrow I shall see the ships stand away from the land.' She put her hand to her face. 'I will feel nothing, Richard, because my heart, such as it is, will sail with you. *Now go!*'

Then she turned and ran from the shed, her cloak swirling about her until she reached the carriage.

Jenour said huskily, 'I am indeed sorry, Sir Richard –'

Bolitho turned on him. 'It's *time* you grew up, Mr Jenour!'

Jenour hurried after him, his mind still in a whirl from what he had seen and unwillingly shared.

Bolitho paused by the jetty and looked back. The carriage lamps were still motionless, and he knew she was watching him even in the darkness.

He heard the barge moving towards the jetty and was suddenly thankful. The sea had claimed him back.

At noon on the third day at sea Bolitho went on deck and walked along the weather side. It was like the other days, as if nothing, not even the men on watch, had changed.

He shaded his eyes to glance up at the masthead pendant. The wind was steady, as before, across the starboard quarter, creating a long regular swell which stretched unbroken in either direction. He heard the helmsman call, 'Steady as she goes, sir! Sou' west by west!' Bolitho knew it was more for his benefit than the officer-of-the-watch.

He looked at the long swell, the easy way *Hyperion* raised her quarter and allowed it to break against her flank. A few men were working high above the deck, their bodies tanned or peeling according to their time at sea. It never stopped. Splicing and reeving new lines, tarring-down and refilling the boats with water on their tier to keep the seams from opening in the relentless glare.

Bolitho felt the officer-of-the-watch glancing at him and tried to remember what he could about him. In a fight, one man could win or lose it. He paced slowly past the packed hammock nettings. Vernon Quayle was *Hyperion*'s fourth lieutenant, and unless he was checked or possibly killed he would be a tyrant if he ever reached post-rank. He was twenty-two, of a naval family, with sulky good looks and a quick temper. There had been three men flogged in his division since leaving England. Haven should have a word with the first lieutenant. Maybe he had, although the captain and his senior never appeared to speak except on matters of routine and discipline.

Bolitho tried not to think of *Hyperion* as she had once been. If any man-of-war could be said to be a happy ship in days like these, then so she had been then.

58

He walked forward to the quarterdeck rail and looked along the upper deck, the market-place of any warship.

The sailmaker and his mates were rolling up repaired lengths of canvas, and putting away their palms and needles. There was a sickly smell of cooking from the galley funnel, though how they could eat boiled pork in this heat was hard to fathom.

Bolitho could taste Ozzard's strong coffee on his tongue, but the thought of eating made him swallow hard. He had barely eaten since leaving English Harbour. Anxiety, strain, or was it still the guilt of seeing Catherine again?

Lieutenant Quayle touched his hat. '*Upholder* is on station, Sir Richard. The masthead makes a report every half-hour.' It sounded as if he was about to add, 'or I'll know the reason!'

Upholder was hull-down on the horizon and would be the first to signal that she had sighted *Thor* at the rendezvous. *Or not.* Bolitho had placed the brig in the van because of her young commander, William Trotter, a thoughtful Devonian who had impressed him during their first few meetings. It needed brains as well as good lookouts when so much depended on that first sighting.

Tetrarch was somewhere up to windward, ready to dash down if needed, and the third brig, *Vesta*, was far astern, her main role to ensure they were not being followed by some inquisitive stranger. So far they had seen nothing. It was as if the sea had emptied, that some dreadful warning had cleared it like an arena.

Tomorrow they would be near enough to land for the mast-head to recognise it.

Bolitho had spoken to *Hyperion*'s sailing master, Isaac Penhaligon. Haven was fortunate to have such an experienced master, he thought. *So am I.* Penhaligon was a Cornishman also, but in name only. He had been packed off to sea as a cabin-boy at the tender age of seven years, and had walked ashore very little since. He was now about sixty, with a deeply-lined face the colour of leather, and eyes so bright they seemed to belong to a younger person trapped within. He had served in a packet-ship, in East Indiamen, and eventually had, as he had put it, donned the King's coat as a master's mate. His skill and knowledge of the oceans and their moods would be hard to rival, Bolitho thought. An additional piece of luck was that he once sailed in these same waters, had fought off buccaneers and slavers, had done so much that nothing seemed to daunt him. Bolitho had watched him checking the noon sights, his eyes on the assembled midshipmen whose navigation and maritime knowledge lay in his hands, ready to make a rough comment if things went wrong. He was never sarcastic with the *young gentlemen*, but he was very severe, and they were obviously in awe of him.

Penhaligon had compared his charts and notes with Price's own observations and had commented sparingly, 'Knew his navigation, that one.' It was praise indeed.

A petty officer approached the lieutenant and knuckled his forehead. Bolitho was thankful to be left alone as Quayle hurried away. He had seen the petty officer's expression. Not just respect for an officer. It was more like fear.

He stroked the worn rail, hot from the sunlight. He thought of that last meeting in the boatshed, Catherine's voice and fervour. He had to see her again, if only to explain. *Explain what?* It could do nothing but harm to her. To both of them.

She had seemed unreachable, eager to tell him the hurt he had done her, and yet. . . .

He remembered vividly their first meeting, and when she had cursed him for the death of her husband. Her *second* husband. There had also been the one she rarely mentioned, a reckless soldier-of-fortune who had died in Spain in some drunken brawl. Who had she been then, and where had she come from? It was hard to see her, so captivating and striking as she was now, set against the squalor she had once touched on in a moment of intimacy.

And what of Somervell? Was he as cold and indifferent as he appeared? Or was he merely contemptuous; amused perhaps while he watched the reawakening of old memories, which he might use or ignore as he chose?

Would he ever know, or would he spend the rest of his life remembering how it had once been for so short a time, knowing that she was watching from a distance, waiting to learn what he was doing, or if he had fallen in battle?

Quayle had gone to the helm and was snapping something at

60

the midshipman-of-the-watch. Like the others, he was properly dressed, although he must be sweating fire in this heat.

Had Keen been his flag captain he would have – Bolitho called, 'Send for my servant!'

Quayle came alive. 'At *once*, Sir Richard!'

Ozzard emerged from the shadows of the poop and stood blinking in the glare, more mole-like than ever. Small, loyal and ever ready to serve Bolitho whenever he could. He had even read to him when he had been partially blinded, and before, when he had been smashed down by a musket. Meek and timid, but underneath there was another kind of man. He was well-educated and had once been a lawyer's clerk; he had run away to sea to avoid prosecution, and some said the hangman's halter.

Bolitho said, 'Take my coat, if you please.' Ozzard did not even blink as the vice-admiral tossed his coat over his arm and then handed him his hat.

Others were staring, but by tomorrow even Haven might tell his officers to walk the decks in their shirts and not suffer in silence. If it took a uniform to make an officer, there was no hope for any of them.

Ozzard gave a small smile, then scurried thankfully into the shadows again.

He had watched most faces of Bolitho, his moods of excitement and despair. There had been too many of the latter, he thought.

Past the marine sentry and into the great cabin. The world he shared with Bolitho, where rank was of little importance. He held up the coat and examined it for traces of tar or strands of spun yarn. Then he saw his own reflection in the mirror and held the coat against his own small frame. The coat hung almost to his ankles and he gave a shy smile.

He gripped the coat tightly as he saw himself that terrible day when the lawyer had sent him home early.

He had discovered his young wife, naked in the arms of a man he had known and respected for years.

They had tried to bluff it out and all the while he had been *dying* as he had stared at them.

Later, when he had left the small house on the Thames at

Wapping Wall, he had seen the shopkeeper's name opposite. *Tom Ozzard*, Scrivener. He had decided then and there it was to be his new identity.

Never once had he looked back to the room where he had stopped their lies with an axe, had hacked and slashed until there was nothing recognisable in human form.

On Tower Hill he had found the recruiting party; they were never far away, always in the hopes of a volunteer, or some drunkard who would take a coin and then find himself in a man-of-war until he was paid off or killed.

The lieutenant in charge had regarded him with doubt and then amusement. Prime seamen, strong young men, were what the King needed.

Ozzard carefully folded the coat. It was different now. They would take a cripple on two crutches if they got the chance.

Tom Ozzard, servant to a vice-admiral, afraid, no, terrified of battle when the ship quaked and reeled around him, a man with no past, no future.

One day, deep in his heart, Ozzard knew he would go back to that little house at Wapping Wall. Then, only then, he would give in to what he had done.

From the masthead lookout, curled up in the cross-trees, to Allday, sprawled in his hammock while he slept off the aftermath of several *wets*, from Ozzard to the man in the great cabin whom he served, most thoughts were on tomorrow.

Hyperion in all her years, and over the countless leagues she had sailed, had seen many come and go.

Beyond the figurehead's trident lay the horizon. Beyond that, only destiny could identify.

5

Leadership

Bolitho walked up the wet planking to the weather side of the quarterdeck and steadied himself by gripping the hammock nettings. It was still dark, with only spectres of spray leaping over the hull to break the sea's blackness.

Darker shadow moved across the quarterdeck to merge with a small group by the rail, where Haven and two of his lieutenants received their reports and passed out new orders.

Voices murmured from the gundeck, and Bolitho could picture the hands at work around the invisible eighteen-pounders, while on the deck below the heavier battery of thirty-two pounders, although equally busy, remained silent. Down there, beneath the massive deckhead beams, the gun crews were used to managing their charges in constant gloom.

The hands had been piped to an even earlier breakfast, probably an unnecessary precaution because when dawn found them they would still be out of sight of land – except, with any luck, by the masthead lookouts. In the past hour *Hyperion* had altered course, and was heading due west, her yards close-hauled with their reduced canvas of forecourse and topsails. It explained the uneasy, turbulent motion, but Bolitho had noticed the difference in the weather as soon as his feet had touched the damp rug by his cot.

The wind was steady but had risen; not much, but after the seemingly constant calm or glassy swell, it seemed violent by comparison.

Everyone nearby knew he was on deck and had discreetly crossed to the lee side to give him room to walk if he chose. He looked up at the rigging and saw the braced topsails for the first time. They were flapping noisily, showing their displeasure at being so tightly reined.

He had been awake for most of the night, but when the hands were called, and the work of preparing the ship for whatever lay ahead begun, he had felt a strange eagerness to sleep.

Allday had padded into the cabin, and while Ozzard had magicked up his strong coffee, the big coxswain had shaved him by the light of a spiralling lantern.

Allday had still not unburdened himself about his son. Bolitho could remember his elation when he had discovered he had a son of twenty, one he had known nothing about, who had decided to join him when his mother, an old love of Allday's, had died.

Then aboard the cutter *Supreme* after Bolitho had been cut down and almost completely blinded, Allday had nursed an anger and a despair that his son, also named John, was a coward, and had run below at the very moment when Bolitho had needed him most.

Now he knew differently. Afraid of the fire of battle perhaps, but no coward. It took a brave heart to disguise fear when the enemy's iron raked the decks.

But his son had asked to leave the ship when they had docked. For Allday's sake and for everyone's peace of mind Bolitho had spoken to the officer in charge of the coastguard near Falmouth, and asked him to find a place for him. His son, John Bankart as he was named after his mother, had been a good seaman, and could reef, splice and steer with the most experienced Jack. He had been performing the duties of second-coxswain in the prize *Argonaute* to help Allday, who was too proud to admit that his terrible wound was making things hard for him. Also, Allday had been able to keep an eye on him, until the day when Bolitho had been wounded whilst aboard the little cutter.

Bolitho disliked asking favours of anyone, especially because of his rank, and now he was unsure that he had done the right thing. Allday brooded about it, and when not required on duty spent too much time alone, or sitting with a tot in his hand in Ozzard's pantry.

64

We are both in need. Like dog and master. Each fearful that the other would die first.

A youthful voice exclaimed, 'Sunrise, sir!'

Haven muttered something, then crossed to the weather side. He touched his hat in the darkness.

'The boats are ready for lowering, Sir Richard.' He seemed more formal than ever. 'But if *Upholder* is on station we should get plenty of warning if we need to clear for action.'

'I agree.' Bolitho wondered what lay behind the formality. Was he hoping to see *Upholder*'s signal flying to announce she had *Thor* in sight? Or was he expecting the sea to be empty, the effort and the preparation a waste of time?

He said, 'I never tire of this moment.' Together they watched the first glimpse of sunlight as it rimmed the horizon like a fine gold wire. With *Hyperion* on her present tack the sun would rise almost directly astern, to paint each sail by turn then reach out far ahead, as if to show them the way to the land.

Haven commented, 'I just hope the Dons don't know we're so near.'

Bolitho hid a smile. Haven would make Job seem like an optimist.

Another figure crossed the deck and waited for Haven to see him. It was the first lieutenant.

Haven moved a few paces away. 'Well? What now?' His voice was hushed, but the hostility was obvious.

Parris said calmly, 'The two men for punishment, sir. May I tell the master-at-arms to stand over their sentence until —'

'*You shall not*, Mr Parris. Discipline is discipline, and I'll not have men escape their just deserts because we may or may not be engaging an enemy.'

Parris stood his ground. 'It was nothing that serious, sir.'

Haven nodded, satisfied. 'One of them is from your part-of-ship, am I right? Laker? Insolent to a petty officer.'

Parris's eyes seemed to glow from within as the first weak sunlight made patterns on the planking.

'They both lost their tempers, sir. The petty officer called him a whore's bastard.' He seemed to relax, knowing the battle was already lost. 'Me, sir, I'd have torn out his bloody tongue!'

65

Haven hissed, 'I shall speak with *you* later! Those men will be seized up and flogged at six bells!'

Parris touched his hat and walked away.

Bolitho heard the captain say, '*Bloody hound!*'

It was no part of his to interfere. Bolitho looked at the sunrise, but it was spoiled by what he had heard.

He would have to speak to Haven about it later when they were alone. He glanced up at the mizzen topmast as a shaft of light played across the shrouds and running rigging. If he waited until action was joined it might be too late.

The words seemed to echo around his mind. *If I should fall . . .* Every ship was only as strong as her captain. If there was something wrong . . . He looked round, Haven brushed from his thoughts, as the masthead yelled, 'Sail in sight to the sou'-west!'

Bolitho clenched his hands into fists. It must be *Upholder*, right on station. He had been right in his choice for the van.

He said, 'Prepare to come about, Captain Haven.'

Haven nodded. 'Pipe the hands to the braces, Mr Quayle.'

Another face fitted into the pattern; Bolitho's companion of the forenoon watch the day before. The sort of officer who would have no compassion when it came to a flogging.

Bolitho added, 'Do you have a good man aloft today?'

Haven stared at him, his face still masked in shadow. 'I – I believe so, sir.'

'Send up an experienced hand. A master's mate for my money.'

'Aye, sir.' Haven sounded tense. Angry with himself for not thinking of the obvious. He could scarcely blame Parris for that.

Bolitho glanced around as the shadows nearby took on shape and personality. Two young midshipmen, both in their first ship, the officer-of-the-watch, and below the break in the poop he saw the tall, powerful figure of Penhaligon the master. If he was satisfied with their progress you would never know, Bolitho thought.

'Deck there! *Upholder* in sight!'

Bolitho guessed the voice was that of Rimer, master's mate of the watch. He was a small, bronzed man with features so creased that he looked like some seafarer from a bygone age. The other vessel was little more than a blur in the faint daylight, but Rimer's experience and keen eye told him all he needed to know.

Bolitho said, 'Mr Jenour, get aloft with a glass.' He turned aside as the young lieutenant hurried to the shrouds. 'I trust you climb as fast as you ride?'

He saw the flash of teeth as Jenour grinned back at him. Then he was gone, his arms and legs working with all the ease of a nimble maintopman.

Haven crossed the deck and looked up at Jenour's white breeches. 'It will be light enough soon, sir.'

Bolitho nodded. 'Then we shall know.'

He bunched his fists together under his coat-tails as Jenour's voice pealed down.

'Signal from *Upholder*, sir! *Thor in company!*'

Bolitho tried not to show excitement or surprise. Imrie had done it.

'*Acknowledge!*' He had to cup his hands to shout above the slap of canvas and rigging. There was no further signal from *Upholder*. It meant nothing had gone wrong so far, and that the ungainly lighter was still safely in tow.

He said, 'When the others are in sight, Captain Haven, signal them to proceed while we are all of one mind. There is no time for another conference. Even now there is a chance we might be discovered before we are all in position.'

He walked to the nettings again. There was no point in showing doubt or uncertainty to Haven. He looked aloft as more and more of the rigging and spars took shape in the sunlight. It was strange that he had never mastered his dislike of heights. As a midshipman he had faced each dash aloft to help shorten or make more sail as a separate challenge. At night in particular, with the yards heeling over towards the bursting spray and the deck little more than a blur far beneath his feet, he had felt an enduring terror.

He saw some Royal Marines on the mizzen-top, their scarlet coats very bright while they leaned over the barricade to watch for the brig *Upholder*. Bolitho would have dearly liked to climb up past them without caring, as Jenour had done. He touched his left eyelid, then blinked at the reflected sunlight. Deceptively clear, but the worry was always there.

67

He looked along the upper deck, the gun crews standing down to go about their normal tasks as the first tension disappeared with the night.

So many miles. Too many memories. During the night when he had lain awake in his cot listening to the sluice and creak of the sea around the rudder he had recalled another time when *Hyperion* had sailed this far, while he had been her captain. They had slipped past the Isles of Pascua in the darkness and Bolitho could remember exactly that dawn attack on the French ships anchored there. And it was nine years ago. The same ship. But was he still the same man?

He glanced up at the mizzen top and was suddenly angry with himself.

'Hand me that glass, if you please.' He took it from a startled midshipman and walked purposefully to the weather shrouds. He could feel Haven watching him, saw Parris trying not to stare from the larboard gangway where he was in discussion with Sam Lintott, the boatswain. Probably telling him when to rig the gratings so that punishment could be carried out as ordered.

Then he saw Allday squinting up from the maindeck, his jaw still working on a piece of biscuit while he, too, stared with astonishment. Bolitho swung himself up and around the shrouds and felt the ratlines quiver with each step while the big signals telescope bounced against his hip like a quiver of arrows.

It was easier than he would have believed, but as he clambered into the top he decided it was far enough.

The marines stood back, nudging and grinning to each other. Bolitho was able to recall the name of the corporal, a fierce-looking man who had been a Norfolk poacher before he signed on with the Corps. Not before time, Major Adams had hinted darkly.

'Where is she, Corporal Rogate?'

The marine pointed. 'Yonder, sir! Larboard bow!'

Bolitho steadied the long telescope and watched as the brig's narrow poop and braced yards leapt into view. Figures moved about *Upholder*'s quarterdeck, steeply angled as the ship heeled over to show her bright copper to the early sunshine.

Bolitho waited for *Hyperion* to sway upright and for the

mizzen topmast to restrain its shivering, and beyond *Upholder* he saw a tan-coloured pyramid of sails. *Thor* was ready and waiting.

He lowered the glass as if to bring his thoughts into equal focus. Had he decided from the very beginning that he would lead the attack? If it failed, he would be taken prisoner, or. . . . He gave a grim smile. The *or* did not bear thinking about.

Corporal Rogate saw the secret smile and wondered how he would describe it to the others during the next watch below. How the admiral had spoken to him, just like another Royal. *One of us.*

Bolitho knew that if he sent another officer and the plan misfired, the blame would be laid at his door anyway.

They had to trust him. In his heart Bolitho knew that the next months were crucial for England, and for the fleet in particular. Leadership and trust went hand in hand. To most of his command he was a stranger and their trust had to be earned.

He considered his argument with sudden contempt. *Death-wish*. Was that a part of it too?

He concentrated on the brig's sturdy shape as she ducked and rose across steep waves. In his mind's eye he could already see the land as it would appear when they drew nearer. The anchorage at La Guaira consisted mainly of an open roadstead across the front of the town. It was known to be heavily defended by several fortresses, some of which were quite newly constructed because of the comings and goings of treasure-ships. Although La Guaira was just six miles or so from the capital, Caracas, the latter could only be reached by a twisting, mountainous road some four times that distance.

As soon as *Hyperion* and her consorts were sighted the Spanish authorities would send word to the capital with all the haste they could manage. Because of the time it would take on that precarious road, La Guaira might just as well be an island, he thought. All the intelligence they had been able to gather from traders and blockade-runners alike pointed to the captured frigate *Consort* being at Puerto Cabello, eighty miles further westward along the coast of the Main.

But suppose the enemy did not fall for the ruse, would not

believe that the British men-of-war were intending to cut out the new addition to their fleet?

So much depended on Price's maps and observations, and above all, luck.

He looked down at the deck far below and bit his lip. He knew he would never have sent a subordinate to carry out such a mission even nine years back when he had commanded the old *Hyperion*. He glanced at the marines. 'There's work for all of you soon, my lads.'

He swung himself down on to the futtock shrouds, more conscious of their faces split into huge grins than of the wind which flapped around his coat as if to fling him to the deck. *It was so easy.* A word, a smile, and they would die for you. It made him feel bitter and humble at the same time.

By the time he had reached the quarterdeck his mind had cleared. 'Very well. In one hour we shall alter course to the sou' west.' He saw the others nod. 'Have *Upholder* and *Tetrarch* tack closer to the land. I don't want the Dons to get near enough to see our strength.' He saw Penhaligon the sailing master give a wry smile and added, 'Or our lack of it. *Thor* will hold to windward of us in company with *Vesta*. Let me know when it is light enough to make signals.' He turned towards the poop and then paused. 'Captain Haven, a moment if you please.'

In the great cabin the strengthening sunlight made strange patterns on the caked salt which had spattered the stern windows. Most of the ship had been cleared for action before dawn. Bolitho's quarters were like a reminder of better times, until these screens were taken down, and the cabin furniture with all traces of his occupation here were taken to the security of the hold. He glanced at the black-barrelled nine-pounders which faced their closed ports on either side of the cabin. Then these two beauties would have the place to themselves.

Haven waited for Ozzard to close the screen door and withdraw, then stood with his feet apart, his hat balanced in both hands.

Bolitho looked at the sea beyond the smeared glass. 'I intend to shift to *Thor* at dusk. You will take *Hyperion* with *Vesta* and *Tetrarch* in company. By first light tomorrow you should be in sight of Puerto Cabello and the enemy will be convinced that you intend to attack. They will not know your full strength – we have been lucky in reaching this far undetected.' He turned in time to see the captain gripping his hat so fiercely that it buckled in his fingers. He had expected an outburst or perhaps the outline of an alternative strategy. Haven said nothing, but stared at him as if he had misheard.

Bolitho continued quietly, 'There is no other way. If we are to capture or destroy a treasure-ship it must be done at anchor. We have too few ships for an extended search if she slips past us.'

Haven swallowed hard. 'But to go *yourself*, sir? In my experience I have never known such a thing.'

'With God's help and a little luck, Captain Haven, I should be in position in the shallows to the west of La Guaira at the very moment you are making your mock attack.' He faced him steadily. 'Do not risk your ships. If a large enemy force arrives you will discontinue the action and stand away. The wind is still steady at north-by-west. Mr Penhaligon believes it may back directly which would be in our favour.'

Haven looked around the cabin as if to seek an escape.

'He may be wrong, sir.'

Bolitho shrugged. 'I would not *dare* to disagree with him.'

But his attempt to lighten the tension was lost as Haven blurted out, 'If I am forced to withdraw, who will believe –'

Bolitho looked away to hide his disappointment. 'I will have new orders written for you. No blame will be laid at your door.'

Haven said, 'I was not suggesting it merely for my own benefit, sir!'

Bolitho sat down on the bench seat and tried not to think of all those other times when he had sat here. Hopes, plans, anxieties.

He said, 'I shall want thirty seamen from your company. I would prefer an officer whom they know to command them.'

Haven said instantly, 'May I suggest my first lieutenant, sir?'

Their eyes met. *I thought you might.* He nodded. 'Agreed.'

Calls trilled from the quarterdeck and Haven glanced at the door.

Bolitho said abruptly, 'I have not yet finished.' He tried to remain calm but Haven's behaviour was unnerving. 'If the enemy

71

does throw a force against you there is no way that you can cover my withdrawal from La Guaira.'

Haven lifted his chin slightly. 'If you say so, Sir Richard.'

'I do. In which case you will assume command of the flotilla.'

'And may I ask what you would do, sir?'

Bolitho stood up. 'What I came to do.' He sensed that Allday was waiting close by the door. Another argument, when he told him he was not coming over to *Thor* with him.

'Before you leave, Captain Haven.' He tried not to blink as the mist filtered persistently across his left eye. 'Do not have those men flogged. I cannot interfere, because everyone aboard would know that I had taken sides, as you already knew when you crossed swords with your senior in my presence.' He thought he saw Haven pale slightly. 'These people have little enough, God knows, and to see their messmates flogged before being ordered into battle can do nothing but harm. Loyalty is all-important, but remember that while you are under my flag, loyalty goes both ways.'

Haven backed away. 'I hope I know my duty, Sir Richard.'

'So do I.' He watched the door close, then exclaimed, '*God damn him!*'

But it was Jenour who entered, wiping tar from his fingers with a piece of rag.

He watched as if to gauge Bolitho's mood, and said, 'A fine view from up there. I have come to report that your signals have been made and acknowledged.' He glanced up as feet thudded overhead and voices echoed from the maindeck. 'We are about to change tack, Sir Richard.'

Bolitho barely heard. 'What is the matter with that man, eh?'

Jenour remarked, 'You have told him what you intend.'

Bolitho nodded. 'I'd have thought any captain would have jumped at the chance to cast his admiral adrift. I know I did.' He stared round the cabin, searching for ghosts. 'Instead, he thinks of nothing but –' He checked himself. It was unthinkable to discuss the flag captain with Jenour. Was he so isolated that he could find no other solace?

Jenour said simply, 'I am not so impertinent as to say what I think, Sir Richard.' He looked up and added, 'But I would stand by whatever you ordered *me* to do.'

Bolitho relaxed and clapped him on the shoulder. 'They say that faith can move a mountain, Stephen!'

Jenour stared. Bolitho had called him by name. It was probably a mistake.

Bolitho said, 'We will transfer to *Thor* before dusk. It must be smartly done, Stephen, for we have a long way to travel.'

It was not a mistake. Jenour seemed to glow. He stammered, 'Your coxswain is waiting outside, Sir Richard.' He watched as Bolitho strode across the cabin, then chilled as he cannoned into a chair which Haven must have moved.

'Are you all right, Sir Richard?' He fell back as Bolitho turned towards him. But this time there was no anger in his sensitive features. Bolitho said quietly, 'My eye troubles me a little. It is nothing. Now send in my cox'n.'

Allday walked past the lieutenant and said, 'I have to speak my piece, Sir Richard. When you goes across to that bomb,' he almost spat out the word, 'I'll be beside you. Like always, an' I don't give a bugger, beggin' your pardon, Sir Richard.'

Bolitho retorted, 'You've been drinking, Allday.'

'A bit, sir. Just a few wets afore we leave the ship.' He put his head on one side like a shaggy dog. 'We *will*, won't we, sir?'

It came out surprisingly easily. 'Yes, old friend. Together. One more time.'

Allday regarded him gravely, sensing his despair. 'Wot is it, sir?'

'I nearly told that youngster, Jenour. Nearly came right out with it.' He was talking to himself aloud. 'That I'm terrified of going blind.'

Allday licked his lips. 'Young Mr Jenour looks on you as a bit of a hero, sir.'

'Not like you, eh?' But neither of them smiled.

Allday had not seen him like this for a long while, not since. . . .

He cursed himself, took the blame for not being here when he was needed. It made him angry when he compared Haven with Captain Keen, or Herrick. He looked around the cabin where they had shared and lost so much together. Bolitho had nobody to share it with, to lessen the load. On the messdecks the Jacks thought the admiral wanted for nothing. By Jesus, that was just what he had. Nothing.

Allday said, 'I know it's not my place to say it, but –'

Bolitho shook his head. 'When did that ever stop you?'

Allday persisted, 'I don't know how to put it in officers' language like.' He took a deep breath. 'Cap'n Haven's wife is havin' a baby, probably dropped it by now, I shouldn't wonder.'

Bolitho stared at him. 'What of it, man?'

Allday tried not to release a deep breath of relief as he saw the impatience in Bolitho's grey eyes.

'He thinks that someone else may be the father, so to speak.'

Bolitho exclaimed, 'Well, even supposing –' He looked away, surprised, when he ought not to have been, at Allday's knowledge. 'I see.' It was not the first time. A ship in dock, a bored wife and a likely suitor. But it had taken Allday to put his finger on it.

Bolitho eyed him sadly. How could he leave him behind? What a pair. One so cruelly wounded by a Spanish sword thrust, the other slowly going blind.

He said, 'I shall write some letters.'

They looked at each other without speaking. Cornwall in late October. Grey sky, and rich hues of fallen leaves. Chipping-hammers in the fields where farmers took time to repair their walls and fences. The elderly militia drilling in the square outside the cathedral where Bolitho had been married.

Allday moved away towards Ozzard's pantry. He would ask the little man to write a letter for him to the innkeeper's daughter in Falmouth, though God alone knew if she would ever get it.

He thought of Lady Belinda and the time they had found her in the overturned coach. And of the one named Catherine who might still harbour feelings for Bolitho. A fine-looking woman, he thought, but a lot of trouble. He grinned. A sailor's woman, no matter what airs and graces she hoisted at her yards. And if she was right for Bolitho, that was all that mattered.

Alone at his table Bolitho drew the paper towards him and watched the sunlight touch the pen like fire.

In his mind he could see the words as he had written them before. '*My dearest Belinda.*'

At noon he went on deck for his walk, and when Ozzard entered the cabin to tidy things he saw the paper with the pen nearby. Neither had been used.

6

'In War There Are No Neutrals –'

The transfer from *Hyperion* to the bomb-vessel *Thor* was carried out just before sunset, without mishap. Men and weapons with extra powder and shot were ferried across, the boats leaping and then almost disappearing between the crests of a deep swell.

Bolitho watched from the quarterdeck while *Hyperion* lay hove-to, her canvas booming in protest, and once again marvelled at the sunset's primitive beauty. The long undulating swell, like the boats and their labouring crews, seemed to glow like rough bronze, while even the faces around him looked unreal; like strangers.

With two of *Hyperion*'s boats and thirty of her men safely transferred, Bolitho made the final crossing in a jolly boat.

He had barely been received aboard *Thor* before he saw *Hyperion*'s yards swinging round, her shadowed outline shortening as she turned away to follow the two brigs into the last of the sunset.

If Commander Ludovic Imrie was bothered by having his flag officer coming aboard his modest command, he did not show it. He displayed more surprise when Bolitho announced that he did not intend to wear his epaulettes, and suggested that Imrie, as *Thor*'s commander, should follow his example.

He had remarked calmly, 'Your people know you well enough. I trust that they will know me too when this affair is finished!'

Bolitho was able to forget *Hyperion* and the others as they headed further and further away towards Puerto Cabello. He could feel the tension mount around him as *Thor* made more sail and steered, close-hauled, towards the invisible shoreline.

Hour followed hour, with hushed voices calling from the chains where two leadsmen took regular soundings, so that their reports could be checked carefully against the chart and the notes Bolitho had made after his meeting with Captain Price.

The noise was loud, but deceptive. Astern on its tow-line, the clumsy lighter was pumped constantly in a battle which Imrie had admitted had begun within hours of leaving harbour. Any rise in the sea brought instant danger from flooding, and now, with both *Thor*'s heavy mortars and their crews on board, the lighter's loss would spell disaster.

Bolitho prowled restlessly around the vessel's quarterdeck and pictured the land in his mind, as he had seen it that late afternoon. He had made himself climb aloft just once more, this time to the maintop, and through a rising haze had seen the tell-tale landmarks of La Guaira. The vast blue-grey range of the Caracas Mountains, and further to the west the impressive saddle-shaped peaks of the Silla de Caracas.

Penhaligon could be rightfully proud of his navigation, he thought. Allday barely left his side after they had come aboard, and Bolitho could hear his uneven breathing, his fingers drumming against the hilt of a heavy cutlass.

It made Bolitho touch the unfamiliar shape of the hanger at his belt. The prospect of action right inside the enemy's territory occupied everyone's mind, but Bolitho doubted if Allday had missed his decision to leave the old family sword behind in *Hyperion*. He had almost lost it once before. Allday would be remembering that too, thinking Bolitho had left it with Ozzard only because he believed he might not return.

Adam would wear the sword one day. It would never fall into enemy hands again.

Later, in Imrie's small cabin, they peered at the chart behind shuttered stern windows. *Thor* was cleared for action, but her chance would come only if the first part succeeded. Bolitho traced the twisting shallows with the dividers, as Price must have done before his ship had driven ashore. He felt the others crowding around and against him. Imrie and his senior master's mate,

Lieutenant Parris, and *Thor*'s second lieutenant, who would cover the attack.

Bolitho wondered momentarily if Parris was thinking about the floggings, which had been cancelled at Haven's order. Or of the fact that Haven had insisted that the two culprits should be included in the raiding party. All the bad eggs in one basket maybe, he thought.

He pulled out his watch and laid it beneath a low-slung lantern.

'*Thor* will anchor within the half-hour. All boats will cast off immediately, the jolly boat leading. Soundings must be taken, but not unnecessarily. Stealth is vital. We must be in position by dawn.' He glanced at their grim expressions. 'Questions?'

Dalmaine, *Thor*'s second lieutenant, raised his hand.

'What if the Don has moved, sir?'

It was amazing how easy they found it to speak up, Bolitho thought. Without the intimidating vice-admiral's epaulettes, and in their own ship, they had already spoken of their ideas, their anxieties as well. It was like being in a frigate or a sloop-of-war, all over again.

'Then we will be unlucky.' Bolitho smiled and saw Jenour's eyes watching the brass dividers as he tapped the chart. 'But there have been no reports of any large ships on the move.'

The lieutenant persisted, 'And the battery, sir. Suppose we cannot take it by surprise?'

It was Imrie who answered. 'I would suggest, Mr Dalmaine, that all your pride in your mortars will have been misplaced!'

The others laughed. It was the first healthy sign.

Bolitho said, 'We destroy the battery, then *Thor* can follow through the sandbars. Her carronades will more than take care of any guardboats.' He stood up carefully to avoid the low beams. 'And then we shall attack.'

Parris said, 'And if we are repulsed, Sir Richard?'

Their eyes met across the small table. Bolitho studied his gipsy good looks, the reckless candour in his voice. A West Country man, probably from Dorset. Allday's blunt words seemed to intrude, and he thought of the small portrait in Haven's cabin.

He said, 'The treasure-ship must be sunk, fired if possible. It

78

may not prevent salvage, but the delay will be considerable for the Don's coffers!'

'I see, sir.' Parris rubbed his chin. 'The wind's backed. It could help us.' He spoke without emotion, not as a lieutenant who might well be dead, or screaming under a Spanish surgeon's knife by morning, but as a man used to command.

He was considering alternatives. *Suppose, if, perhaps.*

Bolitho watched him. 'So shall we be about it, gentlemen?' They met his gaze. Did they know, he wondered? Would they still trust his judgment? He smiled in spite of his thoughts. Haven certainly trusted nobody!

Imrie said cheerfully, 'Och, Sir Richard, we'll a' be rich men by noon!'

They left the cabin, stooping and groping like cripples. Bolitho waited until Imrie alone remained.

'It must be said. If I fall, you must withdraw if you think fit.'

Imrie studied him thoughtfully. 'If *you* fall, Sir Richard, it will be because I've failed you.' He glanced around the cramped cabin. 'We'll make you proud, you'll see, sir!'

Bolitho walked out into the darkness and stared at the stars until his mind was steady again.

Why did you never get used to it? The simple loyalty. Their honesty with one another, which was unknown or ignored by so many people at home.

Thor dropped anchor, and as she swung to her cable in a lively current, the boats were manhandled alongside or hoisted outboard with such speed that Bolitho guessed that her commander had been drilling and preparing for this moment since he had weighed at English Harbour.

He settled himself in the sternsheets of the jolly boat, which even in the darkness seemed heavy, low in the water with her weight of men and weapons. He had discarded his coat and hat and could have been another lieutenant like Parris.

Allday and Jenour were crowded against him, and while Allday watched the oarsmen with a critical eye, the flag lieutenant said excitedly, 'They'll never believe this!'

By they, he meant his parents, Bolitho guessed.

It seemed to sum up his whole command, he decided. Captains

or seamen, there were more sons than fathers.

He heard the grind of long sweeps as the lighter was cast adrift from *Thor*'s quarter, spray bursting over the blades until two more boats flung over their tow-lines.

It was a crazy plan, but one which might just work. Bolitho plucked his shirt away from his body. Sweat or spray, he could not be sure. He concentrated on the time, the whispered soundings, the steady rise and fall of oars. He did not even dare to peer astern to ensure that the others were following.

The boats were at the mercy of the currents and tides around the invisible sandbars. One minute gurgling beneath the keel, and the next with all the oars thrashing and heaving to prevent the hull from being swung in the wrong direction.

He pictured Parris with the main body of men, and Dalmaine in the lighter with his mortars, the hands baling to keep the craft afloat. So close inshore he would not dare to use the pumps now.

There was a startled gasp from the bows, and the coxswain called hoarsely, '*Oars!* Easy, lads!'

With the blades stilled and dripping above either beam, the jolly boat pirouetted around in the channel like an untidy sea-creature. A man scrambled aft and stared at Bolitho for several seconds.

He gasped, 'Vessel anchored dead ahead, sir!' He faltered, as if suddenly aware that he was addressing his admiral. 'Small 'un, sir. Schooner mebbee!'

Jenour groaned softly. 'What damned luck! We'd never –'

Bolitho swung round. 'Shutter the lantern astern!' He prayed that Parris would see it in time. An alarm now would catch them in the open. It was too far to pull back, impossible to slip past the anchored ship without being challenged.

He heard himself say, 'Very well, Cox'n. Give way all. Very steady now.' He recalled Keen's calm voice when he had spoken with his gun crews before a battle. Like a rider quieting a troubled mount.

He said, 'It's up to us. No turning back.' He made each word sink in but it was like speaking into darkness or an empty boat. 'Steer a little to larboard, Cox'n.' He heard a rasp of steel, and a petty officer saying in a fierce whisper, 'No, don't load! The first man to loose off a ball will feel my dirk in 'is belly!'

And suddenly there she was. Tall, spiralling masts and furled sails, a shaded anchor light which threw thin gold lines up her shrouds. Bolitho stared at it as the boat glided towards her bows and outstretched jib-boom.

Was it to be here, like this?

He heard the oars being hauled inboard with elaborate care, the sudden scramble in the bows where the keen-eyed seaman had first sighted this unexpected stranger.

Allday muttered restlessly, 'Come on, you buggers, let's be 'avin' you!'

Bolitho stood up and saw the jib-boom swooping above him as the current carried them into the hull like a piece of driftwood. Jenour was crouching beside him, his hanger already drawn, his head thrown back as if expecting a shot.

'Grapnel!'

It thudded over the bulwark even as the boat surged alongside.

'*At 'em, lads!*' The fury of the man's whisper was like a trumpet call. Bolitho felt himself knocked and carried up the side, seizing lines, scrabbling for handholds, until with something like madness they flung themselves on to the vessel's deck.

A figure ran from beneath the foremast, his yell of alarm cut short as a seaman brought him down with a cudgel; two other shapes seemed to rise up under their feet and in those split seconds Bolitho realised that the anchor watch had been asleep on deck.

Around him he could sense the wildness of his men, the claws of tension giving way to a brittle hatred of anything that spoke or moved.

Voices echoed below deck, and Bolitho shouted, 'Easy, lads! Hold fast!' He listened to one voice in particular rising above the rest and knew it was speaking a language he did not recognise.

Jenour gasped, 'Swedish, sir!'

Bolitho watched the boarding party prodding at the schooner's crew, as singly or in small groups they clambered through two hatches to gape at their change of circumstances.

Bolitho heard the stealthy movement of oars nearby and guessed that Parris with one of his boats was close alongside. He had probably been expecting a sudden challenge, the raking murder of swivels.

Bolitho snapped, 'Ask Mr Parris if he has one of his Swedish hands on board!' Like most men-of-war *Hyperion* had the usual smattering of foreign seamen in her company. Some were pressed, others volunteers. There were even a few French sailors who had signed on with their old enemy rather than face the grim prospects of a prison hulk on the Medway.

A figure strode forward until Allday growled, 'Far enough, *Mounseer*, or whatever you are!'

The man stared at him, then spat, 'No need to send for an interpreter. I speak English – probably better than you!'

Bolitho sheathed his hanger to give himself time to think. The schooner was unexpected. She was also a problem. Britain was not at war with Sweden, although under pressure from Russia it had been close enough. An incident now, and. . . .

Bolitho said curtly, 'I am a King's officer. And you?'

'*I* am the master, Rolf Aasling. And I can assure you that you will live to regret this – this act of piracy!'

Parris slung his leg over the bulwark and looked around. He was not even out of breath.

He said calmly, 'She's the schooner *Spica*, Sir Richard.'

The man named Aasling stared. '*Sir* Richard?'

Parris eyed him through the darkness. 'Yes. So mind your manners.'

Bolitho said, 'I regret this inconvenience – Captain. But you are anchored in enemy waters. I had no choice.'

The man leaned forward until his coat was touching Allday's unwavering cutlass.

'I am about my peaceful occasions! You have no right –'

Bolitho interrupted him. 'I have every right.' He had nothing of the kind, but the minutes were dashing past. They must get the mortars into position. The attack had to begin as soon as it was light enough to move into the anchorage.

At any second a picket ashore might notice something was wrong aboard the little schooner. She might be hailed by a guardboat, and even if Parris's men overwhelmed it, the alarm would be raised. The helpless lighter, *Thor* too if she tried to interfere, would be blown out of the water.

Bolitho dropped his voice and turned to Parris. 'Take some

men and look below.' His eyes were growing used to the schooner's deck and taut rigging. She mounted several guns, and there were swivels where they had rushed aboard, more aft by the tiller. They had been lucky. She did not have the cut of a privateer, and the Swedes usually kept clear of involvement with the fleets of France and England. A trader then? But well armed for such a small vessel.

The master exclaimed, 'Will you leave my ship, sir, and order your men to release mine!'

'What are you doing here?'

The sudden question took him off balance. 'I am trading. It is all legal. I will no longer tolerate –'

Parris came back and stood beside Jenour as he said quietly, 'Apart from general cargo, Sir Richard, she is loaded with Spanish silver. For the Frogs, if I'm any judge.'

Bolitho clasped his hands behind him. It made sense. How close they had been to failure. Might still be.

He said, 'You lied to me. Your vessel is already loaded for passage.' He saw the man's shadow fall back a pace. 'You are waiting to sail with the Spanish treasure convoy. *Right?*'

The man hesitated, then mumbled, 'This is a neutral ship. You have no authority –'

Bolitho waved his hand towards his men. 'For the moment, Captain, I have just that! Now answer me!'

Spica's master shrugged. 'There are many pirates in these waters.' He raised his chin angrily. 'Enemy warships too!'

'So you intended to stay in company with the Spanish vessels until you were on the high seas?' He waited, feeling the man's earlier bombast giving way to fear. 'It would be better if you told me now.'

'The day after tomorrow.' He blurted it out. 'The Spanish ships will leave when –'

Bolitho hid his sudden excitement. *More than one ship.* The escort might well come from Havana, or already be in Puerto Cabello. Haven could run right into them if he lost his head. He felt Parris watching him. What would *he* have done?

Bolitho said, 'You will prepare to up-anchor, Captain.' He ignored the man's immediate protest and said to Parris, 'Pass the

83

word to Mr Dalmaine, then bring your boats alongside and take them in tow.'

The Swedish master shouted, 'I will not do it! I want no part in this madness!' A note of triumph moved into his tone. 'The Spanish guns will fire on us if I attempt to enter without orders!'

'You *do* have a recognition signal?'

Aaseling stared at his feet. 'Yes.'

'Then use it, if you please.'

He turned away as Jenour whispered anxiously, 'Sweden may see this as an act of war, Sir Richard.'

Bolitho peered at the black mass of land. 'Neutrality can be a one-sided affair, Stephen. By the time Stockholm is told of it, I hope the deed will be done and forgotten!' He added harshly, 'In war there are no neutrals! I've had a bellyful of this man's sort, so put a good hand to guard him.' He raised his voice so that the master might hear. 'One treacherous sign and I'll have him run up to the yard where he can watch the results of his folly from the end of a halter!'

He heard more seamen clambering aboard with their weapons. What did they care about neutrality and those who hid behind it so long as they could profit from it? To their simple reasoning, either you were a friend, or you were just as much a foe as Allday's *mounseers*.

'Space out your men, Mr Parris. If we are driven off at the first attempt —'

Parris showed his teeth in the darkness. 'After this, Sir Richard, I think I'd believe anything.'

Bolitho massaged his eye. 'You may have to.'

Parris strode away and could be heard calling out each man by name. Bolitho noticed the familiar way they responded. No wonder the schooner's small company were so cowed. The British sailors bustled about on the unfamiliar deck as if they had been doing it all their lives.

Bolitho remembered what his father had once told him, with that same grave pride he had always displayed when it came to his seamen.

'Put them on the deck of any ship in pitch darkness and they will be tripping aloft in minutes, so well do they ply their trade!'

What would he make of this, he wondered?

'Capstan's manned, sir!'

That was a midshipman named Hazlewood, who was aged thirteen, and on his first commission in *Hyperion*.

Bolitho heard Parris telling him sharply to stay within call. 'I don't want any damned heroes today, Mr Hazlewood!'

Like Adam had once been.

'Heave away, lads!'

Some wag called from the darkness, 'Our Dick'll get us Spanish gold for some grog, eh?' He was quickly silenced by an irate petty officer.

Bolitho stood beside the vessel's master and tried to contain the sympathy he really felt for the man.

After this night his life would be changed. One thing was certain; he would never command any vessel again.

'Anchor's aweigh, sir!'

'Braces, lads!' Bare feet skidded on damp planking as the schooner curtsied round, freed from the seabed, her mainsail filling above their crouched figures to make the stays hum and shiver to the strain.

Bolitho clung to a backstay and made himself remain patiently silent until the schooner had gathered way, and with the boats veering astern, pointed her bowsprit to the east.

Parris seemed to be everywhere. If the attack was successful, he might end up as the senior survivor. Bolitho was surprised that he could consider the possibility of dying without dispute.

Parris crossed the deck to join him. 'Permission to load, Sir Richard? I thought it best to double-shot the six-pounders, and it all takes time.'

Bolitho nodded. It was a sensible precaution. 'Yes, do it. And, Mr Parris, impress on your people to watch the crew. In all conscience, I could not batten them below in their own hull in case the batteries fire on us before we can fight free, but I'd not trust any man of them one inch!'

Parris smiled. 'My boatswain's mate Dacie is a good hand at that, Sir Richard.'

Figures flitted about the guns, and Bolitho heard some of the seamen whispering to one another as they rammed home the charges and shot. They were doing something they understood, which had been drummed into them every working day since they had walked or been dragged aboard a King's ship.

Jenour seemed to have a smattering of Swedish, and was speaking jerkily to the *Spica*'s mate. Eventually two large flags were produced, and quickly bent on to the halliards by Midshipman Hazlewood.

Bolitho moved across the deck, picking out faces, watching where each man had been stationed. Above, *Spica*'s wide topsail was now set and billowing out from its yard, and Bolitho could feel a rising excitement which even the nervous chant of the leadsman could not disperse. He could picture the schooner's slender hull as she plunged so confidently along the channel amongst the lurking sandbars, sometimes with only a few feet beneath her keel. If it was broad daylight they would be able to see *Spica*'s shadow keeping company with them on the bottom.

'All guns loaded, sir!'

'Very well.' He wondered how the abandoned Lieutenant Dalmaine was getting on with his two thirteen-inch mortars. If the attack failed, and *Thor* was unable to recover the men from the lighter, Dalmaine had orders to make his way ashore and surrender. Bolitho grimaced. He knew what he would do in those circumstances; what any sailor would attempt. Sailors mistrusted land. When others saw the sea as an enemy or a final barrier against escape, men like Dalmaine would take a chance, even in something as hopeless as a lighter.

Jenour joined them by the tiller and said, 'I was speaking with the Swedish mate, Sir Richard.'

Bolitho smiled. The lieutenant could barely suppress his eagerness.

'We are all ears.'

Jenour pointed into the darkness. 'He says we are past the battery. The biggest treasure-ship is anchored in line with the first fortress.' He added proudly. 'She is the *Ciudad de Sevilla*.'

Bolitho touched his arm. 'That was well done.' He pictured the marks on the chart. It was exactly as Price had described it, and the newly constructed fortress, which rose from the sea on a bed of rocks.

The leadsman called sharply, 'By th' mark two!'

Parris murmured, 'Christ Almighty.'

Bolitho said, 'Let her fall off a point.' He peered into the black cluster of shapes by the compass box. 'Who is that?'

'Laker, sir!'

Bolitho turned away. It would be. The seaman who was to have been flogged.

Laker called, 'Steady as she goes, sir! East-by-south!'

'By th' mark seven!'

Bolitho clenched his fists. In the time it had taken for the leadsman to recover and then cast his line from the chains, the *Spica* had ploughed out of the shallows and into deeper water. But if the chart with its sparse information was wrong . . .

'By th' mark fifteen!' Even the leadsman's voice sounded jubilant. It was not wrong. They were through.

He walked aft to the taffrail and peered at the boats astern, the gurgle of spray around each stem where lively phosphorescence painted the sea.

Allday said, 'Sun-up any minute, Sir Richard.' He sounded on edge. 'I'll be fair glad to see it go down again, an' that's no error.'

Bolitho loosened the hanger in its scabbard. It felt strange without the old sword. He pictured Adam wearing it as his own, Belinda's perfect face when she received the news that he had fallen.

He said harshly, 'Enough melancholy, old friend! We've faced worse odds!'

Allday watched him, his craggy face hidden in darkness.

'I knows it, Sir Richard. It's just that sometimes I get –'

His eyes shone suddenly and Bolitho grasped his thick forearm.

'The sun. Friend or foe, I wonder?'

'Stand by to come about!' Parris sounded untroubled. 'Two more hands on the forebrace, Keats.'

'Aye, aye, sir.'

Bolitho tried to recall the petty officer's face, but instead he saw other, older ones. *Hyperion*'s ghosts come back to watch him. They had waited over the years after their last battle. To claim him as their own, perhaps?

87

The thought made a chill run down his spine. He unclipped the scabbard and tossed it aside while he tested the hanger's balance in his hand.

More light, seeping and spreading across the water. There was the land to starboard, sprawling and shapeless. The flash of sunlight on a window somewhere, a ship's masthead pendant lifting to the first glow like the tip of a knight's lance.

The fortress was almost in line with the jib-boom, a stern, square contrast with the land beyond.

Bolitho let the hanger drop to his side and found that he had thrust his other hand inside his shirt. He could feel his heart pounding beneath the hot, damp skin, and yet his whole being felt cold; raw like steel.

'And there she lies!' He had seen the mastheads of the great ship below the fortress. She could be nothing else but Somervell's galleon. But instead of Somervell he saw Catherine's eyes watching him. Proud and captivating. Distant.

To tear himself from the mood he slowly raised his left arm, until the early sunlight spilled down the hanger as if he had dipped it into molten gold.

The sea noises intruded from every side. Wind and spray, the lively clatter of rigging and shrouds while the deck tilted to the change of tack.

Bolitho called, 'Look yonder, my lads! A reckoning indeed!'

But nobody spoke, for only *Hyperion*'s ghosts understood.

7

Perhaps The Greatest Victory

Bolitho held up the folded chart and strained his eyes in the faint sunlight. He would have wished to take more time to study it in the security of the schooner's tiny cabin, but every second was precious. It was all happening so swiftly, and when he glanced up again from the tilting compass-box he saw the grand roadstead opening up like some vast amphitheatre. More anchored shipping, the distance making them appear to be huddled together near the central fortress, then the coast itself, with white houses and the beginning of the twisting road which eventually led inland. Each mountain was brushed with sunshine, their blue-grey masses overlapping and reaching away, until they faded into mist and merged with the sky.

He stared for several seconds at the big Spanish ship. In size she matched *Hyperion*. It must have taken a month or more to load her with the gold and silver which had been brought overland on pack-mules and in wagons, guarded every mile of the way by soldiers.

At any minute now Lieutenant Dalmaine would open fire on the battery, before the sunlight reached out and betrayed *Thor* at her anchorage.

He tore his eyes away to look along the schooner's deck. Most of the *Spica*'s crew were sitting with their backs against the weather bulwark, their eyes fixed on the British seamen. No wonder they had offered no resistance. By contrast with the neat shirts of the Swedes, *Hyperion*'s men looked like pirates. He saw

Dacie the boatswain's mate, his head twisted at an angle so that he could watch his men and the *Spica*'s master at the same time. Dacie wore an eye patch to cover an empty socket; it gave him a villainous appearance. Parris had every right to have such confidence in him. Near the helm, Skilton, one of *Hyperion*'s master's mates, in his familiar coat with the white piping, was the only one who showed any sort of uniformity.

Even Jenour had followed his admiral's example and had discarded his hat and coat. He was carrying a sword which his parents had given him, with a fine blue blade of German steel.

Bolitho tried to relax as he studied the big Spanish ship. It was a far cry from that quiet room at the Admiralty when this plan had been discussed with all the delicacy of a conference at Lloyds.

He looked at Parris, his shirt open to the waist, his dark hair streaming above his eyes in the lively offshore breeze. Was Haven right to suspect him, he wondered? It certainly made sense that any woman might prefer him to his colourless captain.

A gull dived above the topsail yard, its mewing cry merging with the far-off blare of a trumpet. Ashore or at anchor, men were stirring, cooks groping for their pots and pans.

Parris stared at him across the deck and grinned. 'Rude awakening, Sir Richard!'

The crash when it came was still a surprise. It was like a double thunderclap which echoed across the water and then rolled back from the land like a returned salute.

Bolitho caught a sudden picture of Francis Inch when he had been given his first command of a bomb like Imrie's. He could almost hear his voice, as with his horse-face set in a frown of concentration he had walked past his mortars, gauging the bearing and each fall of shot.

'*Run the mortar up! Muzzle to the right! Prime! Fire!*'

As if responding to the memory both mortars fired again. But it was not Inch. He was gone, with so many others.

The double explosions sighed against the hull, and Bolitho tightened his grip on the hanger as flags broke from the big Spaniard's yards. They were awake now, right enough.

'Make the recognition signal, Mr Hazlewood!'

The two flags soared aloft and broke stiffly to the wind. All

90

they needed now was for it to drop and leave them helpless and becalmed.

Parris yelled, 'Jump about, you laggards! Wave your arms and point astern, damn your eyes!' He laughed wildly as some of the seamen capered around the deck.

Bolitho waved. 'Good work! We are supposed to be running from the din of war, eh?'

He snatched up a glass and levelled it towards the anchored ship. Beyond her, about half a cable distant, was a second vessel. Smaller than the one named *Ciudad de Sevilla* but probably carrying enough booty to finance an army for months.

Parris called, 'She's got boarding nets rigged, Sir Richard!'

He nodded. 'Alter course to cross her bows!' It would appear that they were heading towards the nearest fortress for protection.

'Helm a-lee, sir!'

'Steady as she goes, Nor' east by east!'

Bolitho gripped a stay and watched the sails flapping and banging as the schooner lurched close to the wind; but she answered well. He winced as the mortars fired yet again, and still the shore battery remained silent. It seemed likely that the first shots had done their work, the massive balls falling to explode in a lethal flail of iron fragments and grape.

Astern there was a lot of smoke, haze too, so that the shallows where they had felt their way into the anchorage had completely vanished. It might delay *Thor*'s entrance, but at least she would be safe from the battery.

He said, 'Keep those other hands out of sight, Mr Parris!'

He saw Jenour watching him, remembering everything and perhaps feeling fear for the first time.

A man yelled, '*Guardboat*, starboard bow, sir!'

Bolitho trained his glass and watched the dark shape thrusting around the counter of an anchored merchantman.

Just minutes earlier each man would have been thinking of his bed. Then some wine perhaps in the sunshine before the heat drove them all to their siesta.

He saw the oars, painted bright red, pulling and backing to bring the long hull round in a tight turn.

91

And far beyond he could make out the shape of a Spanish frigate, her masts like bare poles while she completed a refit, or like the *Obdurate*, repairs after a violent Caribbean storm.

'Two points to starboard, Mr Parris!' Bolitho tried to steady the glass as the deck tilted yet again. He could hear more trumpet calls, most likely from the new fortress, and could imagine the startled artillerymen running to their stations, still unaware of what was happening.

Explosions maybe, but there was nothing untoward immediately obvious, except for the appearance of the Swedish schooner which was, reasonably, running for shelter. No enemy fleet, no cutting-out raid, and in any case the other fortresses would have taken care of such daring stupidity.

Bolitho watched the jib-boom swinging round until it seemed to impale the treasure-ship's forecastle, although she still stood a cable away. The guardboat was pulling towards them unhurriedly, an officer rising now to peer towards the smoke and haze.

Bolitho said, 'Pass the word. The guardboat will stand between us. Make it appear we are shortening sail.'

Jenour stared at him. '*Will* we, Sir Richard?'

Bolitho smiled. 'I think not.'

A sudden gust filled the topsail and a line parted high above the deck like a pistol shot.

Dacie, the formidable boatswain's mate, jabbed a seaman with his fist. 'Aloft with ye, boy! See to it!'

It took just a second and yet as Dacie peered aloft, the Swedish master sprang forward and seized a musket from one of the crouching sailors. He pointed it above the bulwark and fired towards the guardboat. Bolitho saw the musket smoke fan away even as the master hit the deck, felled by one of the boarding party.

The guardboat was frantically backing water, her blades churning the sea into a mass of foam. There was no time left.

Bolitho shouted, 'Run her down! *Lively!*' He forgot the shouts, even the crack of a solitary musket as the schooner tacked round and drove into the guardboat like a Trojan galley.

It felt like hitting a rock, and Bolitho saw oars and pieces of planking surging alongside, men floundering, their cries lost in the rising wind and the boom of canvas.

92

The treasure-ship seemed to tower above them, individual figures which moments earlier had been staring transfixed towards the explosions, running along the gangways, others pointing and gesticulating as the schooner charged towards them.

'*Stand by to board!*' Bolitho gripped the hanger and tightened the lanyard around his wrist. He had forgotten the danger, even the fear of his eye's treachery, as the last half-cable fell away.

'Down helm! Take in the tops'l!'

Shots whimpered overhead and one gouged a tall splinter from the deck like a clerk's quill.

'Hold your fire!' Parris strode forward, his eyes narrowed against the glare while he watched his men, as they hunched down close to the point of impact.

Bolitho saw the sagging boarding nets, faces peering through them at the schooner, one solitary figure reloading a musket, his leg wrapped around the foremast shrouds.

Halfway down the Spaniard's side a port-lid rose like an awakened man opening one eye.

Then he saw the gun muzzle lumber into view, and seconds later the livid orange tongue, followed by the savage bang of an explosion. It was a wild gesture and nothing more; the ball eventually hit open water like an enraged dolphin.

As the last of the sails were freed to the wind, the *Spica*'s jib-boom plunged through the Spaniard's larboard rigging and shivered to splinters. Broken cordage and blocks showered down on the forecastle before both ships jarred finally together with a terrible crash. *Spica*'s foretopmast fell like a severed branch, but men ran amongst torn canvas and snakes of useless rigging, oblivious to everything but the need to board the enemy.

'*Swivels!*' Bolitho dragged the midshipman aside as the nearest swivel jerked back on its mounting and blasted the packed canister across the other ship's beakhead. Men fell kicking into the sea, their screams lost as Parris signalled the six-pounders to add their weight to the attack.

Allday ran, panting at Bolitho's side as he leapt on to the bulwark, the hanger dangling from his wrist. To board her from aft would have been impossible; her high stern, a mass of gilded carving, rose above her reflection like an ornate cliff.

The forecastle was different. Men clambered across the beak-head, hacking aside resistance, while others slashed and cut their way through the nets.

A pike darted through a net like a serpent's tongue and one of Parris's men fell back, clutching his stomach, his eyes horrified as he dropped into the water below.

Another turned to stare after him then gurgled as a pike thrust into him, withdrew and struck again, the point taking him in the throat and reappearing through his neck.

But Dacie and some of the seamen were on deck, pausing to fire into the defenders before slashing aside the remaining nets. Bolitho felt someone seize his wrist and haul him through a hole in the netting. Another toppled against him, his eyes glazing as a ball smashed into his chest like the blow of a hammer.

'To me, Hyperions!' Parris waved his hanger and Bolitho saw it was running with blood. '*Starboard gangway!*'

Shots banged and whimpered over their heads, and two more men fell writhing and gasping, their agony marked by the stains across the planking.

Bolitho stared round wildly as some swivels blasted the Spaniard's high poop, cutting down a handful of men who had appeared there as if by magic. Mere seconds, and yet his mind recorded that they were only partly dressed or stark naked; probably some of the ship's officers roused from their sleep by the sudden attack.

Parris's men were on the starboard gangway, where another swivel was seized and depressed towards an open hatch as more faces peered up at them.

The remainder of Parris's boarders were already leaving the little schooner, and Bolitho heard the thud of axes as the Swedes took the opportunity to hack their vessel clear of the treasure-ship, complete with *Hyperion*'s longboats.

Dacie brandished his boarding axe. 'At 'em, you buggers!'

Every man Jack would know now that there was no retreat. It was victory or death. They would receive no quarter from the Spaniards after what they had done.

Bolitho paused on the gangway, his eyes watering from drifting smoke as the scrambling seamen spread out into purposeful patterns. Two to the big double-wheel below the poop, others already swarming aloft to loose the topsails while Dacie rushed forward to cut the huge anchor cable.

Shots cracked from hatchways to be answered instantly by reloaded swivels, the packed canister smashing into the men crammed on the companion ladders and turning them into flailing, bloody gruel. One Spaniard appeared from nowhere, his sword cutting down a seaman who crouched on all fours, already badly wounded from the first encounter.

Bolitho saw the little midshipman, Hazlewood, staring at the wild-eyed sailor, his dirk gripped in one hand while the Spaniard charged towards him.

Allday stepped between Bolitho and the enemy and shouted hoarsely, 'Over here, matey!' He could have been calling a pet dog. The Spaniard hesitated, his blade wavering, then saw his danger too late.

Allday's heavy cutlass struck him across the collar-bone with such force it seemed it might sever the head from his body. The man swung round, his sword clattering to the deck below as Allday struck him again.

Allday muttered, 'Get yerself a proper blade, *Mr* Hazlewood! That bodkin couldn't kill a rat!'

Bolitho hurried aft to the wheel, and watched as the bows appeared to swing towards the nearest fort with the cry, '*Cable's cut!*'.

'Loose tops'ls! Lively, you scum!' Dacie was peering aloft, his single eye gleaming like a bead in the sunlight.

Parris wiped his mouth with a tattered sleeve. 'We're under way! Put your helm down!'

There were unexplained splashes alongside, then Bolitho saw some Spanish seamen swimming away from the hull, or floundering in the current like exhausted fish. They must have clambered from the gun-ports to escape; anything rather than face the onslaught they had heard on deck.

Midshipman Hazlewood walked shakily beside Bolitho, his eyes downcast, fearful of what terrible scene he might witness next. Corpses sprawled in the scuppers who had been caught by the double-shotted six-pounders, and others who had been running to repel boarders when the swivels had scoured the decks with their murderous canister shot.

One jibsail cracked out to the wind and the great ship began to gather way. She appeared to be so loose in stays that she must be fully loaded with her precious cargo, Bolitho thought. What would the fort's battery commander do? Fire on her, or let her steal away under his eyes?

Bolitho saw the second treasure-ship as she appeared to glide towards them. Pin-pricks of light flashed from her tops, but at that range it would need a miracle to hit any of *Hyperion*'s topmen or those around the helm.

Bolitho snapped, 'Hand me the glass!' He saw Hazlewood fumbling with it, his mouth quivering from shock as he stared at the vivid splashes of blood across his breeches. He had been within a hair's breadth of death when Allday's cutlass had hacked the man down.

Bolitho took the glass and levelled it on the other ship. She lay between them and the fort. Once clear of her, every gun on the battery would be brought to bear.

If I were that commander I would shoot. To lose the ship was bad enough. To do nothing to prevent their escape would get little mercy from the Captain-General in Caracas.

There was a ragged cheer and Parris exclaimed, 'Here comes Imrie, by God!'

The *Thor* had spread every stitch of canvas so that her sails seemed to make one great golden pyramid in the early sunlight. All her snub-nosed carronades were run out like shortened teeth along her buff and black hull, and Bolitho saw the paintwork shine even more brightly as the helm went over and she tacked round towards the two treasure-ships. Compared with the *Ciudad de Sevilla*'s slow progress, *Thor* seemed to be moving like a frigate.

It must have taken everyone in the forts and ashore completely by surprise. First the Swedish schooner, and now a man-of-war, running it would appear from inshore, their own heavily-defended territory. Bolitho thought briefly of Captain Price. This would have been his moment.

'Signal *Thor* to attack the other treasure-ship.' They had discussed this possibility, even when it was originally intended to be a boat attack. Bolitho glanced at the bloodstained deck, the gaping corpses and moaning wounded. But for falling upon the schooner it now seemed unlikely they would have succeeded.

Bolitho trained the glass again and saw tiny figures stampeding along the other ship's gangways, sunlight flashing on pikes and bayonets. They expected *Thor* to attempt a second boarding, but this time they were ready. When they realised what Imrie intended it was already too late. A trumpet blared, and across the water Bolitho heard the shrill of whistles and saw the running figures colliding with each other, like a tide on the turn.

Almost delicately, considering her powerful timbers, *Thor* tacked around the other ship's stern, and then with a deafening, foreshortened roar so typical of the heavy 'smashers', the carronades fired a slow broadside, gun by gun as *Thor* crossed the Spaniard's unprotected stern.

The poop and counter seemed to shower gold as the bright carvings splashed into the sea or were hurled high into the air, and when a down-draft of wind carried the smoke clear, Bolitho saw that the whole stern had been blasted open into a gaping black cave.

The heavy grape would have cut through the decks from stern to bow in an iron avalanche, and anyone still below would have been swept away.

Thor was turning, and even as someone managed to cut the stricken ship's cable, she came about and fired another broadside from her opposite battery.

There was smoke everywhere, and the men trapped below Bolitho's feet must have been expecting to share the same fate. The other ship's mizzen and main had fallen in a tangle alongside, and the rigging trailed along the decks and in the water like obscene weed.

Bolitho cleared his throat. It was like a kiln.

'Get the forecourse on her, Mr Parris.' He gripped the midshipman's shoulder and felt him jump as if he had been shot. 'Signal *Thor* to close on me.' He retained his grip for a few seconds, adding, 'You did well.' He glanced at the staring eyes of the men at the wheel, their smoke-grimed faces and bare feet, the blood still drying on their naked cutlasses. 'You *all* did!'

The big foresail boomed out and filled to the wind, so that the deck tilted very slightly, and a corpse rolled over in the scuppers as if it had only feigned death.

He saw Jenour on the maindeck where two armed seamen were standing guard over an open hatch, although it was impossible to know how many of the enemy were still aboard. Jenour seemed to sense that he was looking at him, and raised his beautiful sword. It was like a salute. Like the thirteen year-old Hazlewood, it was probably his first blooding.

'*Thor* has acknowledged, sir!'

Bolitho made to sheathe his hanger and remembered he had dropped the scabbard before the fight. It was lying in the little schooner which even now was fading in sea-mist, like a memory.

'Steady as she goes, sir! Nor'-east by east!'

The open sea was there, milky-blue in the early light. Men were cheering, dazed, with joy or disbelief.

Bolitho saw Parris grinning broadly, gripping the master's mate's hand and wringing it so hard the man winced.

'She's *ours*, Mr Skilton! God damn it, we took her from under their noses!'

Skilton grimaced. 'We're not in port yet, sir!'

Bolitho raised the glass yet again; it felt like lead. And yet it had been less than an hour since they had driven into the anchored treasure-ship.

He saw a host of small boats moving out from the land, a brig making sail to join them as they all headed for the shattered treasure-ship. That last broadside must have opened her like a sieve, he thought grimly. Every boat and spare hand would be used to salvage what they could before she keeled over and sank. A worthwhile sacrifice. To try and take two such ships would have meant losing both. The master's mate was right about one thing. They still had a long way to go.

He dropped the hanger to the deck and looked at it. Unused. Like the midshipman's dirk; you never really knew what you could do until called to fight.

He examined his feelings and only glanced up as the main

topsail boomed out to the wind.

Death-wish? He had felt no fear. Not for himself. He looked at the sweating seamen as they slid down the backstays and rushed to the next task, where a hundred men should have been ready at halliards and braces.

They trusted him. That was perhaps the greatest victory.

Bolitho picked up a coffee cup and then pushed it away. Empty. Something Ozzard would never allow to happen in these circumstances. Wearily he rubbed his eyes and looked around the ornate cabin, palatial when compared with a man-of-war. He smiled wryly. Even for a vice-admiral.

It was mid-afternoon, and yet he knew that if he had the will to go on deck again and climb to the maintop he would still be able to see the coast of the Main. But in this case speed was as important as distance, and with the wind holding steady from the north-west he intended to use every stitch of canvas the ship would carry. He had had a brief and hostile interview with the ship's captain, an arrogant, bearded man with the face of some ancient *conquistador*. It was hard to determine which had angered the Spaniard more. To have his ship seized under the guns of the fortress, or to be interrogated by a man who proclaimed himself to be an English flag-officer, yet looked more like a vagrant in his tattered shirt and smoke-blackened breeches. He seemed to regard Bolitho's intention to sail the ship to more friendly waters as absurd. When the reckoning came, he had said in his strangely toneless English, the end would be without mercy. Bolitho had finished the interview right there by saying quietly, 'I would expect none, since you treat your own people like animals.'

Bolitho heard Parris shouting out to someone in the mizzen top. He seemed tireless, and was never too proud to throw his own weight on brace or halliard amongst his men. He had been a good choice.

Thor had placed herself between the ponderous treasure-ship and the shore, probably as astonished as the rest of them by their success. But great though that success had been it was not without cost, or the sadness which followed any fight.

Lieutenant Dalmaine had died even as his men had been hoisted into *Thor* from the waterlogged lighter. The two mortars had had to be abandoned, and their massive recoil had all but knocked out the lighter's keel. Dalmaine had seen his men to safety and had apparently run back to retrieve something. The lighter had suddenly flooded and taken Dalmaine and his beloved mortars to the bottom.

Four men had died in the attack, three more had been seriously wounded. One of the latter was the seaman named Laker, who had lost an arm and an eye when a musketoon had been discharged at point-blank range. Bolitho had seen Parris kneeling over him and had heard the man croak, 'Better'n bein' flogged, eh, sir?' He had tried to reach out for the lieutenant's hand. 'Never fancied a checkered shirt at th' gangway, 'specially for 'is sake!'

He must have meant Haven. If they met with *Hyperion* soon, the surgeon might be able to save him.

Bolitho thought of the holds far below his feet. Cases and chests of gold and silver plate. Jewel-encrusted crucifixes and ornaments – it had looked obscene in the light of a lantern held by Allday, who had never left his side.

So much luck, he thought wearily. The Spanish captain had let slip one piece of information. A company of soldiers were to have boarded the ship that morning to guard the treasure until they unloaded it in Spanish waters. A company of disciplined soldiers would have made a mockery of their attack.

He thought of the little schooner, *Spica*, and her master, who had tried to raise the alarm. Hate, anger at being boarded, fear of reprisal, it was probably a bit of each. But his ship was intact, although it was unlikely that the Spaniards would divert other vessels to convoy him to safer waters as intended. They might even blame him. One thing was certain; he would not want to trade with the enemy again, neutral or not.

Bolitho yawned hugely and massaged the scar beneath his hair. *Hyperion*'s imposing boatswain, Samuel Lintott, would have a few oaths to offer when he discovered the loss of the jolly boat and two cutters. Maybe the chance of prize-money would soften his anger. Bolitho tried to stop his head from lolling. He could not remember when he had last slept undisturbed.

100

This ship and her rich cargo would make a difference only in the City of London, and of course with His Britannic Majesty. Bolitho smiled to himself. The King who had not even remembered his name when he had lowered the sword to knight him. Perhaps it meant so little to those who had so much.

He knew it was sheer exhaustion which was making his mind wander.

There was more than one way of fighting a war than spilling blood in the cannon's mouth. But it did not feel right, and left him uneasy. Only pride sustained him. In his men, and those like Dalmaine who had put their sailors first. And the one called Laker, who had fought shoulder-to-shoulder with his friends, simply because it meant far more to him and to them than any flag or the cause.

He allowed his mind to touch on England, and wondered what Belinda was doing with her time in London.

But like a salt-blurred telescope her picture would not settle or form clearly, and he felt a pang of guilt.

He turned his thoughts to Viscount Somervell, although he knew it was a coward's way of opening the door to Catherine. Would they leave the Indies now that the treasure, or a large part of it, was taken?

His head touched his forearm and he jerked up, aware of two things at once. That he had fallen asleep across the table, and that a masthead lookout had pealed down to the deck.

He heard Parris call something and found himself on his feet, his eyes on the cabin skylight as the lookout shouted again.

'Deck there! Two sail to the nor'-west!'

Bolitho walked through the unfamiliar doors and stared at the deserted ranks of cabins. With the remaining crew members battened below where they could neither try to retake the ship nor damage her hull without risking their own lives, it was like a phantom vessel. All *Hyperion*'s hands were employed constantly on deck; or high above it amongst the maze of rigging, like insects trapped in a giant web. He noticed a portrait of a Spanish nobleman beside a case of books, and guessed it was the captain's father. Perhaps like the old grey house in Falmouth, he too had many pictures to retell the history of his family.

He found Parris with Jenour and Skilton, the master's mate, grouped by the larboard side, each with a levelled telescope.

Parris saw him and touched his forehead. 'Nothing yet, Sir Richard.'

Bolitho looked at the sky, then at the hard horizon line. Like the top of a dam, beyond which there was nothing.

It would not be dark for hours yet. Too long.

'*Hyperion*, maybe, Sir Richard?'

Their eyes met. Parris did not believe it either. Bolitho replied, 'I think not. With the wind in our favour we should have made contact by noon.' He ceased thinking out loud. 'Signal *Thor*. Imrie may not have sighted the ships as yet.' It gave him time to think. To move a few paces this way and that, his chin digging into his stained neckcloth.

The enemy then. He made himself accept it. The *Ciudad de Sevilla* was no man-of-war, nor did she have the artillery and skills of an Indiaman. The cannons with their ornate mountings and leering bronze faces were impressive, but useless against anything but pirates or some reckless privateer.

He glanced at some of the seamen nearby. The fight had been demanding enough. Friends killed or wounded, but survival and the usual dream of prize-money had left them in high spirits. Now it was changing again. It was a wonder they didn't rush the poop and take all the bullion for themselves. There was precious little Bolitho and his two lieutenants could do to prevent it.

The lookout yelled down, 'Two frigates, sir! Dons by the cut o' them!'

Bolitho controlled his breathing as some of the others looked at him. Somehow he had known Haven would not make the rendezvous. It was an additional mockery to recall he himself had given him the honourable way out.

Parris said flatly, 'Well, they say the sea is two miles deep under our keel. The Dons'll not get their paws on the gold again, unless they can swim that far down!' Nobody laughed.

Bolitho looked at Parris. *The decision is mine.* Signal *Thor* to take them and their Spanish prisoners on board? But with only half their boats available it would take time. Scuttle the great ship

102

and all her wealth, and run, hoping *Thor* could outsail the frigates, at least until nightfall?

A victory gone sour.

Jenour moved closer. 'Laker just died, sir.'

Bolitho turned towards him, his eyes flashing. 'And for what – is that what you're asking? Must we all die now because of your vice-admiral's arrogance?'

Jenour, surprisingly, stood his ground. 'Then let's fight, Sir Richard.'

Bolitho let his arms fall to his sides. 'In God's name, Stephen, you mean it – don't you?' He smiled gravely, his anger spent. 'But I'll have no more dying.' He looked at the horizon. Is this how he would be remembered? He said, 'Signal *Thor* to heave-to. Then muster the prisoners on deck.'

The lookout yelled, 'Deck there! Two Spanish frigates an' another sail astern o' them!'

Parris muttered, 'Christ Almighty.' He attempted to smile. 'So, Mr Firebrand, will you still stand and fight the Dons?'

Jenour shrugged, then gripped his beautiful sword. It said more than any words.

Allday watched the officers and tried to fathom out what had gone wrong. It was not just failure which bothered Bolitho, that was as plain as a pikestaff. It was the old *Hyperion*. She had not come for him. Allday ground his teeth together. If ever he reached port again he would settle that bloody Haven once and for all, and swing for him to boot.

Bolitho must have felt it all the while in his blood. Why he had left the old sword behind. He *must* have known. Allday felt a chill run down his spine. *I should have guessed.* God alone knew it had happened to others.

They all stared up as the foremast lookout, forgotten until now, yelled down, 'Sail to the nor'-east, sir!'

Bolitho gripped his fingers together behind him. The newcomer must have run down on them while every eye was on the other strange sails.

He said, 'Get aloft, Stephen! Take a glass!'

Jenour paused just a few seconds as if to fix the importance and the urgency of the moment. Then he was gone, and was soon swarming hand over hand up the foremast shrouds to join the lookout on his precarious perch in the crosstrees.

It felt like an eternity. Other hands had climbed up to the tops or merely clung to the ratlines to stare at the eye-searing horizon. Bolitho felt a lump in his throat. It was not *Hyperion*. Her masts and yards would be clearly visible by now.

Jenour yelled down, his voice almost lost amongst the clatter of blocks and the slap of canvas.

'She's English, sir! Making her number!'

Parris climbed on to one of the poop ladders and levelled his own glass on the pursuers.

'They're fanning out, Sir Richard. They must have seen her too.' He added savagely, 'Not that it matters now, God damn them!'

Jenour called again, 'She's *Phaedra*, sloop-of-war!'

Bolitho felt Parris turning to watch him. Their missing sloop-of-war had caught up with them at last, only to be a spectator at the end.

Jenour shouted, faltered, then tried again, his voice barely audible. But this time it was not only because of the shipboard sounds.

'*Phaedra* has hoisted a signal, sir! *Enemy in sight!*'

Bolitho looked at the deck, at the blackened stain where a Spanish sailor had died.

The signal would be being read and repeated to all the other ships. He could picture his old *Hyperion*, her men running to quarters, clearing for action again to the beat of the drums.

Parris exclaimed with quiet disbelief, 'The Dons are standing away, Sir Richard.' He wiped his face, and perhaps his eyes. 'God damn it, old lady, don't cut it so fine next time!'

But as the Spanish topsails melted into the sea-mist, and the smart sloop-of-war bore down on the treasure-ship and her sole escort, it soon became obvious that she was quite alone.

The ill-assorted trio rolled in the swell, hove-to as *Phaedra*'s youthful commander was pulled across in his gig. He almost bounded up the high tumblehome, and doffed his hat to Bolitho, barely able to stop himself from grinning.

'There are no others?' Bolitho stared at the young man. 'What of the signal?'

The commander recovered his composure very slightly. 'My name is Dunstan, Sir Richard.'

Bolitho nodded. 'And how did you recognise *me*?'

The grin came back like a burst of sunlight.

'I had the honour to serve in *Euryalus* with you, Sir Richard.' He looked at the others with exclusive pride. 'As a midshipman. I recalled how you had used that deception yourself to confuse the enemy.' His voice trailed away. 'Although I was not sure it might work for *me*.'

Bolitho gripped his hand and held it for several seconds.

'Now I *know* we shall win.' He turned away and only Allday saw the emotion in his eyes.

Allday glanced across at the eighteen-gun *Phaedra*.

Perhaps after this Bolitho would accept what he had done for others. But he doubted it.

8

A Bitter Departure

The Right Honourable the Viscount Somervell looked up from the pile of ledgers and eyed Bolitho curiously.

'So you accepted Captain Haven's explanation, what?'

Bolitho stood beside a window, his shoulder resting against the cool wall. The air was heavy and humid although the wind which had stayed with them all the way to English Harbour remained quite firm. The small breakers near the harbour were no longer white, but in the sun's glare sighed over the sand like molten bronze.

He could see the great ship clearly from here. After the tumultuous welcome when they had sailed into harbour, the serious work of unloading her rich cargo had begun immediately. Lighters and boats plied back and forth, and Bolitho had never seen so many redcoats as the army guarded the booty every yard of the way, until, as Somervell had explained, it would be transferred and divided amongst several smaller vessels as an extra precaution.

Bolitho half-turned and glanced at him. Somervell had already forgotten his question about Haven. It was only yesterday morning that they had dropped anchor, and for the first time since he had met Somervell, Bolitho had noticed that he still wore the same clothes as when he had come out to the *Ciudad de Sevilla*. It was as if he could not bear leaving these detailed ledgers even to sleep.

They had met *Hyperion* and two of the brigs only a day out of

106

Antigua. Bolitho had decided to send for Haven rather than shift to his flagship, where there must have been speculation enough already.

Haven had been strangely confident as he had made his report. He had even presented it in writing to explain fully, if not excuse his action.

Hyperion and the little flotilla had closed with Puerto Cabello, and had even drawn the fire of a coastal battery when it had seemed they were about to force their way into harbour. Haven was certain that the captured frigate *Consort* was still there, and had sent the brig *Vesta* under the guns of a battery to investigate. The Spaniards had rigged a long boom from one of the fortresses and *Vesta* had run afoul of it. In minutes one of the batteries, using heated shot, had found *Vesta*'s range, and the helpless onlookers had seen her burst into flames before being engulfed in one devastating explosion.

Haven had said in his unemotional voice, 'Other enemy ships were heading towards us. I used my discretion,' his eyes had watched Bolitho without a flicker, 'as so ordered by you, Sir Richard, and withdrew. I considered that you would have succeeded or pulled back by that time, as I had offered the diversion required, with some risk to my command.'

After what they had done in taking the rich prize it was like a personal loss instead of a victory.

Haven could not be blamed. The presence of a boom might be expected or it might not. As he had said, he had used his discretion.

Tetrarch, another of the brigs, had risked sharing the same fate to sail amongst the smoke and falling shot to rescue some of her companion's people. One of the survivors had been her captain, Commander Murray. He was in an adjoining building with *Hyperion*'s wounded from the boarding party, and the remainder of the brig's company who had been plucked from the sea and the flames, a sailor's two worst enemies.

He said, 'For the moment, my lord.'

Somervell smiled as he turned over another leaf; he was gloating. 'Hell's teeth, even His Majesty will be satisfied with this!' He looked up, his eyes opaque. 'I know you grieve for the brig; so

107

may the navy. But set against all this it will be seen as a noble sacrifice.'

Bolitho shrugged. 'By those who do not have to risk their precious skins. In truth I'd rather have cut out *Consort*, damn them!'

Somervell folded his arms reluctantly. 'You have been lucky. But unless you contain your anger or direct it elsewhere, I fear that same luck will desert you.' He put his head on one side. Like a sleek, fastidious bird. 'So make the most of it, eh?'

The door opened an inch and Bolitho saw Jenour peering in at him. Bolitho began, 'Excuse me, my lord. I left word with –' He turned away. Somervell had not heard; he was back again in the world of gold and silver.

Jenour whispered, 'I fear Commander Murray is going fast, Sir Richard.'

Bolitho fell into step beside him and they strode across the wide, flagged terrace to the archway which led to the temporary hospital. Bolitho had been grateful for that at least. Men who were suffering from their wounds should not share a place with garrison soldiers who died from yellow fever without ever hearing the sounds of war.

He glanced shortly at the sea before he entered the other building. Like the sky, it looked angry. A storm perhaps; he would have to consult with *Hyperion*'s sailing master.

Murray lay very still, his eyes closed as if already dead. Even though he had been on the West Indies station for two years, his features were like chalk.

Hyperion's surgeon, George Minchin, a man less callous than most of his trade, had remarked, 'A miracle he survived this far, Sir Richard. His right arm was gone when they pulled him from the sea, and I had to take off a leg. There is a chance, but –'

That had been yesterday. Bolitho had seen enough faces of death to know it was almost over.

Minchin rose from a chair near the bed and walked purposefully to a window. Jenour studied the sea through another window, thinking perhaps that Murray must have been staring at it too, like a handhold to life itself.

Bolitho sat beside the bed. 'I'm here –' He remembered the

108

young commander's name. 'Rest easy if you can, James.'

Murray opened his eyes with an effort. 'It was the boom, sir.' He closed his eyes again. 'Nearly tore the bottom out of the poor old girl.' He tried to smile but it made him look worse. 'They never took her though – never took her –'

Bolitho groped for his remaining hand and held it between his own.

'I shall see that your people are taken care of.' His words sounded so empty he wanted to cry out, to weep. 'Is there anyone?'

Murray tried again, but his eyes remained like feverish slits.

'I – I – ' his mind was clouding over. 'My mother – there's nobody else now –' His voice trailed away again.

Bolitho made himself watch. Like candles being snuffed out. He heard Allday outside the door, Jenour swallowing hard as if he needed to vomit.

In a remarkably clear voice Murray said, 'It's dark now, sir. I'll be able to sleep.' His hand bunched between Bolitho's. 'Thank you for –'

Bolitho stood up slowly. 'Yes, you sleep.' He pulled the sheet over the dead man's face and stared at the hard sunlight until he was blinded by it. *It's dark now.* For ever.

He crossed to the door by the terrace and knew Jenour was going to say something, to try and help when there was none to offer.

'Leave me.' He did not turn. '*Please.*'

Then he walked to the terrace wall and pressed both hands upon it. The stone was hot, like the sun on his face.

He raised his head and stared again at the glare. He could remember as a small boy seeing the family crest, carved in stone above the great fireplace at Falmouth. He had been tracing it with one finger when his father had entered and had picked him up in his arms.

The words below the crest stood out in his mind. *Pro Libertate Patria. For my country's freedom.*

What young men like Murray, Dunstan and Jenour all believed.

He clenched his fists until the pain steadied him.

They had not even begun to live yet.

He turned sharply as he heard footsteps to his left and seemingly below him. He had been staring so hard at the glare that he could see nothing but a vague shadow.

'Who is that? What do you want?' He twisted his head further, unaware of the edge to his voice or its helplessness.

She said, 'I came to find you.' She stood quite still at the top of some rough stone steps which led down to a small pathway. 'I heard what happened.' Another pause, which to Bolitho seemed endless, then she added quietly, 'Are you all right?'

He looked at the flagstones and saw the image of his shoes sharpen as the pain and mist in his eye slowly withdrew.

'Yes. One of my officers. I barely knew him –' He could not continue.

She remained at her distance as if afraid of him or what she might cause.

She said, 'I know. I am so sorry.'

Bolitho stared at the nearest door. 'How could you marry that man? I've met some callous bastards in my time, but –' He struggled to recover his composure. She had done it again. Like being stripped naked, with neither defence nor explanation.

She did not answer directly. 'Did he ask about the second treasure galleon?'

Bolitho felt the fight draining from him. He had almost expected Somervell to ask him just that. Both of them would have known where that might lead.

He said, 'I apologise. It was unforgivable of me. I had no right to question your motives, or his for that matter.'

She watched him gravely, one hand holding a lace mantilla in place over her dark hair as the hot wind whipped across the parapet. Then she stepped up on to the terrace and faced him. 'You look tired, Richard.'

He dared at last to look at her. She was wearing a sea-green gown, but his heart sank when he realised that her fine features and compelling eyes were still unclear. He must have been half-crazy with despair to stare at the sun. The surgeon in London had declared it to be his worst enemy.

He said, 'I hoped I would see you. I have thought of you a great

110

deal. More than I should; less than you deserve.'

She flicked open her fan and moved it in the wind like a bird's wing.

'I shall be leaving here quite soon. Perhaps we ought never to have met. We must both try –'

He reached out and took her wrist, not caring who might see, conscious only that he was about to lose even her, when he had lost everything else.

'I cannot try! It is hell to love another man's wife, but that is the truth, in God's name it is!'

She did not pull away, but her wrist was rigid in his grasp.

She answered without hesitation, '*Hell?* You can never know what that is unless you are a woman in love with another woman's husband!' Her voice threw caution aside. 'I told you, I would have died for you once. Now, because you seem to think your chosen life is in ruins you can turn again to me! Don't you know what you're doing to me, damn you? Yes, I married Lacey because we needed one another, but not in a fashion you would ever understand! I cannot have a child, but then you probably know that too. Whereas *your wife* has given you a daughter I believe, so where's the rub, eh?' She tore her arm away, her dark eyes flashing as loose strands of hair broke from under the mantilla. 'I shall never forget you, Richard, God help me, but I pray that we never meet again, lest we destroy even that one moment of joy I held so dear!'

She turned and almost ran through the door.

Bolitho walked into the adjoining building and received his hat from a footman without even noticing. He saw Parris walking towards him and would have passed without a word had the lieutenant not touched his hat and said, 'I have been supervising the last of the treasure-chests, Sir Richard. I can still barely believe what we went through to get them!'

Bolitho looked at him vaguely. 'Yes. I shall note your excellent behaviour in my report to their lordships.' Even that sounded hollow. The aftermath. Letters to Murray's mother and Dalmaine's widow, arrangements for prize-money to be paid to the dependents of those others killed or discharged. His despatch would at least guarantee that.

111

Parris eyed him worriedly. 'I did not speak to you for praise, Sir Richard. Is something wrong?'

Bolitho shook his head, and felt the wind in his face, just as he could still sense her wrist under his fingers. In hell's name, what had he expected?

'No. Why should there be? It will be known as a noble sacrifice, I am given to understand, so be grateful that you serve and do not command!'

He walked away and Parris turned and saw Allday striding out into the angry sunlight.

'Sir Richard will require the barge, Cox'n.'

Allday shook his head. 'No, he'll walk a piece. When he's wore himself out, then he'll want the barge.'

Parris nodded, understanding perhaps for the first time. 'I envy the both of you.'

Allday walked slowly to the balustrade that overlooked the main anchorage. The sea was getting up right enough. He bit on an apple he had obtained from the commodore's cook. Bloody good job. Blow some of the bitterness clean out of sight.

He saw his barge standing off from the jetty to avoid scraping the paintwork as lively catspaws spattered the stone stairs with spray. Bolitho was all aback, just when he had believed things were getting better. Bloody women. He had said as much to Ozzard when they had returned in triumph with the treasure-ship. Ozzard had made one of his defensive remarks and Allday, too tired and angry to care, had exclaimed, 'What the hell do you know? You've never been married!' Strange how it had upset the little man. Allday had decided he would give him one of his precious bone carvings to make up for it. He tossed the apple core into the sun-dried grass and turned to leave. Then he saw her, standing on the terrace, watching him with those eyes of hers. That look could make a man turn to water.

She met his gaze and said, 'Do you remember me? You are Mr Allday.'

Allday replied carefully, 'Why, o' course I remember *you*, Ma'am. Nobody could forget what you done for the Captain, as he was then.'

She ignored the unspoken suggestion in his voice. 'I need your

112

help. Will you trust me?'

Allday felt his defences slipping. She was asking him to trust *her*. The wife of the high and mighty Inspector General, a man who needed watching if half what he had heard was true. But she had paid out her line first. She was the one who was taking all the risks.

He grinned slowly. *A sailor's woman.* 'I will.'

She moved towards him, and Allday saw the quick movement of her breasts beneath the fine gown. Not so cool and calm as she wanted to appear, he thought.

'Vice-Admiral Bolitho is not himself.' She hesitated; perhaps she had already gone too far. She had seen the grin fade, the instant hostility in the big man's eyes.

'I – I wish to help him, you see –' She dropped her gaze. 'In God's name, Mr Allday, must I beg of you?'

Allday said, 'I'm sorry, Ma'am. We've had a lot of enemies over the years, see.' He weighed it up. What was the worst thing that could happen? He said abruptly, 'He was nearly blinded.' He felt like ice despite the searing wind, but now he could not stop. 'He thinks he's losing the use of his left eye.'

She stared at him, the picture leaping into her mind like a stark dream. He had been staring at the sky or the sea when she had found him. Bolitho had looked so defeated, so lost that she had wanted to run to him and take him in her arms, forget security, life itself if only she could comfort and keep him a few moments more. She recalled his voice, the way he had looked at her without seeming to see her.

She heard herself whisper, 'Oh, dear God!'

Allday said, 'Remember, I've told you nothin', Ma'am. I'm often in hot water as it is without you adding more coals to it.' He hesitated, moved by her distress, her sudden loss of poise before him, a common seaman. 'But if you *can* help –' he broke off and touched his hat quickly. He whispered hoarsely, 'I sees yer husband hull-down on th' horizon, Ma'am. I'll be off now!'

She stared after him, a great, loping figure in flapping blue jacket and nankeen breeches, one scarred and hurt so badly she could see it on his homely features. But a man so gentle that she wanted to cry for him, for all of them.

113

But her husband did not come to her; she saw him walking along the terrace with the lieutenant called Parris.

When she looked down the sloping pathway which led to the harbour she saw Allday turn and lift his hat to her.

Just a small gesture, and yet she knew that he had accepted her as a friend.

The deckhead lanterns in *Hyperion*'s great cabin spiralled wildly, throwing insane shadows across the checkered deck covering and across the tightly lashed nine-pounders on either side.

Bolitho sipped a glass of hock, and watched while Yovell finished yet another letter and pushed it across the table for him to sign. Like actors on a stage, he thought, as Ozzard busied himself refilling glasses, and Allday entered and left the cabin like a player who had been given no lines to learn.

Captain Haven stood by the stern windows, now half-shuttered as the wind, made more fearsome by the darkness, broke the crests from the inshore waves, and flung spray over the anchored ships.

Bolitho felt the whole ship trembling as she tilted to her cable, and remembered the feeling of disbelief when Dacie had severed the Spaniard's mooring.

Haven concluded, 'That is everything I can determine, Sir Richard. The purser is satisfied with his storing, and all but one working party has been withdrawn from the shore.' He was speaking carefully, like a pupil repeating a hard-learned lesson to his teacher. 'I have been able to replace the three boats too, although they will need some work done on them.'

An observation, a reminder that it had been his admiral who had abandoned them. Haven was careful not to display his true feelings.

'Who is in charge of the last party?'

Haven looked at his list. 'The first lieutenant, Sir Richard.'

Always the title now, after their last clash. Bolitho swilled the hock around his glass. So be it then. Haven was a fool and must know that his admiral, any flag officer for that matter, could make or destroy his career. Or was it his way of exploiting Bolitho's sense of fairness?

114

Yovell looked over his steel-rimmed spectacles. 'I beg your pardon, Sir Richard, but did you intend this despatch to *Obdurate* to read in this fashion?'

Bolitho gave a wry smile. 'I did.' He did not need to be reminded.

You are directed and commanded to make ready for sea. Captain Robert Thynne of the other seventy-four could think what he liked. *Obdurate* was needed now more than ever. The vessels carrying the bulk of the treasure would have to be escorted clear of dangerous waters until they met with ships of Sir Peter Folliot's squadron, or until they could have the sea-room to manage for themselves. Bolitho would have preferred to bide his time until his own small squadron arrived, but the change of weather had altered all that.

He turned away from the others, glad of the lanterns' mellow light as he massaged his eye. It was still aching from his stupid contest with the sun. Or was it another snare of his imagination? He was glad to be aboard this old ship again. Somervell had guessed as much when he had said his farewell.

Somervell had explained that he and his lady were leaving after the main exodus, aboard a large Indiaman which was daily expected here. Personal comfort rated very high with Somervell.

Bolitho had seen the other side of the man when he had asked, 'I should like to take my leave of Lady Somervell.'

'Impossible.' Somervell had met his gaze insolently. Bolitho could well imagine those same cold eyes staring along the barrel of a duelling pistol in the dawn light, although it was known he favoured swords for such settlements.

He had added, 'She is not here.'

Antigua was a small island. If she had wanted to see him she could. Unless Somervell had grown tired of the game and had prevented it. Either way it did not matter now. It was over.

There was a tap at the door and Lieutenant Lovering, who was the officer-of-the-watch, took a pace into the cabin and reported, 'I beg your forgiveness for this intrusion, Sir Richard,' his eyes flickered between Bolitho and Haven, 'but a courier-brig has been reported running for harbour.'

Bolitho lowered his eyes. Maybe from England. Letters from

home. News of the war. Their lifeline. He thought of Adam, in command of his own brig, probably still carrying despatches for Nelson. Another world away from the heat and fever of the Indies.

Haven leaned forward. 'If there is any mail –' He recovered himself, and Bolitho recalled what Allday had said about his wife expecting a baby.

Bolitho signed more letters. Recommendations for promotion, for bravery, for transfers to other ships. Letters to the bereaved.

The lieutenant hesitated. 'Will you have any letters for the shore, Sir Richard?'

Bolitho looked at him. Lovering was the second lieutenant. Waiting for promotion, the chance to prove himself. If Parris fell . . . He shut the idea from his mind. 'I think not.' It came out easily. Was it that simple to end something which had been so dear?

Haven waited until the lieutenant had withdrawn. 'First light then, Sir Richard.'

'Yes. Call the hands as you will, and signal your intentions to *Obdurate* and the Commissioner of the Dockyard.'

When *Hyperion* returned to Antigua the Indiaman would have gone. Would they ever meet again, even by accident?

'It will take all day to work out of harbour and muster our charges into a semblance of order. This wind will decide then whether to be an ally or a foe.'

If the treasure-ships and their escort were contained in the shelter of English Harbour for much longer, the Spaniards and perhaps their French allies might even try to counter-attack before the new squadron arrived.

Left alone in the cabin Bolitho drank some more hock, but although his stomach was empty he was unable to face Ozzard's meal. With the old ship swaying and groaning around him, and the duty watch being mustered every few minutes, or so it appeared, to secure and lash down some loose gear, it was impossible to rest.

The hock was good, and Bolitho found time to wonder how Ozzard managed to keep it so cool even in the bilges.

He toyed with the idea of sending a note to Catherine and dismissed it immediately. In the wrong hands it could ruin her.

What it might do to his own career did not seem to matter any longer.

He heard the clank of pumps and remembered what he had been told about *Hyperion*'s age and service. It was like an additional taunt.

He lolled in his favourite chair but was awakened, it seemed within seconds, by Ozzard shaking his arm.

Bolitho stared at him. The ship was still in darkness, the din and movement as before.

'The first lieutenant wishes to see you, Sir Richard.'

Bolitho was wide awake. Why not the captain?

Parris entered, soaked with spray. He looked flushed despite his tan, but Bolitho knew he had not been drinking.

'What is it?'

Parris steadied himself against a chair as the deck swayed again. 'I thought you should know, Sir Richard. The guardboat reported earlier that a schooner left harbour. One of the commodore's own vessels, it seems.'

'Well?' Bolitho knew there was worse to come.

'Lady Somervell was on board.' He recoiled slightly under Bolitho's grey stare. 'I discovered that she intends to sail round to St John's.'

Bolitho stood up and listened to the wind. It was a gale now, and he heard the water surging against the hull like a flood tide.

'In *this*, man!' He groped round for his coat. 'Viscount Somervell must be informed.'

Parris watched dully. 'He knows. I told him myself.'

Haven appeared in the screen door, his sleeping attire covered by a boat-cloak. 'What's this I hear?' He glared at Parris. 'I shall speak to you later!'

Bolitho sat down. How could Somervell let her do it? He must have known when he had said it was impossible for her to make her farewell. A small schooner could founder if wrongly handled. He tried to remember who commanded Glassport's vessels.

Even in calm weather it was dangerous to make casual passages amongst the islands. Pirates were too commonplace to mention. For every one rotting in chains, or on the gallows, there were a hundred more in these waters.

117

He said, 'I can do nothing until daylight.'

Haven regarded him calmly. 'If you ask me –'

He fell silent then added, 'I must attend the watch on deck, Sir Richard.'

Bolitho sat down very slowly. *I did this to her.* He did not know if he had spoken aloud or not, but the words seemed to echo around the cabin like a shot.

He called to Ozzard, 'Rouse my flag lieutenant, if you please.'

He would send him ashore with a message for Somervell, in bed or not.

He stood up restlessly and walked to an unshuttered window.

If I go myself one of us will surely die.

9

A Sloop Of War

Bolitho strode out on to the quarterdeck and felt the wind lift under his boat-cloak, and the spray which burst over the weather quarter like tropical rain.

He held on to the nettings and slitted his eyes against the gale. It was strong but clammy, so that it did nothing to refresh his tired limbs. Two days since they had clawed their way out of English Harbour to assemble their small but priceless convoy. In that time they had barely logged fifty miles.

By night they rode out the storm under a reefed maintopsail and little else, while the four transports and the smaller vessels lay hove-to as best they could under savage conditions.

Secrecy was now of secondary importance and *Hyperion* burned flares and her vice-admiral's top-lights to try and hold the ships together. Then as each dawn found them it had taken a full day to reassemble the badly scattered ships and to begin the formation all over again. Everything was wet, and as the men toiled aloft to fight the wind-crazed sails or stumbled to replace their companions on the bilge-pumps, many must have wondered what was keeping them afloat.

Bolitho stared abeam and saw the faint sheen of the sloop-of-war's topgallants. *Phaedra* was standing up to windward, heeling every so often as the waves lifted her slender hull like a toy. The brig *Upholder* was invisible, far ahead in the van, and the other brig *Tetrarch* was an equal distance astern.

Bolitho climbed up a few steps on a poop ladder and felt the cloak stream away from him, his shirt already soaked with spray and spindrift. There was *Obdurate*, half-a-mile astern, her black and buff bows shining like glass as the waves burst into her. It felt strange to have another third-rate in company again, although he doubted if Thynne was thanking him for it. After a long stay in harbour, repairing the last storm battering she had suffered, it was likely that *Obdurate*'s people were cursing their change of roles.

Bolitho climbed down to the deck again. There were four seamen at the big wheel, and nearby Penhaligon the master was in deep conversation with one of his mates.

The wind had backed decisively to the south-west and they had been blown many miles off their original course. But if the sailing master was troubled he did not show it.

All around, above and along the maindeck, men were working to repair any storm damage. Lines to be replaced or spliced, sails to be sent down, to be patched or discarded.

Bolitho glanced at the nearest gangway where a boatswain's mate was supervising the unrigging of a grating.

Another flogging. It had been worse than usual, even after Ozzard had closed the cabin skylight. The wild chorus of the wind through stays and shrouds, the occasional boom of reefed topsails, and all the while the rattle of drums and the sickening crack of the lash across a man's naked back.

He saw blood on the gangway, already fading and paling in the flung spray. Three dozen lashes. A man driven too far in the middle of the storm, an officer unable to deal with it on the spot.

Haven was in his quarters writing his log, or re-reading the letters which had been brought in the courier bag.

Bolitho was glad he was not here. Only his influence remained. The men who hurried about the decks looked strained, resentful. Even Jenour, who had not served very much at sea, had remarked on it.

Bolitho beckoned to the signals midshipman. 'The glass, if you please, Mr Furnival.' He noticed the youth's hands, raw from working all night aloft, and then trying to assume the dress and bearing of a King's officer by day.

Bolitho raised the glass and saw the sloop-of-war swim sharply into focus, the creaming wash of sea as she tilted her gunports into a deep swell. He wondered what her commander, Dunstan, was thinking as he rode out the wind and waves to hold station on his admiral. It was a far cry from *Euryalus*'s midshipman's berth.

He moved the glass still further and saw a green brush-stroke of land far away on the larboard bow. Another island, Barbuda. They should have left it to starboard on the first day. He thought of the schooner, of Catherine who had asked the master to take her around Antigua to St John's instead of using the road.

A small vessel like that would stand no chance against such a gale. Her master could either run with the wind, or try to find shelter. Better ships would have suffered in the storm; some might have perished. He clenched his fingers around the telescope until they ached. Why did she do it? She could be lying fathoms deep, or clinging to some wreckage. She might even have seen *Hyperion*'s toplights, have known it was his ship.

He heard the master call to the officer-of-the-watch, 'I would approve if you could get the t'gallants on her, Mr Mansforth.'

The lieutenant nodded, his face brick-red from the salt spray. 'I – I shall inform the Captain.' He was very aware of the figure by the weather side, with the boat-cloak swirling around him. Hatless, his black hair plastered to his forehead, he looked more like a highwayman than a vice-admiral.

Jenour emerged from the poop and touched his hat. 'Any orders, Sir Richard?'

Bolitho returned the glass to the midshipman. 'The wind has eased. Please make a signal to the transports to keep closed up. We are not out of trouble yet.'

The four ships which were sharing most of the treasure were keeping downwind of the two seventy-fours. With a brig scouting well ahead, and the other trailing astern like a guard-dog, they should be warned in time should a suspicious sail show itself. Then *Hyperion* and *Obdurate* could gauge their moment before running down on the convoy, or beating up to windward to join *Phaedra*.

Flags soared up to the yards and stiffened to the wind like painted metal.

'Acknowledged, Sir Richard.' Then in a hushed voice Jenour added, 'The Captain is coming.'

Bolitho felt the bitterness rising within him. They were more like conspirators than of one company.

Haven walked slowly across the streaming planking, his eyes on the gun-breechings, flaked lines, coiled braces, everything.

He was apparently satisfied that he had nothing to fear from what he saw, and crossed the deck to Bolitho.

He touched his hat, his face expressionless while his eyes explored Bolitho's wet shirt and spray-dappled breeches.

'I intend to make more sail, Sir Richard. We should carry it well enough.'

Bolitho nodded. 'Signal *Obdurate* so that they conform. I don't want us to become separated.' Captain Thynne had lost two men overboard the previous day and had backed his mizzen topsail while he had attempted to send away the quarter boat. Neither of the luckless men was recovered. They had either fallen too far from aloft and been knocked senseless when they hit the sea, or like most sailors, were unable to swim. Bolitho had not intended to mention it.

But Haven snorted, 'I will make the signal *at once*, Sir Richard. Thynne wants to drill his people the better, and not dawdle about when some fool goes outboard through his own carelessness!'

He gestured to the lieutenant of the watch.

'Hands aloft and loose t'gan'sls, Mr Mansforth!' He looked at the midshipman. 'General signal. *Make more sail.*' His arm shot out across the quarterdeck rail. '*That man!* Just what the bloody hell is he about?'

The seaman in question had been wringing out his checkered shirt in an effort to dry it.

He stood stockstill, his eyes on the quarterdeck, while others moved aside in case they too might draw Haven's wrath.

A boatswain's mate yelled, ''Tis all right, sir! I told him to do it!'

Haven turned away, suddenly furious.

But Bolitho had seen the gratitude in the seaman's eyes and knew that the boatswain's mate had told him nothing of the kind. Were they all so sick of Haven that even the afterguard were against him?

'Captain Haven!' Bolitho saw him turn, the anger gone. It was unnerving how he could work up a sudden rage and disperse it to order. 'A word, if you please.'

The midshipman called, 'All acknowledged, sir.'

Bolitho said, 'This ship has never been in action under your command or beneath my flag. I'll trouble you to remember it when next you berate a man who has been running hither and thither for two days and nights.' He was finding it hard to keep his voice level and under control. 'When the time comes to beat to quarters in earnest, you will expect, nay, demand instant loyalty.'

Haven stammered, 'I know some of these troublemakers –'

'Well, hear me, Captain Haven. All these men, good and bad, saints and *troublemakers*, will be called on to fight, do I make myself clear? Loyalty has to be earned, and a captain of your experience should not need to be told! Just as you should not require me to remind you that I will not tolerate senseless brutality from anyone!'

Haven stared back at him, his eyes sparking with indignation.

'I am not supported, Sir Richard! Some of my wardroom are as green as grass, and my senior, Mr Parris, is more concerned with gaining favour for himself! By God, I could tell you things about that one!'

Bolitho snapped, 'That is enough. You are my flag captain, and you have my support.' He let the words sink in. 'I know not what ails you, but if you abuse my trust once again, I shall put you in the next ship for England!'

Parris had appeared on deck and as the calls trilled to muster the topmen once again for making more sail, he glanced at Bolitho, then at his captain.

Haven tugged his hat more firmly over his ginger hair and said, 'Carry on, Mr Parris.'

Bolitho knew Parris was surprised. There was no additional threat or warning.

As the seamen poured up the ratlines like monkeys, and the masthead pendant whipped sharply for the first time to prove that the wind was indeed easing, Haven said stiffly, 'I have standards too, Sir Richard.'

Bolitho dismissed him and turned again towards the far-off

island. Allday stood a few paces away. He never seemed to trust him alone any more, Bolitho thought.

Allday said, 'Them island schooners is hardy craft, Sir Richard.'

Bolitho did not turn but touched his arm. 'Thank you, old friend. You always know what I'm thinking.' He watched two gulls rising above the wave crests, their wings spread and catching a brighter sunlight as it broke through the clouds. Like Catherine's fan.

He said desperately, 'I feel so helpless.' He looked at Allday's strong profile. 'Forgive me. I should not pass my burden to you.'

Allday's eyes narrowed as he stared at the leaping waves, their long crests curling over to the wind's thrust.

It was like gauging the fall of shot. Up one. Down one. The next would hit home.

He said, 'Matter of fact, she spoke to me afore we left harbour.'

Bolitho stared. 'To *you*?'

Allday sounded ruffled. 'Well, some women feels free to speak with the likes o' me.'

Bolitho touched his arm again. 'Please, no games, old friend.'

Allday said, 'Told me she was fair bothered about you. Wanted you to know it, like.'

Bolitho banged his fist on the weathered rail. 'I didn't even try to understand. Now I've lost her.' It was spilling out of him, and he knew that only Allday would understand, even if he did not always agree.

Allday's eyes were faraway. 'Knew a lass once in a village where I was livin'. She was fair taken with the squire's son, a real young blade 'e was. She was made for him, an' he never even knew she was alive, the bastard, beggin' your pardon, Sir Richard.'

Bolitho watched him, wondering if Allday had wanted that girl.

Allday said simply, 'One day she threw herself down in front of the squire's coach. She couldn't take no more, I 'spect, and wanted to *show him*.' He looked at his scarred hands. 'She was killed.'

Bolitho wiped the spray from his face. To *show him*. Was that what Catherine had done because of him?

Why had he not seen it, accepted that love could never be won the easy way? He thought of Valentine Keen, and his girl with the moonlit eyes. He had risked so much, and won everything because of it.

He heard Allday move away, probably going below for a *wet* with his friends, or with Ozzard in his pantry.

He walked towards the poop and saw Mr Penhaligon watching the set of each sail, his beefy hands on his hips. Haven pouting as he peered at the compass, Parris watching him, waiting to dismiss the watch below.

Bolitho listened to the regular clank of pumps; the old *Hyperion* carried all of them. She had seen hundred of hopes dashed, bodies broken on these same decks.

Bolitho's ears seemed to fasten on to a new intrusion.

He exclaimed, '*Gunfire!*'

Several men jumped at the sharpness in his voice; Allday, who was still on the ladder, turned and looked towards him.

Then the signals midshipman said excitedly, 'Aye, I hear it, sir!'

Haven strode to the quarterdeck rail, his head moving from side to side, still unable to hear the sound.

Jenour came running from the poop. 'Where away?' He saw Bolitho and flushed. 'I beg your pardon, Sir Richard!'

Bolitho shaded his eyes as the midshipman yelled, 'From *Phaedra*, sir! *Sail to the nor'-west!*'

Bolitho saw men climbing into the shrouds, their discomfort forgotten. For the moment.

Jenour asked anxiously, 'What does it mean, Sir Richard?'

Bolitho said, 'Signal *Phaedra* to investigate.' Minutes later when the midshipman's signalling party had run the flags up to the yard Bolitho replied, 'Small cannon, Stephen. Swivels or the like.'

Why had he heard, when so many others around him had not?

He said, 'Signal *Tetrarch* to close on the flag.'

Allday said admiringly, 'God, look at 'er go!' He was watching the sloop-of-war turning away, showing her copper in the misty

125

sunlight, as she spread more canvas and rounded fiercely until she was close-hauled on the larboard tack.

Allday added, 'Like your *Sparrow*, eh, Cap'n?' He grinned awkwardly. 'I *mean* Sir Richard!'

Bolitho took a telescope from the rack. 'I remember. I hope young Dunstan appreciates the greatest gift as I once did.'

None of the others understood and once again Allday was moved by the privilege.

Bolitho lowered the glass. Too much spray and haze, whirling in the wind like smoke.

A privateer perhaps? Crossing swords with a Barbuda trader. Or one of the local patrols braving the wind and sea to chase an enemy corvette? *Phaedra* would soon know. It might also be a decoy to draw their flimsy defences away from the gold and silver.

He smiled bitterly. How would Haven react to that, he wondered?

'Nor'-west-by-north, sir!' The helmsman had to yell to make himself heard above the roar of wind through the canvas and rigging, pushing the sloop-of-war hard over until it was impossible to stand upright.

Commander Alfred Dunstan gripped the quarterdeck rail and tugged his cocked hat more firmly over his wild auburn hair. He had been *Phaedra*'s captain for eighteen months, his first command, and with luck still on his side might soon be transferring his single epaulette to his right shoulder, the first definite step to post-rank.

He shouted, 'Bring her up two points to wind'rd, Mr Meheux! God damn it, we'll not let it escape, whatever it is!'

He saw the first lieutenant exchange a quick glance with the sailing master. *Phaedra* seemed to be sailing as close to the wind as she dared, so that her braced yards and bulging sails appeared to be almost fore-and-aft, thrusting her over, the sea boiling around her gunports and deluging the bare-backed seamen until their tanned bodies shone like crude statuary.

Dunstan strained his eyes aloft to watch every sail, and his topmen straddled out along the yards, some doutbless remem-

126

bering *Obdurate*'s hands who had been lost overboard in the storm.

'Full-an'-bye, sir! Nor'-west-by-west!'

The deck and rigging protested violently, the shrouds making a vibrant thrumming sound as the ship heeled over still further.

The first lieutenant, who was twenty-three, a year younger than his captain, shouted, 'She'll not take much more, sir!'

Dunstan grinned excitedly. He had a sensitive, pointed face and humorous mouth, and some people had told him he looked like Nelson. Dunstan liked the compliment, but had discovered the resemblance himself long ago, even as a midshipman in Bolitho's big first-rate *Euryalus*.

'A plague on your worries! What are you, an old woman?'

They laughed like schoolboys, for Meheux was the captain's cousin, and each knew almost what the other was thinking.

Dunstan tightened his lips as a line parted on the foretopsail yard with the echo of a pistol shot. But two men were already working out to repair it, and he replied, 'We must beat up to wind'rd in case the buggers show us a clean pair of heels an' we lose them!'

Meheux did not argue; he knew him too well. The sea boiled over the gangway and flung two men, cursing and floundering, into the scuppers. One came up against a tethered cannon and did not move. He had been knocked senseless, or had broken a rib or two. He was dragged to a hatchway, the others crouching like athletes as they gauged the moment to avoid the next incoming torrent of water.

Meheux enjoyed the excitement, just as Dunstan was never happier than when he was free of the fleet's apron strings or an admiral's authority. They did not even know the meaning or source of the gunfire; they might discover that it was another British man-of-war engaged in taking an enemy blockade-runner. If so, there was no chance of sharing the prize-money this time. The other captain would see to that.

Dunstan climbed up the ratlines of the lee shrouds, the waves seeming to swoop at his legs as he hung out to train his telescope while he waited for the next cry from the masthead.

The lookout yelled, 'Fine on the starboard bow, sir!' He broke off as the ship lifted then plunged deeply into a long trough, hard down until her gilded figurehead was awash, as if *Phaedra* was on her way to the bottom. The crash must have all but shaken the lookout from his precarious perch.

Then he called, 'Two ships, sir! One dismasted!'

Dunstan climbed back again and grinned as he poured water from his hat. 'Fine lookout, Mr Meheux! Give him a guinea!'

The first lieutenant smiled. 'He's one of *my* men, sir.'

Dunstan was wiping his telescope. 'Oh, good. Then you give the feller a guinea!'

There was more sporadic firing, but because of the lively sea and the drifting curtains of spray it was impossible to determine the other vessels, except from the masthead.

Phaedra heeled upright, and the main topsail boomed and thundered violently as the wind went out of it.

'Man the braces there! Let her fall off three points!' Dunstan released his grip on the rail. The wind was dropping significantly so that the hull had to be brought under command to take advantage of it.

'Nor'-nor'-west, sir! Steady as she goes!'

Meheux gasped, 'By God, there they are.'

Dunstan raised his glass again. 'Hell's teeth! It's that damn schooner we were looking for!'

Meheux studied his profile, the wild hair flapping beneath the battered hat which Dunstan always wore at sea. Once, in his cups, Dunstan had confided, 'I'll get meself a new hat when I'm posted, not before!'

Meheux said, 'The one with the Inspector General's lady aboard?'

Dunstan grinned broadly. Meheux was a reliable and promising officer. He was a child where women were concerned.

'I can see why our vice-admiral was so concerned!'

A man yelled, 'They're casting adrift, sir! They've seen us, by God!'

Dunstan's smile faded. 'Stand by on deck! Starboard battery load, but don't run out!' He gripped the lieutenant's arm. 'A bloody pirate if I'm any judge, Josh!'

The first lieutenant's name was Joshua. Dunstan only used it

128

when he was really excited.

Dunstan said urgently, 'We'll take him first. Put some good marksmen in the tops. She's a fancy little brigantine, worth a guinea or two, wouldn't you say?' He saw Meheux hurry away, the glint of steel as a boarding party was mustered clear of the gun crews and their rammers.

The schooner was dismasted although someone had tried to put up a jury rig. In that gale it must have been a nightmare.

Meheux came back, strapping on his favourite hanger.

'What about the others, sir?'

Dunstan trained the glass, then swore as a puff of smoke followed by a sharp bang showed that the pirate had fired on his ship.

'God blast their bloody eyes!' Dunstan raised his arms as he had seen Bolitho do when they had prepared for battle, so that his coxswain could clip on his sword. 'Open the ports! *Run out!*'

He recalled what Meheux had just asked him. 'If they're alive we'll take them next, if not —' He shrugged. 'One thing is certain, they're not going anywhere!'

He glanced around and winced as the pirate fired again and a ball slapped down alongside. The stage was set.

Dunstan drew his sword and held it over his head. He felt the chill run down his arm, as if the blade was made of ice. He remembered crouching with another midshipman on *Euryalus*'s quarterdeck, sick with terror, yet unable to tear his eyes away as the enemy's great mountain of sails had towered above the gangway. And Bolitho standing out on the exposed deck, his sword in the air, each gun-captain watching, sweating out the agonising seconds whch had been like hours. Eternity.

Dunstan grinned and brought his arm down with a flourish.

'*Fire!*'

The small brigantine came up floundering into the wind, her foremast gone, her decks covered with torn canvas and piles of rigging. That well-aimed broadside had also shot away the helm, or killed the men around it. The vessel was out of control, and one man who ran on to the poop with a raised musket was shot down instantly by *Phaedra*'s marksmen.

'*Hands aloft! Shorten sail!* Take in the main-course!' Dunstan

129

sheathed his sword and watched the other vessel reeling under *Phaedra*'s lee. The fight was already over. 'Stand by to board!' Some of the seamen were clambering into the shrouds, their muskets cocked and ready, while others waited like eager hounds to get to grips. It was rare to catch a pirate. Dunstan watched his first lieutenant bracing his legs to jump as the sloop-of-war sidled heavily alongside. He knew it would be a madman who put up a defence. This was what his sailors did best. They would offer no quarter if one of their own was cut down.

There was a ragged cheer as the red ensign was hoisted up the brigantine's mainmast.

Dunstan glanced at the low-lying shape of the schooner. She must be badly holed, and looked ready to capsize.

It would mean risking a boat despite the lively waves.

He called, 'Mr Grant! Jolly boat, lively with you! Stand clear if the buggers fire on you!'

The boat lifted and dipped away from the side, the other lieutenant trying to stay upright as he looked towards the schooner. Once he stared astern, then gestured wildly towards *Phaedra*.

Dunstan stared up and then laughed aloud, feeling some of the tension draining out of him.

Bolitho would have had something to say about that. He shouted, 'Run up the Colours!' He saw Meheux clambering inboard again. 'We fought under no flag, dammit!'

He saw his cousin's face and asked, 'How was it, Josh?'

The lieutenant sheathed his hanger and let out a long sigh.

'One of the bastards had a go at us, slashed poor Tom Makin across the chest, but he'll live.'

They both watched as a corpse splashed down between the two hulls.

'He'll not try that again!'

Leaving the prize crew on board, *Phaedra* cast off, and under reduced canvas, edged towards the listing schooner.

Dunstan watched as the boarding party climbed across her sloping deck. Two men, obviously pirates who had been left stranded by the brigantine, charged to the attack. Lieutenant Grant shot one with his pistol; the other ducked and retreated

130

towards the companionway. A seaman balanced his cutlass and then flung it like a spear. In the telescope's lens everything was silent, but Dunstan swore he could hear the scream as the man tumbled headlong, the blade embedded in his back.

'I'll not go alongside. Stand by to come about! Ready on deck!'

Dunstan lowered the glass, as if what he saw was too private. The woman, her gown almost torn off her back, yet strangely proud as she allowed the sailors to guide her towards the jolly boat. Dunstan saw her pause just once as she passed the dead pirate, shot down by Lieutenant Grant. He saw her spit on him and kick the cutlass from his hand. Hate, contempt and anger; but no sort of fear.

Dunstan looked as the first lieutenant. 'Man the side, Josh. This is something we shall all remember.'

Then later, when *Phaedra* with her prize making a painful progress astern, sighted the flagship, Dunstan discovered another moment which he would never forget.

She had been standing beside him, wrapped in a tarpaulin coat which one of the sailors had offered her, her chin uplifted and her eyes wide while she had watched *Hyperion*'s yards swinging, her sails refilling on to the tack which would bring them together.

Dunstan had said, 'I'll make a signal now, my lady. May I order my midshipman to spell out your name?'

She had shaken her head slowly, her eyes on the old two-decker, her reply almost lost in the crack of sails and rigging.

'No, Captain, but thank you.' Quieter still, 'He will see me. I know it.'

Only once had Dunstan seen her defences weaken. The master's mate had shouted, 'There, lads! The old girl's goin'!'

The schooner had lifted her stern and was turning in a circle of foam and bubbles, like a pale hand revolving in a chandler's butt of grain. The hull was surrounded by bobbing flotsam and a few corpses when suddenly it dived, as if eager to be gone from those who had wronged her.

Dunstan had glanced at her and had seen her clutching a fan to her breast. He could not be certain but he thought he saw her

131

speak two words. *Thank you.*

Afterwards Dunstan had said, 'Make it *two* guineas, Josh. It was more important than either of us realised.'

10

Harbour

Two weeks after *Phaedra*'s capture of the pirate brigantine and
the release of the captives, *Hyperion* and *Obdurate* returned to
Antigua.

The island was sighted at dawn, but as if to taunt their efforts,
the wind all but died completely and it was nearly dusk before
they edged their way into English Harbour and dropped anchor.

Bolitho had been on the quarterdeck for most of the afternoon,
idly watching the hands trimming the sails while the island
seemed to stand away at the same distance.

Any other time it would have been a proud moment. They had
met with ships of Sir Peter Folliot's squadron, which even now
would be escorting the treasure convoy all the remainder of the
way to England.

The lookouts had eventually reported that there were three
ships-of-the-line in harbour and Bolitho guessed they were the
other vessels of his squadron, with each captain doubtless wondering about his immediate future under Bolitho's flag.

That too should have been like a tonic, after the strain of escorting
the treasure and fighting a daily battle with the weather. Now,
Bolitho was somehow grateful that it would not be until the next day
that he could meet his new captains and while they studied him, he
would measure the men who would be serving him.

When both the two-deckers finally dropped their anchors
Bolitho had gone aft to his quarters where the great cabin was
already transformed by several cheerful lanterns.

He walked to the stern windows and leaned out over the darkening water to watch a full-blooded sunset, but his mind was still hanging on to that moment when Catherine had been hoisted up the ship's side in the rough tarpaulin coat.

It did not seem possible that she had been here in this same cabin, alone with him.

Alone with him and yet still at a measured distance. He walked around the cabin and looked at his sleeping quarters, which he had given her during her brief stay on board. There should still be some sign of her presence. A breath of her perfume, a garment forgotten perhaps when she had been carried over to Admiral Folliot's flagship when the two formations of ships had found each other.

Bolitho crossed to the fine mahogany wine cabinet and ran his fingers along it. Made by one of the best craftsmen, it had been her gift to him after he had left her in London, where he had last seen her until Antigua. He smiled sadly as he remembered his old friend Thomas Herrick's disapproval when the cabinet had been brought aboard his *Lysander*, after he had been appointed Bolitho's flag captain.

Herrick had always been a loyal friend, but had mistrusted anything and anyone he thought might damage Bolitho's name and career. Even young Adam had been involved because of the so-called liaison between them for that short, precious time. He had fought a duel with another hot-headed lieutenant at Gibraltar in defence of his uncle's reputation. It seemed as if everyone Bolitho cared for was hurt or damaged by the contact.

He turned and looked along the cabin, and saw the marine sentry's shadow through the screen door. She had stood here, quite still, only her breathing rapid and uncontrolled as she had stared around, the coat bunched to her throat as if she was cold.

Then she had noticed the cabinet, and for just a moment he had seen her mouth quiver.

He had said quietly, 'It goes everywhere with me.'

Then she had walked right up to him and had laid her hand on his face. When he had made to put his arms round her she had shaken her head with something like desperation.

'*No!* It is hard enough to be here like this. Do not make it

134

worse. I just want to look at you. To tell you how much it means to be alive because of you. God, Fate, I know not which, once brought us together. And now I fear what it might do to us.'

He had seen the great rent in her gown and had asked, 'Can I not have it mended? Your maid, where is she?'

She had walked away but had kept her eyes on him. 'Maria is dead. They tried to rape her. When she fought them with her bare hands they killed her, cut her down like some helpless animal.' She added slowly, 'Your little ship came just in time. For me, that is. But I made sure that some of those filthy pigs never breathe the same air again.' She had looked at her hands, at the soiled fan which she still grasped in one of them. 'I wish to God I could be there when they make those vermin dance on their ropes!'

The screen door opened slightly and Jenour looked in at him. 'The Commodore's boat has been sighted, Sir Richard.' His eyes moved around the cabin. Maybe he could see her too.

'Very well.' Bolitho sat down and looked at the deck between his feet. Glassport was the last man he wanted to see just now.

He thought of that final moment when he had accompanied her across to Sir Peter Folliot's big three-decker.

The admiral was a slight, sickly man, but there was nothing wrong with his quick mind. Despite the poor communications he seemed to know all about the preparations for the raid on La Guaira, and the actual amount of booty down to the nearest gold coin.

'Quite an escapade, eh?' He had greeted Catherine with lavish courtesy, and had announced that he would place her in the care of one of his best frigate captains, who would make all speed to return her to her husband in Antigua.

Maybe he knew something about that as well, Bolitho thought.

He had watched the powerful forty-four gun frigate making sail to take her away from him for the last time, and had stayed on deck until only the topgallant sails showed above the evening horizon like pink shells.

The big Indiaman had gone from the harbour, and he had pictured Catherine with her husband drawing further and further away with each turn of the glass.

The door opened again and Captain Haven took a few paces into the cabin.

'I am about to greet the Commodore, Sir Richard. May I signal your captains to repair on board tomorrow forenoon?'

'Yes.' It was all so empty, so coldly formal. Like a great wall between them.

Bolitho tried again. 'I did hear your wife was expecting a child, Captain Haven.' He recalled how tense Haven had been since he had received his letters from the courier brig. Like a man in a trance; he had even allowed Parris to manage the ship's affairs for him.

Haven's eyes narrowed. 'From whom, Sir Richard, may I ask?'

Bolitho sighed. 'Does it matter?'

Haven looked away. 'A baby boy.'

Bolitho saw his fingers clench around his cocked hat. Haven was driving himself mad.

'I congratulate you. It must have been on your mind a great deal.'

Haven swallowed hard. 'Yes, er, thank you, Sir Richard –'

Mercifully, shouted orders floated from the quarterdeck and Haven almost fled from the cabin to meet Commodore Glassport as he came aboard.

Bolitho stood up as Ozzard entered with his dress coat. Was it really Parris's child, he wondered? How would they settle it?

He looked down at Ozzard. 'Did I thank you for taking good care of our guest while she was amongst us?'

Ozzard brushed a speck of dust from the coat. He had mended Catherine's torn gown. There seemed no end to his skills.

The little man gave a shy smile. 'You did, Sir Richard. It was a pleasure.' He reached into a drawer and pulled out the fan she had brought with her from the sinking schooner.

'She left this.' He flinched under Bolitho's stare. 'I – I cleaned it up. There was some blood on it, y'see.'

'*Left it?*' Bolitho turned the fan over in his hands, remembering it, seeing her expression above it. He turned aside from a lantern as his eye misted over very slightly. He repeated, 'Left it?'

Ozzard watched him anxiously. 'All the rush. I expect she forgot.'

136

Bolitho gripped the fan tightly. No, she had not forgotten it.

Feet tramped towards the door and then Commodore Glassport, followed by the flag captain and Jenour, entered the cabin. Glassport's features were bright scarlet, as if he had been running uphill.

Bolitho said, 'Be seated. Some claret perhaps?'

Glassport seemed to revive at the word. 'I'd relish a glass, Sir Richard. Dammee, so much excitement, I think I should have retired long since!'

Ozzard filled their glasses and Bolitho said, 'To victory.'

Glassport stuck out his thick legs and licked his lips.

'A very fair claret, Sir Richard.'

Haven remarked, 'There are some letters, Sir Richard; they came in the last packet ship.' He watched as Jenour brought a small bundle and laid it on the table by Bolitho's elbow.

Bolitho said, 'See to the glasses, Ozzard.' Then, 'If you will excuse me, gentlemen.'

He slit open one letter. He recognised Belinda's handwriting immediately.

His glance moved rapidly across the letter, so that he had to stop and begin again.

My dear husband. It was as if the letter was for someone else. Belinda wrote briefly of her latest visit to London, and that she was now staying in a house which she had leased to await his approval. Elizabeth had had a cold, but was now well and had taken to the nurse whom Belinda had hired. The rest of the letter seemed to be about Nelson, and how the whole country was depending on him as he stood between the French and England.

Jenour asked quietly, 'Not bad news, Sir Richard?'

Bolitho tucked the letter into his coat. 'Really, Stephen, I wouldn't know.'

There had been nothing about Falmouth and people there he had known all his life. No concern, not even anger or remorse at the way they had parted.

Glassport said heavily, 'It is a mite quieter here now that the King's Inspector General is departed.' He gave a deep chuckle. 'I would not wish to get on the wrong side of that one.'

137

Haven said primly, 'His is another world. It is certainly not mine.'

Bolitho said, 'I shall see my captains tomorrow –' He looked at Glassport. 'By how much was the Indiaman delayed?'

Glassport peered at him, his mind already blurred by several large glasses of claret.

'When the gale eased, Sir Richard.'

Bolitho stood up without realising it. He must have misheard. 'Without waiting for Lady Somervell? By what vessel did she take passage after she arrived in the frigate?' Surely even Somervell, so eager to present the treasure to His Majesty in person, would have waited to be assured of Catherine's safety?

Glassport sensed his sudden anxiety and said, 'She did not leave, Sir Richard. I am still awaiting her instructions.' He seemed confused. 'Lady Somervell is at the house.'

Bolitho sat down again, then glanced across at the fan which lay on the wine cabinet.

He said, 'Once again, please excuse me, gentlemen. I will speak with you tomorrow.'

Later, as he listened to the trill of calls and the thud of Glassport's launch alongside, he walked to the stern windows and stared at the land. Pinpricks of light from the harbour and the houses behind it. A slow, glassy swell which tilted *Hyperion*'s heavy bulk just enough to make the rigging and blocks stir uneasily. A few pale stars. Bolitho took time to count them, to contain the sudden realisation which moments earlier had been disbelief.

Would you risk everything? The voice seemed to speak out loud.

Jenour re-entered silently and Bolitho saw his reflection in the thick glass beside him.

Bolitho said, 'Fetch Allday, if you would, Stephen, and call away my barge. I am going ashore directly.'

Jenour hesitated, unwilling to pit his beliefs against Bolitho's sudden determination.

Jenour had watched him when Glassport had blurted out about the woman *Phaedra* had snatched from the sea and the nearness of brutal rape and death. It had been like seeing a light rekindled. A cloud passing away.

He said, 'May I speak, Sir Richard?'

'Have I ever prevented you from doing so, Stephen?' He half turned, feeling the young lieutenant's uncertainty and discomfort. 'Is it about my leaving the ship?'

Jenour replied huskily, 'There is not a man under the flag who would not die for you, Sir Richard.'

Bolitho said, 'I doubt that.' He immediately sensed Jenour's dismay and added, 'Please continue.'

Jenour said, 'You intend to visit the lady, Sir Richard.' He fell silent, expecting an instant rebuff. When Bolitho said nothing he continued, 'By tomorrow the whole squadron will know. This time next month, all England will hear of it.' He looked down and said, 'I – I am sorry to speak out in this fashion. I have no right. It is just that I care very much.'

Bolitho took his arm and shook it gently. 'It took courage to speak as you did. An old enemy, John Paul Jones, was quoted as saying that "he who will not risk cannot win". Whatever his other faults may have been, a lack of courage was not one of them.' He smiled gravely. 'I *know* the risk, Stephen. Now fetch Allday.'

On the other side of the pantry door Ozzard withdrew his ear from the shutter and nodded very slowly.

He was suddenly grateful he had discovered the fan.

Bolitho barely noticed anything as he strode through the shadows to leave the harbour behind him. Only once he paused to regain his breath, and to try and test his feelings and the depth of his actions. He watched the anchored ships, their open gunports glittering across the even swell, the heavier, darker shape of the captured *Ciudad de Sevilla*. What would become of her? Would she be commandeered or sold to some wealthy merchant company, or even offered in trade to the Spaniards in an attempt to recover *Consort*? The latter was unlikely. The Dons would be humiliated enough at losing the treasure-ship and having another destroyed under their own fortress without adding to it.

When he arrived at the white walls of the house he paused again, conscious of his heart against his ribs, of the realisation that he had no plan in mind. Perhaps she would not even see him?

He walked up the carriage-drive and entered the main door, which was open to tempt any sea-breeze into the house. A sleeping servant, curled in a tall wicker chair by the entrance, did not even stir as Bolitho passed.

He stood in the pillared hall, staring at the shadows, some heavy tapestry glowing in the light from two candelabra. It was very still, and there seemed to be no air at all.

Bolitho saw a handbell on a carved chest by another door and played with the idea of ringing it. In that last fight aboard the treasure-ship, death had been a close companion, but it was no stranger to him. He had felt no fear at all, not even afterwards. He gripped his sword tightly. Where was that courage now that he really needed it?

Maybe Glassport had been mistaken and she had gone from here, overland this time to St John's. She had friends there. He recalled Jenour's anxiety, Allday's watchful silence as the barge had carried him to the jetty. Some Royal Marines on picket duty had scrambled into a semblance of attention as they realised that the vice-admiral had come ashore without a word of warning.

Allday had said, 'I shall wait, Sir Richard.'

'No. I can call for a boat when I need one.'

Allday had watched him leave. Bolitho wondered what he thought about it. Probably much the same as Jenour.

Who is that?

Bolitho turned and saw her on the curved stairway, framed against another dark tapestry. She wore a loose, pale gown, and was standing very still, a hand on the rail, the other concealed in the gown.

Then she exclaimed, 'You! I – I did not know –'

She made no move to come down and Bolitho walked slowly up the stairway towards her.

He said, 'I have just heard. I believed you gone.' He paused with one foot on the next step, afraid she would turn away. 'The Indiaman sailed without you.' He was careful not to mention Somervell by name. 'I could not bear to think of you here. Alone.'

She turned and he realised that she was holding a pistol.

He said, 'Give it to me.' He moved closer and held out his hand. 'Please, Kate.'

140

He took it from her fingers and realised it was cocked, ready to fire. He said quietly, 'You are safe now.'

She said, 'Come to the drawing room.' She might have shivered. 'There is more light.'

Bolitho followed her and waited for her to close the door behind them. It was a pleasant enough room, although nothing looked personal; it was occupied too often by visitors, strangers.

Bolitho laid the pistol on a table and watched her draw shutters across the window, where some moths were tapping against the glass, seeking the light.

She did not look at him. 'Sit there, Richard.' She shook her head vaguely. 'I was resting. I must do something to my hair.' Then she did turn to study him, a lingering, searching glance, as if she was seeking an answer to some unspoken question.

She said, 'I knew he would not wait. He took his mission very seriously. Put it above all else. It was my fault. I knew the matter was so dear to him, so urgent once you had made the plan into reality. I should not have gone in the schooner.' She repeated slowly, 'I knew he would not wait.'

'Why did you do it?'

She looked away and he saw her hand touch the handle on the other door, which was in deep shadow, away from the lights.

She replied, 'I felt like it.'

'You might have been killed, and then –'

She swung round, only her eyes flashing in the shadows. 'And *then*?'

She tossed her head with something like anger. 'Did you ask yourself that question too when you went after the *Ciudad de Sevilla*?' The ship's name seemed to intrude like a person. It had rolled so easily off her tongue, a cruel reminder that she had been married to a Spaniard. She continued, 'Someone of *your* value and rank, you of all people must have realised that you were taking a terrible risk? You knew that, I can see it on your face – must have known that any junior captain could have been sent, just as you once seized the ship I was aboard, when I first laid eyes on you!'

Bolitho was on his feet and for several seconds they stared at each other, both hurt and vulnerable because of it.

141

She said abruptly, 'Do not leave.' Then she vanished through the other door although Bolitho did not even see it open and close.

What had he expected? He was a fool, and looking a worse one. He had harmed her enough, too much.

Her voice came from beyond. 'I have put down my hair.' She waited until he faced the door. 'It is not quite right yet. Yesterday and today I walked along the foreshore. The salt air is cruel to vain women.'

Bolitho watched the long, pale gown. In the deep shadows she appeared to be floating like a ghost.

She said, 'You once gave me a ribbon for it, remember? I have tied it around my hair.' She shook her head so that one shoulder vanished in shadow, which Bolitho knew was her long dark hair.

'Do you see it, or had you forgotten that?'

He replied quietly. 'Never. You liked green so much. I had to get it for you —' He broke off as she put out her arms and ran towards him. It seemed to happen in a second. One moment she was there, pale against the other door, and the next she was pressed against him, her voice muffled while she clutched his shoulders as if to control her sudden despair.

She exclaimed, 'Look at me! In God's name, Richard, I *lied* to you, don't you see?'

Bolitho took her in his arms and pressed his cheek into her hair. It was not the ribbon he had bought in London from the old lady selling lace. This one was bright blue.

She ran her hand up to his neck and then laid it against his face. When she raised her eyes he saw that they were filled with emotion, pity.

She whispered, 'I did not *know*, Richard. Then, before you sailed with the convoy, I — I heard something about it — how you —' She held his face between her hands now. 'Oh, dearest of men, I had to be sure, to know!'

Bolitho pulled her closer so that he could hide his face above her shoulder. It must have been Allday. Only he would take the risk.

He heard her whisper, 'How bad is it?'

He said, 'I have grown used to it. Just sometimes it fails me.

Like the moment you stood there in the shadows.' He tried to smile. 'I was never able to outwit you.'

She leaned back in his arms and studied him. 'And the time you came to the reception here, when you almost fell on the stair. I should have known, ought to have understood!'

He watched the emotions crossing her face. She was tall and he was very aware of her nearness, of the trick which had misfired.

He said, 'I will leave if you wish.'

She slipped her hand through his arm. She was thinking aloud as they walked around the room, like lovers in a quiet park.

'There are people who must be able to help.'

He pressed her wrist to his side. 'They say not.'

She turned him towards her. 'We will *go on trying*. There is always hope.'

Bolitho said, 'To know that you care so much means every-thing.' He half-expected her to stop him but she remained quite still, her hands in his, so that their linked shadows appeared to be dancing across the walls.

'Now that we are together I never want to lose you. It must sound like madness, the babbling of some besotted youth.' The words were flooding out of him and she seemed to know how he needed to speak. 'I thought my life was in ruins, and knew that I had done a terrible harm to yours.' Then she made to speak but he shook her hands in his. 'No, it is all true. I was in love with a ghost. The realisation ripped me apart. Someone suggested I had a death-wish.'

She nodded slowly. 'I can guess who that was.' She met his gaze steadily, without fear. 'Do you really understand what you are saying, Richard? How high the stakes may be?'

He nodded. 'Even greater for you, Kate. I remember what you said about Nelson's infatuation.'

She smiled for the first time. 'To be called a whore is one thing; to be one is something very different.'

He gripped her hands even tighter. 'There are so many things —'

She twisted from his grip. 'They must wait.' Her eyes were very bright. 'We cannot.'

He said quietly, 'Call me what you did just now.'

'Dearest of men?' She pulled the ribbon from her hair and shook it loose across her shoulder. 'Whatever I have been or done, Richard, you have always been that to me.' She looked at him searchingly. 'Do you want me?'

He reached for her but she stepped away. 'You have answered me.' She gestured towards the other door. 'I need just a moment, *alone.*'

Without her the room seemed alien and hostile. Bolitho removed his coat and sword, and as an afterthought slid the latch on the door. His glance fell on the pistol and he uncocked it, seeing her face when she had discovered him. Knowing that she would have fired at the first hint of danger.

Then he walked to the door and opened it, the shadows and the fears forgotten as he saw her sitting on the bed, her hair shining in the candlelight.

She smiled at him, her knees drawn up to her chin like a child.

'So the proud vice-admiral has gone, and my daring captain has come in his place.'

Bolitho sat beside her, and then eased her shoulders down onto the bed.

She wore a long robe of ivory silk, tied beneath her throat by a thin ribbon. She watched him, his eyes as they explored her body, remembering perhaps how it had once been.

Then she took his hand and pulled it to her breast, tightening his fingers until he thought he must hurt her.

She whispered, 'Take me, Richard.' Then she shook her head very slowly. 'I know what you fear now, but I tell you, it is not out of pity, it is from the love I have never given to another man.'

She thrust her hands out on either side like one crucified and watched as he untied the ribbon and began to remove the robe.

Bolitho could feel the blood rushing through his brain; while he too felt momentarily like an onlooker as he bared her breasts and her arms until she was naked to the waist.

He gasped, 'Who did this to you?'

Her right shoulder was cruelly discoloured, one of the worst bruises he had ever seen.

But she reached up with one hand and dragged his mouth down to hers, her breathing as wild as his own.

144

She whispered, 'A Brown Bess has a fearsome kick, like a mule!'

She must have been firing a musket when the pirates had attacked the schooner. Like the pistol.

The kiss was endless. It was like sharing everything in a moment. Clinging to it, never wanting it to finish, but unable to hold on for a minute longer.

He heard her cry out as he threw the robe on the floor, saw her fists clench as he touched her, then covered her in his hand as if to prolong the need they had for each other.

She watched him tear off his clothes and touched the scar on his shoulder, remembering that too, and the fever she had held at bay.

She said huskily, 'I don't care about *afterward*, Richard.'

He saw her looking at him as his shadow covered her like a cloak. She said something like 'It's been so long –' Then she arched her body and gave a sharp cry as he entered her, her fingers pulling at him, dragging him closer and deeper until they were one.

Later, as they lay spent in each other's arms and watched the smoke standing up from the guttering candles, she said softly, 'You needed love. *My* love.' He held her against him as she added, 'Who cares about the tomorrows.'

He spoke into her hair. 'We shall make them ours too.'

Down on the jetty Allday seated himself comfortably on a stone bollard and began to fill his new pipe with tobacco. He had sent the barge back to the ship.

Bolitho would not be needing it for a bit yet, he thought. The tobacco was rich, well dampened with rum for good measure. Allday had dismissed the barge but found that he wanted to remain ashore himself. *Just in case.*

He put down a stone bottle of rum on the jetty and puffed contentedly on his new clay.

Perhaps there was a God in Heaven after all. He glanced towards the darkened house with the white walls.

Only God knew how this little lot might end, but for the present, and that was all any poor Jack could hope for, things were looking better for Our Dick. He grinned and reached down for the bottle. *An' that's no error.*

Gibraltar
1805

11

The Letter

His Britannic Majesty's Ship *Hyperion* heeled only very slightly as she changed tack yet again, her tapering jib-boom pointing almost due east.

Bolitho stood by the quarterdeck nettings and watched the great looming slab of Gibraltar rise above the larboard bow, misty-blue in the afternoon glare. It was mid-April.

Men moved purposefully about the decks, the lieutenants checking the set of each sail, conscious perhaps of this spectacular landfall. They had not touched land for six weeks, not since the squadron had quit English Harbour for the last time.

Bolitho took a telescope from the rack and trained it on the Rock. If the Spaniards ever succeeded in retaking this natural fortress, they could close the Mediterranean with the ease of slamming a giant door.

He focused the glass on the litter of shipping which seemed to rest at the foot of the Rock itself. More like a cluster of fallen moths than ships-of-war. It was only then that a newcomer could realise the size of it, the distance it still stood away from the slow-moving squadron.

He looked abeam. They were sailing as close as was prudently safe to the coast of Spain. Sunlight made diamond-bright reflections through the haze. He could imagine just how many telescopes were causing them as unseen eyes watched the small procession of ships. *Where bound? For what purpose?* Riders would be carrying intelligence to senior officers and lookout stations. The Dons could study the comings and goings with ease here at the narrowest part of the Strait of Gibraltar.

As if to give weight to his thoughts he heard Parris say to one of the midshipmen on the quarterdeck, 'Take a good look, Mr Blessed. Yonder lies the enemy.'

Bolitho tucked his hands behind him and thought over the past four months, since his new squadron had finally assembled at Antigua. Since Catherine had taken passage for England. The parting had been harder than he had expected, and still hurt like a raw wound.

She had sent one letter in that time. A warm, passionate letter, part of herself. *He was not to worry. They would meet again soon. There must be no scandal.* She was, as usual, thinking of him.

Bolitho had written back, and had also sent a letter to Belinda. The secret would soon be out, if not already; it was right if not honourable that she should hear it from him.

He moved across the quarterdeck and saw the helmsmen drop their eyes as his glance passed over them. He climbed a poop ladder and raised the glass again to study the ships which followed astern. It had kept his mind busy enough while the squadron had worked up together, had got used to one another's ways and peculiarities. There were four ships-of-the-line, all third-rates which to an ignorant landsman would look exactly like *Hyperion* in the van. Apart from *Obdurate*, the others had been new to Bolitho's standards, but watching them now he could feel pride instead of impatience.

Holding up to windward in the gentle north-westerly breeze he saw the little sloop-of-war *Phaedra*, sailing as near as she dared to the Spanish coast, Dunstan hoping possibly for a careless enemy trader to run under his guns.

Perhaps the most welcome addition was the thirty-six gun frigate *Tybalt*, which had arrived from England only just in time to join the squadron. She was commanded by a fiery Scot named Andrew McKee, who was more used to working independently. Bolitho understood the feeling even if he could not condone it. The life of any frigate captain was perhaps the most remote and monastic of all. In a crowded ship he remained alone beyond his cabin bulkhead, dining only occasionally with his officers, completely cut off from other ships and even the men he commanded. Bolitho smiled. Until now.

They had achieved little more in the Caribbean. A few indecisive attacks on enemy shipping and harbours, but after the reckless cutting-out of the treasure-ship from La Guaira all else seemed an anti-climax. As Glassport had said when the squadron had set sail for Gibraltar. *After that, life would never be the same.*

In more ways than one, Bolitho thought grimly.

It had been a strange feeling to quit Antigua. He had the lurking belief that he would never see the islands again. The Islands of Death, as the luckless army garrisons called them. Even *Hyperion* had not been immune from fever. Three seamen employed ashore had been taken ill, and had died with the disbelief of animals at slaughter.

He stepped from the ladder as Haven crossed the deck to speak with Penhaligon the master.

The latter remarked confidently, 'The wind stands fair, sir. We shall anchor at eight bells.'

Haven kept very much to himself, and apart from a few fits of almost insane anger, seemed content to leave matters to Parris. It was a tense and wary relationship, which must affect the whole wardroom. And yet the orders when they came by courier brig had been welcome. The storm was still brewing over Europe, with the antagonists watching and waiting for a campaign, even a single battle which might tip the balance.

The captured frigate *Consort*, renamed *Intrépido*, had slipped out of port unseen and unchecked. It was said that she too had left for Spain, to add her weight to His Catholic Majesty's considerable navy. She would be a boost to public morale as well. A prize snatched from the English, who were as ever desperate for more frigates.

Bolitho stared at the towering Rock. *Gibraltar for orders.* How many times had he read those words? He looked along the busy maindeck, the hands trimming the yards, or squinting up at the restless sails. It had been in Gibraltar that he had first met with *Hyperion*, when this endless war had barely begun. Did ships wonder about their fates? He saw Allday lounging by the boat tier, his hat tilted down to shade his eyes from the hard glare. He would be remembering too. Bolitho saw the coxswain put one hand to his chest and grimace, then glance suspiciously around to make sure nobody had noticed. He was always in pain, but would never rest. Thinking about his son, of the girl at the Falmouth inn; of the last battle, or the next one.

Allday turned and looked up at the quarterdeck. Just a brief glance of recognition, as if he knew what Bolitho was thinking.

Like that dawn when he had gone to the jetty after leaving Catherine.

Allday had been there, had put his fingers to his mouth to give his piercing whistle which dismissed any boatswain's call to shame, to summon a boat.

When he had last seen Catherine he had argued with her, tried to persuade her to move away from London until they could face the storm together. She had been adamant. She intended to see Somervell, to tell him the truth. *Our love must triumph.*

When Bolitho had voiced his fears for her safety she had given the bubbling, uninhibited laugh he remembered so well. 'There has been no love between us, Richard. Not as you thought it was. I wanted a marriage for security, Lacey needed my strength, my backing.'

It still hurt to hear her use his name.

He could see her now, on that last evening before she had sailed. Those compelling eyes and high cheekbones, her incredible confidence.

He heard Jenour's footsteps on the worn planking. Ready to convey his orders to the other captains.

Bolitho saw a brig riding untidily on the blue water, her yards alive with flags as she conveyed news of the squadron to the Rock fortress. There might even be word from Catherine. He had reread her only letter until he knew each line perfectly.

Such a striking, vibrant woman. Somervell must be mad not to fight for her love.

One night when they had been lying together, watching the moonlight through the shutters, she had told him something of her past. He already knew about her first marriage to an English soldier-of-fortune who had died in a brawl in Spain before the

Franco-Spanish Alliance. She had been just a young girl at the time, who had been raised in London, *a part you would not dare to believe, dear Richard!* She had laughed, and nuzzled his shoulder, but he had heard the sadness too. Before that she had been on the stage. When she was fourteen. A long hard journey to become the wife of the Inspector General. Then there had been Luis Pareja, who had been killed after Bolitho had taken their ship as a prize, then defended it against Barbary pirates.

Pareja had been twice her age, but she had cared for him deeply; for his gentle kindness above all, something which until then had been denied her.

Pareja had provided for her well, although she had had no idea that she owned anything but some jewellery she had been wearing aboard that ship when Bolitho had burst into her life.

Their first confrontation had been one of fire. She had spat out her bitter despair and hate. It was still hard to fathom when all that had changed to an equally fiery love.

He took the telescope again and trained it on the brig.

Catherine had missed the sight she had sworn to witness. Almost the last thing Bolitho had seen when *Hyperion* left English Harbour had been a line of grisly gibbets, their sun-blackened remains left as a reminder and a warning to other would-be pirates.

He saw Parris standing forward along the starboard gangway, to make sure that when they anchored nobody ashore would find even the smallest fault in the manoeuvre.

Parris had taken a working party ashore at Antigua to move Catherine's trunks aboard the packet-ship.

Catherine had slipped her hand through Bolitho's arm while they had watched the sailors carrying the boxes towards the jetty.

She had said, 'I don't like that man.'

Bolitho had been surprised. 'He's a good officer, brave too. What don't you like about him?'

She had shrugged, eager to change the subject. 'He gives me the shivers.'

Bolitho glanced again at the first lieutenant. How simply he could raise a grin from a seaman, or the obvious awe of a midshipman. Maybe he reminded her of someone in her past? It would be easy to picture Parris as a soldier-of-fortune.

Jenour remarked, 'My first time here, Sir Richard.'

Bolitho nodded. 'I've been glad enough to see the Rock once or twice after a rough passage.'

Captain Haven called, 'Stand by to alter course two points to larboard!'

Bolitho watched his shoulders and wondered. Or had Catherine recognised in Parris what Haven obviously believed?

Bolitho took out his watch as the seamen hurried to the braces and halliards.

'General signal. *Tack in succession.*'

The waiting midshipmen bustled amongst a mass of bunting, while their men bent on each flag with the speed of light.

'All acknowledged, sir!'

Haven glowered. 'About time, dammit!'

Jenour said carefully, 'I was wondering about our orders, Sir Richard?'

Bolitho smiled. 'You are not alone. North to Biscay and the damned blockade of Brest and Lorient. Or join Lord Nelson? The dice can fall either way.'

Bolitho shaded his eyes to watch the other ships shortening sail in preparation for the last leg to the anchorage.

Astern of *Obdurate* was another veteran, *Crusader*. Twenty-five years old, and like most third-rates she had tasted the fire of battle many times. Bolitho had seen her at Toulon and in the West Indies, seeking French landings in Ireland, or standing in the blazing line at the Nile. *Redoubtable* and *Capricious* completed the squadron, the latter being commanded by Captain William Merrye, whose grandfather had once been an infamous smuggler; or so the story had it. Seventy-fours were the backbone of the fleet, any fleet. Bolitho glanced up at his flag at the fore. It looked right and proper there.

Then the drawn-out ceremony of gun-salutes to the Rock, repeated and acknowledged until the anchorage was partly hidden by smoke, the echoes sighing across to Algeciras like an added insult.

Bolitho saw the guardboat with its huge flag and motionless

oars. Marking where they should drop anchor. He thought suddenly of the Spanish boat at La Guaira, smashed apart under the schooner's stem.

'*Anchor!*'

They must make a fine, if familiar, sight to the people on the shore, Bolitho thought.

Leviathans turning into the gentle wind, with all canvas clewed up but for topsails and jibs.

'Tops'l clew lines! *Start that man!* Lively there!'

'Helm a-lee!'

Bolitho clenched his fists as Parris's arm fell. '*Let go!*'

The great anchor threw up a pale waterspout, while high overhead the topsails vanished against their yards as if to a single hand.

Bolitho looked quickly at the other ships, swinging now to their cables, each captain determined to hold a perfect bearing on his vice-admiral.

Boats were already being swayed out, the excitement of seeing the great harbour after weeks at sea contained and suppressed by leather-lunged boatswain's mates and petty officers.

'Gig approaching, sir!'

Bolitho saw the small boat rising and dipping smartly across the slight swell. Their first encounter.

'I shall go aft, Mr Jenour.' He spoke formally in front of Haven. 'As soon as –'

He turned as the quartermaster yelled the age-old challenge.

'Boat ahoy?'

The answer came back from the gig. '*Firefly!*'

Jenour said, 'Someone's captain coming to see us already, Sir Richard.' Then he saw Bolitho's eyes, his look of relief and something more.

Bolitho said, 'I shall greet *Firefly*'s captain myself.'

The young commander almost bounded up *Hyperion*'s tumblehome. Those who did not know stared with astonishment as their admiral threw his arms about the youthful officer who at first glance could have been his brother.

Bolitho held him and shook his shoulders gently. 'Adam. Of all people.'

Commander Adam Bolitho of the brig *Firefly* grinned with delight, his teeth very white in his sunburned face.

All he could say was, 'Well, Uncle!'

Bolitho stood in the centre of his cabin, while Yovell and Jenour sorted through a bag of despatches and letters which Adam had brought from the shore.

Adam said, 'It was amazing bad luck, Uncle. The Frogs put to sea under Admiral Villeneuve, and Our Nel went looking for them. But while the little admiral was searching around Malta and Alexandria, Villeneuve slipped through the Strait and into the Atlantic. In God's name, Uncle, had your orders been sent earlier you might have met up with 'em! Thank the high heavens you did not!'

Bolitho smiled quietly. Adam spoke with the ease and confidence of a seasoned old campaigner, and he was twenty-four years old; twenty-five in two months' time.

Adam said, 'This old ship, Uncle. Look at us now, eh?'

Bolitho nodded as Yovell placed an official Admiralty envelope before him. Adam had joined *Hyperion* as his first ship, a thin, pale youth, but with all the determination and wildness of a young colt.

Indeed, he thought. Look at us now.

So the French had put to sea at last. Past Gibraltar and across the Atlantic with Nelson eventually in hot pursuit. Villeneuve had apparently sailed westward, though for what purpose nobody seemed quite sure. Bolitho read swiftly, aware of Adam watching him. Wanting to talk with him more than anything, but needing to know what was happening; it might affect them all.

Bolitho handed the letter to Yovell and said, 'So the French are on the move. Is it a trick or are they out to divide our forces?'

Adam was right. Had he been ordered to leave Antigua earlier they might well have met up with the enemy. Five third-rates against one of the finest fleets in the world. The outcome would have been in no doubt. But at least they might have delayed Villeneuve until Nelson caught up with them. He smiled. *Our Nel* indeed.

Bolitho took the next letter, already opened by Jenour, who

156

had barely taken his eyes off the young commander since he had stepped aboard. A part of the Bolitho story he did not yet share.

Bolitho said softly, 'Hell's teeth. I am to relieve Thomas Herrick at Malta.' He examined his feelings. He should be happy to see the man who was his best friend. After the court of enquiry into Valentine Keen's behaviour, when only Bolitho's word had prevented a court-martial, he was not so certain. Deep in his heart Bolitho knew Herrick had been in the right. *Would I have twisted the rules in his place?* The question had never been answered.

Adam eyed him gravely. 'But first you sail for England, Uncle.' He forced a grin. 'With me.'

Bolitho took the envelope from him and slit it open. It was strange that of all his people who were dear to him, only Adam had ever met the famous Nelson, had carried more despatches from him in his brig *Firefly* than anybody.

The new squadron would rest and take on victuals at Gibraltar. Nelson had written in his strange sloping hand, 'Doubtless the care and attention of English Harbour will have left much to complain on!' Was there anything he did not know about?

Bolitho was to be released from his command for a brief visit to their Lordships of Admiralty. The letter ended with the barb Nelson so enjoyed. 'There you may discover how well they fight their wars with words and paper instead of ordnance and good steel. . . .'

It was true that the squadron could do with fresh victualling and some spare spars. The blockade was likely to be a lengthy one. The French must return to port, if only to await reinforcements from their Spanish ally. One of which would likely be the *Intrépido*.

Bolitho glanced at the pile of charts on a nearby table. The vastness of a great ocean which could hide or swallow a fleet with ease. Thank God Catherine had written her letter from England, otherwise he would have been fretting that she had been taken by the enemy.

He looked at Adam and saw the sudden apprehension in his eyes.

Bolitho said to the others, 'Please leave us a while.' He touched

Jenour's arm. 'Delve through the rest of the pile, Stephen. I am afraid I have come to rely too much on you.'

The door closed behind them and Adam said quietly, 'That was kindly done, Uncle. The flag lieutenant is another one caught in your spell.'

Bolitho asked, 'What is wrong?'

Adam stood up and crossed to the stern windows. How like his father, Bolitho thought. Hugh would have been proud of him this day, to see him in command of his own ship.

'I know you hate deceit, Uncle.'

'So?'

'I once fought a stupid duel over yonder.'

'I've not forgotten, Adam.'

He shifted his feet on the checkered canvas deck. 'Is it true what they're saying?'

'I expect so. Some of it anyway.'

Adam turned, his hair shining in the sunlight. 'Is it what you want?'

Bolitho nodded. 'I will see that no harm is done to you, Adam. You have been hurt enough, if not by your family then because of it.'

Adam's chin lifted. 'I shall be all right, Uncle. Lord Nelson said to me that England needs all her sons now –'

Bolitho stared. His father had said those same words when he had given him the old sword, which should have been Hugh's but for his disgrace. It was uncanny.

Adam continued, 'If one man can love another, then you have mine, Uncle. You know that already, but you may wish to remember it when others turn against you, which they will. I do not know the lady, but then I do not really know the Lady Belinda.' He looked down, embarrassed. 'In God's name, I am out of my depth!'

Bolitho walked to the windows and stared hard at the nearest ship's motionless reflection.

'She has my heart, Adam. With her I am a man again. Without her I am like a ship denied sails.'

Adam faced him. 'I believe this call to London is for you to settle matters. To clear the air.'

'By denying the truth?'

'It is what I think, Uncle.'

He smiled sadly. 'So wise a head on so young a pair of shoulders.'

Adam shrugged, and appeared suddenly vulnerable. Like the fourteen-year old midshipman who had once walked all the way from his home in Penzance to join Bolitho's *Hyperion* after the death of his mother. A whore she might have been, but she had tried to care for the boy. And Hugh had known nothing about it, not until it was all too late.

Adam said, 'At least we will keep one another company. I have more despatches from Lord Nelson.' He eyed him steadily. 'I am to carry you back to the squadron when your affairs in London are settled.'

Who had decided that, Bolitho wondered? Nelson himself, getting his own back on those who despised his infatuation with Emma Hamilton, and showing them he had a kindred spirit? Or someone more highly placed, who would use family unity to make him change his mind? He could still not accept that he was going to see Catherine again so soon. Even the news of a temporary French breakout seemed unimportant by comparison.

He recalled the others to the cabin and said, 'I shall require you to remain here in my absence, Stephen.' He shook his head to cool down the protests and added, 'I need you in *Hyperion*; do you know what I am saying?'

He saw understanding clearing the disappointment from the lieutenant's eyes.

Bolitho said, 'An ally, if you like, someone who will send me word if anything untoward happens.'

He looked at Yovell. 'Help the flag lieutenant all you can.' He forced a smile. 'A rock in stormy seas, eh?'

Yovell did not smile. 'I'm worried about *you*, Sir Richard.'

Bolitho looked at them. 'Good friends, all of you. But just now and then I have to act alone.'

He thought suddenly of the livid scar on Somervell's neck. Was that what was intended to settle the matter? A duel?

He dismissed the idea immediately. Somervell was too anxious to please the King. No, it was to be a skirmish of a different kind.

159

He said, 'I shall take Allday with me.'

Adam clapped one hand over his hair and exclaimed, 'I am an idiot! I completely forgot it!' He pointed vaguely through the windows. 'I have taken young Bankart as my own coxswain! He marched aboard *Firefly* at Plymouth when I called there for orders.'

'That was good of you, Adam.'

He grinned but it did not reach his eyes. 'Only right that one bastard should help another!'

The little brig *Firefly* weighed and put to sea the following day. It was a rush from the moment Bolitho had read the despatches, and he barely had time to summon his captains and to tell them to use the next weeks to supply and refurbish their ships.

Haven had listened to the instructions without any show of surprise or excitement. Bolitho had impressed on him more than any other, that as flag captain it was his obliged duty to watch over the squadron, and not merely the affairs of his own command. He had also made it very clear that no matter what impressive plan Captain McKee of the frigate *Tybalt* should put forward as an excuse to steal away and regain his independence, it was to be denied. *I need that frigate as much, if not more than I need him.*

After *Hyperion*'s cabin, the brig's quarters seemed like a cupboard. Only beneath the skylight could Bolitho stand upright, and he knew that the ship's company had to exist in some parts where the deckhead was only four feet six inches high.

But the vessel seemed as lively inboard as out, and Bolitho quickly noticed that there was a very relaxed feeling between afterguard and forecastle, and was secretly proud of what his nephew had done.

He was disturbed by the fact there had been no more news from Catherine and had told himself she was trying to keep up normal appearances until the gossip died, or was transferred to another. But it worried him nevertheless, especially after reading the one letter which had been sent by Belinda.

It was a cool, and what his mother would have called a *sensible* letter. She referred only briefly to the infatuation with *this woman*, something which could be forgiven if not understood. Nothing would be allowed to stand between them. *I shall not tolerate it.* Had she written in anger he might have felt less troubled. Perhaps she had already met Catherine at one of the receptions which attracted Belinda so much. But that also seemed unlikely.

Once into the Western Ocean *Firefly* began to live up to her name. Adam kept her standing well out and away from land as day by day they beat their way around the southern shores of Portugal, then north towards the Bay of Biscay. When he asked Adam why he was standing so far out from land he explained with an awkward grin that it was to avoid the weatherbeaten ships of the blockading squadrons. 'If any captain sees *Firefly* he'll make a signal for me to heave-to so that he can pass over mail for England! This time, I do not have an hour to waste!'

Bolitho found time to pity the men of the blockading squadrons. Week in and week out they tacked up and down in all weathers, while the enemy rested safely in harbour and watched their every move. It was the most hated duty of all, as *Hyperion*'s newer hands would soon appreciate.

The passage of twelve hundred miles from Gibraltar to Portsmouth was one of the liveliest Bolitho could recall. He spent much of the time on deck with Adam, shouting to each other above the roar of spray and wind as the brig spread her canvas to such a degree that Bolitho wondered why the sticks were not torn out of her.

It was exhilarating to be with him again, to see how he had changed from the eager lieutenant to a man in command. Who knew the strain of every piece of cordage and canvas, and could give confidence to those who did not. Sometimes he liked to quote Nelson, the hero he so obviously admired. His first lieutenant, quite new to Bolitho, had asked him nervously about reefing when the Biscay gales had sprung up suddenly like some fierce tribe.

Adam had called above the din, 'It is time to reef when you *feel* like it!'

Another time he had quoted his uncle when a master's mate had asked about getting the men fed, before or after changing tack?

Adam had glanced across at Bolitho and smiled. 'The people come first this time.'

Then into the Western Approaches and up the Channel, exchanging signals with watchful patrols, and then on a glorious spring morning they sighted the Isle of Wight. Five and a half days from Gibraltar. They had flown right enough.

Bolitho and Adam went to a smaller inn, and not the George, to await the *Portsmouth Flier* to London. Perhaps they had both spoken so much about the last time they had left Portsmouth together. Too many memories, maybe? Like being cleansed of something bad.

It had been like a tonic to see Allday with his son throughout the lively passage. Now they too were saying their farewells, while young Bankart remained with his ship and Allday boarded the coach. Bolitho protested that Allday had to be an outsider, because the coach was filled to capacity.

Allday merely grinned and looked scornfully at the plump merchants who were the other passengers.

'I want to see the land, Sir Richard, not listen to th' bleatings o' th' likes o' them! I'll be fine on the upper deck!'

Bolitho settled in a corner, his eyes closed as a defence against conversation. Several people had noticed his rank, and were probably waiting to ask him about *the war*. At least the merchants appeared to be doing well out of it, he thought.

Adam sat opposite him, his eyes distant as he watched the rolling Hampshire countryside, his reflection in the coach window like the portraits at Falmouth.

On and on, stops for fresh horses, tankards of ale from saucy wenches at the various coaching inns. Heavy meals when they halted so that the passengers could ease their aching muscles and test their appetites on anything from rabbit pie to the best beef. The further you went from the sea, the less sign of war you found, Bolitho decided.

The coach ground to a halt at the final inn at Ripley in the county of Surrey.

Bolitho walked along the narrow street, his cloak worn to conceal his uniform although the air was warm and filled with the scent of flowers.

162

England. *My England.*

He watched the steaming horses being led to their stables and sighed. Tomorrow they would alight at the George in Southwark. *London.*

Then she would give him back his confidence. Standing there, without a uniform in sight, and the sound of laughter from the inn he found he was able to say it out loud.

'*Kate. I love thee.*'

12

The One-Legged Man

Admiral Sir Owen Godschale watched while his servant carried a decanter of claret to a small table and then withdrew. Outside the tall windows the sun was shining, the air hot and dusty, remote like the muffled sounds of countless carriage wheels.

Bolitho took time to sip the claret, surprised that the Admiralty could still make him ill-at-ease and on the defensive. Everything had changed for him; it should be obvious, he thought. He and Adam had been ushered into a small, comfortably furnished library, something quite different from the large reception room he had seen earlier. It had been crowded with sea-officers, mostly captains, or so it had appeared. Restlessly waiting to meet a senior officer or his lackey, to ask favours, to plead for commands, new ships, almost anything. *As I once was*, he had thought. He still could not get used to the immediate respect, the servility of the Admiralty's servants and guardians.

The admiral was a handsome, powerfully built man who had distinguished himself in the American Revolution. A contemporary of Bolitho's, they had in fact been posted on the same day. There was little to show of that youthful and daring frigate captain now, Bolitho thought. Godschale looked comfortably sleek, his hands and features pale as if he had not been at sea for years.

He had not held this high appointment for very long. It seemed likely he would discourage anything controversial which might delay or damage his plans to enter the House of Lords.

164

Godschale was saying, 'It warms the heart to read of your exploits, Sir Richard. We in Admiralty too often feel cut adrift from the actual deeds which we can only plan, and which with God's guidance, can be brought to a victorious fruition.'

Bolitho relaxed slightly. He thought of Nelson's wry comment on wars fought with words and paper. Across the room, his eyes alert, Adam sat with an untouched glass by his side. Was it a courtesy, or part of a plot to include him in this meeting?

Godschale warmed to his theme. 'The treasure-ship was one such reward, *although.* . . .' his voice dragged over the word. 'There are some who might suggest you took too much upon yourself. Your task is to lead and to offer the encouragement of your experience, but that is in the past. We have to think of the future.'

Bolitho asked, 'Why was I brought here, Sir Owen?'

The admiral smiled and toyed with his empty glass. 'To put you in the position of knowing what is happening in Europe, and to reward you for your gallant action. I believe it is His Majesty's pleasure to offer you the honorary rank of Lieutenant Colonel in the Royal Marines.'

Bolitho looked at his hands. When was Godschale getting to the point? An honorary appointment to the Royal Marines was only useful if you were faced by a confrontation between Army and Navy in some difficult campaign. It was an honour, of course, but it hardly warranted bringing him away from his squadron.

Godschale said, 'We believe that the French are gathering their fleet in several different areas. Your transfer to the flag at Malta will enable you to disperse your squadron to best advantage.'

'The French are said to be at Martinique, Sir Owen. Nelson declares —'

The admiral showed his teeth like a gentle fox. 'Nelson is not above being wrong, Sir Richard. He may be the country's darling; he is not immune to false judgement.'

The admiral included Adam for the first time. 'I am able to tell your nephew, and it is my honour so to do, that he is appointed captain from the first of June.' He smiled, pleased with himself. 'The *Glorious* First of June, eh, Commander?'

Adam stared at him, then at Bolitho. 'Why, I thank you, Sir Owen!'

The admiral wagged his finger. 'You have more than earned your promotion. If you continue as you have I see no reason for your advancement to falter, eh?'

Bolitho saw the mixed emotions on Adam's sunburned features. Promotion. Every young officer's hope and dream. Three years more and he could be a post-captain. But was it a just reward, or a bribe? With the rank would come a different command, maybe even a frigate, what he had always talked about; as his uncle had once been, his father too, except that Hugh had fought on the wrong side.

Godschale turned to Bolitho. 'It is *good* to be here with you today, Sir Richard. A long, long climb since the Saintes in eighty-two. I wonder if many people realise how hard it is, how easy to fall from grace, sometimes through no fault of ours, eh?'

He must have seen the coldness in Bolitho's eyes and hurried on, 'Before you quit London and return to Gibraltar, you must dine with me.' He glanced only briefly at Adam. 'You too, of course. Wives, a few friends, that kind of affair. It does no harm at all.'

It was not really a request, Bolitho thought. It was an order.

'I am not certain that Lady Belinda is still in London. I have not had the time yet to –'

Godschale looked meaningly at a gilded clock. 'Quite so. You are a busy man. But never fear, my wife saw her just a day back. They are good company for one another while you and I deal with the dirtier matters of war!' He chuckled. 'Settled then.'

Bolitho stood up. He would have to see her anyway, but why no word from or about Catherine? He had gone alone to her house against Adam's wishes, but had got no further than the entrance. An imposing footman had assured him that his visit would be noted, but Viscount Somervell had left the country again on the King's service, and her ladyship was most likely with him.

He knew a lot more than he was saying. And so did Godschale. Even the cheap comment to Adam had an edge to it. The promotion was his right; he had won it without favour and against all prejudice.

Outside the Admiralty building the air seemed cleaner, and Bolitho said, 'What did you make of that?'

Adam shrugged. 'I am not that much of a fool that I could not recognise a threat, Uncle.' His chin lifted again. 'What do you want me to do?'

'You may become involved, Adam.'

He grinned, the strain dropping away like an unwanted mask. 'I *am* involved, sir!'

'Very well. I shall go to the house I mentioned.' He smiled at a memory. 'Browne, once my flag lieutenant, placed it at my disposal whenever I needed it.' *Browne with an 'e'*. Since the death of his father, he had succeeded to the title and had taken his place well ahead of Godschale in the House of Lords.

Adam nodded. 'I will put the word about.' He glanced at the imposing buildings and richly dressed passers-by. 'Though this is not some seaport. A man could be lost forever here.'

He glanced at him thoughtfully, 'Are you quite sure, Uncle? Maybe she *has* gone, thinking it best for you,' he faltered, 'as it might well be. She sounds like a most honourable lady.'

'I am sure, Adam, and thank you for that. I know not where Valentine Keen is at present, and there is no time to reach him by letter. I have days, not weeks.'

He must have displayed his anxiety, and Adam said, 'Rest easy, Uncle. You have many friends.'

They fell into step and walked into the sunshine. There were some people watching the passing carriages and one turned as the two officers appeared.

He called, 'Look, lads, 'tis 'im!' He waved a battered hat. 'God bless you, Dick! Give the Frogs another drubbin'!'

Someone gave a cheer and shouted, 'Don't you listen to them other buggers!'

Bolitho smiled, although his heart felt like breaking.

Then he said quietly, 'Yes, I do have friends after all.'

True to the promise of his one-time flag lieutenant, Bolitho was warmly received at the house in Arlington Street. The master was away in the North of England, the housekeeper explained, but she had her instructions, and conducted them to a suite of

167

pleasant rooms on the first floor. Adam left almost at once to see friends who might be able to shed some light on Catherine's disappearance; for Bolitho was now convinced that she had vanished. He dreaded that Adam might be right, that she had gone away with Somervell for appearance's sake, to save their reputations.

On the first morning Bolitho left the house. He had an immediate clash with Allday, who protested at being left behind.

Bolitho had insisted. 'This is not the quarterdeck with some Frenchie about to board us, old friend!'

Allday had glared out at the busy street. 'The more I'm in London, the less I trust th' place!'

Bolitho had said, 'I need you here. In case someone comes. The housekeeper might turn him away otherwise.'

Or her, Allday thought darkly.

It was not a long walk to the quiet square of which Belinda had written in her letter.

He paused to look at some children who were playing in the grassy centre of the square, their nursemaids standing nearby; gossiping about their respective families, he thought.

One of the little girls might be Elizabeth. It brought him all aback to realise that she must have changed a lot since he had last seen her. She would be three soon. He saw two of the nursemaids curtsy to him, and touched his hat in reply.

Another sailor home from the sea. It seemed ironic now. How would he conduct the next moments in his life?

The house was tall and elegant, like many which had been built in His Majesty's reign. Wide steps flanked by ornate iron railings, with three stories above to match the houses on either side. A servant opened the door and stared at him for several seconds. Then she bobbed in a deep curtsy, and, stammering apologies, took his hat and showed him into a pillared hall with a blue and gilt-leafed ceiling.

'This way, sir!'

She opened a pair of doors, and stood aside while he walked into an equally fine drawing-room. The furniture looked foreign to him, and the curtains and matching carpets were, he guessed, newly made. He thought of the rambling grey house in Falmouth. Compared with this it was like a farm.

He caught sight of himself in a tall, gilded mirror, and automatically straightened his shoulders. His face looked deeply tanned above his spotless waistcoat and breeches, but the uniform made him look like someone he did not know.

Bolitho tried to relax, to pitch his ear to the muted sounds above him in the house. Another world.

The doors opened suddenly and she walked quickly into the room. She was dressed in dark blue which almost matched his own coat, and her hair was piled high to show her small ears and the jewellery around her neck. She looked very composed, defiant.

He said, 'I sent a note. I hope this is convenient?'

She did not take her eyes from him; she was examining him as if to seek some injury or disfigurement, or that he had changed in another way.

'I think it absurd that you should be staying in somebody else's house.'

Bolitho shrugged. 'It seemed best until –'

'Until you saw how I would behave to you, is that it?'

They faced each other, more like strangers than husband and wife.

He replied, 'I tried to explain in my letter –'

She waved him down. 'My cousin is here. He begged me to forgive your foolishness, for all our sakes. I have been much embarrassed by your reckless affair. You are a senior officer of repute, yet you behave like some foul-mouthed seaman with his doxy on the waterfront!'

Bolitho looked around the room; his heart, like his voice, was heavy.

'Some of those foul-mouthed sailors are dying at this very moment to protect houses like this.'

She smiled briefly, as if she had discovered what she had been seeking. 'Tut, Richard! Your share of prize money from the Spanish galleon will more than cover it, so do not lose the issue in hypocrisy!'

Bolitho said flatly, 'It is not an affair.'

'I see.' She moved to a window and touched a long curtain. 'Then where is this woman you seem to have lost your mind to?' She swung round, her eyes angry. 'I shall tell you! She is with her

169

husband Viscount Somervell, who is apparently more willing to forgive and forget than I!'

'You saw him?'

She tossed her head, her fingers stroking the curtain more quickly to reveal her agitation.

'Of course. We were both very concerned. It was humiliating and degrading.'

'I regret that.'

'But not what you did?'

'That is unfair.' He watched her, amazed that his voice was calm when his whole being was in turmoil. 'But not unexpected.'

She looked past him at the room. 'This belonged to the Duke of Richmond. It is a fine house. Suitable for us. For you.'

Bolitho heard a sound and saw a small child being led past the doors. He knew it was Elizabeth despite her disguise of frothy lace and pale blue silk.

She turned just once, hanging to the hand of her nursemaid. She stared at him without recognition and then walked on.

Bolitho said, 'She knew me not.'

'What did you expect?' Then her voice softened. 'It can and must change. Given time –'

He looked at her, hiding his despair. 'Live here? Give up the sea when our very country is in peril? What is this madness, when people cannot see the danger?'

'You can still serve, Richard. Sir Owen Godschale commands the greatest respect both at Court and in Parliament.'

Bolitho rested his hands on the cool marble mantel. 'I cannot do it.'

She watched him in the mirror. 'Then at least escort me to Sir Owen's reception and dinner. I understand we shall receive notice of it this day.' She hesitated for the first time. 'So that people can see the emptiness of the gossip. She has gone, Richard. Have no doubt of that. Maybe it was an honest reaction, or perhaps she saw where her best fortune lies.' She smiled as he turned hotly towards her. 'Believe what you will. I am thinking of you now. After all, I do have the *right*!'

Bolitho said quietly, 'I shall stay at the other house until tomorrow. I have to think.'

170

She nodded, her eyes very clear. 'I understand. I know your moods. Tomorrow we shall begin again. I shall forgive, while you must try to forget. Do not damage your family name because of a momentary infatuation. We parted badly, so I must carry some of the blame.'

She walked beside him to the entrance hall. At no time had they touched, let alone embraced.

She asked, 'Is everything well with you? I did hear that you had been ill.'

He took his hat from the gaping servant. 'I am well enough, thank you.'

Then he turned and walked out into the square as the door closed behind him.

How could he go to the reception and act as if nothing had happened? If he never saw Catherine again, he would never forget her and what she had done for him.

Almost out loud he said, 'I cannot believe she would run away!' The words were torn from him, and he did not even notice two people turn to stare after him.

Allday greeted him warily. 'No news, Sir Richard.'

Bolitho threw himself into a chair. 'Fetch me a glass of something, will you?'

'Some nice cool hock?'

Allday watched worriedly as Bolitho replied, 'No. Brandy this time.'

He drank two glasses before its warmth steadied his mind.

'In God's name, I am in hell.'

Allday refilled the glass. It was likely the best thing to make him forget.

He stared round the room. Get back to the sea. *That* he could understand.

Bolitho's head lolled and the empty glass fell unheeded on the carpet.

The dream was sudden and violent. Catherine pulling at him, her breasts bared as she was dragged away from him, her screams probing at his brain like hot irons.

He awoke with a start and saw Allday release his arm, his face full of concern.

171

Bolitho gasped, 'I – I'm sorry! It was a nightmare –' He stared round; the room was darker. 'How long have I been here?'

Allday watched him grimly. 'That don't matter now, beggin' yer pardon.' He jabbed his thumb at the door. 'There's someone here to see you. Wouldn't talk to no one else.'

Bolitho's aching mind cleared. 'What about?' He shook his head. 'No matter, fetch him in.'

He got to his feet and stared at his reflection in the window. *I am losing my sanity.*

Allday pouted. 'Might be a beggar.'

'Fetch him.'

He heard Allday's familiar tread, and a strange clumping step which reminded him of an old friend he had lost contact with. But the man who was ushered in by Allday was nobody he recognised, nor was his rough uniform familiar.

The visitor removed his outdated tricorn hat to reveal untidy greying hair. He was badly stooped, and Bolitho guessed it was because of his crude wooden leg.

He asked, 'Can I help you? I am –'

The man peered at him and nodded firmly. 'I knows 'oo you are, zur.'

He had a faint West Country accent, and the fashion in which he touched his forehead marked him as an old sailor.

But the uniform with its plain brass buttons was like nothing Bolitho had ever seen.

He said, 'Will you be seated?' He gestured to Allday. 'A glass for – what may I call you?'

The man balanced awkwardly on a chair and nodded again very slowly. 'You won't recall, zur. But me name's Vanzell –'

Allday exclaimed, 'Bless you, so it is!' He stared at the one-legged man and added, 'Gun-captain in th' *Phalarope.*'

Bolitho gripped the back of a chair to contain his racing thoughts. All those years, and yet he could not understand why he had not recognised the man called Vanzell. A Devonian like Yovell. It was over twenty years back, when he had been a *boy-captain* like Adam would soon be.

The Saintes Godschale had dismissed as a sentimental memory. It was not like that to Bolitho. The shattered line of battle, the roar of cannon fire while men fell and died, including his first coxswain, Stockdale, who had fallen protecting him. He glanced at Allday, seeing the same memory on his rugged features. He had been there too, as a pressed man, but one who was still with him as a faithful friend.

Vanzell watched their recognition with satisfaction. Then he said, 'I never forget, y'see. 'Ow you helped me an' th' wife when I was cast ashore after losin' me pin to a Froggie ball. You saved us, an' that's a fact, zur.' He put down the glass and stared at him with sudden determination.

'I 'eard you was in London, zur. So I come meself. To try an' repay what you did for me an' th' wife, God rest her soul. There's only me now, but I'll not forget what 'appened after them bastards raked our decks that day.'

Bolitho sat down and faced him. 'What are you doing now?' He tried to conceal the anxiety and urgency in his bearing. This man, this tattered memory from the past, was frightened. For some reason it had cost a lot for him to come.

Vanzell said, 'It will lose me me job, zur.' He was thinking aloud. 'They all knows I once served under you. They'll not forgive me, not never.'

He made up his mind and studied Bolitho searchingly. 'I'm a watchman, zur, it was all I could get. They've no time for half-timbered Jacks no more.' His hand shook as he took another glass from Allday. Then he added huskily. 'I'm at th' Waites, zur.'

'What is that?'

Allday said sharply, 'It's a prison.'

Vanzell downed the glass in one gulp. 'They got 'er there. I know, 'cause I saw 'er, an' I 'eard what the others was sayin' about you both.'

Bolitho could feel the blood rushing through his brain.

In a prison. It was impossible. But he knew it was true.

The man was saying to Allday, 'It's a filthy place full o' scum. Debtors an' lunatics, a bedlam you'd not believe.'

Allday glanced tightly at Bolitho. 'Oh, yes I would, matey.'

Bolitho said, 'Tell the housekeeper I shall need a carriage at once. Do you know where this place is?' Allday shook his head.

Vanzell said, 'I – I'll show 'ee, zur.'

'Good.' Bolitho's mind was suddenly clear, as if it had been doused in icy water.

He asked, 'Would you care to work for *me* at Falmouth? There'll be a cottage.' He looked away, unable to watch the gratitude. 'There are one or two old *Phalaropes* working there. You'll feel at home.'

Allday came back and handed him his cloak. Bolitho saw that he had donned his best blue coat with the gilt buttons, and he carried a brace of pistols in his other hand.

Allday watched him while he clipped on his sword. 'It might still be a mistake, Sir Richard.'

'Not this time, old friend.' He looked at him for a few seconds. 'Ready?'

Allday waited for the other man to lead the way to a smart carriage standing outside the door.

The words kept repeating themselves over and over again. *She did not run away. She had not left him.*

The Waites prison was just to the north of London and it was almost dark by the time they got there.

It was a grim, high-walled place, and would look ten times worse in daylight.

Bolitho climbed down from the coach and said to Vanzell, 'Wait here. You have done your part.' To Allday he added shortly, 'So let's be about it.'

He hammered on a heavy door and after a long pause it was opened just a few inches. An unshaven man, wearing the same uniform as Vanzell, peered out at them.

'Yeh? 'Oo calls at this late hour?' He held up a lantern, and at that moment Bolitho let his cloak fall from his shoulders so that the light glittered on his epaulettes.

'Tell the governor, or whoever is in charge, that Sir Richard Bolitho wishes to see him.' He stared at the man's confusion and added harshly, '*Now!*'

They followed the watchman up a long, untidy pathway to the main building and Bolitho noticed that he was limping. They evidently found it cheaper to employ unwanted ex-servicemen, he thought bitterly. Another door, and a whispered conversation while Bolitho stood in a dank room, his hand on his sword,

174

aware of Allday's painful breathing close behind him.

Allday gasped as a piercing scream, followed by shouts and thuds, echoed through the building. Other voices joined in, until the place seemed to cringe in torment. More angry yells, and someone banging on a door with something heavy; and then eventual silence again.

The door opened and the watchman waited to allow Bolitho to enter. The contrast was startling. Good furniture, a great desk littered with ledgers and papers, and a carpet which was as much out of place here as the man who rose to greet him.

Short, and jolly-looking, with a curly wig to cover his baldness, he had all the appearances of a country parson.

'Sir Richard Bolitho, this is indeed an honour.' He glanced at a clock and smiled, like a saucy child. 'And a *surprise* at this late hour.'

Bolitho ignored his out-thrust hand. 'I have come for Lady Somervell. I'll brook no argument. Where is she?'

The man stared at him. 'Indeed, Sir Richard, I would do anything rather than offend such a gallant gentleman, but I fear that someone has played a cruel game with you.'

Bolitho recalled the terrible scream. 'Who do you hold here?'

The little man relaxed slightly. 'Lunatics, and those who plead insanity to avoid their debts to society –'

Bolitho walked around the desk and said softly, 'She is here and you know it. How could you hold a lady in this foul place and not know? I do not care what name she is given, or under what charge. If you do not release her into my care I will see that you are arrested and tried for conspiracy to conceal a crime, and for falsifying the deeds of your office!' He touched the hilt of his sword. 'I am in no mood for more lies!'

The man pleaded, 'Tomorrow perhaps I can discover –'

Bolitho felt a strange calm moving over him. *She is here.* For just a moment the man's confidence had made him doubt.

He shook his head. 'Now.' By tomorrow she would have been taken elsewhere. Anything could have happened to her.

He said curtly, 'Take us to her room.'

The little man pulled open a drawer and squeaked with fright as Allday responded instantly by drawing and cocking a pistol in one movement. He raised a key in his shaking hands.

'Please, *be careful!*' He was almost in tears.

Bolitho caught his breath as they walked into a dimly lit corridor. There was straw scattered on the flagstones, and one of the walls was dripping wet. The stench was foul. Dirt, poverty and despair. They stopped outside the last door and the little governor said in a whisper, 'In God's name I had naught to do with it! She was given in my charge until a debt was paid. But if you are certain that –'

Bolitho did not hear him. He stared in through a small window which was heavily barred, each one worn smooth by a thousand desperate fingers.

A lantern shone through a thick glass port, like those used in a ship's hanging magazine. It was a scene from hell.

An old woman was leaning against one wall, rocking from side to side, a tendril of spittle hanging from her mouth as she crooned some forgotten tune to herself. She was filthy, and her ragged clothes were deeply soiled.

On the opposite side Catherine sat on a small wooden bench, her legs apart, her hands clasped between her knees. Her gown was torn, like the day she had come aboard *Hyperion*, and he saw that her feet were shoeless. Her long hair, uncombed, hung across her partly bared shoulders, hiding her face completely.

She did not move or look up as the key grated in the lock and Bolitho thrust open the door.

Then she whispered very quietly, 'If you come near me, I shall kill you.'

He held out his arms and said, 'Kate. Don't be frightened. Come to me.'

She raised her head and brushed the hair from her eyes with the back of her hand.

Still she did not move or appear to recognise him, and for a moment Bolitho imagined that she had been driven mad by these terrible circumstances.

Then she stood up and stepped a few paces unsteadily towards him.

'Is it you? Really you?' Then she shook her head and exclaimed, 'Don't touch me! I am unclean –'

Bolitho gripped her shoulders and pulled her against him, feeling her protest give way to sobs which were torn from each awful memory. He felt her skin through the back of the gown; she wore nothing else beneath it. Her body was like ice despite the foul, unmoving air. He covered her with his cloak, so that only her face and her bare feet showed in the flickering lanterns.

She saw the governor in the doorway and Bolitho felt her whole body stiffen away from him.

Bolitho said, 'Remove your hat in the presence of my lady, *sir*!' He found no pleasure in the man's fear. 'Or by God I'll call you out here and now!'

The man shrank away, his hat almost brushing the filthy floor.

Bolitho guided her along the corridor, while some of the inmates watched through their cell doors, their hands gripping the bars like claws. But nobody cried out this time.

'Your shoes, Kate?'

She pressed herself against his side as if the cloak would protect her from everything.

'I sold all I had for food.' She raised her head and studied him. 'I have walked barefoot before.' Her sudden courage made her look fragile. 'Are we really leaving now?'

They reached the heavy gate and she saw the carriage, with the two stamping horses.

She said, 'I will be strong. For you, dear Richard, I —' She saw the shadowy figure inside the coach and asked quickly, 'Who is that?'

Bolitho held her until she was calm again.

He said, 'Just a friend who knew when he was needed.'

13

Conspiracy

Belinda dragged the doors of the drawing room shut behind her and pressed her shoulders against them.

'Lower your voice, Richard!' She watched his shadow striding back and forth across the elegant room, her breasts moving quickly to betray something like fear. 'The servants will hear you!'

Bolitho swung round. 'God damn them, and you too for what you did!'

'What is the matter, Richard? Are you sick or drunk?'

'It is fortunate for both of us that it is not the latter! Otherwise I fear what I might do!'

He stared at her and saw her pale. Then he said in a more controlled voice, 'You knew all the time. You connived with Somervell to have her thrown into a place which is not even fit for pigs!' Once again the pictures flashed across his mind. Catherine sitting in the filthy cell, and later when he had taken her to Browne's house in Arlington Street, when she had tried to prevent him from leaving her.

'Don't go, Richard! It's not worth it! We're together, that's all that matters!'

He had turned by the waiting carriage and had replied, 'But those liars intended otherwise!'

He continued, 'She is no more a debtor than you, and you knew it when you spoke with Somervell. I pray to God that he is as ready with a blade as he is with a pistol, for when I meet with him –'

She exclaimed, 'I have never seen you like this!'

'Nor will you again!'

She said, 'I did it for *us*, for what we were and could be again.'

Bolitho stared at her, his heart pounding, knowing how close he had come to striking her. Catherine had told him in jerky sentences as the coach had rolled towards the other house, an unexpected rain pattering across the windows.

She had loaned Somervell most of her own money when they had married. Somervell was in fear of his life because of his many gambling debts. But he had friends at Court, even the King, and a government appointment had saved him.

He had deliberately invested some of her money in her name, then left her to face the consequences when he had caused those same investments to fail. All this Somervell had explained to Belinda. It made Bolitho's head swim to realise just how close to success the plan had been. If he had moved into this house, and then been seen at Admiral Godschale's reception, Catherine would have been told that they were reconciled. A final and brutal rejection.

Somervell had left the country; that was the only known truth. When he returned he might have expected Catherine half-mad or even dead. Like a seabird, Catherine could never be caged.

He said, 'You have killed that too. Remember what you threw in my face on more than one occasion after we were married? That because you *looked* like Cheney, it did not mean that you had anything in common. By God, that was the truest thing you ever said.' He stared round the room and realised for the first time that his uniform was soaked with rain.

'Keep this house, by all means, Belinda, but spare a thought sometimes for those who fight and die so that you may enjoy what they can never know.'

She moved away, her eyes on him as he wrenched open the doors. He thought he saw a shadow slip back from the stairway, something for the servants to chew on.

'You will be ruined!' She gasped as he stepped towards her as if she expected a blow.

'That is my risk.' He picked up his hat. 'Some day I shall speak with my daughter.' He looked at her for several seconds. 'Send

179

for all you need from Falmouth. You rejected even that. So enjoy your new life with your proud friends.' He opened the front door. 'And God help you!'

He walked through the dark street, heedless of the rain which soothed his face like a familiar friend. He needed to walk, to marshal his thoughts into order, like forming a line of battle. He would make enemies, but that was nothing new. There had been those who had tried to discredit him because of Hugh, had even tried to hurt him through Adam.

He thought of Catherine, where she should stay. Not at Falmouth, not until he could take her himself. If she would come. Would she see double-meanings in his words because of what had happened? Expect another betrayal?

He dismissed the thought immediately. She was like the blade at his hip, almost unbreakable. Almost.

One thing was certain. Godschale would soon hear what had happened, although no one would speak openly about it without appearing like a conspirator.

He gave a bleak smile. It would be Gibraltar for orders very soon.

His busy mind recorded a shadow and the click of metal. The old sword was in his hand in a second and he called, '*Stand!*'

Adam sounded relieved. 'I came looking, Uncle.' He watched as Bolitho sheathed his blade.

'It's done then?'

'Aye. 'Tis done.'

Adam fell into step and removed his hat to stare up into the rain. 'I heard most of it from Allday. It seems I cannot leave you alone for a moment.'

Bolitho said, 'I can still scarce believe it.'

'People change, Uncle.'

'I think not.' Bolitho glanced at two army lieutenants walking unsteadily towards St James's. 'Circumstances may, but not people.'

Adam tactfully changed the subject. 'I have discovered Captain Keen's whereabouts. He is in Cornwall. They had gone there to settle some matters relating to Miss Carwithen's late father.'

Bolitho nodded. He had been afraid that Keen would be married without his being there to witness it. How strange that such a simple thing could still be so important after all which had happened.

'I sent word by courier, Uncle. He *should* know.'

They fell silent and listened to their shoes on the pavement.

He probably did already. The whole fleet would by now. Offensive to many, but a welcome scandal as far as the overcrowded messdecks were concerned.

They reached the house, where they found Allday sharing a jug of ale with Mrs Robbins, the housekeeper. She was a Londoner born and bred in Bow and despite her genteel surroundings had a voice which sounded like a street trader's. Mrs Robbins got straight down to business.

'She's in bed now, Sir Richard.' She eyed him calmly. 'I give 'er a small guest room.'

Bolitho nodded. He had taken her point. There would be no scandal in this house, no matter how it might appear.

She continued, 'I stripped 'er naked as a brat and bathed 'er proper. Poor luv, she could do wiv it an' all. I burned 'er clothes. They was alive.' She opened her red fist. 'I found these sewn in the 'em.'

They were the earrings he had given her. The only other time they had been in London together.

Bolitho felt a lump in his throat. 'Thank you, Mrs Robbins.'

Surprisingly, her severe features softened.

'It's nuffink, Sir Richard. Young Lord Oliver 'as told me a few yarns about when you saved 'is rump for 'im!' She went off chuckling to herself.

Allday and Adam entered and Bolitho said, 'You heard all that?'

Allday nodded. 'Best to leave her. Old Ma Robbins'll call all hands if anything happens in the night.'

Bolitho sat down and stretched his legs. He had not eaten a crumb since breakfast but he could not face it now.

It had been a close thing, he thought. But perhaps the battle had not even begun.

＊   ＊   ＊

181

Catherine stood by a tall window and looked down at the street. The sun was shining brightly, although this side of the street was still in shadow. A few people strolled up and down, and very faintly could be heard the voice of a flower-girl calling her wares.

She said quietly, 'This cannot last.'

Bolitho sat in a chair, his legs crossed, and watched her, still scarcely able to believe it had ever happened, that she was the same woman he had snatched from squalor and humiliation. Or that he was the man who had risked everything, including a court-martial, by threatening the governor of the Waites jail.

He replied, 'We can't stay here. I want to be alone with you. To hold you again, to tell you things.'

She turned her head so that her face too was in shadow. 'You are still worried, Richard. You have no need to be, where my love for you is concerned. It never left me, so how can we lose it now?' She walked slowly around his chair and put her hands on his shoulders. She was dressed in a plain green robe, which the redoubtable Mrs Robbins had bought for her the previous day.

Bolitho said, 'You are protected now. Anything you need, all that I can give, it is yours.' He hurried on as her fingers tightened their grip on his shoulders, glad that she could not see his face. 'It may take months longer even to retrieve what he has stolen from you. You gave him everything, and saved him.'

She said, 'In return he offered me security, a place in society where I could live as I pleased. Foolish? Perhaps I was. But it was a bargain between us. There was no love.' She laid her head against his and added quietly, 'I have done things I am too often ashamed of. But I have never sold my body to another.'

He reached up and gripped her hand. 'That, I know.'

A carriage clattered past, the wheels loud on the cobbles. At night, this household, like others nearby, had servants to spread straw on the road to deaden the sound. London never seemed to sleep. In the past few days Bolitho had lain awake, thinking of Catherine, the code of the house which kept them apart like shy suitors.

She said, 'I want to be somewhere I can hear about you, what you are doing. There will be more danger. In my own way I shall share it with you.'

Bolitho stood up and faced her. 'I will likely receive orders to return to the squadron very soon. Now that I have declared myself, they will probably want rid of me from London as soon as possible.' He smiled and put his hands on her waist, feeling her supple body beneath the robe, their need for each other. There was colour in her cheeks now, and her hair, hanging loose down her back, had recovered its shine.

She saw his eyes and said, 'Mrs Robbins has taken good care of me.'

Bolitho said, 'There is my house in Falmouth.' Instantly he saw the reluctance, the unspoken protest, and added, 'I *know*, my lovely Catherine. You will wait until –'

She nodded. 'Until you carry me there as your kept woman!' She tried to laugh but added huskily, 'For that is what they will say.'

They stood holding hands and facing each other for a full minute.

Then she said, 'And I'm not lovely. Only in your eyes, dearest of men.'

He said, 'I want you.' They walked to the window and Bolitho realised that he had not left the house since that night. 'If I cannot marry you –'

She put her fingers on his mouth. 'Enough of that. Do you think I care? I will be what you wish me to be. But I shall always love you, be your tiger if others try to harm you.'

A servant tapped on the door and entered with a small silver salver. On it was a sealed envelope with the familiar Admiralty crest. Bolitho took it, felt her eyes on him as he slit it open.

'I have to see Sir Owen Godschale tomorrow.'

She nodded. 'Orders then.'

'I expect so.' He caught her in his arms. 'It is inevitable.'

'I know it. The thought of losing you –'

Bolitho considered her being alone. He must do something.

She said, 'I keep thinking, we have another day, one more night.' She ran her hands up to his shoulders and to his face. 'It is all I care for.'

He said, 'Before I leave –'

She touched his mouth again. 'I know what you are trying to say. And yes, dearest Richard, I want you to love me like you did

183

in Antigua, and all that time ago here in London. I told you once that you needed to be loved. I am the one to give it to you.'

Mrs Robbins looked in at them. 'Beg pardon, Sir Richard.' Her eyes seemed to measure the distance between them. 'But yer nephew is 'ere.' She relented slightly. 'You're lookin' fair an' bright, m'lady!'

Catherine smiled gravely. 'Please, Mrs Robbins. Do not use that title.' She looked steadily at Bolitho. 'I have no use for it now.'

Mrs Robbins, or 'Ma' as Allday called her, wandered slowly down the stairway and saw Adam tidying his unruly black hair in front of a looking-glass.

It was a rum do, she thought. God, everyone in the kitchen was talking about it. It had been bad enough for Elsie, the upstairs maid, when her precious drummer-boy had gone off with a blackie in the West Indies. Not what you expected from the quality; although old Lord Browne had been one for the ladies before he passed on. Then she thought of Bolitho's expression when she had given him the earrings she had rescued from the filthy gown. There was a whole lot more to this than people realised.

She nodded to Adam. ' 'E'll be down in a moment, sir.'

Adam smiled. It was strange, he thought. He had always loved his uncle more than any man. But until now he had never envied him.

Admiral Sir Owen Godschale received Bolitho immediately upon his arrival. Bolitho had the impression that he had cut short another interview, perhaps to get this meeting over and done with without further delay.

'I have received intelligence that the French fleet outran Lord Nelson's ships. Whether he can still call them to battle is doubtful. It seems unlikely that Villeneuve will be willing to fight until he has combined forces with the Spaniards.'

Bolitho stared at the admiral's huge map. So the French were still at sea but could not remain so for long. Nelson must have believed the enemy's intention was to attack British possessions and bases in the Caribbean. Or was it merely one great exercise in strength? The French had fine ships, but they had been sealed up in harbour by an effective blockade. Villeneuve was too experienced to make an attack up the English Channel, to pave the way for Napoleon's armies, with ships and men whose skills and strength had been sapped by inactivity.

Godschale said bluntly, 'So I want you to hoist your flag again and join forces with the Maltese squadron.'

'But I understood that Rear-Admiral Herrick was to be relieved?'

Godschale looked at his map. 'We need every ship where she can do the most good. I have sent orders today by courier-brig to Herrick's command.' He eyed him impassively. 'You know him, of course.'

'Very well.'

'So it would appear that the reception I had planned must now be postponed, Sir Richard. Until quieter times, eh?'

Their eyes met. 'Would I have been invited to attend *alone*, Sir Owen?' He spoke calmly but the edge was clear in his voice.

'Under the circumstances I think that would have been preferred, yes.'

Bolitho smiled. 'Then under those same circumstances I am glad it is postponed.'

'I resent your damned attitude, sir!'

Bolitho faced his bluff. 'One day, Sir Owen, you may have cause to remember this disgraceful conspiracy. The last time we met you told me that Nelson was not above being wrong. And neither, sir, are you! And should you too fall from grace you will most certainly discover who your true friends are!' He strode from the room, and heard the admiral slam a door behind him like a thunderclap.

Bolitho was still angry when he reached the house. Until he saw Catherine speaking with Adam, and heard a familiar voice from the adjoining study.

Then Allday stepped out of the passageway which led from the kitchen, his jaw still working on some food. They were all staring at him.

Bolitho said, 'I am to return to the squadron as soon as is convenient.'

A shadow fell across the passage, and Captain Valentine Keen stepped into the light.

Bolitho clasped his hands. 'Val! This is a miracle!'

Beyond his friend he saw the girl Zenoria, exactly as he had remembered her. Both of them were travel-stained, and Keen explained, 'We have been on the road for two days. We were already on our way back from Cornwall and by a stroke of fate we met with the courier at a small inn where he was changing his mount.'

Fate. That word. Bolitho said, 'I don't understand.' He saw the girl's face as she walked up to him and held him, while he kissed her on the cheek. Something more had happened.

Keen said, 'I am to be your flag captain, Sir Richard.' He gave Zenoria a despairing glance. 'I was asked. It seemed right.' He handed Bolitho a letter. 'Captain Haven is under arrest. The day after you left in *Firefly* he attacked another officer and attempted to kill him.' He watched Bolitho's face. 'The commodore at Gibraltar awaits your orders.'

Bolitho sat down while Catherine stood beside him, her hand on his shoulder.

Bolitho looked up at her. *My tiger*. That poor, wretched man had broken under the strain. There was nothing much in the letter, but Bolitho knew the other officer must be Parris. He at least was alive.

Keen looked from one to the other. 'I was about to suggest that your lady might care to share my home with Zenoria and my sister until we return.'

Bolitho clasped Catherine's hand; he could tell from the way the dark-haired girl from Cornwall was looking at her that it was a perfect arrangement. God alone knew they both had plenty in common.

Keen had rescued Zenoria from the transport ship *Orontes* after she had been wrongly charged and convicted of attempted murder. She had been trying to defend herself from being raped. Transportation to the penal colony in New South Wales; and she had been innocent. Keen had boarded the transport and cut her down when she was about to be flogged at the ship's master's command. She had taken one blow across her naked back before

Keen had stopped the torment. Bolitho knew she would carry the scar all her life. It made him go cold to realise that the same fate could have been thrown at Catherine, but for different reasons. Jealousy and greed were pitiless enemies.

He said, 'What say you, Kate?' The others seemed to fade away as if his damaged eye would only focus on her. 'Will you do it?'

She said nothing but nodded very slowly. Only a blind man would have failed to see the light, the communion, between them.

'It's settled then.' Bolitho looked at their faces. 'Together again.'

It seemed to include them all.

Lieutenant Vicary Parris sat in his cabin only half paying attention to the ship noises above and around him. Compared with the upper deck the cabin with its open gunport seemed almost cool.

The fifth lieutenant, *Hyperion*'s youngest, stood beside the small table and stared at the open punishment book.

Parris asked again, 'Well, do you think it fair, Mr Priddie?'

It was chilling, Parris thought. The vice-admiral had barely quit the Rock in *Firefly* when Haven had gone on the rampage. At sea, fighting the elements and working the ship, men were often too busy or desperate to question the demands of discipline. But *Hyperion* was in harbour, and in the hot sunshine, work about the ship and taking on fresh stores made its own slower and more comfortable routine, when men had the time to watch and to nurse resentment.

'I – I am not certain.'

Parris swore under his breath. 'You wanted to pass for lieutenant, but now that you share the wardroom you seem prepared to accept any excuse for a flogging without care or favour?'

Priddie hung his head. 'The Captain insisted –'

'Yes, he would.' Parris leaned back and counted seconds to restore his temper. At any other time he would have requested, even demanded a transfer to another ship, and to hell with the consequences. But he had lost his last command; he wanted, no, he *needed* any recommendation which might offer the opening to another promotion.

187

He had served under several captains. Some brave, some too cautious. Others ran their ships like the King's Regulations and would never take a risk which might raise an admiral's eyebrow. He had even served under the worst kind of all, a sadist who punished men for the sake of it, who had watched every breath-stopping stroke of the cat until the victim's back had been like seared meat.

There was no defence against Haven. He simply hated him. He used the weapon of his complete authority to punish seamen without proper consideration as if to force his first lieutenant to challenge it.

He touched the book. 'Look at this, man. Two dozen lashes for fighting. They were skylarking in the dog watches, nothing more; you must have seen that?'

Priddie flushed. 'The Captain said that discipline on deck was lax. That eyes ashore would be watching. He would tolerate no more slackness.'

Parris bit off a harsh retort. Priddie had not yet forgotten what it was like to be a midshipman. As first lieutenant he should do something. He could appeal to no one; the other captains would see his behaviour as betrayal, something which might rebound on their own authority if encouraged. Right or wrong, the captain was like a god. Only one man cared enough to stop it, and he was on passage for England with trouble enough of his own if he did not bow down to threats. It seemed unlikely that Bolitho would bend a knee to anyone if he believed what he was doing was right.

Parris considered the ship's surgeon, George Minchin. But he had tried before to no avail. Minchin was a drunkard like so many ships' surgeons. Butchers, at whose hands more men died than ever did because of their original injury or wound.

Hyperion was supposed to be getting a senior surgeon, one of several being sent into the various squadrons to observe and report on what they discovered. But that was later. It was now he was needed.

Parris said, 'Leave it to me.' He saw the lieutenant's eyes light up, thankful that he was no longer involved.

Parris added angrily, 'You'll never hold a command, Mr Priddie, unless you face up to the rank you carry.'

He climbed to the quarterdeck and watched the seamen swaying up new rigging to the mizzen top. There was a strong smell of fresh tar for blacking-down, the sounds of hammers and an adze as Horrocks the carpenter and his mates completed work on a new cutter, built from materials to hand. They worked well, he thought, would even be happy, but for the cloud which always hung over the poop.

With a sigh he made his way aft and waited for the Royal Marine sentry to announce him.

Captain Haven was sitting at his desk, papers arranged within easy reach, his coat hanging from the chairback as he fanned his face with his handkerchief.

'Well, Mr Parris? I have much to do.'

Parris made himself ignore the obvious dismissal. He noticed that the pens on the desk were all clean and dry. Haven had written nothing. It was as if he had prepared for this, had been expecting his visit despite the hint of rejection.

Parris began carefully, 'The two men for punishment, sir.'

'Oh, which two? I was beginning to believe that the people did much as they pleased.'

'Trotter and Dixon, sir. They have not been in any trouble before. Had the fifth lieutenant come to me –' He got no further.

Haven snapped, 'But you were not aboard, sir. No, you were elsewhere, I believe?'

'Under your orders, sir.'

'Don't be impertinent!' Haven shifted on his chair. It reminded Parris of a fisherman he had watched when he had felt something take the hook.

Haven said, 'They were behaving in a disgusting and disorderly fashion! I saw them. As usual I had to stop the rot!'

'But two dozen lashes, sir. I could give them a week's extra work. Discipline would be upheld, and I think Mr Priddie would learn from it.'

'I see, you are blaming the junior lieutenant now.' He smiled. Parris could feel the strain clutching at him like claws. 'Men will be flogged, and Mr Priddie will take the blame for it. God damn your eyes, sir! Do you think I give a sniff for what they think? I

189

command here, they will do my bidding, *do I make myself clear?*' He was shouting.

Parris said, 'You do, sir.'

'I am glad to hear it.' Haven watched him, his eyes slitted in the filtered sunlight. 'Your part in the cutting-out will be known at the Admiralty, I have no doubt. But you can crawl after our admiral's coat-tails as long as you like. I shall see that your disloyalty and damned arrogance are noted fully when your case for promotion is considered again!'

Parris felt the cabin sway. 'Did you call me disloyal, sir?'

Haven almost screamed at him. 'Yes, you lecherous swine, I bloody well did!'

Parris stared at him. It was worse than anything which had happened before. He saw the sunlight at the bottom of the captain's door blackened in places by feet. There were men out there listening. God, he thought, despairingly, what chance do we have if we stand into battle?

He said, 'I think we may both have spoken out of turn, sir.'

'Don't you ever dare to reprimand me, blast you! I suppose that when you lie in your cot you think of me down aft, sneer because of the foul deed you committed – well, answer me, you bloody hound!'

Parris knew he should summon another officer, just as he knew he would strike Haven down in the next few seconds. Something, like a warning in his sleep, seemed to stay his anger and resentment. *He wants you to strike him. He wants you as his next victim.*

Haven slumped back in his chair, as if the strength and fury had left him. But when he looked up again Parris saw it was still there in his eyes, like fires of hate.

In an almost conversational voice Haven said, 'You really thought I would not find you out? Could you be *that* stupid?'

Parris held his breath, his heart pounding; he had believed that nothing more could unseat him.

Haven continued, 'I know your ways and manners, the love you bear for yourself. Oh yes, I am not without some wit and understanding.' He pointed at the portrait of his wife but kept his eyes on Parris.

190

He said in a hoarse whisper, 'The guilt is as plain as day on your face!'

Parris thought he had misheard. 'I met the lady once, but –'

'Don't you dare to speak of her in my presence!' Haven lurched to his feet. 'You with your soft tongue and manners to match, just the sort she'd listen to!'

'*Sir*. Please say nothing more. We may both regret it.'

Haven did not appear to be listening. 'You took her when I was occupied in this ship! I worked myself sick pulling this damned rabble into one company. Then they hoisted the flag of a man much like you, I suspect, who thinks he can have any woman he chooses!'

'I can't listen, sir. It is not true anyway. I saw –' He hesitated and finished, 'I did not touch her, I swear to God!'

Haven said in a small voice, 'After all that I gave her.'

'You are wrong, sir.' Parris looked at the door. Someone must come surely? The whole poop must hear Haven's rantings.

Haven shouted suddenly, 'It's *your child*, you bloody animal!'

Parris clenched his fists. So that was it. He said, 'I am leaving now, sir. I will not listen to your insults or your insinuations. And as far as your wife is concerned, all I can say is that I am sorry for her.' He turned to go as Haven screamed, 'You'll go nowhere, God damn you!'

The roar of the pistol in the confined space was deafening. It was like being struck by an iron bar. Then Parris felt the pain, the hot wetness of blood even as he hit the deck.

He saw the darkness closing in. It was like smoke or fog, with just one clear space in it where the captain was trying to ram another charge into his pistol.

Before the pain bore him into oblivion Parris's agonised mind was able to record that Haven was laughing. Laughing as if he could not stop.

14

For Or Against

It was early morning on a fine June day when Bolitho rehoisted his flag above *Hyperion*, and prepared his squadron to leave the Rock.

During *Firefly*'s speedy passage to Gibraltar, Bolitho and Keen had had much to discuss. If Keen had been unsettled at being made flag captain of a squadron he knew nothing about he barely showed it, while for Bolitho it was the return of a friend; like being made whole again.

At the commodore's request he had visited Haven at the place where he was being confined ashore. He had expected him to be in a state of shock, or at least ready to offer something in the way of a defence for shooting Parris down in cold blood.

A garrison doctor had told Bolitho that Haven either did not remember, or did not care about what had happened.

He had risen as Bolitho had entered his small room and had said, 'The ship is ready, Sir Richard. I took steps to ensure that old or not, *Hyperion* will match her artillery against any Frenchman when called to!'

Bolitho had said, 'You are relieved. I am sending you to England.'

Haven had stared at him. 'Relieved? Has my promotion been announced?'

Upon returning to the ship Bolitho had been handed a letter addressed to Haven, which had just been brought by a mail schooner from Spithead. Under the circumstances Bolitho

192

decided to open it; he might at least be able to spare someone in England the bitter truth about Haven, until the facts were released at his inevitable court-martial.

Afterwards, Bolitho was not certain he should have read it. The letter was from Haven's wife. It stated in an almost matter-of-fact fashion that she had left him to live with a wealthy mill-owner who was making uniforms for the military, where she and her child would be well cared for.

It seemed that the mill-owner was the father of the child, so it was certainly not Parris's. When Haven eventually came to his senses, if he ever did, that would be the hardest cross to bear.

The first lieutenant must be born lucky, Bolitho thought. The pistol ball had lifted too much in the short range of the cabin, and had embedded itself in his shoulder and chipped the bone. He must have suffered terrible agony as Minchin had sought to probe it out. But the shot had been intended for his heart.

Keen had asked Bolitho, 'Do you wish to keep him aboard? The wound will take weeks to heal, and I fear it was roughly treated.' He had probably been remembering how a great splinter had speared into his groin; rather than allow him to face the torture of a drunken surgeon, it had been Allday who had cut the jagged wood away.

'He is an experienced officer. I have hopes for his promotion. God knows we can use some skilled juniors for command.'

Keen had agreed. 'It will certainly put the other lieutenants on their mettle!'

And so with mixed feelings the squadron sailed and headed east into the Mediterranean, the sea which had seen so many battles, and where Bolitho had almost died.

With *Hyperion* in the van, Bolitho's flag at the fore, and the other third-rates following astern, heeling steeply to a lively north-westerly, their departure probably roused as much speculation as their arrival. Bolitho watched the Rock's famous silhouette until it was lost in haze. The strange cloud of steam rising against an otherwise clear sky was a permanent feature when the wind cooled the overheated stones, so that from a distance it appeared like a smouldering volcano.

Most of *Hyperion*'s company had grown used to one another

since the ship had commissioned, and Keen was almost the only stranger amongst them.

As day followed day, and each ship exercised her people at sail or gun drill, Bolitho was thankful for the fates which had brought Keen back to him.

Unlike Haven, he did know Bolitho's ways and standards, had served him both as a midshipman and lieutenant before eventually becoming his flag captain. The ship's company seemed to sense the bond between their captain and admiral, and the older hands would note and appreciate that if Keen did not know something about his ship he was not too proud to ask. It never occurred to Bolitho that Keen had perhaps learned it from him.

It had been sad to part with *Firefly*, but she had bustled on to deliver more despatches to admirals and captains who were eagerly awaiting the latest news of the French. Amongst *Firefly*'s mountain of despatches there would doubtless be a few like the one which Haven had still not read. War was as cruel in the home as it was on the high seas, he thought.

When he met with Adam again his promotion would have been confirmed. It seemed strange to consider it. He could imagine what they would think and say at Falmouth when the latest Captain Bolitho came home. Unless Adam eventually met and married the girl of his choice, he would be the last captain to arrive at the house in Cornwall.

He often thought of Catherine and their farewell. They had shared their passion and love equally, and she had insisted that she accompany him all the way to Portsmouth to board the little *Firefly*. Keen had said his own goodbyes earlier when he had gone to Portsmouth with Adam in another carriage.

With the horses stamping and steaming in the sunshine Catherine had clung to him, searching his face, touching it with tenderness and then dismay when Allday had told them the boat was waiting at the sally port.

He had asked her to wait by the carriage but she had followed him to the wooden stairs where so many sea-officers had left the land. There had been a small crowd watching the ships and the officers being pulled out to them.

Bolitho had noticed that there were very few of the age for

194

service. It would be a fool who risked the press gang's net if he had no stomach for the fight.

The people had raised a cheer, and some of them recognised Bolitho, as well they might.

One had shouted, 'Good luck, Equality Dick, an' to yer lady as well!'

He had faced her and he had seen tears for the first time.

She had whispered, 'They included *me!*'

As the boat had pulled clear of the stairs Bolitho had looked back, but she had vanished. And yet as they had bumped over a choppy Solent where *Firefly* tugged at her cable, he had sensed that she was still there. Watching him to the last second. He had written to ask her just that, and to tell her what her love meant to him.

He remembered what Belinda had said about their *infatuation*. Allday had described Catherine as *a sailor's woman, an' that's no error*. When he said it, it sounded the greatest compliment of all.

While the frigate *Tybalt* and the sloop-of-war *Phaedra* chased and questioned any coaster or trader foolish enough to be caught under their guns, Bolitho and Keen studied the scanty reports, as day by day they sailed deeper into the Mediterranean.

It was said that Nelson was still in the Atlantic and had joined up with his friend and second-in-command Vice-Admiral Collingwood. Nelson had probably decided that the enemy were trying to divide the British squadrons by ruses and quick dashes from safe harbours. Only when that was achieved would Napoleon launch his invasion across the Channel.

As Yovell had mildly suggested, 'If that is so, Sir Richard, then you are the senior officer in the Mediterranean.'

Bolitho had barely considered it. But if true, it meant one thing to him. When the enemy came his way he would need to ask no one what he must do. It made the weight of command seem more appealing.

One forenoon as he took his walk on the quarterdeck he saw Lieutenant Parris moving along a gangway, his arm strapped to his side, his steps unsteady while he gauged the rise and fall of the hull. He appeared to have withdrawn more into himself since Haven's attack with intent to murder him. Keen had said that he was well content to have him as his senior, but had not known him before so could not make a comparison.

Parris moved slowly to the lee side of the quarterdeck and clung to a stay to watch some seabirds swooping and diving alongside.

Bolitho walked across from the weather side. 'How do you feel?'

Parris tried to straighten his back but winced and apologised. 'It is slow progress, Sir Richard.' He stared up at the bulging sails, the tiny figures working amongst and high above them. 'I'll feel a mite better when I know I can climb up there again.'

Bolitho studied his strong, gipsy profile. A ladies' man? An enigma?

Parris saw his scrutiny and said awkwardly, 'May I thank you for allowing me to remain aboard, Sir Richard. I am less than useless at the moment.'

'Captain Keen made the final decision.'

Parris nodded, his eyes lost in memory. 'He makes this old ship come alive.' He hesitated, as if measuring the confidence. 'I was sorry to hear of your trouble in London, Sir Richard.'

Bolitho looked at the blue water and tensed as his damaged eye misted slightly in the moist air.

'Nelson has a saying, I believe.' It was like quoting one of Adam's favourites. 'The boldest measures are usually the safest.'

Parris stood back as Keen appeared below the poop-deck, but added, 'I wish you much joy, Sir Richard. Both of you.'

Keen joined him by the nettings. 'We shall sight Malta tomorrow in the forenoon watch.' He glanced over at the master's powerful figure. 'Mr Penhaligon *assures* me.'

Bolitho smiled. 'I was speaking with the first lieutenant. A strange fellow.'

Keen laughed. 'It is wrong, I know, to jest on it, but I have met captains I would have dearly liked to shoot. But never the other way about!'

Down by the boat-tier Allday turned as he heard their laughter. Keen's old coxswain had been killed aboard their last ship, *Argonaute*. Allday had selected a new man for him, but secretly wished it was his son.

Keen's coxswain was named Tojohns, and he had been captain of the foretop. He glanced aft with him and said, 'A new ship since he stepped aboard.' He studied Allday curiously. 'You've known him a long while then?'

Allday smiled. 'A year or two. He'll do me, an' he's good for Sir Richard, that's the thing.'

Allday thought about their parting at Portsmouth Point. The people cheering and waving their hats, the women smiling fit to burst. It *had* to work this time. He frowned as the other coxswain broke into his thoughts.

Tojohns asked, 'Why did you pick me?'

Allday gave a lazy grin. Tojohns was a fine seaman and knew how to put himself about in a fight. He was not in the least like old Hogg, Keen's original coxswain. Chalk and cheese. *What they said about me and Stockdale.*

Allday said, ' 'Cause you talk too much!'

Tojohns laughed but fell silent as a passing midshipman glanced sharply at him. It was hard to accept his new role. He would no longer have to be up there at the shrill of every call, fighting wild canvas with his foretopmen. Like Allday he was apart from all that. Somebody, for the first time.

'Mind you.' Allday watched him gravely. 'Whatever you sees down aft, you keep it to yerself, right, matey?'

Tojohns nodded. *Down aft.* Yes, he was somebody.

Six bells chimed out from *Hyperion*'s forecastle and Captain Valentine Keen touched his hat to Bolitho, barely able to suppress a smile.

'The master was right about our arrival here, Sir Richard.'

Bolitho raised his telescope to scan the familiar walls and batteries of Valletta. 'Only just.'

It had been a lengthy passage from Gibraltar, over eight days to log the weary twelve hundred miles. It had given Keen time to impress his methods on the whole ship, but had filled Bolitho with misgivings at the forthcoming meeting with Herrick.

He said slowly, 'Only three ships-of-the-line, Val.' He had recognised Herrick's flagship *Benbow* almost as soon as the masthead lookouts. Once his own flagship, and like *Hyperion*,

197

full of memories. Keen would be remembering her for very different reasons. Here he had faced a court of enquiry presided over by Herrick. It could have ruined him, but for Bolitho's intervention. Past history? It seemed unlikely he would ever forget.

Bolitho said, 'I can make out the frigate yonder, anchored beyond *Benbow*.' He had been afraid that she would have been sent elsewhere. She was named *La Mouette*, a French prize taken off Toulon while Bolitho had been at Antigua. She was a small vessel of only twenty-six guns, but beggars could not be choosers. Any frigate was welcome at this stage of the war against the new cat-and-mouse methods used by the French.

Keen said, 'But it raises our line of battle to eight.' He smiled. 'We have managed with far less in the past.'

Jenour stood slightly apart, supervising the signals midshipmen with their bright flags strewn about in apparent disorder.

Bolitho crossed to the opposite side to watch as the next astern, Thynne's *Obdurate*, took in more sail and tacked slowly after her admiral.

He pictured Herrick in *Benbow*, watching perhaps as the five major ships of Bolitho's squadron moved ponderously on a converging tack in readiness to anchor. It was very hot, and Bolitho had seen the sunlight flash on many telescopes amongst the anchored ships. Would Herrick be regretting this meeting, he wondered? Or thinking how their friendship had been born out of battle and a near mutiny in that other war against the American rebels?

He said, 'Very well, Mr Jenour, you may signal now.'

He glanced at Keen's profile. 'We shall just beat eight bells, Val, and so save Mr Penhaligon's reputation!'

'All acknowledged, sir!'

As the signal was briskly hauled to the deck, the ships faced up to the feeble breeze and dropped anchor.

Bolitho said, 'I have to go aft. I shall require my barge directly.'

Keen faced him. 'You'll not wait for the rear-admiral to come aboard, Sir Richard?'

Keen must have guessed that he was going to visit *Benbow* mainly to avoid having to greet Herrick with all the usual formalities. Their last meeting had been across the court's table. When next they met it would have to be as man-to-man. For both their sakes.

'Old friends do not need to rest on tradition, Val.' Bolitho hoped it sounded more convincing than it felt.

He tried to push it from his mind. Herrick had been here a long time; he might well have news of the enemy. Intelligence was everything. Without the little scraps of information gathered by the patrols and casual encounters they were helpless.

He heard Allday calling hoarsely to his barge crew, the creak of tackles as the boat, soon followed by others, was swayed up and over the gangway.

A few local craft were already approaching the ships, their hulls crammed with cheap wares to tempt the sailors to part with their money. Like Portsmouth and any other seaport, there would be women too for the land-starved men if the captains turned a blind eye. It must be hard for any man to accept, Bolitho thought. The officers came and went as duty permitted, but only trusted hands and those of the press-gangs were ever allowed to set foot ashore. Month in and year out, it was a marvel there had not been more outbreaks of rebellion in the fleet.

He thought of Catherine as he had left her. Keen would be thinking the same about Zenoria. It would be ten thousand times worse if they could not meet until the war had ended, or they had been thrown on the beach as rejected cripples, like the one-legged man.

He went to his cabin and collected some letters which had been brought on board *Firefly* at the last moment. For Herrick. He gave a grim smile. Like bearing gifts.

Ozzard pattered round him, his eyes everywhere, to make sure that Bolitho had forgotten nothing.

It made Bolitho think of Catherine's face when he had presented her with the fan Ozzard had cleaned.

She had said, 'Keep it. It is all I have to give you. Have it by you. Then I shall be near when you need me.'

He sighed and walked out past the sentry and Keen's open cabin door, where fresh white paint disguised where Haven's pistol had been fired. Haven was lucky that Parris was still alive.

Or was he? His career was wrecked, and there would be nothing waiting for him when he eventually reached his home.

He walked into the bright sunlight and saw the Royal Marines assembled at the entry port, boatswain's mates with their silver calls, Keen and Jenour ready to pay their respects.

Major Adams of the Royal Marines raised his sword and barked:

'Guard ready, *sir!*'

Keen looked at Bolitho. 'Barge alongside, Sir Richard.'

Bolitho raised his hat to the quarterdeck and saw bare-backed seamen working aloft on the mizzen yard peering down at him, their feet dangling in space.

One ship. One company.

Bolitho hurried down to the barge. The memories would have to wait.

Rear-Admiral Thomas Herrick stood with his hands grasped behind his back and watched the other ships anchoring, while the wind fell away to leave their sails almost empty. Gunsmoke from exchanged salutes drifted towards the shore, and Herrick tensed as he saw the green barge being lowered alongside *Hyperion* almost as soon as the Jack was hoisted forward.

Captain Hector Gossage remarked, 'It seems that the vice-admiral is coming to us immediately, sir.'

Herrick grunted. There were so many new faces in his command, and his flag captain had only been with him for a few months. His predecessor, Dewar, had gone home in ill health and Herrick still missed him.

Herrick said, 'Prepare to receive him. Full guard. You know what to do.'

He wanted to be left alone, to think. When he had received his new orders from Sir Owen Godschale at the Admiralty, Herrick had thought of little else. The last time he had met Bolitho had been here in the Mediterranean when *Benbow* had been under heavy attack from Jobert's squadron. Re-united in battle, friends meeting against the heartless terms of war. But afterwards, when Bolitho had sailed for England, Herrick had thought a great deal about the court of enquiry, how Bolitho had cursed them after he had heard of Inch's death. Herrick still believed that Bolitho's hurt and anger had been directed at him, not the anonymous court.

He thought of Godschale's personal letter, which had accompanied the changed orders. Herrick had already learned of the liaison between Bolitho and the woman he had known as Catherine Pareja. He had always felt ill-at-ease with her, out of his depth. A proud, uninhibited woman. In his eyes she lacked modesty, humility. He thought of his dear, loving Dulcie at their new house in Kent. Not a bit like her at all.

How brave Dulcie had been when she had been told finally that she could not bear him any children. She had said softly, 'If only we had met earlier, Thomas. Maybe we would have had a fine son to follow you into the navy.'

He thought of Bolitho's life in Falmouth, the same old grey house where he had been entertained when Bolitho had commanded *Phalarope*, and he had risen to become his first lieutenant. It seemed like a century ago.

Herrick had always been stocky, but he had filled out comfortably since he had married Dulcie, and had risen to the unbelievable height of rear-admiral as well. He had been out here so long that his round, honest face was almost the colour of mahogany, which made his bright blue eyes and the streaks of grey in his hair seem all the more noticeable.

What could Richard Bolitho be thinking of? He had a lovely wife and daughter he could be proud of. Any serving officer could envy his record, fights won at cost to himself, but never failing to hold his men's values close to his heart. His sailors had called him Equality Dick, a nickname taken up by the popular newsheets ashore. But some of those were telling a very different story now. Of the vice-admiral who cared more for a lady than his own reputation.

Godschale had skirted round it very well in his letter.

'I know you are both old friends, but you may find it difficult now to serve under him when you were expecting quite rightly to be relieved.'

By saying nothing, Godschale had said everything. A warning or a threat? You could take it either way.

He heard the marines falling in at the entry port, their officer snapping out commands as he inspected the guard.

Captain Gossage rejoined him and watched the array of anchored ships.

He said, 'They look fine enough, sir.'

Herrick nodded. His own ships needed to be relieved, if only for a quick overhaul and complete restoring. He had only been able to release one vessel at a time for watering or to gather new victuals, and the sudden change of orders to place him under Bolitho's flag had left everyone surprised or resentful.

Gossage was saying, 'I served with Edmund Haven a few years ago, sir.'

'Haven?' Herrick pulled his mind back. 'Bolitho's flag captain.'

Gossage nodded. 'A dull fellow, I thought. Only got *Hyperion* because she was little more than a hulk.'

Herrick dug his chin into his neckcloth. 'I'd not let Sir Richard hear you say that. It is not a view he would share.'

The officer-of-the-watch called, 'The barge is casting off, sir!'

'Very well. Man the side.'

In her last letter Dulcie had said little about Belinda. They had been in touch, but it seemed likely that any confidences would be kept secret. He smiled sadly. Even from him.

Herrick thought too of the girl Bolitho had once loved and married – Cheney Seton. Herrick had been at the marriage. It had been his terrible mission to carry the news of her tragic death to Bolitho at sea. He had known that Belinda was not another like her. But Bolitho had seemed settled, especially after he had been presented with a daughter. Herrick tried to keep things straight. It had nothing to do with the cruel fact that Dulcie was beyond the age to give him children. Even as he arranged his thoughts he recognised the lie. Could almost hear the comparison. *Why them and not us?*

And now there was Catherine. Rumours were always blown up out of all proportion. Like Nelson's much-vaunted affair. Later, Nelson would regret it. When he laid down his sword for the last time, there would be many old enemies eager to forget his triumphs and his worth. Herrick came of a poor family and knew how hard it was to rise above any superior's dislike, let alone outright hostility. Bolitho had saved him from it, had given him the chance he would otherwise never have had. There was no denying that. And yet –

Gossage straightened his hat. 'Barge approaching, sir!'

A voice yelled, 'Clear the upper deck!'

It would not look right to have the gundeck and forecastle crowded with idlers when Bolitho came aboard. But they were there all the same, despite some tempting smells from the galley funnel.

Herrick gripped his sword and pressed it to his side. Old friends. None closer. How could it happen like this?

The calls shrilled and the Royal Marine fifers struck into *Heart of Oak*, while the guard slapped their muskets to the present in a small cloud of pipeclay.

Bolitho stood framed against the sea's silky blue and doffed his hat.

He had not changed, Herrick thought. And as far as he could see, he had no grey hairs, although he was a year older than Herrick himself.

Bolitho nodded to the Royal Marines and said, 'Smart guard, Major.' Then he strode across to Herrick and thrust out his hand.

Herrick seized it, knowing how important this moment was, perhaps to Bolitho as well.

'Welcome, Sir Richard!'

Bolitho smiled, his teeth white against his sunburned skin.

'It is good to see you, Thomas. Though I fear you must hate this change of plans.'

Together they walked aft to the great cabin while the guard was dismissed, and Allday cast off the barge to idle comfortably within *Benbow*'s fat shadow.

In the cabin it seemed cool after the quarterdeck, and Herrick watched as Bolitho seated himself by the stern windows, saw his eyes moving around while he recalled it as it had once been. His own flagship. There had been other changes too. That last battle had made certain of that.

The servant brought some wine and Bolitho said, 'It seems that Our Nel is still in the Atlantic.'

Herrick swallowed his wine without noticing it. 'So they say. I have heard that he may return to England and haul down his flag, as it looks unlikely that the French will venture out in strength. Not this year anyway.'

'Is that what you think?' Bolitho examined the glass. Herrick was on edge. More than he had expected. 'It is possible, of course, that the enemy may slip through the Strait again and run for Toulon.'

Herrick frowned. 'If so, we shall *have 'em*. Caught between us and the main fleet.'

'But suppose Villeneuve intends to break out from another direction? By the time their lordships got word to us, he would be beating up the Channel, while we remain kicking our heels in ignorance.'

Herrick stirred uneasily. 'I am keeping up my patrols –'

'I knew you would. I see you are short of a ship?'

Herrick was startled. '*Absolute*, yes. I sent her to Gibraltar. She's so rotten, I wonder she remains afloat.' He seemed to stiffen. 'It was my responsibility. I did not know then that you were assuming total command.'

Bolitho smiled. 'Easy, Thomas. It was not meant as a criticism. I might have done the same.'

Herrick looked at the deck. *Might*. He said, 'I shall be pleased to hear of your intentions.'

'Presently, Thomas. Perhaps we might sup together?'

Herrick looked up and saw the grey eyes watching him. Pleading with him?

He replied, 'I'd relish that.' He faltered. 'You could bring Captain Haven if you wish, although I understand –'

Bolitho stared at him. Of course. He would not have heard yet.

'Haven is under arrest, Thomas. In due course I expect he will stand trial for attempting to murder his first lieutenant.' He almost smiled at Herrick's astonishment. It probably sounded completely insane. He added, 'Haven imagined that the lieutenant was having an affair with his wife. There was a child. He was wrong, as it turned out. But the damage was done.'

Herrick refilled his glass and spilled some wine on the table without heeding it.

'I have to speak out, Sir Richard.'

204

Bolitho watched him gravely. 'No rank or title 'twixt us, Thomas – unless you need a barricade for your purpose?'

Herrick exclaimed, 'This woman. What can she mean to you except –'

Bolitho said quietly, 'You and I are friends, Thomas. Let us remain as such.' He looked past him and pictured Catherine in the shadows. He said, 'I am in love with her. Is that so hard to understand?' He tried to keep the bitterness from his tone. 'How would you feel, Thomas, if some stranger referred to your Dulcie as *this woman*, eh?'

Herrick gripped the arms of his chair. 'God damn it, Richard, why do you twist the truth? You know, you *must* know what everyone is saying, that you are besotted by her, have thrown your wife and child to the winds so that you can lose yourself, and to hell with all who care for you!'

Bolitho thought briefly of the grand house in London. 'I've thrown nobody to the winds. I *have* found someone I can love. Reason does not come into it.' He stood up and crossed to the windows. 'You must know I do not act lightly in such matters.' He swung round. 'Are you judging me too? Who are you – Christ?'

They faced each other like enemies. Then Bolitho said, 'I need her, and I pray that she may always need me. Now let that be an end to it, man!'

Herrick took several deep breaths and refilled both glasses.

'I shall never agree.' He fixed Bolitho with the bright blue eyes he had always remembered. 'But I'll not let it put my duty at risk.'

Bolitho sat down again. 'Duty, Thomas? Don't speak to me of that. I've had a bellyful of late.' He made up his mind. 'This combined squadron is our responsibility. I am not usurping your leadership and that you must know. I don't share their lordships' attitude on the French, that is if they indeed have one. Pierre Villeneuve is a man of great intelligence; he is not one to go by the book of fighting instructions. He needs to be cautious on the one hand, for if he fails in his ultimate mission to clear the Channel for invasion, then he must die at the guillotine.'

Herrick muttered, '*Barbarians!*'

Bolitho smiled. 'We must explore every possibility and keep

our ships together except for the patrols. When the time comes, it will be a hard sail to find and support Nelson and brave Collingwood.' He put down his glass very slowly. 'You see, I do not believe that the French will wait until next year. They have run the course.' He looked through the sun's glare towards the anchored ships. 'So have we.'

Herrick felt safer on familiar ground. 'Who do you have as flag captain?'

Bolitho watched him and said dryly, 'Captain Keen. There is none better. Now that you are promoted beyond my reach, Thomas.'

Herrick did not hide his dismay. 'So we are all drawn together?'

Bolitho nodded. 'Remember Lieutenant Browne — how he called us *We Happy Few*?'

Herrick frowned. 'I don't need reminding.'

'Well, think on it, Thomas, my friend, there are even fewer of us now!'

Bolitho stood up and reached for his hat. 'I must return to *Hyperion*. Perhaps later —' He left it unsaid. Then he placed the packet of letters for Herrick on the table.

'From England, Thomas. There will be more *news*, I expect.' Their eyes met and Bolitho ended quietly, 'I wanted you to hear it from me, as a friend, rather than assault your ears with more gossip from the sewers.'

Herrick protested, 'I did not mean to hurt you. It is for you that I care.'

Bolitho shrugged. 'We will fight the war together, Thomas. It seems that will have to suffice.'

They stood side-by-side at the entry port while Allday manoeuvred the barge alongside once again. Allday had never been caught out before and would be fuming about it.

Like everyone else he must have expected him to remain longer with his oldest friend.

Bolitho walked towards the entry port as the marine guard presented their muskets to the salute, the bayonets shining like ice in the glare.

He caught his shoe in a ring-bolt, and would have fallen but for a lieutenant who thrust out his arm to save him.

'Thank you, sir!'

He saw Herrick standing at him with sudden anxiety, the major of marines swaying beside the guard with his sword still rigid in his gloved hand.

Herrick exclaimed, 'Are you well, Sir Richard?'

Bolitho looked at the nearest ship and gritted his teeth as the mist partly covered his eye. A close thing. He had been so gripped with emotion and disappointment at this visit that he had allowed his guard to fall. As in a sword-fight, it only took a second.

He replied, 'Well enough, thank you.'

They looked at one another. 'It shall not happen again.'

Some seamen had climbed into the shrouds and began to cheer as the barge pulled strongly from the shadow and into the sunlight. Allday swung the tiller bar and glanced quickly at Bolitho's squared shoulders, the familiar ribbon which drew his hair back above the collar. Allday could remember it no other way.

He listened to the cheers, carried on by another of the seventy-fours close by.

Fools, he thought savagely. What the hell did they know? They had seen nothing, knew even less.

But he had watched, and had felt it even from the barge. Two friends with nothing to say, nothing to span the gap which had yawned between them like a moat around a fortress.

He saw the stroke oarsman watching Bolitho instead of his loom and glared at him until he paled under his stare.

Allday swore that he would never take anyone at face value again. *For or against me, that'll be my measure of a man.*

Bolitho twisted round suddenly and shaded his eyes to look at him.

'It's *all right*, Allday.' He saw his words sink in. 'So be easy.'

Allday forgot his watching bargemen and grinned awkwardly. Bolitho had read his thoughts even with his back turned.

Allday said, 'I was rememberin', Sir Richard.'

'I know that. But at the moment I am too full to speak on it.'

The barge glided to the main chains and Bolitho glanced up at the waiting side-party.

207

He hesitated. 'I sometimes think we may hope for too much, old friend.'

Then he was gone, and the shrill of calls announced his arrival on deck.

Allday shook his head and muttered, 'I never seen him like this afore.'

'What's that, Cox'n?'

Allday swung round, his eyes blazing. 'And *you*! Watch your stroke in future, or I'll have the hide off ye!'

He forgot the bargemen and stared hard at the towering tumblehome of the ship's side. Close to, you could see the gouged scars of battle beneath the smart buff and black paintwork.

Like us, he thought, suddenly troubled. Waiting for the last fight. When it came, you would need all the friends you could find.

15

A Time For Action

Bolitho leaned on one elbow and put his signature on yet another despatch for the Admiralty. In the great cabin the air was heavy and humid, and even with gunports and skylight open, he felt the sweat running down his spine. He had discarded his coat, and his shirt was open almost to his waist, but it made little difference.

He stared at the date on the next despatch which Yovell pushed discreetly before him. September; over three months since he had said his farewell to Catherine and returned to Gibraltar. He looked towards the open stern windows. *To this.* Hardly a ripple today, and the sea shone like glass, almost too painful to watch.

It seemed far longer. The endless days of beating up and down in the teeth of a raw Levantine, or lying becalmed without even a whisper of a breeze to fill the sails.

It could not go on. It was like sitting on a powder-keg and worse. Or was it all in his mind, a tension born of his own uncertainties? Fresh water was getting low again, and that might soon provoke trouble on the crowded messdecks.

Of the enemy there was no sign. *Hyperion* and her consorts lay to the west of Sardinia, while Herrick and his depleted squadron maintained their endless patrol from the Strait of Sicily to as far north as Naples Bay.

The other occupant of the cabin gave a polite cough. Bolitho glanced up and smiled. 'Routine, Sir Piers, but it will not take much longer.'

209

Sir Piers Blachford settled down in his chair and stretched out his long legs. To the officers in the squadron his arrival in the last courier-brig had been seen as another responsibility, a civilian sent to probe and investigate, a resented intruder.

It had not taken long for this strange man to alter all that. If they were honest, most of those who had taken offence at his arrival would be sorry to see him leave.

Blachford was a senior member of the College of Surgeons, one of the few who had volunteered to visit the navy's squadrons, no matter at what discomfort to themselves, to examine injuries and their treatment in the spartan and often horrific conditions of a man-of-war. He was a man of boundless energy and never seemed to tire as he was ferried from one ship to the other, to meet and reason with their surgeons, to instruct each captain on the better use of their meagre facilities for caring for the sick.

And yet he was some twenty years older than Bolitho, as thin as a ramrod, with the longest and most pointed nose Bolitho had ever seen. It was more like an instrument for his trade than part of his face. Also, he was very tall, and creeping about the different decks and peering into storerooms and sickbays must have taxed his strength and his patience, but he never complained. Bolitho would miss him. It was a rare treat to share a conversation at the end of a day with a man whose world was healing, rather than running an elusive enemy to ground.

Bolitho had received two letters from Catherine, both in the same parcel from a naval schooner.

She was safe and well in the Hampshire house which was owned by Keen's father. He was a powerful man in the City of London, and kept the country house as a retreat. He had welcomed Catherine there, just as he had Zenoria. The favour went two ways, because one of Keen's sisters was there also, her husband, a lieutenant with the Channel Fleet, having been lost at sea. A comfort, and a warning too.

He nodded to Yovell, who gathered up the papers and withdrew.

Bolitho said, 'I expect that your ship will meet with us soon. I hope we have helped in your research?'

Blachford eyed him thoughtfully. 'I am always amazed that

casualties are not greater when I see the hell-holes in which they endure their suffering. It will take time to compare our findings at the College of Surgeons. It will be well spent. The recognition of wounds, the responses of the victims, a division of causes, be they gunshot or caused by thrusting or slashing blades. Immediate recognition can save time, and eventually lives. Mortification, gangrene and the terror it brings with it, each must be treated differently.'

Bolitho tried to imagine this same, reedy man with the wispy white hair in the midst of a battle. Surprisingly, it was not difficult.

He said, 'It is something we all dread.'

Blachford smiled faintly. 'That is very honest. I am afraid one tends to think of senior officers as glory-seeking men without heart.'

Bolitho smiled back. 'Both our worlds appear different from the outside. When I joined my first ship I was a boy. I had to learn that the packed, frightening world between decks was not just a mass, a mindless body. It took me a long time.' He stared at the glittering reflections that moved across one of the guns which shared the cabin, as *Hyperion* responded to a breath of wind. 'I am still learning.'

Through the open skylight he heard the shrill of a call, the slap of bare feet as the watch on deck responded to the order to man the braces yet again, and retrim the great yards to hold this cupful of wind. He heard Parris, too, and was reminded of a strange incident when one of the infrequent Levantine gales had swept down on them from the east, throwing the ship into confusion.

A man had gone overboard, probably like Keen's sister's husband, and while the ship forged away with the gale, the sailor had floundered astern, waiting to perish. For no ship could be brought about in such a blow without the real risk of dismasting her. Some captains would not even have considered it.

Keen had been on deck and had yelled for the quarter-boat to be cast adrift. The man overboard could obviously swim; there was a chance he might be able to reach the boat. There were also some captains who would have denied even that, saying that any boat was worth far more than a common seaman who might die anyway.

211

But Parris had shinned down to the boat with a handful of volunteers. The next morning the wind had backed and dropped, its amusement at their efforts postponed. They had recovered the boat, and the half-drowned seaman.

Parris had been sick with pain from his wounded shoulder, and Blachford had examined it afresh, and had done all he could. Bolitho had seen respect on Keen's face, just as he had recorded Parris's fanatical determination to prove himself. Because of him, there was one family in Portsmouth who would not grieve just yet. Blachford must also have been thinking of it, as well as all the other small incidents which when moulded into one hull made a fighting ship.

He remarked, 'That was a brave thing your lieutenant did. Not many would even attempt it. It can be no help to see your own ship being carried further and further away until you are quite alone.'

Bolitho called for Ozzard. 'Some wine?' He smiled. 'You are only unpopular aboard this ship if you ask for water!'

The joke hid the truth. They had to divide the squadron soon. If they did not water the ships. . . . He shut it from his mind as Ozzard entered the cabin.

And all the time he felt Blachford watching him. He had only once touched on the subject of his eye, but had dropped the matter when Bolitho had made light of it.

Blachford said abruptly, 'You must do something about your eye. I have a fine colleague who will be pleased to examine it if I ask him.'

Bolitho watched Ozzard as he poured the wine. There was nothing on the little man's face to show he was listening to every word.

Bolitho spread his hands. 'What can I do? Leave the squadron when at any moment the enemy may break out?'

Blachford was unmoved. 'You have a second-in-command. Are you afraid to delegate? I did hear that you took the treasure galleon because you would not risk another in your place.'

Bolitho smiled. 'Perhaps I did not care about the risk.'

Blachford sipped his wine but his eyes remained on Bolitho. Bolitho was reminded of a watchful heron in the reeds at Falmouth. Waiting to strike.

'But that has changed?' The heron blinked at him. 'You are playing games with me.'

'Not really. To cure the sick is one thing. To understand the leaders who decide if a man shall live or die is another essential part of my studies.'

Bolitho stood up and moved restlessly about the cabin. 'I am the cat on the wrong side of every door. When I am at home I fret about my ships and my sailors. Once here and I yearn for just a sight of England, the feel of grass underfoot, the smell of the land.'

Blachford said quietly, 'Think about it. A raging gale like the one I shared with you, the sting of salt spray and the constant demands of duty are no place for what you need.' He made up his mind. 'I tell you this. If you do not heed my warning you will lose all sight in that eye.'

Bolitho looked down at him and smiled sadly. 'And if I hand over my flag? Can you be sure the eye will be saved?'

Blachford shrugged. 'I am certain of nothing, but –'

Bolitho touched his shoulder. 'Aye, the *but*; it is always there. No, I cannot leave. Call me what you will, but I am *needed* here.' He waved his hand towards the water. 'Hundreds of men are depending on me, just as their sons will probably depend on your eventual findings, eh?'

Blachford sighed. 'I call you stubborn.'

Bolitho said. 'I am not ready for the surgeon's wings-and-limbs tub just yet, and I do not yearn for glory as some will proclaim.'

'At least think about it.' Blachford waited and added gently, 'You have another to consider now.'

Bolitho looked up as a far-off voice cried out, 'Deck there! Sail on the lee bow!'

Bolitho laughed. 'With luck that will be your passage to England. I fear I am no match for your devious ways.'

Blachford stood up and ducked his head between the massive beams. 'I never thought it, but I'll be sorry to go.' He looked at Bolitho curiously. 'How can you know that from a masthead's call?'

Bolitho grinned. 'No other ship would dare come near us!'

Later, as the newcomer drew closer, the officer-of-the-watch reported to Keen that she was the brig *Firefly*. The vessel which, like the old *Superb* in Nelson's famous squadron, sailed when others slept.

Bolitho watched as Blachford's much-used chests and folios were carried on deck and said, 'You will meet my nephew. He is good company.'

But *Firefly* was no longer captained by Adam Bolitho; it was another young commander who hurried aboard the flagship to make his report.

Bolitho met him aft and asked, 'What of my nephew?'

The commander, who looked like a midshipman aping his betters, explained that Adam had received his promotion. It was all he knew, and was almost tongue-tied at meeting a vice-admiral face to face. Especially one who was now well known for reasons other than the sea, Bolitho thought bleakly.

He was glad for Adam. But he would have liked more than anything to see him.

Keen stood beside him as *Firefly* spread more sails, and tacked around in an effort to catch the feeble wind.

Keen said, 'It seems wrong without him in command.'

Bolitho looked up at *Hyperion*'s braced yards, the masthead pendant lifting and curling in the glare.

'Aye, Val, I wish him all the luck –' he faltered and remembered Herrick's Lady Luck. 'With men like Sir Piers Blachford taking an interest at long last, maybe Adam's navy will be a safer one for those who serve the fleet.'

He watched the brig until she was stern-on and spreading more canvas, and her upper yards were touched with gold. In two weeks' time *Firefly* would be in England.

Keen moved away as Bolitho began to pace up and down the weather side of the quarterdeck.

In his loose, white shirt, his lock of hair blowing in the breeze, he did not look much like an admiral.

Keen smiled. *He was a man.*

A week later the schooner *Lady Jane*, sailing under Admiralty warrant, was sighted by the frigate *Tybalt*, whose captain immediately signalled his flagship.

214

The wind was fair but had veered considerably, so that the smart schooner had to beat back and forth for several hours before more signals could be exchanged.

On *Hyperion*'s quarterdeck, Bolitho stood with Keen and watched the schooner's white sails fill to the opposite tack, while Jenour's signals party ran up another acknowledgement.

Jenour said excitedly, 'She is from Gibraltar with despatches, Sir Richard.'

Keen remarked, 'They must be urgent. The schooner is making heavy weather of it.' He gestured to Parris. 'Prepare to heave-to, if you please.'

Calls trilled between decks and men swarmed through hatchways and along the upperdeck to be mustered by their petty officers.

Bolitho touched his eyelid and pressed it gently. It had barely troubled him since Sir Piers Blachford had left the ship. Was it possible that it might improve, despite what he had said?

'*Lady Jane*'s hove-to, Sir Richard. She's putting down a boat.'

Someone chuckled, 'Gawd, her captain looks about twelve years old!'

Bolitho watched the small boat rising and dipping over the smooth-sided swell.

He had been in his cabin when the hail had come from the masthead about *Tybalt*'s signal. He had been composing fresh orders for Herrick and his captains. *Divide the squadron. Delay no longer.*

Bolitho glanced at the nearest gangway, the bare-backed seamen clinging to the nettings to watch as the boat pulled nearer. Was it wrong to curse boredom when the alternative could be sudden death?

'Heave-to, if you please!'

Parris raised his speaking trumpet. 'Main tops'l braces!' Even he seemed to have forgotten his wound.

Hyperion came slowly into the wind, while Bolitho kept his gaze on the approaching boat.

Suppose it was just one more despatch, which in the end meant nothing? He swung away to hide the anger he felt for himself. In God's name, he should be used to that by now.

215

Lady Jane's captain, a pink-cheeked lieutenant named Edwardes, clambered through the entry port and stared around like someone trapped.

Keen stepped forward. 'Come aft, sir. My admiral will speak with you.'

But Bolitho stared at the second figure who was being hauled unceremoniously on deck, accompanied by grins and nudges from the seamen.

Bolitho exclaimed, 'So you could not stay away!'

Sir Piers Blachford waved a warning hand as a sailor made to drop his case of instruments on the deck. Then he said simply, 'I had reached Gibraltar. There I was told that the French are massed at Cadiz with their Spanish allies. I could not see my way to joining the fleet, so I decided to return here in the schooner.' He smiled gently. 'I have the blessing of authority behind me, Sir Richard.'

Keen smiled wryly. 'You are more likely to get sunburn or dry rot if you stay with *us*, Sir Piers!' But his eyes were on Bolitho, seeing the change in him. It never failed to move him, just to watch his expression, the sudden glint in his dark grey eyes.

In the cabin Bolitho slit open the weighted canvas envelope himself. The shipboard sounds seemed to be muffled, as if *Hyperion* too was holding her breath.

The others stood around like unrehearsed players. Keen, feet astride, his fair hair and handsome features picked out in a bar of sunlight. Yovell by the table, a pen still gripped in his hand. Sir Piers Blachford, sitting down because of his height, but unusually subdued, as if he knew this was a moment he must share and remember. Jenour by the table, close enough for Bolitho to hear his rapid breathing. And Lieutenant Edwardes who had carried the despatches under all sail from the Rock, gulping gratefully from a tankard which Ozzard had put into his hand.

And of course, Allday. Was it by chance, or had he taken his stance by the rack with its two swords to mark the moment?

Bolitho said quietly, 'Last month Lord Nelson hauled down his flag and returned home after failing to bring the French to battle.' He glanced at Blachford. 'The French fleet is at Cadiz, so too the Spanish squadrons. Vice-Admiral Collingwood is blockading the enemy in Cadiz.'

216

Jenour whispered, 'And Lord Nelson?'

Bolitho looked at him. 'Nelson has rejoined *Victory*, and is now doubtless with the fleet.'

For a long moment nobody spoke. Then Keen asked, 'They will break out? They must.'

Bolitho gripped his hands behind him. 'I agree. Villeneuve is ready. He has no choice. Which way will he head? North to Biscay, or back here, Toulon perhaps?' He studied their intent faces. 'We shall be ready. We are ordered to prepare to join Lord Nelson, to blockade or to fight; only Villeneuve knows which.'

He felt every muscle relax, as if a weight had been lifted from his shoulders.

He looked at the pink-cheeked lieutenant. 'So you are on your way?'

'Aye, Sir Richard.' He waved vaguely. 'First to Malta, and then. . . .'

Bolitho watched the sparkle in his eyes; he was planning how he would relate to his friends, how he had carried the word to the rest of the fleet.

'I wish you Godspeed.'

Keen left to see the young man over the side and Bolitho said, 'Make a signal to *Tybalt*, repeated to *Phaedra*. Captain to close the Flag and repair on board without delay.'

Jenour wrote in his book and said, 'Immediately, Sir Richard.' He almost ran from the cabin.

Bolitho looked at Blachford. 'I shall send *Phaedra* to recall the rest of the squadron. When Herrick joins me, I intend to move to the west. If there is to be a fight, then we shall share it.' He smiled and added, 'You will be more than welcome here if that happens.'

Keen came back and asked, 'Will you send *Phaedra*, Sir Richard?'

'Yes.'

Bolitho thought, Val's mind matches my own. He is thinking it a pity it could not be Adam going to tell Herrick the news.

Blachford remarked, 'But it may end in another blockade?'

Keen shook his head. 'I think not, Sir Piers. There is too much at stake here.'

217

Bolitho nodded. 'Not least, Villeneuve's honour.'

He walked to the stern windows and wondered how long it would take Dunstan to work his sloop-of-war back to the squadron.

So Nelson had quit the land to rejoin his *Victory*? He must feel it too. Bolitho ran his palms over the worn sill of the stern windows and watched the sea rise and fall beneath the counter. Two old ships. He thought of the sally port where he had released his hold on Catherine that last time. Nelson would have used those same stairs. One day they would meet. It was inevitable. Dear Inch had met him, and Adam was on speaking terms. He smiled to himself. *Our Nel.*

There were whispers at the screen door, then Keen said, '*Phaedra* is in sight, Sir Richard.'

'Good. We'll send her on her way before dusk with any luck.'

Bolitho threw off his gold-laced coat and sat at the table. 'I shall write my orders, Mr Yovell. Tell your clerk to prepare copies for every captain.'

He stared at the sun glinting across the fresh ink.

Upon receipt of these orders you are to proceed with all despatch – Right or wrong, it was a time for action.

Herrick sat squarely in *Hyperion*'s stern cabin and grasped a tankard of ginger-beer with both hands.

'It feels strange.' He dropped his eyes. 'Why should that be?'

Bolitho walked about the cabin, remembering his own feelings when the lookouts had sighted *Benbow* and her two consorts in the dawn light.

He could understand Herrick's feelings. Two men drawn together like passing ships on an ocean. Now he was here, and not even the coolness Bolitho had seen between him and Keen as the latter had greeted his arrival on board could dispel a sense of relief.

Bolitho said, 'I have decided to head west now that we are joined, Thomas.'

Herrick looked up, but his eyes seemed drawn to the elegant wine cabinet in the corner of the cabin. He probably saw Catherine's hand here too.

218

'I am not certain it is wise.' He pouted, and then shrugged. 'But if we are called to support Nelson, then the closer we are to the Strait the better, I suppose.' He did not sound very certain. 'At least we can face the enemy if he comes our way in the narrows.'

Bolitho listened to the tramp of feet as the afterguard manned the mizzen braces for changing tack again. Eight ships-of-the-line, a frigate and a small sloop-of-war. It was no fleet, but he was as proud of them as a man could be.

Only one was missing, the little prize frigate *La Mouette* which Herrick had sent further north to scout for any coastal shipping from which she might glean some information.

Herrick said, 'If the Frogs decide not to venture out, we shall remain in ignorance of their next plan of attack. What then?' He waved Ozzard aside as he made to bring the tray and some claret. 'No, I would relish some more ginger-beer.'

Bolitho turned away. Was it really that, or had Herrick become so rigid in his bias against Catherine that he would take nothing from her cabinet? He tried to dismiss the thought as unworthy, petty, but it still persisted.

He said, 'We'll move in separate formations, Thomas. If the weather remains our ally, we shall stand two miles or more apart. It will give our mastheads a better scan of the horizons. If the enemy is chased our way, we should have good warning of it, eh?' He made to smile. 'It is never wise to stand in the path of a charging bull!'

Herrick said abruptly, 'When we return home, what will you do?' He moved his shoes on the deck. 'Share your life with another?'

Bolitho braced his legs as the ship heeled slightly to an extra thrust in her canvas.

He replied, 'I share nothing. Catherine *is* my life.'

'Dulcie said –' The blue eyes lifted and watched him stubbornly. 'She believes you will regret it.'

Bolitho glanced at the wine cabinet, the folded fan lying on top of it.

'You can go with the stream, Thomas, or fight against it.'

'Our friendship means a lot to me.' Herrick frowned as Ozzard padded in with a fresh tankard. 'But it gives me the right to speak my mind. I can never accept this –' he licked his lips, 'this lady.'

Bolitho faced him sadly. 'Then you have made your decision, Thomas.' He sat down and waited for Ozzard to refill his glass. 'Or have you had it made by others?' He watched Herrick's angry reaction and added, 'Perhaps the enemy will decide our future.' He raised the glass. 'I give you a sentiment, Thomas. May the best man win!'

Herrick stood up. 'How can you jest about it!'

The door opened and Keen peered in. 'The rear-admiral's barge is standing by, Sir Richard.' He did not glance at Herrick. 'The sea is getting up, and I thought –'

Herrick looked round for his hat. Then he waited for Keen to withdraw and said flatly, 'When we meet again –'

Bolitho held out his hand. 'For friendship?'

Herrick grasped it, his palm as hard as it had ever been.

He said, 'Aye. Nothing can break that.'

Bolitho listened to the calls as Herrick was piped over the side for the lively pull to his flagship.

Allday lingered in the other doorway, his rag moving up and down on the old sword.

Bolitho said wearily, 'They say love is blind, old friend. It seems to me that only those who have never known it are blind.'

Allday smiled and replaced the sword on its rack.

If it took war and the risk of a bloody fight to make Bolitho's eyes shine again, then so be it.

He said, 'I knew a lass once –'

Bolitho smiled, and recalled his thoughts when he had written his orders.

A time for action. It was like an epitaph.

16

Articles Of War

The twenty-six gun frigate *La Mouette* was completely shrouded in a heavy sea-mist. The lookouts could barely see more than a few yards on either beam, and from the deck the upper shrouds and limp sails were invisible.

There was a slow, moist breeze, but the mist kept pace with the ship to add a sense of being motionless.

Occasionally the disembodied voice of a leadsman floated aft, but the water was deep enough, although if the mist suddenly lifted the ship might be close inshore, or completely alone on an empty sea.

Aft by the quarterdeck rail the first lieutenant, John Wright, stared at the dripping maincourse until his eyes smarted. It was eerie, like thrusting into something solid. He could picture the jib-boom feeling the way like a blind man's stick. There was nothing beyond the pale patch of the figurehead, a fierce-looking seagull with its beak wide in anger.

Around and behind him the other watchkeepers stood about like statues. The helmsman, the sailing master close by. The midshipman of the watch, a boatswain's mate, their faces shining with moisture, as if they had been standing in a rainfall.

Nobody spoke. But that was nothing new, Wright thought. He longed for the chance of a command for himself. Anything. It had meant the next step on the ladder just being first lieutenant. He had not bargained for a captain like Bruce Sinclair. The captain was young, probably twenty-seven or so, Wright decided. A man with fine cheekbones, his chin always high, like a haughty pose, someone who was always quick to seek out slackness and inefficiency in his command.

A visiting admiral had once praised Sinclair for the smartness of his ship. Nobody ever walked on the upper deck, orders were carried out at the double, and any midshipman or petty officer who failed to report a man for not doing so would also face punishment.

They had been in several single-ship actions with privateers and blockade runners, and Sinclair's unyielding discipline had, on the face of it, worked well enough to satisfy any admiral.

The master joined him at the rail and said in a low voice, 'This mist can't last much more, Mr Wright.' He sounded anxious. 'We could be miles off course by now. I'm not happy about it.'

They both looked at the gundeck as a low groan made the men on watch glance uneasily at each other.

Like all the other ships in the squadron *La Mouette* was short of fresh water. Captain Sinclair had ordered it to be severely rationed for all ranks, and two days ago had cut the ration still further. Wright had suggested they might call at some island provided there was no sign of an enemy, if only to replenish a portion of the water supply. Sinclair had studied him coldly. 'I am ordered to seek information about the French, Mr Wright. I cannot spare any time for spoonfeeding the people merely because their lot is not to their taste!'

Wright stared at the man by the larboard gangway. He was quite naked, his legs braced apart by irons, his arms tied back to a gun so that he looked as if he had been crucified. The man occasionally rolled his head from side to side, but his tongue was too swollen in his blistered mouth to make sense of his pleas.

Aboard any King's ship a thief was despised. The justice meted out by the lower deck against such an offender was often far harsher than that of a proper authority.

The seaman McNamara had stolen a gallon of fresh water one night, when a Royal Marine sentry had been called away by the officer-of-the-watch.

He had been caught by a boatswain's mate, drinking the rancid water in secret while his messmates had slept in their hammocks.

Everyone had expected his punishment to be severe, especially as McNamara was a regular defaulter, but Sinclair's reaction had taken even the most hardened sailor aback. For five days he had been in irons on the upper deck, in blazing sunlight, and in the chill of the night. Naked, and in his own filth, he had been doused with salt water by other hands under punishment, to clean up the deck rather than afford him any relief from his torment.

Sinclair had turned up the hands to read the relevant sections of the Articles of War, and had ended by saying that McNamara would be awarded three dozen lashes when the example of his theft was completed.

Wright shivered. It seemed unlikely that McNamara would live long enough to face the flogging.

The master hissed, 'Cap'n's comin' up, Mr Wright.'

It was like that. Whispers. Fear. Smouldering hatred for the man who ruled their daily lives.

Sinclair, neatly dressed, his hand resting on his sword hilt, strode first to the compass, then to the quarterdeck rail to study the set of any visible sails.

'Nor'-west-by-west, sir!'

Sinclair waited as Wright made his report, then said, 'Direct a boy to fetch your hat, Mr Wright.' He smiled faintly. 'This is a King's ship, not a Bombay trader!'

Wright flushed. 'I'm sorry, sir. This heat –'

'Quite.' Sinclair waited until a ship's boy had been sent below for the hat and remarked, 'Deuced if I know how much longer I can waste time like this.'

The wretched man on the gundeck gave another groan. It sounded as if he was choking on his tongue.

Sinclair snapped, 'Keep that man silent! God damn his eyes, I'll have him seized up and put to the lash here and now if I hear another squeak from him!' He looked aft. 'Bosun's mate! See to it! I'll have no bleatings from that bloody thief!'

Wright wiped his lips with his wrist. They felt dry and raw.

'It *is* five days, sir.'

'I too keep a log, Mr Wright.' He moved to the opposite side and peered down at the water as it glided past. 'It may help others to think twice before they follow his miserable example!'

223

Sinclair added suddenly, 'My orders are to rendezvous with the squadron.' He shrugged, the dying seaman apparently forgotten. 'The meeting is overdue, thanks to this damnable weather. Doubtless Rear-Admiral Herrick will send someone to seek us out.'

Wright saw the boatswain's mate merge with the swirling mist as he hurried towards the naked man. It made him feel sick just to imagine what it must be like. Sinclair was wrong about one thing. The anger of the ship's company had already swung to sympathy. The torture was bad enough. But Sinclair had stripped McNamara of any small dignity he might have held. Had left him in his own excrement like a chained animal, humiliated before his own messmates.

The captain was saying, 'I'm not at all sure that our gallant admiral knows what he is about.' He moved restlessly along the rail. 'Too damn cautious by half, if you ask me.'

'Sir Richard Bolitho will have his own ideas, sir.'

'I wonder.' Sinclair sounded faraway. 'He will combine the squadrons, that is my opinion, and then –' He looked up, frowning at the interruption as a voice called, 'Mist's clearin', sir!'

'God damn it, make a proper report!' Sinclair turned to his first lieutenant. 'If the wind gets up, I want every stitch of canvas on her. So call all hands. Those idlers need work to keep their fingers busy!'

Sinclair could not restrain his impatience and strode along the starboard gangway, which ran above a battery of cannon and joined quarterdeck to forecastle. He paused amidships and looked across at the naked man. McNamara's head was hanging down. He could be dead.

Sinclair called, 'Rouse that scum! *You*, use your starter, man!'

The boatswain's mate stared up at him, shocked at the captain's brutality.

Sinclair put his hands on his hips and eyed him with contempt.

'Do it, or by God you'll change places with him!'

Wright was thankful as the hands came running to halliards and braces. The muffled stamp of bare feet at least covered the sound of the rattan across McNamara's shoulders.

The second lieutenant came hurrying aft and said to the

master, 'Lively, into the chartroom. We shall be expected to fix our position as soon as we sight land!'

Wright pursed his lips as the master's mate of the watch reported the hands ready to make more sail.

If there was no land in sight, God help them all, he thought despairingly.

He watched some weak sunshine probing through the mist and reaching along the topsail yards, then down into the milky water alongside.

The leadsman cried out again, 'No bottom, sir!'

Wright found that he was clenching his fingers so tightly that he had cramp in both hands. He watched the captain at the forward end of the gangway, one hand resting on the packed hammock nettings. A man without a care in the world, anyone might think.

'Deck there! Sail on the weather bow!'

Sinclair strode aft again, his mouth in a thin line.

Wright ran his finger round his neckcloth. 'We'll soon know, sir.' Of course, the lookout would be able to see the other ship now, if only her topgallant yards above the creeping mist.

The lookout shouted again, 'She's English, sir! Man-o'-war!'

'Who is that fool up there?' Sinclair glared into the swirling mist.

Wright answered, 'Tully, sir. A reliable seaman.'

'Hmph. He had better be.'

More sunlight exposed the two batteries of guns, the neatly flaked lines, the pikes in their rack around the mainmast, perfectly matched like soldiers on parade. No wonder the admiral had been impressed, Wright thought.

Sinclair said sharply, 'Make sure our number is bent on and ready to hoist, Mr Wright. I'll have no snooty post-captain finding fault with my signals.'

But the signals midshipman, an anxious-looking youth, was already there with his men. You never fell below the captain's standards more than once.

The foretopsail bellied out from its yard and the master exclaimed, 'Here it comes at last!'

'Man the braces there!' Sinclair pointed over the rail. 'Take

225

that man's name, Mr Cox! God damn it, they are like cripples today!'

The wind tilted the hull, and Wright saw spray lift above the beakhead. Already the mist was floating ahead, shredding through the shrouds and stays, laying bare the water on either beam.

The naked seaman threw back his head and stared, half-blinded, at the sails above, his wrists and ankles rubbed raw by the irons.

'Stand by on the quarterdeck!' Sinclair glared. 'Ready with our number. I don't want to be mistaken for a Frenchie!'

Wright had to admit it was a wise precaution. Another ship new to the station might easily recognise *La Mouette* as French-built. Act first, think later, was the rule in sea warfare.

The lookout called, 'She's a frigate, sir! Runnin' with the wind!'

Sinclair grunted, 'Converging tack.' He peered up to seek out the masthead pendant, but it was still hidden above a last banner of mist. Then like a curtain rising the sea became bright and clear, and Sinclair gestured as the other ship seemed to rise from the water itself.

She was a big frigate, and Sinclair glanced above at the gaff to make certain his own ensign was clearly displayed.

'She's hoisting a signal, sir!'

Sinclair watched as *La Mouette*'s number broke from the yard.

'You see, Mr Wright, if you train the people to respond as they should –'

His words were lost as somebody yelled, 'Christ! *She's runnin' out!*'

All down the other frigate's side the gunports had opened as one, and now, shining in the bright sunshine, her whole larboard battery trundled into view.

Wright ran to the rail and shouted, '*Belay that! Beat to quarters!*'

Then the world exploded into a shrieking din of flame and whirling splinters. Men and pieces of men painted the deck in vivid scarlet patterns. But Wright was on his knees, and some of the screams he knew were his own.

His reeling mind held on to the horrific picture for only seconds. The naked man tied to the gun, but no longer complaining. He had no head. The foremast going over the side, the signals midshipman rolling and whimpering like a sick dog.

The picture froze and faded. He was dead.

Commander Alfred Dunstan sat cross-legged at the table in *Phaedra*'s cramped cabin and studied the chart in silence.

Opposite him, his first lieutenant Joshua Meheux waited for a decision, his ear pitched to the creak and clatter of rigging. Astern through the open windows he could see the thick mist following the sloop-of-war, heard the second lieutenant calling another change of masthead lookouts. In any fog or mist even the best lookout was subject to false sightings. After an hour or so he would see only what he expected to see. A darker patch of fog would become a lee shore, or the topsail of another vessel about to collide. He watched his cousin. It was incredible how Dunstan was able to make his ship's company understand exactly what he needed from them.

He glanced round the small cabin, where they had had so many discussions, made plans, celebrated battles and birthdays with equal enthusiasm. He looked at the great tubs of oranges and lemons which filled most of the available space. *Phaedra* had run down on a Genoese trader just before the sea-mist had enveloped them.

They were short of water, desperately so, but the mass of fresh fruit which Dunstan had *commandeered*, as he had put it, had tilted the balance for the moment.

Dunstan glanced up from the chart and smiled. 'Smells like Bridport on market day, don't it?'

His shirt was crumpled and stained, but better that than have the ship's company believe that water rationing did not apply to the officers as well.

Dunstan tapped the chart with his dividers. 'Another day, and I shall have to come about. We are sorely needed with the squadron. Besides, Captain Sinclair will have an alternative rendezvous. But for this mist, I'd wager we would have sighted his ship days ago.'

227

Meheux asked, 'Do you know him?'

Dunstan lowered his head to peer more closely at his calculations. 'I know *of* him.'

The lieutenant smiled to himself. Dunstan was in command. He would go no further in discussing another captain. Even with his cousin.

Dunstan leaned back and ruffled his wild auburn hair. 'God, I itch like a poxed-up whore!' He grinned. 'I think Sir Richard intends to join the fleet under Nelson. Though he will take all the blame if the French outpace him and slip back into port in these waters.'

He reached under the table and then produced a decanter of claret. 'Better than water anyway.' He poured two large glasses. 'I'll bet that our vice-admiral will be in enough hot water as it is! God damn it, any man who can accept the wrath of Admiralty and that of the dandified Inspector General must be made of stern stuff.'

'What was he like as a captain?'

Dunstan looked at him, his eyes distant. 'Brave, courteous. No conceit.'

'You liked him?'

Dunstan swallowed the claret; the casual question had slipped through his guard.

'I worshipped the deck he walked on. All of us in the gunroom did, I believe.' He shook his head. 'I'd stand beside him any day.'

There was a tap at the door and a midshipman, dressed in an even grubbier shirt than his captain's, peered in at them.

'The second lieutenant's respects, sir, and he thinks the mist may be clearing.'

They looked up as the deck quivered very slightly, and the hull murmured a gentle protest at being disturbed again.

'By God, the wind *is* returning.' Dunstan's eyes gleamed. 'My compliments to the second lieutenant, Mr Valliant. I shall come up presently.' As the boy left he winked at Meheux. 'With a name like his he should go far in the navy!'

Dunstan held up the decanter and grimaced. It was almost empty.

He remarked, 'It will be a drier ship than usual, I fear.' Then he became serious again. 'Now this is what I intend –'

Meheux stared at the decanter as the glass stopper rattled for several seconds.

Their eyes met. Meheux said, 'Thunder?'

Dunstan was groping for his shabby hat. 'Not this time, by God. That came from iron guns, my friend!'

He slipped his arms into his coat and climbed up the companion ladder to the deck.

He glanced through the drifting mist, seeing his seamen standing and listening. Such a small vessel, yet so many men, he thought vaguely. He tensed as the booming roar sighed through the mist and imagined he could feel the sullen vibration against the hull. Faces had turned aft towards him. Instantly he remembered Bolitho, when they had all stared at him as if expecting salvation and understanding, because he had been their captain.

Dunstan tucked one hand into his old seagoing coat with the tarnished buttons. *I am ready. Now they look to me.*

Meheux was the first to speak.

'Shall we stand away until we are sure what is happening, sir?'

He did not reply directly. 'Call all hands. Have the people lay aft.'

They came running to the pipe, and when they were all packed from side to side, with some clinging to the mizzen shrouds and on the upturned cutter, Meheux touched his hat, his eyes curious.

'Lower deck cleared, sir.'

Dunstan said, 'In a moment we shall clear for action. No fuss, no beat of a drum. Not this time. You will go to quarters in the manner you have learned so well.' He looked at those nearest him, youngsters like their officers, grizzled old hands such as the boatswain and the carpenter. Faces he had taught himself to know and recognise, so that he could call any one of them by name even in pitch darkness. At any other time the thought would have made him smile. For it was often said that his hero Nelson had the same knack of knowing his people, even now that he had reached flag rank.

But he did not smile. 'Listen!' The booming roar echoed through the mist. Each man would hear it differently. Ships at war, or the sound of enraged surf on a reef. Thunder across the hills in a home land which had produced most of these men.

'I intend to continue on this tack.' His eyes moved over them. 'One of those ships must be a friend. We shall carry word of our finding to Sir Richard Bolitho and the squadron.'

A solitary voice raised a cheer and Dunstan gave a broad grin. 'So stand-to, my lads, and God be with you all!'

He stood back to watch as they scattered to their various stations, while the boatswain and his own party broke out the chain slings and nets for the yards to offer some protection to the gun crews should the worst happen.

Dunstan said quietly, 'I think we may have found *La Mouette*.' He kept the other thought to himself. That he hoped Sinclair was as ready for a fight as he was with the lash.

The thuds of screens being taken down, stores and personal belongings being lowered to the orlop deck, helped to muffle the occasional sound of distant thunder.

Lieutenant Meheux touched his hat and reported, 'Cleared for action, sir.'

Dunstan nodded and again recalled Bolitho. 'Ten minutes this time. They take fairly to their work.' But the mood eluded him and he smiled. 'Well done, Josh!'

The sails billowed out loudly, like giants puffing their chests. The deck canted over and Dunstan said, 'Bring her up a point! Steer nor'-nor'-west!'

He saw Meheux clipping on his hanger and said, 'The people are feeling this.' He looked at the crouching gun crews, the ship's boys with their buckets of sand, the others at the braces or with their fingers gripping the ratlines, ready to dash aloft when the order was piped to make more sail.

Dunstan made up his mind. 'Load if you please, I –'

There was a great chorus of shouts and Dunstan stared as the mist lifted and swirled to one violent explosion.

He said sharply, '*Load*, Mr Meheux! Keep their minds in your grasp!'

Each gun captain faced aft and raised his fist.

'All loaded, sir!'

They looked aloft as the mist faded more swiftly and laid bare the rippling ensign above the gaff.

Dunstan plucked his chin. 'We are ready this time anyway.'

All eyes turned forward as the mist lost its greyness. Something like a fireball exploded through it, the sound going on and on until eventually lost in the beat of canvas, the sluice of water alongside.

'Ship on the starboard bow, sir!'

Dunstan snatched a glass. 'Get aloft, Josh. I need your eyes up there today.'

As the first lieutenant swarmed up the mainmast shrouds a warning cry came from the forecastle.

'Wreckage ahead!'

The master's mate of the watch threw his weight onto the wheel with that of the two helmsmen but Dunstan yelled, 'Belay that! Steady as you go!' He made himself walk to the side as what appeared to be a giant tusk loomed off the bow. It was always best to meet it head on, he thought grimly. *Phaedra* did not have the timbers of a liner, nor even a frigate. That great pitching spar might have crashed right through the lower hull like a ram.

He watched the severed mast pass down the side, torn shrouds and blackened canvas trailing behind it like foul weed. There were corpses too. Men trapped by the rigging, their faces staring through the lapping water, or their blood surrounding them like pink mist.

Dunstan heard a boatswain's mate bite back a sob as he stared at one of the bobbing corpses. It wore the same blue jacket with white piping as himself.

There was no more doubt as to who had lost the fight.

Some of the small waves crumpled over as the rising wind felt its way across the surface.

Dunstan watched the mist drawing clear, further and further, leaving the sea empty once again. He stiffened as more shouts came from forward.

Something long and dark which barely rose above the uneasy water. There was much weed on it. One of the vessels which should have been released for a much needed overhaul. Surrounded by giant bubbles and a great litter of flotsam and charred remains, it was a ship's keel.

231

Dunstan said, 'Up another point. Hands aloft, Mr Faulkner! As fast as you like!'

High above it all, Lieutenant Meheux clung to the main crosstrees beside the lookout and watched the mist rolling away before him. He saw the other ship's topgallant masts and braced yards, and then as the mist continued to outpace the thrust of the sails, the forepart of the hull and her gilded figurehead.

He slid down a backstay and reached Dunstan in seconds.

Dunstan nodded very slowly. 'We both remember *that* ship, Josh. She's *Consort* – in hell's name I'd know her anywhere!'

He raised his telescope and studied the other vessel as more sails broke to the wind, and her shining hull seemed to shorten while she leaned over on a fresh tack. Towards *Phaedra*.

The midshipman was pointing wildly. 'Sir! There are men in the water!' He was almost weeping. 'Our people!'

Dunstan moved the glass until he saw the thrashing figures, some clinging to pieces of timber, others trying to hold their comrades afloat.

Dunstan climbed into the shrouds and twisted his leg around the tarred cordage to hold himself steady.

The masthead lookout yelled, 'Ships to the nor'-east!'

But Dunstan had already seen them. With the mist gone, the horizon was sharp and bright; it reminded him of a naked sword.

Someone was shouting, 'It'll be th' squadron! Come on, lads! Kill them buggers!'

Others started to cheer, their voices broken as they watched the survivors from *La Mouette*. Men like themselves. The same dialects, the same uniforms.

Dunstan watched the ships on the horizon until his eye ached. He had seen the red and yellow barricades around their fighting-tops in the powerful lens, something the lookout had not yet recognised.

He lowered the glass and looked sadly at the midshipman. 'We must leave those poor devils to die, Mr Valliant.' He ignored the boy's horrified face. 'Josh, we will come about and make all haste to find Sir Richard.'

Meheux waited, dazed by the swiftness of disaster.

His captain gestured towards the horizon. 'The Dons are

coming. A whole bloody squadron of them.'

The air cringed as a shot echoed across the sea. The frigate had fired a ranging ball from one of her bow chasers. The next one –

Dunstan cupped his hands. 'Hands aloft! Man the braces! Stand by to come about!' He bit his lip as another ball slammed down and threw up a waterspout as high as the topsail yard. Men ran to obey, and as the yards swung round *Phaedra*'s lee bulwark appeared to dip beneath the water.

Another shot pursued her as the frigate made more sail, her yards alive with men.

Meheux was waving to his topmen with the speaking trumpet. He shouted breathlessly, 'If they reach our squadron before we can warn them –'

Dunstan folded his arms and waited for the next fall of shot. Any one of those nine pounders could cripple his command, slow her down until she reeled beneath a full broadside as Sinclair had done.

'I think it will be more than a squadron at stake, Josh.'

A ball crashed through the taffrail and seared across the deck like a furnace bar. Two men fell dead, without even uttering a cry. Dunstan watched as two others took their place.

'Run, my beauty, *run*!' He looked up at the hardening sails, the masts curving like coachmen's whips.

'Just this once, you are the most important ship in the fleet!'

17

Prepare For Battle!

Captain Valentine Keen walked up the slanting deck and hunched his shoulders against the wind. How quickly the Mediterranean could change her face at this time of year, he thought. The sky was hidden by deep-bellied clouds, and the sea was no longer like blue silk.

He stared at the murky horizon, at the endless serried ranks of short, steep white horses. It looked hostile and without warmth. There had been some heavy rain in the night and every available man had been roused on deck to gather it in canvas scoops, even in humble buckets. A full glass, washed down with a tot of rum for all hands, seemed to have raised their spirits.

The deck heaved over again, for *Hyperion* was butting as close to the wind as she dared, her reefed topsails glinting with spray as she held station on the other ships astern.

For as Isaac Penhaligon, the master, had commented, with the wind veered again to the nor'-east, it was hard enough to dawdle until Herrick's ships joined them, without the additional problem of clawing into the wind, watch in and watch out. For if they were driven too far to the west, they would find it almost impossible to steer for Toulon should the enemy try to re-enter that harbour.

Keen pictured the chart in his mind. They were already at that point right now, another cross, a new set of bearings and the noon sights. With such poor visibility they could be miles off their estimated course.

Keen walked to the quarterdeck rail and stared along the maindeck. As usual it was busy despite the weather. Trigge the sailmaker with his assistants, squatting on the deck, their needles and palms moving intricately like parts of a mill as they repaired heavy-weather canvas brought up from below.

Trigge was experienced enough to know that if they entered the Atlantic in search of the enemy, every spare sail would be needed.

Sheargold the purser, his unsmiling features set in a permanently suspicious frown, was watching as some casks of salt-beef were hoisted through another hatch. Keen did not envy anyone in that trade. Sheargold had to plan for every league sailed, each delay or sudden change of orders which might send the ship in an opposite direction without time to restock his provisions.

Hardly anybody ever felt grateful to Sheargold. It was generally believed between decks that most pursers retired rich, having won their fortunes by scrimping on the sailors' meagre rations.

Major Adams was up forward, standing at an angle on the tilting deck while he studied a squad of marines being put through their paces. How bright the the scarlet coats and white cross belts looked in the dull light, Keen thought.

He heard the boatswain, Sam Lintott, discussing the new cutter with one of his mates. The latter was the villainous-looking one named Dacie. Keen had been told of his part in the cutting-out of the Spanish treasure-ship. He could believe all that he had heard. With his eye patch, and crooked shoulder, Dacie would frighten anybody.

Lieutenant Parris approached the rail and touched his hat.

'Permission to exercise the quarterdeck guns this afternoon, sir?'

Keen nodded. 'They will not thank you, Mr Parris, but I think it a good idea.'

Parris looked out to sea. 'Shall we meet the French, sir?'

Keen glanced at him. Outwardly easy and forthcoming with the sailors, there was something else within the man, something he was grappling with, even in casual conversation. Getting his

235

command? Keen did not know why he had lost it in the first place. He had heard about Haven's animosity towards him. Maybe there had been another superior officer with whom he had crossed swords.

He replied, 'Sir Richard is torn between the need to watch the approaches to Toulon, and the strong possibility we will be called to support the fleet.' He thought of Bolitho in the cabin, dictating letters to Yovell or his clerk, telling young Jenour what might be expected of him if they met with the enemy. Keen had already discussed the possibility with Bolitho.

Bolitho had seemed preoccupied. 'I do not have the time to call all my captains aboard. I must pray that they know me well enough to respond when I so order.'

I do not have the time. It was uncanny. Bolitho seemed to accept it, as if a battle was inevitable.

Parris said, 'I wonder if we shall see Viscount Somervell again.'

Keen stared at him. 'Why should that concern you?' He softened his tone and added, 'I would think he is better off away from us.'

Parris nodded. 'Yes, I – I'm sorry I mentioned it, sir.' He saw the doubt in Keen's eyes. 'It is nothing to do with Sir Richard's involvement.'

Keen looked away. 'I should hope not.' He was angry at Parris's interest. More so with himself for his instant rush of protectiveness. *Involvement.* What everybody was probably calling it.

Keen walked to the weather side and tried to empty his mind. He took a telescope from the midshipman-of-the-watch and steadied it on the ships astern.

The three seventy-fours were somehow managing to hold their positions. The fourth, Merrye's *Capricious*, was almost invisible in spray and blown spume. She was far astern of the others, while work was continued to replace the main topgallant mast which had carried away in a sudden squall before they could shorten sail.

He smiled. A captain's responsibility never ceased. The man who was seen by others as a kind of god, would nevertheless pace his cabin and fret about everything.

A lookout yelled, 'Deck there! *Tybalt* is signallin'!'

Keen looked at the midshipman. 'Up you go, Mr Furnival. *Tybalt* must have news for us.'

Later, Keen went down to the cabin and reported to Bolitho.

'*Tybalt* has the rest of the squadron in sight to the east'rd, Sir Richard.'

Bolitho glanced across his scattered papers and smiled. He looked and sounded tired.

'That is something, Val.' He gestured to a chair. 'I would ask you to join us, but you will need to be on deck until the ships are closer.'

As he left, Sir Piers Blachford said, 'A good man. I like him.' He was half-lying in one of Bolitho's chair. *The heron at rest.*

Yovell gathered up his letters and the notes he would add to his various copies.

Ozzard entered to collect the empty coffee cups, while Allday, standing just inside the adjoining door, was slowly polishing the magnificent presentation sword. Bolitho's gift from the people of Falmouth for his achievements in this same sea and the events which had led up to the Battle of the Nile.

Bolitho glanced up. 'Thank you, Ozzard.'

Blachford slapped one bony fist into his palm.

'Of course. I remember now. Ozzard is an unusual name, is it not?'

Allday's polishing cloth had stilled on the blade.

Blachford nodded, remembering. 'Your secretary and all the letters he has to copy must have brought it back to me. My people once used the services of a scrivener down by the London docks. Unusual.'

Bolitho looked at the letter which he might complete when the others had left him. He would share his feelings with Catherine. Tell her of his uncertainty about what lay ahead. It was like speaking with her. Like the moments when they had lain together, and she had encouraged him to talk, had shared those parts of his life which were still a mystery to her.

He replied, 'I've never asked him about it.'

But Blachford had not heard. 'I don't know how I could have forgotten it. I was directly involved. There was the most dastardly

237

murder done, almost opposite the scrivener's shop. How could one forget that?'

There was a crash of breaking crockery from the pantry and Bolitho half-rose from his chair.

But Allday said quickly, 'I'll go. He must have fallen over.'

Blachford picked up a book he had been reading and remarked, 'Not surprised in this sickening motion.'

Bolitho watched him, but there was nothing on his pointed face to suggest anything other than passing interest.

Bolitho had seen Allday's expression, had almost heard his unspoken warning.

Coincidence? There had been too many of those. Bolitho examined his feelings. *Do I want to know more?*

He stood up. 'I am going to take my walk.'

He could feel Blachford's eyes following him as he left the cabin.

It was not until the next day that Herrick's three ships were close enough to exchange signals.

Bolitho watched the flags soaring aloft, Jenour's unusual sharpness with the signals midshipmen, as if he understood the mood which was gripping his vice-admiral.

Bolitho held on to a stay and studied the new arrivals, the way they and his own seventy-fours lay about haphazardly under reduced canvas, as if they and not their captains were awaiting instructions.

The weather had not improved, and overnight had built the sea into a parade of steep swells. Bolitho covered his damaged eye with one hand. His skin was wet and hot, indeed like the fever which had brought him and Catherine together.

Keen crossed the slippery planking and stood beside him, his telescope tilted beneath his arm to keep the lens free of salt spray.

'The wind holds steady from the nor'-east, Sir Richard.'

'I know.' Bolitho tried not to listen to the clank of pumps. The old ship was working badly, and the pumps had continued all through the night watches. Thank God Keen knew his profession and the extent of his complete authority. Haven would have been flogging his luckless sailors by now, he thought bitterly. Hardly an hour had passed without the hands being piped aloft to make or shorten sail. Manning the pumps, lashing loose gear in the uncomfortable motion – it took patience as well as discipline to keep men from flying at each other's throats. The officers were not immune to it. Tempers flared out of all proportion if a lieutenant was just minutes late relieving his opposite number; he had heard Keen telling one of them to try and act up to the coat he wore. It was not easy for any of them.

Bolitho said, 'If it gets any worse we'll not be able to put down any boats.' He studied his scattered ships. *Waiting for his lead.* He saw *Benbow* swaying steeply as she hove-to, her sails billowing and cracking, shining in the filtered glare like buckled breastplates.

Herrick was coming to see him. Face-to-face. It was typical of him.

Herrick's barge had to make three attempts before the bowman could hook on to the main chains.

In the cabin the sounds faded, and only the sloping horizon, blurred by the thick glass of the stern windows, appeared to be swaying, as if to tip the weatherbeaten ships into a void.

Herrick got straight to the point.

'I wish to know what you intend.' He shook his head as Ozzard hovered nearby with a tray in his hand. 'No, but thank you.' To Bolitho he added, 'I'd not want to be marooned here, away from my flagship.' He glanced at the spray running down the glass. 'I don't like this at all.'

Bolitho said, 'No sign of *La Mouette*, Thomas?' He saw Herrick shake his head. 'I sent *Phaedra* to hunt for her.'

Herrick leaned forward in his chair. 'Captain Sinclair knows what he is about. He will find the squadron.'

Bolitho said, 'I will use every vessel which can scout for us. It was not a criticism.'

Herrick settled back again. 'I think we should stand towards Toulon. Then we shall know, one way or the other.'

Bolitho rested his hands on the table. He could feel the whole ship shivering through it, the rudder jerking against helm and wind.

'If the enemy intend to re-enter the Mediterranean, Thomas,

we could lose them just as easily as Nelson lost contact when they ran to the west.' He made up his mind. 'I intend to head for Gibraltar. If we still have no news we shall proceed through the Strait and join the fleet. I see no other choice.'

Herrick eyed him stubbornly. 'Or we can stay here and wait. No one can blame us. We shall certainly be damned if we miss the enemy when they break through to Toulon.'

'I would blame *myself*, Thomas. My head tells me one thing, instinct directs me otherwise.'

Herrick cocked his head to listen to the pumps. 'Is it that bad?'

'She will stand more of it.'

'I sent *Absolute* into harbour because she was too rotten.'

Bolitho retorted, 'I could use her too, rotten or not.'

Herrick stood up and walked to the stern windows. 'I should leave. I mean no disrespect, but my barge will have a hard pull as it is.'

Bolitho faced him. '*Listen to me*, Thomas. I don't care what you think about my private life, for private it is not apparently. I need your support, for fight we shall.' He clapped his hand to his heart. 'I know it.'

Herrick watched him as if seeking a trap. 'As your second-in-command I will be ready *if* we are called to battle. But I still believe you are misguided.'

Bolitho said despairingly, 'You are not listening, man! I am not commanding you, I am asking for your help!' He saw Herrick's astonishment as he exclaimed, 'In God's name, Thomas, must I plead? *I am going blind*, or did that piece of gossip rouse no interest amongst you?'

Herrick gasped, 'I had no idea –'

Bolitho looked away and shrugged. 'I will trouble you to keep it to yourself.' He swung round, his voice harsh. 'But if I fall, you must lead these men, you will make them perform miracles if need be – are you listening now?'

There was a tap at the door, and Bolitho shouted, '*Yes?*' His anguish tore the word from his throat.

Keen entered and glanced between them. 'Signal from *Phaedra*, sir, repeated by *Tybalt*.'

Herrick asked quickly, 'What of *La Mouette*?'

Keen was looking only at Bolitho. He guessed what had happened, and wanted to share it with him.

He answered abruptly, 'She is down.'

Bolitho met his gaze, grateful for the interruption. He had almost broken that time.

'News, Val?'

'There is an enemy squadron on the move, Sir Richard. Heading west.'

Herrick asked, 'How many?'

Still Keen avoided his eyes. '*Phaedra* has not yet reported. She is damaged after a stern-chase.' He took a step towards him, then let his arms fall to his sides. 'They are Spanish, Sir Richard. Sail of the line, that we do know.'

Bolitho ran his fingers through his hair and asked, 'How many ships does Nelson have?'

Keen looked at him, and then his eyes cleared with understanding.

'It was last reported as two dozen of the line, Sir Richard. The French and their Spanish ally are said to have over thirty, which will include some of the largest first-rates afloat.'

Bolitho listened to the moan of the wind. *Divide and conquer.* How well Villeneuve had planned it. And now with this new formation of ships, discovered only accidentally by *Phaedra*, Nelson's fleet would be overwhelmed and hopelessly outnumbered.

He said simply, 'If they slip through the Strait we may never catch them in time.' He looked at Keen. 'Signal *Phaedra* to close on the Flag.' He caught his arm as he made to leave. 'When that brave little ship draws close enough, spell out *well done*.'

When Keen left Herrick said with sudden determination, 'I am ready. Tell me what to do.'

Bolitho stared through the stained windows. 'Minimum signals, Thomas. As we discussed.'

'But your eyesight?' Herrick sounded wretched.

'Oh no, *not any more*, Thomas. Little *Phaedra* has lifted my blindness. But hear me. If my flag comes down, *Benbow* will take the van.'

Herrick nodded. 'Understood.'

Bolitho said, 'So hold back your conscience, my friend, and together we may yet win the day!'

He turned to look at the breaking wave-crests, and did not move until he heard the door shut.

Bolitho put his signature to his final letter and stared at it for several minutes.

The swell was as steep as before, but the wind had lessened, so that the hull seemed to rise and fall with a kind of ponderous majesty. He glanced at the quarter windows as a pale shaft of sunlight penetrated the sea-mist and showed up the salt stains on the glass like ice-rime. He hoped the sun would break through completely before the day ended. The air was heavy with damp; hammocks, clothing, everything.

He reread the last of the letter which *Phaedra* would carry to the fleet. He tried to picture Nelson eventually reading it, understanding as a sailor, better than any other, what Bolitho's ships and men were trying to do.

He had finished with, '*And I thank you, my lord, for offering my nephew, who is most dear to me, the same inspiration you have given to the whole fleet.*'

He pushed it aside for Yovell to seal and turned the other letter over in his fingers, while he imagined Catherine's dark eyes as she read the words, his declaration of love *which now can never die.* There would be many letters going in *Phaedra*. What would Herrick say to his Dulcie, he wondered? Their parting yesterday had left a bad taste. Once, such a thing would have seemed impossible. Maybe people did change, and he was the one who was mistaken.

Keen would have written to his Zenoria. It was a great comfort that she would be with Catherine. He stood up, suddenly chilled to the marrow despite the damp, humid air. *Nothing must happen to Val.* Not after what they had shared. The pain and the joy, the fulfilment of a dream which had been snatched from Keen and had left him like half a man. Until Zenoria. The girl with the moonlit eyes; another whose love had been forged from suffering.

Keen looked in. '*Phaedra*'s captain is come aboard, Sir Richard.'

Bolitho faced the door as Dunstan almost bounded into the cabin.

A young man of tireless energy, and certainly one of the scruffiest captains Bolitho had ever laid eyes on.

'It was good of you to come.' Bolitho held out his hand. 'I believe it was intended we should pass the despatches over by line and tackle.'

Dunstan beamed and looked around the cabin. 'I thought, damn the sea, Sir Richard. I'll go myself.'

Bolitho gestured to the letters. 'I place these in your hands. There is one for Lord Nelson. When you have run him to ground I would wish you to present it to him personally.' He gave a quick smile. 'It seems I am fated not to meet him in person!'

Dunstan took the letter and stared at it as if he expected it to look different from all the others.

Bolitho said, 'I am told that you had some casualties.'

'Aye, Sir Richard. Two killed, another pair cut down by splinters.'

For just a moment Bolitho saw the young man behind the guise of captain. The memory and the risks, the moment of truth when death sings in the air.

Dunstan added, 'I am only sorry I could not linger to estimate the full array of Spanish vessels.' He shrugged. 'But that damn frigate was at my coat-tails, and the mist hid many of the enemy.'

Bolitho did not press him. Keen would have laid all of his findings and calculations alongside his own on *Hyperion*'s charts.

Dunstan said, 'It struck me that war is an odd game, Sir Richard. It was just a small fight by today's standard, but how strange the contestants.'

Bolitho smiled. 'I know. A captured British frigate fighting under Spanish colours against a French prize beneath our own flag!'

Dunstan looked at him squarely. 'I would ask that you send another to seek out Lord Nelson. My place is here with you.'

Bolitho took his arm. 'I need the fleet to know what is happening, and my intention to prevent these ships of yours from joining with Villeneuve. It is vital. In any case I can spare nobody else.'

He shook his arms gently. '*Phaedra* has done enough. For me, and for us all. Remember that well and tell your people.'

Dunstan nodded, his eyes searching Bolitho's face as if he wanted to remember the moment.

He said, 'Then I shall leave, Sir Richard.' Impetuously he thrust out his hand. 'God be with you.'

For a long while afterwards Bolitho stood alone in the cabin, watching the sloop-of-war as she went about, her gunports awash as she took the wind into her courses and topsails.

He heard distant cheers, from *Phaedra* or the other ships he could not tell.

He sat down and massaged his eye, hating its deception.

Allday clumped into the cabin and regarded him dubiously.

'She's gone then, Sir Richard?'

'Aye.' Bolitho knew he must go on deck. The squadron was waiting. They must assume their proper formation long before dusk. He thought of his captains. How would they react? Perhaps they doubted his ability, or shared Herrick's opposition to his intentions.

Allday asked, 'So, it's important?'

'It could well be, old friend.' Bolitho looked at him fondly. 'If we head them off, they *must fight*. If they have already outrun us then we shall give chase.'

Allday nodded, his eyes faraway. 'Nothin' new then.'

Bolitho grinned, the tension slipping away like soft sand in a glass.

'No, nothing new! My God, Allday, they could do with you in Parliament!'

By the next morning the weather had changed yet again. The wind had veered and stood directly from the east. That at least put paid to any hope of beating back to Toulon.

The squadron, lying comfortably on the starboard tack, headed north-west with the Balearic Islands lying somewhere beyond the starboard bow.

Sixth in the line leading his own ships, Rear-Admiral Herrick had been up since dawn, unable to sleep, and unwilling to share his doubts with Captain Gossage.

244

He stood in one corner of *Benbow*'s broad quarterdeck and watched the ships ahead. They made a fine sight beneath an almost clear sky, broken only by fleecy patches of cloud. His face softened as he remembered his mother, in the little house where he had been born in Kent.

Watch the big sheep, Tommy! She had always said that.

Herrick looked around at the busy seamen, the first lieutenant in a close conversation with several warrant officers about today's work.

What would that dear, tired old lady think of her Tommy now?

Captain Gossage crossed the deck, his hat tilted at the jaunty angle which he seemed to favour.

Herrick did not wish to pass the time in idle conversation. Each turn of the log was taking his ships further westward. He felt uneasy, as if he had suddenly been stripped of his authority. He shaded his eyes to peer across the starboard nettings. Their one remaining frigate was far away from the squadron. *Tybalt* would be the first to sight any enemy shipping. He bit his lip until it hurt. If the enemy had not already slipped past them. Slamming a door after the horse had bolted.

Gossage remarked, 'I suppose that *Phaedra*'s captain was not mistaken, sir?'

Herrick glared. 'Well, somebody sunk *La Mouette*, he did not imagine that!'

Gossage grunted. 'Had we been relieved from the Maltese station we would have been at Gibraltar anyway, sir. Then our ships would have had the honour –'

Herrick snapped, 'Honour be damned! Sir Richard Bolitho is not the kind of man to seize glory for himself!'

Gossage raised his eyebrows, 'Oh, I see, sir.'

Herrick turned away, quietly fuming. *No, you don't.* Try as he might he could not tear his thoughts from the twenty-odd years that he had known Bolitho.

All the battles, some hard-won, others surprisingly kind to them. Bad wounds, old friends lost or maimed, sea-passages and landfalls when at times they had wondered if they might ever walk ashore again. Now it had gone rotten, thrown away because of –

Gossage tried again. 'My wife wrote to me and says that there is talk of Sir Richard being relieved.'

Herrick stared at him. Dulcie had said nothing of the kind. 'When?'

Gossage smiled. He had caught his admiral's attention at last. 'Next year, sir. The fleet will be reformed, the squadrons allocated differently. In this article she read –'

Herrick gave a cold grin. 'Bloody rubbish, man! Sir Richard and I have been hearing the bleats of shorebound experts all our lives. God damn it, the day we –'

The masthead yelled, 'Deck there! Signal from *Flag*!'

A dozen telescopes rose as one and the signals midshipman called, '*General*, sir! Have *Tybalt* in sight to the north!'

Gossage hissed to the officer-of-the-watch, 'Why in hell's name did they sight her first?'

Herrick smiled wryly. 'Acknowledge it.' To the first lieutenant he called, 'Send a good master's mate aloft, Mr O'Shea!'

The lieutenant turned as if to confirm the order with Gossage but Herrick snapped, 'Just do it!'

He moved away, his hands grasped behind his back. He had never got used to flag rank, nor had he expected it, no matter what flattering things Dulcie had said about the matter.

He knew he was being petty but he felt better for it. At heart he would always remain a captain and not leave it to others to carry out his plans.

All down the line of eight ships, the air would be buzzing with speculation. Herrick thought of the missing third-rate *Absolute*. He had done the right thing. One great gale like the last one, and that poor, rotten ship would surely have foundered.

Bolitho's refusal to accept his action still rankled deeply. He took his own telescope, the latest and most expensive one which Dulcie could find, and trained it on the ships astern. In perfect formation, their masthead pendants licking out like serpents' tongues, the sunlight glistening on the checkered patterns of gunports.

The new voice hailed from the masthead. '*Tybalt* in sight, sir!'

Herrick climbed up the starboard poop ladder and levelled his beautiful telescope. He could just make out the frigate's top-

246

gallant sails, like the fleecy clouds, pink-edged and delicate against the hard horizon. The edge of the sea, he thought. Deep, dark blue. Still no sign of rain. Perhaps Bolitho would decide after all to send some of the ships to seek fresh water.

He saw the tiny pin-pricks of colour rise against the frigate's pyramid of sails. Herrick blinked his eyes. His vision was not as good as it had been, although he would never admit it. He thought of Bolitho's expression, the anguish when he had revealed to him about his damaged eyesight.

It troubled Herrick for several reasons, not the least being that he had failed Bolitho when he had most needed him.

Herrick's flag lieutenant, a willowy young man called De Broux, called, 'From *Tybalt*, sir!'

Herrick waited impatiently. He had never really liked his flag lieutenant. He was soft. Even had a Frenchie-sounding name.

Unaware of Herrick's distaste De Broux said, '*Strange sail bearing north-east!*'

Several of the officers nearby chuckled amongst themselves and Herrick felt his face smart with anger, and embarrassment too for Bolitho.

Gossage said cheerfully, 'A strange sail, eh? Damn my eyes if I don't think that our eight *liners* can't take care of it, what?' He turned to his officers. 'We can leave *Tybalt* outside to act as umpire!'

Herrick said harshly, 'Hold your damn noise!' He spoke to the lieutenants. It was meant for Gossage.

'From *Flag*, sir. *General. Make more sail.*'

Herrick watched the acknowledgement dashing aloft.

Gossage, sulking slightly, called, 'Hands aloft, Mr O'Shea! Shake out all reefs!' His tone suggested it was merely to cover Bolitho's confusion.

Herrick raised the telescope and climbed up two more steps.

She had been so proud when she had bought it for him, from one of the best instrument makers in London's Strand. His heart sank. She had gone there with Belinda.

De Broux shouted suddenly, '*Tybalt* to *Flag*, sir!' For once he seemed unsure of himself. Then he stammered, '*Estimate twelve sail-of-the-line!*'

247

Herrick climbed down to the quarterdeck again. He was uncertain how he felt. Resigned, or stunned by the last signal.

Gossage was staring at him, and made to speak as De Broux called desperately, '*General signal*, sir. *Prepare for battle!*'

Herrick met Gossage's disbelief with something close to complete calm. To feel that way under such circumstances was almost unnerving.

Herrick asked coolly, 'Well, Captain Gossage, how do the odds appeal to you now?'

18

In Danger's Hour

Bolitho held out his arms and tried to contain his impatience as Ozzard nimbly buttoned his white waistcoat. After all the shortages it felt strange to be dressed from head to toe in clean clothing. Over Ozzard's shoulder he watched Keen, who was standing just inside the cabin so that he could still hear the shouted commands and replies from the quarterdeck.

Hyperion had not yet cleared for action; he would leave it to Herrick and the individual captains to do it when they were ready, and in their own time.

Hyperion's company were snatching a last hasty meal, although how the average sailor managed to eat anything before a fight was beyond Bolitho.

Keen said, 'If the Dons continue that approach, Sir Richard, neither of us will hold the wind-gage. It would seem that the enemy is on a converging tack.' His eyes were clouded with concentration as he tried to picture the distant ships. A day later and the enemy would have slipped past them to close with the coast of Spain before a final dash through the Strait.

Bolitho said, 'I must take the wind-gage from them. Otherwise, ship-to-ship they will swamp us.' He could feel Keen watching him as the plan formed itself so that they could both see it. As if it was here and now. 'We shall hold our forces together until the last moment. I intend to alter course to starboard and form two columns. Herrick knows what to do. His will be the shorter line, but no matter. Once battle is joined we may throw

249

the Dons into confusion.' He allowed Ozzard to offer him his coat and hat.

Keen said, 'I must protest, Sir Richard.' He looked at the gold lace, the Nile medal which Bolitho would hang about his neck. 'I know your custom. I have shared this suspense too many times to forget.'

Allday entered by the other door and reached up for the old sword. Over his shoulder he remarked, 'You're wastin' your time, with all respect, Cap'n Keen.'

Keen and Allday looked at one another. Allday recalled better than any how he had seen Bolitho on board the embattled *Phalarope* at the Saintes. In his best uniform, a ripe target for any sharp-eyed marksman, *so that the people should see him*. Oh yes, Allday knew it was impossible to talk him out of it.

Bolitho slipped his arms into the coat and waited for Ozzard to stand on tip-toe to adjust the bright epaulettes with the twin silver stars.

'This will not be a battle to test each other's mettle, Val. We must not even consider losing it. It is vital; you accept that now.'

Keen smiled sadly. 'I know it.'

There was a muffled hail from the masthead, and a lieutenant came running from the quarterdeck.

He stared at Bolitho and then said, 'The first lieutenant's respects, sir.' He tore his eyes from his vice-admiral and faced Keen. 'The mainmast lookout has just reported the enemy in sight. Steering south-west.'

Keen glanced at Bolitho, who nodded, then said, 'General signal. Enemy in sight.'

As the lieutenant hurried away Keen said, 'Brief and to the point. As you like it, Sir Richard.'

Bolitho smiled, and beckoned to Ozzard. 'You may clear the cabin. The bosun's party is waiting to carry the bits and pieces to the hold.' He rested his hand on Ozzard's bony shoulder. 'Go with them. No heroics today.' He saw his wistful gaze and added, 'I know not what ails you, but I will deal with it. Remember that, eh?'

As Ozzard made to pick up some small items Bolitho called, '*No!* Not that!' He took the fan from Ozzard's hand and looked at it. Remembering.

Keen watched as Bolitho slipped the fan into his coat-pocket.

Bolitho reached for his hat. 'A small thing, I know, Val. But it is all I have of hers.'

Allday followed them from the cabin, then he paused, the old sword over one arm as he stared back at the place he knew so well. Why should this time be any different? The odds were bad, but that was nothing new, and the enemy were Dons. Allday felt he wanted to spit. Even the Frogs were better fighters than them. He took a last glance round, then touched his chest where the Spanish blade had thrust into him.

The cabin was deserted. He turned away, angry with the thought. For it looked as if it would remain empty forever.

On deck Bolitho walked to the centre of the quarterdeck rail and took a telescope from the senior midshipman. He looked at him more closely, then at the other officers and master's mates near the wheel. Everyone appeared to be dressed in his best clothing.

Bolitho smiled at the midshipman. 'That was nicely done, Mr Furnival.'

He raised the glass and found *Tybalt*'s sails almost immediately. He moved it still further and saw the dark flaws on the horizon, like the rippling edge of some distant tidal wave.

Bolitho returned the glass and looked up at the sky. The pendant was still pointing towards the larboard bow. The wind held steady, but not too strong. He recalled something his father had said. *A good wind for a fight.* But out here that could easily change, if the mood took it.

Keen stood watching him, his fair hair ruffling beneath the brim of his hat, even though it had been cut in the modern fashion. Bolitho gripped the rail with both hands. *Like Adam's.*

He felt the old wood, hot in the sunshine. So dented and pitted with the years, yet worn smooth by all the hands which had rested here.

He watched Major Adams with his lieutenant, Veales, standing below the quarterdeck. The major was frowning with concentration as he pulled on a fresh pair of white gloves.

Bolitho said, 'It is time.' He saw Keen nod, the lieutenants glance at one another, probably wondering who might still be here when the smoke cleared.

Keen said, 'The wind is firm, Sir Richard. They'll be up to us before noon.'

Penhaligon remarked indifferently, 'Fine day for it anyway.'

Bolitho drew Keen to one side. 'I have to say something, Val. We must clear for action directly; after that we shall be divided by our duties. You have come to mean a great deal to me, and I think you must know it.'

Keen answered quietly, 'I understand what you are trying to say, Sir Richard. But it will not happen.'

Bolitho gripped his arm tightly. 'Val, Val, how can we know? It will be a hard fight, maybe the worst we have endured.' He gestured towards the ships astern. '*All these men* following like helpless animals, trusting the Flag to carry them through, no matter what hell awaits them.'

Keen replied earnestly, 'They will be looking to you.'

Bolitho gave a quick smile. 'It makes it less easy to bear. And you, Val, what must you be thinking as the Dons draw to an embrace? That but for me you would be at home with your lovely Zenoria.'

Keen waited while Allday stepped up with the sword.

Then he said simply, 'If I never lived beyond this day I have still known true happiness. Nothing can take that away.'

Allday clipped on the old sword and loosened it in its scabbard.

He said gruffly, 'Amen to that, I says, Cap'n.'

Bolitho looked at both of them. 'Very well. Have the marines beat to quarters.' He touched his pocket and felt the fan inside. Her presence. 'You may clear for action, Captain Keen!'

They faced each other, and Keen formally touched his hat.

He smiled, but it did not reach his eyes. 'So be it.'

The stark rattle of drums, the rush of feet from every hatch and along both gangways made further speech impossible. Bolitho watched the gun crews throwing themselves around their charges, topmen swarming aloft to rig the slings and nets, ready to whip or splice their repairs even in the carnage of a broadside.

Jenour appeared on deck, his hat tugged well down on his forehead, the beautiful sword slapping against his hip. He looked stern, and somehow older.

252

As the ship fell silent once more, Parris strode aft and faced up to the captain. He wore a pair of fine hessian boots.

'Cleared for action, sir. Galley fire doused. Pumps manned.'

Keen did not take out his watch but said, 'Nine minutes, Mr Parris. The best yet.'

Bolitho smiled. Whether it was true or not, those who had heard Keen's praise would pass it on to each deck. It was little enough. But it all helped.

Keen came aft. 'Ready, Sir Richard.'

Bolitho saw him hesitate and asked, 'What is it, Val?'

'I was wondering, Sir Richard. Could we have the fifers strike up? Like we did in *Tempest*?'

Bolitho looked at the sea, the memory linking them once again. 'Aye, make it so.'

And as the old *Hyperion* leaned over to the same starboard tack, and while the edge of the horizon broke into more silhouettes and mastheads, the Royal Marine fifers struck up a lively march. Accompanied by the drums from the poop, and the seamen's bare feet stamping on the sanded planking, they strode up and down as if they were on parade at their barracks.

Bolitho met Keen's glance and nodded. *Portsmouth Lass*. It was even the same tune.

Bolitho raised his telescope and slowly examined the Spanish line from end to end. The two rearmost ships were well out of formation, and Bolitho suspected that the very end vessel was standing away so that the other one could complete some repairs as *Olympus* had done.

He shifted his gaze to the solitary frigate. It was easy to see why *La Mouette*'s captain had been deceived. It took much more than a foreign ensign to disguise an English-built frigate.

He knew that *Consort* had been launched on the Medway, near Herrick's home. Would he be thinking of that now, he wondered?

Twelve sail-of-the-line. The flagship in the van had already been identified by Parris, who had met with her before. She was the ninety-gun *San Mateo*, flagship of Almirante Don Alberto Casares, who had commanded the Spanish squadrons at Havana.

253

Casares would know all about *Hyperion*'s part in the attack on Puerto Cabello. Some of these very ships had probably been intended to escort the treasure galleons to Spain.

Bolitho watched the *Intrépido*. At least the two squadrons had something in common, two frigates between them.

He heard Parris saying to the signals midshipmen, 'It will be a while yet.'

Bolitho glanced at the two youths, who could barely drag their eyes from the enemy. How much worse for anyone who had never faced a line of battle, he thought. It could take hours to draw together. At the Saintes it had taken all day. First the few mastheads topping the horizon, then they had risen and grown until the sea's face had seemed to be covered.

A lieutenant who had written home after the Saintes had described the French fleet as 'rising above the horizon, like the armoured knights at Agincourt'. It had been a fair description.

Bolitho walked forward to the rail and looked along the maindeck. The men were ready; the gun captains had selected the best-fashioned balls and grape for the first, double-shotted broadside. This time they would need to fight both sides of the ship at once, so there would be no extra hands to spare. They had to break through the line – after that, it was every ship for herself.

The Royal Marines were in the fighting tops, the best marksmen Major Adams could find, with some others to man the vicious swivels. The bulk of the marines lined the poop, not yet standing to the packed hammock nettings to mark down their targets, but waiting in gently swaying ranks, Sergeant Embree and his corporals talking to each other without appearing to move their mouths.

Penhaligon and his master's mates were near the wheel, with two extra hands at the helm in case of casualties.

Apart from the sea noises and the occasional slap of the great driver sail above the poop, it seemed quiet after the fifers had stopped playing. Bolitho raised his glass yet again and saw a seaman turn from a maindeck eighteen-pounder to watch him.

The enemy flagship was much nearer. He could see the glint of sunlight on swords and fixed bayonets, men swarming up the

254

ratlines of her foremast, others rising from their guns to watch the approaching squadron.

The Spanish admiral might expect his opposite number to fight ship-to-ship. His ninety guns against this old third-rate. Bolitho smiled grimly. It would even be unwise to cross *San Mateo*'s ornate stern in the first stage of the engagement. To be crippled breaking the line would throw the following ships into disorder, and Herrick would be left to attack on his own with just three ships.

Bolitho said, 'Signal *Tybalt* to take station astern of *Olympus*. It might add some weight to Herrick's line.' He heard the flags rushing aloft but continued to watch the big Spanish flagship.

Keen must have read his thoughts. 'May I suggest we break the line astern of the third or fourth ship, as it may present itself?'

Bolitho smiled. 'The further away from that beauty the better. Until we have lessened the odds anyway.'

Jenour was standing near the signals party and heard Bolitho's casual comment. Was it all a bluff, or did he really believe he could win against so many? Jenour tried to concentrate on his parents, how he would word his next letter. His mind reeled when he realised that the concept eluded him. Perhaps there would *be* no more letters. He felt a sudden terror and stared up at the wispy clouds directly above Bolitho's flag at the foremast truck. *He was going to be killed.*

Midshipman Springett, who was the youngest in the ship, appeared on deck. His station was on the lower gundeck, to relay messages back and forth to the poop. In the bright sunlight he had to blink several times after the gloom of the sealed gundeck.

Bolitho saw the boy turn, watched his expression as he gazed at the enemy ships, seeing them probably for the first time.

For those few moments his uniform and the proud, glinting dirk at his belt meant nothing. He drove his knuckles into his mouth as if to hold back a cry of fear. He was a child again.

Jenour must have seen him, and strode across. 'Mr Springett, isn't it? I could do with you assisting me today.' He gestured to the two signals midshipmen, Furnival, the senior, and Mirrielees, who had red hair and a face covered with freckles. 'These *old men* are getting past it, I fear!' The two in question grinned and nudged one another as if it were all a huge joke.

The boy stared at them. Mesmerised. He whispered, 'Thank you, sir.' He held out a paper. 'Mr Mansforth's respects, sir.' He turned and trotted back to the ladder without once looking at the imposing ranks of sails.

Keen said quietly, 'Your flag lieutenant just about saved that lad from bursting into tears.'

Bolitho watched more flags rising and dipping above the *San Mateo*. To himself he said, 'And it saved Stephen Jenour, I suspect.'

Even across the expanse of glistening swell you could hear the slow rumble of gun trucks, while something like a sigh came from the waiting sailors as shadows painted the *San Mateo*'s tall side. All her larboard battery had been run out. It was like looking into the mouth of every one of them.

Bolitho heard the blare of a trumpet, and pictured the enemy gun crews at their quarters. Eyes peering over the muzzles, the next shots and charges already to hand.

'Hoist *Benbow*'s number.' Bolitho took Keen aside as the flags were swiftly bent on to the halliards. 'I dare not wait too much longer, Val.' They both stared at the converging lines of ships, like one great arrowhead which must soon meet at some invisible westerly point.

There was a dull bang and Bolitho saw a puff of smoke drifting away from *San Mateo*'s side. The ball hit the sea, rebounded and smacked down, flinging a ragged waterspout half a cable clear. A ranging shot? Or was it merely to raise the spirits of the Spanish seamen who had been sharing the same agony of suspense as *Hyperion*'s?

'*Benbow*'s acknowledged, sir!'

Make the signals as few as possible. Bolitho had always believed it a good idea in principle. It was not difficult for an enemy to guess or determine the next move from another's signals. It was likely too that the prize, *Intrépido*, had been captured with some secret signals still intact.

When poor Captain Price had run his ship aground he could never have visualised any of this.

Bolitho looked at Keen and his first lieutenant. 'We will alter course in succession. *Hyperion* and *Benbow* will lead the two divisions.' He saw them nod; Parris was watching his lips as if to read what he had not said.

'It will be as close to the wind as she can lie, so it will reduce our progress.' He saw their understanding. It might also mean that it would give the enemy more time to traverse his guns. Bolitho walked to the starboard side and stood on the truck of a quarterdeck nine-pounder, his hand gripping the bare shoulder of one of its crew.

He could see *Benbow*'s masts beyond the others astern, Herrick's flag rippling out from the mizzen. *Benbow* was still flying her acknowledgement, just as *Hyperion* had kept her number hoisted close-up. Like a trumpet signalling a cavalry charge into the jaws of hell. A charge which cannot be halted once it has been urged to attack. Bolitho felt the man's shoulder tense as he turned to stare up at him. Bolitho looked at him. About eighteen. The sort of face you saw around the farms and lanes of Cornwall. But not in times of war.

He said, 'Naylor, am I right?'

The youth grinned while his mates winked at each other. 'Aye, Sir Richard!'

Bolitho kept his eyes on him, thinking of the terrified midshipman, and Jenour, who was more frightened of showing fear than of fear itself.

'Well, Naylor, there is our enemy. What say you?'

Naylor stared at the nearest ships with their trailing banners and curling pendants, some of which almost touched the water. 'I reckon we can take 'em.' He nodded, satisfied. 'We can clear the way for t'others, Sir Richard!'

Some of the gun crews cheered and Bolitho climbed down, afraid that his eye might choose this moment to betray him.

Just an ordinary sailor, who if he survived today, would likely end in another battle before he was a year older.

He thought suddenly of the grand London house, and Belinda's scathing words to him.

He nodded to the bare-backed seaman called Naylor. 'So we shall!' He turned quickly. 'Captain Keen!' Again, time seemed to stop for both of them. Then Bolitho said in a more level tone,

'Alter course three points to starboard, steer nor'-by-west!' He waved to Jenour. '*Now! Execute!*'

Every man in Herrick's flagship must have been poised for the moment. For as the flags were hauled down *Benbow* appeared to swing immediately out of the line, as if she, and she alone, was mounting a solitary attack on the enemy.

Keen watched closely, as pursued by Parris's speaking trumpet the scrambling seamen hauled on the braces, while others freed the big maincourse even as the yards creaked round.

Penhaligon spread his legs while the deck leaned to larboard, as the wind explored the braced sails and thrust the ship over.

Then Keen was at the compass, although Bolitho had not seen him move.

'*Meet her!* Steady as you go!'

The sails boomed and thundered in protest, and the driver rippled from peak to foot as if it was about to tear apart. She could stand no closer to the wind, and from the Spanish line it must appear as if all her sails were overlapping fore-and-aft.

Bolitho clutched the rail and stared at the enemy. Someone was firing, but the nets rigged above the maindeck gunners, and the huge billowing maincourse hid the flashes.

Bolitho saw *Benbow* drawing level abeam, barely three cables away. The others astern of her were already following round, with *Tybalt* tacking wildly to take station as the last of the line.

Keen exclaimed, 'The Dons are taken aback, by God!'

Bolitho looked at the Spanish flagship. Now she seemed to be heading away from *Hyperion*'s larboard bow, two others still following her as before.

Bolitho shouted, 'Load and run out, Captain Keen!'

The order was repeated to the deck below, and it seemed barely a minute had passed before each gun captain was faced aft, his fist above his head.

'All loaded, sir!'

'Open the ports! Run out!'

Squeaking noisily, the guns were hauled up to their ports. On the lee side the sea appeared to be curling up to the black muzzles as if to drive them inboard again.

Hyperion's deck shivered violently as the nearest enemy ships opened fire. But the two small divisions had taken the Spanish admiral by surprise, and most of his guns could not be brought to bear. Several tall waterspouts shot above the gangways, and Bolitho felt the tell-tale crash of a ball hitting *Hyperion*'s lower hull.

'Brail up the courses!'

Shots whimpered overhead, and the gun crews crouched even lower, their faces running with sweat as each group peered through their open port, waiting for a target.

As the forecourse was brailed up the scene opened on either bow as if a giant curtain had been raised.

Bolitho heard one of the midshipmen gasp with alarm as the stern of the nearest Spaniard appeared from nowhere, or from the depths – her high, ornate gallery, stabbing musket fire from above, and her name, *Castor*, reflecting the spray beneath her counter.

'Stand by to larboard!' Lovering, the second lieutenant, was striding inboard from the first division of guns. 'As you bear!'

Keen raised his sword, then sliced it down. '*Fire!*'

The larboard carronade on the forecastle hurled its huge ball into *Castor*'s stern with terrible effect. Bolitho heard the roar of its explosion within the other ship's hull, could imagine the scything horror of the packed grape as it swept through the ship. Cleared for action, any man-of-war was most vulnerable when an enemy was able to cross her stern.

The ship on the other side was looming through the smoke, her guns shooting out vivid orange tongues.

'*Fire!*'

Bolitho was deafened by the roar of guns as both sides vanished in swirling smoke and charred fragments from the charges. The ship to starboard was already being engaged by *Obdurate*, and Bolitho could see just her mastheads rising above the dense smoke like lances. He felt the deck jar again and again, Parris yelling, 'On the uproll, lads!' Then the next division fired as one, and Bolitho saw the *Castor*'s mizzen mast topple, suspended momentarily in the rigging and stays before going over the side with a sound like thunder.

'*Fire!*'

259

Keen strode across the quarterdeck, his eyes streaming, as the upper battery recoiled singly and in pairs on their tackles, the crews leaping forward with sponges and rammers, ready to tamp home the next ball. To do what they had been taught, to keep on firing no matter what was happening about them.

Jenour coughed in the smoke, then shouted, '*Obdurate* is in collision with a Spaniard, Sir Richard!' He winced as a musket ball slammed into the deck nearby and added, 'She requests assistance!'

Bolitho shook his head.

Keen said tersely, '*Inability!*'

The flags bearing Keen's curt signal lifted and vanished into a great pall of smoke which came surging inboard as the lower battery roared out to starboard.

Parris shouted, 'We're through, we're through!' He waved his hat wildly. 'Huzza, lads! *We've broken the line!*'

More sails loomed like giant ghosts astern. *Crusader*, and *Redoubtable*, the latter almost colliding with another Spaniard which had either lost her steering or had her helmsmen shot down.

'Stand by to alter course to larboard!' Bolitho tossed his telescope to one of the midshipmen. 'I don't need this now!' He could feel his lips set in a grin.

'Deck there!' Someone up there above the smoke and shrieking iron was keeping his head. '*Benbow*'s through the line!'

There were more wild cheers and coughs as the larboard battery fired a full broadside through the smoke, some into the *Castor*'s side, while the rest fell on and around the second ship in the enemy column.

'Lay her on the larboard tack, Mr Penhaligon! Afterguard, man the mizzen braces there!' Selected marines put down their muskets and ran to help, while some of their comrades squinted above the hammocks, their weapons cradled to their cheeks, seeking a target.

Bolitho looked up and saw lengths of severed cordage dangling on the protective nets, while above it all there was still the same peaceful sky.

A ball slammed into the larboard side, and crashed amongst

the men by one of the forward eighteen-pounders. Bolitho gritted his teeth as two were smashed to bloody ribbons, and another rolled across the deck, his leg held on by a thread of skin.

He tried to concentrate. All his ships must be engaged now. The roar of battle seemed to roll all around, as if vessels were on every hand, masked from each other by their own smoke. Sharper gunfire, like the staccato beat of drums, echoed over the water, as if it were another part of destiny.

Bolitho shouted, '*General signal. Close on the Flag. Reform line of battle!*'

How they could work with their flags was a miracle, Bolitho thought.

'All acknowledged, Sir Richard!' Jenour tried to grin. 'I think!'

'No matter!' Bolitho strode to the rail as he saw a Spanish two-decker standing out from the others as she made more sail. Her captain either wished to rejoin his own flagship, or he had increased sail to avoid hitting the crippled *Castor*.

Bolitho pointed, 'There, Val! Engage her!'

Keen yelled, 'Stand by to starboard!'

The newcomer seemed to gather speed as the distance fell away, but Bolitho knew it was the illusion made by smoke. He watched the Spaniard changing tack so that she would cross *Hyperion*'s bowsprit; he could see the scarlet and gold banner of Spain, the huge cross on her forecourse.

Keen's sword rose in the air. '*As you bear!*'

The other ship fired almost at the same time. Iron and wooden splinters flew across the maindeck, while overhead the sails flailed and kicked, shot through so many times that some could not hold a cupful of wind. Bolitho wiped his face and saw the other ship's foremast going down in the smoke, rigging and pieces of canvas vanishing into bursting spray alongside.

But he could ignore even that. *Hyperion* had been badly wounded. He had felt part of the enemy's broadside crash into the lower hull with the weight of a falling cliff.

He made to cross the deck but something held his shoe. He looked down and saw it was the young seaman, Naylor. He was lying against his upended gun, and was trying to speak, his face creased with pain, and the effort to find words.

Keen called, 'Over here, Sir Richard! I think we may –' He stopped, his feet slipping on blood as he saw Bolitho drop to his knee beside the dying seaman.

Bolitho took the youth's hand. The Spaniards must have used extra grape in their broadside. Naylor had lost half of his leg, and there was a hole in his side big enough for a fist.

'Easy, Naylor.' Bolitho held his hand tightly as the deck seemed to leap beneath him. He was needed, probably urgently. Around them the battle raged without let-up. Obeying his instruction. *No matter what.*

The seaman gasped, 'I – I think I'm dyin', sir!' There were tears in his eyes. He seemed oblivious to his blood, which poured unchecked into the scuppers. It was as if he was puzzled by what was happening. He almost prized his broken body away from the gun, and Bolitho felt a sudden strength in his grip.

The youth asked, 'Why me, sir?' He fell back, blood making a thin line from a corner of his mouth. '*Why me?*'

Keen waited while Bolitho released his hand and let it fall to the deck.

Keen said, '*Capricious* is in support, Sir Richard! But there is another Don breaking through yonder!' He stared at his own raised arm. There was a strip torn from his sleeve. Yet he had not even felt the ball hiss past.

Bolitho hurried to the side and saw the second ship already overhauling the one which had fired the last broadside.

Bolitho nodded. 'Trying to join her admiral.'

Keen waved his hand. 'Mr Quayle! Pass word to the lower battery! We will engage this one immediately!'

The fourth lieutenant was no longer pouting disdainfully. He was almost beside himself with terror.

Keen turned. 'Mr Furnival!' But the midshipman had fallen too, while his companion stood rigidly beside Jenour, his eyes on the flags where his dead friend lay as if resting from the heat of battle.

Bolitho snapped, 'Get below, Mr Quayle! That is an order!'

Keen dashed the hair from his forehead and realised that his hat had been plucked away.

'God damn,' he said.

'*Ready*, sir!'

Keen sliced down with his sword. '*Fire!*'

Gun by gun the broadside painted the heaving water between the ships in the colours of the rainbow. It was possible to hear *Hyperion*'s weight of iron as it crashed into the other ship's side, smashing down men and guns in a merciless bombardment.

The smoke swirled away in a rising breeze and Keen exclaimed, 'She'll be into us! Her rudder's shot away!'

Bolitho heard a splash and when he turned his head he saw some of the boatswain's party hurrying from the upended gun. Naylor's corpse had gone over the side. There was only blood left to mark where he had fought and died.

Bolitho could still hear his voice. *Why me?* There were many more who would ask that question.

He saw Allday with a bared cutlass in his fist, watching the oncoming Spaniard with a cold stare.

Parris yelled, 'Stand by to repel boarders!'

Major Adams went bustling forward, as the other ship's tapering jib-boom rose through the smoke and locked into *Hyperion*'s bowsprit with a shudder which made even the gun crews pause at their work.

Keen shouted, '*Continue firing!*'

Hyperion's lower battery of thirty-two pounders fired relentlessly across the littered triangle of smoky water. Again, and yet once more, before the enemy's jib-boom shattered to fragments and with a great lurch she began to sidle alongside, until the gun muzzles of both friend and enemy clashed together.

Muskets cracked from the tops and a dozen different directions. Men dropped at their guns, or collapsed as they ran to hack away fallen rigging and blocks.

The swivels barked out from *Hyperion*'s maintop, and Bolitho saw a crowd of Spanish sailors blasted away even as they swung precariously across the boarding nets.

Keen shouted, 'We've lost steerage way, Sir Richard! We'll have to fight free of this one, and I think the other two-decker is snared into *her*!'

'Clear the lower battery, Val. Seal the ports! I want every spare hand up here!'

They dared not fire into the ship alongside now. They were locked together. It only needed one flaming wad from a gun to turn both ships into an inferno.

The seamen from the lower battery, their half-naked bodies blackened by the trapped smoke, surged up to join Major Adams's men as they charged to meet the attack.

Keen tossed his scabbard aside and tested the balance of his sword in his hand. He stared around in the drifting smoke, picking out his lieutenants amongst the darting figures. 'Where's my bloody coxswain?' Then he gave a quick grin as Tojohns ran to join him, his cutlass held high to avoid the other hurrying seamen.

'Here, sir!' He glanced at Allday. 'Ready when you are, sir!'

Keen's eyes settled on Parris by the rail. 'Stay here. Hold the quarterdeck.' Just the flicker of a glance towards Bolitho. It was as if they had clasped hands.

Then he too was up and running along the starboard gangway, as the enemy clambered aboard, or fired down from their own ship. Lieutenant Lovering pointed with his hanger and yelled, 'To the fo'c'stle, lads!' Then he fell, the hanger dangling from his wrist as an unseen marksman found his victim.

Dacie the one-eyed boatswain's mate was already there on the beakhead, swinging a boarding axe with terrible effect, cutting down three of the enemy before some of Adams's marines jumped down to join him, their bayonets licking through the nets, hurling aside the men caught there like flies in a web.

The swivels in the maintop banged out again, and some of Spanish sailors about to join the first boarders were scattered in a deadly hail of canister. Those already aboard *Hyperion* fell back, one throwing away his cutlass as the marines cornered him on the forecastle, but it was already too late for quarter. Gunsmoke drifted over the deck and when it cleared, there were only corpses as the jubilant marines fought their way across to the other ship's deck.

Jenour stood close beside Bolitho, his sword drawn, his face like one already dead. He shouted, 'Two of the Dons have struck, Sir Richard!'

Despite the clash of steel and the sporadic bang of muskets, there were faint cheers from another ship, and Bolitho imagined he could hear drums and fifes.

He climbed up the poop ladder and rubbed his eyes before peering through the enveloping smoke. He could just make out *Obdurate*, now completely dismasted and lashed alongside the Spanish two-decker she had collided with. A British ensign flew above the other vessel's deck, and Bolitho guessed it was Captain Thynne's men who were cheering.

Then he saw *Benbow*, pushing past another crippled Spaniard, pouring a slow broadside into her as she moved by. Masts toppled like felled trees, and Bolitho saw Herrick's flag curling above the smoke, so bright in the mocking sunlight.

He thought wildly, *Hyperion* had cleared the way, just as Naylor had promised she would.

Allday shouted, 'Here, watch out!'

Bolitho turned and saw a group of Spanish seamen clamber up over the starboard gangway, slashing aside the nets before anyone had noticed them. They must have climbed from the main chains; they could have been creatures from the sea itself.

Bolitho drew his sword, and saw some of Adams's red-coated marines already hacking their way aft on the other ship. These boarders had no chance at all. Their own vessel would have to strike unless the other two-decker could come to her aid. But another broadside hurled smoke and debris high in the air and even on to *Hyperion*'s maindeck, as one of Bolitho's squadron, probably *Crusader*, raked her from stern to bow.

There was a lieutenant leading the small group, and as he saw Bolitho he brandished his sword and charged to the attack.

Jenour stood his ground, but the Spaniard was a fine swordsman. He parried the blue blade aside as if it was a reed, twisted it with his hilt and sent it flying. He drew back to balance himself for a last thrust, then stared with horror at the boarding pike which lunged up through the quarterdeck ladder. The seaman gave an insane yell, tugged the pike free and drove it into the lieutenant's stomach.

Bolitho faced another Spaniard who was armed only with a heavy cutlass.

Bolitho yelled, 'Surrender, *damn you*!'

265

But whether he understood or not the seaman showed no sign of giving in. The wide blade swung in a bright arc and Bolitho stepped aside easily, then almost fell as a shaft of sunlight probed through the smoke haze and touched his injured eye. It was like that other time. Like being struck blind.

He felt himself swaying, the old sword held straight out, pointing uselessly at nothing.

Parris yelled, '*Stop that man!*' Bolitho could only guess what was happening, and waited for the searing agony of the cutlass he could not see. Someone was screaming, and occasional yells told Bolitho that more of Keen's men were running to vanquish the last of the attackers.

Allday sliced his blade at an angle, his mind numb as he saw the other man lunging towards Bolitho, who was apparently unable to move. The blade took the man on one side of his head, a glancing blow, but it had Allday's strength and memory behind it. As he pivoted round, squinting into the sudden glare, he saw Allday looming towards him.

Jenour heard the next blow even as he scrabbled in the blood-stained scuppers to retrieve his sword. Parris, who was sobbing with pain from a slash across his wounded shoulder, saw the cutlass hit the Spaniard on the forearm; could only stare as the arm, complete with cutlass, clattered across the deck.

Allday spat, 'An' this is for *me*, matey!' He silenced the man's scream with one final blow across the neck.

He grasped Bolitho's arm. 'You all right, Sir Richard?'

Bolitho took several deep breaths. His lungs felt as if they were filled with fire; he could barely breathe.

'Yes. Yes, old friend. The sun. . . .'

He looked for Jenour. 'You have true courage, Stephen!'

Then he saw Jenour's features change yet again and thought for an instant he had already been wounded. There were wild cheers from the ship snared alongside by a tangle of fallen rigging, but as a freak gust of wind drove the smoke away Bolitho knew the reason for Jenour's stunned look of dismay.

He turned, covering his left eye with his hand, and felt his body cringe.

The Spanish admiral's flagship *San Mateo* had stayed clear of the close-action, or maybe it had taken her this long to put about. She seemed to shine above her own tall reflection; there was not a scar or a stain on her hull or a shot hole in her elegant sails. She was moving very slowly, and Bolitho's mind recorded that there were many men aloft on her yards. She was preparing to change tack again. Away from the battle.

Bolitho could feel his limbs quivering, as if they would never stop. He heard Parris shout, 'In Christ's name! She's going to fire!'

San Mateo had run out every gun, and at the range of some fifty yards could not miss with any of them, even though two of her own consorts lay directly in the path of her broadside.

Bolitho's mind refused to clear. It was *Hyperion* they wanted. The defiant ship with his flag still at the fore which had somehow broken their line, and inspired the others to follow. He looked at Allday but he was staring at the enemy flagship, his cutlass hanging loosely from his fist.

Together. Even now.

Then the flagship fired. The sound was deafening, and as the weight of the broadside smashed into the drifting *Hyperion*, Bolitho felt the deck rear up as if the ship was sharing their agony.

He was thrown to the side of the quarterdeck, his ears deaf to the thundering roar of falling spars, of men crying and screaming before the torn rigging dragged them over the side like corpses in a huge net.

Bolitho crawled to Midshipman Mirrielees and dragged at his shoulder to turn him on to his back. His eyes were shut tight, and there was moisture like tears beneath the lids. He was dead. He saw Allday crouching on his knees, his mouth wide as he sucked in the air. Their eyes met and Allday tried to grin.

Bolitho felt someone pulling him to his feet, his eyes blinded again by the sunlight as it laid bare the destruction.

Then the smoke drifted lower and hid *San Mateo* from view.

19

The Last Farewell

Sir Piers Blachford steadied himself against the makeshift table while the guns thundered out yet again and shook the whole ship. He wiped his streaming face and said, 'Take this man away. He's dead.'

The surgeon's assistants seized the naked corpse and dragged it away into the shadows of the orlop deck.

Blachford reached up and felt the massive beam by his head. If there was really a hell, he thought, it must surely look like this.

The swinging lanterns which dangled above the table made it worse, if that were possible, casting shadows up the curved sides of the hull one moment, and laying bare the huddled or inert shapes of the wounded who were being brought down to the orlop with hardly a let-up.

He looked at his companion, George Minchin, *Hyperion*'s own surgeon, a coarse-faced man with sprouting grey hair. His eyes were red-rimmed, and not only from fatigue. There was a huge jug of rum beside the table, to help ease the agony or the passing moments of the pitiful wounded who were brought to the table, stripped, then held like victims under torture until the work was done. Minchin seemed to drink more than his share.

Blachford had seen the most terrible wounds. Men without limbs, with their faces and bodies burned, or clawed by flaying splinters. The whole place, which was normally the midshipmen's berth, where they slept, ate and studied their manuals by the dim light of their glims, was filled with suffering. It stank of blood, vomit and pain. Each thundering roar of a broadside, or the sickening crash of enemy balls hitting the ship around them, brought cries and groans from the figures who waited to be attended.

Blachford could only guess what was happening up there, where it was broad daylight. Here on the orlop, no outside light ever penetrated. Below the waterline it was the safest place for this grisly work, but it revolted him none the less.

He gestured to the obscene tubs below the table, partly filled with amputated limbs, a stark warning to those who would be the next to be carried to endure what must be an extension of their agony. Only death seemed like a blessed relief here. 'Take them out!'

He listened to the beat of hammers in the narrow carpenter's walks, which ran around the ship below the waterline. Like tiny corridors between the inner compartments and the outer hull, where the carpenter and his mates repaired shot holes or leaks as the iron smashed again and again into the side.

There was a long drawn out rumbling directly overhead, and Blachford stared at the red-painted timbers as if he expected them to cave in.

A frightened voice called from the shadows. 'What's that, Toby?'

Someone replied, 'They're runnin' in the lower battery, that's what!'

Blachford asked quickly, 'Why would they do that?'

Minchin took a cupful of rum and wiped his mouth with a blood-stained fist.

'Clearing it. We're alongside one o' the buggers. They'll need every spare Jack to fight 'em off!'

He shouted hoarsely, 'Next one, Donovan!'

Then he eyed Blachford with something like contempt. 'Not quite what you're used to, I expect? No fancy operating rooms, with lines of ignorant students hanging on your every word.' He blinked his red-rimmed eyes as smoke eddied through the deck. 'I hope you learn something useful today, *Sir Piers*. Now you know what we have to suffer in the name of medicine.'

A loblolly boy said, 'This one's an officer, sir.'

Blachford leaned over the table as the lieutenant was stripped of his torn shirt and pressed flat on the table.

It was the second lieutenant, Lovering, who had been shot down by a Spanish marksman.

Blachford studied the terrible wound in his arm. The blood looked black in the swinging lanterns, the skin ragged where the ball had split apart upon hitting the bone.

Lovering stared at him, his eyes glazed with pain. 'Oh God, is it bad?'

Minchin touched his bare shoulder. It felt cold and clammy. 'Sorry, Ralph.' He glanced at Blachford. 'It's got to come off.'

Lovering closed his eyes. 'Please God, not my arm!'

Blachford waited for an assistant to bring his instruments. He had had to order them to to be cleaned again and again. No wonder men died of gangrene. He said gently, 'He's right. For your own sake.'

The lieutenant rolled his head away from the nearest lantern. He was about twenty-two, Blachford thought.

Lovering said in a whisper, 'Why not kill me? I'm done for.'

More crashes shook the hull and several instruments fell to the deck. Blachford stooped to retrieve one of them and stared, sickened, as a rat scurried away into the shadows.

Minchin saw his disgust and set his teeth. Coming here with all his high-and-mighty talk. What did he know about war?

From one corner of his eye he saw the lamplight glint on Blachford's knife.

'Here, Ralph.' He placed a wedge of leather between his jaws before he could protest. 'I'll give you some proper brandy after this.'

A voice yelled through the misty smoke. 'Another officer, sir!'

An assistant held up his lantern and Blachford saw Lieutenant Quayle slipping down against one of the massive timbers, trying to cover his face with his coat.

A seaman protested angrily, ' 'E's not even marked!'

Lieutenant Lovering struggled on the table, and but for the assistant holding his uninjured arm, and Minchin's hands on his shoulders, would have fought his way to his feet.

'You bloody bastard! You cowardly –' His voice trailed away

as he fell back in a faint on the table.

Blachford glanced again at Quayle; he was gripping his fingers and whimpering like a child.

'Call him what you will, but he's as much a casualty as any of them!'

Minchin replaced the leather wedge between Lovering's jaws. Brutal, callous; they were the marks of his trade. He held Lovering's shoulders and waited for him to feel the first incision of the knife. With luck he might lose consciousness completely before the saw made its first stroke.

Minchin could dismiss what Blachford and others like him thought about the navy's surgeons. He could even ignore Lovering's agony, although he had always liked the young lieutenant.

Instead he concentrated on his daughter in Dover, whom he had not seen for two years.

'Next.' Lovering was carried away; the amputated limb fell into the tub. The *wings and limbs* tub as most of them called it. Until it was their turn.

Blachford waited for a seaman whose foot had been crushed beneath a careering gun-truck to be laid before him. Around him the loblolly boys and their helpers held the flickering lanterns closer. Blachford looked at his own arms, red to the elbows, like Minchin's and the rest. *No wonder they call us butchers.*

The man began to scream and plead but sucked greedily on a mug of rum which Minchin finished before laying bare the shattered foot. The hull quivered again, but it felt as if the battle had drawn away. There seemed to be cannon fire from all directions, occasional yells which were like lost spirits as they filtered through the other decks.

Hyperion might have been boarded, Blachford thought, or the enemy could have drawn away to reform. He knew little about sea-warfare other than what he had been told or had read about in the *Gazette*. Only since his travels around the fleet had he thought about the men who made victories and defeats real, into flesh and blood like his own.

'*Next!*' It never stopped.

This time a marine ran down a ladder and called, 'We've taken the Don alongside, lads!' He vanished again, and Blachford was

271

amazed that some of the wounded could actually raise a weak cheer. No wonder Bolitho loved these sailors.

He looked down at the young midshipman. A child.

Minchin probed open part of his side where the ribs showed white through the blood.

Blachford said quietly, 'God, he looks so young.'

Minchin stared at him, wanting to hurt him, to make him suffer.

'Well, Mr Springett won't be getting any older, Sir Piers. He's got a fistful of Spanish iron inside him!' He gestured angrily. 'Take him away.'

'How old was he?'

Minchin knew the boy was thirteen, but something else caught his attention. It was the sudden stillness, which even the far-off gunfire could not break. The deck was swaying more slowly, as if the ship was heavier in the water. But the pumps were still going. God, he thought, in this old ship they never seemed to stop.

Blachford saw his intent expression. 'What is it?'

Minchin shook his head. 'Don't know.' He glanced at the dark shapes of the wounded along the side of the orlop. Some already dead, with no one to notice or care. Others waiting, still waiting. But this time. . . . He said harshly, 'They're all sailors. They *know* something is wrong.'

Blachford stared at the smoke-filled ladder which mounted to the lower gundeck. It was as if they were the only ones left aboard. He took out his watch and peered at it. Minchin reached down and refilled his cup with rum, right to the brim.

He had seen the fine gold timepiece with the crest engraved on its guard. God rot him!

The roar of the broadside when it came was like nothing Minchin had ever experienced. There must have been many guns, and yet they were linked into one gigantic clap of thunder which exploded against the ship as if the sound, and not the massive weight of metal, was striking into the timbers.

The deck canted right over, shivered violently as it reared against the ship alongside, but the din did not stop. There was an outstanding, splitting crack which seemed to come right through the deck; it was followed immediately by a roar of crashing spars

272

and rigging, and heavy thuds which he guessed were guns being hurled back from their ports.

The wounded were shouting and pleading, some dragging themselves to the ladder, their blood marking the futility of their efforts. Blachford heard the broken spars thudding against the hull, then sudden screams from the carpenter's walk, men clawing their way in darkness as the lanterns were blown apart.

Minchin picked himself up from the deck, his ears still ringing from the explosion. He saw some rats scurrying past the bodies of those who were beyond pain, and shook his head to clear it.

As he brushed past, Blachford called, 'Where are you going?'

'My sickbay. All I own in this bloody world is in there.'

'In Heaven's name, *tell me*, man!'

Minchin steadied himself as the deck gave another great shudder. The pumps had finally stopped. He said savagely, 'We're going down. But I'm not staying to watch it!'

Blachford stared round. *If I survive this*. . . . Then he took a grip on his racing thoughts.

'Get these men ready to move on deck.' The assistants nodded, but their eyes were on the ladder. *Going down*. Their life. Their home, whether from choice or impressment; it could not happen. Shoes clattered on the ladder, and Dacie, the one-eyed boatswain's mate, peered down at them.

'Will you come up, Sir Piers? It's a bloody shambles on deck.'

'What about these wounded?'

Dacie gripped the handrail and wiped his remaining eye. He wanted to run, run, keep on running. But all his life he had been trained to stand fast, to obey.

'I'll pass the word, Sir Piers.' Then he was gone.

Blachford picked up his bag and hurried to the ladder. As he climbed the first steps he felt they were different. At an angle. He sensed the chill of fear for the first time.

He thought of Minchin's anger.

Going down.

Lieutenant Stephen Jenour retained his grip on Bolitho's arm even after he had pulled him from the deck. He was almost incoherent in his relief and horror. 'Thank God, oh thank God!'

273

Bolitho said, 'Take hold, Stephen.' His eyes moved across the quarterdeck and down to the awful spread of destruction. No wonder Jenour was close to a complete breakdown. He had probably imagined himself to be the only one left alive up here.

It was as if the whole ship had been stripped and laid bare, so that no part of her wounds should be hidden. The mizzen mast had gone completely, and the whole of the foretopmast had been severed as if by some gigantic axe, and was pitching alongside with all the other wreckage. Spars, ropes, and men. The latter either floated in the weed of rigging, or floundered about like dying fish.

Jenour gasped, 'The first lieutenant, Sir Richard!' He tried to point, but his body was shaking so violently he almost fell.

Bolitho forgot his own despair as he hurried down a splintered ladder to the maindeck. Guns lay up-ended and abandoned, their crews strewn around them, or crawling blindly for the nearest hatch to hide. Parris was pinned beneath an overturned eighteen-pounder, his eyes staring at the sky until he saw Bolitho.

Bolitho dropped beside him. To Jenour he said, 'Send some one for the surgeon.' He held his coat. 'And Stephen, remember to *walk*, will you? Those who have survived will need all their confidence in us.'

Parris reached up to touch his arm. Through gritted teeth he gasped, 'God, that was bad!' He tried to move his shoulders. 'The *San Mateo*, what of her?'

Bolitho shook his head. 'She has gone. There was no point in continuing the fight after this.'

Parris released a great sigh. 'A victory.' Then he looked at Bolitho, his eyes pleading. 'My face – is it all right, sir?'

Bolitho nodded. 'Not a mark on it.'

Parris seemed satisfied. 'But I can't feel my legs.'

Bolitho stared at the overturned gun. The barrel was still hot from being fired, yet Parris could feel nothing. He could see his hessian boots protruding from the other side of the truck. Both legs must have been crushed.

'I'll wait here until help comes.' He looked along the shattered deck. Only the foremast still stood as before, with his flag rippling from the truck above the shredded sails.

He felt the deck quiver. The pumps had stopped, probably choked or smashed apart. He made himself face the truth. *Hyperion* was dying, even while he waited. He glanced across at the dead midshipman Mirrielees, whose body had been hurled down from the quarterdeck where he had been killed. He was sixteen. *I was just his age when Hyperion's keel tasted salt water for the first time.*

He heard voices and hurrying feet and saw seamen and marines returning from the Spanish two-decker alongside. It was strange, but Bolitho had not even glanced at their battered prize.

He saw Keen, an arm wrapped around Tojohns' shoulders, a bloody bandage tied about one leg, limping anxiously towards him.

'I died a dozen times back there, Sir Richard. I – I thought you must have fallen in that broadside.' He saw Parris and said, 'We should move him.'

Bolitho took his arm. 'You *know*, don't you, Val?'

Their eyes met. Keen replied, 'Yes. She's sinking. There's little we can do.' He stared at the abandoned cannon, unable to watch Bolitho's pain. 'Even if we could cast these guns overboard. But time is against us.'

Parris gave a groan and Bolitho asked, 'Is the prize safe, Val?'

'Aye. She's *Asturias* of eighty guns. She took much punishment too from that battering, as did her neighbour. But she is useful for repeating signals.'

Bolitho tried to clear his throbbing mind; his ears were still aching from that terrible broadside.

'Signal *Benbow* to secure the prizes and then give chase with whatever forces we have still seaworthy. The Dons will doubtless be running for the nearest Spanish port.' He stared at the bloody decks. 'Leaving their friends as well as their enemies to manage for themselves!'

Keen tightened his hold on his coxswain. 'Come, Tojohns! We must muster the hands!'

Bolitho said to Jenour, 'Go below and take charge of the boatswain's party. Can you do that?'

Jenour stared at Parris. 'What about him, Sir Richard?'

'I'll wait for the surgeon.' Bolitho lowered his voice. 'He will want to amputate both legs, I fear.'

Parris said vaguely, 'I am sorry about this, Sir Richard.' He gasped as a great pain went through him. 'I – I could have helped. Should have come to you earlier when I learned about your troubles in London.'

He was rambling. Bolitho leaned over him and grasped his hand. *Or was he?*

Parris continued in the same matter-of-fact tone, 'I *should* have known. I wanted a new command so much, just as I hated to lose the other. I suppose I didn't want it quite enough.'

Figures were clambering over from the other ship, voices of command emerged from chaos, and he saw Penhaligon, the master, with one of his mates coming from the wrecked poop, carrying the ship's chronometer, the same one she had carried in all her years of service. He half-listened to Parris's vague sentences but he was thinking of this ship he had known better than any other. *Hyperion* had carried three admirals, served fifteen captains, and countless thousands of sailors. There had been no campaign of note she had missed except for her time as a hulk.

Parris said, 'Somervell became very dear to me. I fought against it, but it was no use.'

Bolitho stared at him, for a moment not understanding what he was saying.

'You and Somervell – is *that* how it was?' It came at him like a blow, and he was stunned at his own blindness. Catherine's dislike for Parris, not because he was a womaniser as Haven had believed, but because of his liaison with her husband. *There was no love between us.* He could almost hear her words, her voice. It must have been why Parris had lost his only command, the matter dropped by some authority which required the scandal to be buried.

Parris gazed at him sadly. 'How it was. I wanted to tell you – you of all people. After what you did for me and this ship what you had to endure because of my folly.'

Bolitho heard Blachford hurrying along the deck. He should have felt anger or revulsion, but he had been in the navy since he had been twelve years old; what he had not seen in that time he had soon learned about.

He said quietly, 'Well, you've told me now.' He touched his shoulder. 'I shall speak with the surgeon.'

The deck gave a shudder, and broken blocks and discarded weapons clattered from a gangway like so much rubbish.

Blachford looked as white as a sheet, and Bolitho could guess what it had been like for him in the cockpit.

'Can you do it here on deck?'

Blachford nodded. 'After this I can do anything.'

Keen came limping down from the quarterdeck and called, '*Benbow* has acknowledged, Sir Richard. Rear-Admiral Herrick wishes you well, and offers you all assistance!'

Bolitho smiled sadly, 'Tell him no, but thank him.' Dear Thomas was alive, unharmed. Thank God for that.

Keen watched Blachford stooping to open his bag. His eyes said, *it could have been either of us, or both*. He said, 'Six of the Dons have struck, Sir Richard, including *Intrépido* which was the last to haul down her colours to *Tybalt*.'

There was the crack of a line parting and Keen added, 'She drags heavily on *Asturias*, Sir Richard.'

'I know.' He stared round. 'Where's Allday?'

A passing seaman called, 'Gone below, Sir Richard!'

Bolitho nodded. 'I can guess why.'

Blachford said, 'I'm ready.'

There was another loud crack but this time it was a pistol shot. Bolitho and the others stared at Parris as his arm fell to the deck, the pistol he always carried still smoking in his fingers.

Blachford closed his bag, and said quietly, 'Perhaps his was the best way, better than mine. For such a courageous young man, I think living as a cripple would have proved unbearable.'

Bolitho removed his hat and walked to the quarterdeck ladder. 'Leave him there. He will be in good company.'

Afterwards he thought it sounded like an epitaph.

Scarlet coats moved into the ship, and Major Adams, hatless but apparently unmarked, was bellowing orders.

Bolitho said, 'The wounded first, Major. Over to the Spaniard. After that –' He did not finish.

Instead he turned to watch as *Benbow*, accompanied by *Capricious*, passed down the opposite side. There were no cheers this

277

time, and Bolitho could envision how *Hyperion* must look. Was it imagination, or were the figurehead's muscled shoulders already closer to the sea? He stared until his damaged eye throbbed.

He could think of nothing else. *Hyperion* was settling down. They could not even anchor, for here the sea had no bottom, so her exact position could never be marked.

Men moved briskly around him, but like the moment he had hoisted his flag aboard, the faces he saw were different ones.

He touched the fan in his pocket. *Sharing it with her.*

He saw Rimer, the wizened master's mate who had accompanied him on the cutting-out of the treasure galleon. He was sitting against a bollard, his eyes fixed and unmoving, caught at the moment the shot had cut him down. Loggie the ship's corporal, sprawled headlong across another marine he had been trying to haul to safety when a marksman had found him too.

The first of the wounded were being swayed up through one of the hatchways. A few cried out as their wounds touched the coaming or the tackles, but most of them just stared like the dead Rimer; they had never expected to see daylight again.

Allday reappeared by his side; he had brought Ozzard with him.

He said, 'He was still in the hold, Sir Richard.' He forced a grin. 'Didn't know the fight was over, bless 'im!' He did not say that he had found Ozzard sitting on the hold's ladder, Bolitho's fine presentation sword clutched against his chest, staring at the last lantern's reflections on the black water which was creeping slowly towards him. He had not intended to leave.

Bolitho touched the little man's shoulder. 'I am very glad to see you.'

Ozzard said, 'But all that furniture, the wine cabinet from her ladyship –' He sighed. 'All gone.'

Keen limped over and said, 'I hate to trouble you, Sir Richard, but –'

Bolitho faced him. 'I know, Val. You continue your work. I shall attend the ship.' He saw the protest die on Keen's lips as he added, 'I know her somewhat better than you.'

Keen stood back. 'Aye, aye, Sir Richard.' He glanced at the

tautening hawsers to the ship alongside. 'There may not be long.'

'I know. Single-up your lines.' Then almost to himself he added, 'I have never lost a ship before.'

He saw Minchin coming on deck with one of his assistants, their clothing dark with blood, each carrying a bag.

Minchin approached Bolitho and said, 'Permission to leave with the wounded, Sir Richard?'

'Yes, and thank you.'

Minchin forced a grin to his ruined face. 'Even the rats have gone.'

Bolitho said to Ozzard, 'Leave with the others.'

Ozzard clutched the bright sword. 'No, Sir Richard, I'm staying –'

Bolitho nodded. 'Then remain here, on deck.'

He looked at Allday. 'Are you coming with me?'

Allday watched him despairingly. *Must you go down there?* Aloud he said, 'Have I ever left you?'

They walked beneath the poop and down the first companionway to the lower gundeck. The ports were still sealed, but most of those on the larboard side had been blasted open, their guns hurled from their breechings. There were few dead here. Mercifully Keen had cleared the deck to storm the Spaniard alongside. But there were some. Lolling figures, eyes slitted as if because of the smoky sunlight, watching as they passed. Half a man, chopped neatly in two by a single ball even as he had run with his sponge to the nearest gun. Blood everywhere; no wonder the sides were painted red, but it still showed itself. Lieutenant Priddie, second-in-command of the lower gundeck, lay face down, his back pierced with long splinters which had been blasted from the planking. He was still holding his sword.

Down another ladder, to the orlop, where Bolitho had to duck beneath each low beam. There were still one or two lanterns alight here. The dead lay in neat rows covered by sail-cloth. Others remained around the bloodied table, where they had died while they waited. Above their heads a heavy object fell to the deck, and then after a few seconds began to rumble along the scarred planking, like something alive.

Allday whispered, 'In the name of Christ!'

279

Bolitho looked at him. It must be a thirty-two pounder ball which had broken free of its garland and was now rolling purposefully down towards the bows.

They paused by the last hatchway and Allday dragged back the cover. It was one of the holds, where Ozzard always kept his vigil when the ship was in action.

Bolitho dropped to his knees and peered down while Allday lowered a lantern beside him.

He had expected to see water amongst the casks and crates, the chests and the furniture, but it was already awash from side to side. Barrels floated on the dark water, and lapped around a marine who had been clinging to a ladder when he had died. A sentry put to guard against terrified men running below in battle. He might have been killed by one of them, or like Ozzard had been trying to find refuge from the hell on deck.

The deck quivered again, and he heard heavy fragments booming against the carpenter's walk where more of his men had been trapped and drowned.

The orlop, and the holds and magazines beneath it, places which had remained in total darkness for all of *Hyperion*'s thirty-three years. When they had returned the old ship to service after a hasty refit, it was more than likely the dockyard had missed something. Probably down there, where the first heavy broadside had smashed into the hull, there had still been some rot, unseen and undiscovered. Gnawing at the timbers and frames as far down as the keelson. *San Mateo*'s last bombardment had dealt the mortal blow.

Bolitho watched Allday shut the hatch and made his way back to the ladder.

So many memories would go with this ship. Adam as a midshipman; Cheney whom he had loved in this same hull. So many names and faces. Some would be out there now in the battered squadron where they waited to secure the prizes after their victory. Bolitho thought of them watching *Hyperion*, remembering her perhaps as she had once been, while the younger ones like Midshipman Springett. . . . He cursed and held his hand to his eyes. No, he was gone too, with so many others he could not even remember.

Allday murmured, 'I think we'd better get a move on, sir.'

The hull shook once more, and Bolitho thought he saw the gleam of water in the reflected light, creeping through the deck seams; soon it would cover the blood around Minchin's table.

They climbed to the next deck, then threw themselves to one side as a great thirty-two pounder gun came to life and squealed down the deck, as if propelled by invisible hands. *Load! Run out! Fire!* Bolitho could almost hear the orders being screamed above the roar of battle.

On the quarterdeck once more Bolitho found Keen and Jenour waiting for him.

Keen said quietly, 'The ship is cleared, Sir Richard.' His eyes moved up to the flag, so clean in the afternoon sunlight.

'Shall I have it hauled down?'

Bolitho walked to the quarterdeck rail and grasped it as he had so many times as captain and now as her admiral.

'No, if you please, Val. She fought under my flag. She will always wear it.'

He looked at the Spanish *Asturias*. He could see much more of her damage, her side pitted by *Hyperion*'s own broadsides. She appeared much higher in the water now.

Bolitho looked at the sprawled figures, Parris's outflung arm with the pistol he had chosen as his final escape.

They had succeeded in driving off and scattering the enemy. Looking at the drifting ships and abandoned corpses, it seemed like a hollow victory.

Bolitho said, '*You are my ship.*'

The others stood near him but he seemed quite alone as he spoke.

'No more as a hulk. This time with honour!' He swung away from the rail. 'I am ready.'

It took another hour for *Hyperion* to disappear. She dipped slowly by the bows, and standing on the Spaniard's poop Bolitho heard the sea rushing through the ports, sweeping away wreckage, eager for the kill.

Even the Spanish prisoners who gathered along the bulwarks to watch were strangely silent.

Hammocks floated free of the nettings, and a corpse by the

wheel rolled over as if it had been only feigning death.

Bolitho found that he was gripping his sword, pressing it against the fan in his pocket with all his strength.

They were all going with her. He held his breath as the sea rolled relentlessly aft towards the quarterdeck until only the poop, and the opposite end of the ship, his flag above the sinking masthead, marked her presence.

He remembered the words of the dying sailor.

Hyperion cleared the way, as she always had.

He said aloud, 'There'll be none better than you, old lady!'

When he looked again she had gone, and only bubbles and the scum of flotsam remained as she made her last voyage to the seabed.

Keen glanced at the stricken survivors around him and was inclined to agree.

Epilogue

Bolitho paused near the edge of the cliff and stared hard across Falmouth Bay. There was no snow on the ground, but the wind which swept the cliffs and hurled spume high above the rocks below was bitterly cold, and the low dark-bellied clouds hinted at sleet before dusk.

Bolitho felt his hair whipping in the wind, drenched with salt and rain. He had been watching a small brig beating up from the Helford River, but had lost sight of her in the wintry spray which blew from the sea like smoke.

It was hard to believe that tomorrow was the first day in another year, that even after returning here he was still gripped by a sense of disbelief and loss.

When *Hyperion* had gone down he had tried to console himself that she had not made a vain sacrifice, nor had the men who had died that day in the Mediterranean sunshine.

Had the Spanish squadron been able to join with the Combined Fleet at Cadiz, Nelson might well have been beaten into submission.

Bolitho had transferred to the frigate *Tybalt* for passage to Gibraltar and had left Herrick in command of the squadron, although most of the ships would need dockyard care without delay.

At the Rock he had been stunned by the news. The Combined Fleet had broken out without waiting for more support, but outnumbered or not, Nelson had won a resounding victory; in a single battle had smashed the enemy, had destroyed or captured two-thirds of their fleet, and by so doing had laid low any hope Napoleon still held of invading England.

But the battle, fought in unruly seas off Cape Trafalgar, had cost Nelson his life. Grief transmitted itself through the whole fleet, and aboard *Tybalt* where none of the men had ever set eyes on him, they were shocked beyond belief, as if they had known him as a friend. The battle itself was completely overshadowed by Nelson's death, and when to Bolitho eventually reached Plymouth he discovered it was the same wherever he went.

Bolitho watched the sea boil over the rocks, then tugged his cloak closer about his body.

He thought of Nelson, the man he had so wanted to meet, to walk and talk with him as sailor to sailor. How close their lives had been. Like parallel lines on a chart. He recalled seeing Nelson just once during the ill-fated attack on Toulon. It was curious to recall that he had seen Nelson only at a distance aboard the flagship; he had waved to Bolitho, a rather shabby young captain who was to change their world. Stranger still, the flagship Nelson had been visiting for orders was that same *Victory*. He thought also of the few letters he had received from him, and all in the last months aboard *Hyperion*. Written in his odd, sloping hand, self-taught after losing his right arm, *There you may discover how well they fight their wars with words and paper instead of ordnance and good steel*. He had never spared words for pompous authority.

And the words which had meant so much to Bolitho when he had asked for, and had been reluctantly given, *Hyperion* as his flagship. *Give Bolitho any ship he wants. He is a sailor, not a landsman*. Bolitho was glad that Adam had met him, and been known by him.

He glanced back along the winding cliff path towards Pendennis Castle. The battlements were partly hidden by mist, like low cloud; everything was grey and threatening. He could not remember how long he had been walking or why he had come. Nor did he remember when he had ever felt so alone.

Upon returning to England he had paid a brief visit to the Admiralty with his report. No senior had been available to see him. They were all engaged in preparing for Nelson's funeral, apparently. Bolitho had ignored the obvious snub, and had been glad to leave London for Falmouth. There were no letters for him from Catherine. It was like losing her again. But Keen would see her when he joined Zenoria in Hampshire.

Then I shall write to her. It was surprising how nervous it made him feel. Unsure of himself, like the first time. How would she see him after their separation?

He walked on into the wind, his boots squeaking in the sodden grass. Nelson would be buried at St Paul's, with all the pomp and ceremony which could be arranged.

It made him bitter to think that those who would be singing hymns of praise the loudest, would be the very same who had envied and disdained him the most.

He thought of the house now hidden by the brow of the hill. He had been glad that Christmas had been over when he reached home. His moods of loneliness and loss would have cast a wet blanket over all festivities. He had seen no one, and he imagined Allday back at the house, yarning with Ferguson about the battle, adding bits here and there as he always did.

Bolitho had thought often of the battle. At least there had been no mourning in Falmouth. Only three of *Hyperion*'s company had come from the port, and all had survived.

There had been a letter from Adam waiting for him. The one shining light to mark his return.

Adam was at Chatham. He had been appointed captain, in command of a new fifth-rate now completing in the Royal Dockyard there. He had got his wish. He had earned it.

He stopped again, suddenly tired, and realising he had eaten nothing since breakfast. Now it was afternoon, and darkness would soon arrive to make this path a dangerous place to walk. He turned, his cloak swirling about him like a sail.

How well his men had fought that day. *The Gazette* had summed it up in a few lines, overshadowed by a nation's sense of mourning. *On 15th October last, some hundred miles to the East of Cartagena ships of the Mediterranean squadron under the flag of Vice-Admiral Sir Richard Bolitho KB encountered a superior Spanish force of twelve sail-of-the-line. After a fierce engagement the enemy withdrew, leaving six prizes in British hands. God Save The King.* Hyperion was not mentioned, nor the men who now lay with her in peace. Bolitho quickened his pace and almost stumbled, not from any blindness, but because of the emotion which blurred his eyes.

God damn them all, he thought. Those same hypocrites would praise the little admiral now that they no longer had to fear his honesty. But the true people would remember his name, and so would ensure that it lived forever. For Adam's new navy, and the ones which would follow.

A figure was approaching by way of the path which ran closest to the edge. He peered through the mist and rain and saw the person wore a blue cloak like his own.

In an hour, maybe less, it would be dangerous here. A stranger perhaps?

. . . She came towards him very slowly, her hair, as dark as his own, streaming untied in the bitter wind off the sea.

Allday must have told her. He was the only one in the house who knew about this walk. This *particular* walk they had both taken after his fever, a thousand years ago.

He hurried towards her, held her at arms' length and watched her laughing and crying all in one. She was dressed in the old boat-cloak he kept at the house for touring the grounds in cold weather. A button missing, a rent near the hem. When it lifted to the wind he saw she was wearing a plain dark red gown beneath. So far a cry from the fine carriage and the life she had once shared.

Then Bolitho clutched her against his body, feeling her wet hair on his face, the touch of her hands. They were like ice, but neither of them noticed.

'I was going to write –' He could not go on.

She studied him closely, then gently stroked his brow near his injured eye.

'Val told me everything.' She pressed her face against his, while the wind flung their cloaks about them. 'My dearest of men, how terrible it must have been. For you and your old ship.'

Bolitho turned her and put his arm over her shoulders. As they mounted the path over the hill he saw the old grey house, light already gleaming in some of the windows.

She said, 'They say I am a sailor's woman. How could I stay away?'

Bolitho squeezed her shoulder, his heart too full to speak.

Then he said, 'Come, I'll take you home.'

He paused at the bottom to help her over the familiar old stile-gate where he had played as a child with his brother and sisters.

She looked down at him from the stile, her hands on his shoulders. 'I love thee, Richard.'

He made the moment last, sensing that peace like a reward had come to them in the guise of fate.

He said simply, 'Now it's your home, too.'

The one-legged ex-sailor named Vanzell touched his hat as they passed; but they did not see him.

Fate.

The Only Victor

For Maurice and Geraldine FitzGerald,
with our love and thanks

'We few, we happy few, we band of brothers;
For he today that sheds his blood with me
Shall be my brother . . .'

Henry V

Contents

1

'In the Name of Duty'

Captain Daniel Poland of His Britannic Majesty's frigate *Truculent* stretched his arms and stifled a yawn, while he waited for his eyes to accustom themselves to the darkness. As he gripped the quarterdeck rail and the dim figures around him took on identity and status, he was able to accept the pride he felt for this command, and the fashion in which he had moulded his company into a team, one that would react to his wishes and orders with little room for improvement. He had been in command for two years, but would not be fully 'posted' for a further six months. Then, and only then, would he feel safe from disaster. A fall from grace, an unfortunate mistake or misunderstanding of some senior officer's despatches – any of these could hurl him down the ladder of promotion, or worse. But once a post-captain with matching epaulettes on his shoulders, little could shift him. He gave a brief smile. Only death or some terrible wound could do that. The enemy's iron was no respecter of the hopes or ambitions of its victims.

He moved to the small table by the companion way and raised its tarpaulin hood so that he could examine the log by the light of a small shaded lamp.

Nobody on the quarterdeck spoke or disturbed him; every man was well aware of his presence and, after two years, his habits.

As he ran his eyes along the neatly written comments of the most recent officers-of-the-watch he felt his ship lift and plunge beneath him, spray whipping across the open deck like cold hail.

1

In an hour all would be different. Again he felt the same twinge of pride, *cautious* pride, for Captain Poland trusted nobody and nothing which might bring displeasure from his superiors, and which in turn might damage his prospects. But if the wind held they would sight the coast of Africa, the Cape of Good Hope, perhaps at first light.

Nineteen days. It was probably the fastest passage ever made by a King's ship from Portsmouth. Poland thought of the England they had seen fall into a rain squall as *Truculent* had thrust her way down-channel for open waters. Cold. Wet. Shortages and press-gangs.

His gaze fastened on the date. The first of February, 1806. Perhaps that was the answer. England was still reeling from the news of Trafalgar, which had exploded less than four months ago. It seemed people were stunned more by the death of Nelson, the nation's hero, than the crushing victory over the French and Spanish fleets.

Even aboard his own ship, Poland had sensed the change, the damage to morale amongst his officers and seamen. *Truculent* had not even been in the same ocean at the time of the great battle, and to his knowledge none of the people had ever laid eyes on the little admiral. It irritated him, just as he damned the luck which had taken his ship so far from a fight out of which only glory and reward could result. It was typical of Poland that he had not considered the awesome lists of dead and wounded after that memorable day off Cape Trafalgar.

He peered up at the pale shape of the bulging mizzen topsail. Beyond it there was only darkness. The ship had rid herself of her heavy canvas and changed every sail to the pale, light-weather rig. She would make a fine sight when the sunlight found her again. He pictured her rapid passage south, with the mountains of Morocco misty blue in the far distance, then south-east across the Equator with the only landfall the tiny island of St Helena, a mere speck on the chart.

It was no wonder that young officers prayed for the chance to gain command of a frigate, where once free of the fleet's apron strings and the interference of one admiral or another, they were their own masters.

He knew that to his company a captain was seen as some kind

2

of god. In many cases it was true. He could punish or reward any soul aboard with impunity. Poland considered himself a just and fair captain, but was sensible enough to know that he was feared rather than liked.

Each day he had made certain that his men were not lacking in work. No admiral would find fault with his ship, either her appearance or efficiency.

His eyes moved to the cabin skylight. It was already sharper in the gloom, or maybe his eyes had become completely used to it. *And there would be no mistakes on this passage*, not with such an important passenger down there in the captain's quarters.

It was time to begin. He walked to the rail again and stood with one foot on the truck of a tethered nine-pounder.

The ship's second lieutenant appeared as if by magic.

'Mr Munro, you may muster the Afterguard in fifteen minutes, when we shall wear ship.'

The lieutenant touched his hat in the darkness. 'Aye, aye, sir.'

He spoke almost in a whisper, as if he too were thinking of the passenger, and the noise of the Royal Marines' boots above his sleeping cabin.

Poland added irritably, 'And I don't want any slackness!'

Munro saw the sailing-master, who was already at his place near the big double-wheel, give what might have been a shrug. He was probably thinking that the captain would blame him if the dark horizon was as empty as before.

A burly figure moved to the lee side of the deck and Poland heard him fling some shaving-water into the sea. The passenger's personal coxswain, a powerful man by the name of John Allday. One who seemed to have little respect for anyone but his vice-admiral. Again, Poland felt a sense of irritation – or was it envy? He thought of his own coxswain, as smart and reliable as anyone could wish, one who would take no nonsense from his crew. But never a friend, as Allday appeared to be.

He tried to shrug it off. Anyway, his coxswain was only a common seaman.

He snapped, 'The vice-admiral is up and about, apparently. Call the Afterguard, then pipe the hands to the braces.'

Williams, the first lieutenant, clattered up the ladder and tried to button his coat and straighten his hat when he saw the captain already on deck.

3

'Good morning, sir!'

Poland replied coldly, 'It had better be!'

The lieutenants glanced at each other and grimaced behind his back. Poland was usually realistic in his dealings with the people, but he had little sense of humour, and as Williams had once put it, divided his guidance evenly between the Bible and the Articles of War.

Calls shrilled between decks and the watch below came thudding along the glistening planking, each man bustling to his familiar station where petty officers stood with their lists, and boatswain's mates were waiting to 'start' any laggard with rope's end or rattan. They were all aware of the importance of the man who wore his reputation like a cloak, and who for most of the lively passage had remained aft in Poland's quarters.

'There she comes, lads!'

Poland snapped, 'Take that man's name!'

But he looked up nevertheless and saw the first frail glow of light as it touched the whipping and frayed masthead pendant, then flowed down almost like liquid to mark the shrouds. Delicate, salmon-pink. Soon it would spread over the horizon, expand its colour, give life to a whole ocean.

But Poland saw none of these things. Time, distance, logged speed, they were the factors which ruled his daily life.

Allday lounged against the damp nettings. They would be packed with hammocks once the ship lay on her new course. Landfall? It seemed likely, but Allday could sense the captain's unease, just as he was aware of his own private anxieties. Usually, no matter how bad things had been, he was glad, if not relieved, to quit the shore and get back to a ship again.

This time it was different. Like being motionless with only the ship's wild movements to give the sensation of life around them.

Allday had heard them talking about the man he served and loved as he loved none other. He had wondered what he had really been thinking as *Truculent* had ploughed through each long day. *Something apart.* Not their ship. He let his mind explore the thought, like fingers probing a raw wound. *Not like the old Hyperion.*

October 15th, less than four months ago. Was that all it was? In his heart he could still feel the crash and roar of those terrible

4

broadsides, the screams and the madness, and then – The old pain lanced through his chest and he clutched it with his fist and gasped in great mouthfuls of air, waiting for it to ease. Another sea, a different battle, but always a reminder of how entwined their lives had become. He could guess what the stiff-faced Poland thought. Men like him could never understand Richard Bolitho. Nor would they.

He massaged his chest and gave a little, private smile. Yes, they had seen and done so much together. Vice-Admiral Sir Richard Bolitho. Even their paths had been spliced by fate. Allday wiped the spray from his face and shook his long pigtail over his collar. Most folk probably believed that Bolitho wanted for nothing. His last exploits had swept the seaports and taverns of England. A ballad had been composed by Charles Dibdin or one of his fellows: '*How Hyperion Cleared The Way!*' The words of a dying sailor whose hand Bolitho had held on that awful sunlit day, although he had been needed in a hundred other places at once.

But only those who had shared it really knew. The power and the passion of the man behind the gold lace and gleaming epaulettes, who could lead his sailors, be they half mad, half deafened by the hellish roar of battle; who could make them cheer even in the face of the Devil and the moment of certain death.

And yet he was the same one who could turn up the noses of London society, and invite gossip in the coffee houses. Allday straightened and sighed. The pain did not return. Yet. They would all be surprised if they knew just how little Bolitho did have, he thought.

He heard Poland snap, 'A good man aloft, Mr Williams, *if* you please!'

Allday could almost feel pity for the first lieutenant, and hid a grin as he replied, 'Already done, sir. I sent a master's mate to the foremast when the watch came aft.'

Poland strode away from him and glared when he saw the vice-admiral's coxswain loitering.

'Only the Afterguard and my officers –' He shut his mouth and moved instead to the compass.

Allday stamped down the companion ladder and allowed the smells and sounds of the ship to greet him. Tar, paint, cordage

5

and the sea. He heard the bark of orders, the squeal of braces and halliards through their blocks, the thud of dozens of bare feet as the men threw themselves against the tug of rudder and wind and the ship began to change tack.

At the door of the great cabin a Royal Marine sentry stood near a wildly spiralling lantern, his scarlet coat angled more steeply as the helm went hard over.

Allday gave him a nod as he thrust open the screen door. He rarely abused his privileges, but it made him proud to know he was able to come and go as he pleased. Something else to gall Captain Poland, he thought with a grim chuckle. He nearly collided with Ozzard, Bolitho's small, mole-like servant, as he scuttled away with some shirts to wash.

'How is he?'

Ozzard glanced aft. Beyond the sleeping quarters and Poland's swaying cot the cabin was almost in darkness again, but for a single lantern.

He murmured, 'Not moved.' Then he was gone. Loyal, secretive, always there when he was needed. Allday believed Ozzard was still brooding about the October day when their old *Hyperion* had given up her last fight and gone down. Only Allday himself knew that it had been Ozzard's intention to stay and go with her to the seabed, with all the dead and some of the dying still on board. Another mystery. He wondered if Bolitho knew or guessed what had almost happened. To speculate why, was beyond him.

Then he saw Bolitho's pale figure framed by the broad stern windows. He was sitting with one knee drawn up on the bench seat, his shirt very white against the tumbling water beyond.

For some reason Allday was moved by what he saw. He had seen Bolitho like this in so many of the ships they had shared after that first meeting. So many mornings. So many years.

He said uncertainly, 'I'll fetch another lantern, Sir Richard.'

Bolitho turned his head, his grey eyes in dark shadow. 'It will be light enough soon, old friend.' Without noticing it he touched his left eyelid and added, 'We may sight land today.'

So calmly said, Allday thought, and yet his mind and heart must be so crammed with memories, good and rotten. But if there was bitterness he gave no hint of it in his voice.

6

Allday said, 'Reckon Cap'n Poland will cuss an' swear if there ain't, an' that's no error!'

Bolitho smiled and turned to watch the sea as it boiled from the rudder, as if some great fish was about to break surface in pursuit of the lively frigate.

He had always admired the dawn at sea. So many and such different waters, from the blue, placid depths of the Great South Sea to the raging grey wastes of the Western Ocean. Each unique, like the ships and men who challenged them.

He had expected, hoped even, that this day might bring some relief from his brooding thoughts. A fine, clean shirt, one of Allday's best shaves; it often gave a sense of well-being. But this time it eluded him.

He heard the shrill of calls again and could picture the orderly bustle on deck as the sails were sheeted home, the slackness shaken from braces and halliards. At heart he was perhaps still a frigate captain, as he had been when Allday had been brought aboard as a pressed man. Since then, so many leagues sailed, too many faces wiped away like chalk off a slate.

He saw the first hint of light on the crests, the spray leaping away on either quarter as the dawn began to roll down from the horizon.

Bolitho stood up and leaned his hands on the sill to stare more closely at the sea's face.

He recalled as if it were yesterday an admiral breaking the painful truth to him, when he had protested about the only appointment he could beg from the Admiralty after recovering from his terrible fever.

'You *were* a frigate captain, Bolitho . . .' Twelve years ago, maybe more.

Eventually he had been given the old *Hyperion*, and then probably only because of the bloody revolution in France and the war which had followed it, and which had raged almost without respite until this very day.

And yet *Hyperion* was the one ship which was to change his life. Many had doubted his judgment when he had pleaded for the old seventy-four as his last flagship. From captain to vice-admiral; it had seemed the right choice. The only choice.

She had gone down last October, leading Bolitho's squadron

in the Mediterranean against a much more powerful force of Spanish ships under the command of an old enemy, Almirante Don Alberto Casares. It had been a desperate battle by any standards, and the outcome had never been certain from the first broadsides.

And yet, impossibly, they had beaten the Dons, and had even taken some prizes back to Gibraltar.

But the old *Hyperion* had given everything she had, and could offer no further resistance. She was thirty-three years old when the great ninety-gun *San Mateo* had poured the last broadside into her. Apart from a short period as a mastless stores hulk, she had sailed and fought in every sea where the flag was challenged. Some rot in her frames and timbers, deep down in her worn hull, undiscovered by any dockyard, had finally betrayed her.

In spite of everything Bolitho had witnessed and endured during a lifetime at sea, it was still to hard to accept that she was gone.

He had heard some say that but for his judgment in holding and defeating the Spanish squadron, the enemy would have joined with the Combined Fleet off Trafalgar. Then perhaps even brave Nelson could not have triumphed. Bolitho had not known how to react. More flattery? After Nelson's death he had been sickened to watch the same people who had hated him and despised him for his liaison with *that Hamilton woman* sing his praises the highest, and lament his passing.

Like so many he had never met the little admiral who had raised the hearts of his sailors even in the squalor most of them endured on endless blockade duty, or firing gun-to-gun with an enemy. Nelson had *known* his men, and given them the leadership they understood and needed.

He realised that Allday had padded from the cabin, and hated himself for bringing him out here on a mission which was probably fruitless.

Allday would not be moved. *My English oak*. Bolitho would only have hurt and insulted him if he had left him ashore at Falmouth. They had got this far together.

He touched his left eyelid and sighed. How would it torment him in the bright African sunlight?

He could recall the exact moment when he had faced the sun and his damaged eye had clouded over, as if a sea-mist had crept

8

across the deck. He felt the chill of fear as he relived it: the Spaniard's sharp breathing as he lunged forward with a cutlass. The unknown sailor must have realised the fight was over, that his own shipmates were already flinging down their weapons in surrender. Maybe he had simply seen Bolitho's uniform as the enemy, *all authority everywhere*, which had brought him to this place of certain death.

Jenour, Bolitho's flag-lieutenant, attempting to defend him, had had his sword struck from his hand, and there was nothing to stop the inevitable. Bolitho had waited for it, his old sword held out before him, and unable to see his would-be assassin.

But Allday had been there, and had seen everything. The Spaniard's cutlass had gone clattering across the blood-stained deck, his severed arm with it. Another blow had finished him. Allday's own revenge for the wound which had left him almost constantly in pain, unable to act as swiftly as he once did.

But abandon him, even out of kindness? Bolitho knew that only death would ever part them.

He pushed himself away from the window and picked up the fan from his sea-chest. Catherine's fan. She had made certain he had had it with him when he had boarded *Truculent* at Spithead.

What was she doing now, all those six thousand miles astern? It would be cold and bleak in Cornwall. Crouching cottages beyond the big grey house below Pendennis Castle. Winds from the Channel to shake the sparse trees on the hillside, the ones Bolitho's father had once called 'my ragged warriors'. Farmers making good damage to walls and barns, fishermen at Falmouth repairing their boats, grateful for the written protection which kept them safe from the hated press-gangs.

The old grey house would be Catherine's only sanctuary from the sneers and the gossip. Ferguson, the estate's one-armed steward, who had originally been pressed into naval service with Allday, would take good care of her. But you never knew for certain, especially in the West Country.

Tongues would wag. *Bolitho's woman. Wife of a viscount, who should be with him and not living like some sailor's whore.* They had been Catherine's own words, to prove to him that she did not care for herself but for *his* name and *his* honour. Yes, the ignorant ones were always the most cruel.

9

The only occasion when she had revealed bitterness and anger had been when he was called to London, to receive his orders. She had stared at him across the room they shared which overlooked the sea, that constant reminder, and had exclaimed, 'Don't you *see* what they are doing to us, Richard?'

In her anger she was beautiful in a different way, her long dark hair in disorder across her white gown, her eyes blazing with hurt and disbelief. 'It is Lord Nelson's funeral in a few days time.' She had stepped back from him as he had made to calm her. 'No, listen to me, Richard! We shall have less than two weeks together, and much of that time spent on the road. You are worth a hundred of any of them, though I know you would never say it . . . *Damn their eyes!* You lost your old ship, you have given *everything*, but they are so afraid that you will refuse to attend the funeral unless you can take *me* with you, when they are expecting Belinda!'

Then she had broken and had let him hold her, his cheek in her hair like the time they had watched the first dawn together in Falmouth.

Bolitho had stroked her shoulders and had replied gently, 'I would never allow anyone to insult you.'

She had not seemed to hear. 'That surgeon who sailed with you – Sir Piers Blachford? He could help you, surely?' She had pulled his face to hers and kissed his eyes with sudden tenderness. 'Dearest of men, you *must* take care.'

Now she was in Falmouth. Despite all the offered protection and love, a stranger nonetheless.

She had accompanied him to Portsmouth on that cold blustery forenoon; so much to say still unsaid. Together they had waited by the old sally-port, each aware that these same worn stairs had been Nelson's last contact with England. In the background, the carriage with the Bolitho crest on its doors waited with Matthew the coachman holding the horses' heads. The carriage was streaked with mud, as if to mark the time that they had spent together in its secret privacy.

Not always so secret. Passing through Guildford on the way to London, some idlers had raised a cheer. 'God bless you, Our Dick! Don't you mind they buggers in Lonnon, beggin' yer pardon, Ma'am!'

10

She had watched his reflection in the carriage window and had said quietly, 'See! I am not the only one!'

As the frigate's gig had pulled strongly towards the sally-port she had clasped her arms around his neck, her face wet with rain and drifting spray.

'I love thee, dearest of men.' She had kissed him hard, unable to release him until the boat had hooked on with a noisy clatter. Then, and only then, had she turned from him, pausing just briefly to add, 'Tell Allday I said to take good care of you.'

The rest was lost as if darkness had suddenly descended.

There was a sharp tap at the screen door.

Captain Poland stepped into the cabin, his cocked hat jammed beneath one arm.

Bolitho saw his eyes flit around the shadows, as if he expected to see his quarters completely changed or gutted.

Bolitho sat down again, his hands on the edge of the bench seat. *Truculent* was a fine ship, he thought. He pictured his nephew, Adam, and wondered if he had yet accepted the greatest gift, the command of his own frigate. His ship was probably commissioned by now, even at sea like this one. He would do well.

He asked, 'News, Captain?'

Poland looked at him squarely. 'Land in sight, Sir Richard. The Master, Mr Hull, thinks it is a perfect completion.'

Always the caution. Bolitho had noticed it before when he had asked Poland to sup with him a few times during the voyage.

'And what do *you* think, sir?'

Poland swallowed hard. 'I believe it to be true, Sir Richard.' He added as an afterthought, 'The wind has dropped – it will take most of the day to stand close to the mainland. Even Table Mountain is only plainly visible from the fore-topmast.'

Bolitho reached for his coat, but decided against it. 'I shall come up. You have performed a fast and exceptional passage, Captain. I shall say as much in my final despatches.'

It would have been comic at any other time to see the swift changes of thought and expression on Poland's sun-reddened features. A written compliment from the vice-admiral, *the hero*, which might facilitate an even quicker advancement for the captain.

11

Or might it be seen differently by those in office? That Poland had found favour with the same man who had flouted authority, left his wife for another and tossed honour to the winds . . .

But it was not *any other time*, and Bolitho said sharply, 'So let us be about it, eh?'

On the quarterdeck Bolitho saw Jenour, his flag-lieutenant, standing with the ship's officers, and marvelled at the change he had seen in him since his flag had been hoisted above *Hyperion*. A keen, likeable young man – the first in his family to enter the navy – Bolitho had once doubted if he would survive the campaign, and the battles they would have to share together. He had even heard it said that some of the 'hard men' of the old ship's company had taken bets on how long Jenour would live.

But survive he had – more than that, he had come through it a man, a veteran.

It had been Jenour's beautiful sword, a gift from his father, which had been parried aside and jerked from his grip as he had run to Bolitho's aid, before Allday could bound forward and deliver the fatal stroke. Jenour had learned from that experience, and many others. Bolitho had noticed that since *Hyperion*'s last fight, whenever the young man wore his sword, it carried a strong lanyard for his wrist as well as its decorative knot.

It was interesting, too, to see the respect with which *Truculent*'s officers treated Jenour, although most of them were older and by far more senior. The thirty-six gun frigate had been on constant patrol and convoy duty since Poland had taken command. But there was not a member of her wardroom who had ever been in a major fleet action.

Bolitho nodded to the officers and walked to the larboard gangway which, like the one on the opposite side, joined the quarterdeck with the forecastle. Beneath it the vessel's main armament was already being checked and inspected by the gunner and one of his mates. Poland was certainly thorough, Bolitho thought. He was by the rail now, his eyes on the bare-backed seamen as they packed home the hammocks in the nettings like neat lines of pods. Some bodies were already brown, some showing a painful rawness from too much exposure to the unaccustomed glare.

12

The sun was rising as if from the ocean itself, the lines of low rollers curling away like molten copper. *Truculent* was already steaming, despite the lingering chill of night. She would look like a ghost-ship when the heat really enfolded her and every sail dried out in its intensity.

Bolitho pitied the officers on watch in their hats and heavy coats. Poland obviously believed that there was never a proper moment to relax any show of authority, no matter how uncomfortable. He wondered what they thought of his own casual rig. There would be time enough for pomp and tradition when he made contact with the fleet, which was allegedly assembled off the coast. For all they had seen on passage they could have been the only ship afloat.

Immersed in his thoughts, he began to walk slowly up and down, a measured distance between the wheel and the taffrail. Sailors working on the ever-necessary repairs and maintenance, splicing, replacing frayed cordage, painting and washing down, glanced up as his shadow passed over them. Each man looked quickly away if their eyes chanced to meet.

Mr Hull, the frigate's taciturn sailing-master, was watching three midshipmen who were taking turns to prepare a chart. Beside him, as officer-of-the-watch, the second lieutenant was trying not to yawn, with his captain in such an uncertain mood. There was a smell of cooking from the galley and the lieutenant's stomach contracted painfully. It was still a long wait before the watch changed and he could be relieved.

Hull asked quietly, 'What d'ye reckon 'e thinks about, Mr Munro?' He gestured shortly towards the tall figure in the white shirt, whose dark hair, tied to the nape of his neck, lifted in the light breeze as he strode unhurriedly up and down.

Munro lowered his voice. 'I know not, Mr Hull. But if half of what I hear about him is true, then he has plenty to choose from!' Like the others, Munro had seen little of the vice-admiral, except for one meal together, and once when he and the captain had summoned the lieutenants and senior warrant officers to explain the purpose of his mission.

Two strong forces of ships had been ordered to the Cape of Good Hope with soldiers and marines for the sole purpose of landing and laying siege to Cape Town, with the intention of retaking it from the Dutch, Napoleon's unwilling ally.

13

Then, and only then, would the shipping routes around the Cape be safe from marauding men-of-war and French privateers. There was also a dockyard which, once repossessed, would be vastly improved and expanded, so that never again would English ships be forced to fend for themselves, or waste valuable months beating back and forth seeking other suitable anchorages.

Even Captain Poland had seemed surprised at Bolitho's open confidence with subordinates he did not know, especially when most flag-officers would have considered it none of their business. Munro glanced at the flag-lieutenant and recalled how Jenour had described that last battle, when *Hyperion* had led the squadron and broken through the enemy's line, until both sides had been broadside to broadside.

You could have heard a pin fall, he thought, as Jenour had described the death of the old two-decker, the ship which Bolitho had twice made into a legend.

Jenour had looked down at the wardroom table and had said, 'Her stern was rising all the time, but at her foremast the admiral's flag was still close-up. He had ordered them to leave it there. A lot of good men went with her. They could have no better company.' Then he had raised his head and Munro had been shocked to see the tears in his eyes. 'Then I heard him say, just as if he was speaking to the ship, *There'll be none better than you, old lady*. And then she was gone.'

Munro had never been so moved before by anything; neither had his friend the first lieutenant.

Poland's voice cut through his thoughts like a dirk.

'Mr Munro! I would trouble you to cast an eye over those idle roughknots who are supposed to be working on the second cutter – they seem more intent on gaping at the horizon than using their skills! Maybe they should not be blamed if the officer-of-the-watch is day-dreaming, what?'

Mr Hull bared his teeth in an unfeeling grin.

'Got eyes everywhere, 'e 'as!' He swung on the midshipmen to cover Munro's embarrassment. 'An' wot d'you think you're a-doin' of? Gawd, you'll never make lieutenants, nary a one o' ye!'

Bolitho heard all of it, but his mind was elsewhere. He often

14

thought of Catherine's despairing anger. How much of what she said was true? He knew he had made enemies down the years, and many had tried to hurt and damage him because of his dead brother, Hugh, who had gone over to the other side during the American Revolution. Later they had used young Adam for the same purpose, so it was likely that the enemies were truly there, and not merely in his mind.

Did they really need him to come to the Cape so urgently; or was it true that Nelson's victory over the Combined Fleet had changed strategy out of all recognition? France and Spain had lost many ships, destroyed or taken as prizes. But England's fleet had been badly battered, and the essential blockading squadrons outside enemy ports were stretched to the limit. Napoleon would never give up his vision of a mighty empire. He would need more ships, like the ones which were building at Toulon and along the Channel coast, vessels of which Nelson had spoken many times in his written duels with the Admiralty. But until then, Napoleon might look elsewhere – perhaps to France's old ally, America?

Bolitho plucked at the front of his shirt, one of the elegant selection Catherine had bought for him in London while he had been with Their Lordships.

He had always hated the capital, its false society, its privileged citizens who damned the war because of its inconvenience to them, without a thought for the men who daily gave their lives to protect their liberty. Like – He thrust Belinda from his mind, and felt the locket which Catherine had given him. Small, silver, with a perfect miniature of her inside, her dark eyes, the throat bared as he had known and loved it. In a compartment at the back was a compressed lock of her hair. That was new, but he could only guess how long she had owned the locket, or who had given it to her. Certainly not her first husband, a soldier of fortune who had died in a brawl in Spain. Perhaps it had been a gift from her second, Luis Pareja, who had died trying to help defend a merchantman taken by Bolitho and then attacked by Barbary pirates.

Luis had been twice her age, but in his own way he had loved her. He had been a Spanish merchant, and the miniature had all the delicacy and finesse he would have appreciated.

15

So she had come into Bolitho's life; and then, after a brief affair, she had gone. Misunderstanding, a misguided attempt to preserve his reputation – Bolitho had often cursed himself for allowing it to happen. For letting their tangled lives come between them.

And then, just two years ago when *Hyperion* had sailed into English Harbour, they had found one another again. Bolitho leaving behind a marriage which had soured, and Catherine married, for the third time, to the Viscount Somervell, a treacherous and decadent man who, on learning of her renewed passion for Bolitho, had attempted to have her dishonoured and thrown into a debtor's prison, from which Bolitho had saved her.

He heard her voice now as clearly as if she were standing here on this rapidly drying deck. '*Keep this around your neck, darling Richard. I shall take it off again only when you are lying by my side as my lover.*'

He felt the engraving on the back of the locket. Like the small wisp of hair, it was new, something she had caused to be done in London while he had been at the Admiralty.

So simply said, as if she were speaking to him even as he recalled it.

May Fate always guide you. May love always protect you.

He walked to the nettings, and shaded his eyes to watch some gulls. It made him tremble merely to think of her, how they had loved in Antigua and in Cornwall for so short a time together.

He moved his head slightly, holding his breath. The sun was strong but not yet high enough to – He hesitated, then looked hard at the horizon's glittering line.

Nothing happened. The mist did not edge out like some evil disease to mock his left eye. *Nothing.*

Allday was looking aft and saw Bolitho's expression, and felt like praying. It was like seeing the face of a man on the scaffold when given a last-minute reprieve.

'*Deck there!*' Every face looked up. 'Sail on the starboard quarter!'

Poland called sharply, 'Mr Williams, I'd be obliged if you would take a glass aloft!'

The first lieutenant seized a telescope from the midshipman

16

on watch and hurried to the main shrouds. He looked surprised: Bolitho guessed it was at his captain's unusual courtesy, rather than the task.

Truculent's sails were barely filling, and yet the stranger's topgallants seemed to be speeding down on a converging tack at a tremendous rate.

He had seen it many times. The same stretch of ocean, with one ship all but becalmed, and another with every stitch of canvas filled to the brim.

Poland glanced at Bolitho, his features expressionless. But his fingers were opening and closing at his sides, betraying his agitation.

'Shall I clear for action, Sir Richard?'

Bolitho raised a telescope and levelled it across the quarter. A strange bearing. Perhaps not one of the local squadron after all.

'We will bide our time, Captain Poland. I have no doubt you can be ready to run out in ten minutes, if need be?'

Poland flushed. 'I – that is, Sir Richard –' He nodded firmly. 'Indeed, in less!'

Bolitho moved the glass carefully, but could only make out the mastheads of the newcomer; saw the bearing alter slightly as they drew into line to swoop down on *Truculent*.

Lieutenant Williams called from the mainmast crosstrees, 'Frigate, sir!'

Bolitho watched tiny specks of colour rising to break the other ship's silhouette as she hoisted a signal.

Williams called down the recognition and Poland could barely prevent himself from tearing the signals book from the midshipman's fingers. '*Well!*'

The boy stammered, 'She's the *Zest*, sir, forty-four. Captain Varian.'

Poland muttered, 'Oh yes, I know who *he* is. Make our number – lively now!'

Bolitho lowered the glass and watched. *Two faces*. The midshipman's confused, perhaps frightened. One moment he had been watching the first hump of land as it eased up from the sea-mist, and the next he had probably seen it all vanish, the prospect of an unexpected enemy, death even, suddenly laid before him.

The other was Poland's. Whoever Varian was he was no friend, and was doubtless much senior, to command a forty-four.

Lieutenant Munro was in the shrouds, his legs wrapped around the ratlines, heedless of the fresh tar on his white breeches, and even thoughts of breakfast forgotten.

'Signal, sir! *Captain repair on board!*'

Bolitho saw the crestfallen look on Poland's face. After his remarkable passage from England without loss or injury to any man aboard, it was like a slap in the face.

'Mr Jenour, lay aft if you please.' Bolitho saw the flag-lieutenant's mouth quiver as though in anticipation. 'I believe you have my flag in your care?'

Jenour could not contain a grin this time. 'Aye, *aye*, sir!' He almost ran from the quarterdeck.

Bolitho watched the other frigate's great pyramid of sails lifting and plunging over the sparkling water. Maybe it was childish, but he did not care.

'Captain Poland, for convenience's sake, yours is no longer a private ship.' He saw doubt alter to understanding on Poland's tense features. 'So please make to *Zest*, and spell it out with care, *The privilege is yours*.'

Poland turned as Bolitho's flag broke at the foremast truck, and then gestured urgently to the signals party as bunting spilled across the deck in feverish confusion.

Jenour joined Munro as he clambered back to the deck.

'That is what you wanted to know. *There* is the real man. He'd not stand by and see any of his people slighted!' *Not even Poland*, he almost added.

Bolitho saw sunlight reflecting from several telescopes on the other frigate. *Zest*'s captain would not know anything about Bolitho's mission, nor would anyone else.

He tightened his jaw and said gently, 'Well, they know now.'

2

Remember Nelson

'May I assure you, Sir Richard, that no disrespect was intended . . .'

Bolitho walked to the cabin stern windows, half listening to the clatter of blocks and the surge of water alongside as *Truculent* rolled, hove-to in the swell. This would need to be quick. As predicted by Poland's sailing-master, the wind would soon return. He could not see the other frigate, and guessed that she was standing slightly downwind of her smaller consort.

He turned and sat on the bench seat, gesturing to a chair. 'Some coffee, Captain Varian?' He heard Ozzard's quiet footsteps and guessed that the little man was already preparing it. It gave Bolitho time to study his visitor.

Captain Charles Varian was a direct contrast to Poland. Very tall and broad-shouldered, self-confident: probably the landsman's idea of a frigate captain.

Varian said, 'I was eager for news, Sir Richard. And seeing this ship, well –' He spread his big hands and gave what was intended as a disarming smile.

Bolitho watched him steadily. 'It did not occur to you that a ship from the Channel Squadron might not have time to waste in idle gossip? You could have closed to hailing distance, surely.'

Ozzard pattered in with his coffee pot and peered unseeingly at the stranger.

Varian nodded. 'I was not thinking. And *you*, Sir Richard – of all people, to be out here when you must be needed else-where . . .' The smile remained, but his eyes were strangely opaque. *Not a man to cross*, Bolitho decided. By a subordinate, anyway.

'You will need to return to your command directly, Captain. But first I would appreciate your assessment of the situation here.' He sipped the hot coffee. *What was the matter with him? He was on edge, as he had been since* . . . After all, he had done it himself as a young commander. So many leagues from home, and then the sight of a friendly ship.

He continued, 'I have come with new orders.'

Varian's inscrutable expression sharpened immediately.

He said, 'You will know, Sir Richard, that most of the force intended for retaking Cape Town from the Dutch is already here. They are anchored to the north-west, near Saldanha Bay. Sir David Baird commands the army, and Commodore Popham the escorting squadron and transports. I have been told that the landings will begin very shortly.' He hesitated, suddenly uncertain under Bolitho's level gaze.

'You are with the supporting squadron.' It was a statement, and Varian shrugged while he moved his cup across the table.

'That is so, Sir Richard. I am still awaiting some additional vessels to rendezvous as planned.' When Bolitho said nothing he hastened on, 'I had been patrolling in the vicinity of Good Hope and then your topsails were sighted. I thought a straggler had finally arrived.'

Bolitho asked quietly, 'What of *your* senior officer – Commodore Warren? I am surprised that he would release his biggest fifth-rate at a time when he might need your full support.'

He had a vague picture of Commodore Warren in his mind, like a faded portrait. He had known him briefly during the ill-fated attempt by the French Royalists to land and retake Toulon from the Revolutionary army. Bolitho had been a captain then like Varian, and his ship had been *Hyperion*. He had not seen Warren since. But the navy was a family and he had heard of him serving on various stations in the West Indies and the Spanish Main.

Varian said abruptly, 'The Commodore is unwell, Sir Richard. In my opinion he should never have been given –'

Bolitho said, 'As the senior captain you have assumed overall charge of the supporting squadron; is that it?'

'I have made a full report, Sir Richard.'

'Which I shall read in due course.' Bolitho moved his hand consciously away from his eyelid and added, 'It is my intention to hasten the attack on Cape Town. Time is of the essence. Which is why this fast passage was of the utmost importance.' He saw the shot go home but continued, 'So we will return to the squadron in company. I intend to see Commodore Warren without delay.'

He stood up and walked to the quarter windows to watch the crests beginning to ruffle like crisp lace in the wind. The ship was rising to it. Eager to move again.

Varian tried to recompose himself. 'The other vessels, Sir Richard?'

Bolitho said, 'There are none. There will be none. As it is I am authorised to dispatch several of the ships here directly to England.'

'Has something happened, sir?'

He said quietly, 'Last October our fleet under Lord Nelson defeated the enemy off Cape Trafalgar.'

Varian swallowed hard. 'We did not know, Sir Richard!' For once he seemed at a loss. 'A victory! *By God*, that is great news.'

Bolitho shrugged. 'Brave Nelson is dead. So the victory is a hollow one.'

There was a tap at the door and Poland stepped into the cabin. The two captains glanced at one another and nodded like old acquaintances, but Bolitho sensed they were completely divided as if by the bars of a smithy's furnace.

'The wind is freshening from the nor'-west, Sir Richard.' Poland did not look again at the other man. '*Zest*'s gig is still hooked on to the chains.'

Bolitho held out his hand. 'I shall see you again, Captain Varian.' He relented slightly. 'The blockade continues around all enemy ports. It is vital. And though heartened by our victory at Trafalgar, our own forces are weakened by it nonetheless.'

The door closed behind them and Bolitho heard the shrill of calls as Varian was piped over the side into his gig.

He moved restlessly about the cabin, remembering one of the meetings he had had with Admiral Sir Owen Godschale at the Admiralty. The last one, in fact, when he had outlined the need for urgency. The Combined Fleets of France and Spain had been thoroughly beaten, but the war was not won. Already it had been reported that at least three small French squadrons had broken through the tightly-stretched blockade, and had seemingly vanished into the Atlantic. Was this to be Napoleon's new strategy? To raid ports and isolated islands, to prey upon supply ships and trade routes, to give the British squadrons no rest while they, the French, gathered another fleet?

He could almost smile at Godschale's contemptuous dismissal of the enemy's strength. One group which had outwitted the blockading squadron off Brest had been under the veteran Vice Amiral Leissègues, and his flagship was the 120-gun first-rate *Impérial*. Hardly small.

The French might even have their eye on Cape Town. It was impossible to guess at the havoc they could create there. They could sever the routes to India and the East Indies as surely as the blade of an axe.

He remembered the studied coolness between Godschale and himself. The admiral had been a contemporary of his; they had even been posted together on the same date. There was no other similarity.

Bolitho was suddenly conscious of the distance between himself and Catherine. Godschale, like so many others, had tried to keep them apart, may even have plotted with Belinda to have Catherine dishonoured and lost in lies. But Bolitho doubted that. The admiral was too fond of his own power and comfort to risk a scandal. Or was he? It was openly said that Godschale's next step was to the House of Lords. There might be others there who would wish to destroy them through Godschale.

Catherine's words rang in his ears. *Don't you see what they are doing to us?*

Perhaps this mission to the Cape was merely a beginning. To keep him employed without respite, knowing that he would never resign, no matter what they did.

He crossed to the rack and touched the old family sword, dull by contrast with the fine presentation blade below it. Other Bolithos had worn it, proved it, and sometimes had fallen with it still gripped in a dead hand. He could not see any of them giving

22

up without a fight. The thought gave him comfort, and when Allday came into the cabin he saw him smiling, the first time for a long while.

Allday said, 'The whole squadron will know about Lord Nelson by now, Sir Richard. It'll take the heart out of some.' He gestured towards the nearest gunport as if he could already see the African mainland. 'Not worth dyin' for, they'll say. Not like standing 'twixt the *mounseers* and England, clearin' the way like we did!'

Bolitho was moved beyond his own anxieties and said, 'With old oaks like you about, they'll soon take heed!'

Allday gave his slow grin. 'I'll wager two o' the cap'ns will have some grief afore long as well.'

Bolitho eyed him severely. 'You damned fox! What do *you* know of it?'

'At present, not much, Sir Richard. But I does know that Cap'n Poland was once the other gentleman's first lieutenant.'

Bolitho shook his head. Without Allday he would have nobody to share his feelings or fears. Others looked to him only for leadership – they wanted nothing more.

Allday took down the sword and wrapped it in his special cloth.

'But it's what I always says, Sir Richard, and every true Jack knows it.' He gave another grin. 'It's aft the most honour may be, but forrard you finds the better men. An' that's no error!'

After Allday had gone Bolitho seated himself at the table and opened his personal log. Inside it was the letter he had started when England's mist and drizzle had faded astern, and the long passage had begun.

When she would read it, or if it even reached her, he would not know until she was in his arms. Her skin against his, her tears and her joy mingled with his own.

He leaned over the letter while he touched the locket through his new shirt.

Another dawn, dearest Kate, and how I long for thee . . .

He was still writing when the ship changed tack yet again, and from the high masthead came the cry that the assembled ships had been sighted.

Bolitho went on deck at noon, and felt the sun strike his face

23

and shoulders like fire; his shoes stuck to the deck-seams as he strode to the hammock-nettings with a telescope from the rack.

Mountains, red and pink in the harsh, misty glare, and over all the sun, which was like burnished silver, strong enough to drain all colour from the sky around it.

He shifted the glass slightly, his legs braced as the lazy offshore swell lifted the keel and rolled noisily down either beam. Table Mountain, a paler wedge, but still shrouded in haze and mystery like some giant's altar.

There were the ships. His eyes moved professionally across the mixed collection. The elderly sixty-four *Themis*, which he knew was Commodore Warren's ship. Warren was ill. How ill? He had not enquired further of Varian. It would show his hand, or display uncertainty when he must soon need these unknown men to trust him without question.

Another frigate, some schooners and two large supply vessels. The cream of the attacking force would be as Varian had described, to the north-west where the ships could anchor well offshore, whereas here there was only one natural bank shallow enough to ride at their cables. Beyond the hundred-fathom line the sea's bed fell away to infinity, a black oblivion where nothing moved.

He saw sunlight flashing on glass and knew they were watching *Truculent*'s slow approach, as surprised by his flag at the fore as Varian had been.

Captain Poland joined him by the side.

He said, 'Do you think it will be a long campaign, Sir Richard?'

He spoke with elaborate care, and Bolitho guessed he was probably wondering what had passed between himself and Varian in the cabin. Bolitho lowered the telescope and faced him.

'I have had some dealings with the army in the past, Captain. They are more used to campaigns than I care for. A battle is one thing – you win or you strike. But all this drawn-out business of supplies and marching is not for me.'

Poland gave a very rare smile. 'Nor me, Sir Richard.'

Bolitho turned to look for Jenour. 'You may signal for water lighters when you are anchored, Captain. A word of praise to

24

your people will not come amiss either. It was an *admirable passage.*'

A shaft of sunlight like the blade of a lance swept down on them as the Afterguard hauled over the great driver-boom.

Bolitho gritted his teeth. *Nothing.* They had to be wrong. There was nothing. He could see the other ships plainly in spite of the unwavering glare.

Jenour watched him and felt his heart thumping against his ribs. Then he saw Allday coming aft, the old sword protruding from his polishing cloth.

Their exchange of glances was swift but complete. Was it too soon to hope? For all their sakes?

The two frigates rounded-up and anchored in the late afternoon considerably earlier than even the taciturn Mr Hull had predicted. As signals were made and exchanged, boats lowered and awnings spread, Bolitho watched from the quarterdeck, his mind exploring the task which lay ahead.

It was strange how the land never seemed to draw any closer, and because of the difficult anchorage it gave an impression of brooding defiance. The point to the north-west which had been selected for the first assault was a good choice, possibly the only one. Bolitho had examined the charts with great care, as well as the maps supplied to him by the Admiralty. Up there at Saldanha Bay the coastal waters were shallow and protected enough to land soldiers and marines under the cover of men-of-war, which could offer fire. But once ashore the true difficulty would begin. Saldanha Bay was one hundred miles from Cape Town. Foot soldiers, some sick and weary from weeks and weeks at sea in their cramped quarters between decks, would be in no fit state to march and skirmish all the way to Cape Town. The Dutch were excellent fighters and would harry rather than confront them every mile. When they finally reached the Cape, the enemy would be ready and waiting. It seemed unlikely that any large force of Dutch soldiers would be sent to contest the landings. It would leave them in danger of being cut off by this supporting squadron.

Bolitho felt his impatience returning. A campaign then,

lengthy and costly. A war of supply-lines, to be fought by soldiers, many of whom had been confined to garrison duties in the Indies. The Islands of Death, as the army called them, where more men died of fever than under the enemy's fire.

Jenour strode aft and touched his hat. 'Your despatch to the general has gone, Sir Richard, taken by the courier schooner *Miranda* this moment.'

Bolitho shaded his eyes to watch the small and graceful schooner tacking away from the other vessels, her commander doubtless grateful to be free of other authority, albeit for only a few days.

Bolitho watched the redness of evening spreading along the glittering horizon, the masts and yards of the small squadron suddenly like bronze. Ashore telescopes would have observed *Truculent*'s arrival as they had doubtless studied all the others.

He remarked, 'You are in irons, Stephen, so why not spit out what you think?'

But for his self-control, Jenour would have blushed. Bolitho always knew. It was pointless to pretend.

'I – I thought –' He licked his dry lips. 'I would have thought that the Commodore might have requested to come aboard.' He fell silent under Bolitho's scrutiny.

Bolitho said, 'In his place I would have done just that.' He recalled Captain Varian's tactless remark. 'Call away the gig, Stephen. My compliments to Captain Poland and explain that I am going across to *Themis*.'

Fifteen minutes later, sweating steadily in his dress coat and hat, he sat in the gig's sternsheets with Jenour beside him, and a critical Allday crouching with the boat's coxswain.

As they pulled slowly abeam of the other ships, Bolitho saw officers-of-the-watch doffing their hats, motionless figures in shrouds and rigging staring in silence, their bare arms and shoulders like parts of the bronze around them.

Allday leaned forward, his mouth just inches from Bolitho's ear.

'Y'see, they *knows*, Sir Richard. Only here an hour an' the word has gone through the whole squadron!' He saw one of the oarsmen staring at him and scowled over Bolitho's epaulette. The man dropped his gaze and almost lost the stroke. He had

26

probably been surprised at seeing a seaman, even an admiral's personal coxswain, chatting with his master, while the latter even turned his head to listen.

Bolitho nodded. 'Lord Nelson will be sadly missed. We'll not see his like in our lifetime.'

Allday leaned back again and rolled his tongue inside his cheek to restrain a grin. *I'm not too sure o' that*, he thought.

Bolitho watched the *Themis*'s bowsprit and tapering jib-boom sweeping out to greet them. She was an old ship and had been employed on every sort of duty other than the line of battle. Originally a sixty-four, she had been stripped of some of her armament while she was carrying soldiers from one trouble spot to the next; she had even been to the penal colony in New South Wales. Transport, receiving ship, and now with the war demanding everything that would stay afloat, she was here, part of the invading force.

Jenour bit his lip and tried to relax. He had seen the assembled guard at the entry port, the glitter of red sunlight on drawn swords. An air of wariness.

Bolitho waited while the bowman hooked on to the main chains, then pulled himself up to the entry port, immediately deafened by the bark of commands, the chorus of squealing calls, which sailors termed 'Spithead Nightingales'. He no longer needed to look for Allday to know he was there, ready to reach out if he lost his footing, or if his eye . . . *No. He would not think about it.*

The din faded away and he raised his hat to the poop, where the White Ensign made a lively dance against the hot sky.

The officer who stepped forward to present himself wore the epaulette of commander. He was old for his rank and had possibly been passed over for captain.

'I bid you welcome, Sir Richard.'

Bolitho smiled briefly. Allday was right. There were no secrets.

'Where is the Commodore?' He glanced up at the curling pendant. 'Is he unwell?'

The commander, whose name was Maguire, looked uncomfortable. 'He sends his apologies, Sir Richard. He awaits you in his cabin.'

27

Bolitho nodded to the other officers and turned aside to Jenour. 'Remain here. Discover what you can.' He patted his arm but did not smile. 'I am certain Allday will do likewise!'

Maguire led the way to the companion ladder and almost bowed as Bolitho walked aft, where a Royal Marine sentry drew his heels together with the precision of a bolt snapping shut.

There was nothing slack about the old *Themis*. It was just as if she did not belong. Maybe too many tasks in far-flung stations, too long away from home. As far as Bolitho could gather, the ship had not returned to England for fifteen years, so God alone knew what state her lower hull was in.

The screen doors were opened by a black servant and Bolitho received another surprise. During her role as accommodation ship they must have removed some of the armament from aft to enlarge the officers' quarters. Now, with her gunports filled only with wooden 'quakers', the shortened muzzles of which might deceive another vessel at long-range, or even a landsman walking on a dockside, the after accommodation was huge, and contained nothing more war-like than furniture and a stand of muskets.

Commodore Arthur Warren walked from a screened-off cabin and exclaimed, 'Sir Richard. What must you think of me?'

Bolitho was shocked by what he saw. He had never really known Warren as a friend, but he guessed him to be about his own age. But the officer in the loose-fitting coat, whose lined face had somehow defied the suns of so many fierce climates, was an old man.

The door closed, and apart from the watchful servant, who wore a red waistcoat above his duck trousers, they were alone. The elderly commander had taken his leave without dismissal. It was no wonder that the confident Captain Varian had seen this squadron as his own future responsibility.

Bolitho said, 'Please be seated.' He waited while the other officer beckoned to his servant and some finely-cut Spanish goblets were filled with red wine. Warren then seated himself. One leg was thrust out, as if in pain, his left hand hidden beneath his coat. He was not sick, Bolitho thought. He was dying.

Bolitho raised his goblet. 'Your health, sir. Everyone seems to know I am here, even though the news of Trafalgar has not reached them.'

28

The wine was rough and brackish, but he barely noticed it.

Once he had been a flag-captain to Rear-Admiral Sir Charles Thelwall in the big three-decker *Euryalus*. Bolitho had been made to work doubly hard because his admiral's health had deteriorated over the months at sea. He had admired Thelwall and had been saddened to see him step ashore for the last time with only a short while left to live. Bolitho was only glad that the admiral had been spared what had happened that year, the mutinies throughout the fleet at the Nore and Spithead, Plymouth and Scotland. No captain had ever forgotten. Nor would they, unless they were inviting disaster.

But the admiral had looked and sounded like Warren now. As he swallowed some wine he struggled to contain a deep, tearing cough, and when he took his handkerchief from his lips Bolitho knew the stains on it were not all wine.

'I would not trouble you, sir, but if you wish I could send for another surgeon from *Truculent*. He seems an excellent man from the talks I had with him.'

Warren's face stiffened with pathetic determination. 'I am well enough, Sir Richard. I know my duty!'

Bolitho looked away. *This ship is all he has. The temporary title of commodore the only triumph he has known*. He tried to harden his mind, to shut out the pity he could feel and understand.

He said, 'I have sent a despatch to the main squadron. I am ordered here to withdraw certain ships for service in home waters.' He thought he saw a small gleam of hope in Warren's faded eyes and added gently, '*Frigates*, not this ship. There has to be a strategy for taking and then defending Cape Town, without prolonging it into a siege which only the Dutch can win.'

Warren said huskily, 'The army won't like that, Sir Richard. Sir David Baird is said to be a forceful general.'

Bolitho thought of the letter locked in his strong-box aboard *Truculent*. Not signed by some senior Secretary or Lord of Admiralty; not this time. It was signed by the King, and even though the uncharitable hinted amongst themselves that His Majesty often did not know what he was putting his signature to these days, it still held the ultimate power and opened all doors.

'I shall cross that bridge in due course. In the meantime I

29

would like to shift to this ship.' He held up his hand as Warren made to protest. 'Your broad pendant will still fly. But as someone once said, I need room to bustle in!'

Warren held down another bout of coughing and asked, 'What must I do? You have my word that I will serve you well. And if Captain Varian has told you –'

Bolitho retorted calmly, 'I have been in the King's service since I was twelve. Somewhere along the way I learned to form my own opinions.' He stood up and walked to an open port and stared along the false wooden muzzle at the nearest ship, another frigate. 'But I have to tell you, Commodore Warren, I'll not waste anyone's life because we have not tried to do our best. Throughout the navy, loyal seamen and marines, officers too, will be shocked and disappointed that after Trafalgar, victory is not complete. In my view it will take years before the tyranny of France and her jackals is finally routed!'

He realised that Warren and the silent servant were both staring at him and that he had raised his voice.

He forced a smile. 'Now I must ask you to forgive *me*. It is just that I have seen so many fine ships lost, brave men dying for the wrong reasons, some cursing those who despatched them in the first place. While I direct what is to be done here, those who forget the hard lessons of war will answer to me.' He picked up his hat. 'Just as one day I will answer to God, I have no doubt.'

'A moment, Sir Richard!' Warren seized his own hat from the black servant and followed him into the shadows of the half-deck.

Before they reached the entry port he said in his halting tones, 'I am *honoured*, Sir Richard.' His voice was suddenly firmer than Bolitho had heard before. 'I am unused to this sort of work, but I will do all I can. So shall my people!'

Jenour saw Bolitho's grave smile as he walked out into the strange sunlight. It gave him a twinge of excitement, like those other times, when up to now he had been expecting a dull and undemanding role for the man he had always looked up to, even before he had laid eyes on him.

When he had told his parents in Southampton that he intended one day to personally serve Bolitho in some capacity, they had chuckled at his innocence. The chuckles had gone now.

30

There was only the concern which was the legacy of all those with young sons away at war.

Commodore Warren walked off to seek his commander; his cut-down *Themis* did not warrant a flag-captain apparently. Bolitho took his flag-lieutenant aside.

'We are coming aboard, Stephen.' He saw no surprise on Jenour's open features. 'For the present at least. Fetch the others from *Truculent* . . . I fear that Mr Yovell will be writing throughout the night. And find a good signals midshipman aboard *this* ship – it does not look well to employ strangers. Tomorrow I want all captains on board at eight bells, so warn them before nightfall. Send the guardboat if you will.'

Jenour could barely keep up with him. Bolitho seemed tireless, as if his mind were breaking out of a self-made prison.

Bolitho added, 'The enemy know we are about – they have all day to watch us. I intend to discover what is happening around the Cape where the other anchorage lies. I feel the remedy may be there, rather than a hundred-mile struggle from Saldanha Bay. I do not know these captains here, and there is little time to do so. As you are aware, Stephen, in my despatch to the army I requested that the attack be delayed.'

Jenour watched the eyes, lighter grey now as he turned towards the open sea. Like the ocean itself, he thought.

He said, 'But you do not believe that the general will agree?'

Bolitho clapped him on the arm like a boyish conspirator. 'We will act independently.' His face was suddenly introspective. 'As this is a day for remembering Nelson, let us use his own words. The boldest measures are usually the safest!'

That night Bolitho sat by the stern windows of the cabin – which had once been used by no less than a governor-general, who had fled on board to escape the plague which had broken out amongst the islands he controlled – and watched the ships' riding lights with no inclination to sleep.

The air was heavy and humid, and as a guardboat pulled slowly amongst the anchored squadron, he thought instead of Cornwall, of the bitter wind on the night when she had come to him. Just over a month ago, no more; and now he was here in the shadow of Africa, and they were separated again at the whim of others.

31

Did they need his skills so much that they could overlook his contempt for them? Or, like Nelson, would they prefer a dead hero to a living reminder of their own failings?

The deck quivered as the anchor cable took the sudden strain of a faster current. Allday had not been very optimistic about shifting to the old sixty-four. The company had been aboard too long, pressed from passing merchantmen in the Caribbean, survivors from other vessels, even pardoned prisoners from the courts of Jamaica.

Like Warren, the ship was worn out, and suddenly thrust into a role she no longer recognised. Bolitho had seen the old swivel-gun mountings on either gangway. Not facing a possible enemy but pointing inboard, from the time when she had carried convicts and prisoners-of-war from a campaign already forgotten.

He thought he heard Ozzard pattering about in his newly-occupied pantry. So he could not sleep either. Still remembering *Hyperion*'s last moments – or was he nursing his secret, which Bolitho had sensed before that final battle?

Bolitho yawned and gently massaged his eye. It was strange, but he could not clearly remember why Ozzard had not been on deck when they had been forced to clear the ship of the survivors and the wounded.

He thought too of his flag-captain and firm friend, Valentine Keen, his face full of pain, not at his own injury but for his vice-admiral's despair.

If only you were here now, Val.

But his words went unspoken, for he had fallen asleep at last.

3

The Albacora

An onlooker, had there been one, might have compared the little topsail schooner *Miranda* with a giant moth. But apart from a few screaming and wheeling gulls, there was none to see her as she came about in a great welter of bursting spray, her twin booms swinging over to refill the sails on the opposite tack.

She leaned so far to leeward that the sea was spurting through her washports, rising even above her bulwark to surge along the streaming planking, or breaking over the four-pounder guns like waves on rocks.

It was wild and exhilarating, the air filled with the din of sea and banging canvas, with only the occasional shouted command, for nothing superfluous was needed here. Each man knew his work, aware of the ever-present dangers: he could be flung senseless against some immovable object to suffer a cracked skull or broken limbs, or be pitched overboard by a treacherous wave as it burst over the bows and swept along like a mill-race. *Miranda* was small and very lively, and certainly no place for the unwary or the inexperienced.

Aft by the compass box her commander, Lieutenant James Tyacke, swayed and leaned with his ship, one hand in his pocket, the other gripping a slippery backstay. Like his men he was soaked to the skin, his eyes raw from spray and spindrift as he watched the tilting compass card, the flapping mainsail and pendant while his command plunged again, her bowsprit pointing due south.

33

They had taken all night and part of the day to claw out of Saldanha Bay, away from the impressive formations of anchored men-of-war, supply ships, bombs, army transports and all the rest. Lieutenant Tyacke had used the time to beat as far out as possible, to gain the sea-room he needed before heading back to Commodore Warren's small squadron. There was another reason, which probably only his second-in-command had guessed. He wanted to put as much ocean as possible between *Miranda* and the squadron before someone signalled him to repair aboard the flagship yet again.

He had done what he had been ordered, delivered the despatches to the army and the commodore. He had been glad to leave.

Tyacke was thirty years old and had commanded the speedy *Miranda* for the last three of them. After her grace and intimacy, the flagship had seemed like a city, with the navy seemingly outnumbered by the red and scarlet of the military and the marines.

It was not that he did not know what a big ship was like. He tightened his jaw, determined to hold the memory and the bitterness at bay. Eight years ago he had been serving as a lieutenant aboard the *Majestic*, a two-decker with Nelson's fleet in the Mediterranean. He had been on the lower gundeck when Nelson had finally run the French to earth at Aboukir Bay, the Battle of the Nile as it was now called.

It was too terrible to remember clearly, or to arrange the events in their proper order. With the passing of time they eluded him, or overlapped like insane acts in a nightmare.

At the height of it his ship, *Majestic*, had come up against the French *Tonnant* of eighty guns, which had seemed to tower over them like a flaming cliff.

The noise was still there to remember, if he let himself, the awful sights of men, and pieces of men, being flung about the bloody litter and gruel of the gundeck, a place which had become a hell all of its own. The wild eyes of the gun crews, white through their filthy skins, the cannon firing and recoiling, no longer as a controlled broadside but in divisions, then in ones and twos, while the ship shook and quaked around and above them. Unbeknown to the demented souls who sponged out,

34

loaded and fired because it was all that they knew, their captain, Westcott, had already fallen dead, along with so many of his men. Their world was the lower gundeck. Nothing else mattered, could matter. Guns were upended and smashed by the enemy's fire; men ran screaming to be driven back by equally terrified lieutenants and warrant officers.

Run out! Point! Fire!

He heard it still. It would never leave him. Others had told him he was lucky. Not because of the victory – only ignorant landsmen spoke of such things. But because he had survived when so many had fallen, the lucky to die, the others to cry out their lives under the surgeon's saw, or to be pathetic cripples whom nobody wanted to see or remember.

He watched the compass card steady and felt the keel slicing through the steep rollers as if they were nothing.

He touched his face with his hand, feeling its roughness, seeing it in his mind as he was forced to do each day when he shaved himself.

Again he could remember nothing. A gun had exploded, or a flaming wad had come inboard from one of *Tonnant*'s lower battery and sparked off a full charge nearby. It could have been either. Nobody had been left to tell him.

But the whole of the right side of his face had been scored away, left like charred meat, half a face which people turned their heads not to see. How his eye had survived was the real miracle.

He thought of his visit to the flagship. He had not seen the general or even the commodore, just a bored-looking colonel who had been carrying a glass of hock or something cool in one elegant hand. They had not even asked Tyacke to be seated, let alone to take a glass with them.

As he had gone down the great ship's side to his own longboat, that same aide had come dashing after him.

'I say, Lieutenant! Why did you not tell me the news? About Nelson and the victory?'

Tyacke had looked up the ship's curving black and buff hull and had not tried to conceal his contempt.

''Cause nobody asked me, *sir!*' God damn their eyes.

Benjamin Simcox, master's mate and acting-master of the

schooner *Miranda*, lurched along the treacherous planking to join him. He was the same age as his captain, a seaman through and through who originally, like the schooner, had been in the merchant service. In such a small vessel – she was a bare sixty-five feet long with a company of thirty – you got to know a man very well. Love or hate and not much in between. With Bob Jay, another master's mate, they ran the schooner to perform at her best. It was a matter of pride.

Usually one of them was on watch, and when Simcox had spent a few watches below with the tall lieutenant he had got to know him well. Now, after three years, they were true friends, their separate ranks only intruding in rare moments of formality. Like Tyacke's visit to the flagship for instance.

Tyacke had looked at him, momentarily forgetting his hideous scars, and had said, 'First time I've buckled on a sword for over a year, Ben!' It was good to hear him joke about it. It was rare too.

Did he ever think about the girl in Portsmouth, Simcox wondered? One night in harbour he had been awakened in his tiny cabin by Tyacke's pitiful, dreaming entreaties to the girl who had promised to wait for him, to marry him. Rather than wake the whole ship, Simcox had shaken his shoulder, but had not explained. Tyacke had understood, and had fetched a bottle of brandy which they had taken off a runner. When dawn had broken the bottle had been empty.

Tyacke had not blamed the girl he had known for most of his life. Nobody would want to see his face every morning. But he had been deeply hurt; wounded no less severely than others at the Nile.

Simcox shouted above the din, 'Runnin' well!' He jerked a thumb at a slight figure who was clinging to the companion hatch, a lifeline tied around his waist, his breeches and stockings soiled with vomit. 'He's not so good, though!'

Mister Midshipman Roger Segrave had been in *Miranda* since they had taken on stores at Gibraltar. At the request of his captain he had been transferred from a big three-decker to complete his time as midshipman in a vessel where he might learn something more about practical seamanship and self-reliance. It had been said that the midshipman's uncle, an admiral at Plymouth, had arranged the transfer, not merely for the youth's sake but also for the family name. It would not look good to fail the lieutenant's examination, especially in time of war when chances of promotion lay on every hand.

Tyacke had made it clear he disliked the idea. Segrave's presence had upset their tight routine, an intrusion, like an unwanted visitor.

Simcox was one of the old school; the rope's end or a clip round the ear were, in his book, worth far more than lengthy discussions on tradition and discipline.

But he was not a hard man, and tried to explain to the midshipman what he might expect. Lieutenant Tyacke was the only commissioned officer aboard. He could not be expected to live in total isolation in a ninety-two ton schooner; they were a team. But he knew that Segrave did not really understand. In the teeming world of a ship-of-the-line everything was divided and sub-divided by rank, status and experience. At the top there was the captain, usually so remote he seemed like a god. The rest, though crammed together out of necessity, were totally separated.

Segrave rolled over and leaned back against the hatchway with a deep groan. He was sixteen years old with fair, almost girlish good looks. He had perfect manners, was careful, even shy when dealing with the hands – not like some little monsters Simcox had heard about. And he tried hard at everything but, even Simcox had to agree, with very little success. He was staring up at the sky, seemingly oblivious to the spray which ripped over the deck like pellets, or the filthy state of his clothing.

Lieutenant Tyacke looked at him coldly. 'Free yourself and go below, *Mr* Segrave, and fetch some rum from the clerk. I can't afford to let anyone useful stand-down until I change tack again.'

As the youth clambered wretchedly down the ladder, Simcox grinned.

'Bit hard on the lad, James.'

Tyacke shrugged. 'You think so?' He almost spat. 'In a year or two he'll be sending men to the gratings for a striped shirt, just for looking at him!'

37

The master's mate yelled, 'Wind's veered a piece!'

'Bring her up a point. I think this is going to blow over. I want to get the tops'l spread if it does, and run with the wind under our coat-tails.'

There was a sound of breaking pottery and someone vomiting from the deck below.

Tyacke murmured, 'I swear I shall kill that one.'

Simcox asked, 'What d'you reckon to Vice-Admiral Bolitho, James?'

The lieutenant gripped the stay again and bent from the waist as the sea boiled over the weather bulwark in a solid flood. Amongst the streaming water and foam he saw his men, like half-naked urchins, nodding and grinning to each other. Making certain that no one had gone over.

He replied, 'A good man to all accounts. When I was at the –' He looked away, remembering the cheers despite the hell when Bolitho's ship was reported engaging. He changed tack. 'I've known plenty who've served with him – there used to be an old fellow who lived in Dover. I used to speak with him when I was a lad, down by the harbour.' He smiled suddenly. 'Not far from where they built this schooner, as a matter of fact . . . He was serving under Richard Bolitho's father when he lost his arm.'

Simcox watched his strong profile. If you did not see the other side of his face, he was handsome enough to catch any girl's fancy, he thought.

He said, 'You should tell him that, if you meet.'

Tyacke wiped the spray from his face and throat. 'He's a vice-admiral now.'

Simcox smiled but was uneasy. 'God, you make him sound like the enemy, James!'

'Do I? Well, there's a thing!' He touched his dripping sleeve. 'Now rouse these layabouts and stand by to change tack. We will steer south by east.'

Within the hour the squall had fallen away, and with all sails filling well, their dark shadows riding across the waves alongside like huge fins, *Miranda* responded with her usual disdain.

She had started life as a Dover mail packet, but had been taken by the navy before she had completed more than a few passages. Now at seventeen years, she was one of the many such vessels working under a naval ensign. She was not only a lively sailer; she was a delight to handle because of her simple sail-plan and deep keel. A large mainsail aft, with a forestaysail and jib and the one topsail on her foremast, she could out-manoeuvre almost anything. The deep keel, even when she was close-hauled, prevented her from losing leeway like a cutter or something heavier. Armed with only four four-pounders and some swivels, she was meant for carrying despatches, rather than taking part in any real skirmish.

Smugglers and privateers were one thing; but half a broadside from some enemy frigate would change her from a lean thoroughbred to a total wreck.

Between decks there was the strong smell of rum and tobacco, and the greasy aroma of the noon meal. As the watch below scrambled down to their messdeck, Tyacke and Simcox sat wedged on either side of the cabin table. Both men were tall, so that any movement in the cabin had to be performed bent double.

The midshipman, repentant and anxious, sat at the other end of the table. Simcox could pity him, for even under reefed canvas the motion was violent, the sea surging astern from the sharply raked counter, the prospect of food another threat for any delicate stomach.

Tyacke said suddenly, 'If I *do* see him, the admiral I mean, I shall ask him about getting some beer. I saw some of the soldiers drinking their fill when I visited the flagship. So why not us? The water out here will kill more good sailors than Johnny Dutchman!'

They both turned as the midshipman spoke up.

Segrave said, 'There was a lot of talk in London about Vice-Admiral Bolitho.'

Tyacke's tone was deceptively mild. 'Oh, and what sort of talk was that?'

Encouraged, his sickness momentarily quiescent, Segrave expounded willingly.

'My mother said it was disgraceful how he behaved. How he left his lady for that woman. She said London was up in arms about it –' He got no further.

'If you speak like that in front of the people I'll put you under

39

arrest – *in bloody irons if need be*!' Tyacke was shouting, and Simcox guessed that many of the offwatch seamen would hear. There was something terrible about his rage; pathetic too.

Tyacke leaned over towards the pale-faced youth and added, 'And if you speak such shite to me, I'll damn well call you out, young and useless though you may be!'

Simcox rested his hand on his wrist. 'Be easy, James. He knows no better.'

Tyacke shook his hand away. 'God damn them, Ben, what do they want of us? How dare they condemn men who daily, hourly risk their lives so that *they* –' he pointed an accusing finger at Segrave '– can sip their tea and eat their cakes in comfort.' He was shaking, his voice almost a sob. 'I've never met this Richard Bolitho, but God damn me, I'd lay down my life for him right now, if only to get back at those useless, gutless bastards!'

In the sudden silence the sea intruded like a soothing chorus.

Segrave said in a whisper, 'I am very sorry, sir.'

Surprisingly, Tyacke's hideous face moved in a smile. 'No. I abused you. That is wrong when you are unable to answer back.' He mopped his forehead with a crumpled handkerchief. 'But I meant every bloody word, so be warned!'

'Deck thar!' The masthead's cry was shredded by the brisk north-westerly. 'Sail on th' starboard bow!'

Simcox thrust his mug into a safe corner and began to slide towards the door.

No matter what this proved to be, he thought, it had come along just in time.

'Sou'-West-by-South, sir! Full an' bye!'

The *Miranda*'s deck tilted even more steeply as she responded to her rudder and the great span of main and staysails, water cascading around the bare-backed seamen while they sheeted home swollen halliards and dug with their toes at anything which would hold them.

Lieutenant Tyacke lurched up to the weather rail, and watched the surf and spray leaping high from the stem to make the flapping jib glint in the sunshine like polished metal.

Simcox nodded with approval as George Sperry, the tub-shaped boatswain, put two extra hands on the tiller. *Miranda* did not boast a wheel but had a long, ornately carved tiller bar, which took some handling in the brisk wind sweeping down on the starboard quarter.

He saw Midshipman Segrave standing in the shadow of the heavily raked mainmast, his eyes wary as he tried to avoid men dashing past to take up the slack of the forebrace.

Simcox called, 'Over here!' He sighed when the youth all but fell, as a wave curled lazily over the lee bulwark and broke around him, leaving him spluttering and gasping, water pouring from his shirt and breeches as if he had just been pulled from the sea.

'Just bide along o' me, young feller, and watch the mains'l an' compass. Get th' *feel* of 'er, see?'

He forgot Segrave as a line high above the deck cracked like a whip, and instantly began to unreeve itself as if it were alive.

A sailor was already swarming aloft, another bending on some fresh cordage so that no time would be lost in repairs.

Segrave clung to the bitts beneath the driver-boom and stared dully at the men working on the damaged rigging, paying no heed to the wind which tried to pluck them down. He could not recall when he had felt so wretched, so utterly miserable, and so unable to see his way out of it.

Tyacke's words still stung, and although it was not the first time the captain had given him the sharp side of his tongue, the boy had never seen him so angry: as if he had lost control and wanted to strike him.

Segrave had earnestly tried not to rouse Tyacke's ire; had wanted nothing more than to keep out of his way. Both were impossible in so small a ship.

He had nobody to talk to, really talk and understand. There had been plenty of midshipmen aboard his last ship – his *only* ship. He shuddered. What must he do?

His father had been a hero, although Segrave could barely remember him. Even on his rare returns to their home he had seemed distant, vaguely disapproving, perhaps because he had but one son and three daughters. Then one day the news had been brought to that far-off Surrey house. Captain Segrave had been killed in battle, fighting under Admiral Dundas at Camperdown. His mother had told them, her face sad but

41

composed. By then it was already too late for Roger Segrave. His uncle, a retired flag-officer in Plymouth, had decided to offer him his patronage – for his father's memory, for the honour of the family. As soon as a ship could be found he was kitted out and packed off to sea. For Segrave it had been three years of hell.

He looked despairingly at Simcox. His rough kindness had almost finished him. But he would understand no better than Segrave's lieutenant in the three-decker. What would he say if he knew that Segrave hated the navy, and had never wanted to follow the family tradition. *Never.*

He had intended to tell his mother on that last leave, when she had taken him to London to stay with some of her friends. They had clucked over him like hens. *So sweet in his uniform* as one of them had exclaimed. That had been when he had heard them discussing Nelson and another name, Richard Bolitho.

Now the unthinkable had happened. Brave Nelson was dead. And the other name was here, with the squadron.

Before he had left for Portsmouth to take passage to the Mediterranean, he had tried to explain to his mother.

She had hugged him, and then held him at arm's length. She had sounded hurt. 'After all the Admiral has done for you and the family –' It was strange, but Segrave could never recall his uncle being called by name. He was always *the Admiral*.

'Be brave, Roger. Make us proud of you!'

He tensed as the captain turned aft towards him. If only his face were not like that. Segrave was not too immature not to know how Tyacke must hate and loathe his own appearance. And yet he could not stop himself from staring at his disfigurement, even when he was trying to prevent himself from doing so.

If he passed his examination . . . Segrave ducked as a curtain of spray soaked into him again. *If* – he would be appointed as a lieutenant, the first real step, to share a wardroom with other officers who would see him as the weak link, a danger whenever they were called to action.

But suppose – he found he was clenching his fists until they ached – he ended up with a terrible wound like Tyacke? He felt the bile in his throat, choking him.

Simcox slapped him on the shoulder. 'Let her fall off a point.

Steer sou'-sou'-west.' He watched as Segrave relayed his order to the helmsman, but saw the senior hand at the tiller glance at him, not the boy, to make certain it was correct.

'Deck thar! She's standin' away, sir, an' makin' more sail!'

Tyacke tucked his thumbs into his belt. 'So he wants to play games, does he?' He cupped his hands and called, 'Would you take a glass aloft, Mr Jay?' As the master's mate hurried to the shrouds he said, 'Hands aloft, and loose tops'l, Ben!' He gave a rare grin. 'I'll wager he'll not outreach *Miranda*!'

Then he appeared to notice the midshipman for the first time. 'Go with him and learn something!' He dismissed him immediately as the topsail suddenly boomed out from its yard and then hardened like a breastplate.

Simcox eyed the set of the sails. 'We must catch him afore dusk. Sir Richard Bolitho'll not thank us for keepin' him waiting!'

Segrave finally reached the top of the quivering ratlines and joined the master's mate by the foot of the fidded topmast. Heights did not trouble him, and he gazed across the endless dark blue desert with its ranks of yellow-crested waves. The ship was momentarily forgotten; he stared wide-eyed at the spray as it drifted up from the plunging stem, felt the mast shaking and jerking, every brace and shroud catching the wind in a wild chorus which drowned out the men on the deck far below.

'Take a look.' Jay handed him the telescope before bellowing to the deck, 'Schooner, sir! Flies no flag!'

Tyacke's voice carried effortlessly from aft. 'She running?'

'Aye, sir!'

They heard the squeal of a block, and seconds later a huge White Ensign floated from *Miranda*'s gaff.

Jay chuckled. 'That'll show the buggers!'

But Segrave was peering at the other vessel as she heeled over to an angle that matched *Miranda*'s. The vessel seemed to leap out of the distance so that he could see the patched and dirty sails, even some loose trailing cordage awaiting repair, *Irish pendants* as he had heard the old sailors call them. The hull was originally black but was scored, and in places worn bare by wind and weather. It would not be tolerated in a King's ship, no matter how hard she was worked.

43

'What d'you think, Mr Jay?'

The man looked at him before raising the glass again. 'At a guess she's a bloody blackbirder.' He saw the uncertainty on the youth's face. 'Slaver, lad.'

Segrave looked away and did not see the other man's pitying stare. 'Will we catch her?'

Jay was watching the other vessel with professional interest. 'We'll *catch* the bastard right enough.'

There was a hail from the deck. 'Clear for action! Mr Archer, lay aft if you please!'

Archer was the gunner, so there could be little doubt about it now.

Tyacke's voice seemed to be right beside him.

'*Mr Segrave!* Down here at the double!'

Jay watched him clambering down the ratlines, his fair hair rippling in the wind.

There was nothing to dislike about the midshipman, but Jay knew the dangers. In small ships like *Miranda* it was one hand for the King, t'other for yourself. There was no room for passengers and mother's boys.

Simcox faced Segrave as he reached the bulwark. 'Keep with Mr Archer. He will personally lay and point a four-pounder. You will do well to watch him!'

The tub-like boatswain grinned and showed him broken teeth.

'I knowed Elias Archer knock an apple off a tree at a 'undred paces!'

The other man who waited by halliards and braces grinned as if it was a huge joke.

Segrave saw Tyacke turn to speak with the helmsmen. In the sun's angry glare his face looked as if it had just been clawed away.

Then he followed the gunner to the foremost starboard side port and tried not to think about it. He felt like running below to hide, anything but being made to bare his fear before the others.

Elias Archer, *Miranda*'s master gunner, was a grizzled little man and stood effortlessly on the pitching foredeck, his arms folded while he waited for his men to clear away the four-pounder nearest to the bows.

44

'Done much of this, 'ave yer?' He glanced briefly at the midshipman, then returned his gaze to the other vessel. She was larger than *Miranda*, and might yet outsail them until nightfall made a further chase impossible.

Segrave shook his head. His body was like ice in spite of the sun's high glare across his neck and shoulders; and each time the schooner dipped her stem the bursting spray made him shiver uncontrollably.

He replied, 'Not like this. My last ship engaged a French two-decker, but she ran aground and caught fire before we could take her.'

'This is different.' Archer took a shining black ball from the shot garland and felt it in his hard palms. 'Ships like this 'un 'ave to be quick an' nimble. But without the likes o' us the fleet would be all aback fer news, an' without *that* even Our Nel couldn't move.' He nodded to one of his crew. 'Right, Mason, open the port.'

Segrave watched as other men ran to the halliards and braces and the deck canted over again. The other schooner must have headed away a point or so, but it was hard to tell from where they stood now, here in the eyes of the ship.

Archer leaned over to supervise as the charge was carefully tamped home. He said, 'Some 'otheads double-shot their guns. But not me. Not in a little piece like this 'un.'

Segrave heard the captain call, 'Signal that bastard to heave-to!'

Archer chuckled, ''*E* won't take no notice!'

Segrave was puzzled. 'Maybe he cannot read our signals?'

A seaman with the rammer grinned and pointed at the gun. 'He'll understand this, right enough.'

The other schooner was showing her bilge as she heeled over to the press of canvas. There were several heads above her bulwark, but there was no response to the signal.

Lieutenant Tyacke shouted, 'Load and run out!'

The shot was thrust down the muzzle with a wad to keep it secure. Then, with the hands hauling on the tackles, the little gun was run up to the open port.

Archer explained, 'Y'see, my lad, that bugger yonder has the wind-gage, but it will help us to put a shot down where we wants it.'

45

Jay, the forgotten master's mate, called from the foremast: 'They've just pitched a corpse over the side, sir! There goes another!'

Tyacke lowered his telescope, his eyes hard. 'That last one was still alive, Mr Simcox.' The sudden formality seemed to add menace to the moment.

'Beyond her if you can, Mr Archer!'

Archer was crouching like an athlete, the trigger-line pulled taut as he peered over the barrel.

He jerked the line and the gun hurtled inboard on its tackles, smoke fanning through the port even as they began to sponge out for the next shot.

Segrave saw a sudden confusion of spray to starboard and for an instant thought that Archer's aim had failed him. But the ball hit the water just a few yards from the schooner's lee bow and ricocheted across the waves like a jubilant dolphin. Segrave pointed at the other disturbance which was already settling again.

'What's *that*?'

Sperry the boatswain, who had sauntered forward to watch, said harshly, 'Sharks.'

Segrave felt the nausea returning. Those two unknown people had been cast outboard like so much rubbish; torn to pieces while he had watched.

'Bosun! Stand by to sway out the boat!'

Segrave raised his eyes again. The other vessel was heaving-to, her patched sails in wild confusion as she rounded-up into the wind.

Segrave had the feeling that *Miranda*'s people were used to this kind of thing. The arms chest was already on deck and open, and Jay came slithering down a back stay with a grunt, his hands already reaching for a hanger while someone passed him his pistol.

Tyacke was saying, 'I shall stand off. Board the schooner and search her. Don't take any insolence from any of them. You know what to do.'

Simcox beckoned to the midshipman. 'You go with Mr Jay, lad. If that bastard *is* full of slaves we'll have to release him. There's no law against blackbirdin', not yet anyways, an' we'd

46

get precious few thanks from the commodore if we return to th' squadron with a load o' slaves. Me, I'd hang the bastards an' to hell with the law an' th' right o' it!'

Tyacke crossed the deck. 'Help Mr Jay all you can. Arm yourself – they're as treacherous as snakes.'

Small though she was, *Miranda* appeared to tower over them as they tumbled into the longboat and cast off.

'*Give way all!*' Jay grasped the tiller bar and watched narrowly as the men pulled strongly towards the other schooner.

Sperry was in the boat too, a boarding axe and a heavy cutlass in his belt.

'No slaves,' he said.

Jay asked, 'How so, George?'

'No bloody stench, is there? An' us downwind of 'em an' all!'

Segrave gritted his teeth and gripped the bulwark with all his strength. It was another nightmare. He saw a sudden picture of his mother when she had told them about their father's death. How would she feel about him? Proud? Moist-eyed that her only son had died in battle? He stared wildly at the other vessel, stared until his eyes watered and smarted. *Damn them all.*

Jay cupped his hands. 'We're comin' aboard! In th' King's name!'

Sperry bared his teeth and loosened the axe in his belt.

'Oh, that was *prettily* said, Bob!'

They grinned fiercely at each other while Segrave could only stare at them. At any second they might be fired on; he had heard it said that slavers were often well armed.

Jay was suddenly serious. 'The usual, lads. Take over the helm, an' disarm the crew.' He glanced at Segrave. 'You stick with me, lad. Nowt to it!'

A grapnel flew over the schooner's bulwark and the next second they were clambering aboard, the sea-noises fading slightly as they found themselves on the deck. Segrave stayed close to the master's mate. When he looked at his companions he was not surprised that this vessel had failed to stop. *Miranda*'s White Ensign was genuine but the little boarding party looked more like ragged pirates than the King's seamen.

Jay beckoned to a man in dirty white breeches and a contrasting ruffled silk shirt.

47

'You th' Master?'

Segrave looked at the others. A mixture. The sweepings of the gutter.

'An' wot do we 'ave '*ere*?' The boatswain's thick arm shot out and dragged one of the crew away from the others. With surprising speed for such a squat man, Sperry ripped off the sailor's shirt, then swung him round so that Jay could see the tattoos on his skin. Crossed flags and cannon, and a ship's name: *Donegal*.

Jay rasped, 'A deserter, eh? Looks like the end o' th' roamin' life for you!'

The man cringed. 'For Gawd's sake 'ave some pity. I'm just a poor Jack like yerselves!'

Sperry shook him gently. 'An' soon you'll be a poor *dead* Jack, dancin' at the yardarm, you bastard!'

Segrave had never even tried to understand it. How men who had been taken by the press-gangs as some of *Miranda*'s had, were always outraged by those who had run.

The one who was obviously the master shrugged his shoulders and shook his head.

Jay sighed. 'Don't speak no English.' His eyes gleamed and he pointed at the deserter with his hanger.

'You'll do! You 'elp us an' we'll see you escapes the rope, eh?'

The sailor's gratitude was pathetic to see. He fell on his knees and sobbed, 'I only done one passage in 'er, '*onest*, sir!'

'Wot about the two "burials"?' The point of the hanger lifted suddenly until it rested on the man's throat. 'An' don't lie, or you'll be joinin' them!'

'The master put 'em over, sir!' He was babbling with fear and relief. 'They'd been fighting, and one stabbed t'other.' He dropped his eyes. 'The master was goin' to get rid of 'em anyway. They weren't strong enough for 'ard work.'

Segrave watched the man in the frilled shirt. He seemed calm, indifferent even. They could not hold him, although he had murdered two slaves who were no longer of any use.

Jay snapped, 'Take charge of the deck, George.' He beckoned to a seaman. 'We'll go below.' He added, 'You too, Mr Segrave!'

It was even filthier between decks, the whole hull creaking

and pitching while the sailors, holding lanterns like tin-miners, crept amongst the evidence of the schooner's trade. Ranks of manacles and leg-irons lined and crisscrossed the main hold, with chains to keep each batch of slaves from moving more than a few feet. And this for a voyage across an ocean, to the Indies or the Spanish Main.

Jay muttered, 'That's why they only takes the fit ones. T'others would never last the passage.' He spat. 'Lyin' in their own filth for weeks on end. Don't bear thinkin' about.' He shrugged. 'Still, I suppose it's a livin', like everythin' else.'

Segrave wanted to be sick, but he controlled it and asked timidly, 'That deserter – will he really be pardoned?'

Jay paused and glanced at him. 'Yes, if he's any use to us. Pardoned the rope anyway. He'll likely get two hundred strokes of the cat, just to remind him of 'is loyalties in the future!'

The young seaman named Dwyer said softly, 'What's abaft this lot, Mr Jay?'

Jay forgot Segrave and turned swiftly. 'Th' cabins. Why?'

'I heard something, or *someone* more like.'

'God's teeth!' Jay drew his pistol and cocked it. 'Might be some bastard with a slow-match ready to blow us all to hell! Use yer shoulder, Dwyer!'

The young seaman hurled himself against one of the doors and it burst open, smashed from its hinges by the blow.

The hutchlike cabin was in darkness but for a patch of sunshine which could barely penetrate the filthy glass of a skylight.

On a littered and stained bunk was a young black woman. She was sitting half-upright, propped on her elbows, her lower limbs covered by a soiled sheet. She was otherwise quite naked. There was no fear, not even surprise, but when she tried to move a chain around her ankle restricted her.

Jay said quietly, 'Well, well. Does himself very nicely, does the master!'

He led the way on deck again and shaded his eyes in the glare as *Miranda* changed tack and drew closer to the drifting vessel, which was apparently named *Albacora*.

Tyacke's voice, unreal in a speaking-trumpet, reached them easily.

49

'What is she?'

Jay cupped his hands, 'Slaver, sir. No cargo but for one. We've a deserter on board as well.'

Segrave saw the man bobbing and smiling wretchedly in the background as if Tyacke could see him. But he kept thinking of the black girl. Chained there like a wild animal for the slaver's pleasure. She had a lovely body, despite . . .

Tyacke called over, 'Where bound?'

Jay held up the chart. 'Madagascar, sir.'

A seaman near Segrave murmured, 'We'll have to let 'er go.' He glared around the filthy deck. 'She bain't much but she'd fetch a few shillin's in the prize court!' His mate nodded in agreement.

Tyacke's voice betrayed no emotion. 'Very well, Mr Jay. Return on board and bring the deserter with you.'

The man in question shouted, '*No! No!*' The boatswain cuffed him around the ear and sent him sprawling, but he crawled across the deck and clawed at Jay's shoes like a crippled beggar.

He shouted again, 'He took the chart below when you was sighted, sir! I seen him do it afore. He puts a different one for all to see.'

Jay kicked his hands away. 'Now, why didn't I think of that?' He touched Segrave's arm. 'Come with me.'

They returned to the cabin where the girl still lay propped on her elbows, as if she had not moved.

They searched through the litter of books and charts, discarded clothing and weapons, Jay becoming clumsier by the moment, well aware of Tyacke's impatience to get under way again.

Jay said desperately, ''S no use. I can't find it, an' that bugger don't speak English.' He sounded angry. 'I'll lay odds that the deserter is lyin' to save 'is own skin. He'll 'ave no skin left when I've done with 'im!'

There was a looking-glass leaning against a case of paired pistols. Jay picked it up and searched behind it as a last hope.

'Not a god-damned thing!' He tossed the glass on the table and Segrave snatched it as it slithered towards the deck. As he did so he caught the merest glimpse of the girl behind him, now turned slightly to watch, her breasts shining in the filtered sunlight.

He exclaimed, 'She's lying on something, Mr Jay!'

Jay stared from him to her with stunned amazement. 'By the livin' Jesus!' He sprang across the cabin and seized the girl's naked shoulder to push her across the bunk.

But her body, slippery with sweat, escaped his grasp, and she moved like lightning, a knife appearing in her left hand even as Segrave ran to Jay's assistance.

Jay went sprawling from the impetus of his charge across the cabin and as he pitched to the deck he saw Segrave fall over the girl, and heard his sharp cry of agony.

Segrave felt the blade like fire across his hip, somehow knew that she had raised the knife for another blow at his unprotected back.

There was a cracking sound and the knife went clattering to the deck. The girl lay back, her eyes closed, her mouth bleeding where Jay had punched her.

Another figure ran into the low cabin. It was the seaman named Dwyer.

Jay rasped, ''Ere, give Mr Segrave a hand!' He rolled the girl's body aside and tugged a worn leather pouch from beneath her.

Segrave groaned and tried to move. Then he saw the slash in his breeches where the knife had gone in. There was blood everywhere, and the pain was making him gasp, bite his lip to prevent himself from screaming.

The sailor wrapped what appeared to be a shirt around the wound, but it was soon soaked through with blood.

Jay ripped open the big pouch, his eyes speedily scanning the contents before he opened the chart with trembling fingers.

Then he stood up. 'I must speak with the Cap'n.' He looked at Segrave's contorted face. 'You saved my rump, an' no mistake!' He watched his agony and added kindly, 'Be easy till I come back.'

On deck the sky already seemed darker, the clouds under-bellied with deep gold.

In quick sentences Jay shouted his information across the choppy division of water. 'She was bound for *Cape Town*! There's a despatch, wrote in French it looks.'

Tyacke called, 'How badly is Mr Segrave?' He saw Jay's

shrug. 'Then you had better not move him! Send the vessel's master across with the pouch – the deserter too. I will rejoin the squadron. Are you confident that you can manage?'

Jay grinned and said to himself, 'Manage? They'll not make trouble now.'

The *Albacora*'s master protested violently as a seaman seized his arm.

Jay snarled, 'Put those irons on him! Attempting to murder a King's officer, butchering slaves, to say nothing of trading with the enemy.' He nodded, satisfied as the man fell silent. 'Yes, my friend, you've understood the signal at last.'

As the boat cast off and headed for *Miranda*, Jay positioned his most trusted men with great care.

'We will get under way presently. Watch every move, even if they blinks! Shoot if in any doubt, see?'

With the boatswain, he returned to the cabin where Dwyer was holding the midshipman and trying to staunch the blood.

Dwyer said helplessly, 'Won't let me do it proper, sir!'

Sperry tore his eyes from the sprawled figure on the bunk and licked his lips.

'Now *there's* a thing, Bob.'

Jay was thinking of how close he had been to death. 'Later, George.'

Segrave was weaker but still tried to struggle as Sperry held him on the deck, while Dwyer and Jay began to cut away his bloodied breeches.

Sperry said huskily, 'I'll put a stitch or two in it. Just lay another dressin' on while I –'

Jay exclaimed, 'Who the bloody hell did *that*?'

The midshipman lay quietly now, like a sick or injured animal.

The whole of his buttocks and the backs of his thighs were scarred and bruised as if he had been beaten over and over again with a cord or a whip. Whoever had done this to him it was not in *Miranda*. That meant he had carried these scars for over six weeks, and without a word being said.

Jay thought of the jibes and grins, and all the while he . . .

The boatswain said, 'He's passed out, Bob. I'll fetch me gear.'

'Yeh, an' see if you can find some rum or brandy – anythin'.'

52

He turned back to the midshipman, who lay as if he was dead.

'You poor little bugger,' he said softly. He watched the blood soaking through the makeshift bandages. But for Segrave's unexpected courage it would have been his own blood, and no second chance either.

He saw Dwyer watching him and said harshly, 'And it goes no further, see? This is *Miranda*'s business, no one else's! I reckon 'e's suffered enough in this poxy squadron.'

Midshipman Segrave opened his eyes and was conscious of two things immediately. The sky overhead was dark and dotted with tiny stars; he was wrapped in blankets, a pillow beneath his head.

A shadow bent over him, and Jay asked, 'How is it?'

Then came the pain, throbbing in time with his heartbeats. He could taste brandy on his lips but could only remember the sequence of events like dark pictures. Hands holding him down; sharp stabbing pains; oblivion. Then the girl. He shook violently. *That was it.* When it had happened.

'Am I all right?' His voice sounded weak.

Jay forced a grin. ''Course you are. 'Ero of the hour. Saved my skin, an' gave us cause to 'old this ship.'

He looked across at two kneeling figures. Like some natives at prayer. But he knew they were trying to peer through the dirty skylight. Sperry was down there with the girl, doing what he probably did better than anything, if half his yarns were to be believed.

Then he asked, 'Tell me, lad, who did that to you?'

But Segrave shook his head, his eyes closed with the pain and the emotion.

Jay, the hard-bitten master's mate, had called him a *hero*.

4

Seek and Find

Themis's stern cabin was like a furnace in spite of the open gunports and the windsails rigged to each hatchway, so it was difficult even to think. Bolitho sat at the table, his head resting on one hand while he scanned the contents of the pouch which had been ferried across from the schooner *Miranda*.

Commodore Warren slumped in a high-backed chair, his ashen features turned towards the nearest port, his only movement when he plucked his uniform coat or shirt away from his damp skin.

Seated beside Bolitho, his plump, round-shouldered secretary, Daniel Yovell, had to repeatedly push his gold-rimmed spectacles back into position when they slipped down his nose, as he wrote the notes which Bolitho might require later on.

Warren asked suddenly, 'You are not surprised by the army's reply to your request, Sir Richard?'

Bolitho dragged his thoughts away from the pouch which *Miranda*'s boarding party had discovered. The evidence of the chart was interesting, but the lengthy letter to some French merchant in Cape Town was far more so.

He replied, 'Much what I expected, Commodore Warren. But we have to use the proper channels. By now, Sir David Baird's soldiers will have begun their landings. It is too late to prevent it, even if I could.'

Lieutenant Jenour stood beside the stern windows and watched the *Miranda* as she swung above her reflection, a perfect twin on the calm water. Her commander had been fortunate, he thought. A few hours later and he would have lost the wind completely.

He turned as Bolitho said, 'Your French is excellent, Stephen. When you translated this letter for me, did you notice anything unusual?'

Jenour tried to shake off the torpor. Of them all, Bolitho looked the coolest. Dressed in shirt and breeches, his coat tossed aside on to a chest, he even managed to appear alert, although Jenour knew that he had been pacing the cabin since *Miranda*'s sails had been sighted closing the land. That had been at dawn. It was now high noon. In this oven-heat men trod warily; it was a dangerous time when frayed tempers brought sharp discipline, with an aftermath of resentment. Better to be at sea, with every man too busy to brood.

Jenour screwed up his face. 'If the letter *is* a code I cannot read it, Sir Richard. It is the kind of letter that one merchant might send to another, passed perhaps by one ship on passage to that particular destination. After all, it is quite possible for French merchants to be in Cape Town surely?'

Bolitho massaged his forehead. It *was* a code, and he was surprised that even the quick-witted Jenour had missed a vital clue.

It fell to Yovell, who had been peering at his papers, his fat fingers holding his spectacles in place, to discover it.

He exclaimed, 'The battle off Cape Trafalgar, Sir Richard! The sender mentions it to his friend!'

Bolitho saw their expressions begin to change. 'Quite what you would expect, eh? Except that *Truculent* made a record passage here from England, before anyone in this squadron knew about the battle and Lord Nelson's death. So to have time in hand to pass this letter to a slaver, the sender must have been in these waters ahead of us!'

Warren dabbed his mouth with care. 'A French man-of-war?'

Jenour clenched his fists with disbelief. 'One of those which broke out of Brest?'

Bolitho tugged the chart towards him. 'Cape Town is the clue, my friends, although I fear I cannot determine what it is.'

He made up his mind. 'Make a signal to *Miranda*, Stephen. Summon her commander aboard. I would like to meet him in any case.'

55

As Jenour turned towards the door Commodore Warren said humbly, 'I am sorry. It slipped my mind, Sir Richard. Lieutenant Tyacke has been aboard since he delivered the pouch.'

Bolitho bit back a sharp retort. It was not now the time, but later . . . He sighed. Two frigate captains who disliked one another; their commodore who showed little interest in the whole operation; and a mixed handful of vessels which had barely worked with one another before. Small beginnings.

He said, 'Ask him to come in, Stephen.'

Warren shifted uneasily. 'There is another thing about him . . .'

But Jenour already had the door to the cabin open, so he did not finish it.

Jenour stepped into the other cabin and looked at the tall man who was standing by an open gunport, his hands clasped behind him.

'If you will step aft – Sir Richard Bolitho wishes to speak with you.' He was relieved to see that the lieutenant had at least been given refreshment, and doubtless some of the commodore's terrible wine. 'We were not aware that you were still . . .' The words froze on his lips as the other man turned to stare at him. How could anyone live with a wound like that?

Tyacke said abruptly, 'And who are you, might I ask?' Then he saw the twist of gold lace at Jenour's shoulder. 'I see. Flag-lieutenant.'

Jenour tried again. 'Forgive me. I did not mean –'

Tyacke shifted the sword at his belt and turned his disfigurement aside. 'I am accustomed to it. But I don't have to enjoy it.' He did not attempt to hide his anger and bitterness. *Who did they think they were?*

He lowered his head between the deck beams and stepped into the enlarged cabin. For a few moments he was taken completely off-balance. The commodore he knew slightly by sight, and for some lingering seconds he imagined that the plump man in the plain blue coat must be the much-talked about Bolitho. Not an heroic figure; but then most of the flag-officers Tyacke had met were not.

'Will you accept my apologies, Mr Tyacke?' Bolitho walked

56

from the shadows and crossed beneath a skylight. 'I was not told you had been kept waiting. Please forgive this oversight and take a seat, will you?'

Tyacke sat down awkwardly. Perhaps he had been at sea too long, or had misheard somehow. But the man in the white shirt, with the almost gentle manner of greeting, was not what he had expected. For one thing Bolitho looked no older than himself, although he knew he must be nearer fifty than forty. But for the deep lines around his mouth, and the traces of white in a solitary lock of hair above one eye, he was a young man. Bolitho was looking at him again in that strangely direct and open manner. The eyes were grey, and for a few seconds Tyacke felt tongue-tied, more like Midshipman Segrave than himself.

Bolitho continued, 'Your discovery aboard that slaver may be more useful than any of us realise.' He smiled suddenly, so that he appeared even younger. 'I am trying to fathom how it may help us.'

A door opened, and a very small servant padded across the cabin and paused by Tyacke's chair. 'Some hock, sir?' He watched Tyacke's expression and added mildly, 'It is quite cold, sir.' It sounded as if it was better wine than was usually available in this elderly flagship.

Tyacke swallowed hard. This must be one of Bolitho's men too. He drank deeply, trying to contain something he thought he had lost. *Emotion.* The little man had not even blinked; had shown neither curiosity nor disgust.

Bolitho observed him and saw the lieutenant's hand tremble as his glass was refilled. Another survivor. One more victim which the war had tossed aside, as the sea gave up driftwood.

He asked quietly, 'Where is this *Albacora* now?'

Tyacke seemed to pull himself out of his thoughts with a physical effort.

'She will be here in two days, Sir Richard. I left a small prize-crew aboard and the injured midshipman.'

Bolitho nodded. 'I read of him in your report. He sounds a brave youngster.'

Tyacke dropped his gaze. 'He surprised me.'

Bolitho looked at his secretary. 'I shall require you to write some orders for another of the schooners.' His voice hardened

57

and he saw the commodore watching him anxiously. 'I want the *Albacora* put alongside one of the storeships when she arrives. She must be met at sea, out of sight of prying telescopes ashore, then brought to her moorings at *night*.' He waited for his words to sink in. 'Will you attend to that, Commodore Warren?'

Warren bobbed and fell into a fit of violent coughing.

Bolitho turned his back and studied the tall lieutenant. 'I wish to take passage in your command, Mr Tyacke.' He saw the disbelief, the arguments rushing into the man's eyes. 'I am used to small vessels so have no fear for my – er, dignity!'

When he looked again, the commodore had left the cabin, but he could still hear him coughing. Jenour was at Yovell's shoulder peering at the plump Devonian's neat, round writing.

For a few minutes they were alone, ignored. Bolitho asked softly, 'Where did it happen?' That was all he said, but he saw the words hit Tyacke like a clenched fist.

Then Tyacke met his gaze and said without hesitation, 'The Nile, Sir Richard. The *Majestic*, seventy-four.'

Bolitho nodded very slowly. 'Yes. Captain Westcott. A fine man. Sadly missed.' He touched his left eyelid with one finger and Tyacke imagined that he saw him wince.

Bolitho said, 'Please return to your ship. As soon as the remainder of your people arrive in the prize, *your* prize, Mr Tyacke, be prepared to weigh anchor again.'

Tyacke glanced at the others but Jenour was studying some papers; or perhaps he simply could not face him.

Bolitho added, 'I shall want you to take me to the Cape itself, beyond if need be. I am doing no good here.'

As Tyacke turned to leave Bolitho called to him, 'There is one more thing.' He walked across the cabin until they faced each other again. 'I would like to shake your hand.' His grasp was firm. 'You are a very brave officer.' For just seconds he hesitated. 'You have given *me* hope. I shall not forget.'

Tyacke found himself in the harsh sunlight and then down in *Miranda*'s longboat before he knew what had happened.

Simcox was in the boat, agog with excitement and questions.

Tyacke watched dully as the boat cast off and the seamen picked up the stroke. Then he said without emphasis, 'He wants us to take him to the Cape.'

58

Simcox stared. 'A vice-admiral! In *Miranda*!'

The lieutenant nodded, remembering, holding on to it. And lastly the handshake, the momentary wistfulness in Bolitho's voice.

Simcox was unnerved by the change in his friend. Something strange and important must have happened aboard the flagship. He hoped that Tyacke had not been hurt again.

He tried to pass it off. 'And I'll bet you forgot to ask him about our beer ration, what say you?'

But Tyacke had not heard him. He repeated, 'Take him to the Cape. By the living God, I'd sail that man to hell and back if he asked me!'

They did not speak again until they reached *Miranda*.

Richard Bolitho wedged himself in one corner of the *Miranda*'s small cabin and then stretched out his legs. The motion was certainly lively, he thought ruefully, and even his stomach, which had been hardened by every sort of sea and under most conditions, was queasy.

Lieutenant Tyacke had been on deck for most of the time since they had hauled anchor, and although he could see nothing apart from the bright blue rectangle through the skylight, Bolitho guessed that once clear of the choppy inshore currents things might be easier.

It seemed odd not to have Ozzard pattering about, anticipating his every need even before he had thought of it himself. But space was precious in the rakish schooner, and in any case it might appear as a slight to *Miranda*'s people if he brought his own servant. It was probably shock enough to see him climb aboard, despite Tyacke's warning beforehand. As he had made his way aft Bolitho had caught glimpses of the varied expressions. Astonishment, curiosity, maybe even resentment. Like Tyacke, whose voice seemed to be everywhere on deck, they might see his presence more as an invasion of their private world than any sort of honour. He had asked Jenour to remain in the flagship, too. His eyes and ears were as useful as *Miranda*'s.

Bolitho had seen the captured slaver alongside one of the transports, but had not gone over to her. He had heard about the woman in the master's cabin, and the deserter who was now

59

under guard in the flagship, awaiting his fate. He guessed there were several other things which had not been mentioned in Tyacke's report.

He heard the boom of canvas as the fore-topsail filled out to the wind, and imagined he could feel the instant response while the schooner settled on her new tack.

He looked around the cramped cabin, hearing once more in his mind Allday's outspoken disapproval.

'Not fit for a vice-admiral, 'specially you, Sir Richard! A collier would offer more comfort!' He was out there somewhere, either quietly fuming, or, having accepted it, sharing a 'wet' with one of the *Miranda*'s senior hands. He usually managed to settle in that way, and gain more information than Bolitho might do in a year.

The cabin was packed with personal belongings, sea chests, clothing and weapons, the latter within easy reach for any occupant.

Tyacke had left the wounded midshipman in the care of *Themis*'s surgeon. There was another story there, too, but Bolitho doubted if Tyacke would share it. The tall, powerful lieutenant discouraged confidences, apart from with his friend, the acting-master. Maybe he had always been a solitary man, and his terrible scars had only increased his isolation.

Bolitho opened his chart and moved it beneath a swaying deckhead lantern. Even it was not spiralling now so violently. These great sails were like wings; could hold the schooner steady on her deep keel when other vessels would be pitching like corks.

Bolitho looked at the chart, the hundreds of tiny soundings, bearings and identifying marks. He found that he was rubbing his injured eye, and stopped instantly, as if someone had called aloud to him.

He could feel sweat on his spine and then knew why Allday had been so insistent about his not boarding *Miranda*.

Bolitho shook his head and peered at the chart again. It was no use. It *was* the cabin. Not so different from the one he had been using in the topsail cutter *Supreme*. October 1803, when the French had found the little cutter and had fired on her; when Bolitho's life had changed. One enemy ball had slammed into some buckets of sand and hurled him to the deck.

It had been noon, but when he had been helped to his feet he had found only darkness. His left eye had plagued him badly since. In his old *Hyperion* it had almost cost him his life. The damage had been like a sea-mist creeping over the eye, rendering him half-blind. He recalled Catherine's pleas before he had left Portsmouth in *Truculent*. Aboard *Hyperion*, at the height of her last-ever voyage, they had carried an eminent surgeon, Sir Piers Blachford, who with others of his profession had been scattered throughout the embattled squadrons of the fleet to discover at first hand what ship's surgeons had to contend with in action. As an eventual result of their findings, it was hoped by the College of Surgeons in London that it would not be left to the butchers of the trade to deal with the appalling wounds and amputations which were the price of any battle.

Blachford, like a tall, reedy heron, had told Bolitho that he would lose the sight of his left eye completely unless he quit the sea for a period of time lengthy enough to afford him the proper examination and perhaps treatment. Even then, he could not be sure . . .

Bolitho stared at the chart's wavering coastline and imagined he could feel the old pain deep inside his eye. It was imagination allied to fear. It had to be. He looked desperately around the cabin again. *Allday had known.* He always did.

But it was not just a question of duty or arrogance. Bolitho did not have the conceit to pretend it was either. There were so few leaders with the experience, the understanding, that were needed so much now, perhaps even more so than before Trafalgar. With Nelson gone, and the enemy forces on land untouched by the victory and his sacrifice, it was just a matter of time before the next blow fell.

The door banged open and Tyacke, bent double, thrust himself on to one of the bench seats. He was breathing hard as if he had been personally fighting his enemy, the sea, and his shirt was blotchy with spray. Bolitho noticed that he sat in the opposite corner where his disfigurement was in the deepest shadow.

Tyacke said, 'We're running due south, Sir Richard. The wind's veered a place, but that's all to the good should we want to come about in a hurry.' He glanced at Bolitho. 'Are you certain this is what you want to do, sir?'

Bolitho smiled and gestured to the clothing which hung from the deckhead. His own sea-going coat was no better than Tyacke's and he had purposely left the epaulettes with Ozzard.

He said, 'I know you cannot always tell the contents of a cask by its label, but at least I would hope that your people will feel more at ease. It was *my* choice, Mr Tyacke, so do not blame yourself.' He changed the subject. 'Is all well with your company?'

Tyacke's eyes sharpened as he replied, 'I have one matter left to deal with, but it must wait until I can speak to the person involved.' He sounded wary. 'It is ship's business, Sir Richard. Nothing which will impair the needs of this passage.'

'I am glad to know it.' Bolitho folded the chart, feeling Tyacke watching him. All *Miranda*'s people were returned on board. But for the midshipman, who had according to Tyacke's report acted with gallantry to save the master's mate's life. *Ship's business*, he had said. He smiled briefly. In other words, *not mine*.

Tyacke saw the smile and relaxed slightly, his hands hidden beneath the table. It was not easy. For him it was more than an intrusion; it was the deprivation of his own freedom to think and act.

He said, 'There will be some food very soon, sir.' He grinned uncomfortably. 'I know you told me not to use your title aboard this vessel, but it comes a bit hard.'

'It should draw us closer.' Bolitho felt his stomach contract. He *was* hungry, in spite of everything. Perhaps Sir Piers Blachford was wrong. It was not unknown. When he returned to England . . . well, perhaps then he would take Catherine's advice.

He recalled one of the transports he had visited while he had been waiting for *Miranda*'s return from Saldanha Bay. It had been unspeakable; and a miracle some of the soldiers had not died of disease already. The stench had been appalling, more like a farmyard than a vessel in the King's service. Men, horses, guns and equipment, packed deck upon deck, with less room than a convict ship.

And so they must wait and endure it, until Sir David Baird's artillery and foot soldiers fought their way to the gates of Cape

Town. But suppose the Dutch were stronger than anyone realised? They might turn the English advance into a rout, in which case there was only Commodore Warren's small force to land soldiers and marines and harass the enemy from the rear. The wretched men he had seen aboard the transport would be no match for the difficult landing, let alone the fighting expected of them.

He heard Allday's deep voice beyond the door and knew he was helping one of Tyacke's men to fetch a meal for the officers.

Bolitho said, 'With your experience, you should have a larger command.' Again he saw the guard drop in the ruined face. 'Your promotion ought to have been immediate.'

Tyacke's eyes flashed. 'I was offered it, sir. I declined it.' There was something like sad pride in his tone. '*Miranda*'s enough for me, and nobody can find cause to complain on her performance.'

Bolitho turned as a seaman bowed through the door with some steaming dishes. A far cry from a ship-of-the-line. From *Hyperion*.

The old ship's name was still hanging in his mind when he saw Allday look at him across the sailor's stooped shoulders. He murmured, 'It is all right, old friend. Believe me.'

Allday responded with a cautious grin, as if he were only half-convinced.

The door closed and Tyacke watched covertly as Bolitho cut through the greasy pork on his plate as if it were some rare delicacy.

Simcox kept asking him what Bolitho was like. *Really* like.

How could he explain? How might he describe a man who refrained from probing with his questions, when anyone else of his rank and fame would have *insisted*? Or how could he begin to tell Simcox about the bond between the admiral and his coxswain? *Old friend*, he had just called him. It was like having a vibrant force in the hull. A new light.

He thought of Simcox's earlier remark and smiled to himself. He poured two goblets of madeira and said, 'I was just thinking, sir. Some beer would not come amiss, if we could lay hands on some.'

Bolitho held up the goblet to the lantern, his face serious for a few seconds until he realised that the glass and not his eye had misted over.

Tyacke, sensing his change of mood, exclaimed, 'I beg your pardon, Sir Rich – er – *sir*!'

It was the first time Bolitho had seen him in irons.

'*Beer*, you say? I will pass the word to the army. It is the very least they can do.' He was still holding the goblet when he asked, 'It is Saturday, is it not? So we shall call a toast.'

Tyacke took up his glass. 'Sweethearts and wives, sir?'

Bolitho touched the locket beneath his shirt and shook his head.

'To loved ones. May they be patient with us.'

Tyacke drank the toast but said nothing, as he had no one to care if he lived or died.

He glanced at Bolitho's expression and was deeply moved nonetheless. For a moment at least he was with her, no matter the many miles which held them apart.

Allday wiped his glittering razor and grunted, 'That should do it, Sir Richard. About all the water *is* fit for in this ship!' He did not conceal his disgust. 'It'll be a fisherman's dory next at this pace, I'm thinking.'

Bolitho sighed and slipped into the same crumpled shirt. It was the luxury he missed the most, a clean shirt when he needed it. Like stockings; they seemed to mark his progress from midshipmen's berth to flag-officer. Even as a lowly lieutenant there had been occasions when he had but two pairs of stockings to his name. But in many ways they had been good times; or maybe they always were, in hindsight – the memories of youth.

He thought of Tyacke's brief mention of his midshipman. Something was wrong there. He glanced up at the pale glow in the skylight. Dawn already; he was surprised that he had slept without waking once.

Allday gestured to the coffee-pot and added, 'Barely kills the taste!'

Bolitho smiled. How Allday could shave him when he could scarcely stand upright beneath the skylight was a marvel. He could never recall him cutting his face once.

He was right about the coffee. He decided to send a despatch regarding beer for the sweltering ships. It would help until they could take on fresh water.

Commodore Warren should have made some arrangements. Perhaps he no longer cared? Bolitho pushed the coffee away. Or maybe somebody wanted *him* out of the way. *Like me.*

He heard the sluice of water and the crank of a pump as the hands washed down the deck for a new day. Like everything else in the sixty-five foot schooner, the sounds were always close, more personal than in any larger craft.

'I'll go up.' He rose from the seat and winced as his head glanced off a deckhead beam.

Allday folded his razor away with great care and muttered, 'Bloody little paintpot, that's all *she* is!' Then he followed Bolitho up the short companion ladder and into the damp wind.

Bolitho walked to the compass box. How much steeper the angle of the deck seemed than when he had been below. There appeared to be people everywhere, swabbing down, working in the shrouds, or engaged in the many tasks with running-rigging and coiled halliards.

Tyacke touched his forehead, 'Morning, sir. Steady at sou'east-by-south.' He raised one arm and pointed over the bulwark. 'That's the beginning of the Cape, sir, 'bout four miles abeam.' He smiled, proud of his little ship. 'I'd not risk weathering it much closer. You have to be careful not to be deceived by the soundings hereabouts. There's no bottom according to some charts, but if you glance yonder you'll see a reef all the same!' It seemed to amuse him. Another challenge perhaps?

Bolitho turned and saw all the watching eyes drop or return to their various tasks. Like pulling on a line of puppets.

Tyacke said quietly, 'Don't mind them, sir. The highest ranking officer who came aboard before you, begging your pardon, was the commander in charge of the guard at Gibraltar.'

Simcox joined them and said, 'Sky's clearin', sir.' It was a totally unnecessary comment and Bolitho knew that he was like the rest, nervous in his presence.

'When do you become appointed Master, Mr Simcox?'

The man shifted his feet. 'Not certain, Sir Richard.' He

65

glanced at his friend and Bolitho could guess what was troubling him. Leaving *Miranda*; taking away Tyacke's only prop.

Bolitho shaded his eyes to watch the sea changing colour in the faint sunshine. Plenty of birds this morning, messengers from the land. He looked abeam and saw the mass of Table Mountain, and another across the larboard bow still wreathed in mist, with only its high, craggy ridges bathed in gold.

Simcox cleared his throat. 'The wind favours us, Sir Richard, but I've known ships caught in a gale to the south'rd o' this point, blown all the way to Cape Agulhas afore they could fight their way back!'

Bolitho nodded. Experience? Or was it a warning? Suppose there were men-of-war around the jutting tusk of the Cape? It was unlikely they would wish to reveal themselves for the sake of one frail schooner. But *Supreme* had been small too when the frigate had run down on her.

Tyacke lowered his telescope and said, 'Call all hands, Ben.' The first name had slipped out by accident. 'We will wear ship and steer due east.' He glanced at Bolitho. 'Into the lion's den!'

Bolitho looked up at the whipping pendant. Yes, Tyacke would miss the acting-master when he was promoted to full warrant rank. He might even see his replacement as another intruder.

He said, 'It is the only way, Mr Tyacke, but I shall not hazard the ship unduly.'

The seamen ran to the braces and halliards, fingers loosening belaying pins, casting off lines from their cleats with such deft familiarity that they needed no shouts or curses to hasten them. The sky was growing brighter by the minute, and Bolitho felt his stomach muscles tighten when he considered what he must do. He could sense Allday gazing at him while he stood ready to assist the helmsmen if needed.

It had not just been stockings which had marked Bolitho's change of fortune. Once he had gained promotion to lieutenant at the tender age of eighteen, he had been freed from the one duty he had feared and hated most. As a lieutenant, no longer did he have to scramble up the treacherous ratlines to his particular station aloft whenever the pipe was shrilled between decks, or while he stood his watch with the others.

66

He had never got used to it. In all weathers, with the ship hidden below by a drifting mist of spray and spindrift, he had clung to his precarious perch, watching his men, some of whom had been sent aloft for the first time in their lives. He had seen sailors fall to an agonising death on the deck, hurled from rigging and yard by the force of a gale, or by billowing canvas which had refused all efforts to quell it.

Others had dropped into the sea, to surface perhaps in time to see their ship vanishing into a squall. It was no wonder that young men fled when the press gangs were on the prowl.

'Stand by aft!' Tyacke wiped the spray from his scarred face with the back of his hand, his eyes everywhere while he studied his men and the set of each sail.

'Let go an' haul! Roundly there! Tom, another hand on th' forebrace!'

The shadows of the main and staysail seemed to pass right over the busy figures as the long tiller bar went down, the canvas and rigging clattering in protest.

Bolitho could feel his shoes slipping, and saw the sea creaming under the lee rail as Tyacke brought her round. He saw too the uneven barrier of land stagger across the bowsprit while the schooner continued to swing.

Allday muttered, 'By God, she can turn on a sovereign!' But everyone was too busy, and the noise too overwhelming, to hear what might be admiration instead of scorn.

'*Meet her!* steady as you go! *Now*, let her fall off a point!'

The senior helmsman croaked, 'Steady she goes, sir! East by north!'

'Secure!' Tyacke peered up into the glare. 'Hands aloft to reef tops'l, Mr Simcox!' A quick grin flashed between them. 'With the wind abeam it'll not do the work intended, and we might lose it.'

The twin masts swayed almost vertical and then leaned over once more to the wind's thrust.

Bolitho said, 'A glass, if you please.' He tried not to swallow. 'I am going to the foremast to take a look.' He ignored Allday's unspoken protest. 'I imagine that there will not be too many watching eyes this early!'

Without giving himself time to change his mind he strode

forward, and after a quick glance at the surging water leaping up from the stem, he swung himself on to the weather bulwark and dug his hands and feet into the ratlines. Up and up, his steps mounting the shivering and protesting shrouds. *Never look down.* He had never forgotten that. He heard rather than saw the topmen descending the opposite side, their work done as quickly as thought. What must they think, he wondered? A vice-admiral making an exhibition of himself, for some reason known only to himself . . .

The masthead lookout had watched him all the way, and as he clambered, gasping, to the lower yard he said cheerfully, 'Foine day, Zur Richard!'

Bolitho clung to a stay and waited for his heart to return to normal. Damn the others who had raced him up the shrouds when they had all been reckless midshipmen.

He turned and stared at the lookout. 'You're a Cornishman.'

The sailor grinned and bobbed his head. He did not appear to be holding on to anything. 'That be roight, zur. From Penzance.'

Bolitho unslung the telescope from around his shoulders. *Two Cornishmen. So strange a meeting-place.*

It took several attempts to train the glass in time with the schooner's lunges into the offshore breakers. He saw the sharp beak of the headland creeping out towards the weather bow, a tell-tale spurt of spray from the reefs Tyacke had mentioned.

It was already much warmer; his shirt clung to him like another skin. He could see the crisscross of currents as the sea contested the jutting land before surging, confused and beaten, around it. As it had since time began. From this point and beyond, two great oceans, the Atlantic and the Indian Ocean, met. It was like a giant hinge, a gateway which gave access to India, Ceylon and all the territories of New South Wales. No wonder Cape Town was so valuable, so cherished. It was like Gibraltar at the gates of the Mediterranean: whoever held the Rock also held the key.

'*Ships, zur!* Larboard, yonder!'

Bolitho did not need to ask how he could already see them without the advantage of a telescope. Good lookouts were born, not trained, and he had always respected such sailors. The ones who were first to sight the dreaded breakers ahead when every chart claimed otherwise. Often in time for the captain to bring his ship about and save the lives of all aboard.

He waited for the glass to steady again and felt his face stiffen.

Two large ships at anchor; or were they moored fore-and-aft? It would seem so, he thought, to offer greater protection, a defence against a cutting-out attempt, and also to provide a fixed battery of guns to fend off attack.

The lookout said, 'Beggin' yer pardon, zur. I reckon they be Dutch Indiamen.'

Bolitho nodded. Like the Honourable East India Company, such vessels were usually well-manned and armed and had proved more than a match for privateers, even men-of-war on occasions.

He turned to watch the sea breaking over some rocks. It was far enough. Further, and Tyacke would be hard put to claw away into open water.

Whatever the ships were doing, they represented a real threat. They had probably brought stores and men for the Dutch garrison, and might well be expecting others to join them.

Bolitho stared down at the deck and almost lost his grip. The mast was so steeply angled to the wind that the topmast leaned right over the blue water. He could even see his own shadow reflected on the crests.

'You may come about, Mr Tyacke!' For a moment he thought he had not heard, then saw the men running to their stations again.

A tall waterspout lifted suddenly abeam and seconds later Bolitho heard the echoing boom of a gun. He had no idea where it came from, but it was too close to ignore.

He made to lower himself to the ratlines again when the lookout said hoarsely, 'There be a *third* 'un, zur!'

Bolitho stared at him, then raised the glass again. He must be quick. Already the jib was flapping wildly, spilling wind and cracking like musket-fire as the helm went over.

Then, for just a few seconds, he saw the masts and furled sails of the other vessel, her hull lower and almost hidden by the two bigger ships. Dutch or French, it did not really matter. Bolitho had been a frigate captain and had commanded three of them in his time; there was no mistaking that familiar rig.

Waiting, maybe, for the letter which Tyacke's men had found aboard the *Albacora*. Bolitho pushed the hair from his eyes as the mast bucked and swayed over again and the spar felt as if it would splinter itself apart. This was a very large bay, according to Tyacke's chart some twenty miles across, far bigger than Table Bay which they had passed before dawn.

Whatever the Dutch commander's motives might be, he obviously considered the bay and the moored ships well worth protecting. A frontal attack by the English squadron would be costly and probably end in disaster.

He touched the man's shoulder. 'Take care of those eyes!' Even as he spoke the words they seemed to come back at him like a mocking threat. He did not hear the lookout's reply; he had begun the difficult climb down to the deck.

Tyacke listened to what he had seen before saying, 'They could divide us until –'

'Until they are reinforced? I agree.' Bolitho made up his mind. 'You will close with the squadron as fast as you wish.' He found that he could look at the lieutenant's terrible scars without steeling himself. 'Then I will need to speak with the general.' He touched Tyacke's arm. 'Sir David will not be too pleased.'

Tyacke strode away, calling commands, watching the compass and rudder while Simcox scrawled his calculations on a slate.

A voice seemed to whisper inside Bolitho's mind. *Why interfere? Why not let others take responsibility – or are you allowing yourself to be taken in a trap like some wild animal?*

He shook his head, as if he was replying to someone else. How could he request Commodore Popham to detach some of his ships, when they might be needed to evacuate the soldiers and marines if the worst happened? And Warren; could he be trusted any more than the arrogant Captain Varian?

He fould Allday waiting near the weather shrouds and said, 'I have been thinking . . .'

Allday faced him. 'You saw th' size o' that ball, Sir Richard? It's a fortress. We'd need more ships, an' even then we'd be hard put to close with the buggers.' Then he gave a great sigh and rubbed his chest, where the pain of a Spanish sword-thrust

70

lurked as a constant reminder. 'But I sees it's no use me arguing – is it, Sir Richard?'

Bolitho eyed him fondly. 'I don't want to see men butchered to no good purpose, old friend.'

'Nor I, but . . .'

'And I want to go home. The two enjoined make only one course to take. And if we delay I fear that we shall lose the both.'

From the opposite side Tyacke watched them thoughtfully.

Simcox joined him and mopped his face with his red handkerchief. 'A close thing, James.'

Tyacke saw Bolitho clap his hand on Allday's thick arm, the same impetuous gesture he had used to himself. The youthful vice-admiral with the wild black hair blowing in the wind, in his soiled shirt and tar-smeared breeches, was actually laughing, until his coxswain responded with a reluctant grin.

Almost to himself Tyacke replied, 'We are not out of the woods yet, Ben.' He tried to hide his relief from his friend as the haze-shrouded headland began to swing away across the quarter. 'But they'll cheer as loud as all the rest when the call comes. They've never seen a real battle, that's why.' But Simcox had gone to supervise his men again, and did not hear.

5

'Must They Die for Nothing?'

'If you would care to follow me, Sir Richard?' The young army captain stared at Bolitho as he strode up the sloping beach, as if he had just dropped from the moon.

Bolitho paused and glanced at the closely anchored vessels in the bay. Between them and the land every sort of boat was pulling back and forth, some disgorging red-coated soldiers into the shallows to wade ashore, others making heavy weather of it. They seemed loaded down with weapons and stores so that one or two looked in some danger of capsizing.

Bolitho saw *Miranda*'s longboat threading her way back to the schooner to await his next instructions. Tyacke would be only too glad to be out of this place, he thought.

If it was hot aboard ship it was doubly so ashore. The heat seemed to rise from the ground like a separate force, so that within minutes Bolitho's clothing was clinging to him. For the army's sake he was fully dressed in the frock coat and gold-laced hat he had collected from *Themis* during their brief pause to inform Warren what was happening, and to pass his orders to the other captains.

He walked behind the young officer, watching for signs of success or delays in the army's progress so far. There were plenty of soldiers in evidence, working to haul powder and shot from the beach while others marched steadfastly in squads and platoons towards the hills. A few glanced at him as they passed, but he meant nothing to them. Some of them were very bronzed, as if they had come from garrisons in the Indies; others looked like raw recruits. Weighed down as they were with packs and weapons, their coats were already darkly patched with sweat.

Allday tilted his hat over his eyes and commented, 'Bloody shambles, if you asks me, Sir Richard.'

Bolitho heard the far-off bang of light artillery – English or Dutch it was impossible to tell. It seemed impartial and without menace, but the canvas-covered corpses awaiting burial along the rough coastal track told a different story.

The captain paused and pointed at some neat ranks of tents. 'My company lines are here, Sir Richard, but the General is not present.' When Bolitho said nothing he added, 'I am sure he will be back shortly.'

Somewhere a man screamed out in agony, and Bolitho guessed there was a field hospital here, too, with the headquarters company. Progress *was* slow. Otherwise the army surgeons would be beyond that forbidding-looking ridge, he decided.

The captain opened a tent flap and Bolitho ducked to enter. The contrast was unnerving. The ground was covered by rugs and Bolitho imagined the challenge it must have been for the orderlies to find somewhere flat enough to lay them, and pitch this large tent so securely.

A grave-faced colonel, who had been seated in a folding campaign chair, rose to his feet and bowed his head.

'I command the Sixty-First, Sir Richard.' He took Bolitho's proffered hand and smiled. 'We knew of your presence here, but not *amongst* us of course!' He looked tired and strained. 'There was no time to receive you with due honours.'

Bolitho looked up and saw a singed hole in the top of the tent.

The colonel followed his glance. 'Last evening, Sir Richard. One of their marksmen got right through our pickets. Hoping for an important victim, no doubt.' He nodded to the orderly who had appeared with a tray of glasses. 'This may quench your thirst while you are waiting for the General.'

'Are the enemy well-prepared?'

'They are, Sir Richard, and they have all the advantages.' He frowned and added disdainfully, 'But they use methods I find unsoldierly. That marksman, for instance, was not in uniform, but dressed in rags which matched his surroundings. He shot two of my men before we ran him to earth. Not the kind of ethics I care for.'

Allday remarked, 'I think I sees him just now, Sir Richard, hanging from a tree.'

The colonel stared at him as if seeing him for the first time. 'What . . . ?'

Bolitho said, 'Mr Allday is with *me*, Colonel.'

He watched as Allday took a tall glass of wine from the orderly and winked at him. 'Don't you stray too far, matey.' In his fist, the glass looked like a thimble.

Bolitho sipped the wine. It, like the General, travelled well.

The colonel walked to a folding table where several maps were laid out.

'The enemy falls back when pressed, Sir Richard – there seems no eagerness to stand and fight. It is a slow business all the same.' He shot Bolitho a direct glance. 'And if, as you say, we can expect no further support in men and supplies, I fear it will be months rather than weeks before we take Cape Town.'

Bolitho heard horses clattering amongst loose stones, the bark of commands and the slap of muskets from the sentries outside the tent. The horses would be glad to be on dry land again, Bolitho thought, even if nobody else was enjoying it.

The General entered and threw his hat and gloves on to a chair. He was a neat man with piercing blue eyes. A no-nonsense soldier who claimed that he asked nothing from his men that he could or would not do himself.

There were instructions; then the General suggested that the others should leave. Allday, with three glasses of wine under his belt, murmured, 'I'll be in earshot if you needs me, Sir Richard.'

As the flap fell across the entrance the General commented, 'Extraordinary fellow.'

'He's saved my life a few times, Sir David; my sanity a few times more.'

Surprisingly, some of the sternness left the General's sun-reddened face.

'Then I could use a few thousand more like him, I can tell you!' The smile faded just as quickly. 'The landings went well. Commodore Popham worked miracles, and apart from the inevitable casualties it was very satisfactory.' He looked at Bolitho severely. 'And now I am told that I shall receive no reinforcements, that you even intend to strip the squadron of some of the frigates.'

Bolitho was reminded vividly of his friend Thomas Herrick. His eyes were that blue. Stubborn, loyal, hurt even. Was Herrick still his friend? Would he never accept his love for Catherine?

He said shortly, 'It is not merely *my* intention, Sir David!' Thinking of Herrick and the gulf which had come between them had put an edge to his voice. 'It is the King's own signature on those orders, not mine.'

'I wonder who guided his hand for him?'

Bolitho replied quietly, 'I did not hear that, Sir David.'

The General gave him a wry smile. 'Hear what, Sir Richard?'

Like two duellists who had changed their minds, they moved to the maps on the table.

Once, the General looked up and listened as distant gunfire echoed sullenly around the tent. It reminded Bolitho of surf on a reef.

Bolitho laid his own chart on top of the others and said, 'You are a soldier, I am not; but I know the importance, the vital necessity of supplies to an army in combat. I believe that the enemy expect to be reinforced. If that happens before you can take Cape Town, Sir David, what chances have you of succeeding?'

The General did not answer for a full minute while he studied Bolitho's chart, and the notes which he had clipped to it.

Then he said heavily, 'Very little.' Some of his earlier sharpness returned. 'But the navy's task is to prevent it! Blockade the port, and fight off any would-be attempt to support the garrison.' It sounded like an accusation.

Bolitho stared at the chart, but saw only Warren's handful of ships. Each captain had his orders now. The three frigates would watch and patrol the Cape and the approaches, while the remaining two schooners maintained contact between them and the commodore. They might be lucky, but under cover of darkness it would not be too difficult for other vessels to slip past them and under the protection of the shore batteries.

75

And then the choice would remain as before. Attack into the bay and risk the combined fire of the batteries and the carefully moored ships – at best it would end in stalemate. The worst did not bear contemplating. If the army was forced to withdraw in defeat because of lack of supplies and the enemy's continued stubborn resistance, the effect would resound right across Europe. The crushing victory over the Combined Fleet at Trafalgar might even be cancelled out by the inability of the army to occupy Cape Town. France's unwilling allies would take fresh heart from it, and the morale in England would crumble with equal speed.

Bolitho said, 'I suspect that neither of us welcomed this mission, Sir David.'

The General turned as the young captain Bolitho had seen before appeared at the entrance. '*Yes*?'

The captain said, 'A message from Major Browning, Sir David. He wishes to re-site his artillery.'

'Send word, will you? Do nothing until I reach there. Then tell an orderly to fetch my horse.'

He turned and said, 'The news you have brought me is no small setback, Sir Richard.' He gave him a level stare. 'I am relying on you, not because I doubt the ability of my officers and men, but because I have no damned alternative! I know the importance of this campaign – all eyes will be watching it as a foretaste of what lies ahead. For make no mistake, despite all the triumphs at sea, they will be as nought until the English foot-soldier plants his boots on the enemy's own shores.'

There were hushed voices outside the tent, the dragging steps of a horse being led reluctantly back to duty.

The General tossed back the glass of brandy someone had brought for him and picked up his hat and gloves. They were probably still warm from his last ride.

He gave a wry smile. 'A bit like Nelson yourself, y'know. He used to think he was just as able a brigadier ashore as he was a good sailor afloat!'

Bolitho said coldly, 'I do recall that he captured Bastia and Calvi with his sailors, and not the army.'

'*Touché!*' The General led the way from the tent and Bolitho saw more soldiers marching past, their boots churning up clouds of red dust.

76

The General said, 'Look at 'em. Must they die for nothing?'

Bolitho saw Allday hurrying down the beach to signal for the boat. He answered, 'If you knew me, Sir David, you would not ask that.'

The blue eyes flashed like ice as the General lifted one foot to the stirrup. 'It is because I know *of* you, Sir Richard; and I am not asking. For the first time in my career, I am *begging*!'

The colonel joined Bolitho near the water's edge, and together they watched the boat pulling strongly around an anchored storeship.

He said, 'I have never seen him like that before, Sir Richard.'

Allday was pointing to where he wanted the boat to come in, but his mind was still with Bolitho. What he had not heard, he could guess. Whoever knew the rights and wrongs of all this must have realised the hopeless task they had given him.

He heard the colonel snap his boots together as he said, 'I hope we shall meet again, Sir Richard.'

Bolitho turned and looked up the shelving beach. 'Be certain of it, Colonel. In Cape Town or in hell, only greater powers will decide which!'

The boat had almost reached the anchored schooner when Bolitho turned and spoke to Allday again.

'You remember *Achates*, Allday?'

The big coxswain grimaced and touched his chest. 'Not likely to forget that little lot, Sir Richard!' He tried to grin, to shrug it off. 'But that were four years past.'

Bolitho touched his arm. 'I did not mean to bring it back, old friend, but I had an idea concerning it. There was a time when I thought we had lost "Old Katie" just as surely as *Hyperion*.'

Allday stared at his grave features, his spine suddenly like ice despite the strong sunlight. 'A *fireship*, d'you mean, sir?' He spoke almost in a croak, then glanced at the stroke oarsman to make certain he was not listening as he threw himself back on his loom.

Bolitho seemed to be thinking aloud. 'It might prove useless. I realise what I am asking others to do.' He stared abeam as a fish leaped from the water. 'But set against the cost in lives and ships . . .'

Allday twisted round and looked at the boat's coxswain. But

the man's eyes were fixed on the final approach, his knuckles whitening on the tiller bar. It was unlikely that *Miranda* would carry a flag-officer again. He would be fully aware of the consequences if he ruined it.

Not one of them in the boat would realise what agony Bolitho was going through, nor understand if they did.

Bolitho said, 'I recall what Mr Simcox said about the wind. Little use to us maybe, but it might entice the enemy to cut and run for it.'

He turned as the schooner's masts swept above them. 'They will have to be volunteers.'

Allday bit his lip. These were not Bolitho's men, but strangers. They had not followed his flag when they had broken the enemy's line with all hell coming adrift around them. He could remember that other time at San Felipe as clearly as yesterday. *Achates* at her moorings, and then suddenly the approaching ship bursting into flames, bearing down on them while they stared with horror at the inferno. There was only one thing worse than being snared by a fireship, Allday thought grimly, and that was being the crew of one. *Volunteers*? They were as likely as a virgin on Portsmouth Hard.

Bolitho reached up for the side as the boat lurched against the hull and the seamen tossed their oars, like white bones in the sunshine.

He looked down at Allday's troubled face and said calmly, 'It is not a question of choice this time. For there is none.' Then he was up and over the bulwark. Allday followed and saw him already talking with Tyacke, who mercifully had his terrible scars turned away.

After what he had suffered, it was unlikely that Tyacke would offer much support.

Commodore Arthur Warren watched with open astonishment, while Bolitho tossed his crumpled shirt to Ozzard before slipping into a clean one. The little servant was fussing round him and almost got knocked over as Bolitho hurried between the table and the stern windows of *Themis*'s great cabin.

Before *Themis* began to swing again to her cable, Bolitho had seen the busy activity aboard the nearest transport. The

78

captured slaver was hidden on her seaward side, and he wondered how long it would take to complete the arrangements he had ordered.

Bolitho had never understood his own instincts; how he could *sense* that time was in short supply. He felt it now, and it was vital that Warren knew what was happening.

He said, 'You will have the schooner *Dove* to repeat your signals to the offshore patrol.' In his mind he could see the thirty-six gun frigate *Searcher* tacking back and forth somewhere beyond the horizon, Warren's first line of defence should an enemy approach from the west. The second schooner was retained to keep the same contact with the main squadron at Saldanha Bay. It was up to each captain, from the senior, Varian, to the lieutenants who commanded the schooners, to use their own initiative if the wind changed against them, or they sighted any vessel which was obviously hostile. In his written orders Bolitho had stressed his requirements precisely and finally. There would be no heroics, no ship-to-ship actions without informing the commodore.

The anchorage looked strangely deserted and even more vulnerable, and he wondered if Warren were regretting the removal of his aftermost cannon to replace them with useless 'quakers'. It was too late for regrets now.

Warren said, 'I don't like it, Sir Richard. If you fall in this venture, or are taken prisoner, how will I explain?'

Bolitho looked at him impassively. *Is that all it means?* Perhaps Varian was right after all.

He answered, 'I have left some letters.' He saw Jenour turn from an open port. 'But have no fear.' He failed to conceal his bitterness. 'There are some who would not grieve too much!'

Allday entered through a screen door and handed Bolitho his old sword. He ran his eyes critically over Bolitho's appearance and nodded.

Bolitho smiled. 'Satisfied?'

'Aye. But it don't signify that I've changed my mind!'

Allday too had changed into his fine blue jacket and nankeen breeches. He glanced at Bolitho's other sword on the rack and remarked to Ozzard, 'Take good care o' that, matey.' He patted the little man's bony shoulder. 'Like the last time, remember?'

Bolitho walked to the table again and stared at the chart. Captain Poland's *Truculent* should be on her station to the west of Table Bay, ready to rendezvous with *Miranda* and her dangerous consort. Varian's *Zest*, the most powerful of the frigates, would be standing to the south-west. If the attack was successful, it would be Varian's task to chase and take any vessels which tried to put to sea to escape the fireship.

Whether the enemy recognised the *Albacora* or not made little difference to the attack. Only to those who remained with the fireship until the last moment would it be important.

The marine sentry called from the door, 'Surgeon, *sir*!'

The man who entered was a thin, unsmiling individual whose skin was as pale as Warren's.

He said abruptly, 'I am sorry to intrude, sir but *Miranda*'s midshipman wishes to return to his ship immediately.'

Warren frowned, irritated by the interruption. 'Well, that is for you to say, surely. I am too busy for –'

Bolitho asked, 'Is he recovered enough?'

Confused by the presence of the admiral dressed as he was now in his proper uniform, instead of the casual open shirt, the surgeon stammered, 'It was a severe wound, sir, but he is young and very determined.' His mouth closed in a thin line, as if he had just decided not to say what he had been about to add. It was not his affair.

'Then he can come over to *Miranda* with us. See to it, Stephen.' Bolitho saw the undisguised relief on the flag-lieutenant's features and added, 'Did you think I would leave you yet again?' He tried to smile. 'If Allday is my right arm, you surely must be my left!'

He thought of Jenour's face when he had boarded the flagship only hours ago. A courier brigantine had paused at the anchorage and had sent over a despatch bag without even stopping long enough to anchor. She had been so fast that it was little wonder *Miranda* had not seen any sign of her.

Jenour had dropped his voice as they had walked aft to the cabin. 'Inside your official envelope there is . . . a letter . . . for you, Sir Richard.'

Bolitho had turned on him. 'Tell me, Stephen – I beg of you!'

Warren had been coming towards them, dragging his feet,

trying to control his painful breathing, and Jenour had answered quickly, 'It is from your lady, Sir Richard.' He had recognised Bolitho's remaining uncertainty and clarified, 'From Falmouth.'

'*Thank God.*' At long last. The first letter. He had half expected it might be from Belinda. With distance to give her confidence she might have been demanding more money, or suggesting another reconciliation for the sake of appearances.

The letter was in his pocket now. Somehow, even in *Miranda*'s crowded world, he would find a private place where he could read it, feel her presence, hear her voice. When this was over he would write to her again, tell her all the longings he had built up since their wretched parting.

He looked towards the glittering water beyond the stern windows. *If I should fall . . .* Then there would be the other letter which was locked in his strongbox.

Bolitho raised his arm to allow Allday to clip the old family sword to his belt. So many times; and too many had seemed like the last.

Bolitho left the cabin and paused where Ozzard was waiting with his hat. 'When we are finished with this matter we shall return to Falmouth.' He saw the anxiety in Ozzard's eyes and added gently, 'You are better off here.' He looked across his rounded shoulders. 'Commodore Warren will see that you are taken care of.'

He hurried to the entry port and glanced at the silent figures who had paused in their work to watch him leave. How different from England, he thought. These men were probably glad to see him go, as if by remaining their own lives would be more at risk.

The sun was dipping very slowly, like a gigantic red ball which quivered above its own reflection and made the horizon glisten like a heated wire.

Commodore Warren doffed his hat and the calls trilled, while the flagship's reduced section of Royal Marines slapped their muskets in salute.

Then he lowered himself to the longboat and got a brief glimpse of the midshipman, who was sitting crammed beside Jenour and Allday.

'Good day – Mr Segrave, is it not?' The youth stammered something, but at that moment the boat was cast off and with oars pulling and backing, steered away from the side.

Jenour peered astern, glad he was not remaining in *Themis* with Yovell and Ozzard. He touched the lanyard on his fine sword and lifted his chin as if in defiance.

Allday was watching the fiery sunset. It had taken on a new meaning, a threatening aspect, with Death the winner one way or the other.

To break the silence Bolitho asked, 'What else do you have in your important-looking bag, Stephen?'

Jenour tore his mind from the letter he was writing in his mind to his parents in Southampton.

'For *Miranda*, Sir Richard.' He could guess what Bolitho was thinking and recalled the letter he had given to him. Bolitho had taken it as if it were life itself. It should have surprised him that his admiral could be two such different men: the one who inspired and commanded, and the other who needed that lady's love so much, but could not hide it as he did his other fears and hopes.

Lieutenant Tyacke waited by the ladder and touched his hat as Bolitho climbed aboard. He even managed an ironic smile as he looked at Jenour and Midshipman Segrave. 'Two bad pennies together, eh, Sir Richard?' He took the package from Jenour and said, 'The *Albacora* is all but ready, sir.' They stared across the darkening water to the other, untidy schooner. In the sunset's glow she looked as if she were already burning from within.

'We did our best, sir. But not being pierced for gunports to draw the flames, we had to cut makeshift ones to the main hold an' the like.' He nodded grimly. 'She'll burn like a torch when need be.'

He turned away; his men were waiting for his attention. Both schooners would sail at nightfall, slink away from the other ships like assassins. Thinking aloud, Tyacke said, 'With God's help we should rendezvous with *Truculent* at dawn. Then you'll have a mite more comfort in *her* than I can offer you, sir!'

Bolitho looked at him and saw the red glow on the ruined face. Like melted wax. As if it had just happened.

He said simply, 'It is not comfort I need. Your ship has offered me what I want most.'

Tyacke asked with a touch of wariness, 'And what may that be, sir?'

'An *example*, Mr Tyacke. How all ships could be, large or small, offered the right trust and leadership.'

'If you will excuse me, sir.' He turned awkwardly. 'There is much to do.'

Bolitho gazed at the sun sliding into the horizon and the sea. There should be steam or an explosion, so powerful was its majesty, and menace.

Midshipman Segrave was groping beneath the companion hatch when Simcox found him and said, 'You'll have to sleep rough tonight, my lad. We're somewhat overfull till I can discover *Truculent*'s whereabouts.' The lighter mood eluded him and he said, 'Bob Jay told me about your other injuries.' He saw the youth staring at him in the gloom. ''E 'ad to. It was 'is duty to me.'

Segrave looked down at his clenched fists. 'You had no right . . .'

'Don't you lecture me about rights, *Mister* Segrave! I've had a bloody gutful o' them since I first donned the King's coat, so let's 'ave no more of 'em, see?' His face was only inches from Segrave's as he added vehemently, 'You was whipped like a dog to have scars like that, Bob Jay said. *Bully you*, did they? Some poxy scum who thought you was lettin' them down, was that it?' He saw the youth bow his head and nod. Afterwards Simcox thought he had never witnessed such despair. He said, 'Well, it's in the past now. Bob Jay'll never forget you saved 'is skin.' He touched his shoulder and added roughly, 'I 'ad to tell the Cap'n.'

Segrave shivered, wiping his face with his forearm.

'That was your *duty* too.' But there was no sarcasm or resentment. There was simply nothing at all.

Simcox watched him with concern. 'All right then, son?'

Segrave looked at him, his eyes very bright in the lantern's glow from the cabin.

'You don't understand. I was told aboard *Themis*. I am to return to my old ship as soon as we leave the Cape.' He got to his feet and made for the companion ladder. 'So you see, it was a lie, like everything else!'

Later, as darkness folded over the anchorage and the stars were still too feeble to separate sea from sky, Bolitho sat at the cabin table, half listening to the muffled commands from the deck, the creak of the windlass as the cable was hove short. Jay, the master's mate, was across in *Albacora* with a small prize crew, so all hands would be working doubly hard and standing watch-and-watch until the rendezvous was made.

Tyacke peered through the door. 'Ready to proceed, Sir Richard.' He waited questioningly. 'Any further orders?'

Something about him was different.

Bolitho asked, 'What is troubling you?'

Tyacke said steadily, 'I received orders in the despatch bag, sir. Both Mr Simcox and Segrave are leaving my command after this is over and done with.' He tried to smile, but it made him look desperate. 'Ben Simcox is a good friend, and I've come to feel differently about the midshipman since . . .' He did not go on.

'I understand.' Bolitho saw the surprise on Tyacke's maimed face.

'Because I am what I am, is that it?' He shook his head and Tyacke caught a quick glimpse of the terrible scar which was only partly hidden by the lock of hair. 'I had another flag-lieutenant once. He used to call me and my captains, *We Happy Few*. By God, Mr Tyacke, there are precious few of us now! Oh yes, I know what it is to find a friend, then lose him in the twinkling of an eye. Sometimes I think it is best to know nobody, and to care for nothing.'

Somebody called from the deck, 'Th' slaver's under way, sir!'

'I – I am sorry, sir.' Tyacke had to leave, but wanted to remain.

'There is no need.' Bolitho met his gaze and smiled. 'And know this. I *do* care. And when I call for volunteers tomorrow –'

Tyacke turned to the ladder. 'You'll not lack them, Sir Richard. Not in this ship.' Then he was gone, and moments later came the cry, '*Anchor's aweigh!*'

Bolitho sat for several minutes, his ears deaf to the din of rudder and canvas as the schooner curtsied round, free of the land once more.

Why had he spoken to Tyacke like that? He smiled at his own answer. Because he needed him and his men more than they would ever know, or understand.

With great care he opened the letter, then stared with surprise as a dried ivy leaf fell to the table.

Her writing seemed to blur as he held the letter closer to the swaying lantern.

My darling Richard,

This leaf is from your house and my home –

It was enough. The remainder he would read later when he was quite alone.

6

While Others Dare . . .

Lieutenant James Tyacke clung to the weather rail and squinted through the spray as Bolitho appeared by the companionway.

'Sail in sight, sir!'

Bolitho clutched a backstay and nodded. 'I heard the call, Mr Tyacke. You've a good man aloft!'

It had been dark to all intents when he had caught the lookout's cry. Even in so small a vessel it had been difficult, and to anyone less experienced the overnight change in wind and weather would have appeared astonishing. The wind had veered several points and now came from the north, or near enough. With her bowsprit pointing due east, *Miranda* appeared to be lying hard over, the sea occasionally licking above the lee bulwark; when it touched your skin it felt like ice.

Bolitho peered to where the horizon should be, but could see nothing. Only the creaming wave-crests and the blacker depths of fast-moving troughs. It would make the two schooners' approach doubly challenging. A lantern was shuttered across the tumbling water, and Bolitho guessed that the captured slaver was less than half a cable away. It was a mark of Tyacke's and Jay's experience that they had managed to keep in close company all through the night. When dawn finally broke the seamen would be at their worst, he thought. Worn out by trimming sails, reefing and changing tack over and over again.

Tyacke shouted, 'Time to close with *Albacora*, sir.' He was watching him in the darkness, his eyes well accustomed to the night while Bolitho was still trying to adjust to it.

It was strange to realise that the lookout could not only see the rising dawn but the sails of another vessel. It had to be *Truculent*. If it was not, it could only be the enemy.

'Deck there! She's a frigate, sir. Hove-to.'

Bolitho heard Simcox release a sigh. So it was *Truculent*. Captain Poland could justly be proud of another successful rendezvous.

Someone called, 'Th' slaver's come about, sir. 'Er boat's in the water.'

Tyacke muttered, 'Lucky it's no further. It'll be a rough haul for the oarsmen.'

Bolitho touched Tyacke's arm and said, 'About the volunteers?'

Tyacke faced him. 'That deserter was sent over from the flagship with the prize crew. There was a Royal Marine too, for all the use *he'll* be.' He spoke with the unreasonable contempt of sailors for members of the Corps.

'Is that all?'

Tyacke shrugged. 'It's better this way, sir. My ship will provide the remainder.' His teeth showed faintly through the shadows as the first hint of light fingered the horizon. 'I spoke to them myself, sir. Men I know and trust.' He added bluntly, 'More to the point, who trust *me*.'

'Mr Simcox knows what he must do?'

Tyacke did not answer directly. He was watching the approaching boat as it lifted and plunged like a winged fish while it fought around the stern to find shelter beneath *Miranda*'s lee. He said, 'Mr Simcox will remain in *Miranda*.' He paused as if expecting to be challenged.

Bolitho said, 'I placed you in charge. It must be your decision.'

Simcox suddenly lurched towards them. '*I must protest!* I know these waters, and in any case –' Tyacke seized his arm and spun him round. 'Do as you're bloody told, man! I command here! Now attend to that boat!'

Bolitho could barely see the acting-master in the gloom, but felt his disbelief and hurt as if Tyacke had struck him.

Tyacke said heavily, 'Ben is a fine sailor. If he survives this bloody war, begging your pardon, sir – and I said *if* – he'll have a

career, something waiting for him even if they pitch him on the
beach with all the others.' He gestured angrily towards the
confusion in the waist of the schooner. 'God damn you,
Morgan, catch a turn there, or you'll stove in the bloody boat!'

Bolitho had not heard him berate any of his seamen before.
He was trying to get it out of himself, to forget what he had said
and done to his only friend.

Figures lurched through the darkness and then Jay, the
master's mate, appeared by the tiller.

'All prepared, sir! Ready to change crews!' He glanced
quickly from Tyacke to Simcox, who was standing by the
foremast, then asked. 'Ben not ready yet, sir?'

Tyacke said harshly, 'I am going in his place. So stay with
him.' For a moment his voice softened. 'And the ship.'

Another figure appeared and Bolitho saw it was the midshipman, Segrave.

Tyacke murmured, 'He volunteered, sir, and I might need
another officer, if things go badly.' He said more loudly, 'Are
you still eager, Mr Segrave? You can still fall out – no one would
blame you after what you did for Mr Jay.'

The youth's face seemed to grow out of the shadows as the
first pale sunlight reflected from the dripping sails and rigging.
He said firmly, 'I *want* to go, sir.'

The lookout's cry made them look up again. 'She's *Truculent*
right enough, sir!' A further pause, then, 'She's shaken out
some reefs an' she's comin' about.'

Tyacke said, 'She'll be sending a boat for you, sir.'

'Yes.' Bolitho saw Allday with the small bag of clothing which
they had brought with them from *Themis*. So like those other
occasions, when suddenly there is no more time left. Lastly
came Jenour, yawning hugely. He had slept through everything.
The other figures had disappeared into the pitching boat
alongside; Tyacke was eager to leave. To get it over.

He said in a calm voice, 'I'll not let you down, sir.'

Bolitho took his hand. It was hard like Thomas Herrick's. He
replied quietly, 'You wouldn't know *how*, Mr Tyacke.'

Tyacke swung one leg over the bulwark, but paused as Simcox
pulled himself along the side heedless of the sea sluicing along
the scuppers, dragging at his legs.

'You want me, Ben?'

Simcox staggered and almost fell headlong, but Tyacke caught him with his arm. Watching from the mainmast bitts Bolitho saw and understood. It was like a last embrace.

Tyacke said roughly, 'You've too much to lose, Ben, and you know it. You'll make a fine Master, with a proper captain to take care of, eh?'

Simcox said something but it was lost in the drumming rigging and the turmoil alongside.

When Bolitho looked again Tyacke had gone and the boat was surging away once more, spray flying from the oar blade like ragged silk.

Bolitho said, 'Get under way, Mr Simcox. The sooner we can meet with *Truculent*, the faster we can –' He left the rest unsaid.

Allday said gruffly, 'He's all aback, an' that's no error!'

Bolitho called, 'Mr Simcox, once I am in *Truculent* you will follow the fireship.' He had not used her name. By accident or design, he wondered? Perhaps to make Simcox accept her brutal role. What it might well mean for her crew.

Simcox stared at him. 'Pretend to give chase, Sir Richard?' He sounded vague.

'Yes. It is an old trick but it may well work, and give Mr Tyacke the opportunity to stand closer to the enemy.'

He glanced at his cuff and saw the gold lace suddenly clear and bright; even felt the first warmth as the sunlight rolled down from the horizon.

Jenour asked, 'What *are* their chances, Sir Richard?'

Bolitho looked at him, steadily. 'Not good. With the wind against them they will have to lose valuable time tacking back and forth. After Mr Tyacke has fired the fuses he will have to pull away in the boat and head for the shore. They will fall into Dutch hands, but with our army so near I feel certain they will not be harmed.' He saw the doubt on Jenour's young face. 'If Mr Tyacke fails and is too late to get away, we will lose twelve good men. In a frontal attack we could lose every ship and every soul in the squadron.'

Allday gazed towards the land. 'Not a choice *I'd* care to make, Sir Richard.'

Bolitho pushed the lock of hair from his forehead. Allday

understood. One man or a thousand; life or death; it was a decision which was damned either way.

Allday added, 'I'll lay odds at the Admiralty they never gives it a thought, nor lose a wink of sleep.'

Bolitho saw patches of cloud scudding out from the land and imagined he could feel dust between his teeth.

Allday was studying him grimly and said, 'I was a mite bothered back there, Sir Richard. Knowin' you, I did think once or twice that *you* might take charge o' the fireship.'

Bolitho looked at Simcox, who was still staring after *Albacora* as she laid herself over on her new course.

'Not this time, old friend.'

Allday watched *Truculent*'s pyramid of pale canvas rising above the departing shadows while she bore down on the schooner.

His worry had been real enough, until he had remembered what Bolitho had said when they had been together. *I want to go home.* It was as if the words had been torn from his throat. Allday had shared most things with Bolitho but he had never heard him speak like that before. He released a huge sigh. But they were still a long way from England.

Even as the deck planking began to steam in the first morning warmth, *Truculent* went about and then lowered the gig smartly from her quarter.

Bolitho waited for Simcox to have his depleted company piped to halliards and braces to heave-to and await the boat, then said, 'I wish you well, Mr Simcox. I have written a report which will not come amiss at your final interview.'

Simcox nodded and replied, 'I am grateful, Sir Richard.' He struggled for the right words. 'Y'see, Sir Richard, we was friends, an' I know why he's doin' this for me.'

Bolitho said, 'If anyone can do it, *he* can.' He thought of that last handshake, firm and hard like Herrick's; and of Herrick's *Lady Luck* in whom he had always believed so fervently.

He saw the frigate's boat pulling strongly towards them, a lieutenant trying to stand upright in the sternsheets while the hull bucked beneath him. So like Poland, he thought, everything correct and beyond criticism.

To Simcox he said, 'I hope we meet again. You have a good

company and a fine little ship.' Even as he spoke he knew what was wrong. It was better not to know them, see and recognise their faces, before you made a decision which could kill them all. He had told himself often enough in the past, and after *Hyperion*'s end he had sworn it to himself again.

'Stand by, on deck!'

Bolitho nodded to those by the bulwark. Old Elias Archer the gunner, Jay the master's mate who would probably take Simcox's place when he quit the ship. Faces he had come to know in so short a while. He noticed that Sperry the boatswain was not here. It was good to know he would be with Tyacke. He wondered why the midshipman had insisted on going with the prize crew when he had just received orders to return to his old ship. Perhaps the one riddle answered the other? In Tyacke's hands they might manage to reach the shore. He shut it from his thoughts like slamming a door.

'And I shall not forget the beer, Mr Simcox!'

Then he was down and into the boat, gripping the lieutenant's shoulder and trying not to allow his legs to be caught by his sword.

Only Allday saw his face when he made that last carefree comment.

He was also the only one who knew what it had cost him.

'So this is where it happened?' Tyacke stooped to peer into the *Albacora*'s cabin. 'It's like a pig-sty!'

Midshipman Segrave darted a quick glance at the bunk as if he expected to see the naked slave-girl still chained there. Like the rest of the crew's quarters, the cabin was full of inflammable material of every sort which had been piled or thrown on top of the original master's possessions. The whole schooner stank of it. Oil, old canvas and oakum soaked in grease, wood dipped in tar which had been gathered from Warren's two transports: anything which would transform *Albacora* into a raging torch. Segrave felt the air playing around his face from one of the jagged vent holes which had been cut in the deck to fan the flames. For the first time since he had pushed himself forward to volunteer he knew true fear.

Tyacke's voice helped to reassure him. He sounded

91

completely absorbed in his own thoughts, almost matter-of-fact. As if he accepted the inevitability of his fate with the same coolness as he had changed roles with Simcox.

Segrave said, 'It seems easier, sir.'

'What?' Again, so distant. 'Yes, we're closer inshore. But the wind's as much an enemy as before.' He sat down unexpectedly on a cask and looked at the youth, his awful wound in shadow. 'Mr Simcox told me about your other injuries.' He eyed him calmly, as if there was nothing to do, with all the time in the world to do it. 'Beat you, did they? Because you were no use on board?'

Segrave clenched his fists. Remembering the first time, and all the others which were to follow. The captain had been uninterested in what went on in the midshipmen's berth, and as he had been heard to tell his first lieutenant on several occasions, he was only concerned with *results*. Another lieutenant had been chosen to divide the midshipmen into teams, and would set one against the other in all drills and exercises in seamanship, gunnery and boatwork. There were penalties for the laggards, minor awards for the winners.

Tyacke was not far from the truth in his casual summing-up. Except that it was persecution of the worst kind. Segrave had been stripped naked and bent over a gun and flogged without mercy either by the lieutenant or some of the midshipmen. They had humiliated him in any way they could, had worked off a kind of madness in their cruelty. It was doubtful if he would ever lose the scars, any more than a sailor flogged at the gratings.

Segrave found that he was blurting it out in short, desperate sentences although he did not recall beginning to speak at all.

Tyacke said nothing until he had fallen silent. Then he said, 'In any ship where such brutality is tolerated it is the fault of her captain. It is the way of things. Disinterest in how his lieutenants administer discipline or enforce his orders must lie at his door. No lieutenant would dare to act in this fashion without the full knowledge of his captain.' His eyes gleamed in the shadows. 'The orders to return to your old ship in due course prompted you to volunteer, is that it?' When Segrave remained silent he said harshly, 'By God, boy, you would have done better to kill that lieutenant, for the end will likely be the same, without the satisfaction!' He reached across suddenly and gripped his shoulder. 'It was your choice.' He turned away and a shaft of sunlight filtered through the filthy skylight to lay bare his disfigurement. 'As it was mine.'

He twisted round as feet pattered along the deck overhead, and the boatswain's hoarse bellow chased some of the crew to their stations for altering course.

Segrave said simply, 'I'm glad I came, sir.'

He did not cringe as Tyacke pushed his face nearer and said, *'Well spoken!'*

They went on deck together, and after the foul stench below the air tasted like wine.

Tyacke glanced at the streaming masthead pendant, then at the compass. The wind was as before, but as the youth had noticed, it was less violent in the shelter of the land.

As he removed a telescope from a rack beside the compass box he glanced quickly at the men on deck. Including himself there were twelve of them aboard. He saw the seaman named Swayne, the deserter, hauling on a halliard to take out some slack. He moved quickly and easily, a proper Jack, Tyacke thought. Now that he had accepted what he had done by coming here with the others, he even looked cheerful. While there was life there was still hope. Aboard the flagship an award of two hundred lashes or more, with the only other alternative being an agonising dance at the yardarm, left no room for hope.

Tyacke stared at the other volunteer, a Royal Marine named Buller, under a similar sentence for striking a sergeant after getting fighting drunk on pilfered rum. When it came to such matters the 'Royals' could be merciless with one of their own.

The other faces he knew well. He saw the squat figure of George Sperry the *Miranda*'s boatswain, calling to two hands who were working with chain slings on the foreyard. Once the fire was started, the tarred rigging would ignite in seconds, the sails too if the deed were done too soon. Chain would keep their sails in place just that much longer. Tyacke's face twisted into a grimace. Or so he had been told. Like all sailors Tyacke hated the danger of fire more than anything. He touched his burned face and wondered if he would break at the last moment; knowing in the same breath he would not.

93

He looked at Segrave, his hair ruffling in the wind, and thought of his faltering voice as he had stammered out his story. Tyacke had found his rage mounting to match the boy's shame. Those others should be the ones to feel shame, he thought. There would always be scum like that, but only where their cruelty was condoned.

Tyacke raised his glass and trained it past the midshipman's shoulder. The land was hard abeam, the very tip of the point which guarded the entrance to the bay reaching out rocky and green in the pale sunshine. He felt the deck planking growing warm again; very soon the whole schooner would be as dry as tinder. God help them if the enemy had sited some long-range guns as far out as the point. He doubted it; it was an impossible place for a landing party to scale or even disembark. But the doubt remained. No ship was a match for land artillery, especially those with heated shot. Tyacke forced his mind away from the picture of a red-hot ball slamming into the crammed hull beneath his shoes.

'Deck there!' The lookout was pointing astern. '*Miranda*'s tackin' to the point, sir!'

Tyacke turned his glass towards the open sea, where the water was a deeper blue as if unwilling to give up the night.

He felt a lump in his throat as he saw *Miranda*'s huge courses swinging above the waves, her single topsail flapping wildly as she began to change tack. To all appearances it might well look as if she was in pursuit of the shabby *Albacora*.

'Shake out all reefs, Mr Sperry! Lively there!' He saw the boatswain give his broken-toothed grin as he added, 'We don't want a King's ship to catch us!' But he turned away in case Sperry saw, and understood, the lie.

He said to Segrave, 'Lend a hand at the helm. As far as I can calculate we shall have to make good some ten miles before we can attempt a final approach.'

Segrave watched him as he voiced his thoughts aloud. He found he could do it now without revulsion. There was something compelling about the tall lieutenant, and something frightening too.

Tyacke waved the telescope towards the full breadth of the bay as the point of land appeared to slide across the larboard quarter, like the opening of a giant gateway.

94

'We shall beat up to the nor'-east where the bottom shelves to a few fathoms. The sort of thing any ship's master might do if he was being chased by a man-o'-war. Then we'll come about and lay her on the starboard tack and run straight for 'em.' He glanced at Segrave's sensitive features. 'That's if they're still there, of course.'

Tyacke rubbed his chin and wished he had had a shave. The idea made him smile. As if it mattered now! He recalled the vice-admiral's coxswain, Allday, with the morning ritual. He thought also of his own private talks with Bolitho. Such an easy man to speak with, to share confidences. Like the time when Bolitho had asked him about his face and the Nile, when he had found himself answering without his usual defence and resentment.

And it was all true. There was no falseness in Bolitho, no using men as mere tools to complete some plan, or hiding indifference behind his rank.

'Stand by to alter course, Mr Segrave.' He saw him start with surprise. 'In a minute or so we shall steer nor'-east, so watch the mains'l no less than the compass!'

Segrave swallowed hard then joined the helmsman who acknowledged him almost shyly. Segrave saw that it was the young seaman named Dwyer, the one who had tried to tie up his wound in the cabin beneath them.

Dwyer said, 'We'll manage well enough, eh, Mr Segrave?'

Segrave nodded and discovered he could even offer a smile. 'We shall.'

Tyacke turned as a shot echoed across the water, and was in time to see a faint puff of smoke shred away from *Miranda*'s bows. Simcox had started to play his part. It was to be hoped he did not over-play it and outrun the *Albacora* as *Miranda* had done before.

Then he returned attention to the sailing of the fireship; but even as he signalled for Sperry to put two of his hard-pressed men on the foremast boom, he found himself thinking of the girl he had known in Portsmouth. *Marion*. He dashed the sweat from his eyes with his grubby shirt sleeve and believed for an instant that he had said her name aloud. *If only* . . . Another shot echoed over the glittering water, and from a corner of his

95

eye Tyacke saw the four-pound ball jag into the sea a good cable astern.

'Steady she goes, sir! Nor'-east it is!' It was strange to hear Segrave call out when he was usually so quiet and withdrawn.

Tyacke glanced at him sadly. *We are both scarred, inwardly or out*.

Spray dashed over the side and swept over the patched and dirty deck like a tide. Tyacke saw the boatswain blink as another shot banged out astern, and the ball ploughed down a bit closer than the previous one. He glanced at the skylight and Tyacke knew he was thinking about the woman he had satisfied his lust with in the cabin. *We all have only memories now*.

Tyacke gazed along the busy deck as the schooner leaned over still further under her full press of sail.

Perhaps Marion would read about it someday. He gave a bitter smile. *My last command*.

Captain Daniel Poland remained a little apart from Bolitho as he stood by the cabin table, and used some dividers to measure off the calculations on his chart.

Bolitho said, half to himself, 'As far as we know, there have been no new arrivals in the bay. If there had been, either you or Captain Varian in *Zest* would likely have sighted them. Likewise, the big ships and frigate must still be at anchor.' He looked up in time to see Poland's doubtful expression. 'Don't you agree?'

Poland responded, 'It is a big area, Sir Richard. Four times the size of Table Bay.' He faltered under the grey stare. 'But as you say, it is perhaps unlikely.'

Bolitho watched the sunlight fanning through *Truculent*'s stern windows, swinging across the cabin like fiery bars as the frigate changed tack yet again.

Poland bit his lip with annoyance as someone or something fell heavily on the deck above. '*Clumsy oafs!*'

Bolitho half-smiled. Maybe it was better to be like Poland. Caring only for the immediate and the things he knew best.

He tugged out his watch and studied it. Tyacke should be standing into his proper position by now, *Miranda* too. It was still stark in his mind, the way Tyacke had changed places with his friend. But it was more than a gesture to save his friend, to cast himself away. It was the act of a leader; what he had seen others do without a thought for the cost of it.

It did not occur to Bolitho that it was exactly what he would have done in Tyacke's position.

Jenour, who had been moving restlessly by the stern windows, straightened up and exclaimed, 'Gunfire, Sir Richard!'

Bolitho gave a last lingering glance over the chart. 'So it was, Stephen.' He looked around the cabin which had been his hiding-place on the passage from England. From Catherine. After *Miranda* it was like a ship-of-the-line. He faced Poland as feet clattered along the passageway towards the screen door.

'While others dare, we must wait, Captain.' His own words depressed him, and he added shortly, 'You may beat to quarters when convenient.' He touched his hip as if to find his sword. 'Tell Allday –'

Allday padded across the cabin. 'I'm here, Sir Richard.' He grinned as Bolitho raised his arm for him to fix the scabbard in place. 'Like always!'

Another far-off shot brought Allday's words into sharp focus and Bolitho said quietly, 'I am depending on it.'

Lieutenant Tyacke reluctantly lowered his glass. It would not be sensible to be seen watching the anchored ships rather than the pursuing *Miranda*. But in those last brief seconds he had seen the two large ships, and they certainly had all the appearances of Dutch Indiamen. The most important factor was that they were not moving with the wind and current. So Bolitho's first impression had been right. They were anchored fore-and-aft to provide two fixed batteries of guns against any attacker, which would be in trouble enough beating against the northerly wind.

Dwyer exclaimed admiringly, 'God, look at 'er *go*, Mr Segrave!' He was staring across the quarter at *Miranda*'s bulging sails as she came up into the wind yet again, cutting away the distance still further so that Segrave imagined he could see Simcox aft by the tiller, his unruly hair waving in the wind.

Another puff of smoke from her bow-chaser and this time the ball slammed down just a boat's length clear. Some of the spray pattered across the deck and Sperry cursed violently. 'God damn you, Elias Archer. If you lays another ball like that I'll not forgive 'ee.'

Segrave licked his dry lips. Like Dwyer, the boatswain seemed to have forgotten for the moment what they were attempting to do; that it was unlikely he would get a chance to argue with *Miranda*'s gunner ever again.

A lookout clinging in the foremast shrouds yelled, '*Guardboat, sir!*'

Tyacke was watching the sails and the masthead pendant. 'Stand by to wear ship, Mr Sperry!' He wiped his face again, gauging the distance and the power of the wind. It had taken over an hour to get this far and penetrate the bay without any apparent opposition, although there must be many glasses trained on the one ship fleeing from another. It seemed likely that the Dutch commander might already know the *Albacora*, while *Miranda*'s streaming ensign left little else to doubt.

Tyacke raised his glass again and peered at the boat just reported by the lookout. A small cutter, under a scrap of sail but with oars already angled from her rowlocks for extra power, was rounding the stern of the nearest merchantman. Metal gleamed in the sunshine, and he saw the gilt buttons of an officer in the sternsheets. The guardboat would challenge their presence. Tyacke frowned. There was only one chance.

He called, 'You! Private Buller!' The marine turned away from his place by the halliards as Tyacke added harshly, 'You're *supposed* to be a bit of a marksman, I'm told?'

Buller met his tone with equal insolence. 'Best shot in the company, *sir*!'

Tyacke grinned. 'Right. Fetch your piece and prepare to mark down the officer in charge of the guardboat. They've got a swivel mounted in the bows, so you must not miss!'

He turned away as Buller stooped down to where his weapons were rolled up inside his telltale scarlet coat.

'All ready, sir!'

Tyacke looked steadily at Segrave. 'Ready aft?'

Segrave nodded jerkily, his face pale despite the sun's glare, but strangely determined.

Tyacke walked to the taffrail and made certain that the

98

longboat was towing clumsily astern. Once again he stared hard at the land, then across the larboard quarter where the moored storeships appeared to be falling away into the distance. Even the guardboat seemed in no hurry to close with them, especially with *Miranda* charging in full pursuit.

'Ready about! Helm a-lee! Let go and haul, lads!' Tyacke's voice harried them until they were sweating and gasping to perform the work normally done by twice the number of hands.

Segrave's shoes slipped, then gripped on the tarred deck-seams while he threw his weight on the tiller, his eyes blind to everything but the great swinging sails and the shriek of blocks, while the schooner continued to tack into and then across the eye of the wind.

Dwyer gasped, 'Come round, you bloody bitch!' But he was grinning as the sails banged out on the opposite tack to thrust the deck over even more steeply. Where there had been empty land there suddenly lay the anchorage, the ships clear and real in the sunlight, even their Dutch ensigns visible against the land mass beyond.

Tyacke was holding on for support but even he gave a quick smile. This was no *Miranda*, but she had been used to fast handling in her rotten trade. He studied the guardboat: her sails were flapping and losing wind, and as he watched he saw the oars begin to move ahead and astern, pulling the hull around until the bow-gun was pointing, not at them but at *Miranda*.

Sperry gasped, '*Miranda*'ll blow 'er clean out of the water. Wot's their game?'

The lookout shouted sharply, 'Deck there! Th' frigate's under way!'

Tyacke swung round, his heart sickened as he saw the frigate's topsails shaking out and hardening to the wind while she glided away from her inshore anchorage.

Sperry said hoarsely, 'We'll not stand a chance, sir.' He rubbed his eyes as if he could not believe what he saw. 'She's got th' wind, God damn her!'

Tyacke said, 'Let her fall off a point, Mr Segrave.' He raised his glass and felt a sudden pain, as if the breath had been knocked out of him. 'It's not us. It's *Miranda* she's going for!' Tyacke waved his arms and yelled at the top of his voice. 'Run for it, Ben! In the name of Christ – come about!' Their very helplessness, and the fact that nobody aboard *Miranda* could possibly hear him, made his voice crack with emotion.

'*Get out of it, Ben!*'

Segrave asked in a whisper, 'What's happening?'

Dwyer flung at him, 'Th' frigate's runnin' for open sea, that's what!'

Segrave watched. *Miranda*'s length began to shorten as she saw her danger and started to come about.

Tyacke trained his glass on the frigate. She was smaller than *Truculent*, but showed all the grace of her class as she changed tack, and her huge fore and main courses filled to the wind, pushing her over until he could plainly see the French Tricolour rippling from her peak. Getting away from the bay before she might be caught defending her ally's supply ships, and be held as much a prisoner as they were.

Sickened, Tyacke saw the frigate's ports open, could almost imagine the orders to aim their broadside. It was over a mile's range, but with a controlled assault it was impossible to miss.

He saw the smoke belch along the frigate's low hull, and even before he could swing his glass across the glistening water he heard the staccato crash of gunfire. The sea around and beyond the little *Miranda* seemed to boil, while spray burst skyward, standing in the sunlight like waterspouts – as if they were suddenly frozen and might never fall.

For one more second Tyacke clung to a spark of hope. At that range *Miranda* had somehow managed to escape the enemy's iron.

He heard some of his men groan as, with the suddenness of a great seabird settling to fold its wings, both of *Miranda*'s masts collapsed, burying the deck under a mass of writhing canvas and splintered spars.

The frigate did not fire again. She was already setting her royals, her yards alive with tiny figures as she pointed her jib boom towards the south-east, the wind carrying her speedily to open sea and freedom.

Tyacke wanted to look away but could not even lower his telescope. No wonder the French frigate had not fired a second broadside. *Miranda*'s hull had been blasted open in several

100

places, and he saw smoke escaping from the fallen canvas to add to the horror of the men pinned beneath.

Then just as suddenly the fire was quenched, as quickly as it had begun.

Tyacke lowered the glass and stared into the sun until he could see nothing. The schooner, his *Miranda*, had gone. In trying to help him she had herself become a victim.

He realised that Segrave and some of the others were watching him. When he spoke again he was stunned by the calmness of his own voice.

'Shorten sail, Mr Sperry. The chase is over.' He pointed at the guardboat, where some of the oarsmen were waving and cheering towards the shabby schooner. 'See? They bid us welcome!'

Slowly, like drunken men, the hands turned to, to give the appearance of reducing sail.

Tyacke stood beside Segrave and rested his hand on the boy's until the tiller brought the bowsprit in line with the space between the two anchored ships.

'Hold her steady.' He looked at those nearest him and added, 'Then you take to the boat.' He studied their faces, but was seeing others in their place. Ben Simcox, who would have been leaving the ship to obtain his position as Master. Bob Jay, and old Archer the gunner. So many faces. Gone in a moment. Those who had not died in the broadside would not escape the sharks.

He said, 'Be ready, lads.' He cocked his head as a trumpet echoed across the water. 'The alarm.' He glanced at the sudden activity in the guardboat as the oar blades churned up the water, and the boat began to swing round towards them.

Tyacke snapped, 'Stand by, Private Buller!' He knew the marine was crouching by the bulwark, his long musket resting beside him. Tyacke said, 'Think of what you just saw, Buller, and of the flogging you deserve but will never receive!

'*Ready, Buller!*'

He watched the officer in the guardboat as he got to his feet, his arm beating out the time to his confused oarsmen.

'*Now!*'

The musket bucked against Buller's powerful shoulder, and

101

Tyacke saw the Dutch officer's arm halt in midair before he pitched over the side and floundered away from the hull.

The boat turned, out of command, while some of the crew attempted to reach their officer with an oar.

Segrave heard the sharp bang of the guardboat's swivel and Dwyer cry out before he slithered to the deck, blood pouring down his neck and side. Buller's musket cracked again and another man vanished inside the boat, its oars now in complete disarray.

Segrave saw Sperry the boatswain down on his knees, his teeth bared like fangs as he clutched his bulging stomach. He must have taken some of the guardboat's deadly canister shot even while he was helping to trim the sails.

Tyacke's eyes narrowed as he stared hard at the two big ships which seemed to lie across the bows barely yards away. In fact they were over half a cable distant – but nothing could save them now.

Segrave tore his eyes away as Sperry rolled kicking on to his back, his blood filling the scuppers while he choked out his life.

The Dutch sailors were probably wondering what the *Albacora* was doing, the boy thought wildly. As if reading his thoughts Tyacke shouted, 'Let's not leave them in suspense, eh?' He took the tiller and drew a pistol from his belt. 'Get below, Mr Segrave and take the slow-match to the fuses!'

Even Segrave could sense the fear which had so suddenly replaced the wildness, the urge to kill. Men Tyacke knew and trusted could soon change once the fuses were lit, and they were standing on their own funeral pyre. Segrave ran past the dying boatswain, realising that his eyes were fixed on his as he hurried by, as if they alone were clinging to life.

In his dazed mind he seemed to hear more trumpets, the far-off squeal of gun-trucks as some of the Indiamen's officers understood at last what they were witnessing.

He was sobbing and could not stop himself as he stumbled down into the stinking hull, still shocked by *Miranda*'s unexpected end, and Tyacke's terrible grief and anger.

The man who had been his only friend and whom he had tried to save was dead, and the little schooner, which had been Tyacke's very life, his one escape, had been sent to the bottom.

Segrave fell back with a gasp as the first fuse hissed into life like a malevolent serpent. He had not even seen himself lighting it. He reached the second one and stared at the slow-match in his fingers. His grip was so firm it did not even quiver when he ignited the fuse.

As he scurried back towards the sunlight at the foot of the ladder, he thought of his mother. Perhaps *the admiral* would be satisfied now. But neither bitterness nor tears would come, and when he reached the tiller he saw Tyacke exactly as he had left him, propped against the tiller as if he were part of the ship.

Tyacke nodded. 'Look at 'em now!'

The Indiamen's decks were swarming with sailors. Some were clambering aloft to the yards, others were in the bows, probably attempting to cut their cables.

There was a dull thud below their feet, and seconds later black greasy smoke surged up through the vents, followed by the first vicious tongues of flame.

Tyacke said, 'Heave the boat alongside, *handsomely* now. I'll shoot the first man who tries a run for it!'

Segrave watched flames darting through the deck-seams, his eyes glazed as he felt the whole hull heating up like a furnace.

A man yelled, 'Ready in the boat, sir!' It was the one named Swayne, the deserter.

Segrave said in a strangely controlled voice, 'Don't stay with her, sir.' He waited for Tyacke to turn his terrible scars towards him. '*Please.*' He tried to shut out the growing roar beneath the deck and added, 'They all died back there, sir. Let it not be a waste, for their sakes!'

Surprisingly, Tyacke stood up and grasped his shoulders. 'I'll see you a lieutenant yet, my lad.'

They clambered down into the boat and cast off. They had barely pulled out of *Albacora*'s shadow when, with a savage hiss of flames, the deck appeared to burst open, fires starting everywhere, as if lit by one man's hand.

Tyacke rested his arm on the tiller bar. '*Pull*, lads. If we reach the headland, we may be able to get ashore and hide until we know what's happening.'

One of the oarsmen exclaimed, '*She's struck*, by Jesus!' His own eyes and face were shining in the reflected glare as the schooner, her rigging and sails already blowing away in ashes, crashed alongside the first Indiaman.

Tyacke swung round as the flames leapt up the moored ship's tarred shrouds and darted out along the yards. Some of the men who had been working feverishly to loose the topsails found themselves trapped by the mounting fires. Tyacke watched without expression as their tiny figures fell to the decks below, rather than face that slower, more horrific death. The second Indiaman had managed to cut her stern moorings but she had freed her cable too late. Fires were already blazing on her forecastle and flowing along her hammock nettings like spurting red liquid.

Nobody spoke in the boat, so that the sounds of creaking oars and the men's rasping breathing seemed to come from somewhere else.

So short a while ago, they had all expected to be dead. Now Fate had decided otherwise.

'Watch out for any place to beach when we get closer.'

Buller the Royal Marine paused, ramming home a ball into his musket, and swore with harsh disbelief. 'You won't need no beach, sir!'

Tyacke stared until his mind throbbed and his eyes were too blind to see; all that remained was the memory. *Miranda*'s sails folding like broken wings.

He gripped Segrave's wrist and said, '*Truculent!* She's coming for us!'

The oars seemed to bend as with sudden hope they threw themselves on the looms. The boat headed away towards the frigate's silhouette while she rounded the point, as they themselves had done just a few hours earlier.

Segrave turned to look astern, but there was only a towering wall of black smoke which appeared to be pursuing them, its heart still writhing with flames. He glanced at Tyacke. He knew the lieutenant had intended to stay at the helm and die. The pistol had been ready to prevent anyone dragging him to the boat by force; and for no other reason.

Then Segrave looked away and watched the frigate standing-off to receive them. His pleas had somehow given Tyacke the will to reach out for another chance. And for that, Segrave was suddenly grateful.

For if Tyacke had changed, so had he.

104

7

A Chance to Live

Bolitho walked to one of *Themis*'s open ports and rested his hand on the wooden muzzle of a quaker. In the afternoon sunlight it felt as hot as iron, as if it were a real gun which had just been fired.

The flagship seemed unusually quiet and motionless, and he could see *Truculent* anchored close by, making a perfect twin of her reflection on the calm water. At the cabin table, Yovell, his secretary, was writing busily, preparing more despatches which would in time reach all the senior officers of both squadrons, and others which might eventually end their journey on Sir Owen Godschale's desk at the Admiralty. As the *Themis* swung very slightly to her cable, Bolitho saw part of the land, the unmoving haze above it, much of it dust. Occasionally he heard the distant bark of artillery and pictured the foot-soldiers pressing on towards Cape Town. The Admiralty seemed a million miles away from this place, he thought.

He saw Jenour dabbing his face and neck with a handkerchief while he leaned over Yovell's plump shoulder to check something. He looked strained, as he had done since *Miranda*'s sudden and violent destruction. After picking up the crew of the fireship, *Truculent* had made off under full sail to seek out the French frigate, or at least to be in time to assist Captain Varian's *Zest* when he confronted her. Placed as he was, Varian should have been in a perfect position to capture or attack any vessel which tried to escape the fireship's terrible devastation.

But there had been no sign of the enemy, and not until three days later had they met up with *Zest*. Varian had explained that another vessel had been sighted approaching from seaward, and he had given chase, but without success. Bolitho had expected Poland to make some criticism once the frigates had separated again, as it was rumoured there was bad blood between the captains. He had said nothing. Nor, upon reflection, had he seemed surprised.

Bolitho tried not to dwell on *Miranda*'s loss. Nor on Tyacke's contained anguish as he had clambered up from the fireship's boat. The column of black smoke above the anchorage had been visible for many hours, long after *Truculent* had headed out to the open sea.

The general's soldiers would see it and take new heart, and the Dutch might realise that there was nothing but their own courage to sustain them. But although he tried, Bolitho could not put the memory from his mind. *He must tell himself*. It had been a remarkable feat, the success far outweighing the cost. But he could not forget. He had once again allowed himself to get too close. To Simcox, and Jay, even to an unknown Cornish lookout who had come from Penzance.

There was a tap at the door and then Commander Maguire entered the cabin, his hat beneath his arm.

'You sent for me, Sir Richard?' His eyes moved to the open stern windows as more gunfire echoed across the flat blue water.

Bolitho nodded. 'Be seated.' He walked past him to the table, each step bringing his body out in a rash of sweat. *Just to be in a moving ship again, to feel the wind. Instead of . . .* He turned over some papers. 'When this campaign comes to a close, Commander Maguire, you will be sailing for England. It is all in your orders. You will place yourself with certain other vessels under the charge of Commodore Popham until that time is suitable.' He saw little response on the man's lined features. Perhaps, like some others in the squadron, he might be thinking that the fireship and *Miranda*'s sacrifice would make no difference; that it would drag on into stalemate. There was a thud from the adjoining cabin, then the sounds of a heavy chest being manhandled across the deck. Only then did Bolitho see some expression on Maguire's face. He had served with Warren for a long time.

On *Truculent*'s return to the anchorage Bolitho had realised that he would never speak with Warren again. He had apparently died even as *Truculent*'s topsails had been sighted standing inshore.

Now Warren's clerk and servant were gathering the last of his belongings for stowage in one of the transports to await passage – *where*, he wondered? Warren had no home but this ship, no relatives apart from a sister somewhere in England, whom he had rarely seen even on his visits to the country he had seemingly rejected for the West Indies.

Maguire frowned and asked, 'What will become of the ship, Sir Richard?'

Bolitho saw Jenour watching them, his eyes fall as their gaze met.

'She will doubtless receive a much needed overhaul and refit.'

'But she's too *old*, Sir Richard!'

Bolitho ignored the protest. 'Not as old as my flagship.' He did not mean to let it come out so sharply, and saw the other man start. 'The war continues, Commander Maguire, and we shall need every ship we can lay hands on. Ships which can stand and fight and still give of their best.' He walked to the stern, and leaned on the heated sill to look down into the clear water as it lifted and gurgled around the rudder. He could see the trailing weed, the copper, which was dull and pitted with constant service. As his *Hyperion* had once been when he had first taken command, in that other world. Over his shoulder he added bitterly, 'We need more than wooden guns in the Channel Fleet too!'

It was a dismissal, and he heard the door close behind him, the sentry's musket coming down to rest again with a sharp tap.

'I suppose you think that was wrong of me?'

Jenour straightened his back. 'There comes a time, sir –'

Bolitho smiled, although he felt drained as well as impatient. 'Well, now. What has my sage to tell me?'

Jenour's open face lit up with a broad grin. Relief, surprise; it was both. 'I know I am inexperienced when compared with some, sir.'

Bolitho held up his hand. 'A damned sight *more* experienced than a few I can mention! I was sorry for Warren, but he did not belong here. Like the ship, he had become a relic. That did not count for much once. But this is no game, Stephen, nor was it even when I entered the King's navy.' He looked at him fondly. 'But it took the blade of the guillotine to make some of our *betters* take heed. This war *must be won*. We have to care about our people. But there is no longer any stowage-space for sentiment.'

Allday entered by the other door and said, 'Some casks of beer have just been brought over, Sir Richard. Seems it was for *Miranda*'s people.' He watched Bolitho, his eyes troubled. 'Otherwise, I wouldn't have said –'

Bolitho loosened his shirt for the thousandth time and shook his head. 'I have been bad company since that day, old friend.' He glanced from one to the other. 'I will try to make amends, for my own sake as well as yours.'

Allday was still watching him warily, like a rider with an unknown mount. What did he mean, he wondered? *Since that day*. *Miranda*, or was he still fretting over his old flagship?

He said, 'There's a pin o' brandy for yourself, Sir Richard. From th' General, no less.'

Bolitho looked towards the land, his fingers playing with the locket beneath his damp shirt. 'Sir David said as much in his letter to me.' He had a sudden picture of Baird somewhere over there: in his tent, on horseback, or studying the enemy's positions. Did *he* ever consider defeat or disgrace? He certainly did not show it.

Of the Dutch defenders he had written, '*They will fight on, or they will surrender very soon. There will be no half measures, on either side.*' Of the fireship he had said, '*Brave men are always missed and then too often forgotten. At least others will not die in vain.*' Bolitho could almost hear him saying it, as he had on the shore when he had begged for his assistance. Baird had finished his letter by describing his opponent, the Dutch general Jansens, as a good soldier, and one not given to senseless destruction. Did that mean that he would capitulate rather than see Cape Town brought down in ruins?

Bolitho clutched his arms across his chest as a cold shiver ran through him, despite the scorching air in the cabin.

Warren had gone, but it felt as if he was still here, watching him, hating him for what he was doing with his ship.

Allday asked, 'All right, Sir Richard?'

Bolitho crossed to the windows and stood in the sunshine until the heat burned the chill out of his body. For an instant he had imagined it was a warning of the old fever. The one which had all but killed him. He smiled sadly. When Catherine had climbed into his bed without him knowing or remembering a thing about it. Her care, and the warmth of her nakedness, had helped to save him.

Maybe Warren *was* watching? After all, they had buried him nearby, weighed with shot, down in the depths where even the sharks would not venture. Maguire had used one of the longboats, and the oarsmen had continued to pull until a leadsman had reported 'no bottom' on his line.

The marine sentry shouted from beyond the screen, 'Officer-o'-the-Watch, *sir*!'

The lieutenant seemed to be walking on tiptoe as he entered the presence of the vice-admiral. Bolitho wondered how much more they knew about him now since his arrival among them.

The lieutenant said, '*Truculent*'s boat has just cast off, Sir Richard.'

'Very well, Mr Latham. Please offer Lieutenant Tyacke all respects when he is come aboard the flagship. He *was* in command, remember.'

The lieutenant almost bowed himself out, his face astonished more by Bolitho's remembering his name than at his instruction.

Ozzard appeared as if spirited by a genie's lamp.

'A fresh shirt, Sir Richard?'

Bolitho shaded his eyes to watch the boat pulling slowly towards *Themis*'s side, pinned down in the hazy glare as if it could scarcely make the crossing.

'I think not, Ozzard.' He thought of the schooner's tiny cabin, where a clean shirt and ample drinking water were both luxuries.

Tyacke would be feeling badly enough as it was. The interview he was about to have with the tall lieutenant was suddenly important. It was not merely something to replace his loss, or to offer him compensation for his terrible wound. It *mattered*; but until now Bolitho had not really known how much.

He said quietly, 'Will you leave me, please?' He watched Yovell gather up his papers, his round features completely absorbed with his inner thoughts. A direct contrast to Allday, and yet . . . Neither would change even at the gates of Heaven.

To Jenour he added, 'I would like to dine with Mr Tyacke this evening, and for you to join us.' He saw Jenour's obvious pleasure and said, 'But for this moment it is better without an audience.'

Jenour withdrew and saw a marine guard presenting arms to the man in question as he climbed aboard and raised his hat to the quarterdeck. *Half a man*, Jenour thought, and now with his dreadful scars turned away he could see what he had once been: perhaps what Bolitho was hoping to restore.

Allday stood his ground as Tyacke walked aft and ducked beneath the poop.

Tyacke halted and said coldly, 'All waiting, are they?' He was very much on the defensive. But Allday knew men better than most, sailors more than any. Tyacke was ashamed. Because of his disfigurement; and because he had lost his ship.

He replied, 'Be easy with him, sir.' He saw the sudden surprise in Tyacke's eyes and added, 'He still feels the loss of his old ship very badly. Like one o' the family, *personal*.'

Tyacke nodded, but said nothing. Allday's casual confidence had unnerved him, scattered all his carefully prepared thoughts, and what he had been about to say.

Allday walked away and stooped thoughtfully over the pin of brandy which had been sent over by the redcoats. It was strange when you thought about it. Bolitho and Tyacke were very much alike. Had things been different for them they might even have changed roles.

He heard Ozzard right behind him. 'You can keep your eyes off that little cask, *Mister Allday*!' He stood, arms folded, his watery eyes severe. 'I *know* you when you get your hooks on some brandy.'

The guns ashore fired a long, unbroken salvo, like thunder echoing around those sombre, alien hills.

Allday put his hand on the little man's shoulder. 'Listen to 'em, matey. Don't even know what they're fighting about!'

Ozzard smiled wryly. 'Not like us, eh? *Heart of Oak*!'

He began to roll the brandy towards the poop's deeper shadow and Allday gave a sigh. A nice 'wet' of brandy would have made a change.

They both made a point of not looking towards the great cabin where Warren had died, and another was about to be given a chance to live.

Tyacke waited while the sentry called out his name, his eyes averted from the lieutenant's face.

He pushed open the door and saw Bolitho by the open stern windows. The cabin was otherwise empty. His eyes moved quickly around it, recalling the few times he had been there. As before, he noticed its total lack of personality. Impossible to judge its previous occupant, although he had lived here for such a long time. Perhaps Warren had had nothing to offer it? He tried not to think of all the clutter, the sense of *belonging* in *Miranda*'s tiny, cramped quarters. It was gone. He had to remember that.

'Please sit down.' Bolitho gestured to a small table with some wine and two glasses. 'It is good of you to come.'

Tyacke straightened his borrowed coat, giving himself time to gather his wits.

'I must apologise for my rig, Sir Richard. *Truculent*'s ward-room had a collection for me, you see?'

Bolitho nodded. 'I do see. All your things rest on the seabed. Like many of my most valued possessions.' He moved to the table and poured two glasses of the hock Ozzard had discovered somewhere. 'I am unused to this vessel, Mr Tyacke.' He paused with the bottle in mid-air, his eyes towards the windows as the air quivered to the distant cannon fire. 'I suppose that is the span between us and the military. Sailors are like turtles, in a way. We carry our homes around with us. They become personal to us; in some ways too much so. Whereas the poor soldier sees only the land in front of him.' He smiled suddenly over the rim of his glass. 'And to think I was lecturing my flag-lieutenant on the folly of sentiment!'

He sat down opposite Tyacke and stretched out his legs. 'Now tell me about the men who were with you. That marine, for instance – has he repented of being a volunteer?'

Tyacke found himself describing the long and difficult process of beating back and forth against the wind to get closer to the merchantmen. Of Buller's insolence, and his superb marksmanship. Of the deserter Swayne, and the midshipman who had somehow found courage when he needed it most. Shadowy figures became real as he told of their courage and their fear.

Bolitho refilled the glasses and doubted if either of them had noticed what they were drinking.

He said, 'You *gave* that boy courage – you know that, don't you?'

Tyacke answered simply, 'But for him I wouldn't be here.'

Bolitho eyed him gravely. 'That was then. This is now. I would wish you to sup with me this evening. No talk of war – we shall let it take us where it fancies. I have enough burdens of my own. It would ease the load if I knew I was to achieve something personal before I leave this place.'

Tyacke thought he had misheard. Sup with the vice-admiral? This was not a lowly schooner, and Sir Richard Bolitho was no longer a tolerant passenger.

He heard himself ask, 'What is it, Sir Richard? If there is something I can do, you have but to ask. I may have been changed by events; my respect and loyalty to you have not. And I am not a man to offer false praise to gain favour, sir.'

'Believe me, I do know what you went through; what you are enduring now. We are both sea-officers. Rank divides us, but we still curse and rave at the incompetence of others, those who care nothing for Poor Jack, until *they* are in risk and danger themselves.' He leaned forward, his voice so quiet that it was almost lost in the gentle ship noises around them. 'My late father once said something to me, when I was younger than you are now, at a time when all things seemed set against us. He said, "England needs all her sons now."'

Tyacke listened, all resentment and despair held at bay, almost fearful of missing something of this reserved, compelling man who could have been his brother, and not an envied flag-officer.

Bolitho's eyes were far away. 'Trafalgar has not changed that. We *need* fine ships to replace our losses and old veterans like this one. But most of all we need officers and seamen of courage and experience. Like yourself.'

'You want me to forget *Miranda*, Sir Richard. To become a serving lieutenant again.' Tyacke's expression had changed. He looked trapped, even afraid. 'For if so –'

Bolitho said, 'Do you know the brig *Larne*, Mr Tyacke?' He watched the man's quiet desperation, his obvious inner struggle. 'She is with Commodore Popham's squadron at present.'

Tyacke said, 'Commander Blackmore. I have seen her on occasion.' He sounded mystified.

Bolitho reached over and picked up a piece of Yovell's hard work. 'Blackmore is fortunate. He is promoted to command a sixth-rate. I want *you* to take her.'

Tyacke stared at him. 'But I cannot – I do not have –'

Bolitho handed him the envelope. 'Here is the commission to take her in your charge. It will be confirmed at Their Lordships' leisure, but you are herewith promoted to the rank of commander.' He forced a smile to cover Tyacke's confusion and undisguised emotion. 'I will see what my aide can do about obtaining some more suitable uniform for you without delay!'

He waited, pouring more wine, then asked, 'Will you do this –for me, if for no other reason?'

Tyacke got to his feet without knowing it. 'I will, Sir Richard, and I'd ask no better reason than that!'

Bolitho stood up, very alert. '*Listen.*'

'What is it, Sir Richard?'

Before he turned away Tyacke saw the emotion clearly in Bolitho's eyes, as clearly as he himself had betrayed his own seconds earlier.

Bolitho said softly, 'The guns. They're silent now.' He faced him and added, 'It means, *Commander* Tyacke, that it's over. The enemy have struck to us.'

There was a brief knock at the door, and Jenour almost burst into the cabin. 'I have just heard, Sir Richard!'

His admiral smiled at him. It was a moment Jenour was to remember for a long while afterwards.

Then Bolitho said, 'Now we can go home.'

Captain Daniel Poland stood, arms folded, and watched the throng of bare-backed seamen hurrying to their stations. From the capstan came the scrape of a fiddle accompanied by

Truculent's shantyman, an old sailor with a surprisingly carrying voice.

> 'When we did bang the damned mounseer,
> You gave us beef an' beer,
> Now we 'ave naught to eat an' drink,
> For you 'ave naught to fear!'

A boatswain's mate bellowed in each interval, '*Heave! Heave! Put yer bloody backs into it if you wants to see old England again!*'

The first lieutenant gave a discreet cough. 'The admiral, sir.'

Poland glanced away from the busy figures on deck and aloft on the yards.

'Thank you, Mr Williams, but we have nothing to hide.'

He touched his hat as Bolitho walked beneath the driver-boom, his face and chest like beaten copper in the dying sunlight.

'We are ready to proceed, Sir Richard.'

Bolitho was listening to the fiddle and the sing-song voice of the shantyman. *For you have naught to fear*. A song which went back a long, long way with slight variations to suit the campaign or the war. Bolitho recalled his own father talking about it when he had described the battle of Quiberon Bay. The sailor's despair of those he fought and died for only too often.

It was an inspiring sunset, he thought; few painters could do it credit. The sea, the distant ridge of Table Mountain and all the anchored ships were glowing like molten metal. Only the offshore wind gave life to the picture, the low rollers cruising towards the shadows to awaken the hull and gurgle around the stem. Bolitho could feel the last heat of the day, like a hot breath, and wondered why Poland could not reveal any excitement at this departure.

He heard the sharp clank of the first capstan pawl, the boatswain's harsh encouragement for the seamen to thrust at the bars with all their might.

Bolitho watched the other ships, their open gunports gleaming like lines of watchful eyes. Their part was over, and as dusk had descended on Table Bay he had taken a telescope to look at the Union Flag which now flew above the main battery. It would remain there.

Some of the squadron had already weighed and headed out of the bay to begin the long passage back to England. Two ships-of-the-line, five frigates including Varian's *Zest*, and a flotilla of smaller, unrated vessels. While England waited for her old enemy's next move, these reinforcements would be more than welcome. Others, including *Themis*, would follow as soon as the army had fully established its control of Cape Town and the anchorages which would sustain them against all comers. The blackened bones of the two Dutch Indiamen would be grim reminders of the price of complacency, he thought.

He remembered Tyacke's face when they had shared a last handshake, his voice when he had said, 'I thank you for giving me another chance to live, Sir Richard.'

Bolitho had said, 'Later you may curse me too.'

'I doubt that. *Larne* is a fine vessel. She'll be a challenge after *Miranda*.' He had spoken her name as a man might dwell on a dead friend. 'But she and I will come to respect one another!'

Larne was already hidden in shadow, but Bolitho could see her riding light, and somehow knew that Tyacke would be over there now, on deck to watch *Truculent*'s anchor break out of the ground.

Shadows ebbed and flowed across the quarterdeck, and Bolitho moved clear to give the captain the freedom he needed to get under way. He saw Jenour by the nettings, a slight figure standing near him. The latter made to leave but Bolitho said, 'How does it feel, Mr Segrave? So short a stay, so much experience?'

The youth stared at him in the strong copper glow. 'I – I am glad I was here, Sir Richard.' He turned, his hair flapping in the hot breeze as the capstan began to clatter more eagerly, the pawls falling while the long cable continued to come inboard.

Bolitho watched him, seeing Tyacke, remembering his own early days at sea, when he had shared the danger and the mirth with other midshipmen like Segrave.

'But you also regret leaving?'

Segrave nodded slowly, and momentarily forgot he was speaking with a vice-admiral, the hero whom others had described in so many different guises. 'I only hope that when I return to my old ship . . .' He did not have to finish it.

Bolitho watched as the guardboat drifted abeam, oars tossed in salute, a lieutenant standing to doff his hat to his flag at the fore. Perhaps to the man as well.

'You can be neither too young nor too old to have your heart broken.' Bolitho sensed Jenour turn to listen. 'Courage is something else. I think you will have little to worry you when you rejoin your ship.'

Jenour wanted to smile but Bolitho's voice was too intense. He knew that Yovell had already copied a letter for Segrave's captain. It would be enough. If it was not, the captain would soon learn that Bolitho could be ruthless where brutality was concerned.

'Thank you, sir.'

Bolitho leaned on the hammock nettings and thought of all the miles which lay ahead. It would be a far cry from the swift passage which had brought him here. What might he discover? Would Catherine still feel the same for him after their separation?

When he looked again, the midshipman had gone.

Jenour said, 'He'll do well enough, Sir Richard.'

'You knew then, Stephen?'

'I guessed. Allday put the rest together. His life must have been hell. He should never have been put to sea.'

Bolitho smiled. 'It changes all of us. Even you.'

Then he felt his heart leap as the cry came from forward.

'Anchor's hove short, sir!'

Calls trilled, and a man grunted as a rope's end hurried him after the others to halliards and braces.

Lieutenant Williams reported, 'Standing by, sir!'

'Loose heads'ls.' Poland sounded calm, remote. Bolitho wondered what did move him, why he disliked Varian, what he hoped for beyond promotion?

He looked up at the yards where the strung-out, fore-shortened bodies of the topmen tensed to release their charges to the wind. On deck, others stood by the braces, ready to transform their anchored ship into a flying thoroughbred. What awaited most of them when *Truculent* reached England? Would

116

they be cooped up aboard while they awaited new orders, or sent to other ships to strengthen the ranks of landmen and newly-pressed hands ignorant of the sea and of the navy? The fiddle was scraping out a livelier tune and the capstan was turning even more quickly, as if to hasten their departure.

Bolitho said, 'It will be summer in England, Stephen. How quickly the months go past.'

Jenour turned, his profile in dark shadow, as if, like Tyacke, he had only half a face. 'A year for victory, Sir Richard.'

Bolitho touched his arm. *The hopes of youth knew no bounds.* 'I am past believing in miracles!'

'*Anchor's aweigh*, sir!'

Bolitho gripped the nettings. The ship seemed to rear away as the anchor was hauled up and secured at the cathead. Even that seemed to symbolise the difference he had felt here. When they anchored once more in England, in another hemisphere, they would drop the one on the opposite side.

Truculent came about, canvas banging in confusion, shadowy figures dashing everywhere to bring her under control. Hull, the sailing master, shouted, 'Steady there! *Hold her!*'

Bolitho watched him and his helmsmen as they clung on the double spokes, their eyes gleaming in the disappearing sun. He thought of Simcox, who would have been like Hull one day. He had wanted it more than anything. But not enough to leave his friend when his life was threatened.

He said, 'Fate is fate.'

Jenour looked at him. 'Sir?'

'Thoughts, Stephen. Just thoughts.'

The topsails hardened to the wind and the deck seemed to hold steady as *Truculent* pointed her bows towards the headland and the empty, coppery wastes beyond.

'West-sou'-west, sir! Full an' bye!'

Poland's mouth was set in a tight line. 'Bring her up a point. As close as she'll bear.' He waited for the first lieutenant to come aft again. 'Get the courses and royals on her as soon as we are clear, Mr Williams.' He glanced quickly at Bolitho's figure by the nettings. 'No mistakes.'

Bolitho remained on deck until the land and the sheltering ships were lost in the swift darkness. He waited until the world had shrunk to the leaping spray and trailing phosphorescence, when the sky was so dark there was no margin between it and the ocean. Only then did he go below, where Ozzard was bustling about, preparing a late meal.

Bolitho walked to the stern windows, which were smeared with salt and dappled in spray, and thought of his years as a frigate captain. Leaving port had always been exciting, a kind of rare freedom. It was a pity that Poland did not see it like that. Or perhaps he was merely counting the days until he could rid himself of his responsibility – looking after a vice-admiral.

He glanced up as feet thudded across the deck, and voices echoed through the wind and the din of sails and rigging. It never changed, he thought, even after all the years. He still felt he should be up there, making decisions, taking charge of the ship and using her skills to the full. He gave a grim smile. No, he would never get used to it.

In the adjoining sleeping-cabin, he sat down by his open chest and stared at himself in the attached looking-glass.

Everyone imagined him to be younger than he really was. But what would *she* think as the years passed? He thought suddenly of the young officers who were probably sitting down to enjoy their first meal out of harbour, sharing their table with Jenour and probably trying to pry out the truth of the man he served. It might make a change from all the plentiful rumours, he thought. He stared at his reflection, his eyes pitiless, as if he were inspecting one of his own subordinates.

He was forty-nine years old. The rest was flattery. This was the bitter truth. Catherine was a lovely, passionate woman, one whom any man would fight and die for, if indeed he was a man. She would turn every head, be it at Court or in a street. There were some who might chance their hand now that they knew something of their love, their *affair* as many would term it.

Bolitho pushed the white lock of hair from his forehead, hating it; knowing he was being stupid, with no more sense than a heartsick midshipman.

I am jealous, and I do not want to lose her love. Because it is my life. Without her, I am nothing.

He saw Allday looking in from the door. He said, 'Shall Ozzard pour the wine, Sir Richard?' He saw the expression on

Bolitho's face and thought he knew why he was troubled. Leaving her had been bad. Returning might be harder for him, with all his doubts.

'I am not hungry.' He heard the sea roar alongside the hull like something wilful, and knew that the ship was ploughing into the ocean, away from the land's last protection.

If only they could move faster, and cut away the leagues.

Allday said, 'You've done a lot, Sir Richard. Not spared yourself a moment since we made our landfall. You'll feel your old self tomorrow, you'll see.'

Bolitho watched his face in the glass. *I never give him any peace.*

Allday tried again. 'It's a nice plate o' pork in proper bread-crumbs, just as you like it. Not get anything as good after a few weeks of this lot!'

Bolitho turned on the chair and said, 'I want you to cut my hair tomorrow.' When Allday said nothing, he added angrily, 'I suppose you think that's idiotic!'

Allday replied diplomatically, 'Well, Sir Richard, I sees that most o' the wardroom bloods affects the newer fashion these days.' He shook his pigtail and added reproachfully, 'Don't see it signifies meself.'

'Can you do it?'

A slow grin spread across Allday's weathered face. 'Course I will, Sir Richard.'

Then the true importance of the request hit him like a block. 'Can I say me piece, Sir Richard?'

'Have I ever prevented you?'

Allday shrugged. 'Well, not hardly ever. That is, not *often*.'

'Go on, you damned rascal!'

Allday let out his breath. That was more like it. The old gleam in those sea-grey eyes. The friend, not just the admiral.

'I saw what you done for Mr Tyacke –'

Bolitho snapped, 'What *anyone* would have done!'

Allday stood firm. '*No*, they wouldn't lift a finger, an' *you knows it*, beggin' your pardon.'

They glared at each other like antagonists until Bolitho said, 'Well, spit it out.'

Allday continued, 'I just think it's right an' proper that you gets some o' the cream for yourself, an' that's no error neither!' He grimaced and put his hand to his chest and saw Bolitho's instant concern. 'See, Sir Richard, you're doing it this minute! Thinking o' me, of anyone but yourself.'

Ozzard made a polite clatter with some crockery in the great cabin and Allday concluded firmly, 'That lady would worship you even if you looked like poor My Tyacke.'

Bolitho stood up and brushed past him. 'Perhaps I shall eat after all.' He looked from him to Ozzard. 'It seems I shall get no rest otherwise.' As Ozzard bent to pour some wine Bolitho added, 'Open the General's brandy directly.' To Allday he said, 'Baird was right about you. We could indeed use a few thousand more like you!'

Ozzard laid the wine in a cooler and thought sadly of the splendid cabinet *she* had given him, which lay somewhere on the sea-bed in the shattered wreck of the *Hyperion*. He had seen the glance which passed between Bolitho and his rugged coxswain. A bond. Unbreakable to the end.

Bolitho said, 'Take some brandy, Allday, and be off with you.'

Allday turned by the screen door and peered aft as Bolitho seated himself at the table. So many, many times he had stood behind him in countless different gigs and barges. Always the black hair tied at the nape of his neck above his collar. With death and danger all around, and in times of rejoicing it had always been there.

He closed the door behind and gave the motionless sentry a wink. Whatever the rights and wrongs of it, no matter how they sorted it out with so many set against them, Bolitho and his lady would come through it. He smiled to himself, remembering when she had taken the time to speak with him. *A real sailor's woman*.

And God help anyone who tried to come between them.

In the days and the weeks which followed, while *Truculent* battled her way north-west towards the Cape Verde Islands, against perverse changes of wind which seemed intent only on delaying her passage, Bolitho withdrew into himself, even more than when outward bound.

120

Allday knew it was because he had nothing to plan or prepare this time, not even the affairs of the ship to divert his attention. Jenour too had seen the change in him when he had taken his daily walks on deck; surrounded by *Truculent*'s people and the busy routine found in any man-of-war, and yet so completely alone.

Each time he came on deck he examined the chart or watched the master instructing the midshipmen with the noon sights. Poland probably resented it, and took Bolitho's regular examinations of the calculations and knots made good as unspoken criticism.

Bolitho had even turned on Jenour over some trivial matter, and just as quickly had apologised. Had stared at the empty sea and said, 'This waiting is destroying me, Stephen!'

Now he was fast asleep in his cot after being awake half the night, tormented by dreams which had left him shaking uncontrollably.

Catherine watching him with her lovely eyes, then laughing while another took her away without even a struggle. Catherine, soft and pliable in his hands, then far beyond his reach as he awoke calling her name.

Seven weeks and two days exactly since Bolitho had seen Table Mountain swallowed up in darkness. He rolled over gasping, his mouth dry as he tried to remember his last dream.

With a start he realised that Allday was crouching by his cot, his figure in shadow as he held out a steaming mug. Bolitho's mind reeled, and all his old senses and reactions put an edge to his voice. 'What is it, man?' With something like terror he clapped his hand to his face, but Allday murmured, ''Tis all right, Sir Richard, your eye ain't playin' tricks.' He stumbled from the cot and followed Allday into the stern cabin, the mug of coffee untouched.

If the ship seemed to be in darkness, beyond the stern windows the sea's face was already pale and hard, like polished pewter.

Allday guided him to the quarter window and said, 'I know it's a mite early, Sir Richard. The morning watch is only lately on deck.'

Bolitho stared until his eyes stung. He heard Allday say harshly, 'I thought you'd want to be called, no matter the hour.'

121

There was no burning sunshine or brilliant dawn here. He wiped the thick, salt-stained glass with his sleeve and saw the first spur of land as it crept through the misty greyness. Leaping waves like wild spectres, their roar lost in far distance.

'You recognise it, old friend?' He sensed that Allday had nodded but he said nothing. Maybe he could not.

Bolitho exclaimed, '*The Lizard*. A landfall – and surely there could be none better!'

He rose from the bench seat and stared around the shadows. 'Though we shall stand too far out to see it, we will be abeam of Falmouth at eight bells.'

Allday watched him as he strode about the cabin, the coffee spilling unheeded on the checkered deck covering. He was glad now that he had awakened to hear the lookout calling to the quarterdeck, '*Land on the lee bow!*'

The Lizard. Not just any landfall but the rocky coast of Cornwall.

Bolitho did not see the relief and the pleasure in Allday's eyes. It was like a cloud being driven away. The threat of a storm giving way to hope. She would be in their room at this very moment, and would not know how close he was.

Allday picked up the mug and grinned. 'I'll fetch some fresh.'

He might as well have said nothing. Bolitho had taken out the locket she had given him, and was staring at it intently as the grey light penetrated the cabin.

Allday opened the door of the little storeroom. Ozzard was curled up asleep in one corner. With elaborate care he lifted one of Ozzard's outflung arms off the brandy cask and gently turned the tap over the mug.

Home again. He held the mug to his lips even as the calls trilled to rouse the hands for the new, but different, day.

And not a moment too soon, matey!

8

Full Moon

Bryan Ferguson dabbed his face with his handkerchief while he leaned against the stile to regain his breath. The wind off the sea was no match for the sun which burned down directly across the grey bulk of Pendennis Castle, and threw back such a glare from the water it was not possible to look at it for long.

It was a view he never got tired of. He smiled to himself. He had been steward of Bolitho's estate for over twenty years now. Sometimes it did not seem possible. The Bolitho house was behind him, down the sloping hillside where the fields were banked with wild flowers, while the long grass waved in the breeze like waves on water.

He squinted into the sunlight and stared towards the narrow winding path which led up and around the cliff. He saw her standing where the path turned and was lost around the bend – a treacherous place in the dark, or at any time if you did not take heed. If you fell to the rocks below there was no second chance.

She had told him to remain by the stile, to recover his breath or because she needed to be alone, he did not know. He watched her with silent admiration. Her hair, loosely tied, was whipping in the wind, her gown pressed to her body, making her look like some enchantress in an old poem or folk-tale, he thought.

The household had accepted her warily, unwilling to discuss her presence here with the local people, but, like Ferguson, prepared to defend her right as Bolitho had instructed.

Ferguson and his wife, who was the housekeeper, had expected Bolitho's lady to remain detached from the estate and its affairs. He shook his head as he saw her turn and begin to descend the pathway towards him. How wrong they had been. Almost from the moment she had returned from Portsmouth after saying farewell to Bolitho, she had displayed an interest in everything. But she had always *asked*, not ordered. Ferguson tried not to think of Lady Belinda who had been rather the opposite. It made him feel uneasy and vaguely disloyal.

She had ridden with him to visit the surrounding cottages which were part of the Bolitho heritage; she had even managed to get him to reveal how much larger the estate had originally been in the days of Bolitho's father, Captain James. Much of it had been sold to clear the debts amassed by his other son Hugh, who had deserted the navy and joined the Americans in their fight against the Crown.

Ferguson glanced down at his empty sleeve. Like John Allday he had been pressed not far from here and taken to the frigate *Phalarope*, Bolitho's own command. Ferguson's arm had been taken off at the Saintes. He gave a wry smile. And yet they were still together.

At other times, like today, she had walked with him, asking about crops, the price of seed, ploughing, and the areas where grain and vegetables from the estate were sold. No, she was like nobody Ferguson had ever met.

He had come to understand her during her first days here, when he had been taking her around the old house, showing and naming the grave-faced portraits of Bolitho's ancestors. From old Captain Julius who had died right in Falmouth trying to break the Roundhead blockade of Pendennis Castle, to the recent past. In a small bedroom, covered by a sheet, she had discovered the portrait of Cheney. She had asked him to put it by the window so that she could see it. In that silent room Ferguson had heard her breathing, watched the quick movement of her breasts while she had studied it before asking, 'Why here?' He had tried to explain but she had interrupted him with quiet emphasis. 'Her Ladyship *insisted*, no doubt.' It had not been a question.

Then, after considering, it, 'We will have it cleaned. All of them.' He had seen a rare excitement in her dark eyes and had known a sort of pride at sharing it. A woman who could make a man's head swim; but he could just as easily picture her with a Brown Bess to her shoulder, the way Allday had described.

She had stepped back to look at Cheney's portrait again. It had been Cheney's gift, as a surprise for Bolitho when he had returned from the war. Instead he found only the portrait waiting. Cheney and their unborn child had been killed in a coaching accident.

Catherine had faced Ferguson when he had tried to tell her about it, had gripped his arm with compassion. '*You* were the one who carried her.' Her eyes had moved to his empty sleeve. 'You did all you could.'

Then she had remarked, 'So when I came here you all decided to conceal it further. What did you expect of me, envy?' She had shaken her head, her eyes misty. 'Like the ocean, *his* ocean, some things are permanent.'

And so the portrait was returned to its original place, facing the window and the sea beyond, the colour of Cheney's eyes.

He straightened his back as she strode down to the stile and held out his hand to steady her while she climbed over. Even now, with her hair breaking away from the ribbon which she had used to control it, with wet sand and dust on her gown, she seemed to give off some inner force. She was taller than Ferguson; there could not be much difference between her and Bolitho, he thought. She squeezed his hand. A casual thing, but again he could feel it; strength, tenderness, defiance, it was all there.

'That land yonder. What has been done with it?'

Ferguson replied, 'Too many rocks washed down from the hill. No place for a plough. There's that old copse too.' He watched her lip curve, and imagined her and Bolitho together. When he spoke again his voice was hoarse, so that she looked directly at him, her eyes like dark pools; as if she saw right through him and into his passing thought.

Then she smiled broadly and said, 'I can see I shall have to watch *you*, Mr Ferguson, one arm or no!'

Ferguson flushed, which after serving at sea and then running the estate for so long, was almost unique.

He stammered, 'I beg your pardon, m'lady.' He looked away. 'We've not the men, you see. All taken by the press, or gone for a soldier. Old men and cripples, that's all we've got.'

125

When he looked at her again he was surprised by the emotion in her eyes.

She said, 'You're no cripple. Together we'll make something of that land.' She was thinking aloud, her voice suddenly fierce. 'I'll not stand by and see him milked by everyone who seems to have lived well off his courage! I don't believe the squire –' her mouth puckered '– *the King of Cornwall* as he is called, I believe? *He* seems to have no difficulty managing his land!'

'French prisoners, m'lady. He is a magistrate, too.' He was glad to change the subject. Again he felt the guilt, when he had known she was referring to Belinda in her great house in London.

She said, 'He is a fair man nevertheless. In any case I like his wife – Sir Richard's favourite sister, is she not?'

Ferguson fell into step beside her, but had to walk fast to keep up. 'Aye, m'lady. Miss Nancy, as she once was, was in love with Sir Richard's best friend.'

She stopped and gazed at him searchingly. 'What a lot you know! I envy you the smallest detail, every hour when you have known him and I have not.' She walked on, more slowly now, plucking a flower from a stone wall as she passed. 'You are very fond of him also?'

Ferguson waved to some workers in the field. 'I'd serve none other.'

She looked at the figures, who were pulling a large cart. Most of them were women, but she caught her breath as she recognised the old sailor, the one-legged man named Vanzell. Even he was adding his strength to the load.

Ferguson saw her face and knew she was remembering how Bolitho had taken her from the filth and horror of the Waites jail in London.

Her husband had connived and lied to have her transported. From what Allday had told him it seemed likely she would have died first. Allday had said that Bolitho had been beside himself, had half-carried her from the jail, bringing old Vanzell who had been a guard there out with him. There were several such on the estate. Men like Vanzell who had once served with Bolitho, or women who had lost husbands or sons under his command.

She said, 'He's done so much. We shall repay some of it by

126

making the land come alive again. There's Scotland – they always need grain, surely?'

Ferguson grinned. 'Ships are expensive, m'lady!'

She looked at him thoughtfully, then gave the bubbling laugh he had heard when Bolitho had been with her. 'There are always –' She broke off as they reached the gate to the stable-yard.

Her skin was still sun-burned despite the winter here, but Ferguson later swore to his wife that she had gone as white as death.

'What is it, m'lady? Is something wrong?'

Her hand went to her breast. 'It's the post-boy!'

The youth in his smart cocked hat and breeches was gossiping with Matthew, the head coachman.

Ferguson said, 'He'll be from the town, m'lady. Unusual time of day though.' He beckoned the youth urgently. 'Here, lad, lively now!'

The post-boy touched his hat and showed a gap-toothed smile. 'Fer 'ee, ma'am.'

Ferguson muttered, 'Show respect, or I'll –'

She said, 'Thank you,' then turned away from the sunlight and stared at the letter. 'It bears no mark!'

Ferguson stood by her elbow and nodded. 'A clerk's hand, I'll wager.'

She gazed at him but he knew she could not see him. '*Something has happened to him.* In God's name, I cannot –'

The youth, who was willing but not very bright, said helpfully, ''Tes off the mail coach, y'see.' He grinned again. 'They 'ad to sign for that 'un.' He looked at their faces and added importantly, ''Tes from Lunnon!'

'Easy, m'lady,' Ferguson took her arm. 'Come into the house.'

But she was tearing open the cover which revealed another sealed letter inside.

Ferguson sensed his wife come down the stone steps to join them and was almost afraid to breathe. This was how it would happen. Those family portraits told the same story. There was not a single male Bolitho buried in Falmouth. All had been lost at sea. Even Captain Julius had never been found when his ship had exploded down there in Carrick Road in 1646.

127

She looked at him and said, 'He is in London.' She looked at the letter as if she were dreaming. 'The fight is over at Good Hope. Cape Town has fallen.' She began to shake but no tears came.

Grace Ferguson put a plump arm round her waist and whispered, 'Thank God! 'Tis only right!'

Ferguson asked, 'What is the date, m'lady?'

She appeared to bring herself under control with a physical effort. 'It does not say.' She stared at his handwriting. So few lines, as if to reveal his haste, his need for her.

She exclaimed, 'I felt it. A few nights ago. I got out of bed and looked out to sea.' When she turned, her eyes were shining with happiness. 'He was there, on passage for Portsmouth. *I knew.*'

Ferguson thrust a coin into the post-boy's grubby hand. It had been a nasty moment. Now he guessed that the outer envelope had been to disguise its true contents from prying eyes. That was what he was returning to this time. What they would have to face together.

The post-boy had not gone, and seemed determined to discover what he had stumbled upon.

He said, 'Th' coachman was a-tellin' Oi, zur, why the mail is late, y'see? One o' they coaches cast a wheel along the way – proper excitin' it were!'

Ferguson glared at him. So the letter was late. He looked at her profile, the joy she had always tried to control while he was away. In case . . .

He said, 'He might be here in a day or so, m'lady.' He ticked off the points in his mind. 'He would have to see them at the Admiralty. There would be a report.' He smiled, remembering Bolitho's constant frustration at the delays which had always followed the heat of action. 'Then, of course . . .' He glanced round at the sound of hooves on the track which led down towards the town square and the church where the Bolithos were remembered.

Matthew said doubtfully, ' 'Tis not one o' *my* horses, m'lady.'

But she was already running, her arms outstretched, heedless of the staring eyes and gaping faces.

It was impossible; it could not be him so soon. Almost blinded, she ran through the gates as the horse and rider clattered over the cobbles towards the yard.

As Bolitho slipped from the saddle and caught her in his arms she pressed her face to his and gasped, 'Oh, dearest of men, what can you think? How must I look – when I wanted to be ready for you!'

He put his hand under her chin and gazed at her for several seconds, perhaps to reassure them both that it was no mistake, nor was it the dream which maybe they had shared.

He said, 'There were delays. I could not wait. I was afraid you might not –'

She put her fingers on his mouth. 'Well, I have, and I want you to know . . .'

The rest was lost as their mouths came together.

'There. I was not too long, was I?'

Bolitho turned from a window and watched her come from the foot of the stairs. Her dark hair was still loose but brushed back across her shoulders, and she had changed into a simple dark green gown.

He walked to meet her and held her at arm's length. 'You would be beautiful if you wore a seaman's smock!'

She turned in his arms. 'When you look at me like that I feel I am about to blush like a silly young girl.' She searched his face. 'How *are* you? Your eye . . .'

He kissed her cheek, his whole being aware of her closeness, the pressure of her body against his. All the doubts, all the misgivings were as if they had never been. Like shadows which die in the dawn. It was as if he had never been away. Holding her, talking with her, seemed so natural that it excluded every other sound and feeling.

'It has improved, I think. Even in the African sun, I was rarely troubled.'

She tried to conceal her relief, so that he should not know how her mind had ached for him while he had been away.

Bolitho asked, 'And you? Has it been too bad?'

She laughed and tossed her hair on her shoulders. 'They do not think I am an ogre – in fact I believe they quite like me.'

She became serious again, putting her arm through his and guiding him through to the adjoining room.

'There was some bad news.' She met his gaze as he stopped

and faced her. 'Your sister Nancy brought it a week ago. Your other sister has returned from India.'

Bolitho held her gently. 'Felicity?' He saw her nod and tried to picture his sister. She was two years his senior, and he had not laid eyes on her since he had been a lieutenant. She was married to an officer in the Eighty-First Foot, who had later been seconded to the service of the Hon. East India Company. It was strange, but he could remember her husband better than he could Felicity. A pleasant, unassuming officer who had met her when his company had been stationed in Truro.

'Her husband is dead, Richard. So she is come to live in Cornwall again.'

Bolitho waited, knowing there was more. 'She has two sons. One in the regiment, the other a sea-officer in John Company's fleet, as I recall. How did he die?'

Catherine replied, 'His horse threw him.'

'Have you met Felicity yet?'

He saw her chin lift, then she said, 'She would not come with Nancy.' She added defiantly, 'Because of me.'

He put his arm about her, hating how it must have been, how unfair. He said, 'I would to God I had been here!'

She touched his face and smiled gently. 'I had to tell you. But I did not want to spoil anything. Not now. Not with you here again . . .'

'Nothing will. Nothing can.' He felt her tremble and held her more tightly. 'It is so good to be home again.'

'How was it out there, Richard?'

He tried to think clearly. All the faces. Commodore Warren, Captains Poland and Varian, Tyacke and all the others. In the halls of Admiralty it was as if nothing had really happened; or so it had felt.

He said slowly, 'We lost some men, but it could have been worse. I saw Admiral Godschale in London.' He smiled, remembering his new pomposity. '*Lord* Godschale as he now is.'

She nodded. 'I know. It seems to pay to remain at home while others fight and dare.'

He gripped her hands in his. 'Nelson once wrote as much to me. I see that my tiger is still ready to leap out and protect me!'

She smiled despite her sudden bitterness. '*Always*.'

Bolitho looked out at the flowers and rustling trees. 'I wanted to get away, to be here with you.' He felt her watching him but hurried on as if to rid himself of a burden. 'I left poor Allday to follow with our baggage. He complained, but I think he understands.'

'It was strange to see you without him, your shadow.'

Bolitho said, 'Homeward bound we laid off Madeira to take on fresh water and supplies. I bought you some lace there. When Allday arrives you will see for yourself if it is any use, or that I am less of a shopper than I am a sailor!' He released her and picked up his coat from a chair where he had thrown it. 'I thought you might like this.' He took out a Portuguese fan of silver filigree and held it out to her. 'To replace the one you gave me and which I always have nearby.' He watched her pleasure, the expert way she flicked open its blades and held it to the sunlight.

'How beautiful!' When she faced him again her expression had changed, her dark eyes very steady. 'Is it so wrong of me, Richard?' She went to him and placed her head on his shoulder as if to hide her feelings. 'I cannot wait. I want you now. It is like a hunger, and I should be ashamed.' She looked at him, her faces inches from his. 'But I am not.'

Then she pirouetted round and walked away from him. 'The sun shines on lovers too, my darling Richard!' He heard her laugh as she ran up the stairway and knew she had understood his uncertainty, his awkwardness when he had returned to her.

He found her by the window which faced the headland, her hands parting the curtains, so that she appeared to be held in the sunlight as if she were floating. She wore a long white robe with a plain gold cord around her throat, her hair hanging down her back. She neither moved nor turned as he came up behind her and after the briefest hesitation put his arms around her, pulling her against him. He stared at the same view and felt her gasp as his hands moved over her body, touching the nakedness of her limbs beneath the thin gown.

She whispered, 'Don't stop, for God's sake. Never cease to love me like this!' She arched her back as he ran his hands up and over her breasts, then she turned and waited for him to find and release the gold cord so that the gown fell about her ankles.

131

He barely remembered the next frantic moments as his shirt and breeches went unseen to the floor.

She was on the bed, her lips moist while she watched him.

'I am so cruel, Richard! You must ache from a dozen horses, and yearn for a good meal and some of your own wine.'

Then he was beside her, his hand exploring her while she returned his kisses, her fingers around his neck, caressing the short hair where his queue had been.

She wanted to ask him why he had done away with it; to learn how long they might be together, so many, many things, but neither her will nor her body could prolong the moment another second.

It was brief; the wild need of each other driving away patience and bringing instead a culmination which made Catherine cry out as if she had no care for those who might hear and wonder.

Later, Bolitho opened his eyes and found himself still in her arms, their bodies entwined as if they had never moved. The room was full of silver light, brighter even than the sun; or so it seemed.

'How long . . . ?'

She kissed him. 'Not long enough. I have been with you all the while. Did you know there is a pale patch on your neck where the skin was shaded by your hair?'

'Don't you like it, Kate?'

She pulled his head down to her breast. 'I will grow used to it. The man I love is unchanged!'

She stroked his hair. 'I must bring you something to eat. The whole house is abed. What must they think of us – of me?'

Bolitho propped himself on one elbow, watching the moonlight, knowing she was staring up at him, knowing that he wanted her again, and again.

'It is so warm.' As if to a secret signal they both left the bed and stood side by side at the window, feeling the soft warm air about their nakedness, the sense of peace as the sea boomed faraway on those hidden rocks which guarded the approaches like black sentinels.

He put his arm around her waist and felt her body respond to his touch. Then he looked up at the moon. It was full, like a great silver dish.

'I need you, Kate.' He was almost afraid to say it. He was unused to speaking out about something so secret and yet so powerful.

'And I you.'

Bolitho hugged her. 'But I will close the windows. There will be no food tonight, dearest Kate, and with that halo around the moon I think it may come on to blow before dawn.'

She drew him down again and without effort roused him to match her own excitement, until they were once again joined, and he lay across her, breathing hard, his heart beating against her body like a hammer.

Only when his breathing became regular and he lay close by her side did she allow the tears to come; she even spoke his name aloud, but he was in a deep sleep once more.

She turned her head to look at the window and felt the wetness of her tears on the pillow. The moon was as bright as before. She felt him stir and held him more tightly as if to protect him even in sleep. *But there was no halo*, and the sky was clear but for its stars.

So it was not over. In spite of his high hopes, the damaged eye was waiting; like a thief in the night.

9

Summer Wine

Bolitho reined his horse to a halt beside a low mossy wall and stared across the fields to a cluster of tiny cottages beside the Penryn road. It had been three days since his unexpected arrival in Falmouth and he had never felt so well nor known such happiness. Every hour seemed to be filled with exciting discoveries, although he knew it was only that he was sharing them with Catherine. He had been born here, had grown up amongst these same villages and farms until, like all the Bolitho ancestors, he had gone off to join his first ship, the old *Manxman* of eighty guns which had been lying at Plymouth.

For England it had then been a rare moment of peace, but to the twelve-year-old Midshipman Bolitho it had been the most awesome experience of his life. The very size of the ship, or so she had appeared at the time, had taken his breath away, the towering masts and spread yards, the hundreds of busy seamen and marines and the terrible thought that he would never be able to find his way about, were unnerving enough.

He was quick to learn and had managed to laugh off, outwardly at least, the usual taunts and the brutal humour which he came to recognise as part of any ship, as much as the tar and cordage which held them together. He had never even laid eyes on an admiral until he had joined his second ship, and at no time had he believed he would reach the lordly heights of lieutenant, let alone live to see his own flag leading the line of battle.

Catherine edged her horse closer to him and asked, 'What are you thinking?' She leaned over to put her gloved hand on his. 'You were so far away from me.'

He looked at her and smiled. She wore a dark green riding habit, and her hair was plaited above her ears, shining in the bright sunshine.

'Memories. All kinds of things.' He squeezed her hand. 'Of the past three days. Of our love.' Their eyes seemed to lock. Bolitho thought of the time they had found a quiet cove and left the horses to graze while they had explored it. By the tiny beach he had uncovered an old rusting and weed-covered ringbolt hammered into the stone. It was where, as a boy, he had come in his little dory, and had once been cut off by the tide and unable to pull the boat clear. They had found him clinging halfway up the cliff, the waves spitting at his ankles as if to pluck him down. His father had been away at sea, otherwise Richard doubted if he would have been able to sit down for a week.

She had listened to him and said, 'We shall make it *our* cove.'

It still made him feel dazed to think about it. How they had made love on that tiny crescent of sand, as if the world were abandoned but for themselves.

She said quietly, 'Then I was sharing your thoughts.'

They sat in silence for a long time while the countryside left them untroubled. The horses nuzzled one another, insects kept up a steady chorus and invisible birds joined in. A church clock seemed to rouse them, and Catherine took her hand away. 'I like your sister Nancy very much. She has been most kind. I suspect she has never met anyone like me before.' She looked up directly at the sprawling house which lay beyond a pair of open gates as if it were waiting for them. 'Her husband, too, has offered his services and advice without my asking.'

Bolitho followed her glance. It was huge, this place which Nancy and Lewis Roxby called their home; it had been in the Roxby family for generations, and yet Bolitho knew that for years Lewis, 'the King of Cornwall', had had his eye on the grey house below Pendennis Castle. His ancestors had perhaps been content to be the landowners and magistrates their position dictated. Not so Nancy's husband. Farming, tin mining, even a local packet company were all a part of his empire. He was a hard-drinking, hunting squire when he was not dealing in

135

business or hanging local felons for their crimes. He had little in common with Bolitho, but he had treated Nancy well and was obviously devoted to her. For that, Bolitho would have forgiven him almost anything.

Bolitho urged his mount forward once more, wondering what awaited them. He had sent a note to Felicity to tell her that they were coming. The horses rather than a carriage had been his idea, to give the impression of a casual visit rather than any sort of formality.

As they clattered into the courtyard two servants ran to take their bridles while another brought a dismounting stool, only to stare with astonishment as Catherine slid easily to the ground.

She saw Bolitho's smile and put her head on one side, the unspoken question in her eyes.

Bolitho put his arm round her shoulders and said, 'I am so proud of you, Kate!'

She stared at him. 'Why?'

'Oh, so many reasons.' He hugged her. 'The things you do, the way you look.'

'And there is someone peeping at us from an upstairs window.' For a brief instant her confidence seemed to falter. 'I am not sure I should have come.'

He looked at her and replied, 'Then here is something more to peep at!' He kissed her hard on the cheek. 'See?'

She seemed to shake it off; and when a footman opened the tall doors and Lewis Roxby, red-faced and rotund, bustled to greet them, she returned his welcome with a warm smile and offered her hand to him.

Roxby turned to Bolitho. 'Dammee, Richard, you're a sly old dog! I'd been hopin' you'd stay away a bit longer so that your lady and I could get the better acquainted, what!'

He put his arms round them and guided them to the great room which overlooked his rose gardens. The doors were open and the room was filled with their scent.

She exclaimed, 'What *perfume*!' She clapped her hands together and Bolitho saw the young girl she had once been in London. Not Belinda's town, but the other London of rough streets and markets, pleasure gardens and bawdy theatres, watermen and beggars. He still knew so little about her, but all

136

he could feel was admiration for her, and a love he had never known before.

Bolitho turned to another glass door and through it watched two women walking up towards the house.

Nancy never seemed to change, except that she was plumper each time he saw her. But with the kind of life she shared with Roxby it would have been surprising otherwise. She was the only one of his family who had their mother's fair looks and complexion; her children were the same. But Bolitho could only stare at her companion with a kind of disbelief. He knew it was Felicity, who would be about fifty-one; she had the same Bolitho eyes and profile, but the dark hair was gone, replaced entirely by grey, while her face and cheeks were ashen as if she had only recently recovered from a fever.

Even when she entered the room and nodded her head to him, very slowly, he could sense no contact. She was a complete stranger.

Nancy ran forward and threw her arms around him, kissing him. She smelt fresh and sweet – like the garden, he thought.

'After all these years, here is our Felicity back home again!' Her voice was too bright, and Bolitho thought he saw a warning glance from her husband.

Bolitho said, 'I should like to introduce you to Catherine.'

Felicity studied her coldly, then gave a brief curtsy. 'My lady. I cannot bid you welcome here, as this is not my house . . . nor do I have one at present.'

Roxby said, 'We'll soon take care of that, what?'

Bolitho said, 'I was sorry to learn of Raymond's death. It must have been a terrible shock.'

She did not appear to hear. 'I have sent word to Edmund by way of the regimental agents, Cox and Greenwood. My other son Miles has returned to England with me.' Her deepset eyes turned to Catherine again and seemed to strip her naked, as she added, 'It was not an easy life. I had a little girl, you know, but she died out there. Her father always wanted a girl, you see.'

Catherine looked at her gravely. 'I am sorry to hear that. I grew up in a demanding climate and I can sympathise.'

Felicity nodded. 'Of course. I had forgotten. You were married to a Spaniard before you met your present husband, the viscount.'

137

Roxby said thickly, 'Some wine, Richard?'

Bolitho shook his head. What had happened to Felicity? Or had she always been like this?

He said, 'Catherine sent word that you were always welcome at our house while you are deciding where to settle. While I was away at sea – and Catherine had no idea when I was returning home – she acted as she knew I would wish.'

Felicity sat down in a high-backed gilt chair. 'It has not been my home since I met and married Raymond. There is certainly no place there for me now.' She turned her gaze on Bolitho. 'But you always were a thoughtless fellow, even as a child.'

Catherine said, 'I find that hard to believe, Mrs Vincent. I know of no one more thoughtful when it comes to others.' Her eyes flashed but her voice remained calm. 'Even when that compassion is not returned.'

'Of course.' Felicity dusted a speck of dust from her sleeve. 'You would be in a better position than anyone to know his qualities, or otherwise.'

Catherine turned away and Bolitho saw her fingers digging into the fold of her riding skirt. It had been a mistake. He would make his excuses to Nancy and leave.

Felicity said, 'However, there is a favour I *will* ask of you, Richard.' She looked at him, her face quite composed. 'My son Miles has quit the East India Company. Perhaps you could arrange for him to be accepted for the King's service? I have but few funds, and he would be quick to gain promotion.'

Bolitho walked across the room and took Catherine's arm. 'I will do what I can for him. Perhaps I could meet him at some time.'

Then he said, 'I can accept the hurt which Raymond's loss has done you. But I cannot, will not, tolerate your rudeness to Catherine. This house is not mine either, otherwise I might forget myself further!'

In those few seconds he saw it all. Catherine, very still, Nancy, fingers to her mouth and near to tears, and Roxby puffing out his cheeks, doubtless wishing he was anywhere else but here. Only Felicity seemed cool and unmoved. She needed a favour of him, but her dislike for Catherine had almost ruined even that.

Outside the tall doors Roxby muttered, 'Sorry about that, Richard. Damn bad business all round.' To Catherine he added, 'She'll come round, m'dear, you'll see. Women are a funny lot, y'know!' He took her proffered hand and touched it with his lips.

She smiled at him. 'Aren't we, though?' Then she turned as the two horses were led around the house from the stable-yard. 'I never knew her poor husband, of course.' When she looked at Roxby again the smile was gone. 'But it sounds as if he is well out of it. And as far as I am concerned I don't care if she *comes round* or not!'

Once outside the gates again Bolitho reached over and took her hand. Her whole body was shaking.

He said, 'I am so sorry, Kate.'

'It wasn't that, Richard. I am used to bitches, but I'll not have her talking to you like that!' The horses waited as if they sensed her anger. Then she looked at him and said, 'She is your sister but I would never have guessed it. After all you have done, for me and everyone else, and how you have paid dearly for it –' She shook her head as if to drive it all away. 'Well, she can just go to hell!'

He squeezed her arm and asked quietly, 'Tiger?'

She nodded and wiped her eyes with the back of her glove.

'Never doubt it!' Then she laughed, 'I'll race you back to the house.' Then she was gone, the horse kicking up dirt from the road before Bolitho could move.

Roxby watched from the steps of his great house until they had both vanished into the fields.

Beside him his groom, who had worked for him for many years, remarked, 'A lively mare an' no mistake, sir.'

Roxby stared at him but the man's eyes were devoid of amusement. 'Er, yes, quite so, Tom.' Then he ambled into the house, adjusting his face for whatever was waiting.

What a woman, he thought. No wonder Bolitho looked so well, so young. He caught sight of himself in a tall mirror as he passed through the hallway. Bolitho was about his own age, and looked years younger. With a woman like that . . . He closed his mind and strode into the room they had just left, and felt a sudden relief at finding his wife alone.

139

'She's gone to lie down, Lewis.'

Roxby gave a noncommittal grunt. But he was angry at seeing the tearstains on her cheeks.

'I'll see what I can manage about finding her a suitable house, m'dear.' He walked round the chair and patted her hair fondly, his mind busy with how soon he could rid the place of her sister.

Then he said abruptly, 'I wonder how she knows so much about Catherine's past? I certainly didn't tell her anything. Don't *know* anythin' neither, dammit!'

Nancy took his hand and kissed it. 'I wondered about that too.' She stood up, the mood passing. 'I'll go and arrange supper for this evening, Lewis.' Then she added, 'Richard looks so much better than when he lost his ship last October. They must be good for one another.'

Roxby made certain there were no servants nearby and patted her buttock as she passed.

'You're not so bad yourself, m'dear!' He saw the flush mount to her cheeks, and the way she tidied her hair. Perhaps she was remembering how they had been before the children, and all the work to increase their wealth and living standards. Maybe like the two people he had seen galloping down the lane as if they hadn't a care in the world.

It did not occur to him that his homely wife might have been thinking back down the years about the young midshipman she had fallen in love with; and had been seeing herself with him.

For two whole weeks life continued for Bolitho and his Catherine in the same unplanned, idyllic fashion. Rides down forgotten lanes, or long walks above the sea, never at a loss for words, each ready to contribute towards their new-found isolation.

It was as if the other world of war and threats of invasion lay out of reach, and only once when they had been standing on the headland above the Helford River had Catherine mentioned it. A frigate had been tacking away from the land, her sails very pale in the bright sunshine, her hull low and sleek like the one which had done for Tyacke's *Miranda*.

'When will you be told?' He had put his arm around her shoulders, his eyes distant as he watched the frigate. Was all this

140

just make-believe after all? At any day he might receive new instructions, perhaps a summons to the Admiralty. He was determined that they would spend every possible minute together until . . .

He had replied, 'There was a hint from Their Lordships about a new squadron. It seems the most likely. Provided enough ships can be found.'

The frigate had been setting her topgallants, shaking them out to the offshore wind like a creature awakening from a brief rest.

He thought suddenly of his nephew, Adam. That was one piece of good news he had come by at the Admiralty. He had commissioned his new command, a fifth-rate of thirty-eight guns named *Anemone*. What a proud moment it must have been for him. Captain of a frigate, his dream, at the age of twenty-six. *Anemone*, Daughter of the Wind. It seemed very suitable. He had Allday's son with him as coxswain exactly as he had promised, and the ship had been ordered to the North Sea to carry out patrols off the Dutch coast.

He had hoped that the news might pull Allday out of his present gloom. When he had reached Falmouth with Ozzard and Yovell with all the baggage which Bolitho had left in London, he had gone straight to the inn to see the landlord's only daughter.

Yovell had mentioned it to Bolitho in confidence. Not only had the inn passed into new ownership, but the young woman in question had gone away and married a farmer in Redruth.

At the end of the second week Bolitho was reading a copy of the *Gazette* where the recapture of Cape Town was mentioned for the first time. Time and distance had sharpened the memory for him, but the *Gazette* seemed to take it as a matter of course. There was no mention of the fireship at all.

Allday entered the room and said, 'There's a young gentleman who wishes to see you, Sir Richard. He is Mr Miles Vincent.'

'Very well. I will receive him now.' Catherine was down at the estate office with Ferguson. Bolitho was still amazed by the way she had sorted out facts and figures, and with Ferguson's ready help had prepared her own ploughing and planting suggestions for the coming year. She had even been making comparisons

141

with local grain sales set against those in the North and as far as Scotland. He had expected that Ferguson might have resented her vigorous ideas for the estate, but like the property itself she seemed to have given him new heart for the future.

He crossed to a window and looked towards the road, now hidden by thick bushes. Eventually they would leave here and face up to the world outside Falmouth. To London, to places where people would turn and stare. Where others might hide their envy behind false smiles.

The door opened and closed and he turned to see Felicity's younger son standing in the dusty sunshine. His dress was simple, a plain blue coat and a frilled white shirt, but he gave the immediate impression of incredible neatness. Except for a certain solemnity for one so young, he might have been like Adam when he had been his age.

'Please sit down.' Bolitho took his hand. 'We were sorry to learn of your father's untimely death. It must have been hard on the family.'

'Indeed yes, Sir Richard.' He arranged himself in the chair, his hands folded in his lap.

Bolitho thought, like a youth about to ask his father for his daughter's hand. Shy, but determined nonetheless. You would have known him for a Bolitho anywhere. He was nineteen years old, and had the same grey eyes, and hair almost as dark as his own. Behind this outer shyness was the barely concealed confidence which must be inevitable in any sea officer, no matter how junior.

'I understand that you intend to seek a King's commission. That being so I can foresee no difficulty. Volunteers for the berth of midshipman, even those forced by proud parents, are plentiful enough. Others with experience such as your own are very thin on the ground.' It was meant to relax him, to draw him out. It could not be easy to sit down with a vice-admiral whose exploits at sea and ashore were food for gossip on all levels. Bolitho had no way of knowing what Felicity might have said, so he had expected Miles Vincent to be on edge.

He had not anticipated the youth's reaction. He exclaimed, 'I am most confused, Sir Richard! I was acting-lieutenant in the H.E.I.C., fully qualified in matters of seamanship and standing

142

a watch. It was only a matter of time before I was advanced. Did you mean that I would be reduced to holding a warrant as a mere midshipman?'

The shyness was gone; instead, he looked closer to righteous indignation.

Bolitho replied, 'Be easy now. You will know, as well if not better than I, that holding a rank in one of John Company's ships is a far cry from the King's service. The pay and conditions are far superior, the ships are not manned by the sweepings of the jails or the press gangs, and they are only called on to fight to defend their own cargoes . . . when I was a captain there was many a time I would have seized a few of their prime seamen for my own.' He paused. 'In the King's ships we are expected to do battle with the enemy, no matter what guise or force he comes in. My people do not serve for the money or the profit which any experienced man can make in the Company's vessels, nor do they for the most part fight for their King and country!' He saw Vincent's eyes widen and continued, 'That surprises you? Then let me explain. They fight for each other, for their ship, which must be their home until they are released from a harsh and demanding service.'

The youth stammered, 'You – make it very clear, Sir Richard.'

Bolitho smiled to himself. The nervous suitor was back again.

He said, 'So if you are still of the same mind I will certainly sponsor your request to a captain who requires young gentlemen. I feel certain that one like yourself, with the qualities you have mentioned, will be promoted to lieutenant in a matter of months, perhaps less. The Fleet *needs* officers as never before. But if they cannot lead or encourage the people they are intended to command, I for one have no time for them.'

'If I may say, Sir Richard, your own gallant examples are much talked of.'

He sprang to his feet as Catherine walked through a garden door.

She stared from Bolitho to the stiff-backed figure in blue and commented, 'You must be Miles.' She tossed a wide-brimmed straw hat onto a chest and kissed Bolitho lightly on the cheek. 'It is such a lovely day, Richard, we must walk along the cliff this evening.' She shot him a questioning glance as the youth sprang forward to hold a chair for her. 'Thank you, young sir.'

Vincent was gazing at the portraits, which marked each section of the staircase like silent onlookers.

'All great sailors, Sir Richard. I would wish nothing more than to be like them.' He glanced at Catherine, his features expressionless. 'To add honour to the name of Bolitho!'

With the same precise care he made his excuses and left the house and Bolitho remarked, 'A pretty speech anyway.' He looked at her and then knelt beside her chair.

'What is it, dearest Kate? Tell me.'

She touched his face with sudden tenderness. 'That young man. His face, those eyes . . . he is so much a part of your family background. Like all the other mysteries I cannot share.'

Bolitho took her hand and tried to make light of it. 'His manners are faultless, but they train them well in the H.E.I.C., so that their young officers may flirt with the ladies of quality and lovesick maidens who take passage to distant parts!' It was not working. 'I want to share everything with you, dearest Kate, and share *you* with nobody.'

Catherine placed her palm on his face and smiled. 'You always *know*, Richard. It is like a bond stronger even than marriage, because it is of our making and choice.' Her dark eyes searched his face feature by feature. 'I will be all that you want me to be. Lover, companion, friend –' She laughed and threw back her head. 'Or the lady for whom young officers carry chairs. What did you make of him?'

'What has Felicity made of him, would be a fairer question!' He took her arm. 'Come – the cliff walk. I never tire of it. You can tell me about your plans for the estate as we go.'

Allday closed the door as they walked out into the garden and down towards the small gate.

He tried not to think about the girl at the inn. What had he expected? How could he have hoped to marry her and still serve Bolitho at sea? The questions were still unanswered when he found Ozzard making his way to the kitchen, where he sometimes helped Mrs Ferguson with her duties.

'Did you see the lad who came about joining the service?'

Ozzard frowned. 'He's a dark one, I shouldn't wonder. Why

144

did he quit the East India Company – that's what I'd like to know before *I* gave him any authority!'

Allday sighed. It had been good to see Bolitho and his lady walking together, but it only added to his own sense of being unwanted, with nothing useful to do until the next orders came. Even that prospect gave him no satisfaction.

He said half to himself, 'If only she'd waited.'

Ozzard turned on him with unexpected fury. '*Wait?* They never bloody well wait, any of 'em, and the sooner you get that through your skull the better – *matey!*'

Allday stared after him with astonishment. Usually there was none milder. So he wasn't the only one with troubles after all.

It was, many proclaimed, one of the best summers anyone could remember. The crops, like the lambing, had done well, and even the coastal fishermen were not heard to complain. But for the absence of young men around the farms and in the streets of Falmouth, they might have been at peace.

The news of the war was sparse and, apart from some reports of French men-of-war being sighted near Biscay, and then only in small numbers, it was as if the whole enemy fleet had been swallowed up. Bolitho sometimes thought of the French frigate which had been sheltering at Good Hope, or the coded letters they had found aboard the slaver *Albacora*. Was it part of an overall plan, or were these ship movements and occasional attempts to breach the tightly-stretched English blockade merely at the whim of their local commanders?

He had spoken infrequently of his thoughts to Catherine because she was preparing herself in her own way for the inevitable. When it came on the last day of August she said quietly, 'It is a part of your life which I cannot share; no woman can. But whatever it is, Richard, wherever duty takes you, *I shall be with you.*'

They had been riding along the cliffs and unlike other times they had said very little, had been content with each other's nearness. They had found the little cove again, where they had made love so passionately and had cast all inhibitions to the sea-breezes. This time they had dismounted but remained on the cliff, holding the horses' heads, then touching hands in silence.

It was as if they had both known. As Catherine had sensed the nearness of his ship when it had sailed on to Portsmouth.

When they had entered the stable-yard Bolitho had seen Allday waiting by the door.

Allday looked first at Catherine, then at him. 'Th' courier's been an' gone, Sir Richard.'

Perhaps he too had been expecting it. He might even have been willing it to come. To be at sea again, serving the one who meant more to him than any other living soul. Doing what he had given his life to.

Now, with the late afternoon sunshine casting almost horizontal beams across the big room, the house seemed strangely silent as Bolitho slit open the heavy, red-sealed envelope with the Admiralty fouled anchor in its corner.

She stood with her back to him, her straw hat dangling from her hand, watching the garden, trying to remain calm perhaps, with the taste of the salt air on her lips. Like dried tears.

He laid down the letter and said, 'Apparently I am being given a squadron.' He watched her turn towards him as he added, '*Eventually*. Also a new flagship.'

She crossed the room in quick strides, her hat falling unheeded to the floor. 'Does that mean we are not to be parted yet?' She waited for him to hold her. 'Just tell me that is so!'

Bolitho smiled. 'I must go to London.' He tightened his hold, feeling the warmth of her body against his own. 'We shall go together, if that is what you want.'

She nodded. 'I understand what you mean. What to expect from some quarters.' She saw the pain in his grey eyes and touched his face. 'I knew your thoughts just now about your next flagship. She will not be your old *Hyperion*. But *she* is safe from those who would dishonour her by turning her into a hulk after all her years of service.'

He stroked her hair. 'You read me like a book, Kate. I was thinking that. The new ship is named *Black Prince* and is completing fitting-out at the Royal Dockyard, Chatham. I will take you there, too . . . I don't want to lose you for a moment!'

She seated herself near the great fireplace, now empty, but with the dark stains of countless winter evenings on the stonework. While Bolitho moved about the room she watched him, saying nothing which might distract him or interrupt his thoughts. This was the other man whom she cherished so dearly, so possessively. Once he paused in his restless pacing and looked at her, but she knew he had not seen her.

He said suddenly, 'I shall ask for a good flag-captain. I will insist.'

She smiled sadly. 'You are thinking of Valentine Keen?'

He walked over to her and took her hands. 'Once more, you are right. He is not yet called into service again; and it is not like Val not to have announced the day chosen for their marriage. Strange, too, that Zenoria has not written to you.' He shook his head, his mind made up. 'No, I would not request that he continues as my flag-captain. Neither of them would thank me for *that*!' He squeezed her hands. 'Like me, Val was late in finding the right woman with whom to share his life.'

She looked up at him, seeing the light in his eyes. 'When we are in London will you promise to see that surgeon? For me, if for no other reason.'

He smiled. It was what he had asked of Tyacke. 'If time allows.' He let out a sigh. 'We have to leave for London in two days. How I loathe that journey . . . the only one in the world which gets longer every time!'

She stood up and looked around the quiet room. 'Such memories. Without these past weeks I do not think I could have faced this news. But now it is home to me. It will always be waiting.' She faced him and added, 'And do not fret over Val and his Zenoria. It is not long since they came together. They will want time to arrange matters, and then they will tell us.'

She dragged him to the window and exclaimed, 'And *if time allows* –' She saw him grin as she attempted to mimic his words, 'I shall show you some different sights in London so that you will not feel so gloomy each time you visit the Lords of Admiralty.'

They walked out into the garden and to the wall where the small gate opened on the path to the stile and the cliff. Where she had come to meet him on that first night.

She said eventually, 'And you must not worry about me while you are gone. I would never stand between you and your ships. You are mine, so I am part of them too.'

Ozzard watched them from an upstairs window where he had

been polishing some pewter dishes for Mrs Ferguson. He did not turn as Allday entered the room but remarked, 'We're off again then?'

Allday nodded and massaged his chest as the old ache returned. 'Aye. 'Tis London first though.' He chuckled. 'Just happened to hear it.'

Ozzard began to polish a dish he had already shone to perfection. He looked troubled, but Allday knew better than to disturb his thoughts. Instead he said, 'She's the *Black Prince*, brand-new second-rate of ninety-four guns. Bit larger than we've got used to, eh? Like a palace, an' that's no error!'

But Ozzard was far away. In that street along the old Wapping Wall where he had blundered from his little house on that hideous day.

He could hear her pleading and screams; and afterwards, when he had hacked his young wife and her lover to death until he had lost all strength in his arm, the terrible silence.

It had been haunting him ever since, revived by a casual comment made by the senior surgeon who had been in *Hyperion* during her last fight. When the old ship had started to go down, Ozzard had wanted to go with her, to stay with Bolitho's things in the hold, where he always went when the ship, any of their ships, had been in action.

But it was not to be. He let out a long sigh.

All he said was, 'It's London, then.'

10

The Way of the World

Admiral the Lord Godschale was doing his best to show cordiality, to forget the coolness between himself and Bolitho when they had last met.

'It is time we had a good talk, Sir Richard. We in admiralty can too often become dry old sticks, missing out on greater deeds which officers like you seem to attract.'

Bolitho stood beside one of the tall windows and looked down at the sunlit roadway and the park beyond. Did London never rest, he wondered? Carriages and smart phaetons bustled hither and thither, wheels seemingly inches apart as their coachmen tried to outdo one another's skill. Horsemen and a few mounted ladies made splashes of colour against the humbler vehicles, carriers' carts and small waggons drawn by donkeys.

Jostling people, some pausing to gossip in the warm September sunshine, and a few officers from the nearby barracks, cutting a dash as they strolled through the park and trying to catch the eye of any likely young lady.

Bolitho said, 'We are only as good as our men.' Godschale meant nothing of the sort. He was well pleased with his appointment and the power it gave him, and very likely believed that no ship or her captain would amount to anything without his guiding hand from afar.

Bolitho studied him as he poured two tall glasses of madeira. It was strange to realise that they once served together, when they had both been frigate captains during the American Revolution. They had even been posted on the same day. There was not much to show of that dashing young captain now, he thought. Tall, powerfully built and still handsome, despite a certain florid complexion which had not been gained on an open deck in the face of a gale. But behind the well-groomed sleekness there was steel too, and Bolitho could still recall how they had parted the previous year when Godschale had attempted to manoeuvre him away from Catherine and back to Lady Belinda.

Bolitho did not believe that Godschale had had any hand in the terrible plan to falsify evidence which had put Catherine in the filthy Waites prison. Sometimes she had awakened at his side, even after all the months which had passed since he had rescued her, and had cried out as if she had been trying to fight off her jailers.

No, Godschale was a lot of things but he would have no stomach for a plan which might cast him down from his throne. If he had a weakness it was conceit, an actual belief in his own shrewdness. He had probably been used by Catherine's husband, convinced, as Belinda had been, that it was the only solution.

Bolitho gritted his teeth. He had no idea where Viscount Somervell was now, although he had heard rumours that he was on another mission for His Majesty in North America. He tried not to think about it, knowing that if ever they came face-to-face again he would call him out. Somervell was a duellist of repute, but usually with a pistol. Bolitho touched the old sword at his side. Perhaps someone else would cheat him of the chance.

Godschale handed him a glass and raised his eyebrows, 'Remembering, eh?' He sipped at his madeira. 'To great days, Sir Richard!' He eyed him curiously. 'To happier ones also.'

Bolitho sat down, his sword resting across one leg. 'The French squadrons which slipped through the blockade – you recall, m'lord? Before I sailed for Good Hope. Were they taken?'

Godschale smiled grimly. He saw the sudden interest, the keenness in Bolitho's eyes, and felt in safer waters. He was well aware that Viscount Somervell's wife was here in London, flaunting her relationship as if to provoke more hostility and rouse criticism. With Nelson it had been embarrassing enough;

150

at least that affair had been allowed to rest. Nobody seemed to know where Emma Hamilton was now, or what had happened since his death at Trafalgar.

Godschale did not care much for Somervell's character and reputation. But he still had friends, some very powerful, at Court, and had been rescued from scandal and far worse by no less than His Majesty himself. But even the King, or more likely his close advisers, had conveniently removed Somervell from London's melting-pot until the problem of Bolitho's involvement was solved, or destroyed.

The admiral was sensible enough to accept that no matter how he felt about it, Bolitho was probably as popular in the country as Nelson had once been. His courage was beyond doubt, and in spite of some unorthodox methods and tactics, he *did* win battles.

In peacetime his affair with Lady Somervell would not be tolerated for an instant: they would both be shunned and barred from society, while Bolitho's own career would fly to the winds.

But it was not peacetime; and Godschale knew the value of leaders who won, and the inspiration they offered their men and the nation.

He said, 'The larger of the two enemy squadrons was under the flag of our old opponent Vice-Admiral Leissègues. He managed to slip through all our patrols – nevertheless Sir John Duckworth, who was cruising off Cadiz, gained some intelligence that a French squadron was at St Domingo. Duckworth had already been chasing Leissègues, but had been about to give up when he had the news. He eventually ran them to ground, and even though the French cut their cables when Duckworth's squadron was sighted, he brought them to close-action. All the enemy were taken, but the hundred and twenty gun *Impérial* went aground and was burned. She would have made a formidable addition to our fleet.' He sighed grandly. 'But one cannot do everything!'

Bolitho hid a smile. It sounded as if the admiral had won the victory from this very room.

Godschale was saying, 'The other French force was brought to battle and lost several ships singly before fleeing back to harbour.'

151

Bolitho put down his glass and stared at it bitterly. 'How I envy Duckworth. A decisive action, well thought out and executed. Napoleon must be feeling savage about it.'

'Your work at Cape Town was no less important, Sir Richard.' Godschale refilled the glasses to give himself time to think. 'Valuable ships were released for the fleet by your prompt intervention. It was why I proposed you for the task.' He gave a sly wink. 'Although I know you suspected my motives at the time, what?'

Bolitho shrugged. 'A post-captain could have done it.'

Godschale wagged an admonitory finger. 'Quite the reverse. They needed inspiration by example. Believe me, I *know*!' He decided to change the subject. 'I have further news for you.' He walked to his table and Bolitho noticed for the first time that he was limping. A problem he shared with Lord St Vincent, he thought. Gout – too much port and rich living.

Godschale picked up some papers. 'I told you about your new flagship, the *Black Prince*. A fine vessel to the highest requirements, I understand.'

Bolitho was glad he was looking at his papers and did not see his own rebellious smile. *I understand*. How like Captain Poland. Just to be on the safe side, in case something was proved to be amiss.

Godschale looked up. 'Chosen your flag-captain yet, or need I ask?'

Bolitho replied, 'Under different circumstances I would have picked Valentine Keen without hesitation. In view of his coming marriage, and the fact that he has been continuously employed under demanding circumstances, I am loath to ask this of him.'

Godschale said, 'My subordinate *did* receive a letter from your last captain, offering his services. I thought it odd. I might have expected him to approach you first.' His eyebrows lifted again. 'A good man, is he not?'

'A fine captain, and a firm friend.' It was hard to think clearly with Godschale talking about the new ship. What had happened to Keen? It made no sense.

Godschale was saying, 'Of course, in these hard times, the lieutenants may be quite junior, and the more seasoned professionals that much older. But then none of us loses any years, what?' He frowned suddenly. 'So I would appreciate a quick decision. There are many captains who would give their lives for the chance to sail *Black Prince* with your flag at the fore.'

'It would be a great favour to me, m'lord, if you would allow me the time to enquire into this matter.' It sounded as if he were pleading. He intended it to.

Godschale beamed at him. 'Of *course*. What are friends for, eh?'

Bolitho saw his quick glance at the ornate clock on the wall, an elaborate affair with gilded cherubs supporting it, their cheeks puffed out to represent the four winds.

He said, 'I shall be in London for the present, m'lord, at the address I have given to your secretary.'

Godschale's humour seemed to have faded; his smile was fixed to his mouth. 'Er, yes, quite so. Lord Browne's town house. Used to be your flag-lieutenant before he quit the navy?'

'Yes. A good friend.'

'Hmm, you don't seem to be lacking in those!'

Bolitho waited. Godschale was picturing it all in his mind. Himself and Catherine together, caring nothing for what people thought. He stood up and readjusted the sword at his hip.

Godschale said heavily, 'I don't wish to fan old flames, but is there any chance of your returning . . . er . . . Dammit, man, you know what I mean!'

Bolitho shook his head. 'None, my lord. It is better you know now – I am aware that your lady is a friend of my wife. It would be wrong to promote feelings which are not to be returned.'

Godschale stared at him as if trying to think of some crushing retort. When it failed him he said, 'We shall meet again soon. When that happens I hope I will have fresh information for you. But until that moment, let me remind you of something. A French ball can maim or kill a man, but ashore, his person can be equally hurt, his reputation punctured in a hundred ways!'

Bolitho walked to the door. 'I still believe the former to be the more dangerous, m'lord.'

As the door closed Admiral the Lord Godschale smashed one fist down on his papers. *'God damn his insolence!'*

Another door opened cautiously and the admiral's secretary peered around it.

'My lord?'

Godschale glared. '*Not a damn thing!*'

The man winced. 'Your next appointment will be here very shortly, m'lord.'

Godschale sat down carefully and poured himself another glass of madeira. 'I shall receive him in half an hour.'

The secretary persisted, 'But there *is* no one else, m'lord, not until . . .'

The admiral exclaimed harshly, 'Does *nobody* in the Admiralty listen to what I say? I *know* all about it! But with luck, Sir Richard Bolitho will renew his acquaintance with Rear-Admiral Herrick in the waiting-room. I wish to give them the opportunity to share *old times*. Do you see?'

The secretary did not see but knew better than to wait for another tirade.

Godschale sighed at the empty room. 'One cannot do everything!'

There were two captains sitting in the outer waiting-room, each avoiding the other's eyes and trying to remain as separate as possible. Bolitho knew they were here to see some senior officer or Admiralty official; he had shared their apprehension and discomfort on more occasions than he could remember. Advancement or a reprimand? A new command, or the first step to oblivion? It was all in a day's work at the Admiralty.

Both captains sprang to their feet as Bolitho walked through the long room. He nodded to them, accepting their recognition and curiosity. Wondering why he was here and what it might indirectly imply for them. More likely they were curious about the man and not the vice-admiral; his reputation, if it were true or false.

Bolitho was more concerned with Godschale's announcement about his flag-captain. He could still scarcely believe it. He had known how worried Keen had been about the age difference between himself and the lovely Zenoria. The girl he had rescued from a transport on her way to Botany Bay. Keen was forty-one years old, and she would be nearly twenty-two. But their love for one another had bloomed so suddenly out of suffering and been visible to everyone who knew them. He must

154

discover what had happened. If Keen had signified his readiness to be his flag-captain merely out of friendship or loyalty, Bolitho would have to dissuade him.

He had almost reached the tall double doors at the far end when they swung open, and he saw Thomas Herrick standing stock-still and staring at him as if he had just fallen from the sky.

Herrick was stocky and slightly stooped, as if the weight of his rear-admiral's responsibilities had made themselves felt. His brown hair was more heavily touched with grey, but he had not changed since he had sailed to support *Hyperion* in that last terrible battle.

His palm was as hard as at their first meeting, when he had been one of Bolitho's lieutenants in *Phalarope*; and the blue eyes were clear and as vulnerable as that very day.

'What are you . . .' They both began at once.

Then Bolitho said warmly, 'It is so good to see you, Thomas!'

Herrick glanced warily at the two captains as if to ensure they were well out of earshot. 'You too, Sir Richard.' He smiled awkwardly. '*Richard*.'

'That is better.' Bolitho watched his old friend's uncertainty. So it was still as before. Because of Catherine. He had refused to come to terms with it, could not bring himself to understand how it had happened between them. Bolitho said, 'I have been given *Black Prince*. I shall hoist my flag as soon as she is fitted-out, whenever that might be. You know the dockyards and their strange customs!'

Herrick was not to be drawn. He studied Bolitho's face and asked quietly, 'Your eye – how is it?' He shook his head and Bolitho saw something of the man he had always known and trusted. 'No, I have told no one. But I still think –'

Bolitho said, 'What are *you* doing?'

Herrick's chin was sunk in his neckcloth, something which had become a habit when he was grappling with a problem.

'I still have *Benbow*.' He forced a smile. 'New flag-lieutenant though. Got rid of that fellow with the Frenchie name, De Broux . . . too soft for my taste!'

Bolitho felt strangely sad. Just a few years since *Benbow* had flown his flag and Herrick had been the captain. Ships, if they

155

could think, must wonder sometimes about the men and the fates which controlled them.

Herrick pulled out his watch. 'I must present myself to Lord Godschale.' He spoke the name with dislike. Bolitho could well imagine how Herrick felt about the admiral.

As an afterthought Herrick said, 'I am to command a squadron in the North Sea patrols.' He gave a genuine smile. 'Adam's new command *Anemone* is my only frigate! Some things never change, but I am well pleased to have him with me.'

Somewhere a clock chimed and Herrick said quickly, 'You know me – I hate not to be punctual.'

Bolitho watched his struggle, but when it burst out it was not what he had been expecting.

'Your new flagship. She is completing at Chatham?' He hurried on as if the thing which troubled him could not be contained. 'When you visit the ship, and I have been your subordinate too many times in the past not to know your habits, would you find time to call upon my Dulcie?'

Bolitho asked gently, 'What is it, Thomas?'

'I am not sure and that is the God's truth. But she has been so tired of late. She works too hard with her charities and the like, and will not rest when I am away at sea. I keep telling her, but you know how they are. I suppose she's lonely. If we had been blessed with children, even the one like you and Lady Belinda –' He broke off, confused by his own revelation. 'It is the way of the world, I suppose.'

Bolitho touched his sleeve. 'I shall call on her. Catherine keeps trying to drag me to a surgeon, so we may discover someone who might help Dulcie.'

Herrick's blue eyes seemed to harden. 'I am sorry. I was not thinking. Perhaps I was too fouled by my own worries and forgot for a moment.' He looked along the room. 'Maybe it would be better if you did not pay Dulcie a visit.'

Bolitho stared at him. 'Is this barrier still between us, Thomas?'

Herrick regarded him wretchedly. 'It is not of my making.' He was going. 'I wish you well, Richard. Nothing can take my admiration away. Not ever.'

156

'*Admiration?*' Bolitho looked after him and then called, 'Is that all it has become, Thomas? God damn it, man, are we so *ordinary?*'

The two captains were on their feet as Herrick strode past them, their eyes darting between the flag-officers as if they could scarcely believe what they were witnessing.

Then Bolitho found himself outside the Admiralty's imposing façade, shivering in spite of the sunshine and strolling people.

'Be off with you, you wretch!'

Bolitho glanced up, still breathing hard, and saw a young man, accompanied by two girls, shaking his fist at a crouching figure by the roadside. The contrast was so vivid it made his head swim . . . the elegantly dressed young blade with his giggling friends, and the stooping figure in a tattered red coat who was holding out a tin cup.

'*Belay that!*' Bolitho saw them turn with surprise while several passers-by paused to see what would happen. Ignoring them all, Bolitho strode to the man in the shabby red coat.

The beggar said brokenly, 'I wasn't doin' no 'arm, sir!'

Someone shouted, 'Shouldn't be allowed to hang about here!'

Bolitho asked quietly, 'What was your regiment?'

The man peered up at him as if he had misheard. He had only one arm, and his body was badly twisted. He looked ancient, but Bolitho guessed he was younger than himself.

'Thirty-First Foot, sir.' He stared defiantly at the onlookers. 'The old Huntingdonshire Regiment. We was doin' service as marines.' His sudden pride seemed to fade as he added, 'I was with Lord Howe when I got this lot.'

Bolitho turned on his heel and looked at the young man for several seconds.

'I will not ask the same of you, sir, for I can see plainly enough what *you* are!'

The youth had gone pale. 'You have no right –'

'Oh, but I do. There is at this very moment a lieutenant of the Tower Hill press gang approaching. A word, *just one word* from me, and you will learn for yourself what it is like to fight for your King and country!'

He was angry with himself for using such a cheap lie. No press gang ever ventured into an area of quality and wealth. But the

157

young man vanished, leaving even his companions to stare after him with surprise and humiliation at being abandoned.

Bolitho thrust a handful of coins into the cup. 'God be with you. *Never think that what you did was in vain.*' He saw the man staring at the golden guineas with astonishment, and knew what he was saying was really for his own benefit. 'Your courage, like your memories, must sustain you.'

He swung away, his eyes smarting, and then saw the carriage pulling towards him. She pushed open the door before the coachman could jump down and said, 'I saw what you did.' She touched his mouth with her fingers. 'You looked so troubled . . . did something happen in there to harm you?'

He patted her arm as the carriage clattered back into the aimless traffic. 'It harms us all, it would appear. I thought I understood people. Now I am not so sure.' He looked at her and smiled. 'I am only certain of you!'

Catherine slid her arm through his and looked out of the carriage window. She had seen Herrick stride up the Admiralty steps. The rest, and Bolitho's angry confrontation with the young dandy, needed no explanation.

She answered softly, 'Then let us make the most of it.'

Tom Ozzard paused to lean against a stone balustrade to find his bearings, and was surprised he was not out of breath. The little man had been walking for hours, sometimes barely conscious of his whereabouts but at the back of his mind very aware of his eventual destination.

Along the Thames embankment, then crisscrossing through dingy side-streets where the shabby eaves almost touched overhead as if to shut out the daylight. Around him at every turn was the London he remembered as if it were yesterday. Teeming with life and street cries, the air rank with horse dung and sewers. On one corner was a man bawling out his wares, fresh oysters in a barrel, where several seamen were trying their taste and washing them down with rough ale. Ozzard had seen the river several times on his walk. From London Bridge to the Isle of Dogs it was crammed with merchantmen, their masts and yards swaying together on the tide like a leafless forest.

In the noisy inns along the river sailors jostled the painted

158

whores and flung away their pay on beer and geneva, not knowing when or if they might ever return once their ships had weighed. None of them seemed at all perturbed by the grisly, rotting remains of some pirates which dangled in chains at Execution Dock.

Ozzard caught his breath; his feet had brought him to the very street as if he had had no part in it.

He found that his breathing was sharper as he hesitated before forcing his legs to carry him along the cobbled roadway. It was like a part of his many nightmares. Even the light, dusky orange as evening closed in on the wharves and warehouses of London's dockland; it was said that there were more thieves and cutthroats in this part of London than in all the rest of the country. This was or had been a respectable street on Wapping Wall. Small, neat houses owned or rented by shopkeepers and clerks, agents from the victualling yards and honest chandlers.

A shaft of low sunshine reflected from the top window of his old house. He caught his breath. As if it was filled with blood.

Ozzard stared around wildly, his heart thumping as if to tear itself free from his slight body. It was madness; *he was mad*. He should never have come, there might still be folk here who remembered him. But when Bolitho had come to London he had accompanied him in another carriage. Allday, Yovell and himself. Each so different, and yet each one a part of the other.

Hardly daring to move, he turned his head to look at the shop directly opposite the row of neat houses.

On that horrific day when he had run from his home, heedless of the blood on his hands, he had paused only to stare at this same shop. Then it had been titled, *Tom Ozzard, Scrivener*. Now he had enlarged the premises and had added *& Son* to his name.

He thought of the time when the surgeon Sir Piers Blachford had spoken out about this same scrivener, and had remarked that it was the only time he had heard the name Ozzard. He had nearly collapsed.

Why did I come?

'You lookin' fer somethin', matey?'

Ozzard shook his head. 'No. Thank you.' He turned away to conceal his face.

159

'Suit yerself.' The unknown man lurched away towards a tavern which Ozzard knew lay behind the shops. Knew, because he had paused there for a glass of ginger beer on his way home. The lawyer who had employed him as his senior clerk had sent him off early to show his appreciation for all the extra work he had done. *If only he had not stopped for a drink.* Even as the hazy idea formed in his mind he knew he was deluding himself. She must have been laughing at him for months. Waiting for him to go to his office near Billingsgate, then for her lover to come to her. Surely others in the street must have known or guessed what was happening? Why hadn't someone told him?

He leaned against a wall and felt the vomit rising in his throat.

So young and beautiful. She had been lying in her lover's arms when he had walked in unsuspectingly from the street. It had been a sunny day, full of promise, just as today had started out.

The screams began again, rising to a piercing screech as the axe had smashed down on their nakedness. Again, again, and again, until the room had been like some of the sights he had seen since he had met with Richard Bolitho.

He did not hear the heavy tramp of feet and the clink of weapons until a voice shouted, 'You there! Stand and be examined!'

He could barely stop himself shaking as he turned and saw the press gang poised on the corner he had just come around. Not like the ones you saw in fishing villages or naval seaports. These men were armed to the teeth as they hunted for likely recruits in an area which was crammed with sailors, nearly all of whom would have the right papers, the 'Protection' to keep them free of the navy.

A massive gunner's mate, a cudgel hanging from his wrist, a cutlass thrust carelessly through his belt, said, 'Wot's this then?' He peered at Ozzard's blue coat with the bright gilt buttons, the buckled shoes beloved by sailors whenever they had funds enough to buy them. 'You're no sailor, I'll be damn sure o' that!' He put a hand on Ozzard's shoulder and swung him round to face his grinning party of seamen. 'What say you, lads?'

Ozzard said shakily, 'I – I *do* serve –'

'Stand aside!' A lieutenant pushed through his men and regarded Ozzard curiously. 'Speak up, fellow! The Fleet needs

160

more hands.' He ran his eye over Ozzard's frail person. 'What ship, if serve you do?'

'I – I am servant to Sir Richard Bolitho.' He found he was able to look up at the lieutenant without flinching. 'Vice-Admiral of the Red. He is presently in London.'

The lieutenant asked, '*Hyperion* – was she your last ship?' All his impatience had gone. As Ozzard nodded he said, 'Be off with you, man. This is no place for honest people after dark.'

The gunner's mate glanced at his lieutenant as if for consent, then pressed some coins into Ozzard's fist.

''Ere, go an' get a good wet. Reckon you've bloody earned it after wot you must 'er seen an' done!'

Ozzard blinked and nearly broke down. A *wet*. What Allday would have said. His whole being wanted to scream at them. Didn't they see the name on the shop front? What would they have said had he told them how he had run most of the way to Tower Hill to seek out a recruiting party? In those days there was always one hanging around near the taverns and the theatre. Ready to ply some drunken fool with rum before they signed him on in a daze of patriotic fervour. How would they have behaved if he'd described what he had left behind in that quiet little house? He made himself look at it. The window was no longer in the sun.

When he turned the press gang had vanished, and for a second longer he imagined it was another part of the torment, the stab of guilt which left him no peace. Then he looked down at his hand and opened the fingers while his body began to shake uncontrollably. There were the coins the gunner's mate had given him. '*I don't want your pity.*' The coins jangled across the cobbles as he flung them into the lengthening shadows. '*Leave me alone!*'

He heard someone call out, saw a curtain move in the house next to the one which had once been his. But nobody came.

He sighed and turned his back on the place, and the shop with his stolen name on the front.

Somewhere in the warren of alleys he heard a sudden scuffle, someone bellow with pain, then silence. The press gang had found at least one victim who would awake with a bloody head aboard the Thames guardship.

161

Ozzard thrust his hands into his coat pockets and began the long walk back to that other part of London.

His small figure was soon lost in the shadows, while behind him, the house was as before. Waiting.

Just a few miles upstream from Wapping where Ozzard had made his despairing pilgrimage, Bolitho bent over to offer his hand to Catherine, and assist her from the wherry in which they had crossed the Thames. It was early darkness, the cloudless sky pinpointed with countless stars: a perfect evening to begin what Catherine had promised to be 'a night of enchantment'.

Bolitho put some money into the wherryman's hand, with a little extra so that he would be here to carry them back across the swirling black river. The man had a cheeky grin, and had not taken his eyes off Catherine while he had pulled his smart little craft lustily over the choppy water.

Bolitho did not blame him. She had been standing in Lord Browne's hallway beneath a glittering chandelier when he had come down the staircase. In a gown of shot silk, very like the one she had worn that night in Antigua when he had met her again for the first time after so long. Catherine loved green, and her gown seemed to change from it to black as she had turned towards him. It was low-cut to reveal her throat and the full promise of her breasts. Her hair was piled high, and he had seen that she was wearing the same filigree earrings which had been his first-ever gift to her. The ones she had somehow managed to sew into her clothing when she had been forced into the Waites prison.

The wherryman flashed him a broad grin. 'I'll be 'ere, Admiral – nah you go off an' enjoy yerselves!'

Bolitho watched the little boat speed back across the river to seek out another fare.

'I don't understand.' He looked down at his plain blue coat, bought in Falmouth from old Joshua Miller. He and his father had been making uniforms for the Bolitho family and other Falmouth sea-officers longer than anyone could recall. 'How did he know?'

She flicked open her new fan and watched him above it, her eyes shining in the glow of many lanterns. 'More people know

162

about us than I thought!' She tossed her head. 'What do you think, Richard? My little surprise – to take your mind off weightier matters?'

Bolitho had heard of the London pleasure gardens, but had never visited any. This one at Vauxhall was the most famous of all. It certainly looked enchanted. Lantern-lit groves, wild rose hedges, and the sound of birds who enjoyed the merriment and music as much as the visitors.

Bolitho paid the entrance fee of half a crown each and allowed Catherine to guide him into the Grand Walk, a place for promenade, lined with exactly matching elms, and past little gravel walks with secret grottoes and quiet cascades and fountains.

She tightened her grip on his arm and said, 'I knew you'd like it. *My* London.' She gestured with the fan towards the many supper booths where splendidly dressed women and their escorts listened to the various orchestras, sipping champagne, cider or claret as the fancy took them.

She said, 'Many of the musicians are from the finest orchestras. They work here to keep their pockets filled, their bellies too, until the season returns.'

Bolitho removed his hat and carried it. The place was packed with people, the air heavy with perfume to mingle with the flowers and the distant smell of the river.

Catherine had been wearing a broad Spanish-style shawl, for it was known to be cold along the river at night. Now she let it drop to her arms, her throat and breasts shining in lanternlight or changing into provocative depths and shadows as they walked along a path.

It was like an endless panorama, where comic songs and bawdy ballads shared the same status as the work of great composers and lively dancing. There were plenty of uniforms too. Mostly red with the blue facings of the Royal regiments, and some sea-captains from the many ships moored below London Bridge, and the twisting route which would carry them back to the sea once more.

They paused where two paths crossed, so that it was possible to hear the music of Handel from one angle, while from the opposite direction they could listen to someone singing 'Lass of

163

Richmond Hill'. And neither seemed to detract from the other, Bolitho thought. Or perhaps it really was enchanted . . .

On the extreme of the brightly lit gardens was 'The Dark Walk'. Catherine led him into the deep shadows where other couples stood and embraced, or merely held one another in silence.

Then she turned and lifted her face to him, pale in the darkness. 'And *no*, dearest of men, I never walked here with another.'

'I would not have blamed you, Kate. Or the man who would lose his heart to you as I did.'

She said, 'Kiss me. Hold me.'

Bolitho felt her arch towards him; sensed the power of their love which hurled all caution and reserve aside.

He heard her gasp as he kissed her neck and then her shoulder, and pulled her closer without even a glance as a pair of strolling lovers passed by.

He said into her skin, 'I *want* you, Kate.'

She pretended to push him away, but he knew her excitement matched his own.

She touched his mouth with the fan as he released her and said, 'But first we eat. I have arranged for a booth. It will be a private place.' She gave her infectious laugh, something which at times in the past Bolitho had thought never to hear again. 'As private as anything *can* be in Vauxhall Pleasure Gardens!'

The time passed with an impossible speed while they sat in their little flower-bedecked booth, toying with their salads and roasted chicken, enjoying the wine and the music, but most of all each other.

She said, 'You are staring at me.' She dropped her eyes and took his hand in hers across the table. 'You make me feel so wanton – I should be ashamed.'

'You have a beautiful neck. It seems wrong to hide it, and yet . . .'

She watched him wondering.

'I will buy something for it. Just to adorn what is already so lovely.'

She smiled. 'Only in your eyes.' Then she squeezed his hand until it hurt. 'I am so in love with you, Richard. You just don't know.' She touched her eyes with a handkerchief. 'There, see what you've done!' When she looked at him again they were very bright. 'Let us go and find our lecherous wherryman. I have such need of you I can scarcely wait!'

They walked back along the path towards the gates. Catherine pulled her long shawl over her bare shoulders and shivered. 'I never want the summer to end.'

Bolitho smiled, passion and excitement making him light-headed, as if he had had too much wine.

'Wait here in the shelter. I will make certain that the waterman you described so well is alongside.'

She called after him as he turned by the gates. 'Richard, I *do* like your hair like that. You look so . . . *dashing*.'

She watched him pass into the shadows and drew the shawl more tightly around her; then she turned as a voice said, 'All alone, my dear? That's very remiss of somebody!'

She observed him calmly. An army captain; not very old, with a lopsided grin which told of some heavy drinking.

She said, 'Be off with you. I am not alone, and even if I were –'

'Now let's not be hasty, m'dear.' He stepped closer and she saw him stagger. Then he reached out and seized the shawl. 'Such beauty should never be hidden!'

'Take your hand off my lady.' Bolitho had not even raised his voice.

Catherine said shortly, 'He is full to the gills!'

The captain stared at Bolitho and gave a mock bow. 'I did not realise; and in any case she looked like the sort of woman who might favour a poor soldier.'

Bolitho was still very calm. 'I would call you out, sir –'

The captain grinned stupidly. 'And then I would willingly accept your seconds!'

Bolitho opened his plain blue coat. 'You did not let me finish. I would call you out *if* you were a gentleman and not a drunken lout. So we will settle it here.' The old sword simply seemed to materialise in his hand. 'And now!'

Another soldier lurched through some bushes and gaped at the small, tense scene. He was tipsy, but not too drunk to recognise the danger.

'Come away, you damned fool!' To Bolitho he exclaimed, 'On his behalf, Sir Richard, I crave your pardon. He is not normally like this.'

Bolitho looked at the captain, his eyes hard. 'So I would hope, if only for the sake of England's safety!'

He slid the sword into its scabbard and deliberately turned his back on the pair of them. 'The boat is ready and waiting, my lady.'

She took his proffered arm and felt it shaking.

'I have never seen you like that before.'

'I am sorry to behave like some hot-headed midshipman.'

She protested, 'You were wonderful.' She held up the small reticule which hung from her wrist, and added, 'But if he *had* tried to hurt you he would have got a ball in the buttocks to quieten him down. My little carriage pistol is quite big enough for that.'

Bolitho shook his head. 'You are full of surprises!'

By the time the wherry was halfway across the river, weaving expertly through packs of similar craft, he was calm again.

Then he said, 'It really was a night of enchantment, Kate. I shall *never* forget it.'

Catherine glanced at the staring waterman and then allowed the shawl to drop from her shoulders as she leaned against Bolitho and whispered, 'It is not yet over, as you will soon discover.'

The waterman left his wherry to assist them out on to the pier. In his trade he carried them all. Men with other men's wives, sailors and their doxies, young bucks on the hunt for excitement or a brawl which would end blade to blade. But his two fares this evening were like none he had ever carried, and for some strange reason he knew he would always remember them. He thought of the way she had teased him with her shawl and gave a rueful grin. It had been well worth it.

He called after them, 'Any time, Sir Richard! Just ask for Bobby – they all knows me on the London River.'

The carriage which had been put at their disposal was standing in line with many others, the coachmen nodding while they waited for their masters who were still over at Vauxhall.

Bolitho saw Ozzard's gilt buttons glinting in the carriage

lamps. It was like a silent warning, and he felt Catherine's grip tighten on his wrist.

'Is something wrong, Ozzard? There was no need for you to wait with the carriage.'

Ozzard said, 'There was a messenger from the Admiralty, Sir Richard. I told him I didn't know where you were.' His tone suggested he would not have told him anyway. 'He left word for you to present yourself to Lord Godschale at your earliest convenience tomorrow.'

Somewhere in another world a church clock began to chime.

Catherine said in a small voice, '*Today*.'

When they reached the house in Arlington Street, Bolitho said, 'It cannot be so urgent. I have no flagship as yet, and in any case –'

She turned on the stairway and tossed her shawl impetuously over the curving banister rail.

'And *in any case*, my gallant admiral, there is still the night!'

He found her waiting for him beside one of the windows from which, in daylight, you could see the park. She looked at him, her face almost impassive as she said, 'Take me, use me any way you will, but always love me.'

Down in the deserted kitchen Allday sat at the scrubbed table and carefully filled a new clay pipe. It had cost him a fortune in London but he doubted if it would last any longer.

He had heard the carriage return and had seen Ozzard going quietly to his bed. Something was troubling him sorely; pulling him apart. He would try and find out what it was.

He lit the pipe and watched the smoke rising in the still air. Then he pulled a tankard of rum towards him and tried not to think of them upstairs.

All the same, he thought, it would make everything just perfect. To feel her defences giving way.

Allday snatched the tankard and took a great swallow.

Aloud he said thickly, 'Just watch out for squalls, that's all I asks of 'em!'

But as he thought of them up there together, he knew that nothing would make any difference.

11

The Mission

Bolitho pushed open the tall doors of the drawing room and stood for a few moments in silence.

Catherine was by one of the windows, looking down at the street, waiting as he was for the inevitable departure.

Then he crossed the room and put his hands on her shoulders, and touched her hair with his mouth. 'It is nearly time.'

She nodded and seemed to lean back against him. 'I will not let you down, Richard. We have been free to love these past weeks, free from everything. For that I can only be grateful.' She twisted round in his arms and searched his face despairingly. 'But perhaps I am greedy, and want so much more.'

Bolitho heard someone bumping his chest down the stairs and stared past her at the empty street. The shadows were lengthening already, each evening drawing in – an early autumn then.

He said, 'At least there is no danger. I am to go on a mission –' He hesitated, hating the secrecy. 'Should anything go amiss, I have taken care of –'

She pressed her hand over his lips. 'Say no more. I *do* understand. If secrecy is necessary, then I'll not plead to share it. But come back to me.'

Bolitho embraced her. Just a few days since his summons to the Admiralty. Maybe the secrecy was necessary; or was it merely another ruse to keep him out of the country? The latter was hard to believe. It all took organisation and trust. He was to go to Dover, not Portsmouth or Chatham as might be expected, and from there take passage to Copenhagen. He would be met at Dover and the rest of his mission explained.

As if to dispel his own doubts he said, 'It will not take long. Perhaps two weeks, certainly no longer. And then –'

She looked at him and asked, 'What would you have me do?'

'Oliver Browne has said that this house is ours for as long as we require it. His lordship is visiting his family estate in Jamaica.' He smiled. 'It is hard not to think of him still as my flag-lieutenant!'

'What of Lieutenant Jenour?' She too smiled, remembering. 'A fellow conspirator and a good friend.'

'He will already be at Dover waiting for me.'

'Then he is luckier than I!'

He felt her tense as iron-shod wheels rolled along the street and halted outside the house.

Bolitho spoke hurriedly. 'Ozzard will tend to your needs, Kate, and Yovell will apprise you of everything you wish to know. I am leaving you in their care. I would offer Allday's services but –'

She smiled. 'No. He would never allow it, and besides I need your "oak" to protect you!'

The doors opened a few inches and one of the servants said, 'The carriage is here, Sir Richard. Your chest is inside.' The doors closed silently. It was as if the house, even the street was holding its breath for these last, fleeting moments.

'Come.' Bolitho put his arm around her shoulders and together they descended to the hallway. 'I have so much to say, and it will all come flooding out once we are parted.'

She looked back up the staircase, thinking perhaps of the night she had been carried here in her filthy clothing, her feet bare from her experiences in the Waites prison. Recalling their love and moments of tender passion. Now she would be looking at her other man, the King's officer; the service which would always be a rival if given the chance.

The front doors were wide open and there was a chill in the evening air. She clutched his arm and said, 'I cause such trouble for you, when I would do anything but harm you. I have even come between you and your friends, and all because of our love!'

Bolitho held her. Somehow he had known that she had guessed or understood what had happened with Herrick that day at the Admiralty.

He replied, 'Nothing separates us.' He looked into the street, the house lights already reflecting on the side of the carriage. 'Except what I must do.' He had noticed that the carriage was unmarked by any crest or recognition. A secret indeed.

One of the horses stamped its feet, and the coachman murmured something to soothe its impatience. Behind the rear wheels Bolitho could see Allday's thick shadow waiting, as he had so many times.

Bolitho said, 'I wrote to Val Keen. It is all I *can* do. If you are staying here until I return it is possible he might come to see you.'

'It still troubles you?'

'Yes.' He smiled distantly. 'A war raging all about us while we stumble in personal crossfire. I suspect that has always been my real weakness.'

She shook her head. '*Strength*. I hear people talking of you as a man of war, and yet with you I have never before known such peace.'

He wrapped his boat-cloak around her shoulders as they walked down the steps together, then she stooped to pick up a dead leaf which had blown against her shoe.

When she faced him again her eyes were dark and shining. 'Remember when I sent you the ivy leaf from *our* house?'

'I still have it.'

'And now here is a messenger of another coming winter. Please God we may not be parted for too long.' She was speaking quickly as if fearful he would interrupt. 'I know I promised – I vowed to you I should be brave, but I have only just found you again.'

He said quietly, 'There is none braver than you, Kate.' He *had* to leave; it was best to do it quickly, for both their sakes. 'Kiss me.'

He felt her mouth mould into his body as if to hold them together for ever. Then they were just as suddenly apart. Allday held open the carriage door and raised his hat.

She handed him Bolitho's cloak and stood very upright on the bottom step, her body framed against the chandelier-lit hallway.

170

She said, 'I ask of you again, Mr Allday. Take the best care of him!'

Allday grinned, but felt the sadness like his own. 'We'll be back afore you knows it, m'lady.' He went around the carriage so that Bolitho could watch her from the window.

Bolitho said, 'You hold my heart, dear Kate!' He might have said something more, but freed from the brake and with the sharp crack of the coachman's whip, the words were lost in the din of wheels and the jangle of harness.

The carriage had been out of sight for some time before she eventually turned, oblivious to the cool air, and entered the house. How empty and alien it seemed without him.

She had considered returning to Falmouth, but something, a hint in his tone had made her believe that her place was here. Was it only a short distance he was going this time? She thought of his sea-chest, the fine new shirts she had forced him to buy in London. She smiled, remembering again. *Her* London. He certainly was not carrying enough baggage for a lengthy mission.

She found Yovell waiting for her, to discover her requirements.

'Why *him*, Mr Yovell? Can you tell me that? Is there no limit to what they can demand?'

Yovell removed his small gold-rimmed spectacles and polished them vigorously with his handkerchief.

'Because he is usually the only one for the task, m'lady.' He smiled as he replaced his glasses. 'Even I do not know what he is about this time!'

She looked at him proudly. 'Will you sup with me tonight, Mr Yovell? I would take it as a favour.'

He stared at her, trying not to let his eyes stray over her hair, the way she lifted her chin, the very presence of her.

'It would be a privilege indeed, m'lady!'

She made for the staircase. 'There is a *price*, Mr Yovell. I will wish to hear everything you know about the man I love, more than life itself.'

Yovell was glad she did not press him further. Her frankness, the light of defiance which seemed to shine from her eyes, was like nothing he had ever experienced.

He took off his glasses and polished them again without even realising what he was doing.

And she trusted him. The woman who had created the gossip and lies but had just spoken so fervently of her love, could have done the round-shouldered secretary Daniel Yovell no greater honour.

It was four o'clock in the morning when, stiff and painfully aware of the fast drive from London, Bolitho finally stepped down from the unmarked carriage and tasted the salt air in his mouth.

It was pitch dark as, followed by Allday and two seamen who were waiting to carry his chest, he walked towards the gates of the guardhouse. When he looked up at the low clouds he saw just a hint of the castle's solid silhouette. It could easily have been a ridge of rock, a miniature Table Mountain.

He heard Allday cough, then stifle it with his hand. His coxswain was probably as glad as he was to have arrived in one piece. Thank God the Dover Road had been deserted, because the coachman had driven like a soul possessed. Bolitho had the feeling he was well used to this kind of work.

'*Halt!* Who goes there?'

Bolitho tossed his boat-cloak back from one epaulette and walked into a circle of lantern-light.

He heard Jenour's familiar voice, saw his pale breeches as he hurried out to greet him.

'Bravo, Sir Richard! You must have been blessed with wings!'

Bolitho shook his hand. It was cold, like his own, and he was reminded of Catherine's words about the coming winter.

Allday muttered, 'That bugger nearly did what the Dons an' the Frogs has failed to do many times!'

The Officer-of-the-Guard joined them and doffed his hat. 'Welcome to Dover, Sir Richard.'

Bolitho could feel the lieutenant's scrutiny even in the dark. Recognition again, curiosity too.

Bolitho had never really liked Dover. He found it difficult to forget the months before the outbreak of war – what was it? Thirteen years ago? It did not seem possible. He had been unemployed, still weakened by the fever which had struck him

172

down so cruelly in the Great South Sea, and which had all but killed him. Too many captains, too few ships. In peacetime the fleet had been cut to the bone, sound vessels laid up to neglect and rot, sailors thrown on the beach unwanted with no jobs to go to.

Bolitho was still very bitter about it. Like the shantyman's song which had ended on that same note, *Now we have naught to eat and drink, For you have naught to fear. . .* Would it be the same when this war was finally won, and a part of history?

More than anything he had wanted a ship then. To forget his experiences in the Great South Sea, to begin all over again with another fine frigate like his *Tempest* had been. Instead he had been offered the thankless task of recruiting men at the Nore and the Medway towns, and at the same time seeking out deserters who had fled the navy for the more lucrative and brutal trade of smuggling.

His work had sometimes brought him to Dover. To see a smuggler kick out his life on the gallows, or to pit his wits against the authorities, the men of power who were hand-in-glove with the Brotherhood, as it was called. But the guillotine's blade which had fallen on the neck of France's king had changed all that overnight. Not a frigate; they had given him the old *Hyperion*. It was as if she had been destined for him. Now like so many faces, she too had gone to the bottom.

He realised that the others were waiting and he said, 'What ship?'

The lieutenant swallowed apologetically. 'My orders are –'

Bolitho snapped, 'Don't waste my time, man!'

'She lies out at anchor, Sir Richard. The *Truculent*, Captain Poland.' He sounded crushed.

Bolitho sighed. Like a family. You either lost touch completely, or faces and ships reappeared again and again. He knew that both *Zest* and *Truculent* had joined the North Sea squadron and would eventually serve under his flag once *Black Prince* was in full commission. He forced himself from going over the mystery of Keen's silence again and asked, 'Is there a boat waiting?'

'Er, yes, Sir Richard.'

Jenour hid a smile as the lieutenant led the way with a lantern, half-shuttered as if the dock area was filled with spies and French agents. He watched Bolitho's quick stride and was glad to be with him again. Jenour had enjoyed his freedom, which he had spent with his parents in Southampton, and yet when the messenger had brought his orders he had felt something like elation, without even the hesitation which might have been expected after his recent experiences.

Feet shuffled on cobbles, and as they turned a corner around some victualling sheds the sea-breeze swept amongst them like a boisterous greeting.

Bolitho stood on the edge of the jetty and stared past the other moored vessels, the gaunt shadows of rigging and furled sails, to the riding-lights of ships at anchor. He rarely thought about it at sea, but now, standing here on the wet cobbles which would soon reveal themselves in a grey dawn, it was a strange, unnerving feeling. Out there in the darkness, no more than twenty sea-miles away, was the enemy coast. In a man-of-war you could fight or run as your wisdom dictated. Along these shores, thinly protected by gunboats, the sea fencibles or some local militia, the ordinary people had no such choice. They more than any others probably thanked God for the weather-beaten ships of the blockade which day and night rode out storms and calms alike to keep the enemy bottled up in his harbours.

'Boat's ready, Sir Richard.'

Bolitho nodded to the Officer-of-the-Guard. 'How sets the tide?'

The man's face looked paler in the gloom, or was it imagination? He replied, 'It'll be on the ebb in two hours, Sir Richard.'

'Good.' It would mean a quick start. But who was the one chosen to give him the information he needed? He relented slightly. 'You keep a good watch, Lieutenant. It is just as well in this port!'

Then he was down into the boat with unexpected familiarity; even the lieutenant who had been sent in charge of the gig he recognised instantly.

'I'll wager you never expected to see *me* again so soon, Mr Munro?'

Jenour watched it all; as he had tried to describe it to his parents. The way *Truculent*'s young second lieutenant responded with such obvious pleasure. Had it been daylight Jenour was certain he would have been blushing. Just small points, but Bolitho never seemed to forget, nor did he overlook the importance which these brief contacts he had with his men might carry for them when they most needed them later on.

Jenour shivered despite his warm cloak. It was exactly like one of his old storybooks. A secret mission. Jenour was not so naive that he did not see past the excitement to the danger and death which might lie in store. He had witnessed plenty of it since he had joined Bolitho; was still surprised that he had not cracked because of it. Perhaps later? He pushed it aside and said, 'I see her, Sir Richard!'

Bolitho swung round and turned up the collar of his cloak as the spray from the oars spat over the gunwale and stung the tiredness from his mind.

He could guess what Jenour was thinking. But the mission, whatever it was, could already be common gossip on messdecks and in wardrooms alike.

He saw the frigate's spiralling masts cut across the clouds to tower over them, heard the ship's own noises moving out to receive them. Shouted commands carried away by the breeze which might soon be a strong south-westerly wind, the creak of tackles and the urgent shrill of calls. Men feeling their way about the decks or high above them on the treacherous yards and ratlines, slippery with spray; no place for the unskilled. But there were some of the latter, Bolitho thought. A man was calling out in fear, his pleas cut short by a blow. Captain Poland must have put a press gang ashore somewhere away from the port, or else the local flag officer had sent him a few landsmen from the guardship. For them the long, hard lesson was about to begin.

He thought again of Catherine, all that they had done together, all that they had given each other, and still there had not been enough time. He had not found the necklace he wanted for her lovely throat, nor had they been to visit the surgeon, Sir Piers Blachford. He had thought several times of his daughter Elizabeth, who would be four years old. The last occasion when he had seen her was when he had had his first confrontation with

Belinda – she had passed him by with barely a glance. Not like a child at all. A doll in silks, a possession. But it would all have to wait.

'*Boat ahoy?*' Figures jostled around the light at the frigate's entry port.

Before the gig's coxswain could reply to the age-old challenge, Allday cupped his big hands and yelled, '*Flag! Truculent!*'

Bolitho pictured the tension on board. They might have been waiting and wondering for hours. Nobody could have known when his carriage would arrive or even when he had left London. But he had no doubts at all that Captain Poland would have kept every man alert and ready to receive him, if it had taken him another full day!

The gig's bowman managed to hook on to the main chains, while others did their best to control the boat's pitching and swaying as it felt the surge of the current alongside.

Bolitho reached the entry port and saw Poland and his officers waiting to be presented, even at this unearthly hour. As he had expected, they were all smartly dressed for his arrival.

He took Poland's hand and said, 'I see that I must congratulate you, Captain.'

Poland smiled modestly as the swaying lantern threw a glow across his matching pair of epaulettes.

He said, 'And I must *thank* you, Sir Richard. I cannot say how grateful I was to be told that my posting had been confirmed as a result of your report.'

Bolitho paused to watch the gig being hoisted up and over the nettings, then manhandled down on to the boat-tier with the others. A sense of urgency and mystery he had known often enough as a young frigate captain.

He said, 'It will be a mite different from the shores of Africa.'

Poland hesitated, sifting it through as if to seek out any possible traps. Then he admitted, 'I know our eventual landfall, Sir Richard, but in God's name I know nought else.'

Bolitho touched his arm and felt it stiffen. Poor Poland; like so many before him he had imagined that to gain the coveted rank of post-captain was to be beyond the reach of uncertainty, a summit from which nobody could topple you. Bolitho smiled to himself. He was learning otherwise. Like the epaulettes, the responsibility was also doubled. *As I discovered for myself many times*.

Poland glanced quickly at his hovering first lieutenant. 'Have the capstan fully manned, Mr Williams. We shall sail on the tide, or I shall need to know about it!'

To Bolitho he added, 'If you will come aft, Sir Richard, there is a gentleman who is taking passage with us.'

While the ship came alive with the noise of getting under way, Bolitho entered the stern cabin, which he had come to know so well in his solitude. The first thing he saw was a curly wig which stood on its rest by an open chest; the second was the man who walked unsteadily from the shadows by the stern window, his legs as yet unused to the uncomfortable motion of a ship eager to tear free from the ground.

He was older, or appeared so, perhaps more stooped in the light of the spiralling lanterns. Sixty at a guess, his head almost bald so that his old-fashioned queue hung down over his collar like a rope's end.

He put his head on one side and regarded Bolitho like a quizzical bird. 'It's a long while, Sir Richard, and many miles since we last met.'

Bolitho clasped both his hands in his own.

'Of course I remember. Charles Inskip! You guided me when I strained our country's diplomacy – that was in Copenhagen too!' They studied one another, their hands still gripped together as the memories flooded back. Bolitho had been sent to Denmark to help parley with the Danes after Napoleon had demanded that they hand over their fleet to his French admirals. The failure then to reach an agreement had led to the Battle of Copenhagen, when Nelson had defied his admiral's order to discontinue the action, and had forced the attack alone. The memories were flooding back. Keen had been there in his own command. Herrick had been Bolitho's flag-captain in *Benbow*, which was now his own flagship. Such was fate and the ways of the navy.

It had been a bloody battle between nations who had nothing against one another but for their fear of the French obtaining the upper hand over them both.

Inskip gave a small smile. 'Like you, Sir Richard, I, too, am honoured. *Sir* Charles, by His Majesty's gracious consent.'

They both laughed and Bolitho said, 'An unnerving experience!' He did not add that the King had forgotten his name at the moment of knighting him.

More cries echoed from the deck above, and then the thrashing thunder of freed canvas. They could not hear the cry of *'Anchor's aweigh!'* but Bolitho braced his legs and felt *Truculent* respond like a released stallion, free of the halter, and responsible only to her captain's skills.

Inskip was watching him thoughtfully. 'You still miss it, don't you? Being up there with the people, pitting your wits against the sea? I saw it in your eyes, as I did those six years back in Copenhagen.'

He moved carefully to a chair as a servant entered with some glasses on a tray.

'Well, we are returning there, Sir Richard.' He sighed and patted his side pockets. 'In one I carry a promise, in t'other a threat. But sit you down and I'll tell you what we are about –' He broke off and covered his mouth as the deck reeled over to the thrust of the helm. 'I fear I have been too long in the comforts of London. My damned stomach defies me yet!'

Bolitho watched the servant's expressionless face – one of Inskip's men – as he poured the wine with some difficulty.

But he was thinking of Catherine and the London she had given him. *Enchantment*. Not at all like the one Inskip was already regretting leaving astern.

He leaned forward and felt her fan press against his thigh. 'I am all attention, Sir Charles, though what part I can play is still beyond me.'

Inskip held his glass up to the light and gave a nod of satisfaction. He was probably one of the most senior government officials employed on Scandinavian affairs, but at this moment he looked more like a village schoolmaster.

He said, 'Nelson is gone, alas, but the Danes know you. It is little enough, but when I explain further you will see we have no room for choices. There are sensible men in Copenhagen, but there are many who will see the value of *compromise*, another word for surrender, with Napoleon's army at the frontier.'

Bolitho glanced down at the gold lace on his sleeve. He was back.

178

Bolitho stood on the weather side of *Truculent*'s quarterdeck and strained his eyes through the first grey light of morning. Around him the ship reeled and plunged to a lively quarter-sea, spray and sometimes great surges of water dashing over the decks or breaking through the rigging where spluttering, cursing seamen fought to keep everything taut and free.

Captain Poland lurched up the slippery planking towards him, a tarpaulin coat flapping about him and running with water.

He shouted above the din, 'We should sight the narrows when daylight finds us, Sir Richard!' His eyes were red-rimmed with strain and lack of sleep, and his normally cool composure was less evident.

It had been a long, hard passage from Dover for him, Bolitho thought. No empty expanse of ocean with kind skies and prevailing winds, and Table Mountain as a mark of achievement at the end of it. *Truculent* had thrashed through the Channel and then north-east across the North Sea towards the coast of Denmark. They had sighted very little except for an English schooner and a small frigate which exchanged recognition signals before vanishing into a violent rain squall. It needed constant care with the navigation, especially when they altered course through the Skagerrak, then finally south, so close-hauled that the lee gunports had been awash for most of the time. It was not merely cold; it was bitter, and Bolitho was constantly reminded of the last great battle against the Danes at Copenhagen, with Nelson's flag shifted to the *Elephant*, a smaller seventy-four than his proper flagship, so that he could pass through the narrows close inshore and so avoid the enemy batteries until the final embrace.

Bolitho thought too of Browne's apt quotation for his own captains: *We Happy Few*. To think of it now only saddened him. So many had gone, returning only in memory at times like this while *Truculent* completed that very same passage. Captain Keverne of *Indomitable*, Rowley Peel and his fine frigate *Relentless*, Veitch in the little *Lookout*, and so many others. More were to fall from Browne's 'Few' in the following months and years. Firm friends like dear Francis Inch, and the

179

courageous John Neale who had once been a midshipman in Bolitho's *Phalarope*, only to die a captain when they had been taken prisoner by the French after the loss of his frigate *Styx*. Bolitho and Allday had done all they could to save him and ease his agony; but he had joined all the others where nothing further could hurt him.

Bolitho shivered inside his boat-cloak and said, 'A difficult passage, Captain.' He saw the red-rimmed eyes watching him guardedly, probably seeking out some sort of criticism in his remark. Then he pictured Catherine as he had last seen her. She would be wondering while she waited. It might be longer than he had promised. By the time *Truculent*'s anchor splashed down it would have taken them a full week to reach their goal. He added, 'I'm going below. Call me if you sight anything useful.'

Poland let out a sigh as Bolitho disappeared down the companion hatch. He called sharply, 'Mr Williams! Change the lookouts, if you please. When they sight land I want to know about it!'

The first lieutenant touched his dripping hat. No matter how worried the captain was he usually managed to find time for a little stab of sharp encouragement.

Below the quarterdeck it seemed suddenly quiet after the beat and bluster of the biting wind and spray. Bolitho made his way aft, past the sentry and into the cabin. Everything was damp and cold, and the bench seats below the stern windows were bloomed with moisture as if they had been left out on deck.

Sir Charles Inskip was sitting at the table, his head resting on one hand while his secretary, a Mr Patrick Agnew, turned over papers for him to examine by the light of a lantern which he held above them.

Inskip looked up as Bolitho seated himself, and waited for Allday to appear with his razor and hot water from the galley.

'Will this ship *never* be still?'

Bolitho stretched his arms to relieve the ache of clinging to one handhold or another, while trying to keep away from the watchkeepers bustling around him.

He said, 'Look at the chart. We are entering the narrows where I made my mark yesterday. We should sight Helsingør presently –'

'Hmmm. We are being met by a Danish escort at that point.' Inskip did not sound too certain. 'After that, we are in their hands.' He glanced at his reedy secretary. 'Not for too *long* I trust, Mr Agnew?'

They both looked up as a shout probed thinly through the sealed skylight before being lost in the wind.

'What was that?' Inskip turned as usual to Bolitho. 'Did you hear?'

Bolitho smiled. 'Land.'

Allday padded through the door of the sleeping cabin and wedged his steaming bowl on a chair before stropping his deadly-looking razor.

Inskip was calling for his servant and searching for a heavy coat. 'We had better go on deck.'

Allday tucked a cloth around Bolitho's neck and could almost have winked. Poland would make damn certain that it was the right landfall before he reported as much to his admiral.

Bolitho closed his eyes while Allday prepared to shave him. Like the first strong coffee of each new day, it was a moment to think and contemplate.

Allday poised the razor and waited for the deck to steady again. He was still unused to seeing Bolitho's hair cut in the modern fashion. What her ladyship apparently admired. He smiled to himself as he remembered her pleasure when he had fumbled with the package he had brought home to Falmouth. He heard himself muttering, 'Sorry about the smell of baccy, m'lady. 'Twas all I had fit to carry it in without him seeing it, so to speak!'

He had been astonished by her reaction, the poignant pleasure in those dark eyes, which Allday knew had said it all.

He had saved most of Bolitho's queue after his sudden insistence on having it cut off. After seeing her face he was glad.

Captain Poland entered the cabin just as Allday stood back and folded his razor.

'We are in sight of Helsingør, Sir Richard.' He waited, a puddle forming around his boots.

'I shall come up directly, Captain.' He smiled at him. 'Well done.'

The door closed and Bolitho allowed Allday to help him into

his coat. Simple words of praise, yet Poland still frowned. When invited through the gates of Heaven he would likely seek out a reason before entering, he thought. Another hail floated down.

Bolitho looked up at the salt-stained skylight. 'That poor wretch must be frozen to the masthead!'

'Shouldn't wonder.' Allday grimaced. Not many captains would care about a lowly seaman, never mind a vice-admiral.

The door banged open and Inskip and his secretary rushed into the cabin. It was all confusion as they tore open their chests and called for the servant, while trying to find what they needed to wear.

Inskip gasped, '*A ship*, Sir Richard! It will be the Danish escort.'

Bolitho heard the sullen rumble of gun trucks as some of the main armament was freed from the breechings and loaded. Poland again. *Just in case.*

'Then we had best attend to our business.' He gave a wry smile. '*Whatever* it proves to be!'

'A moment, Sir Richard.' Allday plucked a shred of spunyarn from Bolitho's fine coat. What little Ozzard would have seen to. Then he stood back and nodded with approval. The bright gold lace, the Nile medal which he always wore with such pride, and the old sword. Like one of the portraits, he thought. No wonder she loved him like she did. How could you not?

He said roughly, 'None better, Sir Richard, an' that's no error!'

Bolitho eyed him gravely. 'Then we are well matched, old friend.' He stepped aside as Inskip's servant dashed past with a crumpled shirt.

'So let us be about it, eh?'

12

Storm Warning

Sir Charles Inskip peered gloomily from a narrow window and shivered as a sudden squall rattled the thick glass.

'This is hardly the treatment I had been expecting!'

Bolitho put down his empty coffee cup and joined him to look across the harbour at some of the vessels which lay at anchor. He had not failed to notice the thick bars across the window, nor the way they had been kept in semi-isolation since they had stepped ashore. Their quarters in what appeared to be a part of a fortress were comfortable enough, but the door was locked at night all the same. He saw *Truculent* tugging at her cable, her furled canvas quivering as the wind ruffled up the surface of the anchorage and pounded against her hull and rigging. She, too, appeared isolated and vulnerable. The big Danish frigate *Dryaden*, which had met and then escorted them into Copenhagen, lay some two cables clear. Bolitho gave a grim smile. That was not a sign of trust, but to make sure she would suffer no damage if Captain Poland tried to cut and run. *Truculent* was lying directly beneath the guns of one of the main batteries. It would be an unhealthy place to be if it was forced to open fire.

Seven days. Bolitho tried not to let his mind linger on it. Inskip had told him repeatedly that they were here at the suggestion of a senior Danish minister named Christian Haarder. A man dedicated to keeping Denmark out of the war and safe from attack either by France *or* England.

Bolitho looked towards the array of anchored men-of-war,

183

their scarlet flags with the distinctive white crosses taut and bright in the stiff wind. It amounted to quite a fleet despite the savage losses in this very harbour some five years back. The Danes had probably mustered all their available warships from the mainland to place them under a single command. It made good sense, no matter what happened.

Inskip said irritably, 'I have sent two messages with no effect. Out of courtesy the palace was informed, and my own letters should have made further delays totally unnecessary.'

'People must be wondering about the presence of one of His Majesty's frigates in the harbour.' Bolitho watched a long-oared galley pulling slowly past the *Truculent*, the red blades rising and falling gracefully like a relic of ancient Greece. But Bolitho knew from hard experience that they were not simply for decoration. They could outmanoeuvre almost any ship under sail, and for armament they carried a solitary, heavy cannon with which they could maul a vessel's stern and pound her into submission while her prey was unable to bring a single gun to bear. To be attacked by several at once, as the flagship had been, was like being a beast torn apart by fleet-footed wolves.

Inskip said, 'They'll soon find out if they keep us waiting much longer.'

Bolitho saw Allday gathering up the cups although Inskip's own servant was in an adjoining room. He glanced at his watch. Jenour should have returned long ago. Inskip had sent him with another letter which he had written himself. Bolitho bit his lip. Too many secrets. Like trying to carry sand in a fishing-net.

He asked, 'Do you think the French may be involved at this stage?'

Inskip wrenched his thoughts into perspective. 'The *French*? Dammit, Bolitho, you see the Frenchman's fingers in everything! But I believe –' He broke off as Agnew, his long nose red from the cold, peered around the door and whispered, 'The lieutenant has returned, Sir Charles.'

Inskip adjusted his wig and glared at the main doorway. 'Not alone by the sound of it, by God!'

The door swung inwards and Bolitho saw Jenour, accompanied by the *Dryaden*'s captain and a tall man in a dark velvet coat whom he guessed was the minister named Haarder.

184

Bows were exchanged and to Inskip Haarder offered his hand. Like old antagonists, Bolitho thought, rather than friends. A sort of familiar wariness which he guessed was as much a part of them as their political evasiveness.

Haarder looked steadily at Bolitho and said, 'You I know from your last visit to my country.'

Bolitho searched for hostility but found none. 'I was treated with great courtesy.' He did not add, *unlike this time*. He did not need to.

Haarder shrugged. 'We are under no illusions here, Admiral. The Danish fleet is once again a rich prize to those who would seize it for their own cause.' His eyes flickered in amusement. 'Or those who might wish to destroy it for another reason, yes?' He glanced at their faces and said, 'My associates are hard to convince. Either way they lose –' He raised one hand as Inskip seemed about to argue. 'If, as your government is suggesting, the French intend to demand authority over our fleet, what will we do? Deny them, face them in battle? How could we survive when your own powerful nation has been at war with the same enemy for over twelve years? Think what you are asking before you condemn our uncertainty. We want only peace, even with our old foes in Sweden. Trade, not war – is that so alien that you cannot envisage it?'

Inskip sat back wearily and Bolitho knew he had given up before he had had a chance to negotiate.

Inskip said, 'Then you cannot, or *will* not help us in this matter? I had hoped –'

Haarder eyed him sadly. 'Your hope was mine also. But my voice is only one against many.'

Bolitho said, 'On my last visit I saw the Crown Prince, although his identity was kept secret from me until later.'

' Haarder smiled. 'It is often better for royalty to stay removed from affairs of state, Admiral. I think I will have your agreement on *that* at least.'

Bolitho knew that Inskip was watching him anxiously, as if he expected him to rise to the bait.

Bolitho replied, 'I am a sea-officer, sir, not a politician. I came here to advise, if required, on the balance of naval power in a very small area. But in all honesty I would not wish to see

185

Denmark suffer the same terrible losses as before. I believe I have *your* agreement on that!'

Haarder stood up and said heavily, 'I will keep trying. In the meantime I am instructed to end this attempted interference in Danish neutrality. Captajn Pedersen of the *Dryaden* will escort you to open waters.' He held out a sealed envelope and handed it to Inskip. 'For your Prime Minister, from someone far more senior than I.'

Inskip stared at the envelope. 'Lord Grenville dislikes being threatened no less than Mr Pitt did.' He straightened his back and smiled, the old antagonist once again. 'But it is not over.'

Haarder shook his hand gravely. 'Nor is it yet begun, my old friend.'

To Bolitho he said simply, 'I have long admired your achievements.' Again the twinkle of a smile. 'Ashore as well as afloat. Be assured that my King would have wished to receive you but –' He shrugged. 'We are in a vice. To show favour to one is to open the gates to another, yes?'

More bows and solemn handshakes and then Haarder took his leave.

The Danish captain said politely, 'If you will permit?' Some armed seamen entered the outer room and waited to collect their belongings. 'I will have a boat waiting to take you to your ship. After which,' he spoke haltingly but clearly, 'you will please obey my directions.'

The captain walked from the room and Inskip said, 'I wonder why they kept Haarder waiting so long. Just to tell me that he could do nothing?' It was the first time Bolitho had heard him sound puzzled.

Bolitho turned as if to watch Allday directing the Danish seamen into the other room for his sea-chest.

But he did not want Inskip to see his face, as his simple remark seemed to explode in his thoughts like a mortar shell.

Was it just imagination, a twist of words? Or had the tall Dane been trying to warn him, knowing at the same time that Inskip would not recognise it, or might challenge even a hint of suggestion?

Lieutenant Jenour remarked quietly, 'At least we shall be back in England before the winter gales return to the North Sea, Sir Richard.'

Bolitho took his arm and felt him tense as he said, 'I think *we* were delayed deliberately, Stephen, not the other way round.' He saw the understanding in Jenour's eyes. 'And it is a long way yet to England, remember?' He heard Inskip calling to his secretary and added sharply, 'Not a word. Just hurry our departure as much as you can without causing a stir.' He shook his arm lightly. 'Something else to tell your parents about, eh?'

Allday watched their exchange. Bolitho's alertness, like a reawakening, and the young lieutenant's sudden excitement. Jenour had never been able to hide his feelings anyway.

He walked across and clipped the old sword to Bolitho's belt. Like the moment when they had prepared to leave *Truculent* and transfer to the Danish frigate for the final approach to Copenhagen. Something unspoken seemed to pass between them.

Bolitho looked at him searchingly until Allday murmured, 'Seems we might soon be needing this old blade again, Sir Richard?'

Inskip bustled into the room. 'A good hot tub and a fine English serving of roast beef, that's what I –' His eyes flashed between them and he asked suspiciously, 'I suppose you think it was all a waste of time, what?'

Bolitho faced him grimly, the first elation of danger already contained. 'Indeed, Sir Charles, I hope that *is* all it was!'

The same short journey in a sealed carriage as when they had arrived, and then on to the wet, windswept jetty, where a boat was hooked on waiting for them. Inskip pulled his heavy coat around his body and gave the Danish captain a curt nod before he clambered down into the boat.

His face was a mask, his mind already grappling with what he had heard and probably with what had remained unsaid.

Bolitho waited for the others to fit themselves amongst the baggage in the sternsheets and turned to look across at the city, now blurred with rain like a painting left out in bad weather. He was moved by what he saw. The familiar green spires and handsome buildings, none of which he had been allowed to revisit. Catherine would love it.

He realised that the Danish captain was waiting. To make certain that he shared no contact with anyone; or was he merely curious to discover more about the man whose cannon had once pounded their ships into submission? Richard Bolitho, next to Nelson the youngest vice-admiral on the Navy List. Now, with Nelson gone – Bolitho shook it from his thoughts. Perhaps this very captain was a part of some scheme to delay them.

The captain said, 'I wish you God's speed, Sir Richard. Perhaps we shall meet again?'

No, he was not part of some sinister plot. Bolitho smiled, remembering his own remark to Haarder. *I am a sea-officer, sir.*

He replied, 'In fairer times, Captajn Pedersen, when you and I are no longer needed.'

He climbed down into the boat, one hand gripping Allday's shoulder as the hull lurched against the piles.

Apart from an occasional command from the boat's cox-swain, nothing was said by the passengers huddled in the sternsheets. Bolitho glanced at a passing guardboat, the lieutenant rising to doff his hat as he passed. All the correct courtesies, he thought, and was suddenly saddened by it. Like *in fairer times*. It was more than likely that the next time he met with that captain or any other, it would be across the muzzles of a full broadside.

Captain Poland was waiting with his side-party to greet them as they climbed aboard and the Danish longboat backed away from the chains in a welter of icy spray.

Poland began, 'I hope all is well, Sir Richard?' He stared after Inskip as he pushed past the reception and hurried aft to the poop.

Bolitho said, 'Prepare to get under way immediately, Captain Poland. We are to be escorted by *Dryaden* as before, but yours is the faster ship. Once clear of the narrows I want you to sail *Truculent* like you did to Good Hope!' He wished that Poland would stop staring at him. 'I shall explain why, directly, but I believe we may have to fight before we are much older.'

Poland was at last coming out of his daze. 'Er, *yes*, Sir Richard. I shall attend to it –' He peered round for his first lieutenant. 'If fight we must then my ship will give good account –' But when he looked again, Bolitho had vanished. He cupped his hands, his voice shattering the stillness of the side-party while they shivered in the intermittent rain.

188

'Mr Williams! Prepare to get the ship under way! Have the master lay aft!' He swung round, rain water running from his hat. 'Mr Munro, be so good as to pipe all hands, unless of course you are too engrossed in staring at the city yonder. I daresay you'll see more than *that* before long!' He watched the lieutenant as he fled from the quarterdeck. Then he snapped, 'Once clear of land we shall exercise gun crews, Mr Williams.' He derived some pleasure from the lieutenant's surprise. 'It seems we are a passenger-vessel no longer!'

Lieutenant Williams watched him stride away, his hat and coat shining in the downpour like wet coal. Poland never explained anything until he was himself absolutely certain. Williams gave a wry grin, then picked up his speaking-trumpet as the midshipman of the watch reported that the Danish frigate was already shortening her cable.

Why should he anyway? He was, after all, the captain!

As the calls shrilled and echoed between decks and the seamen came pouring from every hatch and along each gang-way, *Truculent*'s first lieutenant felt the excitement run through him like heady wine. Then he took a deep breath and raised his speaking-trumpet.

'*Man the capstan!*' He squinted through the rain. '*Hands aloft, loose tops'ls!*'

He saw his friend gazing at him, grinning despite the captain's sarcasm. 'Remember, lads, they're all watching us over yonder. Let's show 'em that nobody can weigh faster than *Truculent*!'

In the stern cabin Bolitho paused over the chart, the rain still dropping from his coat and hair on to his calculations.

The clank of the capstan, the surge of water alongside which drowned the sounds of shantyman or violin, and the feeling of life running through the hull like no other sensation.

He knew Poland would be down shortly to report that the anchor was hove short. That part of it was no longer his concern. Bolitho sighed and leaned over the chart again. *Then so be it.*

Bolitho felt Jenour's hand on his shoulder and was instantly awake. A second earlier and he had been trudging up the hill towards the house, his eyes searching for her, his legs refusing to carry him any closer. Now as his eyes took in the faint grey light from the stern windows he saw Jenour holding on to the swaying cot, his face wet as if he had been in the rain.

Jenour gasped, 'First light, Sir Richard!' He swallowed and clenched his jaws. 'I – I've been sick, sir!'

Bolitho listened to the roar of water against the side, the heave and groan of timbers as the frigate fought her way through the gale. He could also hear someone vomiting and guessed it was Inskip. Seasoned traveller in his country's service he might be; frigate sailor he was not.

Bolitho saw Allday's dark shadow edging down the cabin towards him, his body leaning over like a tree in the wind.

Allday showed his teeth in the gloom and held out a mug of steaming coffee. He said above the chorus of sea and wind, 'Last coffee for a bit, Sir Richard. Th' galley's flooded!' He looked unsympathetically at the flag-lieutenant. 'Nice bit o' salt pork is what you needs, sir.'

Jenour ran down the sloping deck and disappeared.

Bolitho sipped the coffee and felt it restoring him, driving sleep and dreams into memory.

'What's happening?'

Allday reached up and steadied himself by gripping the edge of a deckhead beam. 'We're still under reefed tops'ls an' jib, 'though the Cap'n was fair reluctant to shorten anything 'til the main t'gallant blew to ribbons! I heard the master say that the Danish ship is preparing to go about.'

Bolitho slid carefully to the deck as he had done ten thousand times, in so many vessels from topsail-cutter to a lordly first-rate. Allday unshuttered a lantern and held it over the table while he peered at his chart. Poland was doing well in spite of the savage weather which had plagued them since they had left the sheltered narrows. *Truculent* would now be at the northern limits of the Kattegat and would soon be changing tack to head south-west through the Skagerrak – more sea room, less chance of running afoul of any fishermen who were mad enough to be out in weather like this.

Allday said helpfully, 'Wind's shifted since the first watch, Sir Richard. A real nor'-easter, blowin' fit to bust every spar. Straight down from the Arctic if you asks me.'

He produced a heavy tarpaulin coat, knowing Bolitho would

190

want to see for himself. As the deck rose and plunged down again, Allday held on to one of the tethered nine-pounders to meet the violent motion. He felt the old wound in his chest come to life, sear his insides until he could scarcely stop himself from calling out.

Bolitho watched him and held out his hand. 'Here, hold on!'

Allday felt the pain recede as if it was reluctant to offer him peace. He shook himself like a great dog and forced a grin. 'Not too bad, sir. Comes at you when you're least ready, the bugger!'

Bolitho said, 'You know what I told you before. I meant it then, I mean it still.' He saw Allday stiffen, ready to argue. 'You deserve it anyway, after what you've done for your country.' He dropped his voice. 'For me.'

Allday waited for the deck to sway upright again and replied, 'An' what'd I do then, Sir Richard? Stand around the inn tellin' lies like all the other old tars? Be a sheep-watcher again? Or marry some rich widow-woman, an' God knows there are enough of *them* around with this war goin' on an' on!'

Bolitho lurched towards the screen door and saw the marine sentry clinging to a stanchion, his face no better than Jenour's. It was useless to try and convince Allday, he thought.

Water tumbled over the companion-way coaming and down to the deck below, and when Bolitho managed to reach the top of the ladder the wind nearly took his breath away.

Both watches were on deck, the air filled with shredded shouts and the slither of feet in water as it surged over the lee side.

Poland saw him and pulled himself along the quarterdeck rail to join him.

'I am sorry you were disturbed, Sir Richard!'

Bolitho smiled at him, his hair already thick with salt spray. 'You cannot be blamed for the weather!' He was not sure if Poland heard him. 'What is our position?'

Poland pointed across the lee bow. 'The last point of land, Skagen's Horn. We will change tack in about half an hour.' His voice was hoarse from shouting into the gale and the cold spray. 'I have barely lost an hour, Sir Richard!'

Bolitho nodded. 'I know. You are doing well.' Always the uncertainty, the search for criticism. It was a pity he did not remember that when he was berating his lieutenants.

191

Poland added, '*Dryaden* split a tops'l yard and most of her driver during the night.' He sounded pleased. 'We'll be leaving her soon.'

Bolitho shivered and was glad that he had had the last coffee as Allday had put it.

Poland had done what he had asked of him. Had kept *Truculent* in the lead all the way. *Dryaden* was not even in sight now except possibly from the masthead. He stared up through the shining black web of rigging and felt his head swim. Who would be a lookout in this gale?

Poland muttered something as several men ran to secure one of the boats on the tier; they were wading waist deep in water one moment, then seeming to rise higher than the quarterdeck the next.

Poland shouted, 'I've three men below with injuries. I ordered the surgeon to make certain they were real and proper – no malingerers, I told him!'

Bolitho looked away. *I'm sure of that*, he thought.

Aloud he said, 'Once clear of the Skaggerak we can use this nor'-easterly to good advantage.' He saw Poland nod, not yet committed. 'We will have a companion for the final passage across the North Sea. You can reduce sail then if need be to carry out repairs and relight the galley fire.'

Poland showed no surprise that Bolitho should know about the galley. Instead he said bluntly, 'You ordered *Zest* to make the rendezvous, Sir Richard? I make no secret of it – Captain Varian and I do not see eye to eye.'

'I am aware of it. I am also conscious that even with our reinforcements from Cape Town and the Caribbean we are pitifully short of frigates.' He did not add *as usual* although it had always been so; he had heard his father complaining about it often enough. 'So you had best forget your private differences and concentrate on the task in hand.'

In the bitter wind, with sea and spindrift reaching further out on either beam as the grey light continued to expand, it was hard to think of plots and schemers in high places. This was the place which truly counted. If England lost command of the seas she would surely lose everything else, with freedom at the top of the tally.

He was glad all the same that he had taken every precaution he could think of. If he was to be proved mistaken he would have lost nothing. But if not – He turned as the lookout yelled, 'Deck there! Th' Dane's gone about!'

Poland staggered as another sea lifted and burst over the beakhead, his hands gripped behind him, his body responding to the deck's movements with the ease of a rider on a well-trained stallion.

Bolitho moved away, his eyes slitted against the weather as he watched a faint blur of land seemingly far away to larboard. In fact he knew it was probably less than two miles distant. Poland was staying as close-hauled as he dared, using the north-east wind to weather the headland, The Skaw as it was respectfully called. He thought suddenly of his own elation when he had been roused by Allday on that other occasion when they had sighted The Lizard; what Catherine had later told him about her certainty that he had been near, although she could not possibly have known.

'All hands! All hands! Stand by to wear ship!'

Red-eyed and sagging with fatigue, their bodies bruised and bloodied by their fight with wind and sea, *Truculent*'s seamen and marines staggered to their stations at halliards and braces like old men or drunkards.

Poland called sharply, 'Get your best topmen aloft, Mr Williams – I want the t'gan's'ls on her as soon as we are on the new course.' He glared at Hull, the sailing master. 'This must be smartly done, sir!' It sounded like a threat.

Williams raised his speaking-trumpet. How his arm must ache, Bolitho thought. 'Stand by on the quarterdeck!' He waited, judging the moment. 'Alter course three points to larboard!' He gestured angrily with the speaking-trumpet as a wave swept over the nettings and hurled several men from their positions, while others stood firm, crouching and spitting out mouthfuls of water.

'Mr Lancer! More hands on the lee braces there!'

Poland nodded, his chin close to his chest. 'Put up your helm!'

With a thunder of canvas and the squeal of blocks *Truculent* began to pay off to the wind, so that the sails refilled and held the ship almost upright instead of lying over to the mercy of the gale.

193

Poland consulted the compass and said, 'Hold her *steady*, Mr Hull.'

Bolitho saw the master glare at his back as he replied smartly, 'Steady she goes, sir! West-by-north.'

'*Deck there!*'

Poland peered up at the scudding, full-bellied clouds, his features raw from endless hours on deck. 'What does that fool want?'

The lookout called again, 'Sail on the starboard quarter!'

Poland looked along the length of his ship where men bustled about amidst the confusion of water and broken rigging, while they carried out repairs as they would perform under fire. Duty, discipline and tradition. It was all they knew.

He said, 'Get somebody aloft with a glass, Mr Williams.' Poland darted a quick glance at Bolitho by the weather rail. How could he have known?

Bolitho saw the glance. It was as if Poland had shouted the question out loud. He felt the tension draining out of him, the uncertainty replaced by a cold, bitter logic.

A master's mate, Hull's best, had been sent to the masthead, and soon he bellowed down in a voice which had become as hardened to a sailor's life as a cannon which has seen a world of battles.

'Deck thar! Man-o'-war, zur!' A long pause while *Truculent* surged and dipped her jib-boom into a mountainous wave. It felt like striking a sandbar. Then he yelled, 'Small 'un, zur! Corvette, aye, 'tis a corvette!'

Hull muttered, 'If 'e says she's a corvette, then *that she be!*'

Poland walked unsteadily towards Bolitho and touched his hat with stiff formality. 'Frenchman, Sir Richard.' He hesitated before adding, 'Too small to hamper us.'

'Big enough to seek us out, Captain Poland, to hang to our coat-tails until –' He shrugged and said, 'Whatever it is we shall soon know.'

Poland digested it and asked, 'Orders, Sir Richard?'

Bolitho looked past him at the listless exhausted seamen. Poland was right. No corvette would dare to challenge a thirty-six gun frigate. So her captain must know that he would not be alone for much longer; and then . . .

He heard himself reply, 'Have the boatswain's party clear out the galley and relight the fires immediately.' He ignored Poland's expression. His face was full of questions; the galley had obviously not been high on his list. 'Your people are in no state to fight – they are worn out. A good hot meal, and a double ration of rum, and you will have men who will follow your orders and not give in at the first whiff of grape.' He saw Poland nod and said, 'I must see Sir Charles Inskip. I fear he is in for another unpleasant surprise.'

Allday was standing close by and saw one of the seamen nudge his companion with a grin. 'See, Bill? Our Dick's not bothered, so why should we be, eh?'

Allday sighed. *Our Dick.* Now they were his men too.

Then he thought about the rum and licked his lips in anticipation. A good 'wet' was always welcome. Especially when it might be your last.

Catherine paused at the foot of the steps and glanced along the street with its tall elegant houses and leafless trees. It was late afternoon and already dark enough for the carriages to show their lamps. She had been shopping in some of the adjoining streets with Yovell as her companion, and sometimes adviser, especially on matters concerning the man he served so loyally.

She waved to the coachman, still called Young Matthew even though his grandfather Old Matthew, who had been the Bolitho coachman for many years, was long dead. It was good to have the light, elegant carriage here, she thought. A part of home. It seemed strange that she could think of Falmouth and the old grey house as *home.*

'You can go to the mews, Young Matthew, I'll not need you again today.' He grinned down at her and touched his hat with his whip. 'Very well, m'lady.' One of Lord Browne's servants had come down the steps and she curtsied, her apron ribbons whipping out in the cold wind, before going to help Yovell with their many parcels.

'Oh, m'lady!' The girl called after her but Catherine was already in the hall. She stood stock-still with surprise, even shock, as she saw a uniformed figure standing inside the book-lined library, his hands held out to the fire.

She waited a few seconds, her hand to her breast, until her breathing became steady again. It was foolish, but just for a moment she had believed – But the tall captain had fair hair and blue eyes: a friend for so many reasons. Captain Valentine Keen took her hand and kissed it. 'I beg your pardon, m'lady, for coming unannounced. I was at the Admiralty, too near to miss the chance of seeing you.'

She slipped her hand through his arm and together they walked towards the fire.

'You are always welcome, Val.' She studied him thoughtfully. He too had known Richard a long time and had served him as midshipman and lieutenant, until he had eventually become his flag-captain. She said quietly, 'Please call me Catherine. We are friends, remember?' She seated herself opposite and waited for him to follow suit. 'What ails you, Val? We have been worried. About you and Zenoria. Is there something I can do?'

He did not reply directly. 'I heard about Sir Richard at the Admiralty.' He glanced around as if expecting to see him. 'He is not returned yet?'

She shook her head. 'It is far longer than we supposed. Four weeks today.'

Keen watched her as she turned to stare into the fire. A beautiful, sensuous woman. One whom men would fight over, one who could excite the one she loved to do almost anything. But she was deeply troubled, and was not trying to hide it.

He said, 'I was told by one of Lord Godschale's aides that he had been on a mission of some importance. But the weather is foul, especially in our waters. I daresay they are riding it out.' He felt her gaze settle on him and he said, 'Zenoria was staying with my sisters. Perhaps they smothered her with too much kindness . . . maybe she felt she no longer cared about me –'

Catherine said, 'The marriage – is it not agreed upon?'

'She left to return to the West Country. There is an uncle, apparently, in whom she used to confide when she was a child, before he went to the Indies. Now he is back in Cornwall – I know not where. She is with him.'

Catherine watched his despair. She knew it, remembered it.

'But you *love* her?' She saw him nod. It made him look like a young boy. 'And I do know she loves you, for many, many

196

reasons. You saved her life, you cared for her when others would have turned their backs. Believe me, Val, I know about such matters at first hand!'

'That is partly why I came. I received a letter from Sir Richard. Did you know . . . Catherine?'

She smiled despite her anxiety. 'That is better. Yes, I knew. About his new flagship, the *Black Prince*. He wants you as his captain, but I will lay odds that he spoke only of your hoped-for marriage?'

'You know him well.' He smiled ruefully. 'It is why I went to see Lord Godschale. He was becoming impatient.'

She touched her throat and remembered what Bolitho had said about it.

'That is not so unusual, I believe.'

Keen faced her resolutely. 'I have made it clear. I *will* serve as his flag-captain.' He was surprised at her reaction, as if some sort of threat had been removed. 'Are you pleased?'

'Of course I am. Who better to stand by my man's side in times of peril? He loves you in the same way he cares for young Adam. I was afraid he would have some stupid captain like –' She dropped her eyes. 'That is another matter.' When she looked up again her dark eyes were flashing. 'And have no fear about your Zenoria. I will find her, although I suspect she will find me first once I am returned to Falmouth. We understand one another. She *shall* be your bride, Val, but you must be gentle with her. I know from what Richard tells me that you are a decent man, and have only loved one other in your life.' She watched the memories clouding his eyes. 'This will be different, more wonderful than you can conceive. But as *she* will learn to accept your calling as a sailor, so must you be patient with her.' She let each word sink in. 'Remember what happened to her. A young girl. Taken and used, with no hope, and nothing to live for.'

He nodded, seeing her naked back as the whip had laid it open from shoulder to hip. The way she had withdrawn when he had spoken of marriage and how it would be for them.

'I never thought. Or perhaps I did not want to think about it. How she would feel, or if she was tormented that she might never be able to accept –' He could not continue.

She stood up and walked to his chair, and laid her hand on his shoulder, touching his epaulette. Each time she saw a sea-officer she thought of him. What he might be doing; whether or not he was in any danger.

'There, Val. You feel better now? And so do I.' She made light of it. 'After all, I cannot rely on Mr Allday for everything!'

The door opened and she felt a chill draught from the hallway, although she had heard no bell or knock at the street entrance.

'Who is it, Maisie?'

The girl stared at her, then at Keen.

'Beg pardon, m'lady, but 'tis a gentleman for the captain.'

Keen stood up. 'I mentioned I would be here a while. I hope that was acceptable?'

Catherine watched him, her gaze very level. 'What is it? Something has happened.'

He said only, 'Please wait here, Catherine.'

The servant girl gaped at her. 'Would you like some tea, m'lady?'

She realised only vaguely what she had asked. 'No, but thank you.'

The door closed, reluctantly or so it seemed, as if the servant had wanted to share what was happening.

Keen came back, his handsome features grave as he shut the door behind him. He strode across the carpet and took her hands in his. They were like ice. 'It was a messenger from the Admiralty.' He gripped her hands more tightly as she pulled away. 'No, hear me. He will want you to know.' He saw a pulse beating in her throat, saw the way she lifted her chin. Dread, defiance; it was all there.

'There has been a sea-fight. Richard's ship was involved but they know little more as yet. He must have been returning to England from his mission. A schooner brought the news to Portsmouth, and the telegraph sent word from there to the Admiralty.'

She stared round the room like a trapped animal.

'Is he hurt? What must I do? I must be there if –'

He guided her to a chair, knowing it was not strength or courage she was lacking, but a direction to point herself.

'You must wait here, Catherine.' He saw the anxiety change

198

to resistance and refusal, and persisted, 'He will *expect* you to be here.' He dropped on one knee beside her chair. 'You have helped me so much. Let me at least try to do the same for you. I will remain at your service until we learn what is happening.'

'*When?*' One word, which sounded as if it was torn from her.

'It must be soon. Tomorrow, the next day. I felt something was wrong, and yet –' He looked past her into the fire. 'I was too beset with my own troubles.'

Catherine looked at the gold lace on his sleeve. Was this how it was? How it would be? After all their hopes. Their love. So many women must have known it.

She thought suddenly of Nelson, of Bolitho's bitterness at those who had hated him the most but who had mourned his death the loudest. Nobody spoke of Emma Hamilton any more. It was as if she had never been, even though she had given him the things he had lacked and had needed more than anything. Love and admiration. It was rare to have one without the other.

She said quietly but firmly, 'I will never give him up.'

Keen was not certain how it was meant, but he was deeply moved.

She stood up and walked towards the door where she turned, the lights reflecting from her dark hair.

'Please stay, Val.' She seemed to hesitate. 'But I am going to our room for a while. So that we may be together.'

13

No Escape

Bolitho gripped the quarterdeck rail and watched the sky brighten to a harsh intensity. Beneath his fingers the rail was so caked with salt that it felt like rough stone. But the motion was easier as *Truculent*, now with her topgallants filled hard to the wind, plunged over a wild succession of curling wavecrests.

He stared at the sun as it tried to break through the morning haze. It was like a bright silver platter, he thought, while the aimless bunches of cloud reminded him of fog above the Helford River at home in Cornwall. The air was still tinged with the smell of grease from the galley, and he had seen the seamen at work about the upper deck showing less strain than before he had suggested to Poland that a good hot meal was a priority.

He tried to picture the ship as she headed south-west, the wind following her from dead astern so that she seemed to bound over the water. Somewhere, about forty miles across the starboard quarter, were the bleak shores and fjords of Norway, beyond which lay only the Arctic. Part of the Danish coast was still abeam, and according to the sailing master's rough calculations some thirty miles distant. Far enough to be out of sight but still within the range of *Zest*'s patrol area. He thought of Poland's dislike for *Zest*'s captain. If he had had more time in London he might have discovered some reason for it. But he doubted it. It was like some secret held closely by each captain as if for protection, or threat.

He shaded his eyes to stare astern but their pursuer was not in sight from the deck. A lance of silver sunlight touched his eye, and he winced before pressing his hand over it while he took another look.

Inskip had appeared at his side. 'Your eye bothering you?'

Bolitho snatched his hand away. '*No.*' He added in a calmer voice, 'You are feeling more the thing now that we are in open water again?' He must try not to be taken by surprise by such an innocent comment. Inskip had no way of knowing. And besides, there was every hope that his eye would recover completely. Grasping at straws? Perhaps, but it barely troubled him.

Inskip smiled. 'I suspect your man Allday can take more credit than the damned sea.'

Bolitho noticed for the first time that there was an unusually strong smell of rum, and that Inskip's normally pallid features were glowing.

Inskip cleared his throat noisily. 'Damme if he didn't produce a potion he had concocted himself. Hot gruel, rum and brandy seem to be the main ingredients!'

Bolitho glanced at Poland who was deep in conversation with his first lieutenant. They both looked to the mastheads, and after a further discussion a warrant officer was sent aloft to join the lookout, a heavy telescope bouncing from one hip.

Inskip asked worriedly, 'What does it mean?' He gestured vaguely towards the taffrail. 'That Frenchman can't do us any harm, surely?'

Bolitho saw Poland gazing at him across the deck. It was almost like defiance.

'I'd tell the captain to come about and go for that corvette, if I didn't think it would waste valuable time.' He rubbed his chin while he pictured his chart again. 'He's hanging on to the scent. A scavenger – like a wild dog on a battlefield, waiting to pick off the bones.' He heard Poland call, 'Prepare to set the main-course, Mr Williams! I'll not lose this soldier's wind!'

The deck shuddered and the taut rigging seemed to whine as the ship plunged forward under a growing pyramid of canvas.

Bolitho saw Jenour by the compass, and wondered if he had guessed why Poland was piling on more sail.

Inskip said vaguely, 'Funny thing about eyes, though.' He did not see Bolitho glance at him warily. 'When I was honoured by the King, for instance –' His words were becoming slurred;

Allday's cure must be working well – 'His Majesty wore a green eye shield all the while, and they say he cannot recognise a single soul without a strong glass.'

Bolitho recalled the general's dry comment about guiding the King's hand. Truer than he had realised perhaps.

Inskip said abruptly, 'You think we're running into a trap, don't you?' The combined power of rum and brandy had put an aggressive edge to his tone. 'How could that possibly be – and where would be the point?'

Bolitho replied quietly, 'We were delayed a full week. Where would be the point of *that*?'

Inskip brooded on it. 'It was all a secret, and anyway, what could the enemy hope to achieve in a week?'

Bolitho said, 'When the schooner *Pickle* arrived at Falmouth on November fourth last year, her commanding officer, a Lieutenant Lapenotière, was the first man to bring the news of Trafalgar and Nelson's death to England.' He let each word sink in; it was important that Inskip should understand. 'Lapenotière posted all the way from Falmouth to London to carry the word to the Admiralty.'

'*And?*' Inskip was sweating despite the bitter air.

'He reached London on the morning of the sixth. All that way, *in just two days*. Imagine what French intelligence could make of a full week!'

He looked at the sky, a thinning here and there in the clouds revealing slivers of glacier blue.

The senior helmsman called, 'Steady she be, zur! Sou'-west!'

Bolitho added, 'South-west, Sir Charles, but over four hundred miles to make good, unless –' He saw Poland moving towards him. 'What is it?'

Poland turned as if to keep his comments from Inskip's ears. 'May I suggest we alter course and run further to the south'rd, Sir Richard?' He looked towards the misty horizon, the drifting spray like steam over the beakhead. 'It would add to the distance, but –'

Bolitho faced him impassively. 'We should also lose any chance of a rendezvous on *Zest*'s station. But you already knew that?'

It was rare for Poland to offer such a definite suggestion, one which might later lay him open to criticism or worse.

Bolitho persisted, 'Do you have any cause to doubt Captain Varian's intentions?' He watched the emotions, the anxieties troubling Poland's features. 'It is your *duty* to tell me. The responsibility of command which you have earned, and which you obviously cherish, makes that duty unavoidable!'

Poland looked trapped. Alone with his command he was second only to God. Faced by a vice-admiral whose name was known throughout most of the country, he was suddenly stripped of power, endangered by his one, unexpected outburst.

He answered wretchedly, 'I served with Varian some years ago. I was his first lieutenant, and I must admit that out there in the Indies I saw small chance of promotion, let alone a ship to command. We were ordered to Jamaica at the urgent request of the Governor . . . there was a slave uprising with some danger to the residents and the plantations.'

Bolitho could see it. That would have been during the uneasy Peace of Amiens when many had thought the war had ended, that France and her allies, like England, had exhausted themselves in constant battle at sea and on land. As first lieutenant, Poland would have grasped at the chance of action like a drowning man clutching a piece of cork.

'I recall it. There were a lot of killings and some savage reprisals, to all accounts.'

Poland did not seem to have heard him. 'We had word from a trader that a plantation was under siege by a mob of slaves. It was too far inland to quell it with gunfire, so Captain Varian ordered me to take an armed party to rout the slaves.' He wiped his mouth with the back of his hand, oblivious to Jenour and the watchful eyes of Lieutenant Williams by the quarterdeck rail. '*Mob*? By God, when we reached the place it was more like a blood-crazed army!' He shuddered. 'The owners and their people had been hacked to death like ribbons, their wives – well, they must have welcomed death when it came!'

'And Varian weighed anchor, am I right?'

Poland gaped at him. '*Aye*, Sir Richard. He thought we would share the same fate as those poor butchered creatures. Varian could not stand the prospect of failure, or being associated with one. He sailed away and reported to the admiral that he had lost contact with us and had been unable to help.' He added with

203

sudden anger, 'But for the arrival of some local militia, he would have been right too!'

'Deck there! Corvette's makin' more sail!'

Bolitho saw the emptiness in Poland's stare and thought he may not even have heard.

Poland continued in the same flat voice. 'Varian's never been in a big action. Hunting smugglers and chasing privateers were more to his taste.' He seemed to draw himself up as he faced Bolitho with some of his old stiffness. 'I should have denounced him. I am not proud of what I did. He recommended me for command.' He looked along his ship. 'I got *Truculent*, so I said naught.'

Bolitho tugged his hat more firmly over his forehead to give himself time to think. If half of it was true then Varian was a menace to everyone who depended on him. He thought of *Zest*'s being off-station at Good Hope; the terrible end of the little schooner *Miranda* while her executioner sped to safety.

A coward then?

'Deck there!' Bolitho saw Jenour shading his eyes to peer up at the foremast crosstrees. 'Sail on the weather bow!'

Poland stared from the masthead to Bolitho. 'I am sorry, Sir Richard. I spoke too soon!' He was probably seeing his only command already slipping away from his grasp.

Inskip swallowed hard. 'You're *both* wrong, dammit!' He wiped his eyes with his handkerchief. 'I'll wager *Zest* makes that damned Frenchie show a clean pair of heels!'

'Deck there!' The foremast lookout's voice was suddenly loud as wind spilled from the topsails. '*She's a French frigate, sir!*'

Bolitho saw faces turn to look towards him, not at their captain this time. So *Zest* was not waiting for them. Instead, the trap was about to be sprung. Bolitho looked at Inskip's flushed face and kept his voice calm. 'No, Sir Charles, *I fear we were both right*.' He swung on Poland. 'Clear for action, if you please!'

'Deck there!' Someone by the wheel gave a groan as the lookout yelled, '*Second* sail astern of t'other, sir!'

'The corvette has run up her colours, sir!'

Poland licked his lips. Two ships closing on a converging tack, another still hounding them from astern. To starboard was the full power of the wind, on the opposite beam and still out of sight was the Danish coast. In those fleeting seconds he could see it all. Jaws closing around his ship. Be run ashore in a hopeless stern-chase, or stand and be destroyed by overwhelming odds. He looked at his first lieutenant, his eyes dull. 'Beat to quarters, Mr Williams, and clear for action at your convenience.'

The marine fifers ran to the stations, adjusting their drums until they received a curt nod from the Royal Marines sergeant.

Bolitho saw Allday striding across the deck, his cutlass wedged carelessly through his belt. Jenour too, fingering his beautiful sword, his face suddenly determined as the drums commenced their urgent rattle to arms.

Inskip gasped, 'Maybe *Zest* will be here yet?' Nobody spoke, and his voice was almost drowned by the rush of bare feet, the stamp of marines across the poop and the thud and clatter of screens being torn down to clear the ship of obstructions. 'Why such a show of force?' He was almost pleading.

Bolitho watched *Truculent*'s big ensigns mounting to gaff and masthead. A challenge accepted.

He said, 'They *knew*, Sir Charles. One of His Majesty's most important emissaries and a senior officer for good measure! Exactly the excuse the French have been looking for. If we are taken, Napoleon will have all he needs to discredit the Danes for their secret discussions with us, and so weaken Sweden's and Russia's resolution to stand against him! Good God, man, even a child should see that!'

Inskip did not rise to Bolitho's angry contempt. He stared around at the gun-crews, the bustle with tackles and hand-spikes as each weapon was prepared to fight.

Then he peered overhead at the nets which were being rigged across the decks from gangway to gangway to protect these same crews from falling spars and debris. Even the boats were being swayed out and made ready to lower and cast adrift for the victors to recover.

Boats represented survival to most sailors, and Bolitho saw some of them turn from their work to watch, and the grim response from the scarlet squads of marines who fingered their Brown Bess muskets and fixed bayonets. If so ordered, they would shoot down anyone who created a panic or provoked any sort of disorder.

205

It was always a bad moment, Bolitho thought. Survival perhaps; but the peril of razor-sharp splinters hurled from tiered boats once battle was joined was far more dangerous.

Williams touched his hat, his eyes wild. 'Cleared for action, sir!'

Poland looked at him coldly and then said, 'That was smartly done, Mr Williams.' He looked past him and at the lines of watching gun-crews, men who moments before had been thinking only of getting another tot to reward them for their efforts. 'Do not load or run out as yet.' He turned and faced Bolitho. 'We are ready, Sir Richard.' His pale eyes were opaque, like a man already dead.

Inskip touched Bolitho's sleeve. 'Shall you *fight* them?' He sounded incredulous.

Bolitho did not answer. 'You may hoist my flag at the fore, Captain Poland. I think there are no more secrets left to keep.'

Inskip's shoulders seemed to droop. It was perhaps the clearest reply of all.

As the next hour dragged remorselessly past, the sky grew clearer, the clouds breaking up as if to give every light to the scene. But the sun held no warmth, and spray when it flew over the tightly-packed hammock nettings felt like fragments of ice.

Bolitho took the big telescope from the senior midshipman and walked to the mizzen shrouds. Without haste he climbed into the ratlines and steadied himself while he waited for his mind to clear. He could see the leading French frigate quite easily, still holding on to her original converging tack, every sail spread and bulging from the wind. She was big, forty guns or more at a guess, with her Tricolour standing out like bright metal. The other vessel was slightly smaller, but well equal to *Truculent*. Very deliberately he raised the heavy glass and watched the picture sharpen. How near she looked now; he could imagine the sounds of voices and the creak of gun-tackles as the crews waited impatiently for the order to run out. Around and behind his back he could sense a silence, and knew that all eyes were on him as he studied the enemy. Measuring their chances against his confidence. Seeing death in any uncertainty. The French were taking their time despite the great press of canvas. If there was to be any chance . . . he slammed the glass shut with sudden anger. *I must never think like that, or we are already lost.*

He returned to the deck and handed the telescope to the midshipman.

'Thank you, Mr Fellowes.' He did not see the pleased surprise in the youth's eyes at the easy familiarity of his name. He crossed to Poland's side where Inskip and his secretary, the lugubrious Agnew, waited anxiously for his assessment.

Bolitho avoided the others and said, 'Captain Poland, make more sail if you please.' He glanced up at the braced yards and lofty sails framed by the washed-out blue sky. 'The wind has eased somewhat – you will not tear the sticks out of her, I think.'

He expected a protest, even an argument, but before Poland turned away to pass his orders to the first lieutenant, Bolitho thought he saw something like relief on his set features. Calls trilled and once again hands clambered aloft with the agility of monkeys. From the quarterdeck Bolitho saw the great mainyard bending like a bow to the following wind, heard the crack and rattle of canvas as the remaining royals were freed to lend their thrust to the ship.

Poland came back breathing hard. 'Sir?'

Bolitho looked at him searchingly. Not a man who would crack, no matter what he might think of the coming fight and its likely conclusion. 'The French will adopt their usual tactics today. The leading ship will continue to close until she can reach us with her fire.' He saw Poland's bleak eyes following his arm as he pointed over towards the enemy, as if he could already see the lurid flash of cannon fire. 'It is my belief that their senior officer will be confident, perhaps too much so.'

Inskip muttered, 'So would *I* be, in his shoes!'

Bolitho ignored him. 'He will try to cripple *Truculent*, doubtless with chain-shot or langridge, while his consort attempts to rake our stern. A divided attack is commonly used in this way.' He watched his words hitting home. 'It must not happen.' He saw Poland flinch as a line snapped somewhere high above the deck. Like a pistol shot. 'If they are allowed to board us we'll be done for.' He nodded beyond the stern. 'And there is always our little scavenger waiting to lend her weight to the fight.'

207

Poland licked his lips. 'What must we do, Sir Richard?'

Inskip snapped, 'It's hopeless, if you ask me!'

Bolitho turned on him. 'Well, I do *not*, Sir Charles! So if you have nothing sensible to offer I suggest you go below to the orlop and do something useful to help the surgeon!' He saw Inskip flush with anger, and added bitterly, 'And *if* you ever reach London again, may I suggest that you explain to your masters, and mine, what they are asking people to do!' He waved his hand briefly over the crouching gun-crews. 'What *they* face each time a King's ship is called to arms!'

When he turned again Inskip and his secretary had disappeared. He smiled at Poland's surprise and said, 'It were better left to us, I think, eh, Captain?' He felt suddenly calm again, so much so that there was no sensation left in his limbs. 'I ordered more sail so that the French will think we are trying to run for it. They are already following suit, I see, every stitch they can muster, for this is a rich prize indeed. English *plotters* and a fine frigate to boot – no, the Frenchman will not wish to lose out on this!'

Poland nodded with slow understanding. 'You intend to luff and come about, Sir Richard?'

'Aye.' He touched his arm. 'Come walk awhile. The enemy will not be in useful range for half an hour at a guess. I have always found it helps to loosen the muscles, relax the mind.' He smiled at him, knowing how important it was for *Truculent*'s company to see their captain at ease.

Bolitho added, 'It will have to be smartly done, sails reduced instantly as the helm goes over. Then we can tack between them and rake them both.'

Poland nodded jerkily. 'I have always trained them well, Sir Richard!'

Bolitho clasped his hands behind him. That was more like it. Poland rising to any sort of criticism. *He had to believe.* He must think only of the first move.

Bolitho said, 'May I suggest you place your first lieutenant by the foremast so that he can control, even point each gun himself. There will be no time for a second chance.' He saw him nod. 'It is no place for a junior lieutenant.'

Poland called to Williams and while they were in deep

208

discussion, with several meaning glances towards the nearest pyramid of sails, Bolitho said to Jenour, 'Keep on the move, Stephen.' He saw the flag-lieutenant's eyes blink. 'It will be warm work today, I fear.'

Allday massaged his chest with his hand and watched the too familiar preparations, and the way the third lieutenant stared at Williams as he passed him on his way aft. He probably saw his own removal from the forward guns as a lack of confidence in his ability. He would soon know why, Allday decided. He thought suddenly of Bolitho's offer.

Perhaps a little alehouse near Falmouth, with a rosy-cheeked widow-woman to take care of. No more danger, the scream of shot and dying men, the awful crash of falling spars. And pain, always the pain.

'Leadin' ship's runnin' out, sir!'

Poland glanced at Bolitho and then snapped, 'Very well, open the ports. Load and run out the *starboard* battery!'

Bolitho clenched his fist. Poland had remembered. Had he run out the guns on either side it would have shown the enemy what he intended as plainly as if he had spelled out a signal.

'Ready, sir!' That was Williams, somehow out of place up forward instead of on the quarterdeck.

'*Run out!*'

Squealing like disgruntled hogs, the maindeck eighteen-pounders trundled up to their ports, each crew watching the other so that the broadside was presented as one.

There was a dull bang and seconds later a thin waterspout leapt from the sea some fifty yards from the starboard bow. A sighting shot.

Poland wiped his face with his fingers. 'Stand by to come about! *Be ready*, Mr Hull!'

Bolitho saw Munro, the second lieutenant, stride to the chart-table near the companion hatch and pull aside its canvas cover.

Bolitho walked slowly past the tense group around the wheel, the marines waiting at braces and halliards, knowing that with so much canvas above them one error could crush them under an avalanche of broken masts and rigging.

The young lieutenant stiffened as Bolitho's shadow fell across

209

the open log book, in which he had just noted the time of the first shot.

'Is there something I can do, Sir Richard?'

'I was just looking at the date. But no, it's not important.'

He moved away again and knew that Allday had drawn nearer to him.

It was his birthday. Bolitho touched the shape of the locket through his shirt. *May love always protect you.*

It was like hearing her speak those same words aloud.

Poland slammed down his hand. '*Now!*'

In seconds, or so it seemed, the great courses were brailed and fisted to their yards, opening up to the sea around them like curtains on a stage.

'*Helm-a-lee! Hard over, damn your eyes!*'

Voices and calls echoed over the deck as men threw themselves on the braces to haul the yards round while the deck swayed over to the violent change of course. Gun-crews abandoned their charges and ran to the opposite side to supplement the depleted numbers there, and as the ports squeaked open they ran out their eighteen-pounders, aided this time by the steep tilt of the deck. Spray lanced through the ports and over the nettings, and some of the crew gaped in astonishment as the leading French frigate seemed to materialise right before their eyes, when moments earlier she had been on the opposite beam.

'*As you bear!*' Lieutenant Williams held up his sword as he lurched along the deck by the larboard carronade. 'A guinea for the first strike!'

A midshipman named Brown shouted, 'I'll double that, sir!'

They grinned at one another like urchins.

'*Fire!*'

The battery fired as one, the deafening roar of the long eighteen-pounders completely blocking out the sounds of the enemy's response. The French captain had been taken by surprise, and only half of his guns had been brought to bear on the wildly tacking *Truculent*. The enemy's sails were in total chaos as her topmen tried to take the way off her and follow *Truculent's* example.

Aft by the compass box, Bolitho felt the deck shudder as some of the enemy's iron crashed into the hull. The sea's face was feathered with flying chain-shot which had been intended for *Truculent*'s mast and rigging.

Poland yelled, 'Stand by to starboard, Mr Williams!'

Men scampered back to their stations at the other battery, as they had drilled so many times. The range was much greater, and the second French ship lay bows on, her topsails rippling and spilling wind while her captain tried to change tack.

'As you bear, lads!' Williams crouched by the first division of guns, then sliced the air with his sword. '*Fire!*'

Bolitho held his breath as gun by gun along *Truculent*'s side the long orange tongues spat out from this carefully timed broadside. But the enemy was still almost end-on, a difficult target at a range of some two cables. He hid his disbelief as like a great tree the frigate's foremast seemed to bow forward under the pressure of the wind. But it did not stop; and with it went the trailing mass of broken shrouds and running rigging, and then the whole topmast, until the forward part of the vessel was completely hidden by fallen debris. It must have been almost the last shot of the battery. But just one eighteen-pound ball was enough.

Bolitho looked at Poland's smoke-stained features. 'Better odds, Captain?'

The seamen, who were already training the quarterdeck nine-pounders with their handspikes, looked at him and gave a hoarse cheer.

Allday slitted his eyes against the funnelling smoke and watched the leading frigate as she eventually came under command. She lay down to larboard now, her maincourse brailed up, but several others punctured by *Truculent*'s cannon fire. Bolitho had stolen the wind-gage from the Frenchie, but it was all they had. One thing was certain: Poland could never have done it, would never have *tried* to attempt it. He saw Bolitho glance up at the sails and then towards the enemy. As in memory. Like at The Saintes in their first ship together, the *Phalarope*. Bolitho was still that captain, no matter what his rank and title said. He glared at the cheering, capering seamen. *Fools.* They would change their tune damn soon. He gripped his cutlass more tightly. *And here it comes.*

Williams raised his sword and looked aft at the captain. 'Ready to larboard, sir!'

'*Fire!*'

The ship staggered to the thunder and recoil of the guns, while the pale smoke billowed downwind towards the enemy.

It was like grinding over a reef or running into a sandbar, so that for a long moment men seemed to stare at one another as the enemy's broadside crashed into the hull or screamed through the canvas and rigging overhead. The spread nets jumped with fallen cordage and blocks, and a scarlet-coated marine dropped from the maintop before lying spreadeagled above one of the gun-crews.

Bolitho coughed out smoke and thought briefly of Inskip down in the reeling gloom of the orlop. The first wounded would already be on their way there. He looked at the marine's corpse on the nets. It was a marvel nothing vital had been shot away.

He saw Jenour wiping his eyes with his forearm, dazed by the onslaught.

'Captain Poland, prepare to alter course, if you please. We will steer due west!' But when he looked through the thinning smoke he saw that Poland was down, one leg doubled under him, his fingers clutching his throat as if to stem the blood which flooded over his coat like paint. Bolitho dropped on his knee beside him. 'Take him to the surgeon!' But Poland shook his head so violently that Bolitho saw the gaping hole in his neck where a fragment of iron had cut him down. He was dying, choking on his own blood as he tried to speak.

Lieutenant Munro joined him, his tanned face as pale as death.

Very slowly, Bolitho stood up and looked towards the enemy. 'Your captain is dead, Mr Munro. Pass the word to the others.' He glanced down at Poland's contorted features. Even in death his eyes were somehow angry and disapproving. It was terrible to see him die with a curse on his lips, although he guessed that he had been the only one close enough to hear it.

His last words on earth had been, '*God's damnation on Varian, the cowardly bastard!*'

Bolitho saw Williams staring aft towards him, his hat gone but the sword still gripped in his hand.

212

Bolitho watched a seaman cover Poland's body with some canvas, then he walked up to the quarterdeck rail as he had done so many times in the past.

He thought of Poland's despairing curse and said aloud, 'And *my* damnation too!' Then he dropped his hand and felt the ship's anger erupt in another savage broadside.

Jenour called huskily, 'The corvette's closing, sir!'

'I see her. Warn the starboard battery, then pass the word to the marines in the tops. *Nobody will board this ship!*' He stared at Jenour and knew he was speaking wildly. '*Nobody!*'

Jenour tore his eyes away and called to a boatswain's mate. But just for a few seconds he had seen a Bolitho he had not known before. Like a man who faced destiny and accepted it. A man without fear; without hate and maybe without hope either. He saw Bolitho turn away from the drifting smoke and look towards his coxswain. The glance excluded everyone, so that the death and danger seemed almost incidental for that one precious moment. They smiled at each other, and before the guns opened fire once again Jenour tried to recall what he had seen in Bolitho's expression as he had glanced at his friend. If it was anything, it was like an apology, he decided.

Bolitho had seen Jenour's desperate gaze but forgot him as the guns thundered again and recoiled on their tackles. Like demons the crews flung themselves to their tasks of sponging out the smoking muzzles, before ramming home fresh charges and finally the black, evil-looking shot. Their naked backs were begrimed from powder smoke, sweat cutting pale lines through it in spite of the bitter wind and floating droplets of spray.

There was blood on the deck too, while here and there great blackened scores cut across the usually immaculate planking, where French balls had come smashing inboard. One of the larboard eighteen-pounders had been upended and a man lay dying beneath its massive weight, his skin burning under the overheated barrel. Others had been pulled aside to keep the deck clear for the small powder monkeys who scurried from gun to gun, not daring to look up as they dropped their charges and ran back for more.

Two corpses, so mutilated by flying metal that they were barely recognisable, were lifted momentarily above the nettings before being cast into the sea. Burial when it came was as ruthless as the death which had marked them down.

Bolitho took a telescope from its rack and stared at the other frigate until his eye throbbed. Like *Truculent*, she had been hit many times and her sails were shot through, some ripping apart to the pressure of the wind. Rigging, severed and untended, swayed from the yards like creeper, but her guns were still firing from every port, and Bolitho could feel some of the iron hitting the lower hull. In the rare pauses, while men fell about their work like demented souls in hell, he could hear the tell-tale sound of pumps, and almost expected to hear Poland's incisive tones urging one of his lieutenants to bid them work all the harder.

The glass settled on the other frigate's poop and he saw her captain staring back at him through his own telescope. He shifted it slightly and saw dead and dying men around the wheel, and knew that some of Williams' double-shotted guns had reaped a terrible harvest.

But they must hurt her, slow her down before her guns could find some weakness in *Truculent*'s defences.

He lowered the glass and yelled to Williams, 'Point your guns abaft her mainmast and fire on the uproll!'

His words were lost in another ragged barrage, but a petty officer heard them, and knuckled his forehead as he dashed through the smoke to tell the first lieutenant.

He saw Williams peer aft and nod, his teeth very white in his bronzed face. Did he see his real chance of promotion now Poland was dead, as his captain had once done? Or did he only see the nearness of death?

Pieces of gangway burst from the side and scattered ripped and singed hammocks across the deck like faceless puppets. Metal clanged from one of the guns and men fell kicking and writhing as its splinters pitched them down in their own blood. One, the young midshipman named Brown whom Bolitho had seen joking with the first lieutenant, was hurled almost to the opposite side, most of his face shot away.

Bolitho thought wildly of Falmouth. He had seen enough stones there. This young fourteen-year-old midshipman would probably have one too when the news reached England. *Who died for the Honour of his King and Country*. What would his loved ones think if they had seen the 'honour' of his death?

'*Again, on the uproll!*' Bolitho reeled back from the rail while the guns roared out. Some spars fell from the Frenchman's mizzen, and one of her topsails was reduced to floating ribbons. But the flag still flew, and the guns had not lost their fury.

Lieutenant Munro shouted, 'She's closing the range, Sir Richard!'

Bolitho nodded, and winced as a ball slammed through an open port and cut a marine in half while he stood guarding the mainhatch. He saw Midshipman Fellowes stuffing his fist into his mouth to prevent himself from retching or screaming at the sight – he could be blamed for neither.

Munro lowered his glass. 'T'other frigate is still adrift, Sir Richard, but they're cutting the wreckage clear.'

'Yes. If she rejoins the fight before we can cripple the –'

There was a loud crack behind him and he heard more splinters whine through the air and thud into woodwork. He felt something strike his left epaulette, and rip it away to toss it to the deck like a contemptuous challenge. A foot lower, and the iron splinter would have cut through his heart. He reached out as Munro reeled against the side, his hand under his coat. He was gasping as if he had been punched in the stomach, and when Bolitho tore his hand away he saw the bright red blood running from his white waistcoat and breeches, even as Allday caught him and lowered him to the deck.

Bolitho said, 'Easy, I'll have the surgeon attend you.'

The lieutenant stared up at the empty blue sky, his eyes very wide as if he could not believe what had happened.

He gasped, 'No, sir! *Please, no* –' He gasped again as the pain increased and blood ran from one corner of his mouth. 'I – I want to stay where I can see . . .'

Allday stood up and said gruffly, 'Done for, Sir Richard. He's shot through.'

Someone was calling for assistance, another screaming with pain as more shot hammered into the side and through the rigging. But Bolitho felt unable to move. *It was all happening again.* *Hyperion* and her last battle, even to holding the hand of a dying seaman who had asked '*Why me?*' as death had claimed

215

him. Almost defiantly he stooped down and took Munro's bloodied hand, and squeezed it until his eyes turned up to his. 'Very well, Mr Munro. You stay with me.'

Allday sighed deeply. Munro's eyes, which watched Bolitho so intently, were still and without understanding. *Always the pain.*

Hull, the sailing-master who had fought his own battle with wind and rudder throughout the fight, yelled hoarsely, 'Corvette's takin' t'other frigate in tow, sir!'

Bolitho swung round and noticed that Jenour was still staring down at the dead lieutenant. Seeing himself perhaps? *Or all of us?*

'Why so?' He trained the glass, and wanted to cry out aloud as the roar of another disjointed broadside probed his brain like hot irons.

He found the two ships through the pall of drifting smoke and saw the boats in the water as a towline was passed across. There were flags on the corvette's yards, and when Bolitho turned the glass towards the attacking ship he saw a signal still flying above the flash of her armament. She showed no sign of disengaging, so why was the other ship under tow? His reeling mind would make no sense of it. It refused to answer, even to function.

He heard Williams' voice. 'Ready to larboard! Easy, my lads!' It reminded him of Keen with his men in *Hyperion*, quietening them as will a rider with a nervous horse.

Bolitho saw the Frenchman's yards begin to move, while more sails appeared above and below the punctured rags as if by magic.

Jenour cried with disbelief, 'He's going about!'

Bolitho cupped his hands. 'Mr Williams! Rake his stern as he tacks!'

Allday sounded dazed. 'He's breaking off the fight. But why? He's only got to hang on!'

There was a sudden stillness, broken only by the hoarse orders of the gun-captains and the thud of the pumps. From somewhere aloft, from lookout or marine in the fighting tops, nobody knew.

'Deck below! Sail on th' weather bow!'

The Frenchman was gathering way as she continued to turn

216

until the pale sunlight lit up her shattered stern windows, where Williams' carronade had scored the first strike for the price of a midshipman's two guineas; and beneath, across her scarlet counter her name, *L'Intrépide*, was clear to see for the first time.

Bolitho said, 'Aloft, Mr Lancer, as fast as you can. I want to know more of this newcomer!'

The lieutenant bobbed his head and dashed wild-eyed for the shrouds. He faltered only when Williams' guns fired again and then he was up and climbing through the smoke as if the devil was at his heels.

Allday exclaimed, 'By God, the bugger's still making more sail!'

Men stood back from their smoking guns, too stunned or crazed to know what was happening. Some of the wounded crawled about the torn decks, their cracked voices demanding answers when there were none to offer.

Bolitho shouted, '*Stand to!* She's run out her stern chasers!' As he had watched his powerful enemy standing away, he had seen two ports in her mauled stern open to reveal the unfired muzzles pointing straight at *Truculent* even as the range began to open.

Williams yelled, 'Ready on deck!'

As if he was totally unaware of the danger and the battle beneath him, Lieutenant Lancer shouted down in the sudden silence, 'She's making her number, sir!'

Allday whispered harshly, '*Zest*, by God – but too bloody late.'

But he was wrong. Even Lancer, struggling with his telescope and signal book from his precarious perch aloft, sounded confused.

'She's *Anemone*, thirty-eight.' His voice seemed to shake. '*Captain Bolitho*.'

At that very moment *L'Intrépide* fired first one stern chaser then the other. A ball crashed into the quarterdeck and cut down two of the helmsmen, covering Hull with their blood before scything through the taffrail. The last ball struck the mizzen top and brought down a mass of broken woodwork and several blocks. It was a miracle that Lancer had not been hurled down to the deck.

Bolitho was more aware of falling than of feeling any pain. His mind was still grappling with Lancer's report, hanging on although it was getting harder every second.

Hands were holding him with both anxiety and tenderness. He heard Allday rasp, 'Easy, Cap'n!' What he had called him in the past. 'A block struck you –'

Another voice and misty face now, the surgeon. *Have I been lying here that long?*

More probing fingers at the back of his skull; sounds of relief as he said, 'No real damage, Sir Richard. Near thing though. A block like that could crack your head like a nut!'

Men were cheering; some seemed to be sobbing. Bolitho allowed Jenour and Allday to get him to his feet amidst the fallen debris from the last parting shot.

The pain was coming now, and Bolitho felt sick. He touched his hair and felt where he had taken a glancing blow. He rubbed his eyes and saw the dead Munro watching him with an intense stare.

Williams was yelling, 'She's an English frigate, lads! The day is won!'

Allday asked in a whisper, 'Is something wrong, Sir Richard?'

Bolitho covered his left eye and waited for the fog of battle to leave his brain. Adam had come looking for him, and had saved them all.

He turned to Allday as his question seemed to penetrate. 'There was a flash.'

'*Flash*, Sir Richard? I'm not sure I understands.'

'In my eye.' He removed his hand and made himself look towards the distant French ships as they withdrew from their near-victory. 'I can't see them properly.' He turned and stared at him. 'My eye! That blow . . . it must have done something.'

Allday watched him wretchedly. Bolitho wanted him to tell him it would go away, that it would pass.

He said, 'I'll get a wet for you, sir. For me too, I reckon.' He reached out and almost gripped Bolitho's arm as he would a messmate, an equal, but he did not. Instead he said heavily, 'You stay put till I gets back, Sir Richard. There's help a'comin'. Captain Adam'll see us right, an' that's no error.' He looked at Jenour. 'Keep by his side. For all our sakes, see?' Then he groped his way past the dead and dying, the upended guns and bloodstained planking.

It was their world and there *was* no escape. All the rest was a dream.

He heard a man cry out in private torment.

Always the pain.

14

Honour Bound

'Well now, that wasn't too demanding, was it?' Sir Piers Blachford turned up his sleeves and rinsed his long, bony fingers in a basin of warm water which a servant had brought to the spacious, elegant room. He gave a dry smile. 'Not for a seasoned warrior like you, eh?'

Bolitho leaned back in the tall chair and tried to relax his whole body, muscle by muscle. Outside the window the sky was already tinged with the gloom of evening, although it was only three in the afternoon. Rain pattered occasionally against the glass, and he could hear the splash of horses and carriage wheels in the street below.

He moved to touch his eye. It felt raw and inflamed after all the poking Blachford had given it. He had used some liquid too, which stung without mercy, so that he wanted to rub his eye until it bled.

Blachford glared at him severely. 'Don't touch it! Not yet anyway.' He wiped his hands on a towel and nodded to the servant. 'Some coffee, I think.'

Bolitho declined. Catherine was downstairs somewhere in this high, silent house, waiting, worrying, hoping for news.

'I have to go. But first, can you tell me . . .'

Blachford regarded him curiously, but not without affection. 'Still impatient? Remember what I told you aboard your *Hyperion*? How there might have been hope for the eye?'

Bolitho met his gaze. Remember? How could he forget? And this tall, stick-like man with the spiky grey hair and the most

220

pointed nose he had ever seen had been there with him, in the thick of it, until he had been forced to give the order to abandon ship.

Sir Piers Blachford was a senior and most respected member of the College of Surgeons. Despite the privations of a man-of-war, he and some of his colleagues had volunteered to spread themselves throughout the squadrons of the fleet to try and discover measures to ease the suffering of those wounded in combat or cruelly injured in the demanding life of the common seaman. Resented at first as an intruder by some of *Hyperion*'s people, he had won the hearts of nearly all of them before he had left.

A man of boundless energy, he, although being some twenty years Bolitho's senior, had explored the ship from forecastle to hold, and spoken with most of her company, and had, in the ship's final battle, saved the lives of many.

Then, as now, he reminded Bolitho of a heron in the reeds near the house at Falmouth. Waiting patiently to strike.

Bolitho said abruptly, 'I could not be spared then.'

He thought suddenly of the homecoming just two days ago after leaving the battered *Truculent* in the hands of the dockyard. Sir Charles Inskip had left for London with barely another word. Shocked by the grim events, or still smarting from Bolitho's bitter words before the battle, he neither knew nor cared.

For long, long minutes he had held Catherine while she had allowed him to find his composure again in his own time. She had knelt at his feet, the firelight shining in her eyes while he had eventually described the short, savage engagement, of *Anemone*'s arrival when all time had run out. Of Poland's despair and death, of those who had fallen because of the folly and treachery of others.

Only once had she touched on Captain Varian and the *Zest*. She had tightened her grip on his hands as he had answered quietly, 'I want him dead.'

Eventually she had dragged out of him an admission about the falling block which had struck him a glancing blow on the head.

Even now, in this quiet, remote room above Albemarle Street, he could feel her compassion, her anxiety. While he had

221

been at the Admiralty to complete his report to Admiral the Lord Godschale she had come here to see Blachford, to plead for his help in spite of his constantly full programme of interviews and operations.

Blachford had been joined in his probing examinations by a short, intense doctor by the name of Rudolf Braks. The latter had barely said a word but had assisted in the examination with an almost fanatical dedication. He had a thick guttural voice when he did eventually speak with Blachford, and Bolitho thought he might be German, or more likely a renegade Dutchman.

One thing was evident; they both knew a great deal about Nelson's eye injury, and Bolitho imagined that, too, was included in the lengthy volumes of their report to the College of Surgeons.

Blachford sat down and thrust out his long, thin legs.

'I will discuss it further with my eminent colleague. It is more in his field than mine. But I shall need to make further tests. You will be in London for a while?'

Bolitho thought suddenly of Falmouth, with winter closing in from the grey waters below the headland. It was like a desperate need. He had expected to be killed, and had accepted it. Perhaps that was why he had managed to hold *Truculent*'s people together when they had nothing left to give.

'I was hoping to go home, Sir Piers.'

Blachford gave a brief smile. 'A few more days, then. I understand that you have a new flagship to commission?' He did not elaborate on how he knew or why he was interested. But then he never did.

Bolitho thought of Admiral Godschale's sympathy; his anger at what had happened. *One cannot do everything oneself.*

The admiral had probably already selected a flag-officer to replace him if the French plan to take *Truculent* had succeeded, or Bolitho had fallen in battle.

Bolitho replied, 'A few more. Thank you for your help, and especially your courtesy to Lady Catherine.'

Blachford stood up, the heron again. 'Had I been made of stone, and some insist that I am, I would have done what I could. I have never met another like her. I had thought that some of the

222

tales of envy might be overplayed, but now I know differently!'
He held out his bony hand. 'I will send word.'

Bolitho left the room and hurried down the gilded circular
staircase. A grand house and yet somehow spartan, like the
man.

She stood up as a servant opened the doors for him, her dark
eyes filled with questions. He pulled her against him and kissed
her hair.

'He said nothing bad, dear Kate.'

She leaned back in his arms and searched his face. 'I nearly
lost you. Now I know it. It is all there in your eyes.'

Bolitho stared past her at a window. 'We are together. The
rain has stopped. Shall we send Young Matthew away and walk
back? It is not far, and I need to walk with you. It is not the lanes
and cliffs of Cornwall, but with you it is always a kind of
miracle.'

Later, as they lingered together on the wet pavements while
the carriages and carts clattered past, she told him of a report
she had seen in the *Gazette*. 'There was nothing written about
you or Sir Charles Inskip.' It sounded like an accusation.

He held his cloak across her as a troop of soldiers trotted past,
their hooves throwing up muddy water from the many puddles.

He smiled at her. 'My tiger again?' He shook his head. 'No, it
was a pretence that neither of us was aboard at the time. No
longer a secret from our enemies, but it will throw some doubts
amongst them. They will not be able to use it against the Danes,
to bring more threats against them.'

She said softly, 'It tells of Poland fighting his ship against all
odds until your nephew's arrival.' She halted and faced him, her
chin lifted. 'It was you, wasn't it, Richard? *You* beat them off,
not the captain.'

Bolitho shrugged. 'Poland was a brave man. He had it in his
eyes. I think he knew he was going to die . . . he probably
blamed me for it.'

They reached the house just as the rain began again. Bolitho
remarked, 'Two carriages. I'd hoped we might be alone
tonight.'

The door was opened even as their feet touched the first step.
Bolitho was surprised to see the red-faced housekeeper Mrs

223

Robbins peering down at them. She had been away at Browne's big estate in Sussex, but had been here when Bolitho had rescued Catherine from the Waites prison. A formidable Londoner born and bred, who had had some definite ideas about keeping them both apart during their stay in his lordship's house.

Catherine threw the hood back from her head. 'It is good to see you again, Mrs Robbins!'

But the housekeeper peered at Bolitho and exclaimed, 'I didn't know where you was, sir. Your man Allday was out, yer lieutenant gone 'ome to South'ampton to all accounts –'

It was the first time Bolitho had seen her distressed or so anxious. He took her arm. 'Tell me. What has happened?'

She raised her apron and held it to her face. 'It's 'is lordship. He's been callin' for you, sir.' She looked up the stairs as if to see him. 'The doctor's with 'im, so please be quick.'

Catherine made to move to the staircase but Bolitho saw the housekeeper shake her head with quiet desperation.

Bolitho said, 'No, Kate. It were better you stay and look after Mrs Robbins. Send for a hot drink.' He held her gaze with his own. 'I'll be down directly.'

He found an elderly servant sitting outside the double doors of Browne's rooms. He looked too shocked to move, and for some reason Bolitho thought of Allday.

It was dark in the big room except around the bed. There were three men sitting by it; one, apparently the doctor, was holding Browne's hand, perhaps feeling his pulse.

One of the others exclaimed, 'He's here, Oliver!' And to Bolitho, 'Oh, thank God, Sir Richard!'

They made way for him and he sat down on the edge of the bed, and looked at the man who had once been his flag-lieutenant until he had succeeded to his father's role and title.

He was still dressed in his shirt, and his skin was wet with sweat. His eyes as they settled on Bolitho seemed to widen with effort, and he gasped, 'I – I heard you were safe! A while I – I thought –'

'Easy, Oliver, it will be all right.' He shot a glance at the doctor. 'What is it?'

Without a word the doctor raised a dressing from Browne's

224

chest. The shirt had been cut open and there was blood everywhere.

Bolitho asked quietly, 'Who did it?' He had seen enough wounds left by pistol or musket to recognise this one.

Browne said in a fierce whisper, '*No time – no time left.*' His eyes fluttered. '*Closer, please closer!*'

Bolitho lowered his face to his. The young flag-lieutenant who had walked the deck with him, as Jenour had done, with all hell around them. A fine, decent young man who was dying even as he watched him fighting a hopeless battle.

Browne said, 'Somervell. A duel.' Each word was a separate agony but he persisted, 'Your lady – your lady is a widow now.' He clenched his jaw so that his teeth brought blood to his lips. 'But he's done for me all the same!'

Bolitho looked desperately at the doctor. 'Can't you *do* something?'

He shook his head. 'It is a marvel he has lived this long, Sir Richard.'

Browne gripped Bolitho's cuff and whispered, 'That damned rogue killed my brother – like this. I have settled the score. Please explain to –' His head lolled on the pillow and he was still.

Bolitho reached out and closed his eyes. He said, 'I shall tell Catherine. Rest now, Oliver.' He looked away, his eyes smarting worse than before. *Browne with an 'e'.* He walked to the doors and said, 'Tell me when –' But nobody answered him.

In the room where he had told Catherine about the battle, she was waiting for him. She held out a goblet of brandy and said, 'I know. Allday heard it in the kitchen. My husband is dead.' She put her hand up to the goblet to press it to his lips. 'I feel nothing, but for you . . . and your dead friend.'

Bolitho felt the brandy sting his throat, remembering, putting each picture in place.

Then, while she refilled the goblet, he heard himself say, 'Oliver used the phrase, *We Happy Few.* The few are much fewer, and now poor Oliver has paid the price.'

In the kitchen Allday sat with a half-demolished mutton pie and paused to refill his pipe. He said, ''Nother stoup of ale wouldn't go amiss, Ma Robbins.' He shook his head and was surprised how much it ached. 'Second thought, I'll take some more o' that rum yonder.'

The housekeeper watched him sadly, grieving over what had happened, but apprehensive about her own future. Young Oliver, as he had been known in the kitchen, was the last in direct line for the title. There was talk of some distant cousin, but who could tell what might become of her?

She said, 'I'm surprised 'ow you can carry on at a time like this, John!'

Allday focused his red-rimmed eyes with difficulty.

'Then I'll *tell* you, Ma Robbins. It's 'cause I survived!' He gestured vaguely to the room above them. '*We've* survived! I'll shed a tear with the next bugger, beggin' yer pardon, Ma, but it's *us* I cares about, see?'

She pushed the stone jug across to him. 'Just you mind your manners when the men come to take 'is lordship away. Quality or not, it's against the law, wot they done!'

She reached out to save the rum as Allday's head thudded down on the table. In this gracious house the war had always been at a distance. There had never been any shortages, and only when young Oliver had been away at sea had it meant much to those who served belowstairs.

But in Allday's last burst of despairing anger, the war had been right here on the doorstep.

She heard a door close and knew they were going upstairs, perhaps to sit with the body. Her red features softened. Young Oliver would rest easy with the man he had loved more than his own father so close at hand.

The doctor who had attended both participants in the duel scrutinised his watch repeatedly, and made no secret of his eagerness to leave.

Catherine sat by a low fire, one hand playing with her necklace, her high cheekbones adding to her beauty.

Bolitho said, 'So Oliver left a letter. Was he so certain that he was going to die?'

The doctor glanced unhappily at Catherine and murmured, 'Viscount Somervell was a renowned duellist, I understand. It would seem a likely conclusion.'

226

Bolitho heard whispers on the staircase, the sounds of doors opening and closing as they prepared Browne for his final journey to his Sussex home.

Catherine said sharply, 'This waiting! Is there no end to it?' She reached out and took his offered hand, and held it to her cheek as if they were alone in the room. 'Don't worry, Richard. I will not disappoint you.'

Bolitho looked at her and wondered at her strength. Together and with the doctor's aid they had discovered the whereabouts of Somervell's seconds, and his body. It had already been taken to his spacious house in Grosvenor Square. Was she thinking of that? That she would be required to go there and complete the process of her dead husband's burial? He tightened his hold on her fingers. He would be with her. There was already scandal enough; a little more could do no further harm.

When the news got out there were many who might think he had killed Somervell. He looked away, his eyes bitter. *I would that I had.*

Word had been sent to Browne's country estate at Horsham. They would be coming for him. *Today.*

Bolitho said, 'I gather that Oliver's older brother died in a similar affair with Somervell. It was in Jamaica.' Who could have guessed that someone like the outwardly carefree Browne would set out to find Somervell and settle the debt, in the only way he knew?

A red-eyed servant opened the door. 'Beg pardon, but the carriage is 'ere.'

More feet and murmured exchanges, and then a powerfully-built man in sombre country clothing entered to announce he was Hector Croker, the estate manager. Three days since they had sent a message by post-horse. In rain-washed lanes and pitch-dark roads, Croker must have driven without any rest at all.

The doctor handed him some papers, his relief even more obvious. Like a man ridding himself of something dangerous or evil.

He saw Mrs Robbins waiting with her bags and said kindly, 'You'll ride with us, Mrs Robbins. His lordship left word you were to stay in your employment.'

227

Catherine walked to the doorway and gave the housekeeper a hug. 'For caring for me as you did.'

Mrs Robbins gave an awkward curtsy and hurried down the steps, with barely a glance at the house where she had witnessed so much.

From the lower floor Allday peered up through the small window, and watched in silence as Browne's body was carried down the steps to the carriage by several men in dark clothing. Aloud he said, 'An' there's an end to it.'

Bolitho followed the men to the carriage and gave some money to their leader. More quick glances, men who were used to this kind of work. Theirs was not to ask questions.

Bolitho felt her slip her hand through his arm and said, 'Goodbye, Oliver. Rest in peace.'

Rain pattered across their bared heads but they watched until the carriage had turned up towards Piccadilly. In his letter Browne had requested that if the worst should befall him, he was to be buried on the family estate.

Bolitho turned and saw her looking at him. *Now she is free to marry me, but I am not.* The thought seemed to torment him.

She said softly, 'It changes nothing, you know.' She smiled, but her dark eyes were sad.

Bolitho replied, 'I shall be with you until –'

She nodded. 'I know. That is my only concern. What it may do to your reputation.'

Bolitho saw Yovell waiting inside the door. 'What is it?'

'Shall I pack our things, Sir Richard?'

He saw her look up at the staircase. Remembering how this place had been their haven in London. Now they must leave it.

Then she said, 'I shall deal with it, Daniel. You assist Sir Richard.' Her eyes were quite calm. 'You will have letters, I expect. To Val, and perhaps Rear-Admiral Herrick?'

Bolitho thought he saw a message in her eyes but was not sure.

'Yes, Val would wish to know.' He thought how busy Keen would be, preparing to commission the newly completed *Black Prince*. It was a nightmare for any captain of a large man-of-war, let alone one which was to wear a vice-admiral's flag at the fore. Shortage of trained hands and seasoned warrant officers, obtaining raw recruits by any manner or means, always more difficult in a naval port like Chatham where the press-gang would be betrayed by anyone from tailor to beggar. Arguing with the victualling yards and making sure that the ship's purser was not doing deals to procure rotten stores, so that purser and supplier could pocket the difference between them. Making a forest of oak into a fighting ship.

Bolitho smiled grimly. And yet Keen had found the opportunity to visit Catherine until he himself could reach London and report on the battle.

He would also send word to Adam, although his *Anemone* had barely had time to anchor after escorting the leaking *Truculent* to the security of the dockyard. Adam, too, had once been Bolitho's flag-lieutenant. More than most, he would appreciate how closely the appointment joined the man to his admiral.

He heard Allday's heavy tread on the kitchen stair. Except for him, of course.

Catherine said thoughtfully, 'He had no relatives to speak of, and most of them live abroad.'

Bolitho noticed that she never spoke of Somervell by name. 'He had friends at Court, I believe.'

She seemed to become aware of the concern in his voice and looked up. 'Yes, so he did. But even the King was angered by his behaviour – his quick temper and his craving for the tables. He took all that I owned.' She touched his face with sudden tenderness. 'Another of Fate's little whims, is it not? For now, what there is left will come to me.'

That afternoon Jenour arrived quite breathless after changing six horses on the ride from Southampton. When asked why and how he had heard the news, Jenour explained, 'Southampton is a great seaport, Sir Richard. News flies on the wind there, although the circumstances were not known.' He added simply, 'My place is here with you. I know how you valued Lord Browne's friendship, and he yours.'

Catherine had gone to visit a lawyer with Yovell as her escort. She had declined Bolitho's offer to accompany her and had said, 'It is better I do it without you. You might be hurt . . . I could not bear that, dearest of men.'

He said now, 'You are just in time, Stephen. We shall quit this place today.'

Jenour dropped his eyes. 'It will be painful, will it not, Sir Richard?'

Bolitho touched his sleeve. 'So old a head on so young a pair of shoulders!'

Somehow Jenour had guessed his innermost feeling, even though he was young and inexperienced. Catherine was free now, and soon, it seemed, she would be independent again. Might Falmouth and his constant absences at sea seem a poor replacement for the life she had once known, and might want again?

Life was like the ocean, he thought; sunshine one moment, a raging storm the next.

He found that he was touching his eye, and felt his heart sink lower. What might she think of him if the worst happened?

'Is there something you wish me to do, Sir Richard?'

Bolitho had forgotten Jenour was there. 'We shall be going to Kent shortly, to the new flagship.' He let his mind dwell on the prospect. He knew that once he would have been on board immediately, no matter what anybody said or thought. But to be so near to death, and to lose another friend, put caution where recklessness had once ruled.

'And there is something else,' he said.

Jenour said, 'I know, Sir Richard. The court-martial.'

'Aye, Stephen. War is no place for personal greed and selfish ambition, though God knows you might not be blamed for thinking otherwise. Captain Varian betrayed his trust, just as he did those who depended on him in their greatest need.'

Jenour watched his grave profile, the way he occasionally touched his eye. As if he had something in it.

The door opened and Bolitho swung round, ready to greet her. But it was a messenger boy, one of the servants watching him suspiciously from the hall.

'I have brought word from Doctor Rudolf Braks, Sir Richard.' He screwed up his face as if to help memorise his message. 'You may visit him on the morrow at ten o'clock.'

Jenour looked away but was very aware that Bolitho showed no resentment at the curt message. It sounded more like a summons. Jenour had thought Bolitho would be at the Admiralty at about that time. *Braks*. A foreign-sounding name, one he was almost certain he had heard his father mention; but why?

Bolitho gave the boy a coin and thanked him, his voice distant. Then he heard the carriage returning and said abruptly, 'No word of that to Lady Catherine, Stephen. She has enough to face up to as it is.'

'Yes, I see, Sir Richard.'

'Damn it, you don't, my lad!' Then he turned away and when she entered the room, he was smiling.

She gave her hand to Jenour and then embraced Bolitho.

He asked quietly, 'Was it bad?'

She shrugged, that one small gesture which always touched him like a sensitive nerve.

'Enough. But 'tis done for the present. A report will go to the magistrates.' She looked at him steadily. 'But both men are dead. No one can be charged for what happened.'

Jenour discreetly left them alone and she said, 'I know what you are thinking, Richard. You are so wrong. If I did not love you so much I would be angry that you could harbour such ideas. You took care of me when I had nothing . . . now we shall take care of each other.' She gazed at the fire and said, 'We shall leave now. Quit this haven where we shared our love, and the world was a million miles away.'

They looked at the window and the rain which ran down the panes.

'Very apt.' She was speaking to the room. 'There is no more light here.'

The day ended more quickly than either of them had believed possible. There were many comings and goings, friends of the deceased and those who were merely curious, as their stares betrayed.

The same doctor was in attendance, and when he asked if Catherine wished to see where the body of her husband was laid out she shook her head.

'I have been wrong many times, but never, I hope, a hypocrite.'

231

There was only one really unpleasant incident.

The last visitor was introduced as a Colonel Collyear of the King's Household guard. A tall, arrogant soldier with a cruel mouth.

'We meet again, Lady Somervell. I find it grotesque to offer my condolences, but duty requires me to pay my respects to your late husband.'

He saw Bolitho for the first time and said in the same affected drawl, 'At first, I thought perhaps it might have been you, sir. Had it been –'

Bolitho said calmly, 'You will always find me ready enough, and that is a promise. So if you continue to demean an honourable uniform in the presence of a lady, I may forget the solemnity of the occasion.'

Catherine said, 'I would have put it less politely. Please go.'

The man backed away, his spurs and accoutrements jingling as he attempted a dignified retreat.

Bolitho thought suddenly of *Hyperion*'s first lieutenant, Parris, whose mangled body had gone down with the ship after he had shot himself, rather than face the surgeon's saw.

Catherine had recognised him for what he was; and yet Bolitho had not. Only while Parris lay pinned beneath an upended cannon, when he had confessed his passion for Somervell, had he understood. In this very room she had just recognised another in the arrogant colonel.

Jenour hovered by one of the beautiful pillared doorways. 'They are all gone, m'lady.'

Catherine looked at herself in a great gilded mirror. 'I see this woman, and yet I feel another.' She seemed to hear what Jenour had said. 'Then we shall make ourselves as comfortable as we can. Is his steward still in the house?'

'Yes, m'lady.' He glanced at Bolitho as if for assistance. 'I found him weeping in his room.'

She said coldly, 'Send him away. I will not have him here. He will be paid, but that is all.'

As Jenour left she said, 'This is my house now. It will *never* be my home.'

She crossed the room and put her arms around his shoulders, and kissed him very slowly and with great tenderness. Then she

232

said, 'I want you so much that I should feel ashamed.' She shivered. 'But not here, not yet.'

Ozzard padded through yet another door with some fresh coffee. Bolitho noticed that the little man was carrying one of the old silver pots from Falmouth. Only he would have thought of that.

Allday glanced in and said, 'I think I'll pipe down early tonight if you don't need me, m'lady.'

Bolitho smiled. It was easy to forget tomorrow and what the doctor might tell him. He could even forget the corpse which lay upstairs, unloved, and soon forgotten.

She replied, 'Please do, Allday. Take something strong to soothe your aches and pains.'

Allday grinned at them. 'You always knows, m'lady.' He went off chuckling to himself.

Bolitho said, 'An oak indeed.'

'I was thinking.' She laid a hand on his arm. 'Your friend Oliver. He could have been speaking for us. *We Happy Few.*'

When the servants bolted the front doors and laid straw in the roadway to lessen the din of iron-shod wheels, they were still sitting there, close to a dying fire.

Ozzard crept quietly into the room and put some fresh logs on the fire before picking up the cold coffee pot and padding softly away again. Just once he glanced at the couple who slept together, half reclining on one of the great sofas. She was covered with his heavy dress coat, and her hair hung loose and free across his arm, which held her about her waist.

He knew again the sadness and loss that would always stay with him now. At least they had each other; only God knew how long they would be granted such happiness.

He found Allday outside the door and exclaimed, 'I thought you'd piped down with a bottle of rum!'

Allday did not rise to it this time. 'Don't feel much like sleep. Thought you might share a wet or two with me.'

Ozzard regarded him warily. 'Then what?'

'You're an educated fellow. You might read somethin' to me till we feels more like turnin' in.'

Ozzard hid his surprise. *He knows it too.* There was a storm brewing. But he remarked, 'I've found a book about a shepherd – you'd like that one.'

They made for the deserted kitchen, the burly coxswain and the tiny servant who carried his terrible secret like a disease which would eventually destroy him.

But storm or not, they were Bolitho's men, and they would see it through as they always had. Together.

15

Full Circle

Captain Valentine Keen cast a searching glance along the full length of his new command before turning and striding aft where a group of senior officers, Admiralty officials and their ladies, waited beneath the shelter of the poop.

The *Black Prince*, a powerful second-rate of ninety-four guns, had been completed here in the Royal Dockyard, Chatham, several months ahead of schedule.

For the latter weeks, after his appointment had been confirmed, Keen had stayed aboard for most of the time. On this bitter November forenoon he was very aware of the long days, and the constant demands on his services. He could feel the wind off the River Medway cutting through his limbs and body as if he were naked. Now, all but the formalities were over, and this towering three-decker was to be his.

Lying nearby was an old seventy-four like *Hyperion*. It was hard to believe that she had been so much smaller than *Black Prince*, and he found himself wondering if this great ship would ever match her in performance and memory. He had been reminded too that it was in this same dock area that Nelson's last flagship *Victory* had had her keel laid, all of forty-seven years ago. And what might the navy become in the same period which lay ahead?

He doffed his hat to the port admiral and then turned to the man he had come to admire and love.

'The ship is prepared, Sir Richard.' He waited, sensing the silence at his back where the ship's company had been piped to witness the official handing over of the new ship. On nearby walls and slipways the dockyard workers waited in the cold wind to watch. Pride of workmanship; and with the war showing little sign of ending it meant that another great keel would be laid down once *Black Prince* had been worked out to the Medway, and finally to the open sea.

Not so with most of the ship's company, he thought. Some had been transferred from other vessels now laid-up for repair or refit without ever being allowed ashore to see their homes or loved ones. The press-gangs had gathered the sweepings of the dockside and local harbours. Scum to be made, by example or more brutal methods, into seamen who would, when required, fight this ship with the loyalty of seasoned tars.

The assizes had provided a good sprinkling of poachers and petty thieves, and one or two harder men who chose the King's service instead of the gallows.

Bolitho looked strained and tired, Keen thought. That last fight aboard the frigate *Truculent* must have demanded a lot from him. But it had not been difficult to picture Bolitho casting down his flag-officer's rank to replace Poland as captain when he had fallen. Keen had served with Bolitho in frigates as midshipman and lieutenant, and had seen him in action so many times that he often wondered how they had survived this long.

Bolitho smiled at him. 'It is good to be here on this proud day, Captain Keen.'

There was warmth in his voice, and he was probably amused by the formality they must maintain in front of such important visitors.

Keen turned about and walked to the quarterdeck rail, his eyes taking in everything, and marvelling how well his lieutenants and warrant officers had managed to be ready for this day. There had been moments when Keen had believed it would never end. The work, the hull full of carpenters and joiners, sailmakers and painters, while the newly appointed midshipmen were driven from pillar to post by Cazalet, his first lieutenant. Keen knew little of him yet as a man. But as his second-in-command, appointed from another ship-of-the-line, he was beyond value. He never seemed to be without energy or an answer to somebody's problem. Day by day Keen had

236

watched him striding through the piled confusion of rigging and spare cordage, anchors and stores which descended on the dockside like an endless invasion. He looked up at the crossed yards and neatly furled sails, that same tangled cordage now in position, and tarred-down like black glass. On the forecastle he saw the scarlet square of Royal Marines matching their smart lines across the poop behind him.

The lieutenants in blue and white and in strict order of seniority; beyond them the midshipmen and warrant officers. Some of the 'young gentlemen' would see this huge ship as the sure step to a lieutenant's exalted rank, while others, so small they looked as if they should be with their mothers, stared around at the great masts and the double lines of the upper deck twelve-pounders. They would be reminded, no doubt, of the twelve miles of rigging they would have to know by name at first, then by touch if required when called on deck in a raging storm and in pitch darkness.

And there was the company of seamen. Old hands and new, pressed men and vagrants, watching him, knowing that of everyone aboard he could control their lives, while his skill as the captain might well decide if they lived at all.

His voice was clear and steady as he read from the scroll with its round copper-plate writing and the crest of Admiralty at the top. It was like hearing someone else reading it to him, he thought.

'. . . and once satisfied you will go on board and take command of captain in her accordingly . . .'

He heard one of the women give a gentle cough behind him, and recalled how he had seen some of them peering around after Bolitho had stepped aboard. Looking for Catherine, preparing the gossip. But they had been disappointed, for she had remained ashore, although Keen had not yet had time to speak with Bolitho about it.

'. . . all officers and company appointed to said ship shall obey, follow and serve you to this purpose, when His Britannic Majesty King George shall charge to accept the said ship Black Prince into his service . . .'

Keen glanced over the scroll and saw his coxswain Tojohns standing beside the powerful figure of Allday. Their familiar

237

faces gave him strength, a sense of belonging in this teeming world of a ship-of-the-line where every man was a stranger until proved otherwise.

'. . . *hereof, not you nor any of you may fail as you will answer the contrary at your peril and according to the Articles of War* . . . *God Save the KING!'*

It was done. Keen replaced his hat and tucked the scroll inside his coat again while the first lieutenant, Cazalet, stepped smartly from the group of officers and shouted, 'Three cheers for His Majesty, lads!' The response could have been better, but when Keen glanced round he saw that the port admiral was beaming, and there were a lot of handshakes amongst the men who had planned and supervised for this day, and those who would profit by the end of it.

Keen said, 'Dismiss the hands, Mr Cazalet, then come aft to my quarters.'

He thought he saw the other man raise an eyebrow. It was now time to entertain the visitors. By the look of some of them it was going to be difficult to get rid of them. He called after the first lieutenant, 'Tell Major Bourchier to double his marine guard.' He had almost forgotten the major's name. In a few weeks he would know them better than they did each other.

Lieutenant Jenour touched his hat. 'I beg your pardon, sir, but Sir Richard is leaving now.'

'Oh, I had hoped . . .' He saw Bolitho standing apart from the others, as they flowed aft on either side of the great double-wheel which was yet to feel the fury of wind and rudder in contest.

Bolitho said, 'Pay my respects, Val. But I have to go. Lady Catherine . . .' He looked away as some visitors passed by, one of the women staring at him quite unashamedly.

He added, 'She would not come aboard. She thought it best. For me. Later perhaps.'

Keen had heard about Browne's death and the duel which had preceded it. He said, 'She is a wonderful lady, Sir Richard.'

'I cannot thank you enough for standing by her in my absence. My God, Fate soon determines who your true friends are!'

He walked slowly to the quarterdeck to look down at the guns, the neatly-packed hammock nettings.

238

'You have a fine ship, Val. A floating fortress. There's no flag-captain I'd rather have, and you know it. And have faith, as I did, although to others the odds against my finding Catherine again were a million-fold. Zenoria needs time. But I am certain that she loves you.' He clapped his arm. 'So no more melancholy, eh?'

Keen glanced aft where the din of voices and laughter was already growing. 'I'll see you over the side, Sir Richard.'

They went down to the entry port together, and Keen noticed there were already more marines in evidence with their muskets and fixed bayonets and immaculate, pipeclayed, cross-belts. Their major had acted promptly; there were still those who might try to desert before the ship was at sea, and order and discipline took root. Keen was a fair and understanding captain, but he was mindful that he was still fifty men short of his full complement of eight hundred officers, marines and sailors. The sight of the armed sentries might make the foolhardy think twice.

'*Man the side!*' The gleaming new barge was rolling gently in the sluggish confinement of the dockyard, Allday in the sternsheets, the crew neatly turned out in checkered shirts and tarred hats.

Bolitho hesitated. A ship without history, without memory. A new start. Even the idea seemed to mock him.

He said, 'You will receive further orders within the week. Use all the time you can to work the people into a team we can be proud of.'

Keen smiled, although he hated to see him leave after so brief a visit. 'I have had the best of teachers, sir!'

Bolitho turned, then felt himself falling. Keen seized his arm, and there was a clatter as one of the marines dropped his musket with surprise. The lieutenant in charge of the side-party snarled something at the luckless marine and gave Bolitho a few seconds to recover his wits.

'Is it the eye, Sir Richard?' Keen was shocked to see the expression of utter despair on Bolitho's features when he faced him again.

'I've not told Catherine yet. They can do naught to help me, it seems.'

239

Keen stood between him and the guard and boatswain's mates with their silver calls still poised and ready.

'I will lay odds she knows.' He wanted to offer some kind of help so badly that even his own worries seemed beyond reach.

'If that is the case . . .' Bolitho changed his mind and touched his hat to the guard before lowering himself down the stairs from the entry port, where Allday's hand was outstretched to guide him the last few steps into the barge.

Keen watched the boat until it was out of sight beyond a moored transport. He had commanded several ships during his service, and this should have been his greatest reward. Older captains than himself would give their blood for such a command. A new ship, soon to fly a vice-admiral's flag, could only bring honour to the man who controlled her destiny. So why did he feel so little? Was he so affected by the *Hyperion*, or was it that he had been so near to death on too many occasions?

He frowned at the laughter from his quarters. They neither knew nor cared about the people who would serve this ship.

A lieutenant blocked his way and touched his hat. 'I beg pardon, sir, but another lighter is putting off from the victualling pier.'

'Are you the Officer-of-the-Watch, *Mister* Flemyng?' The young lieutenant seemed to shrink as Keen added sharply, 'Then do your work, sir, for if you cannot I will seek out another who can!'

Almost before the lieutenant had made to move away he regretted it.

'That was uncalled for, Mr Flemyng. A captain's rank has privileges, but abuse of them is beyond contempt.' He saw him staring in astonishment. 'Ask as much as you like. Otherwise we may all be the poorer when it concerns something vital. So send for the boatswain and the duty-watch to deal with these stores, eh?'

As the lieutenant almost ran across the quarterdeck, Keen gave a sad smile. How true had his words been just now to Bolitho.

I have had the best of teachers.

The thought seemed to rally him, and he looked along the deck again to the black, armoured shoulder of the proud

240

figurehead. Then he stared aloft at the curling masthead pendant and some gulls which screamed through the rigging with an eye for scraps from the galley. Almost to himself he said, '*My ship.*' Then he spoke her name, 'Zenoria.' Afterwards he thought it had been like releasing a bird from captivity. Would she ever call him in return?

The light carriage, with mud splashed as high as its windows, reached the top of a rise and reined to a halt, the two horses steaming in the cold air.

Yovell groaned and released his grip on a tasselled handle and exclaimed, 'These roads are indeed a disgrace, m'lady.'

But she lowered a window and leaned out regardless of the fine, intermittent drizzle which had followed them all the way from Chatham.

'Where are we, Young Matthew?'

Matthew leaned over from his box and grinned down at her, his face like a polished red apple.

'The house is yonder, m'lady.' He pointed with his whip. ''Tis the only one hereabouts.' He puffed out his cheeks and his breath floated around him like steam. 'A lonely spot, in my opinion.'

'You know these parts, Young Matthew?'

He grinned again, but with a certain wistfulness as the memory clouded his eyes. 'Aye, m'lady. I was here 'bout fourteen years back – I were just a boy then, working for my grandfather who was head coachman for the Bolitho family.'

Yovell said, 'Before my time with Sir Richard, I think.'

'What were you doing in Kent?'

'The master was sent here to hunt down smugglers. I was with him an' helped a bit. Then he sent me back to Falmouth 'cause he said it were too dangerous, like.'

Catherine withdrew her head. 'Drive on, then.' She sat back in the seat as the carriage rolled forward through a succession of muddy ruts. Another part of Bolitho's life she could not share. Allday had made some mention of it. How Bolitho had still been recovering from the terrible fever he had caught in the Great South Sea, but had desperately tried to obtain a ship, *any* ship. War with France had still been just a threat, but England had allowed the fleet to rot, her sailors thrown on the beach. There were few ships, and only Bolitho's persistence, his daily visits to the Admiralty, had found him employment at the Nore. Recruiting, but also hunting smugglers, to stamp out their vicious trade, a far cry from the romantic tales which abounded about their exploits.

But when the blade fell on the King of France's neck everything had changed. Allday had put it in his simple way. 'So they gave us the old *Hyperion*. It were a bit of a shock for the Cap'n, as he was then, him being a frigate man. But that old ship changed our lives, m'lady. He found you, and I found out I had a grown-up son.' He had nodded, his clear eyes faraway. 'Aye, we sailed through some blood and tears together.'

She had pressed him to add, 'That was why he fought *Truculent* like he did. Cap'n Poland could never 'a' done it, not in a thousand years.' He had shaken his head like an old dog. 'There'll not be another like *Hyperion*, I'm thinkin'. Not for us anyways.'

She watched the River Medway in the distance. All the way from Chatham it had barely been out of sight, twisting and turning, a wide stretch of water, sometimes silver, sometimes the colour of lead, as the sky and weather dictated. She had found herself shivering when she had caught sight of some prison hulks moored out in the stream. Mastless and forlorn, and somehow frightening. Full of prisoners-of-war. She had another stark memory of the Waites prison, the degradation and filth. Surely it would be better to die?

Bolitho would be on board his new flagship. After that they would be together again – but for how long? She swore that she would make every moment a precious one.

For a few moments she forgot why she had made this journey, and the fact that Rear-Admiral Herrick's wife might not even allow her in the house. She was back in the small chapel in South Audley Street, then in the adjoining St George's Burial Ground, at any other time just a short walk from the Somervell house.

Nobody had spoken to her except the vicar, and he had been a total stranger. A few faceless people had been in the chapel, but by the graveside there had been only her Richard. There had 'been several carriages, but the occupants had not alighted, content apparently to watch and pass judgment. One figure had hurried away from a wall as she had made to leave. His steward, no doubt, who for whatever true reason had always been with him.

The carriage responded to Matthew's brake, and slowed again while it turned off the road and along a well-laid driveway.

Catherine could feel her heart pumping against her ribs and was surprised at her sudden nervousness. She had come uninvited and without sending word of her intention. To do so would have invited a snub. But she accepted that it was important to Bolitho that she should try to get to know the wife of his old friend. She knew that Herrick would never change towards her and it saddened her, although she had managed to hide it from the one she loved more than life itself.

Yovell groaned; he had obviously suffered from the joltings of the journey. 'A goodly house.' He said it with approval. 'A big step.'

Catherine did not know what Yovell meant but guessed it might be because Herrick had come from humble, even poor beginnings locally, and his marriage to his beloved Dulcie had brought him the comfort and encouragement denied him in his struggle for eventual recognition in the navy. She felt a momentary bitterness as Yovell handed her down from the carriage. Bolitho had given his friend much more than encouragement. This should have been the time to repay him with the loyalty and friendship he needed. Instead . . . She shook her head and said, 'Stay with Young Matthew, will you please, Daniel.' She bit her lip. 'I do not expect to be long.'

Matthew touched his hat. 'I'll take the horses to the yard for some water.' He and Yovell exchanged glances as she mounted the stone steps and lifted a large brass knocker in the shape of a dolphin. The door opened instantly, and she vanished into the interior.

When the carriage reached the stable-yard Yovell, who had climbed up beside the coachman, emitted a grunt of anxiety. Two stable hands were washing down another carriage.

'It's Lady Bolitho's.' Matthew gave it a professional scrutiny. 'No mistakin' that 'un!'

Yovell nodded. 'Too late now. I'd better go round – Sir Richard'll never forgive me.'

Young Matthew climbed down and said, 'Leave 'er be. You can't 'andle two mares at once.' He gave his cheeky smile. 'My money's on our Lady Catherine!'

Yovell stared at him. 'You damned rogue!' But he stood fast all the same.

After the creak of wheels and leather and the occasional slashing rain across the windows, the house felt oppressively still. Like a tomb. Catherine looked at the small servant who had opened the door. 'Is your mistress at home?'

The girl stammered, 'She is, Ma'am. She be in bed.' She peered anxiously at some double doors which led off the hallway. 'They moved 'er downstairs. She got a visitor.'

Catherine smiled. The girl was too open to be a liar. 'Would you please announce me? Catherine Somervell – Lady Somervell.'

She walked into an anteroom and through its misted windows watched two men working in the gardens, in spite of the rain.

But it was getting heavier, and they paused beneath the windows to wait its passing. It was still a few moments longer before she realised they were speaking Spanish.

She heard the doors swing open across the hall and when she turned she saw Belinda, framed in the light from other windows on the far side of the room.

She had never laid eyes on her before, and yet she knew instantly who she was. She had something of the looks in the portrait Catherine had had restored to its place at Falmouth, the hair, the shape of the face – but nothing more.

'I did not know you were here, otherwise –'

Belinda replied sharply, '*Otherwise* you would have stayed in your proper place! I don't know how you have the brazen audacity to come.' Her eyes moved slowly over Catherine from head to toe, lingering on the dull black silk of her mourning gown.

'I am surprised you have the impudence to –'

Catherine heard someone call out in a small voice and said, 'Frankly, your reactions, disgust or otherwise, don't matter a jot to me.' She could feel the anger rising like fire. 'This is not your house, and I shall see whom I intended, if she will allow it!'

244

Belinda stared at her as if she had struck her. 'Don't you *dare* take that tone with me –'

'Dare? You talk of daring after what you tried to do to me when you connived with my husband? I wear these clothes because it shows respect, but it is for Richard's dead friend, not my damned husband!' She strode to the door. 'I notice that you have no difficulty in dressing in the latest, and finest fashion!'

Belinda fell back, her eyes never leaving Catherine's face. 'I shall never . . .'

'Give him up? Is that what you were about to say?' Catherine looked at her coldly. 'He is not yours to give. I suspect he never was.'

The voice called again and Catherine walked past her without another word. Belinda was exactly what she had expected. It made her angrier and sad at the same time. *A woman like that with* – She stopped short of a large bed, and gazed at the woman who was propped there on several pillows and cushions. Herrick's wife studied her much as Belinda had done; but there was no hostility.

Belinda said, 'I shall be back shortly, Dulcie my dear. I need some air.'

Catherine heard the doors close. 'I beg forgiveness for this intrusion.' It no longer seemed to matter, and she could feel her body go cold despite the great fire in the room.

Dulcie placed one hand on the bed and said softly, 'Sit here where I can see you the better. Alas, my dear Thomas has sailed just recently to join his squadron. I miss him so much.' The hand moved towards Catherine and after the slightest hesitation took hers in it. It was hot and dry. She murmured, 'Yes. You *are* very beautiful, Lady Somervell . . . I can see why he loves you.'

Catherine squeezed her hand. 'That is a kind thing to say. Please call me Catherine.'

'I was sorry to hear about your late husband's death. Is it still raining?'

Catherine felt something like fear, usually a stranger to her. Dulcie was rambling, even as she clung to her hand.

She asked carefully, 'Have you seen a doctor recently?'

Dulcie said distantly. 'So much sadness. We couldn't have any children, you know.'

'Nor can I,' she said gently. She tried again. 'How long have you been unwell?'

Dulcie smiled for the first time. It made her look incredibly frail.

'You are like Thomas. Always fussing and asking questions. He thinks I work too hard – he does not understand how empty it can be when he is at sea. I could not be idle, you see.'

Catherine felt terribly alone with her secret. 'Those men working in the gardens. Who are they?'

For a moment she thought Dulcie had not heard, as she whispered, 'Belinda is such a *good* person. They have a little girl.'

Catherine glanced away. *They*. 'The men were speaking Spanish . . .'

She had not heard the door re-open, and Belinda's voice was like a knife. 'Of course, you were also married to a Spaniard at one time, were you not? So *many* husbands.'

Catherine ignored the sneer in her voice and turned back to the bed as Dulcie said wearily, 'They are prisoners. But they are allowed here on trust. They are very good gardeners.' Her eyes flickered. 'I am so tired.'

Catherine released her hand and stood up. 'I will take my leave.' She backed away from the bed, oblivious of Belinda's bitter stare, her hatred for her.

'I would like to talk again with you, dear Dulcie.' She turned away, unable to lie.

Outside the room she faced Belinda. 'She is very ill.'

'And you are concerned, is that it? You came prepared to *win her over* – to prove that you are the only one who really cares!'

'Don't be a fool! Has she seen a doctor?'

Belinda smiled. Arrogantly, she thought. 'But of course. A good local man who has known Dulcie and Rear-Admiral Herrick for years.'

Catherine heard the carriage moving to the front of the house again. Yovell was a good judge.

'I must leave. I will send for a competent doctor from London.'

Belinda said violently, 'How can you speak like this? I can see for myself what you are, but don't you know what you are doing

246

to my husband's career and reputation?' She was spitting out each word, unable to hide her spite. 'He has fought duels over you before, or didn't you know? One day he will pay for it!'

Catherine looked away, and did not see the flash of triumph in Belinda's eyes. She was remembering the Vauxhall Pleasure Gardens, where Bolitho had tossed a contemptuous challenge to the drunken soldier who had fondled her arm as if she was a common whore. And only days ago when he had sent the effeminate Colonel Collyear packing after a similar challenge.

But when she raised her eyes again she saw Belinda's features had gone pale, her sudden confidence evaporated.

Catherine said evenly, 'I know that you have no true pride in Richard. You are not fit to carry his name. And let me assure you that had we two been men I would willingly call you out. Your ignorance is far more offensive than your smugness!'

She walked towards the door. 'Dulcie has a fever. I heard the gardeners speaking of it before you found me.' Her eyes flashed dangerously. 'Yes, being married to a Spaniard does have its advantages!'

Belinda said, 'You are trying to frighten me.' But there was no defiance now.

'There is an outbreak on the hulks – it sounds like jail fever. You should have been told. How long has she been like that?'

Belinda's hands plucked at her rich gown, confused by the swift change of events.

'A few days. After her husband's ship sailed.' Her voice faltered. 'What of it?'

Catherine did not answer immediately. 'Send for Mr Yovell. He must take a message for me. Do not make a stupid scene of it. All the servants will go if they understand. It would be better if they were kept away from this room.'

'Is it so terrible?'

Catherine regarded her thoughtfully; she would be useless. 'I shall stay with her.'

She remembered Belinda's frantic question. 'It is typhus.' She saw the word bring terror to her eyes. 'I fear she will not survive it.'

The door opened and Yovell tiptoed across the hallway, although he had not yet been summoned. He listened, his round face expressionless while Catherine explained what had happened.

'This is bad, m'lady.' He watched her gravely. 'We should send for expert help.'

She saw his anxiety, and laid her hand on his plump arm. 'Even then it will be too late. I have seen it before. Had she been treated earlier . . .' She looked at the windows; a watery sunlight was breaking through. 'Even then I think it would have been hopeless. She is in pain, and there were traces of a rash when her shawl was moved. I must stay with her, Daniel. No one should die alone.'

Belinda crossed the hallway, her hands agitated. 'I will have to return to London. My daughter is there.'

Catherine said, 'Go then.' As Belinda hurried to the stairs she remarked, 'You see, Daniel? I have no choice now, even if I wanted one.'

'What do you wish, m'lady? Anything, and I shall do it.'

She smiled, but her thoughts were once more in the past. When she had climbed naked into Bolitho's bed when he had been dying of fever, to bring warmth to his tormented body. And he had never remembered it.

'Go to Chatham. We have sworn to have no secrets, so I must let him know.'

She smiled again and thought sadly, *As he will eventually tell me about his eye.*

Yovell said, 'I shall do that, m'lady.' Then, with a glance at the closed doors, he hurried away.

Belinda came slowly down the staircase, her eyes all the while on the woman in the dull black gown.

By the door she turned and said, '*I hope you die!*'

Catherine looked after her impassively. 'Even then he would not come to you.' But Belinda had gone; and she heard her carriage moving rapidly over the cobbles towards the road.

The same servant was back, staring at Catherine as if she were some secret force which had suddenly come amongst them.

Catherine smiled at her. 'Fetch the housekeeper and the cook.' She saw her uncertainty, the beginning of fear perhaps. 'What is your name, girl?'

'Mary, m'lady.'

'Well, Mary, we are going to look after your mistress. Make things easier for her – do you understand?'

The girl bobbed and showed her teeth. 'Make 'er better, like?'

'That is so. Now off you go and fetch them, while I make a list of things we shall require.'

Alone once more, Catherine leaned her head in her hands and closed her eyes tightly to hold back the hot tears which were waiting to betray her. She had to be strong, as she had been in the past when her world had turned into a nightmare. Danger and death were not new to her, but the thought of losing him now was far more than she could bear. She heard Dulcie calling for someone; she thought she had spoken Herrick's name. She clenched her fists. *What else can I do?*

She seemed to hear Belinda's hatred hanging in the still air. *I hope you die!*

Curiously, it seemed to give her the strength she needed, and when the two women who controlled Dulcie's household entered she spoke to them calmly and without hesitation.

'Your mistress must be bathed. I shall attend to it. Prepare some nourishing soup, and I will need brandy.' The cook bustled away and the housekeeper said quietly, 'Don't 'ee fear, missus, I'll stay with 'ee till it's over.' She bowed her grey head. 'She's bin good to me since my man died.' She raised her head and looked at Catherine steadily. 'He went for a soldier, missus. Fever took 'im from me in the Indies.'

'So you knew?'

The old housekeeper shrugged. 'Guessed, more like. But 'er ladyship said I was bein' foolish.' She glanced around. 'I see *she's* gone all the same.' Then she looked at Catherine and nodded as if in recognition. 'Your man would know about it, I reckon. Rats leavin' the sinkin' ship.' She unbuttoned her sleeves. 'So let's make a start, shall we?'

'Send someone for the doctor. Good or bad, he *should* know.'

The housekeeper studied Catherine's gown. 'I got some servants' clothin' you could wear. It can be burned afterwards.'

The word *afterwards* was still with Catherine when night, like mourning, eventually covered the house.

249

It was very late by the time Young Matthew turned the carriage through the familiar gates, the air from the sea cold enough for snow. As they had rattled through the town, Bolitho had stared out of the window as if expecting to see changes. He always felt like that when he returned to Falmouth, no matter how long or short his absence had been.

Lights still twinkled from some houses and shops, and when they climbed the hill to his home he saw the cottages, their windows lit by candles, with coloured paper and leaves as decoration. It even felt like Christmas. Catherine, muffled in her cloak and fur-lined hood, watched the passing scene with him; she had never expected to see this place again.

It made Bolitho feel sick just to imagine what could so easily have happened. When Yovell had brought word of Dulcie's terrible illness to the inn where they had been staying near the dockyard, he had been beside himself. More so because the carriage had lost a wheel in the darkness, adding an extra day to her lonely vigil.

Bolitho had not waited for the carriage but had taken a horse, and with Jenour keeping pace beside him had ridden hard all the way to Herrick's house. It had been over even before he reached her. Dulcie had died, mercifully after her heart had failed, so that she was spared the final degradation of the fever. Catherine had been lying on a bed, covered by a blanket but otherwise naked as the old housekeeper had burned her borrowed clothes. How easily she might have been infected; she had tended to Dulcie's most painful and intimate needs to the end, had heard her despairing delirium, when she had called out names Catherine had never heard before.

The doctor had eventually attended, a weak sort of man who had been overwhelmed by the manner of Dulcie's death.

The carriage had followed several hours after Bolitho, when Yovell had commented that Lady Belinda had left since his departure for Chatham. He glanced at Catherine's profile and held her arm even tighter. Not once had she mentioned that Belinda had abandoned her to cope with Dulcie on her own. Almost anyone in her position would have done so, if only to bring contempt and scorn on a rival. It was as if she no longer cared. Only that they were together. Six days on the awful roads, a long and tiring journey, but now they were here.

250

Ferguson and his wife, the housekeeper, were waiting for them, while other familiar faces floated into the carriage lamps, gathering luggage, calling greetings, glad to see them back.

Ferguson had had no idea of the exact date of their return but he had been well prepared. Great fires in every room, even in the stone hallway, so that the contrast with the cold outside was like an additional welcome. Alone at last in their room facing the headland and the sea beyond, Catherine said she would have a hot bath. She looked at him gravely. 'I want to wash it all away.' Then she held him tightly and kissed him.

She said just one word before she prized herself away. '*Home.*'

Ozzard came up to collect his uniform coat and left with it, humming softly to himself.

She called through the door, and Bolitho guessed it had been on her mind for much of the time.

'When will he be told?'

'Thomas?' He walked to the low window and peered out. No stars, so it was still overcast. He saw a tiny light far out to sea. Some small vessel trying to reach port for Christmas. He thought of Herrick coming to him and bringing the news of Cheney's death; it was something he could never forget. He answered quietly, 'Admiral Godschale will send word on the first vessel carrying despatches to the squadron. I sent a letter to go with it. From us both.' He thought he heard a catch in her voice and he said, 'You are not only lovely, you are also very brave. I would have died if anything had happened to you.'

She came out wearing a robe, her face glowing from the bath which was something else Ferguson had thought of.

'Dulcie said something of that to me.' Her lip trembled but she composed herself. 'I think she knew what was happening to her. She called for her husband several times.'

Bolitho held her against him so that she could not see his face. 'I will have to join the *Black Prince* quite shortly, Kate. A few weeks, perhaps less.'

She rested her head against his shoulder. 'I know . . . I am prepared. Don't think of it – take care of yourself as much as you can. For me. For us.'

He stared desperately at the crackling log fire. 'There is

251

something I did not tell you, Kate. There was so much to do, after the duel and . . . everything – then poor Dulcie.'

She leaned back in his arms as she so often did to study him, as if to read his innermost thoughts before he uttered a word.

She whispered, 'You look like a little boy, Richard. One with a secret.'

He said bluntly, 'They can't help me with my eye.' He gave a great sigh, relieved to have got it out at last, fearful what she might think. 'I wanted to tell you, but –'

She broke away from him and took his hand to lead him to the window. Then she thrust it wide open, oblivious to the bitter air. 'Listen, darling – church bells.'

They clung to each other as the joyous peal of bells echoed up the hill from the church of Charles the Martyr, where so many Bolitho memories were marked in stone.

She said, 'Kiss me. It's midnight, my love. Christmas morn.'

Then she closed the window very carefully and faced him.

'Look at me, Richard. What if it were me? Would you cast me aside? Do you think it makes any difference, *could* make any? I love you, so much you'll never know. And there is always hope. We shall keep trying. No doctor is God.'

There was a tap at the door and Ozzard stood there with his tray and some finely cut goblets. He blinked at them. 'Thought it might be proper, m'lady.'

It was champagne, misted over with ice from the stream.

Bolitho thanked the little man and opened the bottle. 'The only thing of any value to come out of France!'

She threw back her head and gave her bubbling laugh, something Bolitho had not heard since the pleasure gardens.

Bolitho said, 'You know, I think this is the first Christmas I have been in Falmouth since I was a midshipman.'

She turned down the bed, the half-empty glass still in her other hand. Then she let her robe fall to the floor and faced him, with pride and love in her dark eyes.

'You are my man. I am your woman. Then let us celebrate.'

Bolitho bent over and kissed her breast, heard her gasp, all else forgotten. And so it would be, he thought. The new flagship, Herrick, a court-martial . . . even the war could wait. He touched her breast with some champagne and kissed it again.

She pulled him down. 'Am I stone that I can wait so long?'

Ferguson and Allday were crossing the yard to share a last drink before the festivities in the house and on the estate commenced in earnest. Allday glanced up at a candlelit window. Ferguson, his friend since being pressed into Bolitho's *Phalarope*, heard him sigh, and guessed what he was thinking. He had known his wife Grace since childhood. Allday had nobody to call his own.

He said, 'Come and tell us all about it, John. We've heard a few rumours, but not much else.'

'I was thinking about Rear-Admiral Herrick. Takes you back, don't it, Bryan? *Phalarope*, the Cap'n, us an' Mr Herrick. Come a long way. Now he's lost *his* wife. Full circle, that's what.'

Ferguson opened the door of his little house and glanced round to make sure Grace had retired at long last.

'Here, I'll fetch some grog from the pantry.'

Allday gave a sad grin. Like them up there in that great bedroom. *A sailor's woman.* 'I'd relish that, matey!' *All of us, holding things at bay, knowing it must end, but making the best of it.*

He coughed on the rum and spluttered, 'God, this is the stuff to fill the sails!'

Ferguson smiled. 'Got it off a trader from Port Royal.' He saw the shadow lifting from Allday's face, and held up his glass.

'Welcome home, old friend!'

Allday's eyes crinkled. What Bolitho called him. 'An' here's to those who won't never come home.' He laughed, and the cat sleeping by the fire opened one eye with irritation. 'Even the officers – well, some of 'em!'

As Ferguson went away to open another bottle, Allday added quietly, 'An' to you both over yonder. May God protect you!'

When he looked out, their window was in darkness and only the distant boom of the sea gave him an answer. Always waiting.

CHAPTER SIXTEEN
The Squadron

His Britannic Majesty's Ship *Black Prince* seemed to hesitate for a moment before plunging her massive one thousand eight hundred tons into the next procession of troughs.

Aft in his spacious day cabin, Bolitho looked up from his final cup of coffee before starting the new day, and was surprised how easily the big second-rate took even the heaviest sea.

It was eight o'clock in the morning, and he could vaguely hear the muffled movements of the forenoon watchkeepers as they relieved the men on deck. Unlike *Hyperion* or any other two-decker, there was a sense of protected remoteness in *Black Prince*. Bolitho's quarters with their own private sternwalk were sandwiched between the wardroom beneath his feet and Keen's own domain directly above.

He shivered and looked at the leaping patterns of salt spray on the stern windows, frozen there like the ramblings of some insane artist. The day cabin was finely painted and moulded with carved panels, the stern bench seat and chairs finished with dark green leather. Catherine could have chosen it herself, he thought. But now it was bloomed with damp, and he could picture without effort the discomfort and as yet unfamiliarity endured by the flagship's company of eight hundred souls, including one hundred Royal Marines. Bolitho had once been a flag-captain in a big first-rate, the *Euryalus*, renamed after being taken as a prize from the French. *Twelve years ago*. At the worst time for England's embattled shores, when the fleet had mutinied at the Nore and Spithead. If ever Napoleon had missed

254

his chance, it had been then. They could be thankful a hundred times over that he was a land-creature and not a sailor.

Allday entered the cabin and regarded Bolitho impassively. 'First day o' February, Sir Richard.' He did not sound very enthusiastic about it. 'Like ice on deck.'

'How are things, Allday?' *My eyes and ears.*

Allday shrugged his broad shoulders and winced. He felt his wound more in cold weather.

'*Things*? I think most o' the people are in irons about the new ship.' He glanced around the magnificent cabin with neither dislike nor contentment. 'You can't find nothing when you needs it. All different from *Hyperion*.' His eyes gleamed momentarily and he added, 'I'll say one thing, Sir Richard, she's a good sailer for a big 'un. A few months' drill and who knows what Cap'n Keen will make her do.'

Bolitho understood. It was often so in a brand new vessel. Everything to be learned from the beginning again. *Black Prince* was no frigate, and with her towering hull and three lines of ports for her total firepower of ninety-four guns and two carronades, she would need firm handling.

'I heard a pipe just now.' Bolitho saw Ozzard pause beside the beautiful wine cooler and cabinet which he had found waiting on board when he had hoisted his flag at the fore. Catherine had made no mention of it. A gift like the previous one which now lay on the bottom with his old flagship. She had taken great care; the mahogany cabinet was perfectly matched, and on the top was an inlaid shield – the Bolitho coat of arms.

Ozzard wiped some of the damp bloom from it with his cloth and nodded approvingly. He had no need for words.

Allday watched him warily. 'It was a pipe to witness punishment in the forenoon watch, Sir Richard.'

Bolitho eyed him steadily. Keen would hate that, even when there was no other obvious solution. Bolitho had known too many captains who had flogged first and sought explanations only when it was too late.

There were voices at the outer screen door and Bolitho heard the marine sentry tap the deck with his musket. Keen, reporting at his usual time after he had checked the log, seen the new watch take over, and discussed the day's work with his first lieutenant.

He entered the cabin and said, 'Fresh nor'westerly, Sir Richard.' He nodded to Allday. 'But the decks are dry. She takes it well.' He looked strained, and there were shadows beneath his eyes. 'I am assured we will make contact with the squadron by noon if the weather holds.'

Bolitho noticed that Allday and Ozzard had quietly departed.

'Be seated, Val. Is something wrong?' He forced a smile. 'Is there ever a time in a sailor's life when there is not?'

Keen stared through the spray-dappled glass. 'There are several familiar faces in the company.' He shot him a quick glance. 'I thought you should know before you have cause to meet them.'

Bolitho watched the sea, silent beyond the thick windows, leaping and breaking, so dark it was almost black. There were always old faces. The navy was like that. A family, or a prison. With faces went memories. It could not be otherwise.

He answered. 'That was thoughtful of you, Val. I have deliberately kept out of your way since I stepped aboard.' He saw a big roller break astern and felt the responding shudder of the tiller-head one deck below. He had been at sea for four days. But for Catherine, it might have seemed that he had never left it.

He asked, 'How has my nephew settled down? With his H.E.I.C. experience he should soon prove ready for a lieutenant's examination, eh?'

Keen frowned. 'I have to speak my mind, Sir Richard. I think I know you too well to do otherwise.'

'I would expect nothing but honesty, Val. Despite demands on our authority, we are friends. *Nothing* can change that.' He paused, seeing the uncertainty on Keen's handsome features. 'Besides which, you command here, not I.'

Keen said, 'I am obliged to order another flogging. A seaman named Fittock, who was allegedly insolent to Mr Midshipman Vincent. The lieutenant of his division is young, perhaps too much so in experience if not in years, and maybe . . .'

'And *maybe*, Val, he thought better than to dispute Midshipman Vincent's testimony. *The vice-admiral's nephew* might do him harm.'

Keen shrugged. 'It is not easy. A new ship, a larger

256

proportion of landsmen than I would wish, and a certain listlessness amongst the people – any kind of weakness would be seen as something to exploit.'

'In other words, Vincent provoked the seaman?'

'I believe so. Fittock is a skilled hand. It's foolish to berate such a man in front of pressed landsmen.'

Bolitho thought of *Hyperion*'s captain before Keen had taken his place. He had been driven mad, and had tried to shoot his first lieutenant. He thought also of the sick and overworked commodore, Arthur Warren, at Good Hope, and of the wretched Varian, now awaiting a court-martial which might easily end with his own sword pointing towards him on the table, and death. Captains all; but all so different.

He suggested, 'It could be inexperience, or a need to impress.'

Keen said softly, 'But you don't think so.'

'It seems unlikely. Either way there is little we can do. If I admonish Vincent –' He saw the unspoken protest on Keen's face and added, 'You are his captain. But *if* I took a hand, they would see it as interference, a lack of trust, perhaps, in you. On the other hand if you quash the sentence the end result would be the same. The people might believe that *no* junior officer, Vincent or any other, is worth the cut of his coat.'

Keen sighed. 'Some would say it was a small thing, Sir Richard, but this ship is not yet of one company and does not have the loyalty which will unite the people, given time.'

Bolitho smiled grimly. 'Aye, that's so. Time is also in short supply.'

Keen prepared to leave. 'I have spoken with my first-lieutenant about it. Mr Cazalet is already my right arm.' He gave a rueful grin. 'But doubtless he will soon be promoted out of my ship for a command of his own.'

'A moment, Val. I merely wanted you to know that Catherine intends to call upon Zenoria. They were very close to one another and their suffering was much the same. So take heart – who would have believed that *I* might find Catherine again?'

Keen was silent, his eyes faraway. He was remembering how she had spoken to him, her sincerity about Zenoria matched only by the passion in her words.

Then he said, 'Shall you visit Rear-Admiral Herrick before *Benbow* quits the station?' When Bolitho did not answer immediately he added, 'I know there was bitterness between us . . . but no man should learn of his wife's death in such a fashion.' He hesitated. 'I beg your pardon, Sir Richard. That was a thoughtless and indiscreet thing to say.'

Bolitho touched his sleeve. 'Indiscretion is not unknown to me.' He became grave. 'But yes, I hope to see him when we meet with the squadron.'

There was a knock at the outer screen door and the marine sentry bawled, 'Midshipman-of-the-Watch, *sir!*'

Bolitho winced. 'God, you would think we were three fields away from the fellow!'

Ozzard had appeared in the other cabin, and opened the door to admit the midshipman.

Keen said quietly, 'Someone else whose life you changed, I think, Sir Richard?'

Bolitho looked at the pale-faced youth who was staring back at him, his eyes shining with a barely-contained recognition.

Bolitho said, 'I am glad you are in this ship, Mr Segrave.' He seemed older than when he had helped the cruelly disfigured Lieutenant Tyacke to steer the blazing *Albacora* into the moored supply ships at Good Hope.

'I – I wrote to you, Sir Richard, to thank you for your sponsorship. My uncle the Admiral was full of admiration!' It sounded as if he was about to add *for once*.

Segrave turned to Keen. 'Mr Cazalet's respects, sir, and the masthead has just sighted a sail to the nor'-east.'

'My compliments to the first lieutenant. I shall come up presently.'

As the door closed Keen said, 'I heard all about that lad, and the bullying he received in his other ship. Your Mr Tyacke has become a bit of a hero in his eyes, I think.' He smiled, so that the strain seemed to fall away. 'Next to *you*, of course, Sir Richard!'

It was good to see him smile again. Perhaps his lovely Zenoria came to him in his dreams and tormented him, as Catherine had done and would do again if they were too long separated.

'Lieutenant Tyacke is a remarkable man. When you meet him there is only pity. Afterwards you can only find admiration, pride, even, at knowing him.'

They went on deck together and walked out on to the broad quarterdeck, where at their approach the watchkeepers and the hands who were working there adopted stances and attitudes as if they were mimers.

Bolitho looked up at the dull sky, the tall masts and rigging dark against it. Under topsails and courses the *Black Prince* was leaning only slightly to leeward, her sails quivering to the wind's wet pressure.

'Deck there!' After *Truculent*, the lookout sounded a mile distant. 'Frigate, zur!'

Keen turned up his collar as the wind probed the rawness of his skin. 'Not a Frog, then. He'd be about and running by now if it was!'

Bolitho tried not to touch his left eye. Many were watching him, some seeing him for the first time. A new ship, a well-known flag-officer; it would be easy to lose their confidence before he had found it.

A tall, dark-haired midshipman whose generally aloof behaviour to the other 'young gentlemen' was obvious even on the busy quarterdeck snapped, 'Aloft, Mr Gough. Take a glass, lively now!' A minute midshipman scampered to the shrouds and was soon lost from view amongst the dark crisscross of rigging. Bolitho smiled to himself. The tall youth was named Bosanquet, the senior member of the gunroom, and next to go for promotion. It was not hard to see him as a lieutenant, or even a captain for that matter.

'*Deck there!*' Several of the seamen exchanged grins at the midshipman's squeaky cry from the crosstrees. '*She's made her number!*'

Cazalet, the first lieutenant, a tough-looking man with dark, bushy eyebrows, raised his speaking-trumpet. 'We are all in suspense, Mr Gough!'

The boy squeaked again, although even from that dizzy height he sounded crushed. '*Number Five-Four-Six*, sir!'

Bosanquet already had his book open. '*Zest* sir, forty-four, Captain Charles Varian!'

Jenour had appeared at his side like a shadow. 'You will need to change the captain's name.' He darted a glance at Bolitho. 'He is no longer in command.'

Keen said, 'Make our reply, if you please.'

Bolitho turned away. Some of the watching faces probably saw him as Varian's executioner, and might judge him accordingly.

He saw the boatswain, whose name was already slotted into his mind as Ben Gilpin, with a small working party, supervising the rigging of a grating on the lee side of the deck. Ready for the ritual of punishment. It would seem so much worse for those who had never been to sea in a King's ship before. And for many of the others, it could only brutalise them further.

Bolitho stiffened as he saw Felicity's son standing nearby, watching with fixed attention. Bolitho touched his eye and did not see Jenour glance across at him. He saw only Vincent's face. For one so young he had an expression of cruel anticipation.

Keen called, 'Alter course two points, Mr Cazalet, we will wait for *Zest* to run down on us!'

Jenour stood apart from the bustling seamen as they manned the braces for retrimming the great yards to hold the wind, immersed in his private thoughts. All of his family were in or connected with the medical profession, and he had mentioned the foreign-sounding doctor Rudolf Braks to his uncle just before leaving to join the flagship.

His uncle, a quiet and much respected physician, had responded instantly.

'Of course – the man who attended Lord Nelson and visits the King because of his failing sight. If he can do nothing to help your admiral, then there is nobody who can.'

The words still hung in his mind like part of a guilty secret.

He heard the first lieutenant ask, 'Pipe the hands aft to witness punishment, sir?' Then Keen's equally taut reply. 'Attend to it, Mr Cazalet, but I want loyalty, not fear!'

Bolitho walked towards the poop and knew Allday was following him. He had sensed the unusual bitterness in Keen's words. Had he perhaps been remembering how he had saved Zenoria from a savage whipping aboard the convict transport, when he had rescued her and helped to confirm her innocence? But not before she had taken one stroke across her naked back from shoulder to hip, something which she would never lose. Was that, too, keeping them apart?

He entered the stern cabin and threw himself on to the bench seat.

A new ship. No experience, unblooded, a stranger to the line of battle. Bolitho clenched his fist as he heard the staccato roll of the Royal Marines' drums. He could barely hear the crack of the lash across the seaman's body, but he felt it as if it were happening to himself.

He thought of Herrick, how he would be; what he was going through. Bolitho had heard from Admiral Godschale that it had been *Anemone*, Adam's command, which had carried the news of Dulcie's death. A double twist, he thought. It would have been better if it had been a total stranger.

He tried to think about the squadron he was taking from Herrick. Five ships of the line and only two frigates. There were never enough.

Allday walked across the cabin, his eyes watchful. 'Punishment's over, Sir Richard.'

Bolitho barely heard. He was thinking of Vincent again, of his sister's reproachful coldness towards Catherine.

He said distantly, 'Never hold out your hand too often, old friend.' Then he turned away and added, 'You can get badly bitten.'

'Watch your stroke!' Allday leaned forward, one hand on the tiller bar, as if he were riding across the choppy water instead of steering the *Black Prince*'s barge. Even with all his experience it was going to be a difficult crossing from one flagship to the other. He knew better than to use some of his stronger language in front of his admiral, but later he would have no such qualms. In their turn, the bargemen put all their weight on the painted looms, conscious more of Allday's threatening gaze, perhaps, than their passenger.

Bolitho turned and looked back at his new flagship. It was the first time he had seen her properly in her own element. The light was dull and grey, but even so the powerful three-decker seemed to shine like polished glass, her black and buff hull and the chequered pattern of gunports making a splash of welcome colour against the miserable North Sea afternoon. Beyond her, and turning away almost guiltily, the *Zest* was standing off to resume her proper station.

Bolitho felt Jenour watching him as the green-painted barge lifted and plunged over the water in sickening swoops.

Keen had done well, he thought. He must have been pulled around the ship before and after he had first taken her to sea. He had checked the trim of the great hull, and had ordered some of the ballast to be moved, and many of the stores shifted to different holds to give the ship the right lift at the stem. He saw the figurehead reaching out with his sword from beneath the beakhead. It was one of the most lifelike he had yet seen, carved and painted more to impress than frighten. The son of Edward III, complete with chain mail, fleur-de-lis and English lions. From the black crowned helmet to the figure's unflinching stare, it could have been a living being. The carver had been one of the most famous of his breed, old Aaron Mallow of Sheerness. Sadly, *Black Prince*'s figurehead had been his last; he had died shortly after the ship had been launched for fitting-out.

Bolitho looked instead at *Benbow*, once his own flagship, when Herrick had been his captain. A seventy-four like *Hyperion* but much heavier, for she had been built much later when there were still the oak forests to provide for her. Now the forests of Kent and Sussex, Hampshire and the West Country were left bare, raped by the mounting demands of a war which never lessened in its ferocity.

He saw the scarlet of the marines, the dull glint of metal in the fading light, and felt a pang of anxiety. Herrick was his oldest friend. Had been until . . . He thought suddenly of what Keen had told him about the man who had been flogged. Stripped and seized up to the grating by wrists and knees, he had taken a dozen lashes without a protest, only the usual sound of the air being beaten from his lungs with each blow of the cat.

It was while he was being cut down that an unknown voice had yelled out from the silent onlookers, 'We'll make it even for you, Jim!'

Needless to say, the ship's corporal and the master-at-arms had been unable to discover the culprit. In a way, Bolitho was glad, but he had shared Keen's uneasiness that anyone should show defiance in front of his captain and the armed marines.

And so the unknown seaman named Jim Fittock had become something of a martyr because of Felicity's son Miles Vincent. Bolitho tightened his jaw. It must not happen again.

The other flagship loomed over him, and he sensed Allday's seething exasperation as the bowman had to make several attempts to hook on to the main chains.

As he clambered up the salt-caked side he was thankful for the dull light. To trip and fall like the other time would not rouse any confidence either.

The quarterdeck seemed quiet and sheltered after the blustery crossing in an open boat, so that the sudden din of drums and fifes, a Royal Marines captain shouting orders to the guard plus the dwindling echo of the calls which had piped him aboard took him by surprise.

In those few moments he saw several familiar faces, suitably expressionless for the occasion, with the flag-captain Hector Gossage standing like a rock in front of his officers. He saw the new flag-lieutenant who had replaced De Broux, the one with the *damned Frenchie name* as Herrick had put it. The newcomer was plump, and his face was empty of animation or intelligence.

Then he saw Herrick and felt a cold hand around his heart.

Herrick's hair, once brown and only touched with grey like frost, was almost colourless, and his bronzed features seemed suddenly lined. He could recall their brief meeting in the Admiralty corridor, the two visiting captains gaping at them as Bolitho had called after Herrick, his voice shaking with anger and with hurt. It did not seem possible a man could change so much in so short a time.

Herrick said, 'You are welcome, Sir Richard.' He shook hands, his palm hard and firm as Bolitho had always remembered. 'You will remember Captain Gossage, of course?'

Bolitho nodded, but did not take his eyes from Herrick. 'My heart is full for you, Thomas.'

Herrick gave what might have been a shrug, perhaps to cover his innermost feelings. He said in a vague tone, 'Dismiss the hands, Captain Gossage. Keep station on *Black Prince*, but call me if the weather goes against us.' He gestured aft. 'Join me, Sir Richard. We can talk a while.' Bolitho ducked beneath the poop and studied his friend as Herrick led the way into the shadows between decks. Had he always been so stooped? He did not recall so. As if he were carrying the pain of his loss like a burden on his back.

In the great cabin where Bolitho had so often paced and fretted over the next action or the enemy's intentions, he looked around as if to see something of himself still lingering here. But there was nothing. It could have been the great cabin of almost any ship-of-the-line, he thought.

A servant he did not recognise brought a chair for him, and Herrick asked in an almost matter-of-fact voice, 'A drink perhaps?'

He did not wait for answer. 'Bring the brandy, Murray.' Then he faced Bolitho and said, 'I received word you were coming. I am relieved so that *Benbow* can have some repairs carried out. We almost lost the rudder in a gale . . . but I expect you were in England at the time. It was bad – the sea took a master's mate and two seamen, poor devils. No chance of finding 'em.'

Bolitho tried not to interrupt. Herrick was coming around to what he wanted to say. He had always been like that. But brandy, that was something else. Wine, yes, ginger beer more likely; he must have been drinking heavily since Adam had brought him the news.

Herrick said, 'I got your letter. It was good of you.' He nodded to the servant and then snapped, 'Leave it, man, I can manage!' That, too, was not like the old Herrick, the champion of the common seaman more than anyone he had known. Bolitho watched the hand shaking as he slopped two huge measures of brandy into the goblets, some of it spilling unheeded on to the black and white chequered deck covering. 'Good stuff this. My patrols took it off a smuggler.' Then he turned and stared at him, his eyes still as clear and blue as Bolitho remembered. It was like seeing someone familiar peering out of another's body.

'God damn it, I wasn't with her when she needed me most!' The words were torn out of him. 'I'd warned her about working amongst those bloody prisoners – I'd hang the lot of them if I had my way!' He walked to a bulkhead where Bolitho had once hung his swords. Herrick's fighting hanger dangled from it, swaying unevenly to the pitch of the ship as she fought to keep station on *Black Prince*. But Herrick was touching the finely finished, silver-mounted telescope, the one which Dulcie had bought for him from the best instrument maker in London's

Strand; Bolitho doubted if he knew what he was doing. He probably touched it for comfort rather than to be reminded.

Bolitho said, 'I could not get to the house in time. Otherwise I would . . .'

Herrick tilted the goblet until it was empty. 'Lady Bolitho told me all about those damned Dons who worked around the house. She would have sent them packing!' He looked at Bolitho and asked abruptly, 'Was it all taken care of?'

'Yes. Your sister was there. A lot of Dulcie's friends too.'

Herrick said in a small voice, 'I wasn't even there to see her buried. *Alone* . . .' The one word echoed around the cabin until he said, 'Your lady tried her best . . .'

Bolitho said quietly, 'Dulcie was not alone. Catherine stayed with her, attended to her every need until she was mercifully released from her suffering. It took courage, for there was no little danger to her.'

Herrick walked to the table and lifted the brandy, then waved it vaguely towards the sea.

'Just her? With my Dulcie!'

'Aye. She'd not even allow your housekeeper in close contact.'

Herrick rubbed his eyes as if they were hurting him. 'I suppose you think that gives you the opportunity to redeem her in my opinion.'

Bolitho kept his voice level. 'I am not here to score points from your grief. I am well reminded when you came to me with terrible news. I grieve for you, Thomas, for I know what it is to lose love – just as I understand how it feels to discover it.'

Herrick sat down heavily and refilled his goblet, his features set in tight concentration, as if every thought was an effort.

Then he said in a thick voice, 'So you've got your woman, and I've lost everything. Dulcie gave me strength, she made me feel somebody. A long, long step from the son of a poor clerk to rear-admiral, eh?' When Bolitho said nothing he leaned over the table and shouted, 'But *you* wouldn't understand! I saw it in young Adam when he came aboard – it's all there in him too, like they speak of it in the news-sheets. The Bolitho charm –isn't that so?'

'I shall leave now, Thomas.' His despair was so destructive it

265

was too terrible to watch. Later Herrick would regret his outburst, his words so bitter that it had sounded like something he had been nursing all down the years. A warmth gone sour; envy where there had once been the strongest bond of true friendship. 'Use your time in England to think and relive the good things you found together – and when next we meet –'

Herrick lurched to his feet and almost fell. For an instant his eyes seemed to clear again and he blurted out, 'Your injury? Is it improved now?' Somehow through the mist of distress and loss he must have recalled when Bolitho had almost fallen on this same vessel.

Then he said, 'Lady Catherine's husband is dead, I hear?' It was a challenge, like an accusation. 'Convenient –'

'Not so, Thomas. One day you might understand.' Bolitho turned and recovered his hat and cloak as the door opened a few inches, and Captain Gossage peered in at them.

'I was about to inform the rear-admiral that the wind is rising, Sir Richard.' His glance moved quickly to Herrick who was slumped down again in his chair, his eyes trying to focus, but without success.

Gossage said swiftly, with what he thought was discretion, 'I will call the guard, Sir Richard, and have you seen over the side.'

Bolitho looked gravely at his friend and answered, 'No, call my barge.' He hesitated by the screen door and lowered his voice, so that the marine sentry should not hear.

'Then attend your admiral. There sits a brave man, but badly wounded now – no less than by the enemy's fire.' He nodded curtly. 'I bid you good-day, Captain Gossage.'

He found Jenour waiting for him on deck and saw a messenger running from Gossage to recall the barge to the chains.

Jenour had rarely seen him look so grim, so sad at the same time. But he was not so inexperienced in Bolitho's ways to ask what had occurred during his visit, or mention the glaring fact that Rear-Admiral Herrick was not on deck to show the proper respect at Bolitho's departure.

Instead he said brightly, 'I heard the sailing-master confide that yonder lies the Dutch coast – but we are losing it fast in another squall.' He fell silent as Bolitho looked at him for the first time.

266

Bolitho touched his eye with his fingers, and felt it sting like a cruel reminder. Then he asked, 'Is the barge alongside, Stephen?'

As Jenour left him he thought he heard him murmur, 'Dear God, I would that it were Cornwall.'

The captain of marines yelled, 'Guard of Honour, pre-sent *arms!*'

The rest was lost as Bolitho swung himself out and down to the pitching barge, as if the sea had reclaimed him.

Lieutenant Stephen Jenour tucked his hat beneath his arm and entered Bolitho's day cabin. Outside on the open deck the air was still very cold, but a lull in the blustery wind had smoothed out the North Sea's short, steep waves and remained with them. The presence of some watery sunlight gave an illusion of warmth in the crowded messes, and here in the great cabin.

Bolitho was leaning over a chart, his hands spread across it as if to encompass the squadron's limits. He looked tired, Jenour thought, but calmer than the moment he had left his friend aboard *Benbow*. He could only guess at what had come between them but knew it had affected Bolitho deeply.

Beyond the tall stern windows he could see two of the squadron's seventy-fours, the *Glorious* and the old *Sunderland*. The latter was so elderly that many aboard *Black Prince* had thought her either hulked or sunk in battle. There were few campaigns she had missed; she would be, Jenour thought, about the same age as *Hyperion*.

With *Benbow* returned to England there were five ships-of-the-line awaiting *Black Prince*'s signals, and two others, the *Tenacious* and the *Valkyrie*, were undergoing repairs in England. Jenour had thought it strange that Rear-Admiral Herrick had detached two of his depleted strength without waiting to hear Bolitho's views on the subject. But he had kept his thoughts to himself. He had learned to recognise most, if not all of Bolitho's moods and sensitivities, and knew that he was occasionally only partly in his flagship, while the rest of the time he was in spirit with Catherine in England.

He realised that Bolitho had raised his eyes from the chart, and was watching him patiently. Jenour flushed, something he still did far too often – much to his own annoyance.

'The captains are assembled on board, Sir Richard. Only *Zest*'s commander is absent and on his patrol area.'

Bolitho nodded. Two weeks since he had parted from Herrick, with too much time to think back over their exchange. Now, for the first time, because of the improved weather conditions, he had drawn the bulk of his squadron together in the hard glare which made the sea look like beaten silver. It was the first time, also, that his captains had managed to reach the flagship.

'What about our courier-brig?'

Jenour flushed still further. How could Bolitho have known that the brig had been reported by *Glorious*'s masthead lookout? He had been here in his quarters since a dawn stroll, not on his private sternwalk, but on the quarterdeck in full view of everyone.

Bolitho saw his confusion and smiled. 'I heard the signal being repeated on deck, Stephen. A sternwalk has its uses – the sound carries quite well.' He added wryly, 'Even the things that people say, when they are being somewhat indiscreet!'

He tried not to hope that the little brig, named *Mistral*, was bringing a letter from Catherine. It was too soon, and anyway she would be very busy. He laid out each careful excuse to hold his disappointment at bay.

He said, 'Signal her commander to report on board when the time comes.'

He thought of the captains who were waiting to meet him. Not one of them a friend; but all were experienced. That would suffice. After Thomas Herrick . . . his mind thrust it away, feeling the same hurt and sense of betrayal. There had been a time when, as a captain himself, he had fretted about meeting a new ship's company. Now he knew from experience that usually they were far more worried than he.

All through the past hour or so, calls had shrilled at the entry port as the various captains had been piped aboard. Each one of them might be thinking more about the rumours of scandal than what lay ahead.

He said, 'Please ask Captain Keen to bring them here.' He had not noticed the sudden edge to his voice. 'He was quite surprised to see his old *Nicator* as one of the squadron . . . he commanded her six or seven years back. We were at Copenhagen together.' His grey eyes became distant. 'I lost some good friends that day.'

Jenour waited, and saw the sudden despair depart from his face like a cloud across the sea.

Bolitho smiled. 'He said to me once that *Nicator* was so rotten there were many times he believed only a thin sheet of copper stood between himself and eternity. Heaven knows what the old ship is like now!'

Jenour paused by the door, hating to break into these confidences. 'Are we so short of ships, Sir Richard?'

Bolitho walked to the quarter galley and watched the uneasy water, the way some circling gulls appeared to change colour as they dipped and drifted through the sunlight.

'I fear so, Stephen. That is why those Danish ships are so important. It might all come to nothing, but I think not. I did not *imagine* Poland's death, nor did I invent the near destruction of *Truculent*. They *knew we were there*.' He remembered how Sir Charles Inskip had scoffed at him because of his suspicions about French intentions. But that had been before the desperate battle; he had not scoffed since.

He became impatient with his memories and said, 'Tell Ozzard to fetch some wine for our guests.'

Jenour closed the door, and saw Ozzard and another servant already preparing goblets and standing them inside the fiddles in case a sudden squall came down on the ship.

Bolitho walked to the wine-cooler and touched the inlay with his fingers. Herrick would be at his home. Remembering how it had been; expecting to see his Dulcie and feel the warmth of her obvious adoration for him. Herrick was probably blaming him too for *Benbow*'s being relieved; as if it had happened because Bolitho wanted the squadron for himself. How little he knew – but it was always easy to find a bitter reason if you wanted it enough.

The door opened and Keen ushered the others inside so that they could introduce themselves to Bolitho on arrival.

He had a mixed impression of experience, competence and curiosity. All were post-captains except the last one to arrive. Ozzard bustled amongst them with his tray, but their eyes were

269

on the captain of the frigate *Anemone* as he reported to their vice-admiral. More like a younger brother than a nephew.

Bolitho clasped Adam's hand but could no longer restrain himself, and put his arm around his shoulder and hugged him.

The dark hair which matched his own; even the restless energy of a young colt when he had first joined *Hyperion* as a skinny midshipman of fourteen years. It was all still there. Bolitho held him at arm's length and studied him feature by feature. But Adam was a man now, a captain of his own frigate; what he had always dreamed about. He was twenty-six years old. Another twist of Fate? Bolitho had been the same age when he had been given command of his first frigate.

Adam said quietly, 'It is *good* to see you, Uncle. We barely had an hour together after *Truculent*'s return to port.'

His words seemed to linger in the air like the memory of a threat. But for *Anemone*'s sudden appearance, the three French vessels would surely have overwhelmed Poland's ship by sheer weight of artillery.

Bolitho thought grimly, *And I would be dead*. He knew he would never allow himself to be taken prisoner again.

Keen had got the others seated and they were watching the reunion, each man fitting it into his own image of the Bolitho they knew, or had only heard about. There was no sort of resentment on their faces; Bolitho guessed that Adam was far too junior to present any kind of threat to their own status in the squadron.

Bolitho said, 'We will talk far longer this time. I am proud to have you under my flag.'

All at once the midshipman with the cheeky grin was back again. Adam said, 'From what I hear and read, it is barely safe to leave you on your own, Uncle!'

Bolitho composed himself and faced Keen and the other captains. There was so much he wanted to tell Adam, *needed* to tell him, so that there would never be any doubts, no secrets to plague them when they were alone.

Adam looked so *right* in his dress coat; but more like a youth playing the part of a hero than the man who held the destiny of a thirty-eight gun frigate and some one hundred and eighty souls in his hands. He thought of Herrick's distress, his scathing

270

comments about *the Bolitho charm*. Maybe he had been right? It was easy to picture Adam's face now in one of the portraits at the house in Falmouth.

'I wanted to meet you as soon as possible, for I have discovered in the past that circumstances often prevent us from taking our time over such matters.' There were several smiles. 'I am sorry that we are short of two in our numbers –' He hesitated as he realised what he had said. It was as if Herrick was right here, watching, resenting the implication; blaming him for sending the two ships into port without waiting. He said, 'This is not a time for loosening our grip on the reins. There are many who saw Trafalgar as a victory which would end all danger at a single stroke. I have seen and heard it for myself, in the fleet and on the streets of London. I can assure you, gentlemen, it is a foolish and misinformed captain who believes this is a time for relaxation. We *need every ship we can get*, and the men who care enough to fight them when the time comes, as come it must. The French will exploit their gains on land and have proved that few troops can withstand them. And who knows what leaders they will put to sea once they have the ships again to use against us? The French navy was weakened by the very force which brought Napoleon to power. During the blood-letting of the Terror, loyal officers were beheaded in the same blind savagery as the so-called aristocrats! But new faces will appear, and when they do we must be ready.' He felt suddenly drained, and saw Adam watching him with concern.

He asked, 'Have you any questions?'

Captain John Crowfoot of the *Glorious*, a tall, stooping figure with the solemn looks of a village clergyman, asked, 'Will the Danes offer their fleet to the enemy, Sir Richard?'

Bolitho smiled. He even sounded like one. 'I think not. But under extreme pressure they might yield. No Dane wants the French army on his soil. Napoleon's armies have a habit of staying put after they have invaded, no matter on what pretext.'

Bolitho saw Keen lean forward to look at the next captain to speak. It was Captain George Huxley who commanded *Nicator*, Keen's old ship. He was probably wondering what kind of man could be expected to hold the rotting seventy-four together.

Huxley was stocky and level-eyed, giving an immediate

271

impression of unwavering self-confidence. A hard man, Bolitho thought.

Huxley insisted, 'We must have more frigates, Sir Richard. Without them we are blind and ignorant of affairs. A squadron, nay, a fleet could pass us in the night, to seaward or yonder along the Dutch coast, and we might never know.'

Bolitho saw one of them glance round as if he expected to see the Dutch coastline, even though it was more than thirty miles abeam.

He said, 'I share that sentiment, Captain Huxley. I have but two under my command. That of my nephew, and the *Zest*, whose captain I am yet to meet.'

He thought of Keen's remark: 'Captain Fordyce has the reputation of a martinet, sir. He is an admiral's son, as you will know, but his methods are hardly mine.' It was rare for Keen to speak out on the subject of a fellow captain. Their lordships probably thought that *Zest* needed a firmer hand after Varian's example.

There were more questions on repairs and supplies, on patrol areas and shortages. Some of the questions were directed at Bolitho's proposed signals and fighting instructions, because of their brevity rather than their context.

Bolitho looked at them thoughtfully. *They do not know me. Yet.*

He replied, 'Too much time is lost, wasted by unnecessary exchanges in the midst of a sea-fight. And time, as you know from experience, is a luxury we may not always have.' He let each word sink in before he added, 'I had correspondence with Lord Nelson, but like most of you, I never had the good fortune to meet him.' He let his gaze rest on Adam. 'My nephew is the exception. He met him more than once – a privilege we can never share. Gone for ever he may be, but his example is still ours to be seized and used.' He had all their attention, and he saw Adam touch his cheek surreptitiously with the back of his hand.

'Nelson once said that in his opinion no captain could do very wrong if he laid his ship alongside that of an enemy.' He saw Crowfoot of the *Glorious* nod vigorously, and knew that by the door Jenour was staring at him as if afraid he might miss something.

272

Bolitho ended simply, 'In answer to some of your questions – I don't think Our Nel's words can ever be improved on.'

It was another two hours before they all departed, feeling better for the plentiful supply of wine, and each man preparing his own version of the meeting for his wardroom and company.

As Ozzard remarked ruefully, 'They certainly made a hole in the cheese Lady Catherine sent aboard!'

Bolitho found some time to speak with the youngest captain in his squadron, *Mistral*'s Commander Philip Merrye, whom Allday later described contemptuously, ''Nother one of those twelve-year-old cap'ns!'

Then under a gentler north-westerly than they had known, the five sail-of-the-line took station on their flagship and brought in another reef for the coming night. Each captain and lieutenant was very aware of the man whose flag floated from *Black Prince*'s foremast, and the need not to lose contact with him in the gathering darkness.

Keen had been going to ask Bolitho to sup with him, but when the brig's commander had produced a letter for him he had decided otherwise.

It was to be a private moment, shared by nobody but the ship around him, and with Catherine. This was a man none of his captains would recognise, as he bent over his table and carefully opened her letter. He knew he would read it many times; and he found he was touching the locket beneath his shirt as he straightened the letter under a deckhead lantern.

Darling Richard, dearest of men, so short a while since we were parted and yet already a lifetime . . .

Bolitho stared around the cabin and spoke her name aloud. 'Soon, my love, soon . . .' And in the sea's murmur, he thought he heard her laugh.

17

'You Hold Their Hearts . . .'

If the officers and men of Bolitho's North Sea squadron had expected a quick relief from the dragging boredom of blockade duty, they were soon to be disappointed. Weeks overlapped into months. Spring drove away the icy winds and constant damp of winter, and still they endured the endless and seemingly pointless patrols. Northward from the Frisian Islands, with the Dutch coast sometimes in view, often as far as the Skagerrak where Poland had fought his last battle.

Better than most Bolitho knew he was driving them hard, more so than they had probably ever endured before. Sail and gun drills, in line ahead or abreast to a minimum of signals. Then he had divided his squadron into two divisions with the clergyman-like Crowfoot's *Glorious* as senior ship of the other line. Bolitho had now been reinforced by the two remaining seventy-fours, *Valkyrie* and *Tenacious*, and a small but welcome addition of the schooner *Radiant*, the latter commanded by an elderly lieutenant who had once been with the revenue service.

Small *Radiant* might be, but she was fast enough to dart close inshore and make off again before an enemy patrol vessel could be roused enough to weigh anchor and come out to discourage her impudence.

Allday was shaving Bolitho one morning and for the first time since they had come aboard, the stern windows were open, and there was real warmth in the air. Bolitho stared up at the deckhead while the razor rasped expertly under his chin.

The blade stilled as he said, 'I suppose they hate my insides for all the drills I am forcing on them?'

Allday waited and then continued with his razor. 'Better this way, Sir Richard. It's fair enough in small craft, but in big ships like this 'un it's wrong to draw officers and sailors too close together.'

Bolitho looked at him curiously. *More wisdom.* 'How so?'

''Tween decks they *needs* someone to hate. Keeps them on edge, like a cutlass to a grindstone!'

Bolitho smiled and let his mind drift again. Cornwall would be fresh again after the drab weather. Bright yellow gorse, sheets of bluebells along the little paths to the headland. What would Catherine be doing? He had received several letters in the courier brig; once he had three altogether, as often happened with the King's ships constantly at sea. Catherine always made her letters interesting. She had dispensed with Somervell's property in London, and after paying off what sounded like a mountain of debts she had purchased a small house near the Thames. It was as if she had felt his sudden anxiety all the miles across the North Sea and had explained, 'When you must be in London, we will have our own haven – we shall be beholden to nobody.' She spoke too of Falmouth, of ideas which she and Ferguson had put in motion to clear more land, to make a profit, and not merely sustain its existence. She never mentioned Belinda, nor did she speak of the enormous amount of money Belinda required to live in the only style she had come to accept.

There was a knock at the outer door and Keen entered and said apologetically, 'I thought you should know, Sir Richard. Our schooner is in sight to the east'rd and is desiring to close on us.'

Allday dabbed Bolitho's face and watched the light in his eyes. There was no sign of injury. No change, he thought. So perhaps after all . . .

Bolitho said, 'News, d'you think, Val?'

Keen said impassively, 'She comes from the right direction.'

In Catherine's last letter she had mentioned her meeting with Zenoria. 'Tell Val to take heart. The love is as strong as before. It needs a sign.' Keen had taken the news without comment. Resigned, hopeful or desperate; whatever his emotions were, he hid them well.

275

When Allday had left them alone Bolitho exclaimed, 'In God's name, Val, how much longer must we beat up and down this barren coast waiting for some word? Every morning the horizon is empty but for our own companions, each sunset brings more curses from the people because of all this futility!'

There were more delays, while the schooner tacked this way and that before she could lie under *Black Prince*'s lee and drop her boat in the water.

Lieutenant Evan Evans had served with the Revenue cutters before joining the King's navy, but he looked more like a pirate than a law-abiding sailor. A great block of a man with rough grey hair which looked as if he cut it himself with shears, a brick-red face so battered and so ruined by hard drinking that he was a formidable presence even in Bolitho's great cabin.

Ozzard brought some wine but Evans shook his shaggy head. 'None o' that, beggin' yer pardon, Sir Richard – it plays hell with my gut!'

But when Ozzard produced some rum Evans drained the tankard in one swallow. 'More like it, see?'

Bolitho said, 'Tell me what you found.'

Together they walked to the table where Bolitho's own chart was spread with his personal log open beside it.

Evans put a finger as thick and as hard as a marlin spike on the chart and said, 'Three days back, Sir Richard. Makin' for the Bay o' Heligoland, she was, leastways 'twas a fair guess at her direction.'

Bolitho contained his impatience. Evans was reliving it. It would destroy the picture in his mind if he was goaded. It was strange to hear the local landmarks described in his rich Welsh accent.

Keen prompted gently, 'She?'

Evans glared at him and continued, 'Big as a cathedral, she was. Ship-o'-th'-line.' He shrugged heavily. 'Then two frigates came from nowhere, out o' th' sun to all intents. One was a forty-four.' He frowned, so that his bright eyes seemed to vanish into thick folds of skin.

Bolitho straightened his back and clasped his fingers together behind him. 'Did you see her name, Mr Evans?'

'Well, we were proper busy when she let fly with a bow-

276

chaser, but my little schooner can show a clean pair o' heels as anyone will tell you . . .'

Bolitho remarked, 'She was *L'Intrépide*, was she not?'

The others stared at him and Keen asked, 'But how could you know, sir?'

'A premonition.' He turned from the table to conceal his face from them. It was here; he could feel it. Not just yet, but soon, quite soon.

'The larger vessel – how big, d'you think?'

Evans nodded to Ozzard and took another tankard of rum. Then he wiped his lips with the back of his rough hand and frowned. It seemed habitual.

'Well, I'm no real judge, but she were a liner right enough.' He glanced professionally around the cabin. 'Bigger'n this 'un, see?'

'*What?*' Bolitho turned back at Keen's sudden surprise and doubt. 'Must be a mistake, sir. I have read every word of those reports from the Admiralty. No ship larger than a seventy-four survived Trafalgar. They were either taken or destroyed in the gale that followed the battle.' He looked almost accusingly towards the wild-haired lieutenant. 'No agent has reported the building of any vessel such as the one you describe.'

The lieutenant grinned. The burden was no longer his, and the rum was very good.

'Well, that's what I saw, Sir Richard, an' I've been at sea for twenty-five year. I were nine when I ran out o' Cardiff. Never regretted it.' He shot Keen a pitying glance. 'Long enough to know which is the sharp end o' a pike!'

Keen laughed, the strain leaving his face as he retorted, 'You are an impudent fellow, but I think I asked for it!'

Bolitho watched him, the news momentarily at arm's length. Only Keen would be man enough to make such an admission to a subordinate. It would never have occurred to Bolitho that he might have learned it from his own example.

Bolitho said, 'I want you to carry a despatch to Portsmouth. It could be urgent.'

Keen said, 'The Nore would be a shorter passage, sir.'

Bolitho shook his head, thinking aloud. 'They have the telegraph at Portsmouth. It will be faster.' He eyed Evans

277

meaningly as he swallowed some more rum. 'I take it you have a reliable *mate*?'

It was not lost on the shaggy Welshman. 'I won't let you down, Sir Richard. My little schooner will be there by Monday.'

'There will be a letter also.' He met Evans' searching stare. 'I would appreciate if you send it by post-horse yourself. I shall pay you directly.'

The man grinned. 'God love you, no, Sir Richard. I know them buggers at Portsmouth Point an' they *owe* me a favour or two!'

Keen seemed to come out of his thoughts. 'I have a letter as well which could perhaps go with it, Sir Richard?'

Bolitho nodded, understanding. If the worst happened he might never know Zenoria's love. It did not bear even thinking about.

'You are doing the right thing, Val,' he said quietly. 'My lady will ensure she receives it.'

By noon the schooner was under way again, watched with envy by those who knew her destination, and wished that their next landfall would be England.

While Bolitho and Keen thought about their respective letters, carried in the schooner's safe with the despatches, other smaller dramas were being enacted deep in the hull, as is the way with all large men-of-war.

Two seamen who had been working under the direction of Holland, the purser's clerk, to hoist a fresh cask of salt pork from the store, were squatting in almost total darkness, a bottle of cognac wedged between them. One of the men was Fittock, who had been flogged for insubordination. The other was a Devonian named Duthy, a ropemaker and, like his friend, an experienced seaman.

They were speaking in quiet murmurs, knowing they should not still be here. But like most of the skilled hands they disliked being cooped up with untrained ignorant landsmen who were *always bleating about discipline*, as Duthy put it.

He said, 'I'll be glad to swallow the anchor when me time's up, Jim, but I'll miss some of it, all the same. I've learned a trade out of the navy, an' provided I can stay in one piece . . .'

Fittock swallowed hard and felt the heat of the spirit run through him. No wonder the wardroom drank it.

278

He nodded. '*Provided*, yes, mate, there's always that.'

'Yew think we'm goin' to fight, Jim?'

Fittock rubbed his back against a cask. The scars of the lash were still sore, even now.

He showed his teeth. 'You knows the old proverb, mate? If death rakes the decks, may it be like prize money.'

His friend shook his head. 'Don't understand, Jim.'

Fittock laughed. 'So that the officers get the biggest share!'

'*Now here's a fine thing!*'

They both lurched to their feet as someone slid the shutter from a lantern, and they saw Midshipman Vincent staring at them, his mouth lifted in a faint smile. Behind him, his cross-belt white in the gloom, was the ship's corporal.

Vincent said coldly, 'Just as well I came to complete the rounds.' The officer-of-the-watch had sent him after seeing the purser's clerk appear on deck alone, but he made it sound as if it was his own idea. 'Scum like you, Fittock, never learn, do you?'

Duthy protested, 'We weren't doin' nothin', sir. We was standin' easy, so to speak!'

'Don't lie to me, you pig!' Vincent thrust out his hand. 'Give me that bottle! I'll see your backbones for this!'

Anger, resentment, the scars on his back, and of course the cognac were part and parcel of what happened next.

Fittock retorted angrily, 'Think you can't do no wrong 'cause yer uncle's the vice-admiral, is that it? Why, you little shite, I've served with 'im afore, an' you're not fit to be in the same ship as 'im!'

Vincent stared at him glassily. It was all going wrong.

'Corporal, seize that man! Take him aft!' He almost screamed. '*That's an order, man!*'

The ship's corporal licked his lips and made as if to unsling his musket. 'Come on, Jim Fittock, you knows the rules. Let's not 'ave any trouble, eh?'

Feet scraped on the gratings between the casks and some white breeches moved into the lantern's glow.

Midshipman Roger Segrave said calmly, 'There'll *be* no trouble, Corporal.'

Vincent hissed, 'What the hell are you saying? They were drinking unlawfully, and when I discovered them –'

279

'They were "insubordinate", I suppose?' Segrave was astonished by his own easy tones. Like a total stranger's.

He said, 'Cut along, you two.' He turned to the corporal, who was staring at him, his sweating face full of gratitude. 'And you. I'll not be needing you.'

Vincent shouted wildly, 'What about the cognac?' But of course, like magic, it had vanished.

Fittock paused and looked him in the eyes, and said softly, 'I'll not forget.' Then he was gone.

'One more thing, Corporal.' The leggings and polished boots froze on the ladder. 'Close the hatch when you leave.'

Vincent was staring at him with disbelief. '*Are you mad?*'

Segrave tossed his coat to the deck. 'I used to know someone very like you.' He began to roll up his sleeves. 'He was a bully too – a petty little tyrant who made my life a misery.'

Vincent forced a laugh. In the damp, cool hold it came back as a mocking echo.

'So it was *all too much for you*, was it?'

Surprisingly, Segrave found that he could answer without emotion.

'Yes. It was. Until one day I met your uncle and a man with only half a face. After that I accepted fear – I can do so again.'

He heard the hatch thud into position. 'All this time I've watched you using your uncle's name so that you can torment those who can't answer back. I'm not surprised you were thrown out of the H.E.I.C.' It was only a guess but he saw it hit home. 'So now you'll know what it feels like!'

Vincent exclaimed, '*I'll call you out –*'

The smash of Segrave's fist into his jaw flung him down onto the deck, blood spurting from a split lip.

Segrave winced from the pain of the blow; all those years of humiliation had been behind it.

'Call me out, *sonny*?' He punched him again in the face as he scrambled to his feet, and sent him sprawling. 'Duels are for *men*, not pigmies!'

Four decks above them Lieutenant Flemyng, who was the officer-of-the-watch, took a few paces this way and that before glancing again at the half-hour glass by the compass box.

He beckoned to a boatswain's mate and snapped, 'Go and

280

find that damned snotty, will you, Gregg? Skylarking somewhere, I shouldn't wonder.'

The man knuckled his forehead and made to hurry away, but
was stopped by the harsh voice of Cazalet, the first lieutenant.

'Not just yet, Mr Flemyng!' He came from Tynemouth and
had a voice which carried above the strongest gale.

Flemyng, who was the ship's third lieutenant, stared at him
questioningly.

Cazalet smiled to himself and trained his glass on the old
Sunderland. 'I think he should have a *mite* longer, don't you?'

Admiral the Lord Godschale flapped a silk handkerchief before
his hawk-like nose and commented, 'The damn river is a bit vile
this evening.'

He looked powerfully magnificent in his heavy dress coat and
shining epaulettes, and as he stood watching the colourful
throng of guests which overflowed the broad terrace of his
Greenwich house he found time to reflect on his good fortune.

But it was extremely hot, and would remain so until night
touched the Thames and brought some cool relief to the officers
in their coats of blue and scarlet. Godschale watched the river
winding its endless journey up and around the curve into
Blackwall Reach, the ant-like movement of wherries and local
craft. It was an imposing house and he was constantly grateful
that the previous owner had sold so eagerly and reasonably. At
the outbreak of war with France, as all the hideous news of the
Terror had insinuated its way across the Channel, the former
owner had taken his possessions and investments and had fled to
America.

Godschale smiled grimly. So much for his faith in his
country's defences at the time.

He saw the slight figure of Sir Charles Inskip threading his
way through the laughing, jostling guests, bobbing here, smiling
there – the true diplomat. Godschale felt the return of his
uneasiness.

Inskip joined him and took a tall glass of wine from one of the
many sweating servants.

'Quite a gathering, m'lord.'

Godschale frowned. He had planned the reception with great

care. People who mattered in society, evenly mixed with the military and those of his own service. Even the Prime Minister was coming. Grenville had only held office for a year and after Pitt, whatever people had said about him, he had been a disaster. Now they had a Tory again, the Duke of Portland no less, who would probably be even more out of touch with the war than Grenville had been.

He saw his wife deeply engaged in conversation with two of her closest friends. The latest gossip no doubt. It was hard to picture her as the lively girl he had first met when he had been a dashing frigate captain. Plain, and rather dull. He shook his head. Where had that girl gone?

He glanced at the other women nearest to him. The hot weather was a blessing as far as they were concerned. Bare shoulders, plunging dampened gowns which would never have been tolerated a few years ago in the capital.

Inskip saw his hungry expression and asked, 'Is it true that you have recalled Sir Richard Bolitho? If so, I think *we* should have been informed.'

Godschale ignored the careful criticism. 'Had to. I sent *Tybalt* for him. He anchored at the Nore two days ago.'

Inskip was unimpressed. 'I don't see how it will help.'

Godschale tore his eyes from a young woman whose breasts would have been bare if her gown had been stitched half an inch lower.

He said in a deep whisper, 'You've heard the news? Napoleon has signed a treaty with Russia and has had the damned audacity to *order*, if you please, *order* Sweden and Denmark to close their ports against us and to sever all trade. In addition France has demanded their fleets to be put at *their* disposal! God damn it, man, that would be close on two hundred ships! Why did nobody see the nearness of this sorry affair? Your people are supposed to have eyes and ears in Denmark!'

Inskip shrugged. 'What shall we do next, I wonder?'

Godschale tugged at his neckcloth as if it was choking him. '*Do?* I'd have thought it was obvious!'

Inskip recalled Bolitho's bitterness and contempt when *Truculent* had sighted the three Frenchmen.

He said, 'So that is why Bolitho will be here?'

Godschale did not answer directly. 'Admiral Gambier is even now assembling a fleet and all the transports we will need to carry an army across to Denmark.'

'*Invade?* The Danes will never be willing to capitulate. I think we should wait –'

'Do you indeed?' Godschale studied him hotly. 'D'you believe Denmark's sensibilities are more important than England's survival? For that is what we are talking about, dammit!' He almost snatched a glass from a servant and drained it in two gulps.

The orchestra had struck up a lively gigue but many of the guests seemed unwilling to leave the great terrace, and Godschale guessed why.

At the Admiralty this morning he had told Bolitho of this reception, how it would prove an ideal setting where deeper matters of state might be discussed without arousing attention. Bolitho had replied calmly enough but had left no doubt as to his conditions.

He had said, 'There will be many ladies there, my lord. You will have not had time to arrange an "official" invitation for me as I am *ordered* here.'

Godschale spoke aloud without realising it. 'He simply stood there and told me he would not come here unless he could bring that woman!'

Inskip let out a deep breath of relief. He had imagined that Bolitho might have brought even worse news with him.

'Are you surprised?' Inskip smiled at Godschale's discomfort; Godschale, whom he had heard had a mistress or two in London. 'I have seen what Lady Somervell has done for Bolitho. I hear it in his voice, in the fire of the man.'

Godschale saw his secretary making signals from beside a tall pillar and exclaimed, 'The Prime Minister!'

The Duke of Portland shook their hands and glanced around at the watching eyes. 'Handsome levee, Godschale. All this talk of gloom – rubbish, is what I say!'

Inskip thought of Bolitho's men, the ordinary sailors he had seen and heard cheering and dying in the blaze of battle. They hardly compared with these people, he thought. His men were real.

The Prime Minister beckoned to a severe-looking man dressed in pearl-grey silk.

'Sir Paul Sillitoe.' The man gave a brief smile. 'My trusted adviser in this unforeseen crisis.'

Inskip protested, 'Hardly unforeseen –'

Godschale interrupted. 'I have had the matter under constant surveillance. There is a new squadron in the North Sea with the sole duty of watching out for some move by the French, any show of force towards Scandinavia.'

Sillitoe's eyes gleamed. 'Sir Richard Bolitho, yes? I am all eagerness to meet him.'

The Prime Minister dabbed his mouth. 'Not *I*, sir!'

Sillitoe regarded him impassively; he had hooded eyes, and his features remained expressionless.

'Then I fear your stay in high office will be as short as Lord Grenville's.' He watched his superior's fury without emotion. 'The French Admiral Villeneuve said after he was captured that at Trafalgar every English captain was a Nelson.' He shrugged. 'I am no sailor, but I know how they are forced to live, in conditions no better than a jail, and I am quite certain that they were inspired more by Nelson – enough to perform miracles.' He looked at them almost indifferently. 'Bolitho may not be another Nelson, but he is the best we have.' He turned as a ripple of excitement ran through the guests. 'Forget that at your peril, my friends.'

Godschale followed his glance and saw Bolitho's familiar figure, the black hair marked now by grey streaks in the lock above that savage scar. Then, as he turned to offer her his arm, Godschale saw Lady Catherine Somervell beside him. The mourning was gone, and the hair which was piled above her ears shone in the sunshine like glass. Her gown was dark green, but the silk seemed to change colour and depth as she turned and took his arm, a fan hanging loosely from her wrist.

She looked neither right nor left, but as her glance fell on Godschale he swore he could feel the force of her compelling eyes, and a defiance which seemed to silence even the whispers which surrounded her and the tall sea-officer by her side.

Godschale took her proffered hand and bowed over it. 'Why, m'lady, *indeed* a surprise!'

She glanced at the Prime Minister and made a slight curtsy. 'Are we to be introduced?'

He began to turn away but Bolitho said quietly, 'The Duke of Portland, Catherine.' He gave a small bow. 'We are honoured.' His grey eyes were cold, and said the opposite.

Sir Paul Sillitoe stepped forward and introduced himself in the same flat voice. Then he took her hand and held it for several seconds, his gaze locked against hers. 'They say you inspire him, m'lady.' He touched her glove with his lips. 'But I believe you inspire England, through your love of him.'

She withdrew her hand and watched him, her lips slightly curved, a pulse flickering at her throat in the strong light. But when she had searched his face and found no sarcasm, she answered, 'You do me a great kindness, sir.'

Sillitoe seemed able to ignore all those around them, even Bolitho, as he murmured, 'The clouds are darkening again, Lady Catherine, and I fear that Sir Richard will be required perhaps more than ever before.'

She said quietly, 'Must it always be him?' She felt Bolitho's warning hand on her arm but gripped it with her own. 'I have heard of Collingwood and Duncan.' Her voice shook slightly. 'There must be others.'

Godschale was poised to interrupt, his carefully prepared words flying to the wind at her sudden, unexpected insistence. But Sillitoe said, almost gently, 'Fine leaders – they have the confidence of the whole fleet.' Then, although he glanced at Bolitho, his voice was still directed to her. 'But Sir Richard Bolitho holds their hearts.'

Godschale cleared his throat, uncomfortable at the turn the conversation had taken and especially because of the watching faces around the terrace. Even the orchestra had fallen silent.

He said too heartily, 'A sailor's lot, Lady Catherine – it demands much of us all.'

She looked at him, in time to see his eyes lift quickly from her bosom. 'Some more than *others*, it would appear.'

Godschale beckoned to a footman to cover his embarrassment. 'Tell the orchestra to strike up, man!' He gave a fierce grin at the Prime Minister. 'Are you ready, Your Grace?'

Portland glared at Sillitoe. 'You attend to it. I have no

stomach for this kind of diplomacy! I will discuss the situation tomorrow, Godschale. There is much I have to do.'

Again he turned to leave but Bolitho said, 'Then I may not see you again before I sail?' He waited for Portland's attention. 'There are some ideas I would like to offer –'

The Prime Minister eyed him suspiciously, as if seeking a double meaning. 'Perhaps another time.' He turned to Catherine. 'I bid you good evening.'

As Godschale hurried after his departing guest Bolitho said in a savage whisper, 'I should never have brought you, Kate! They sicken me with their hypocrisy and over-confidence!' Then he said with concern, 'What is wrong – have I done something?'

She smiled and touched his face. 'One day you are across the sea, and now you are here.' She saw his anxiety and tried to soothe it. 'It is far more important than their false words and posturing. When we drove here today, did you not see the people turn and stare – how they cheered when they saw us together? Always remember, Richard, they *trust* you. They know you will not abandon them without lifting a hand to help.' She thought of the impassive Sillitoe, a strange creature who could be friend or enemy, but who had spoken like a truthful man. 'You hold their hearts, he said.'

There was a small stone-flagged passageway which led out on to a quiet garden, with a solitary fountain in its centre. It was deserted; the music, the dancing and the wine were on the far side of the house.

Bolitho took her arm and guided her around some bushes, then held her closely against him.

'I must speak with them, Kate.' He saw her nod, her eyes very bright. 'And then we shall leave.'

'And *then*?'

He lowered his head and kissed her shoulder until she stirred in his arms, and he felt her heart beating to match his own.

'To the house on the river. Our refuge.'

She whispered, 'I want you. I *need* you.'

When Sir Paul Sillitoe and Inskip returned to the terrace with Godschale they found Bolitho watching a small barge as it was manoeuvred downriver past the Isle of Dogs.

286

Godschale said brightly, 'You are alone?'

Bolitho smiled. 'My lady is walking in the garden . . . she had no wish to go amongst strangers on her own.'

Sillitoe studied him and said without a trace of humour, 'She found it a trifle *stuffy*, I suspect?'

Godschale turned, irritated, as his wife plucked insistently at his gold-laced coat, and drew him aside.

'What *is* it?'

'I saw them! Together, just now, in the pine garden. He was fondling her, kissing her naked shoulder!' She stared at him, outraged. 'It is all true, what they say, Owen – I was so shocked I could not look!'

Godschale patted her arm to reassure her. She had seen quite a lot for one who would not look, he thought.

'Not for long, my dear!' He beamed at her but could not drag his thoughts from Catherine's compelling eyes, and the body beneath her dark green gown.

He saw Sillitoe pause to look back for him and said abruptly, 'I have to go. Important, *vital* matters are awaiting my attention.'

She did not hear. 'I'll not have that woman in my house! If she so much as speaks a word to me –'

Godschale gripped her wrist and said harshly, 'You will return the smile, or I shall know the reason, *my love*! You may despise her, but by God's teeth, she is right for Bolitho –'

She said in a small voice, 'Owen, *you swore*!'

He replied heavily, 'Go amongst your friends now. Leave the war to us, eh?'

'If you're certain, dearest?'

'Society will decide; you cannot flout it as you will. But in time of war –' He turned on his heel and fell in step beside his secretary. 'Anything further I should know?'

The secretary was as aware of his good fortune as his master, and wanted it to remain that way. He said softly, 'That young woman, the wife of *Alderney*'s captain.' He saw the memory clear away Godschale's frown. 'She was here again to crave a favour on his behalf.' He paused, counting the seconds. 'She is a most *attractive* lady, my lord.'

Godschale nodded. 'Arrange a meeting.' By the time he

reached the private study where the others were waiting, he was almost his old self again.

'Now, gentlemen, about this campaign . . .'

Bolitho opened the glass doors and stepped out on to the small iron balcony, watching the lights glittering along the Thames like fireflies. It was so hot and airless that the curtains barely moved. He could still feel the heat of their love, the endless demands they had made on one another.

Her words at Godschale's great house still lingered in his mind, and he knew they would keep him company when they were parted again. *One day you are across the sea, and now you are here.* So simply said, and yet so right. Set against it, even the unavoidable separation seemed less cruel. He thought of the people in their fine clothes, pressing forward to see them, to stare at Catherine as she passed through them. Her composure and grace had made their flushed faces empty and meaningless. He watched a tiny lantern moving across the river and thought of their first visit to Vauxhall Gardens . . . they would return when they had more freedom. The house was small but well-proportioned, one in a terrace with a tree-lined square between it and the Thames-side walk.

Tomorrow he would have to leave for the Nore where *Tybalt* would be waiting. It was merely coincidence that *Tybalt* should be the frigate ordered to collect him from the squadron, then take him back. She had been the same vessel which had brought him home, still shocked by the loss of his old *Hyperion*. All else was different, he thought. The rugged Scots captain had gone to a seventy-four, his officers allotted to other ships where their experience, even among the youngest, would be priceless.

Bolitho was glad. Memories could be destructive, when he might need all his resolution.

He thought too of the squadron, which was still out in the North Sea, beating up and down, back and forth, waiting to learn the enemy's intentions, sifting information as fishermen will search for a good catch.

Whatever lay ahead of them, his experience or intuition must decide how they would all face it. It was like being in the hub of a great wheel. At first he had taught himself to reach out around him from the *Black Prince*'s poop or quarterdeck, placing names and faces, duties and reactions of the men who control a ship in battle. They would all know him by reputation or hearsay, but he must understand those closest to him in case the worst should happen. The sailing-master, and Cazalet the first lieutenant; the other officers who stood their watches day and night in all conditions; the gun-captains and the Afterguard. Like spokes reaching out and away to every deck and cranny in the ship.

And far beyond, to his individual captains in the line of battle, the others like Adam who roamed beyond the vision of the lookouts to find evidence, clues which their vice-admiral might fit into the pattern, if indeed there was one. One thing was quite evident. If Napoleon did succeed in seizing the fleets of Denmark and Sweden, and some said there were over a hundred and eighty ships between them, the English squadrons, still reeling from the damage and demands made upon them since Trafalgar, would be swamped by numbers alone.

He had asked Godschale about Herrick's part in the over-all plan. The admiral had tried to shrug it off, but when he had persisted had said, 'He will be in command of the escorts for the supply ships. A vital task.'

Vital? an old passed-over commodore like Arthur Warren at Good Hope could have done it.

Godschale had tried to smooth things out. 'He is lucky – he still has *Benbow* and his flag.'

Bolitho had heard himself retort angrily, '*Luck?* is that what they call it in Admiralty? He's been a fighter all his life, a brave and loyal officer.'

Godschale had watched him bleakly, 'Highly commendable to hear so. Under the present, um – circumstances – I think it surprising you should speak out in this fashion.'

Damn the man! He gave a bitter smile as he remembered Godschale's confusion when he had told him that Catherine would accompany him to the levee.

The moon slipped out of a long coamer of cloud and brought the river to life, like the shimmering silk of Catherine's gown. In the little square he saw the tops of the trees touched with moonlight as if they were crowned with powdered snow.

He gripped the iron rail with both hands and stared at the moon, which appeared to be moving independently, leaving the clouds behind. He did not blink, but continued to stare until he saw the misty paleness begin to form around and beside it. He dropped his gaze, his mouth suddenly dry. It was surely no worse. Or was that another delusion?

He felt the curtains swirl against his legs like frail webs, and knew she was with him.

'What is it, Richard?' Her hand moved between his shoulders, persuasive and strong, easing away his tension if not the anxiety.

He half-turned and slipped his arm beneath the long shawl which she had had made from the lace he had brought from Madeira. She shivered as if from a chill breeze as his hand moved across her nakedness, exploring her again, arousing her when she had believed it impossible after the fierceness of their passion.

He said, 'Tomorrow, we are separated.' He faltered, already lost. 'There is something I must say.'

She pressed her face to his shoulder and moved so that his hand could complete its exploration.

'At the funeral.' He could feel her looking at him, her breath warm on his neck as she waited for him. 'Before the coffin was covered, I saw you toss your handkerchief into the grave . . .'

She said huskily, 'It was the ring. *His* ring. I wanted no part of it after what happened.'

Bolitho had thought as much, but had been afraid to mention it. Was it that he could still harbour doubts, or had he not believed it possible that she could love him as she did?

He heard himself ask, 'Will you face more scandal and wear *my* ring, if I can find one beautiful enough?'

She caught her breath, surprised at his request, and deeply moved that the man she loved without reservation, and who would be called to battle and possibly death if it was so decided, could still find it so dear and important.

She allowed him to take her inside the windows and stood looking at him while he removed her shawl, her limbs glowing in the light of two bedside candles.

'I will.' She gasped as he touched her. 'For we are one, if only in each other's eyes.' It had always been rare for her to shed tears, but Bolitho saw the wetness beneath her closed lashes as she whispered, 'We will part tomorrow, but I am strong. Now take me as you will. For you, I am *not* strong.' She threw back her head and cried as he seized her, 'I am your slave!'

When dawn broke over London, Bolitho opened his eyes and looked at her head on his shoulder, her hair in disorder and strewn across the pillow beside him. There were red marks on her skin although he could not remember how they had been caused, and her face, when he combed some hair from it with his fingers, was that of a young girl, with no hint of the unspoken anxieties they must always share.

Somewhere a clock chimed, and he heard the grind of iron-shod wheels in the street.

Parting.

18

Fire and Mist

Bolitho stood by the *Black Prince*'s stern windows and half listened to all the familiar sounds as she made more sail again and got under way. In the quarter gallery he could see the ghost-like reflection of the frigate *Tybalt*, as she stood off from the flagship and prepared to return to the Nore for orders.

Her new captain was doubtless relieved to have delivered his passenger without mishap or risk of any blame for delays, and that he could now resume his own individual role.

Bolitho thought of that last farewell in the house on the river. Catherine had wanted to drive with him to Chatham, but she had not pleaded when he had said, 'Go to Falmouth, Kate. You will be amongst friends there.' They had parted as passionately as they had lived together. But he could still see her. Standing on the stone steps, her eyes filling her face, her high cheekbones holding shadows as the sun reflected from the river.

Bolitho heard Ozzard banging about in the sleeping compartment: he seemed to be the only one of his little band who was actually glad to be back with the squadron.

Even Allday was unusually depressed. He had confided that when he had seen his son aboard *Anemone*, the younger man had confessed that he wanted to quit the navy after all. It was like a slap in the face for Allday. To discover a son he had known nothing about, to learn of his courage when he had first suspected him a coward, and then to see him made coxswain to Captain Adam Bolitho – it had been more from life than he had ever hoped.

His son, also named John, had explained that he wanted an end to war. He loved the sea, but he had said that there were other ways of serving it.

Allday had demanded to know what they might be, and his son had replied without hesitation, 'I want to fish, and one day own my own boat. Settle down with a wife – not like so many.'

Bolitho knew that last remark was what had really hurt him. *Not like so many*. His father, perhaps?

Allday had described his son's enthusiasm as he had relived their too-brief encounter after the battle. He had ended by saying, 'When he told me that Cap'n Adam agreed with him, I knew I was beaten.'

Maybe Allday had been comparing his own life, and what might become of him one day.

There was a knock at the outer door, and Keen entered and gave his hat to Ozzard.

'Come in, Val.' He watched him curiously. Keen looked more relaxed than for a long time. Even his face was untroubled by the duties which lay heavily on any squadron's flag-captain. Bolitho had carried a letter for him which Catherine had been holding in her care.

Bolitho said, 'You can scan these papers at your leisure, Val. But to cut it short, it seems that Admiral Godschale's prophesies and plans have been put into motion.' They crossed to the table and looked at the chart. 'A large fleet, including some of the ships released from Good Hope, has been gathered at North Yarmouth in Norfolk. It's about the nearest anchorage of any size to Denmark. Admiral Gambier has hoisted his flag in *Prince of Wales*, and he has some twenty-five sail-of-the-line under his command.'

He smiled at Keen's alert profile. 'I gather the admiral originally intended to take *Black Prince* as his flagship, but he feared she would not be completed in time.' He became serious, thinking suddenly of Herrick as he said, 'There will be many transports and troopships – some will carry all the flat-bottomed boats they will need for landing the army, as well as artillery for laying siege. It will be the biggest combined operation since Wolfe took Quebec in fifty-nine.' He thought of the general at Good Hope and added slowly, 'Lord Cathcart commands the army, and I'm told he has some ten major-generals in company, one of whom is Sir Arthur Wellesley. I believe that Cathcart and many others will see this attack as a preparation for the eventual assault on Europe.'

Keen said gravely, 'Then God help the Danes.'

Bolitho slipped out of his heavy coat and tossed it onto a chair.

'We will remain on station until Gambier's fleet is through the Skagerrak, in case the French attempt to pounce on the supply vessels – it would leave the army high and dry if they succeeded! Then we follow in support.'

'As ordered, sir, Captain Crowfoot's *Glorious* is still with our second division to the north'rd.'

'I know.' He rubbed his chin vigorously. 'Have a signal repeated to *Anemone*, Val. Recall her to the squadron and I will send Adam with my despatches for Crowfoot. I think it best if we stand together until we know what is happening.'

As Keen made for the screen Bolitho asked, 'What *other* news, Val?'

Keen looked at him searchingly and then gave a huge grin. 'I have heard from Zenoria, sir.'

Bolitho gave a wry smile. 'I rather gathered so!'

'The date is arranged.' The words seemed to flood out of him. 'Lady Catherine's hand was in it, it seems. They talked together, and she has asked her to visit her at Falmouth.'

Bolitho smiled. 'I am glad to know it.' He walked around the table and clasped Keen's hands. 'There is nobody who better deserves the love and happiness she will offer.'

When Keen had gone to have the signal made which would eventually be repeated to *Anemone* beyond the horizon, Bolitho wondered what the two women had spoken of. Catherine had said little about it, but had obviously been very pleased about their meeting. Something in her tone had suggested that Zenoria's uncle, newly returned from the Indies, might have tried to discourage the marriage. Had he wanted the lovely girl with the moonlit eyes for himself, perhaps?

He went back to the canvas-covered folder, which he had carried in *Tybalt* in its lead-weighted bag in case they had run into a stronger enemy force again, and turned over the pages. A

294

door opened and closed and he heard Jenour whispering, Yovell's deeper response. They were gathering around the wheel's hub again, the spokes waiting to reach out to other ships and different minds from the man who led them.

But Bolitho was seeing reality in the beautiful writing. Twenty thousand soldiers, artillery and mortars, with all the small vessels like bombs and gun-brigs to support their landings.

They would batter their way ashore between Elsinore and Copenhagen itself. If the Danes persisted against a long siege, that lovely city of green spires would be laid in ruins. It did not seem right. The Danes were good people who wanted only to be left alone.

Bolitho slammed the cover shut. But there was no other way. *So be it then*.

Keen returned and said, 'Signal made, sir. The visibility is good, so *Anemone* should be here before dusk.'

They were still discussing tactics and the correct wording of his orders to the squadron's captains when the midshipman-of-the-watch entered to report that *Anemone*'s topgallants were in sight.

Bolitho realised it was his nephew, and asked, 'How are you settled, Mr Vincent?' Then he saw a dark bruise on his cheek, and several scars around his mouth.

Vincent answered sulkily, 'I am well enough, Sir Richard.'

As he left the cabin Bolitho suggested mildly, 'A little altercation, no doubt?'

Keen shrugged. 'It is difficult sometimes to watch over all the young gentlemen at once, sir.'

Bolitho observed his discomfort and said, 'That young fellow is a bully, with a conceit as wide as this cabin. Because he is related to *me*, it makes no difference in matters of discipline. And I will share something else with you. He will never make lieutenant unless you believe in miracles!'

Keen stared at him, astonished by such frankness, and that Bolitho could still surprise him.

'It was a fight, sir. A sort of gunroom court of law. The other one was Mr Midshipman Segrave.'

Bolitho nodded slowly. 'I should have guessed. No one would understand better how to deal with a petty tyrant!'

295

The mood left him and he touched Keen's arm and grinned. 'Just be thankful you do not have to be the one to tell my sister Felicity!'

Lanterns were being lit when *Anemone* finally hove-to under *Black Prince*'s lee and rounded-up into the wind.

Yovell was sealing the despatches for Captain Crowfoot when the calls trilled at the entry port, and Keen led Adam aft to the great cabin.

Bolitho related the bones of what he had already explained to Keen.

'If the French make any show of strength or attempt to interfere with the attack or our supply vessels, I must know without delay. I will send word to *Zest* and *Mistral* at first light, but our little schooner can do it.'

Adam asked, 'What do they say in London about the big liner *Radiant* sighted?'

Keen said sharply, 'They do not believe it.'

Adam murmured, 'I do, sir.'

Bolitho watched him. Adam must return to his ship before darkness closed in and they took up their stations for the night. But something was wrong. He could hear it in Adam's voice; he had always been very close to this other nephew. He allowed himself to think it. *His brother's son*. There had been many times when Bolitho had wished he had been his own.

He said, 'Perhaps Lieutenant Evans did make a mistake.' He recalled how the Welshman had swallowed the tankards of rum. 'But I trust him.'

Adam stood up. 'I had better go, Uncle.' He faced him, with troubled, restless eyes. 'If we fight, Uncle – you will take good care? For all our sakes?'

Bolitho embraced him. 'Only if you do the same.' He saw Keen leave the cabin to order his men to recall Adam's gig and said quietly, 'You are worried about something, Adam. You may command a King's ship, but to me you are still the midshipman, you know.'

Adam forced a smile but it only made him look more wistful. 'It is nothing, Uncle.'

Bolitho persisted, 'If there is anything, please tell me. I will try to help.'

296

Adam turned aside. 'I know that, Uncle. It has always been my sheet-anchor.'

Bolitho accompanied him to the companion ladder while shadows between decks watched them pass in silence, thinking themselves invisible, or beneath their admiral's notice. How wrong they were.

Bolitho listened to the sea's subdued murmur and was conscious that this might be the last time he saw Adam before the sea-fight which every one of his senses had now warned him was imminent. He felt a sudden chill. *Perhaps the last time ever.*

He said, 'Allday told me about his son.'

Adam seemed to rouse himself from his mood. 'I was sorry, but in truth, he has no place in the line of battle. I understand how Allday must feel, but I also know that his son will fall in battle if he remains. I see the signs.'

Bolitho watched him in silence. It was like hearing somebody much older speaking from past experience. As if his dead father was still a part of him.

'You are his captain, Adam – I suspect you know him much better than his father. A coxswain must be close to his commander. The nearest of all men maybe.' He saw Allday with the side-party, his bronzed face standing out in the slow sunset. *The nearest of men.*

'Side-party, *stand by*!'

That was Cazalet, another link in the chain of command. Keen, Cazalet, and the embattled midshipmen, drawing together as one company; in spite of the ship, or perhaps because of her.

Adam held out his hand. 'My warm wishes to Lady Catherine when next you write to her, Uncle.'

'Of course. We often speak of you.' He wanted to press him further, to drag out of Adam what was weighing him down. But he knew Adam was too much like himself, and would tell him only when he was ready.

Adam touched his hat and said formally, 'Your permission to leave the ship, Sir Richard?'

'Aye, Captain. God's speed go with you.'

The calls shrilled, and the side-boys waited at the foot of the ladder to steady the gig for a departing captain.

'I wonder what ails him, Val?'

Keen walked with him towards the poop, where he knew Bolitho would fret out his worries in a measured walk.

He smiled. 'A lady, I shouldn't wonder, sir. None of us is a stranger to the havoc they can create!'

Bolitho watched *Anemone*'s lower yards change shape in the gold light as her fore and main courses filled to the wind.

He heard Keen add admiringly, 'By God, if he can handle a fifth-rate like that, he should be more than a match for a saucy glance!'

Again he saw Allday standing by a tethered twelve-pounder; alone, despite the bustling shadows around him.

Bolitho nodded to Keen and climbed down to the quarter-deck.

'Ah, there you are, Allday!' Once again he saw the watching eyes, figures still unknown to him. How would he convince them when the time came?

In a quieter voice he said, 'Come aft and share a glass with me. I want to ask you something.'

Somehow he knew Allday was going to refuse; his pride and his hurt would leave him no choice.

He added, 'Come, old friend.' He sensed his uncertainty, even though Allday's features were now lost in shadow. 'You are not the only one who is lonely.'

He turned away, and heard Allday say awkwardly, 'I was just thinkin', Sir Richard. You takes risks all your life at sea – you fight, an' if Lady Luck favours you, you lasts a bit longer.' He gave a great sigh. 'An' then you dies. Is that all there is to a man?'

Lady Luck . . . it reminded him of Herrick, the man he had once known.

He turned and faced him. 'Let us wait and see, eh, old friend?'

Allday showed his teeth in the shadows and shook his head like some great dog.

'I *could* manage a wet, Sir Richard, an' that's no error!'

Lieutenant Cazalet, who was about to do his evening rounds of the ship, paused by Jenour and watched the vice-admiral and his coxswain disappear down the companion ladder. 'A most unusual pair, Mr Jenour.'

298

The flag-lieutenant studied him thoughtfully. Cazalet was a competent officer, just what any captain needed, in a new ship more than ever. Beyond that, he decided, there was not much else.

He replied, 'I cannot ever imagine the one without the other, sir.'

But Cazalet had gone and he was alone again, mentally composing his next letter home about what he had just seen.

Captain Hector Gossage of the seventy-four gun *Benbow* moved restlessly about the ship's broad quarterdeck, his eyes slitted against the hard sunlight. Eight bells had just chimed out from the forecastle and the forenoon watch had been mustered; and yet already the heat seemed intense. Gossage could feel his shoes sticking to the tarred seams and silently cursed their snail's progress.

He stared across the starboard bow and saw the uneven line of twenty store and supply ships reaching away towards the dazzling horizon. A pitifully slow passage – their destination Copenhagen, to join Admiral Gambier's fleet in support of the army.

Gossage was not a very imaginative man but prided himself on *Benbow*, a ship which had been in almost continuous service for several years. Many of the seasoned hands and warrant officers had been in the ship since he had assumed command; it had been, if there was such a creature in the King's navy, a happy ship.

He glanced at the open skylight, and wondered what his rear-admiral's mood would be when he eventually came on deck. Ever since he had received news of his wife's death, Herrick had changed out of all recognition. Gossage was prudent enough not to mention certain things which his rear-admiral had overlooked, or more likely forgotten. As flag-captain he might easily have the blame laid at his own door, and this he intended to avoid at all costs. He was nearly forty, and he had his sights set on a commodore's broad-pendant before another year had passed – the obvious step to flag rank which he cherished more than anything. Rear-Admiral Herrick had always been a reasonable superior, ready to listen, or even to use an idea

299

which Gossage had put forward. Some admirals would bite your head off for so doing, then present the idea as their own. But not Herrick.

Gossage bit his lip and remembered the terrible nights at sea when Herrick had been incapable of speaking with any coherence. A man who had always taken his drink in moderation, and who had been quick to come down hard on any officer who saw wine and spirits as a prop for his own weakness.

He took a glass from the rack and levelled it on the wavering column of ships. Deep-laden, they were barely making a few knots, and with the wind veering due north overnight it would be another day before they entered the Skagerrak. A rich convoy, he thought grimly. Two hundred troopers of the light brigade and their horses, foot guards and some Royal Marines with all the supplies, weapons and powder to sustain an army throughout a long siege. He turned away and felt his shoe squeak free of the melting tar. At this rate, the war would be over before they even reached Copenhagen.

He moved the glass slightly before the sunlight blinded him and made him blink the tears from his eye. He had seen *Egret*, the other escort, an elderly sixty-gun two-decker which had been brought out of retirement after many years as a receiving vessel. Then the sea-mist blotted her out again.

Relics, he thought with bitterness. Anything which would stay afloat long enough for their lordships' purposes.

At first light, the masthead lookout of one of the supply ships had sighted land far off on the starboard bow, a vague purple shadow which was soon hidden by the haze as the August sunshine changed the North Sea to an endless procession of undulating glass humps.

Lieutenant Gilbert Bowater climbed through the companion hatch and touched his hat vaguely.

'Rear-Admiral Herrick is coming up, sir.'

Even the piggy flag-lieutenant had entered into a conspiracy with the other officers to keep out of Herrick's way, and avoid another blistering scene like the time recently when Herrick had berated a midshipman for laughing on watch.

The forenoon watchkeepers straightened their backs and a master's mate peered unnecessarily at the compass.

Gossage touched his hat. 'Wind's still steady from the north, sir. The convoy's closed-up since dawn.'

Herrick walked to the compass box and turned over the limp, damp pages of the log. His mouth and throat were raw, and when he turned towards the sun he felt his head throb without mercy.

Then he shaded his eyes and looked at the ships which they had escorted all the way from North Yarmouth. A meaningless task, a burden more than a duty.

Gossage watched him warily, as a post-boy will study a dangerous hound.

'I have put the boatswain's party to blacking-down, sir. She'll be smart enough when we enter harbour.'

Herrick saw his flag-lieutenant for the first time. 'Nothing to *do*, Bowater?' Then he said, 'Don't let these ships straggle like a flock of sheep, Captain Gossage. Signal *Egret* to come about and take charge of them.' Once again, his anger overflowed like water across a dam. 'You should not need to be *told*, man!'

Gossage flushed and saw some of the men by the wheel glance at one another. He replied, 'There is a thick sea-mist, sir. It is difficult to maintain contact with her.'

Herrick leaned against the nettings and said heavily, 'It will take a month to repeat a signal along this line of grocery captains!' He swung round, his eyes red in the glare. 'Fire a gun, sir! That will wake *Egret* from her dreams!'

Gossage flung over his shoulder, 'Mr Piper! Call the gunner. Then have the larboard bow-chaser cleared away!'

It all took time, and Herrick could feel the heat rising from the deck to match the raw thirst in his throat.

'Ready, sir!'

Herrick gave a sharp nod and winced as the pain jabbed through his skull. The gun recoiled on its tackles, the smoke barely moving in the humid air. Herrick listened to the echo of the shot going on and on as it ricochetted across each line of rollers. The supply ships continued on their haphazard course as if nothing had happened.

Herrick snapped, 'A good man aloft, *if* you please. As soon as *Egret* is in sight I wish to know of it!'

Gossage said, 'If we had retained our frigate –'

301

Herrick looked at him wearily. 'But we did not. *I* did not. Admiral Gambier so ordered it once we had reached this far. The North Sea squadron is also with him by now.' He waved one hand around him. 'So there is only us, and this melancholy collection of patched-up hulks!'

A dull bang echoed over the ship and Gossage said, '*Egret*, sir. She'll soon harry them together!'

Herrick swallowed and tugged at his neckcloth. 'Signal to *Egret* immediately. *Close on the flag.*'

'But, sir –' Gossage glanced at the others as if for support. 'She will lose more time, and so shall we.'

Herrick rubbed his eyes with his hands. He had not slept for so long that he could scarcely remember what it was like. Always he awoke with the nightmare which instantly froze into reality and left him helpless. Dulcie was dead. She would never be there to greet him again.

He said sharply, '*Make the signal.*' He walked to the poop ladder and peered over the side. 'That shot came from yonder, not from *Egret*.' He was suddenly quite calm, as if he was somebody else. The air quivered again. 'Hear it, Captain Gossage? What say you now?'

Gossage gave a slow nod. 'My apologies, sir.'

Herrick eyed him impassively. 'You hear what you want to hear. It is nothing new.'

Lieutenant Bowater murmured nervously, 'The merchantmen are drawing into line, sir.'

Herrick smiled bleakly. 'Aye, they smell the danger.'

Gossage felt that he was going mad. 'But how can it *be*, sir?'

Herrick took Dulcie's telescope and levelled it carefully across the quarter as *Egret*'s topsails appeared to float, unattached, above a bank of white mist. He said, 'Perhaps Sir Richard was right after all. Maybe we were all too stupid, or too stricken to listen to him.' He sounded detached, indifferent even, as a midshipman yelled, '*Egret*'s acknowledged, sir!'

Then he said, 'The North Sea squadron is no longer on station.' He trained the splendid telescope on the nearest merchantman. 'But the convoy is still our responsibility.' He lowered it and added irritably, 'Signal *Egret* to make more sail, and take station ahead of the flag.' He watched as Bowater and the signals midshipman called their numbers and sent the bright bunting soaring up the yards.

One hour, then two dragged past in the melting heat. A faulty challenge? An exchange between privateer and smuggler? Each was a possibility.

Herrick did not glance up as the masthead shouted, 'Deck there! Land on the lee bow!'

Gossage remarked, 'Another hour or so and we shall be in sight of the Skagerrak, sir.' He was beginning to relax, but slowly. Herrick's unpredictable temper was having its effect.

'Deck there! Sail on the starboard quarter!'

Men ran across, and a dozen telescopes probed the blinding mirrors of water and the gentle mist.

There was something like a gasp of relief as the lookout cried, 'Brig, sir! She wears our colours!'

Herrick contained his impatience while he watched the brig as she beat this way and that to close with the flagship.

The signals midshipman called, 'She's the *Larne*, sir. Commander Tyacke.'

Herrick screwed up his eyes to clear his aching brain. *Larne?* Tyacke? They triggered off a memory, but he could not quite grasp it.

Gossage exclaimed, 'God, *she*'s been mauled, sir!'

Herrick raised his telescope and saw the brig rise up as if from the sea itself. There were holes in her fore topsail, and several raw scars in the timbers near her forecastle.

'She's not dropping a boat, sir.' Gossage sounded tense again. 'She's going to close with us to speak.'

Herrick moved the glass still further and then felt the shock run through him. He could see the sunlight glinting on the commander's single epaulette, the way he was clinging to the shrouds, a speaking-trumpet already pointing towards the *Benbow*.

But his face . . . even the distance could not hide its horror. It was like being drenched with icy water as the memory flooded back. Tyacke had been with Bolitho at Cape Town. The fireship, the escaping French frigate – his head reeled with each revelation.

'*Benbow* ahoy!' Herrick lowered the glass and thankfully

allowed the man's identity to fall back into the distance. '*The French are out!* I have met with two sail-of-the-line and three others!'

Herrick snapped his fingers and took a speaking-trumpet from the first lieutenant.

'This is Rear-Admiral Herrick! What ships did you see?' Each shouted word made his brain crack.

The man's powerful voice echoed across the water and Herrick thought it sounded as if he were laughing. A most unseemly sound.

'I didn't wait to discover, sir! They were eager to dampen my interest!' He turned away to call some commands as his brig slewed dangerously across *Benbow*'s quarter. Then he shouted, 'One is a second-rate, sir! No doubt of that!'

Herrick faced inboard and said, 'Tell him to carry word to Sir Richard Bolitho.' He stopped Gossage and revised it. 'No. To Admiral Gambier.'

He walked to the compass and back again, then glanced at the old *Egret*'s pyramid of tanned canvas which seemed to tower directly beyond *Benbow*'s jib-boom. He saw all and none of it. They were things and moments in his life too familiar to comment on. Even the old cry, *The French are out!* could not move him any more.

Gossage came back, breathing hard as if he had just been running.

'The brig's making more sail, sir.' He eyed him despairingly. 'Shall I order the convoy to scatter?'

'Have you forgotten *Zest*'s captain so soon, man? Waiting somewhere for his wretched court-martial? They once executed an admiral for failing to press home an attack – d'you imagine they would even hesitate over Captain Varian?' *Or us*, he thought, but did not say it.

He looked for the little brig but she was already tacking around the head of the column. The man with the horribly disfigured face might find Gambier or Bolitho by tomorrow. It was probably already pointless.

But when he spoke again, his voice was steady and unruffled.

'Signal the convoy to make more sail and maintain course and distance. Spell it out *word by word* if you have to, but I want each master to know and understand the nearness of danger.'

'Very well, sir. And then . . ?'

Herrick was suddenly tired, but knew there would be no respite.

'*Then*, Captain Gossage, you may beat to quarters and clear for action!'

Gossage hurried away, his mind groping for explanations and solutions. But one thing stood out above all else. It was the first time he had seen Herrick smile since his wife had died. As if he no longer had anything to lose.

Captain Valentine Keen held his watch against the compass light, then glanced around at the shadowy figures on the quarterdeck. It was strange and unnerving to hear and see the flash of cannon fire from the land while *Black Prince* lay at anchor, another cable run out from aft so that they could kedge her round to use at least one broadside against attack.

When there was a lull in the bombardment Keen felt blind, and could sense the tension around him. A boat was hooked on to either cable, with Royal Marines crouched over the bulwarks armed with muskets and fixed bayonets in case some mad volunteer attempted to swim out and cut them adrift. Other marines lined the gangways, while the swivel guns were loaded and depressed towards the black, swirling current of Copenhagen's great harbour.

The first part of the attack had gone well. The fleet had anchored off Elsinore on the twelfth of August; there had been no opposition despite the presence of so many men-of-war. Three days later the army had begun to advance on the city. The closer they got the heavier became the Danish opposition, and in the last attack the navy had been savaged by a fleet of *praams*, each mounting some twenty powerful guns, and a flotilla of thirty gunboats. They were eventually driven off after a fierce engagement, and the military and naval batteries ashore were soon repaired.

Keen looked up as Bolitho crossed the quarterdeck, and guessed he had not slept.

'It is timed to begin soon, Val.'

'Aye, sir. The army have got their artillery in position. I heard they have seventy mortars and cannon laid on Copenhagen.'

305

Bolitho looked around in the darkness. *Black Prince* had followed Gambier's main fleet to Elsinore and had soon been engaged with the Danish guns of the Crown Battery. It was not that much different from their other attack on Copenhagen, except that here they were fighting small craft and shadows, while the army pressed forward against persistent and dogged resistance.

Two divisions of sail-of-the-line were anchored between the defenders and the Danish fleet, most of which appeared to be laid up in ordinary or in a state of repair, perhaps to appease the English and French predators.

In the midst of the bombardments and the far-off forays of cavalry and infantry, Lord Cathcart, the commander-in-chief, had found time to grant passports to the Princess of Denmark and the King's nieces to travel safely through the English lines, '*So that they could be spared the horrors of a siege.*'

When Keen had remarked on the effect that might have on Danish morale, Bolitho had answered with sudden bitterness, 'King George the Second was the last British monarch to lead his army into battle – at Dettingen, I think it was. I doubt if we'll ever see such a thing again in our lifetimes!'

He winced as the whole sky burst into flame and the systematic bombardment started. To add to the horror, powerful Congreve rockets were soon falling on the city, disgorging their deadly loads of fire, so that within the hour many of the buildings nearest the waterfront were ablaze.

Keen said between his teeth, 'Why don't the Danes strike? They have no chance!'

Bolitho glanced at him and saw his face flickering in the red and orange reflections, while the hull, deep beneath them, shook to each fall of shot.

The Danes, he thought. No one ever referred to them as the enemy.

'*Boat ahoy! Stand off, I say!*'

Marines ran along the deck and Bolitho saw a boat pause abeam, rocking gently in the current and laid bare by the lurid flash of rockets.

There were white-cross belts visible, and someone yelled at the sentries to hold their fire. Another moment, and the nervous marines would have poured a volley into the boat.

An officer stood in the sternsheets and cupped his hands, pausing between each roar of explosions to make himself understood.

'*Sir Richard Bolitho!*' A pause. 'The Admiral-Commanding sends his compliments, and would you join him in the flagship?'

'What a time to choose!' Bolitho glanced round and saw Jenour with Allday close by. To Keen he said, 'I will go across in the guardboat. It must be urgent not to keep until dawn.'

They hurried to the entry port where the boat had eventually been allowed to hook on.

Bolitho said tersely, 'You know what to do, Val. Cut the cables if you are attacked – use the boats if necessary.'

Then he was down in the guardboat and pressed between Jenour and the officer-of-the-guard.

As they pushed off from *Black Prince*'s massive, rounded hull someone thrust his head through an open gunport and yelled, 'You get us out o' this, eh, Our Dick?'

The officer snapped, 'Damned impertinence!'

But Bolitho said nothing; he was too moved for words. It was like being pulled across liquid fire, with anonymous pieces of charred wood tapping against the hull, and falling ashes hissing into the water.

Admiral Gambier greeted him in his usual distant manner.

'Sorry to drag you over, Sir Richard. Your squadron may be sorely needed tomorrow.'

Bolitho's hat was taken away and replaced by an ice-cold glass of hock.

Admiral Gambier glanced aft towards his quarters. All the screen doors were open to the warm air, and smoke drifted in and out of the gunports as if a fireship were already alongside.

The great cabin seemed to be packed with blue and scarlet coats, and Gambier said with obvious disapproval. 'All congratulating themselves – before the Danes surrender!'

Bolitho kept his face impassive. *The Danes* again.

Gambier jerked his head. 'We are using my captain's quarters. Bit quieter.'

In the cabin, similar but older than Keen's in the *Black Prince*, all but one lantern were extinguished. It made the stern windows burn and spark like the gateway to hell.

Gambier nodded to a midshipman and snapped, 'Fetch him!' Then he said, 'Damned glad of those vessels you managed to poach from Good Hope. The Captain of the Fleet never stops talking about it.'

There were footsteps on the outer deck and Gambier said quietly, 'I must warn you, this officer's face is most hideously wounded.'

Bolitho swung round. 'James Tyacke!'

Gambier muttered, 'Never mentioned that he knew you. Odd fellow.'

Tyacke came into the cabin, ducking beneath the deckhead beams until Bolitho gripped his hands warmly in his.

Gambier watched. If he were impressed he did not reveal it. He said, 'Give Sir Richard your news, Commander.'

As Tyacke described his sighting of the French ships, and his later meeting with Herrick's convoy, Bolitho could feel the anger and dismay crowding in from the flashing panorama beyond the ship.

Gambier persisted, 'You are certain, Commander?'

Tyacke turned from the shadows and momentarily displayed his ravaged face.

'A second-rate, possibly larger, and another sail-of-the-line astern of her. There were others too. I had no opportunity to linger.'

Gambier said, 'This is a small-ship war now that the army is ashore, Sir Richard. I did not anticipate that Rear-Admiral Herrick would need further protection. It seems I was wrong, and should have left your squadron on its station until –'

Bolitho interrupted sharply, 'Do you think they've found the convoy?'

Tyacke shrugged. 'Doubt it. But they will, if they maintain their course and speed.'

Bolitho looked at the admiral. 'I am asking you to allow me to order my squadron to sea, sir.'

Gambier eyed him severely. 'Impossible. Out of the question. In any case, most of your ships are to the east'rd in the Baltic approaches. It would take two days, longer, to get them in pursuit.'

Tyacke said bluntly, 'Then the convoy will perish, sir, as will its escorts.'

308

The admiral frowned as a gust of laughter came up from his quarters. 'People are dying over there! Do they care for no damned thing!'

He seemed to make up his mind. 'I will release your flagship. You can have one other – *Nicator*, as she is moored with you. Poor old girl will probably fall apart if she is called to battle!' Then he exclaimed, 'But there is no one to guide you through the Sound.'

Bolitho said desperately, 'I did it before, under Nelson's flag, sir.'

Tyacke remarked calmly, 'I'll lead the way, Sir Richard. If you'll have me.'

Gambier followed them to the side and said to his own captain, 'Would you say I am an easy man to serve?'

The captain smiled. 'Fair, sir.'

'Not the same.' He watched the guardboat speeding across the water, one minute in total darkness, the next illuminated so brightly in the falling Congreve rockets that he could see every detail.

Then he said, 'Just now, in my own flagship, I felt that *he* was in command, not I.'

The flag-captain followed him aft towards the din of voices. It was a moment he would savour all his life.

Back aboard *Black Prince*, Bolitho rapped off his orders as if they had been lurking there in his mind.

'Send a boat to your old ship, Val. She's to weigh and follow without delay.' He gripped his arm. 'I'll not have any arguments. *Larne* will lead us out. I *said* this might happen, damn them!'

The great three-decker seemed to burst alive as calls trilled between decks and men ran to their stations for leaving harbour. Anything was better than waiting and not knowing. They would not care whatever the reason. They were leaving. Bolitho thought of the unknown wag who had called out in the darkness.

The capstan was clanking busily, and he knew that the kedge-anchor would soon be hoisted inboard.

A lantern moved across the water, and occasionally Bolitho saw the brig's sturdy shadow as she made ready to take the lead.

Two great rockets fell together on the city, lighting up the sky and the ships in a withering fireball.

Bolitho had been about to call for Jenour when it happened. As the fire died away he took his hand from his injured eye. It was like looking through clouded water, or a misted glass. He lowered his head and murmured, '*Not now*. Not yet, dear God!'

'*Cable's hove short, sir!*'

Keen's voice was harsh in the speaking-trumpet. 'How does the cable grow, Mr Sedgemore?' Then he paused until the next flash so that he could see the angle of the lieutenant's arm. There was not much room, especially in the darkness. He needed to know how the ship, *his* ship, would perform when she tore free of the ground.

Cazalet bellowed, '*Loose tops'ls!*' A few paces aft. 'Stand by, the Afterguard!'

Black Prince seemed to tilt her lower gunports close to the black water as the cry came drifting aft.

'*Anchor's aweigh*, sir!'

Bolitho gripped the tarred nettings and tried to massage his eye.

Jenour asked in a whisper, 'May I help, Sir Richard?'

He cringed as Bolitho swung on him, and waited for the stinging retort.

But Bolitho said only, 'I am losing my sight, Stephen. Can you keep a secret so precious to me?'

Overcome, Jenour could barely answer, but nodded vigorously, and did not even notice a boat pulling frantically from under the black figurehead while the ship continued to swing round.

Bolitho said, '*They must not know.*' He gripped his arm until Jenour winced with the pain. 'You are a dear friend, Stephen. Now there are other friends out there who need us.'

Keen strode towards them. 'She answers well, sir!' He glanced from one to the other, and knew what had happened. 'Shall I send for the surgeon?'

Bolitho shook his head. Maybe it would pass; perhaps when daylight found them, it would be clear again.

'No, Val . . . too many know already. Follow *Larne*'s sternlight and put your best leadsmen in the chains.'

Allday materialised from the darkness, holding out a cup. 'Here, Sir Richard.'

Bolitho swallowed it and felt the black coffee, with a mixture of rum and something else, steady his insides so that he could think again.

'That was more than welcome, old friend.' He handed him the cup and thought of Inskip. 'I am over it now.'

But when he looked at the burning city again, the mist was still there.

19

True Colours

With her great yards braced so hard round that to a landsman they might appear to lie fore-and-aft, *Black Prince* steered as close-hauled to the wind as was possible. For most of the previous night they had clawed their way up the narrow Sound from Copenhagen, pursued all the while by the continuous thunder of the bombardment.

Somehow *Nicator* had held station on the flagship, but for *Black Prince*, a powerful three-decker, it had been a trial of nerves as well as skill. Urgent voices had passed each sounding aft from the leadsmen in the forechains, and at one time Bolitho had sensed that only a few feet lay between the ship's great keel and disaster.

Dawn had found them heading out into the Kattegat, still comparatively shallow, but after the Sound it felt like the Western Ocean. Later, when Bolitho watched the pink glow on the choppy water, he knew that darkness would be upon them early that night. A glance at the masthead pendant assured him that the wind was holding steady, north-east. It would help them tomorrow, but had he waited until daylight as Gambier had suggested, the wind's sudden veer would have bottled them up in harbour. He thought of Herrick for the hundredth time. *Lady Luck*.

Keen crossed the deck and touched his hat, his handsome features raw from a full day on deck in chill wind.

'Any further orders before nightfall, sir?'

They looked at one another, like friends across a common garden wall at the close of an ordinary day.

'It will be tomorrow, Val. Or not at all. You know what these supply convoys are like, the speed of the slowest vessel in it, necessary for mutual protection. Rear-Admiral Herrick's convoy apparently numbers some twenty ships, so if there *was* a battle, some of the fastest must surely have reached the Skagerrak at least by now?' He forced a smile. 'I realise you think me morbid, even mad. Herrick will probably doff his hat to us at first light tomorrow, and sail past full of noble contentment!'

Keen watched him, the man he had come to know so well.

'May I ask something, sir?' He glanced round as the calls twittered in the endless daily life of a man-of-war: *Last dogwatchmen to supper!*

'Ask away.' He saw the gulls pausing to rest on the pink water like flower petals and thought of the dead Captain Poland, who had seen nothing but the path to duty.

'If you were in Rear-Admiral Herrick's position, what would *you* do, if an enemy second – or even first-rate as it now appears – and other vessels hove in sight?'

Bolitho looked away. 'I would scatter the convoy.' He looked at him again, his eyes dark in the strange glare. 'Then I would engage the enemy. A waste of time . . . who knows? But some might survive.'

Keen hesitated. 'But you do not think *he* would order them to break formation, sir?'

Bolitho took his arm and guided him a few paces past the big double-wheel, where Julyan the tall sailing-master was speaking to his mates in his deep rumbling tones. *Worth his weight in gold*, Keen had claimed several times; he had certainly proved his skill with wind, tide and rudder when they had struggled up the Sound.

'I am concerned, Val. If the enemy is searching for his ships, he will see it as something . . .' He groped for the word but saw only Herrick's stubborn eyes.

'A personal thing, sir?'

'Aye, that's about the strength of it.'

A sickly smell of pork came from the galley funnel and Bolitho said, 'After both watches have eaten, have the ship cleared for action. But keep the galley in use until the last. More warm bellies than steel have won battles in the past, Val!'

313

Keen gazed along the broad length of his command, seeing it probably already enmeshed in the chaos and destruction of close-action.

'I agree.' He added suddenly, 'Your Mr Tyacke could be right about the largest Frenchman, but then precious few know about *Black Prince* as yet – she is far too new.'

The officer-of-the-watch glanced at Keen and cleared his throat impressively.

'A chill, Mr Sedgemore?' Keen grinned with easy humour. 'You wish to have the watch relieved?'

They both turned, startled, as Bolitho interrupted sharply, *'What did you say?'*

He stared as Keen's bewilderment. 'About *Black Prince*'s unknown strength?'

'Well, I simply thought –'

'And I did *not*.' Bolitho glanced up at the ensign curling above his head. 'You have a good sailmaker?'

The watch was changing, but they stood quite alone in the midst of its quiet disorder.

'Aye, sir.'

'Then please ask him to lay aft.' He watched the soft light of a northern dusk. 'This needs to be quick. I must pass word to Captain Huxley before we adopt night-stations!'

Keen sent a midshipman off at the double. Bolitho would explain. Perhaps when he had decided for himself what he intended.

Black Prince's sailmaker's name was Fudge. He was so like the many of his profession that he might have been cut from the same bolt of canvas. Bushy grey hair and sprouting eyebrows, and the familiar leather jerkin which was hung about with tools, thread, needles and, of course, a palm or two.

'This is he, sir.'

They all looked at him in silence. Keen, the officer-of-the-watch, midshipmen and master's mates.

Fudge blinked his watery eyes.

'Aye, sir?'

Bolitho asked, 'Can you make me a Danish ensign, Fudge – full-scale, not some trifling boat-pendant?'

The man nodded slowly, visualising his stocks, neatly stored in one of the holds.

314

He answered, 'Foreign, then, Sir Richard?'

Lieutenant Sedgemore opened his mouth to add a sharp comment of his own, but Keen's glance left it unspoken.

Bolitho said, 'Foreign. White cross on red ground, with two tails like a commodore's broad-pendant.'

Fudge said, 'I was in *Elephant* with Nelson at Copenhagen, Sir Richard.' The bent back and stiffness of his trade seemed to fall away as he glanced around at the silent watchkeepers. 'I *knows* what a Danish flag look like, sir!'

Bolitho smiled. 'So be it. When can you provide it for me?'

Fudge showed his uneven teeth, surprised at being asked.

'No more'n a couple o' days, Sir Richard!'

'This is very important, Fudge. Can I have it by dawn?'

Fudge studied him feature by feature, as if to find an answer to something.

'I'll begin now, Sir Richard.' He looked around at the seamen and Royal Marines, as if they were of some inferior race. 'Leave it to me!'

As Fudge bustled away Keen asked quietly, 'Some deception, sir?'

'Aye, mebbee.' He rubbed his hands together as if they were cold. 'A favour, Val.' He glanced at the shimmering reflection on the water, the first hint of sunset. He held his hand over his left eye and said, 'I would like to walk through your ship with you, if I may?'

It was like sighting a signal from a far-off frigate. An end to speculation. *It was tomorrow.*

Keen said, 'Of course, sir.'

'But first, please signal *Larne* to close on us. I shall have a written instruction for your old ship, Val – there will be no time later on. *Larne* can then haul up to windward. If the French do come, they will surely recognise Tyacke's brig and may decide to stand away. Whatever that French ship is, *I want her.*'

'I see, sir.' He beckoned to Jenour. 'A signal for you!'

It was a short note, which Bolitho wrote in his own hand while Yovell waited in the pink glow, ready to apply the seal before putting it into an oilskin bag for *Nicator*'s captain.

Then he said to Keen, 'It is fair that you should know a part of what I wrote. Should I fall, you will assume command; and if

Black Prince is overwhelmed, Captain Huxley is to take *Nicator* out of the fight and return to Admiral Gambier.' He watched Keen gravely. 'Did I forget anything?'

'I think not, sir.'

Later, as the last dogwatchmen were finishing their evening meal, Bolitho and Keen, accompanied by the ship's junior lieutenant and, of course, Allday, went slowly along each deck and down every companion ladder into the very bowels of the ship.

Many of the startled seamen at their mess tables started to rise at the unheralded tour, but each time Bolitho waved them down.

He paused to speak to some of them and was surprised at the way they crowded around him. To see what he was like? To assess their own chances of survival; who could tell?

Pressed men and volunteers, hands from other ships, dialects which told their own stories. Men from Devon and Hampshire, Kent and Yorkshire, 'foreigners' too, as Fudge would describe any one from north of the border.

And of course a man from Falmouth, who said awkwardly before his grinning messmates, 'O' course 'ee won't know me, Sir Richard – name o' Tregorran.'

'But I knew your father. The blacksmith near the church.' For a brief instant he laid his hand on the man's shoulder while his mind sped on wings back to Falmouth. The man Tregorran stared at the two lines of gold lace on Bolitho's sleeve as if he had been mesmerised.

'He was a good man.' The mood left him. 'Let's hope we'll all be back home soon after this, lads!'

The overcrowded messdeck was stuffy now with the gunports sealed to contain the familiar smells of tar, bilge and sweat; a place where no tall man could stand upright, where their lives began and too often ended.

He climbed up the last of the companion ladders and some of the men stood to cheer, their voices following him, deck by deck, like other men he had known and commanded over the years; waiting perhaps for him to join them in that other world.

Allday saw his face and knew exactly what he was thinking. Roughknots, thieves and villains, alongside the innocent and

316

the damned. England's last hope. *Only* hope – that was what he was thinking right now.

A midshipman's grubby breeches caught the lamplight on the ladder and there was a quick, whispered conversation, before the lieutenant who had accompanied the unorthodox tour said, 'Mr Jenour's respects, sir!' He was looking at Keen but was very aware of his vice-admiral. 'The signal-bag has been passed to *Nicator.*'

He licked his lips as Bolitho remarked, 'All or nothing.' Then he said, 'You are Lieutenant Whyham, are you not?' He saw the youthful officer nod uncertainly. 'I thought as much, but did not wish to lose the use of memory!' He smiled, as if this were a casual meeting ashore. 'One of my midshipmen in *Argonaute* four years ago, correct?'

The lieutenant was still staring after him as Bolitho and Keen climbed into the cooler air of the upper deck. After the sealed messes it tasted like wine.

Keen said, uncertainly, 'Will you sup with me tonight, sir? Before they pull the ship apart and clear for action?'

Bolitho looked at him calmly, still moved by the warmth of those simple men who had nothing but his word to hold onto.

'I would relish that, Val.'

Keen removed his hat and pushed his fingers through his fair hair. Bolitho half-smiled. The midshipman again, or perhaps the lieutenant in the Great South Sea.

'What you said in your instructions to *Nicator*'s captain. It makes one realise, but not accept, how narrow that margin is. Now when I think I have everything I ever wanted . . .' He did not go on. He did not need to. It was as if Allday had just repeated what he had said before. '*An' then you dies* . . .'

Keen could have been speaking for both of them.

At the very first hint of life in the sky *Black Prince* seemed to come slowly into her own. Like men from forgotten sea-fights and long-lost wrecks, her seamen and marines emerged from the darkness of gundeck, orlop or hold, quitting that last pretence of privacy and peace which is the need of all men before a battle.

Bolitho stood on the quarterdeck's weather side and listened

317

to the awakening thud of bare feet and the clink of weapons around and below him. Keen had done his work well: not a pipe given, no beat of drum to inflame the heart and mind of some poor soul who might imagine it was his last memory on earth.

It was as if the great ship herself was coming alive, her company of eight hundred sailors and sea-soldiers merely incidental.

Bolitho watched the sky, his eye at ease in the darkness. First light was not far off, but for the present it was only anticipation, a sense of uneasiness like the sea's deceptive smile before a raging gale.

He tried to imagine the ship as the enemy would gauge her. A fine big three-decker with her rightful Danish ensign flying directly beneath the English one, to announce her true state to the world. But it needed more than that. Bolitho had used many ruses in his time, especially when employed as a frigate captain, and had been caught out by almost as many triggered against himself. In a war which had lasted so long and killed so many men on all sides and of all beliefs, even the normal could not be accepted at face-value.

If the day went against them, the price would be doubly high. Keen had already passed his orders to the boatswain – no chain-slings could be rigged to yards and spars to prevent them from falling to the deck, to cripple the ship or crush the men at the guns. It would put an edge to their spirits when the time came. There had been no protest from the boatswain about keeping all the boats stacked in their tiers. Bolitho had expected none. For despite the real danger from flying splinters, some like saw-toothed daggers if tiered boats were caught in an attack, most sailors preferred to see them there. The last lifeline.

Keen came up to him. Like all the officers who would be on the upper deck he had discarded his tell-tale captain's coat. Too many clues. Too many easy targets.

Keen stared at the sky. 'It's going to be another clear day.'

Bolitho nodded. 'I had hoped for rain – cloud at least with this nor'-easterly.' He looked towards the empty blanket beyond the bows. 'We shall have the sun at our backs. They must sight us first. I think we should shorten sail, Val.'

Keen was peering around for a midshipman. 'Mr Rooke! Tell

the first lieutenant to pipe the hands aloft, to take in t'gan'sls and royals!'

Bolitho smiled in spite of his dry tension. Two minds working together. If they were sighted first, any enemy would be suspicious of a prize-ship being driven under full sail when there was nothing to fear.

Keen looked at the vague shapes of men rushing aloft up the shrouds, to take in and fist the heavy canvas to the yards.

He said, 'Major Bourchier knows what to do. He will have marines on the forecastle, aft here, and up in the maintop, just as he would if he were controlling a prize with her original company still aboard.'

There was nothing more they could do.

Cazalet called, 'Sailmaker, sir!'

Fudge and one of his mates came through the shadows and held out the makeshift Danish flag between them.

Bolitho said, 'True to your word. A fine job.' He beckoned to Jenour. 'Help Fudge to run up our new flag – *his* should be the honour!'

It would have been something to see it, he thought. But even in the raw darkness, with the spray occasionally pattering over the decks like rain, it was a moment to remember. Men crowding inboard from the guns to peer at the strange flapping ensign as it mounted up to the gaff beneath the ship's true colours.

Someone called out, 'Yew musta used all yer best gear fer that 'un, Fudge!'

The old sailmaker was still staring at the faint, curling shape against the black sky. Over his shoulder he said dourly, 'Got enough to sew you up in after this day's over, mate.'

Keen smiled. 'I've put one of our master's mates in the masthead, sir. Taverner – used to be with Duncan. Eyes like a hawk, mind like a knife. I'll see him made sailing-master even if it does mean losing him!'

Bolitho licked his dry lips. Coffee, wine, even the brackish water from the casks would help just now.

He shut it from his mind. 'We shall soon know.'

Keen said, 'Rear-Admiral Herrick could have taken another course, sir. He may have turned the convoy towards England where he could expect to meet with the patrolling squadron.'

Bolitho imagined he could see Herrick's round, honest features. Turn the convoy? Never. It would be like running away.

Tojohns, the captain's coxswain, was kneeling on the deck to secure Keen's curved hanger, the lightweight fighting sword he always carried in battle. As he had when *Hyperion* had gone down under him.

Bolitho touched the hilt of the old family sword at his hip and shivered. It was like ice. He felt Allday watching him, caught the heady scent of rum as he released a great sigh.

Keen was busy again with his master and lieutenants and Bolitho asked, 'Well, old friend, what say you about this?'

For just a few seconds the darkness was gone, the night torn apart by one great, searing explosion which laid bare the whole ship, the men caught at their guns like statues, the rigging and shrouds sharpened by the glare like the bars of a furnace. Just as suddenly the light vanished, as if snuffed out by a giant's hand. Then, it seemed an eternity later, came the volcanic roar of the explosion, and with it a hot wind which seemed to sear the canvas and throw every sail aback.

Voices called out in every direction as the silence, like the darkness, hemmed them in once more.

Allday said harshly, 'One o' the vessels carryin' powder an' shot, I've no doubt!'

Bolitho tried to imagine if any one had known, be it only for a split second, that his life was ending in such a terrible way. No last cry, no handshake with an old friend to hold back the scream or the tears. *Nothing*.

Keen was shouting, 'Mr Cazalet, send midshipmen to each gundeck to tell the lieutenants what has happened!'

Bolitho looked away. Keen had managed to remember even that, as his ship sailed blindly on . . . into what?

Keen was heard to say, 'God, they must have felt that like a reef on the lower gundeck!'

A small figure emerged from somewhere, groping past the helmsmen and officers, the men at the braces, as if he did not belong here at all.

Allday growled, 'What th' hell are you doin' on deck?'

Bolitho turned. 'Ozzard! What is it? You know your place is

below. You were never a Jack Tar like poor Allday here!' But the old joke fell flat as he realised that Ozzard was quivering like a leaf.

'C-can't, s-sir! In the dark . . . down there. Like last time . . .' He stood trembling, oblivious to the silent men around him. 'Not again. I c-can't do it!'

Bolitho said, 'Of course. I should have thought.' He glanced at Allday. 'Find him a place close to hand.' He knew the words were not reaching the terrified little man. 'Near to us, eh?' He watched their shadows merge with the greater darkness and felt it like an old wound. *Hyperion* again.

Allday returned. 'Snug as a bug, Sir Richard. He'll be all right after what you just said.' *If only you knew the half of it*, he thought.

There were whispers as the upper yards and masthead pendant suddenly appeared against the sky, as if caught in another explosion, or even separate from the ship.

From the foremast cross-trees the master's mate's voice: 'Deck there! Land on the larboard bow!'

Keen exclaimed, 'Excellent, Mr Julyan – that must be The Skaw! Be prepared to alter course to the west'rd within the hour!'

Bolitho could share the excitement in many ways. They would soon be out and into the Skagerrak with sea-room which had no bottom, where it was said that wrecks and drowned sailormen shared the black caverns with blind creatures too terrible to imagine.

Be that as it may . . . when the jib-boom pointed west again, nothing stood between them and England.

The light was spreading down on them to reveal each deck like a layer of a cake. Following astern, the seventy-four *Nicator* was completely laid bare in the weak sunlight, when minutes earlier she had been invisible.

Taverner the master's mate, who was sharing the lookout, yelled, *'Deck there! Ships burnin'!'* He seemed choked for words. *'God, sir, I can't count 'em!'*

Keen snatched a speaking-trumpet. *'This is the Captain!'* A pause, to give the slender link time to fasten, the months of training and years of discipline to reassert themselves. 'What of the enemy?'

Bolitho walked to the quarterdeck rail and watched the upturned faces, the stark contrast with the almost cheerful air when Keen had explained what he had intended for this very moment.

'Two sail-of-the-line, sir! One other dismasted.' He broke off and Bolitho heard the master murmur, 'That's not like Bob. It must be bad then.'

The speed with which daylight was ripping away their defences made every moment worse. The enemy must have stumbled on the convoy before dusk yesterday, while they had been crawling out of the Sound with no thought but rescue in their hearts.

They must have taken or destroyed the whole convoy, leaving the clearing up to do until daylight. Until now.

Keen said in a tired voice, 'Too late after all, sir.'

The sudden echo of cannon fire vibrated over the sea and sighed through the masts and flapping canvas like an approaching squall.

Taverner called, 'Dismasted ship has opened fire, sir! She's not done in after all!' Discipline seemed to leave him and he yelled, '*Hit 'em, lads! Hit th' buggers! We'm comin'!*'

Keen and Bolitho stared at one another. The mastless, helpless ship was *Benbow*. There was no other possibility.

Bolitho said, 'Hands aloft, Val. Full sail. Just as we would if we were a prize and escort.' He saw the eagerness and despair in Keen's eyes and said, 'There is no other way. We must hold the surprise, and we must keep the wind-gage.' He felt his muscles harden as a responding broadside overlapped another and knew that the enemy would divide *Benbow*'s remaining firepower, then board and take her. The ship could not even be manoeuvred to protect her stern from a full broadside. He clenched his fists together until they ached. Herrick would die rather than surrender. He had already lost too much.

Black Prince leaned steadily under the mounting pressure in her sails, and began to turn towards the western horizon beyond the blurred finger of land, a sea where the darkness still lingered.

With every minute the daylight revealed the awful evidence of a lost fight. Spars, hatch-covers, drifting boats, and further out, the long dark keel of a vessel which had capsized under the bombardment. As the darkness continued to retreat they sighted other ships. Some were partly dismasted, others outwardly undamaged. All flew the French Tricolour above their English flags, mocking patches of gaiety in a panorama of disaster.

Of the second escort which Tyacke had described there was no sign at all. Under Herrick's flag she would have gone down, too, rather than strike.

Taverner's voice was controlled again. 'Deck there! They've discontinued their fire!'

Keen raised his speaking-trumpet almost desperately. 'Have they struck?'

Taverner was watching from his private eyrie. All his years in ships under every kind of captain; but always learning, stowing it all away like rhino in a ditty-box.

He called, 'The big ship's standin' away and makin' more sail, sir!'

Bolitho gripped Keen's arm. 'They've sighted us, Val. *They're coming!*'

He saw his nephew, Midshipman Vincent, staring wildly over the nettings as far-off screams ebbed and flowed through the lengthening pall of dense smoke from one or more of the wrecks.

Tojohns said between his teeth, 'What's that, in Hell's name?'

Keen looked at him and answered flatly, 'Horses. Caught below decks when their ship was torn apart.'

He saw Bolitho touch his injured eye. Remembering too. The awful cries of army mounts dying in terror and in darkness until the sea finally ended it.

Bolitho noticed some of the seamen staring at each other with anger and sick dismay. Men who would barely turn a hair when they saw an enemy fall, or even one of their own if the time was wrong. But a helpless animal – that was always different.

'May I, Val?' Then all at once he found himself at the rail again, his voice surprisingly level and controlled as every man turned aft towards him.

'That ship is coming for us, lads! Whatever you may think or feel, you must stay your hand! Behind each port is a double-shotted gun with Englishmen to use them when I give the word!' He hesitated as he saw Ozzard's tiny shape scurrying along the starboard gangway towards the forecastle with one of the big signals telescopes over his shoulder like a mace.

He dragged his mind away from what it must have been like here. Helpless ships; Herrick standing like a rock between them and impossible odds. Perhaps Herrick was dead. In the same breath he knew he was not.

'*Stand together!* This is our ship and those people yonder were our kin! But this is not revenge! It is justice!'

He fell silent, exhausted, empty. He said quietly, 'They don't have the heart for it, Val.'

'*Right, lads! Huzza for Our Dick!*' The ship seemed to shiver to the sudden wild burst of cheering. '*An' huzza for our Cap'n whose bride's waitin' for 'm in England!*'

Keen turned, his eyes full of tears. 'There's your answer – they'll give you all they have! You should never have doubted it!'

Allday seized Ozzard and cursed the men for cheering when they had no minds for what they were facing.

'What the hell were you doin'? I thought you'd run dizzy like them natives do in the sun!'

Ozzard put down the telescope and stared at him. He seemed very composed. More so than Allday could ever recall.

He said, 'I heard what Sir Richard just told them. That it's not revenge.' He looked at the powerful telescope. 'I don't know much about ships, but I know *that one* right enough. How could I forget?'

'How d'you mean, matey?' But the throbbing pain in his chest had already warned him.

Ozzard glanced towards Bolitho and the captain. 'I don't care what they call her or what flag she flies. She's the same one that destroyed our *Hyperion*. It will be revenge all right!' He peered at his friend, his courage gone. 'What shall we do, John?'

For once there was no answer.

Midshipman Roger Segrave pressed his palms on the quarter-deck rail and took in great gulps of air, as if he were being suffocated. His whole body was like taut wire, and when he looked at his hands and arms he expected to see them shaking uncontrollably. He glanced quickly at the figures around him. The master and his mates by the compass, the four helmsmen, with extra hands standing by but pretending to look like men with nothing to do. It was like a madness. The larboard gangway, the one which was nearest to the tall enemy three-decker, was packed with sailors, all unarmed, apparently chatting to each other and occasionally pointing at the other ships as if they were not involved. Segrave dropped his eyes and saw the lie revealed. Beneath the gangway and matched by the two decks below that, the gun crews were crammed against their weapons. Handspikes, rammers and sponges were close to hand, and even the breechings were cast off to avoid even a second's delay.

He looked at Bolitho who was standing with Captain Keen, hands on hips, sometimes pointing at the other ships but mostly keeping his eyes inboard. Even without their uniforms they stood out from the rest, Segrave thought wildly. The lordly Midshipman Bosanquet was speaking with the flag-lieutenant and Segrave saw signal flags rolled and ready to bend on, partly hidden by some hammocks stretched out to dry in the sunshine. Only the marines made no pretence of hiding their true identities. Their scarlet coats filled the maintop by the depressed swivel guns, and two more squads were properly deployed with fixed bayonets on the forecastle and aft near the poop.

Segrave heard Bolitho say, 'Mr Julyan, *you* are supposed to be the captain today!'

The tall sailing-master gave a broad grin. 'I feels different already, Sir Richard!'

Segrave felt his breathing and heartbeat steady. He must accept it, as they did.

Bolitho added in the same easy way, 'I know that our Danish opposites dress somewhat more soberly than we do, but I think a hat might make all the difference.'

More grins as Julyan tried first Keen's cocked hat and then Bolitho's, which fitted him perfectly.

Bolitho glanced around the quarterdeck and Segrave tensed as the grey eyes rested momentarily on him. 'The waiting's over. *Stand by!*'

Segrave looked again at the enemy. The second large ship, a two-decker, was falling downwind and changing tack, flags rising and vanishing from her yards as she exchanged signals with her superior. She would confront *Nicator*, which was making full sail as if to head off any attack on her 'prize'.

Keen watched his former ship and murmured, 'She was a good old girl.' *Was.*

Segrave jumped as the first lieutenant's harsh voice smashed through his thoughts.

'Lower gundeck, Mr Segrave! Report to the third lieutenant there!' He glared round the darkly shadowed deck. 'That bloody Vincent should have been here by now! Tell him I want him if you see him!' His eyes fell on Segrave and something perhaps from an old memory made him say, 'Easy, young fellow. Men will die today, but only if chosen.' His hard features cracked into a smile. 'You've proved your worth – it'll not be your turn yet!'

Segrave ran to the ladder and suddenly remembered the rough kindness shown to him in Tyacke's *Miranda* before she had been blown to pieces. He was a year older. He had lived a full lifetime since then.

He paused for a last glance before losing himself in the hull's darkness. A captured scene, which he would never forget. Bolitho, his frilled shirt blowing in the fresh breeze, one hand on the old sword, with his coxswain just behind him. Keen, Jenour, Bosanquet, master's mates and seamen, people now, more real than any he knew at home.

As he turned he felt his mouth go dry. Beyond the larboard gangway was a solitary flag, like a lance-pendant above an armoured knight in one of his old storybooks.

As close as that. He knew it was the foremast truck of the enemy ship.

Someone shouted, 'She's luffed! She wants to speak!' There was no defiant response, no ironic jeers such as he had heard from sailors in danger. It was like a single animal growl, as if the ship were speaking for them.

He found himself hurrying down, deck by deck, ladder by ladder, past wary marine sentries posted to prevent men from running below, and ship's boys as they ran with fresh powder for the guns which had yet to be fired.

He saw a midshipman cowering by the carpenter's extra stock of wedges and plugs, and knew it was Vincent.

He said, 'Mr Cazalet wants you on deck!'

Vincent seemed to shrink into the heap of repairing gear and sobbed, 'Go away, damn you to hell! I hope they kill you!'

Segrave hurried on, shocked more than anything by what he had seen. Vincent was finished. He had not even begun.

The lower gundeck was in total darkness, and yet Segrave could feel the mass of men who crouched there. In places chinks of sunlight probed down the gunports to touch a naked, sweating shoulder, or a pair of eyes white and staring like a blind man's.

Flemyng, the third lieutenant, commanded here. This was the main power of *Black Prince*'s artillery, where twenty-eight thirty-two pounders and their crews lived, trained and waited for just this moment.

Flemyng was a tall man, and was crouched over with his face pressed against the massive hull by the first division of guns. Only when he looked inboard did Segrave see the small round observation port, no bigger than a sailor's basin, where the lieutenant could watch the nearness of an enemy before any one else.

'Segrave? Stay with me.' His voice was clipped, sharp. He was usually one of the easiest of the lieutenants. 'Gunner's mate! See to Mr Segrave!' He dismissed him and turned back to his little port.

Segrave's eyes were getting used to the darkness and he could see the individual guns nearest him, the black breeches resting on the buff-painted trucks, men crowded around them as if in some strange ceremony, their backs shining like steel.

The gunner's mate said, ''Ere, Mr Segrave.' He thrust two pistols into his hands. 'Both loaded. Just cock an' fire, see?'

Segrave stared at the closed gunports. Would the enemy come swarming in here? Into the ship herself?

The gunner's mate had gone, and Segrave jumped as somebody touched his leg and murmured, 'Come to see 'ow the poor live, Mr Segrave?'

Segrave got down by the gun. It was the man he had saved from a flogging, the one Vincent had discovered in the hold below them at this moment.

He exclaimed, 'Jim Fittock! I didn't know this was your station!'

A voice barked, 'Silence on the gundeck!'

Fittock chuckled. 'You got yer pieces then?'

Segrave thrust them into his belt. 'They'll not be allowed to get that close!'

Fittock nodded to his mates on the opposite side of the great thirty-two pounder. It said that this young officer was all right. The reasons were unnecessary.

'Aye, we'll rake the buggers after what they done!' He saw a sliver of sunlight glance off one of the pistols and gave a bitter smile. How could he explain to such an innocent that the pistols were for shooting any poor Jack who tried to run when the slaughter began?

A whistle shrilled and a voice piped from the companion ladder, 'Right traverse, sir!'

Someone growled, 'She's that close, eh?' Handspikes rasped across the deck to move the guns to a steeper angle; this division would be firing directly from the larboard bow.

Lieutenant Flemyng had drawn his hanger. '*Ready*, lads!' He peered through the darkness as if he were seeing each of his men. 'They've been calling to us to heave-to!' His voice sounded wild. '*All nice and friendly!*' As he turned back to look through his observation port, the sunlight, which had held his face suspended against the darkness like a mask, was cut off. It was as if a great hand had been laid across the port like a shutter.

Fittock hissed, 'Keep with us!'

Segrave heard no more as the whistles shrilled and Flemyng yelled, '*Open the ports! Run out!*'

The air was filled with the squeak of trucks as the seamen threw themselves on their tackles and ran the great, lumbering guns up to the waiting sunshine. Gun-captains crouched and took the slack from their trigger-lines, faces, eyes, hands in various attitudes of hate and prayer while they cringed and waited for the order; it was like one vast incomplete painting.

Segrave stared with disbelief at the high beakhead and ornate gilded carving – a ship's tall side already smoke-stained from bombardment and conquest.

328

It was like being held in time. No voice, nor motion, as if the ship, too, was stricken.

Flemyng's hanger slashed down. '*Fire!*'

As each gun came lurching inboard to be seized, sponged out and reloaded in the only fashion they knew, Segrave stood gasping and retching, the smoke funnelling around him and blotting out everything. And yet it was there. Frozen to his mind. The lines of enemy guns pointing at *him*, some with men peering around them, watching their latest capture until the massive weight of iron smashed into them at less than fifty yards' range.

The ship was swaying over as deck by deck the full broadside was fired across the smoky water. Men were cheering and cursing, racing one another to run out the guns and hold up their hands in the swirling mist of powder smoke.

'*Run out! Aim! Fire!*'

A ragged crash thundered against the side and somewhere a gun rolled inboard and overturned like a wounded beast. Men screamed and fell in the choking mist, and Segrave saw a severed hand lying near the next gun like a discarded glove. No wonder they painted the sides red. It managed to hide some of the horror.

'Cease firing!' Flemyng turned away as another midshipman was dragged towards the hatchway which would take him to the orlop. From what he could see he had lost an arm and a leg. There was not much point . . .

Segrave also tore his eyes away. The same age as himself. The same uniform. *A thing*. Not a person any more.

'*Open the starboard ports!*'

Fittock punched his arm. 'Come on, sir! The Cap'n's comin' about and we'll engage the buggers to starboard!' They scrambled across the deck, stumbling over fallen gear and slipping on blood as sunlight poured through the other ports and the enemy seemed to slide past, her sails in complete disorder. Unless engaged on both sides together, the gun crews usually helped each other to keep the broadsides timed and regular.

'Ready, sir!'

'On the uproll, lads!' Flemyng was hatless and there was blood splashed like paint on his forehead. '*Fire!*'

Men were cheering and hugging each other. ''Er bloody foremast's comin' down!'

By one of the guns a seaman held his mate in his arms, and frantically pushed the hair from his eyes as he babbled, 'Nearly done, Tim! The buggers are dismasted!' But his friend did not respond. Together they had lived and yarned by this one gun. Every waking hour it had been here – waiting.

A gunner's mate said roughly, 'Take that man an' put 'im over! 'E's done for!' He was not an unduly hard man, but death was terrible enough without seeing it lingering on.

The seaman clutched his friend closer to him so that his head lolled across his shoulder as if to confide something. '*You won't put 'im over, you bastards!*'

Segrave felt Fittock's hard hand helping him to his feet as he called, 'Leave them, gunner's mate!' He did not recognise himself. 'There is enough to do!'

Fittock glanced across at his own crew, his teeth very white in his grimy face.

'Told you, eh? Right little terrier!' Then he guided Segrave to the curve of one great timber so that the others should not see his distress. He added, 'One of the best!'

Throughout the ship men stood or crouched at their tasks, bodies streaked with sweat, ears bandaged against the deafening roar of cannon fire, fingers raw from hauling, ramming and running-out again and again.

It took time for the marine's trumpet call to penetrate each deck, and then the cheering clawed its way up towards the smoky sunlight, that other place where it had all begun.

Bolitho stood by the quarterdeck rail and watched the enemy ship. As she drifted downwind she turned her high stern towards him, the name *San Mateo* still so bright in the sunlight. He had thought it would never stop, and yet he knew that the whole action, from the time the Danish flag had been hauled down and his own run up to the fore, had lasted barely thirty minutes.

He said, 'I knew we could do it.' He felt Allday near him, heard Keen yell, 'Stand by to starboard!'

There had been casualties. Men killed when seconds before they had been waiting to start the game.

'*Nicator*'s signalling, sir!' Jenour sounded hoarse.

330

Bolitho raised a hand in acknowledgment. Thank God. Jenour was safe too. *Black Prince* must have fired three broadsides before the enemy had gathered wits enough to return a ragged response. By then it was already too late.

He said, 'Signal *Nicator* to close with the convoy. Make certain that she tells the boarding parties that if they try to scuttle our ships or harm the crews, they will have to swim home!' He heard men muttering with approval and knew that had he so much as suggested it, they would have run every French prisoner up to the mainyard.

It was what war dictated. A madness. A need to hurt and kill those who had brought fear to you.

He thought suddenly of Ozzard. So innocuous, and yet he had known, had recognised that it was that same ship which had so brutally destroyed *Hyperion*. Maybe it was the ship, and not the men who crewed her? French flag, Spanish, and now if she surrendered, an addition to His Britannic Majesty's fleet. Would she, the ship, remain unchanged, like something untamed?

It still sickened him to recall how *San Mateo* had poured her broadsides into *Hyperion*, regardless of the destruction and murder she was causing to her own consorts, which were unable to move clear. *The ship then.*

Keen walked round to face him.

'Sir?' He watched quietly. Feeling it. Sharing it. There was pride too. More than he had dared to hope for.

Bolitho seemed to rouse himself. 'Has she struck yet?' *Is that me? So cold, so impersonal . . . An executioner.*

Keen answered gently, 'I believe her steering is shot away, sir. But their guns are still, and I think many of her people are dead.'

Bolitho said, 'A glass if you please.' He saw their surprise as he crossed to the opposite side and levelled the telescope on Herrick's flagship. Unmoving and heavy in the water, her masts and trailing rigging dragging from either side. Thin scarlet threads ran down from the upper deck scuppers to the littered surface and the ship's unmoving reflection. As if she herself were bleeding to death. He felt his heart leap as he saw the tattered ensign still trailing from the poop where someone had braved hell to nail it there. Beyond *Benbow*, the other vessels

331

drifted to no purpose. Spectators, victims; waiting for it all to end.

He called sharply, 'Prepare all divisions to fire, Captain Keen!' There was no reply, and he could almost feel them holding their breath. 'If they do not strike, *they will die.*' He swung round. '*Is that clear?*'

Another voice; another still alive. Bosanquet called, 'Brig *Larne* is closing, sir!'

Perhaps his meticulous interruption helped. Bolitho said, 'Call away my barge and ask the surgeon to report to me. *Benbow* will need help. Your first lieutenant would be a great asset.' He shook himself and walked to his friend. 'My apologies, Val. I had forgotten.'

Cazalet had fallen to the first exchange. A ball had all but cut him in half while he had been sending men aloft to attend repairs.

They were cheering again; it went on and on and Bolitho believed he could see men in *Nicator*'s yards waving and capering, their voices lost in distance. Like great falling leaves the two French flags drifted down from *San Mateo*'s rigging and men stood back from her guns, silently watching like mourners.

Keen said harshly, '*She's struck!*' He could not contain his relief.

Bolitho saw his barge lifting and then dipping over the nettings, and knew that Keen had been dreading the order to re-open fire, flags or not.

Allday touched his hat. 'Ready, Sir Richard.' He studied him anxiously. 'Shall I fetch a coat?'

Bolitho turned to him and winced as the sunlight pricked at his eye.

'I have no need for it.'

Julyan the sailing-master called, 'What about your hat, Sir Richard?' He was half-laughing, but almost sobbing with relief. Men had died right beside him. He was safe – one more time. Another step up the ladder.

Bolitho smiled through the smoky sunshine. 'You have a son, I believe? Give it to him. It will make a good yarn, one day.'

He turned away from the surprise and gratitude in the man's face and said, 'Let us finish this.'

332

It was a silent crossing, with only the creak of oars and the bargemen's breathing to break the stillness.

As *Benbow*'s great shadow loomed over them, Bolitho did not know where he would find the strength to meet whatever lay ahead. He pinched the locket beneath his filthy shirt and whispered, *'Wait for me, Kate.'*

Followed by the others, he clambered up the side. Shot holes pitted the timbers from gangway to waterline, rigging, some with corpses trapped within it like weed, tugged beneath the sea, pulling her down.

Bolitho climbed faster. But a ship's heart could be saved. He saw faces staring at him from open gunports, some driven half-mad, others probably killed at the outbreak of the battle.

He reached the quarterdeck, so bare now without the main and mizzen to protect it.

He heard *Black Prince*'s surgeon calling out orders, and another boat already hooking alongside with more willing hands; but at this moment he was quite alone.

The centre of any fighting ship, where it all began and ended. The shattered wheel with the dead helmsmen scattered like bloodied bundles, even caught in attitudes of shock and fury when death had marked them down. A boatswain's mate who had been kneeling to fix a bandage to the flag-lieutenant's leg, then both of them killed together by a hail of cannister shot. A sailor still bending on a signal when he had fallen, and the hailliards were torn from his hands as the mast had gone careering overboard.

Propped against the compass box with one leg bent beneath him was Herrick. He was barely conscious, although Bolitho guessed that his pain was deeper than any gunshot wound.

He held a pistol in one hand, and raised his head, holding it to one side as if the broadsides had rendered him deaf.

'Ready, Marines! We've got 'em on the run! *Take aim*, my lads!'

Bolitho heard Allday mutter, 'God, look at it.'

The marines did not stir. They lay, from sergeant to private, like fallen toy soldiers, their weapons still pointing towards an invisible enemy.

Allday said sharply, *'Easy*, sir.'

333

Bolitho stepped over an out-thrust scarlet arm with two chevrons upon it and gently took the pistol from Herrick's hand.

He passed it to Allday, who noted that it was in fact loaded and cocked.

'Rest easy, Thomas. Help is here.' He took his arm and waited for the blue eyes to focus and recover their understanding. 'Listen to the cheering! The battle's o'er – the day is won!'

Herrick allowed himself to be raised to a more comfortable position. He stared at the splintered decks and abandoned guns, the dead, and the scarlet trails which marked the retreat of the dying.

As if speaking from far away he said thickly, 'So you came, Richard.'

He uses my name and yet he meets me as a stranger. Bolitho waited sadly, the madness and the exhilaration of battle already drained from him.

Herrick was trying to smile. 'It will be . . . another triumph for you.'

Bolitho released his arm very gently and stood up, and beckoned to the surgeon. 'Attend to the Rear-Admiral, if you please.' He saw the dead marine corporal's hair blowing in the breeze, his eyes fixed with attention as if he were listening.

Bolitho looked at Jenour, and past him to the waiting, listless ships.

'I think not, Thomas. Here, Death is the only victor.'

It was over.

Epilogue

The relentless bombardment of Copenhagen by day and night brought its inevitable conclusion. On the fifth of September, General Peyman, the governor of the city, sent out a flag of truce. Terms were still to be agreed, if possible with some honour left to the heroic defenders, but all fighting was to end.

While Bolitho and his ships took charge of their prizes and did what they could for the many killed and wounded, the terms of Copenhagen were decided. The surrender of all Danish ships and naval stores, and the removal of any other vessel not yet completed in the dockyard, and the occupation by Lord Cathcart's forces of The Citadel and other fortifications for a period of six weeks while these tasks were carried out, formed the basis of the armistice. It was thought by some that even the skills and experience of the English sailors would be insufficient to complete this great operation within the allotted time, but even the most doubtful critics were forced to show admiration and pride at the Fleet's achievements.

In the allotted span of six weeks, sixteen sail-of-the-line, frigates, sloops and many smaller vessels were dispatched to English ports, and the country's fear that the blockade of enemy ports would collapse due to lack of ships was ended.

The various squadrons were returned to their normal stations and some were disbanded to await further instructions. Perhaps, after the glory of Trafalgar, the second battle of Copenhagen was slow to catch the imagination of a public hungry for victories. But the results, and the severe setback to

Napoleon's last hope of breaking the line of wooden-walls which stretched from the Channel ports to Biscay and from Gibraltar to the shores of Italy, were real enough.

The New Year arrived, and with it some of the victors came home.

For late January it was deceptively mild and peaceful in the little Cornish village of Zennor. Some said it was an omen for such a special occasion, for this part of the county was not noted for its placid weather. Zennor lay on the north shore of the peninsula, as different from Falmouth and its pastoral landscape of low hills, silver estuaries and lovely bays as could be imagined. Here was a savage coastline of cliffs and serried lines of jagged black rocks like broken teeth, where the sea boiled and thundered in constant unrest. In normal times, a bleak, uncompromising shore where many a fine ship had made its last and fatal landfall.

Zennor was a small place, owing its existence mainly to the land, as only the foolhardy sought to live from fishing, and there were many stones in the church to confirm as much.

Despite the chill, damp air, not a villager missed this particular day, when one of their own, the daughter of a respected local man who had been wrongly executed for speaking out on the freedoms of farm workers and others, was to be married.

The village had never seen such an occasion. At first glance there were more expensive carriages and horses than residents. The blue and white of sea officers rubbed shoulders with a few Royal Marines and some of the local garrison, while the gowns of the ladies were of a quality and style rarely seen in this proud but humble place.

The little twelfth-century church, more accustomed to farming festivals and local weddings, was packed. Even with extra chairs and stools brought from the dairy, some of the congregation had to remain outside in the timeless churchyard – as much a part of their heritage as the sea and the rolling fields which surrounded the village.

A young lieutenant bowed to Catherine as she entered the church on the arm of Captain Adam Bolitho. 'If you will follow me, my lady!'

An organ was playing in the background when she reached her allotted place; she had noticed several heads leaning forward to watch her pass, then moving together for a quiet remark, or more gossip perhaps.

Strangely, it no longer mattered. She glanced across the church and thought she recognised some of Bolitho's captains. It must have been difficult for a few of them to reach this remote village, she thought. From Falmouth it was some forty miles, first north and through Truro on the main coaching road, then westward where with each passing mile the roads became narrower and more rutted. She smiled to herself. Nancy's husband, 'The King of Cornwall', had performed magnificently, living up to his name by obtaining the full co-operation of the local squire, willingly or otherwise. He had offered his spacious house, not only for many of the guests to stay overnight, but had also joined with Roxby in providing such a spread of food and drink there that it would be talked about for years to come.

She said quietly, 'I am so glad it is a fine day for them.' She watched Adam's profile and remembered what Bolitho had told her, that he seemed troubled by something. 'Look at poor Val! He would rather face another battle than stand and be still like this!'

Keen was standing by the small altar, with his brother beside him. Like his two sisters in the church, the other man was fair; and it appeared odd, in this gathering, for him not to be wearing uniform, but Catherine knew he was a distinguished barrister in London.

Adam said, 'I shall have to leave soon after the wedding, Catherine.' He glanced at her, and she felt her heart leap at the resemblance as it always did. So like Richard; or perhaps all the Bolithos were cast in the same mold.

'So soon?' She laid her hand on his sleeve. The young hero who had said that he had all he had ever dreamed of; but for a few moments he had looked quite lost, like the boy he had once been.

He smiled at her – Bolitho's smile. 'It is the burden of every frigate captain, I'm told. Turn your back and the admiral will poach your best men for some other captain. You find only the sweepings of the press if you stay away too long.'

It was not the reason, and she knew that he realised she understood as much. He said suddenly, 'I want to tell you, Catherine.' He gripped her hand. 'You of all people – I know you – care.'

She returned the pressure on his hand. 'When you are ready, you will share it perhaps.'

There were more whispers by the altar. She sat silently, studying the ancient ceiling of Cornish barrel vaulting, recalling the famous legend of this place. It was said that a mermaid had once sat in the back of the church and lost her heart to a chorister here. Then one day she had lured him out to the little stream which ran through the village and down into the sea at Pendour Cove. They were never seen again; but even now it was claimed by many that you could hear the lovers singing together when the sea was calm . . . like today.

She smiled wistfully as Keen turned and gazed up the aisle, a brave, distinguished figure in the cool winter light reflecting against these old stone walls. Theirs was a role reversed, surely? Zenoria had been his mermaid, and he had plucked her from the sea to make her his own.

She saw Tojohns, Keen's coxswain, proudly dressed in his best jacket and breeches, wave a signal from the door. It was almost time. Beyond him she had seen Allday's familiar figure. Did he feel a little neglected, she wondered? Or was he, like herself, trying not to think of that other marriage that could never be? She touched her finger where Somervell's ring had been. They must not waste a day or an hour, whenever they were together. All those years which had been denied them could never be lived again.

There was a sound of distant cheering, and someone ringing a cow bell. Then carriage wheels on the rough track, and she felt a burning pride as the cheers grew louder, not for the bride this time but for her man. The hero whom even a stranger could recognise and make his own.

She wished they could be alone afterwards, escape back to Falmouth after the wedding, but it was impossible. Forty miles on these roads in the darkness was a sure way of ending everything.

Catherine turned and watched their shadows shut out the

338

bright sunlight in the ancient doorway, and put her hand to her breast.

'What a lovely creature she is, Adam.' She turned to speak further and then made herself face the aisle, as Bolitho with Zenoria on his arm moved slowly into the body of the church.

It was no imagination. Perhaps another woman might have been mistaken; and Catherine found herself wishing it were so.

But she had seen the look on Adam's face before, on Bolitho's in those difficult, reckless days . . .

Adam was in love all right, with the girl who was about to marry Valentine Keen.

Richard Bolitho looked down at the girl and said, 'A promise kept. I said I would give you away. It is a coming-together of so many hopes!'

What had she been thinking on the endless journey by coach, and now along the aisle's weathered stones where so many generations had trod? There seemed only happiness.

He saw familiar faces and smiles, his sister Nancy already dabbing at her eyes as he had known she would. Ferguson and his wife Grace, people from the estate side by side with officers high and low. Even the port admiral from Plymouth had made an appearance, and was sharing a pew with Midshipman Segrave – a suddenly older and more confident young man who would be standing for lieutenant when he returned to the ship.

He smiled at Allday and knew he would have liked to be in charge today as was Keen's own coxswain, organising a carriage decked with ribbons, to be drawn on boat ropes by some of Keen's midshipmen and petty officers to carry them to the squire's house.

He saw a dark shadow slip along the wall and enter the pew shared by Adam and Catherine; he sat among other shadows with his face half averted and the collar of his boat-cloak turned up. He did not need to be told it was Tyacke, paying his respects in his own special way, no matter what the cost to himself. A true friend, he thought with sudden affection and admiration.

He touched his injured eye and tried to ignore it. It was pricking painfully in the smoke of the many candles which lined the church.

There were many others in the shadows today who would

remain equally silent. Friends he would never see again; would never be able to share with Catherine.

Francis Inch, John Neale, Charles Keverne, Farquhar, Veitch, and now poor Browne . . . with an 'e'. And so many more.

He thought too of Herrick, who would be at his own home recovering from a flesh wound, but with a far harder disablement to endure forever.

He gave his place to Keen as the clergyman, whom he did not know, opened his book and beamed nervously at the unusually illustrious congregation.

Bolitho stood beside Catherine and they clasped hands as the familiar words were spoken and repeated, and the ring was offered and received to seal their vows to one another.

Then the ancient bells were chiming overhead and people were leaning out of the pews to call their best wishes to the bridal couple.

Bolitho said, 'Wait a while, Kate.' He saw that Adam had already gone, and of Tyacke there was no sign, although almost lost in the joyful clamour of the bells he heard the beat of hooves as he galloped away; like the devil's highwayman, he thought.

'Young Matthew will bring the carriage for us after the others have left.'

He looked past her at the empty church, a child's glove fallen between some stacked Bibles.

'What is it?' She watched him, waiting, believing he had seen and recognised Adam's despair.

He said quietly, 'This is for you.' He raised her hand and held the ring above it, a glistening band of diamonds and rubies. 'In the eyes of God we *are* married, dearest Kate. It is right that it should be here.'

Allday watched from the porchway. Like young lovers.

He grinned. And why not? A sailor and his woman. There was no stronger bond.

And he shared their joy: and somehow, it dispelled his own envy.

340